THE EDINBURGH EDITION OF
THE WAVERLEY NOVELS

EDITOR-IN-CHIEF
Dr David Hewitt

VOLUME ELEVEN
KENILWORTH

EDINBURGH EDITION OF THE WAVERLEY NOVELS

to be complete in thirty volumes

Each volume will be published separately but original conjoint publication of certain works is indicated in the EEWN volume numbering [4a, b; 7a, b, etc.]. Where EEWN editors have been appointed, their names are listed

WALTER SCOTT

KENILWORTH
A ROMANCE

Edited by
J. H. Alexander

EDINBURGH
University
Press

© The University Court of the University of Edinburgh 1993
Edinburgh University Press
22 George Square, Edinburgh
Columbia University Press
562 West 113th Street, New York

Typeset in Linotronic Ehrhardt
by Speedspools, Edinburgh
and printed in Great Britain
by Cambridge University Press

ISBN 0 7486 0437 5

Reprinted 2002

British Library Cataloguing in Publication Data
Waverley Novels
Fiction
Scott, Sir Walter 1771–1832
New Edition
Hewitt, David, Editor-in-chief
Kenilworth: a Romance
J. H. Alexander, editor

FOREWORD

THE PUBLICATION of *Waverley* in 1814 marked the emergence of the modern novel in the western world. It is difficult now to recapture the impact of this and the following novels of Scott on a readership accustomed to prose fiction either as picturesque romance, 'Gothic' quaintness, or presentation of contemporary manners. For Scott not only invented the historical novel, but gave it a dimension and a relevance that made it available for a great variety of new kinds of writing. Balzac in France, Manzoni in Italy, Gogol and Tolstoy in Russia, were among the many writers of fiction influenced by the man Stendhal called 'notre père, Walter Scott'.

What Scott did was to show history and society in motion: old ways of life being challenged by new; traditions being assailed by counter-statements; loyalties, habits, prejudices clashing with the needs of new social and economic developments. The attraction of tradition and its ability to arouse passionate defence, and simultaneously the challenge of progress and 'improvement', produce a pattern that Scott saw as the living fabric of history. And this history was rooted in *place*; events happened in localities still recognisable after the disappearance of the original actors and the establishment of new patterns of belief and behaviour.

Scott explored and presented all this by means of stories, entertainments, which were read and enjoyed as such. At the same time his passionate interest in history led him increasingly to see these stories as illustrations of historical truths, so that when he produced his final *Magnum Opus* edition of the novels he surrounded them with historical notes and illustrations, and in this almost suffocating guise they have been reprinted in edition after edition ever since. The time has now come to restore these novels to the form in which they were presented to their first readers, so that today's readers can once again capture their original power and freshness. At the same time, serious errors of transcription, omission, and interpretation, resulting from the haste of their transmission from manuscript to print can now be corrected.

DAVID DAICHES

EDINBURGH
University
Press

CONTENTS

ACKNOWLEDGEMENTS

The Scott Advisory Board and the editors of the Edinburgh Edition of the Waverley Novels wish to express their gratitude to The University Court of the University of Edinburgh *and its Press Committee for their vision in initiating and supporting the preparation of the first critical edition of Walter Scott's fiction. Those Universities which employ the editors have also contributed greatly in paying the editors' salaries, and awarding research leave and grants for travel and materials. Particular thanks are due to* The University of Aberdeen *for its grant towards the development of an electronic concordance of the Waverley Novels, and for the assistance it has given both the Editor-in-Chief and the editor of* Kenilworth *throughout.*

Although the edition is the work of scholars employed by universities, the project could not have prospered without the help of the sponsors cited below. Their generosity has met the direct costs of the initial research and of the preparation of the text of the first six novels to appear in this edition.

BANK OF SCOTLAND
The collapse of the great Edinburgh publisher Archibald Constable in January 1826 entailed the ruin of Sir Walter Scott who found himself responsible for his own private debts, for the debts of the printing business of James Ballantyne and Co. in which he was co-partner, and for the bank advances to Archibald Constable which had been guaranteed by the printing business. Scott's largest creditors were Sir William Forbes and Co., bankers, and the Bank of Scotland. On the advice of Sir William Forbes himself, the creditors did not sequester his property, but agreed to the creation of a trust to which he committed his future literary earnings, and which ultimately repaid the debts of over £120,000 for which he was legally liable.

In the same year the Government proposed to curtail the rights of the Scottish banks to issue their own notes; Scott wrote the 'Letters of Malachi Malagrowther' in their defence, arguing that the measure was neither in the interests of the banks nor of Scotland. The 'Letters' were so successful that the Government was forced to withdraw its proposal and to this day the Scottish Banks issue their own notes.

A portrait of Sir Walter appears on all current bank notes of the Bank of Scotland because Scott was a champion of Scottish banking, and because he was an illustrious and honourable customer not just of the Bank of Scotland itself, but also of three other banks now incorporated within it—the British Linen Bank which continues today as the merchant banking arm of the Bank of Scotland, Sir William Forbes and Co., and Ramsays, Bonars and Company.

Bank of Scotland's *support of the EEWN continues its long and fruitful involvement with the affairs of Walter Scott.*

P.F. CHARITABLE TRUST
The P.F. Charitable Trust is the main charitable trust of the Fleming family which founded and still has a controlling interest in the City firm of Robert Fleming Holdings Limited. *It was started in 1951 by Philip Fleming and has since been added to by his son, Robin, who is now Managing Trustee. The Board and the editors are most grateful to the Trust and Mr Robin Fleming for their generosity to the Edition.*

EDINBURGH UNIVERSITY DEVELOPMENT TRUST
The Edinburgh University General Council Trust, now incorporated within the Edinburgh University Development Trust, derived its funds from the contibutions of graduates of the University. To the trustees, and to all whose gifts allowed the Trust to give a generous grant to the EEWN, the Board and the editors express their thanks.

The Board and editors also wish to thank Sir Gerald Elliot *for a gift from his charitable trust, and the* British Academy *and the* Carnegie Trust *for the Universities of Scotland for grants to facilitate specific aspects of EEWN research.*

LIBRARIES
Without the generous assistance of the two great repositories of Scott manuscripts, the National Library of Scotland *and the* Pierpont Morgan Library, *New York, it would not have been possible to have undertaken the editing of Scott's novels, and the Board and editors cannot overstate the extent to which they are indebted to their Trustees and staffs. In particular they wish to pay tribute to the late* Professor Denis Roberts, *Librarian of the National Library, who served on the Scott Advisory Board, who persuaded many of his colleagues in Britain and throughout the world to assist the Edition, and whose determination brought about the repatriation in 1986 of the Pforzheimer Library's Scott manuscripts and of the Interleaved Set of the Waverley Novels.*

KENILWORTH
The dispersal of Scott materials means that the Scott editor is inevitably indebted to many institutions. Most of the manuscript of Kenilworth *is in* The British Library, *with smaller portions in* Edinburgh University Library *and the* Karpeles Manuscript Library, *Santa Barbara. Their help is gratefully acknowledged.*

Editing Scott requires knowledge and expertise beyond what can be mustered by any one person, and a great many people have assisted the editor of Kenilworth. *He is specifically indebted to the late Dr J. C. Corson for the identification of several quotations, and is grateful to Dr. W. E. K. Anderson, Dr Corson's literary executor, for making Dr Corson's material available.*

Thanks are also due to: Mrs Flora Alexander, Miss Hazel Alexander, Miss Ruth Alexander, many members of the academic, library and secretarial staff of the University of Aberdeen, Dr William Baker, Mr W. R. J. Barron, Professor Geoffrey Barrow, Professor Peter Brand, Professor David Buchan, Dr David Caldwell and Ms Naomi Tarrant (Royal Museum of Scotland), D. H. B. Chesshyre (Chester Herald, College of Arms), Mr Thomas Crawford, Professor D. D. Devlin, Mr Kevin Gallacher, Mr A. P. Gorringe, Professor David Greer, Miss Avril Hart, Mr Theodore Hofmann, Miss Santina M. Levey and colleagues (the Department of Textile Furnishings and Dress, Victoria & Albert Museum), Ms Helen S. Maclean, Dr Murray Pittock, the late Professor Denis Roberts and his colleagues in the National Library of Scotland (especially Dr Robert Donaldson, Mr Patrick Cadell, and Dr Iain G. Brown), Mr William Ruddick, Mr Charles J. Sawyer, Ms Gillean Somerville, Miss Joanna Smith, Miss Margaret A. Tait, Dr Clive Wainwright, Professor Mark Weinstein.

To help editors solve specific problems, the Edinburgh Edition of the Waverley Novels has appointed the following as consultants: Professor David Nordloh, Indiana University (editorial practice); Dr Alan Bruford, University of Edinburgh, (popular beliefs and customs); Dr John Cairns, University of Edinburgh (Scots Law); Professor Thomas Craik, University of Durham (Shakespeare); Mr John Ellis, University of Edinburgh (medieval literature); Dr Caroline Jackson-Houlston, Oxford Polytechnic (popular song); Mr Roy Pinkerton, University of Edinburgh (classical literature); Mrs Mairi Robinson (language); Professor David Stevenson, University of St Andrews (history). Of these the editor of Kenilworth *is particularly grateful for the advice of Dr Bruford, Dr Cairns, Professor Craik, Mr Pinkerton, Mrs Robinson and Professor David Stevenson.*

Thanks are also due to the numerous libraries in the British Isles, North America, and Australasia that have responded to requests for details of their Scott holdings. Particular thanks are due to American Antiquarian Society, Worcester MA; Birkbeck College, London; Bodleian Library, Oxford; Boston Public Library, Boston MA; British Library, London; Cambridge University Library; Edinburgh Public Library; Edinburgh University Library; Karpeles Manuscript Library, Santa Barbara CA; The London Library; London University Library; National Library of Scotland, Edinburgh; New York Public Library; Penfield Library; State University of New York at Oswego NY; Princeton University Library NJ; Selwyn College, Cambridge; University of Stirling Library; Taylor Institution, Oxford; Trinity College, Cambridge; University College, London.

GENERAL INTRODUCTION

The Edinburgh Edition of the Waverley Novels is the first authoritative edition of Walter Scott's fiction. It is the first to return to what Scott actually wrote in his manuscripts and proofs, and the first to reconsider fundamentally the presentation of his novels in print. In the light of comprehensive research, the editors decided in principle that the text of the novels in the new edition should be based on the first editions, but that all those manuscript readings which had been lost through accident, error, or misunderstanding should be restored. As a result each novel in the Edinburgh Edition differs in thousands of ways from the versions we have been accustomed to read, and many hundreds of readings never before printed have been recovered from the manuscripts. The individual differences are often minor, but are cumulatively telling. The return to the original Scott produces fresher, less formal and less pedantic novels than we have known.

Scott was the most famous and prestigious novelist of his age, but he became insolvent in 1826 following the bankruptcy of his publishers, Hurst, Robinson and Co. in London and Archibald Constable and Co. in Edinburgh. In 1827 Robert Cadell, who had succeeded Constable as Scott's principal publisher, proposed the first collected edition of the complete Waverley Novels as one way of reducing the mountain of debt for which Scott was legally liable. Scott agreed to the suggestion and over the next few years revised the text of his novels and wrote introductions and notes. The edition was published in 48 monthly volumes from 1829 to 1833. The full story of the making of the Magnum Opus, as it was familiarly christened by Scott, is told in Jane Millgate's *Scott's Last Edition* (Edinburgh, 1987), but for present purposes what is significant is that the Magnum became the standard edition of Scott, and since his death in 1832 all editions of the Waverley Novels, with the single exception of Claire Lamont's *Waverley* (Oxford, 1981), have been based on it.

Because Scott prepared the Magnum Opus it has long been felt that it represented his final wishes and intentions. In a literal sense this must be so, but all readers who open the pages of any edition published since 1832 and are confronted with the daunting clutter of introductions, prefaces, notes, and appendices, containing a miscellaneous assemblage of historical illustration and personal anecdote, must feel that the creative power which took Britain, Europe and America by storm in the preceding decades is cabin'd, cribb'd, confin'd by its Magnum context. Just as the new matter of 1829–33 is not integral to the novels as they were originally conceived, neither are the revisions and additions to the text.

'Scholarly editors may disagree about many things, but they are in general agreement that their goal is to discover exactly what an author wrote and to determine what form of his work he wished the public to have.' Thus Thomas Tanselle in 1976 succinctly and memorably defined the business of textual editing. The editors of the Edinburgh Edition have made this goal their own, and have returned to the original manuscripts, to the surviving proofs, and to other textually relevant material to determine exactly what Scott wrote; they have also investigated each British edition and every relevant foreign edition published in Scott's lifetime. They have discovered that ever since they were written, the Waverley Novels have suffered from textual degeneration.

The first editions were derived from copies of Scott's manuscripts, but the pressure to publish quickly was such that they are not wholly reliable representations of what he wrote. Without exception, later editions were based on a preceding printed version, and so include most of the mistakes of their predecessors while adding their own, and in most cases Scott was not involved. There was an accumulation of error, and when Scott came to prepare the Magnum Opus he revised and corrected an earlier printed text, apparently unaware of the extent to which it was already corrupt. Thus generations of readers have read versions of Scott which have suffered significantly from the changes, both deliberate and accidental, of editors, compositors and proof-readers.

A return to authentic Scott is therefore essential. The manuscripts provide the only fully authoritative state of the texts of the novels, for they alone proceed wholly from the author. They are for the most part remarkably coherent; the shape of Scott's narratives seems to have been established before he committed his ideas to paper, although a close examination of what he wrote shows countless minor revisions made in the process of writing, and usually at least one layer of later revising. We are closest to Scott in the manuscripts, but they could not be the sole textual basis for the new edition. They give us his own words, free of non-authorial interventions, but they do not constitute the 'form of his work he wished the public to have'.

Scott expected his novels to be printed, usually in three volumes, and he structured his stories so that they fitted the three-volume division of the printed books. He expected minor errors to be corrected, words repeated in close proximity to each other to be removed, spelling to be normalised, and a printed-book style of punctuation, amplifying and replacing the marks he had provided in manuscript, to be inserted. There are no written instructions to the printers to this effect, but his acceptance of what was done implies approval, even although the imposition of the conventions of print had such a profound effect on the evolution of his text that the conversion of autograph text into print was less a question of transliteration than of translation.

This assumption of authorial approval is better founded for Scott than for any other writer. Walter Scott was in partnership with James Ballantyne in a firm of printers which Ballantyne managed and for which Scott generated much of the work. The contracts for new Scott novels were unusual, in that they always stipulated that the printing would be undertaken by James Ballantyne and Co., and that the publishers should have the exclusive right only to purchase and to manage the sales of an agreed number of copies. Thus production was controlled not by the publishers but by James Ballantyne and his partner, Walter Scott. The textually significant consequence of this partnership was a mutual trust to a degree uncommon between author and printer. Ballantyne was most anxious to serve Scott and to assist him in preparing the novels for public presentation, and Scott not only permitted this but actively sought it. Theirs was a unique business and literary partnership which had a crucial effect on the public form of the Waverley Novels.

Scott expected his novels to appear in the form and format in which they did appear, but in practice what was done was not wholly satisfactory because of the complicated way in which the texts were processed. Until 1827, when Scott acknowledged his authorship, the novels were published anonymously and so that Scott's well-known handwriting should not be seen in the printing works the original manuscripts were copied, and it was these copies, not Scott's original manuscripts, which were used in the printing house. Not a single leaf is known to survive but the copyists probably began the tidying and regularising. The compositors worked from the copies, and, when typesetting, did not just follow what was before them, but supplied punctuation, normalised spelling, and corrected minor errors. Proofs were first read in-house against the transcripts, and in addition to the normal checking for mistakes these proofs were used to improve the punctuation and the spelling.

When the initial corrections had been made, a new set of proofs went to James Ballantyne. He acted as editor, not just as proof-reader. He drew Scott's attention to gaps in the text and pointed out inconsistencies in detail; he asked Scott to standardise names; he substituted nouns for pronouns when they occurred in the first sentence of a paragraph, and inserted the names of speakers in dialogue; he changed incorrect punctuation, and added punctuation he thought desirable; he corrected grammatical errors and removed close verbal repetitions; he told Scott when he could not follow what was happening; and when he particularly enjoyed something he said so.

These annotated proofs were sent to the author, who sometimes accepted Ballantyne's suggestions and sometimes rejected them. He made many more changes; he cut out redundant words, and substituted the vivid for the pedestrian; he refined the punctuation; he sometimes reworked and revised passages extensively, and in so doing made the proofs a stage in the composition of the novels.

When Ballantyne received Scott's corrections and revisions, he transcribed all the changes on to a clean set of proofs so that the author's hand would not be seen by the compositors. Further revises were prepared. Some of these were seen and read by Scott but by and large he seems to have trusted Ballantyne to make sure that the earlier corrections and revisions had been correctly executed. When doing this Ballantyne did not just read for typesetting errors, but continued the process of punctuating and tidying the text. A final proof allowed the corrections to be inspected and the imposition of the type to be checked prior to printing.

One might imagine that after all this activity the first editions would be perfect, but this is far from being the case. There are usually in excess of 50,000 variants in the first edition of a three-volume novel when compared with the manuscript. The great majority are in accordance with Scott's general wishes as described above. But the intermediaries, as the copyist, compositors, proof-readers, and James Ballantyne are collectively known, made mistakes; they misread the manuscripts from time to time, and they did not always understand what Scott had written. This would not have mattered had there not also been procedural failures. The transcripts were not thoroughly checked against the original manuscripts. Scott himself does not seem to have read the proofs against the manuscripts and thus did not notice transcription errors which made sense in their context. And James Ballantyne continued his editing in post-authorial proofs; his changes may have been in the spirit of Scott's own critical proof-reading, but it is probable that his efforts were never inspected by the author.

The editors of the Edinburgh Edition of the Waverley Novels have studied every single variant in the first editions of all the novels they have worked on to date. There are a large number of small verbal differences, and the editors have come to the conclusion that the words originally written by Scott, though subsequently changed by the intermediaries, are nearly always justified by colloquial, dialect, or period usage. Similarly the punctuation supplied at times misinterprets the sense of the manuscript or the rhythm of speech, and the substitution of synonyms for repeated words was often effected too mechanically, changing meaning or spoiling rhetoric. It is not surprising that the intermediaries should make mistakes when translating the manuscripts into print. Even James Ballantyne's knowledge of language and history was limited compared to Scott's. He was a trusted and competent editor; he was honest about his likes and dislikes and was useful to Scott in giving voice to them. But his annotations and suggestions show that he did not appreciate the full variety of Scott's language, objected to any suggestion of the indelicate, and tidied the text by rule. Above all, his comments were made as Scott wrote, and without knowing the outcome of the story, and thus he was inevitably unaware of the architectonics of the complete work of art. His views were sometimes wrong, and Scott was sometimes wrong to give way to them.

The editors have normally chosen the first edition of a novel as base-text, for the first edition usually represents the culmination of the initial creative process, and, local failings excepted, usually seems closest to the form of his work he wished his public to have. After the careful collation of all pre-publication materials, and in the light of their invest-igation into the factors governing the writing and printing of the Waver-ley Novels, they have incorporated into the base-text readings which were lost in the production process through accident, error or mis-understanding. In certain cases they have also introduced into the base-texts revisions from printed texts which they believe to have emanated from Scott, or are consistent with the spirit of his own revision during the initial creative process. Only revisions which belong to the process and period of initial creation have been adopted. In addition, they have corrected various kinds of error, such as typographical and copy-editing mistakes including the misnumbering of chapters, inconsistencies in the naming of characters, egregious errors of fact that are not part of the fiction, and failures of sense which a simple emendation can restore. The result is an ideal text, which the first readers of the Waverley Novels would have read had the production process been less pressurised and more considered.

The 'new' Scott will be visible not only in the text but also in the context. The Magnum introductions and notes are not integral to the novels as they were originally conceived, and are therefore reserved for separate publication in the final volumes of the edition where they will be treated as a distinct, final phase of Scott's involvement in his fiction. Thus the novels appear as they were first presented. The Edinburgh Edition of the Waverley Novels offers a clean text; there are no foot-notes or superscripts to detract from the pleasure of reading. It does not remove Scott's own introductions only to replace them with those of modern editors; the textual essays appear at the end, where they will be encountered only after reading Scott. The essays present a detailed history of the genesis and composition of the novel, a history of the evolution of the old text, and a description of the distinguishing features of the new. The textual apparatus does not include a full list of variants because for one of the major early works there would be at least 100,000 to record. Instead, the textual essays analyse and illustrate the evidence gleaned from the collation of the manuscripts and proofs (where these are extant) and of all relevant editions published in Scott's lifetime. All variants from the base-text are listed in the emendation list (but as variants from the Magnum are not, the scale of the change from old editions to the new is not immediately apparent).

And finally, there are explanatory notes and a glossary. Scott's read-ing was wide and voluminous, he was immensely knowledgeable in a range of disciplines, and he had a considerable understanding of the social organisation, customs and beliefs of contemporary and historical societies. Few readers are likely to appreciate the full extent of his learning without some assistance, and the notes at the end of this volume draw on a greater variety of expertise, and are more comprehensive, than any previously published. They are informative rather than expository; for instance, they identify all quotations, from the most obvious passages in the Bible and Shakespeare through to the truly recondite, but they leave the reader to consider their significance in each context. And the glossary for the first time attempts to cover comprehensively all Scott's period, dialectal, foreign, and obscure words.

The Edinburgh Edition of the Waverley Novels aims to provide an authoritative text of Scott's fiction, to give the reader the support required to appreciate the intellectual richness of his work, and to allow a new audience to share the excitement that the novels generated when they were first published. The editors are confident of fulfilling the first two aims. The reader must be judge of their success in the third.

DAVID HEWITT

KENILWORTH

VOLUME I

Chapter One

I am an inn-keeper, and know my grounds,
And study them; Brain o' man, I study them.
I must have jovial guests to drive my ploughs,
And whistling boys to bring my harvests home,
Or I shall hear no flails thwack.
The New Inn

IT IS THE PRIVILEGE of tale-tellers to open their story in an inn, the free rendezvous of all travellers, and where the humour of each displays itself, without ceremony or restraint. This is specially suitable when the scene is laid during the old days of merry England, when the guests were in some sort not merely the inmates, but the messmates and temporary companions of mine Host, who was usually a personage of privileged freedom, comely presence, and good humour. Patronized by him, the characters of the company were placed in ready contrast; and they seldom failed, during the emptying of a six-hooped pot, to throw off reserve, and present themselves to each other, and to their landlord, with the freedom of old acquaintance.

The village of Cumnor, within three or four miles of Oxford, boasted, during the eighteenth of Queen Elizabeth, an excellent inn of the old stamp, conducted, or rather ruled, by Giles Gosling, a man of a goodly person, and of somewhat a round belly, fifty years of age and upwards, moderate in his reckonings, prompt in his payments, having a cellar of sound liquor, a ready wit, and a pretty daughter. Since the days of old Harry Baillie of the Tabard in Southwark, no one had excelled Giles Gosling in the power of pleasing his guests of every description; and so great was his fame, that to have been in Cumnor, without wetting a cup at the Bonny Black Bear, would have been to avouch one's-self utterly indifferent to reputation as a traveller. A country fellow might as well return from London, without looking in the face of majesty. The men of Cumnor were proud of their Host, and their Host was proud of his house, his liquor, his daughter and himself.

It was in the court-yard of the inn which called this honest fellow landlord, that a traveller alighted in the close of the evening, gave his horse, which seemed to have made a long journey, to the hostler, and made some inquiry, which produced the following dialogue betwixt the myrmidons of the Bonny Black Bear.

"What, ho! John Tapster."

"At hand, Will Hostler," replied the man of the spiggot, shewing himself in his costume of loose jacket, linen breeches, and green apron, half within and half without a door, which appeared to descend to an outer cellar.

"Here is a gentleman asks if you draw good ale," continued the hostler.

"Beshrew my heart else," answered the tapster, "since there are but four miles betwixt us and Oxford.—Marry, if my ale did not convince the heads of the scholars, they would soon convince my pate with the pewter flagon."

"Call you that Oxford logic," said the stranger, who had now quitted the rein of his horse, and was advancing towards the inn-door, when he was encountered by the goodly form of Giles Gosling himself.

"Is it logic you talk of, Sir Guest?" said the Host; "why, then, have at you with a downright consequence—

> The horse to the rack,
> And to fire with the sack."

"Amen! with all my heart, my good host," said the stranger; "let it be a quart of your best Canaries, and give me your good help to drink it."

"Nay, you are but in your accidents yet, Sir Traveller, if you call on your host for help for such a sipping matter as a quart of sack—were it a gallon, you might lack some neighbourly aid at my hand, and yet call yourself a toper."

"Fear me not," said the guest, "I will do my devoir as becomes a man who finds himself within five miles of Oxford; for I am not come from the fields of Mars to discredit myself amongst the followers of Minerva."

As he spoke thus, the landlord, with much semblance of hearty welcome, ushered his guest into a large low chamber, where several persons were seated together in different parties; some drinking, some playing at cards, some conversing, and some, whose business called them to be early risers on the morrow, concluding their evening meal, and conferring with the chamberlain about their night's quarters.

The entrance of a stranger procured him that general and careless sort of attention which is usually paid on such occasions, from which the following results were deduced:—The guest was one of those who, with a well-made person, and features not in themselves unpleasing, are nevertheless so far from handsome, that, whether from the expression of their features, or the tone of their voice, or from their gait and manner, there arises, on the whole, a disinclination to their society. The stranger's address was bold, without being frank, and seemed eagerly and hastily to claim for him a degree of attention and deference, which he feared would be refused, if not instantly vindicated as his right. His attire was a riding-cloak, which, when open, displayed a handsome jerkin, overlaid with lace, and belted with a buff girdle, which sustained a broadsword and a pair of pistols.

"You ride well provided, sir," said the host, looking at the weapons as he placed on the table the mulled sack which the traveller had ordered.

"Yes, mine host; I have found the use on't in dangerous times, and I do not, like your modern grandees, turn off my followers the instant they are useless."

"Ay, sir?" said Giles Gosling; "then you are from the Low Countries, the land of pike and caliver?"

"I have been high and low, my friend, broad and wide, far and near; but here is to thee in a cup of thy sack—fill thyself another to pledge me; and, if it is less than superlative, e'en drink as you have brewed."

"Less than superlative?" said Giles Gosling, drinking off the cup, and smacking his lips with an air of ineffable relish,—"I know nothing of superlative, nor is there such a wine at the Three Cranes, in the Vintry, to my knowledge; but if you find better sack than that in Sheres, or in the Canaries either, I would I may never touch either pot or penny more. Why, hold it up betwixt you and the light, you shall see the little motes dance in the golden liquor like dust in the sunbeam. But I would rather draw wine for ten clowns than one traveller.—I trust your honour likes the wine?"

"It is neat and comfortable, mine host; but to know good liquor, you should drink where the vine grows. Trust me, your Spaniard is too wise a man to send you the very soul of the grape. Why, this now, which you account so choice, were counted but as a cup of bastard at the Groyne, or at Port St Mary's. You should travel, mine host, if you would be deep in the mysteries of the butt and pottle-pot."

"In troth, Signior Guest," said Giles Gosling, "if I were to travel only that I might be discontented with that which I can get at home, methinks I should go but on a fool's errand. Besides, I warrant you, there is many a fool can turn his nose up at good drink without ever having been out of the smoke of Old England; and so ever gramercy mine own fire-side."

"This is but a mean mind of yours, mine host," said the stranger; "I warrant me, all your town's-folks do not think so basely. You have gallants among you, I dare undertake, that have made the Virginia voyage, or taken a turn in the Low Countries at least. Come, cudgel your memory. Have you no friends in foreign parts that you would gladly have tidings of?"

"Troth, sir, not I," answered the host, "since ranting Robin of Drysandford was shot at the siege of the Brill. The devil take the caliver that fired the ball, for a blither lad never filled cup at midnight. But he is dead and gone, and I know not a soldier, or a traveller who is a soldier's mate, that I would give a peeled codling for."

"By the mass, that is strange. What, so many of our brave English hearts are abroad, and you, who seem to be a man of mark, have no friend, no kinsman, among them?"

"Nay, if you speak of kinsmen," answered Gosling, "I have one wild slip of a kinsman, who left us in the last year of Queen Mary, but he is better lost than found."

"Do not say so, friend, unless you have heard ill of him lately. Many a wild colt has turned out a noble steed.—His name, I pray you?"

"Michael Lambourne," answered the landlord of the Black Bear; "a son of my sister's—there is little pleasure in recollecting either the name or the connection."

"Michael Lambourne!" said the stranger, as if endeavouring to recollect himself—"What, no relation to Michael Lambourne, the gallant cavalier who behaved so bravely at the siege of Venlo, that Grave Maurice thanked him at the head of the army? Men said he was an English cavalier, and of no high extraction."

"It could scarce be my nephew," said Giles Gosling, "for he had scarce the courage of a hen-partridge for aught but mischief."

"O, many a man finds courage in the wars," replied the stranger.

"It may be," said the landlord; "but I would have thought our Mike more likely to lose the little he had."

"The Michael Lambourne whom I knew," continued the traveller, "was a likely fellow—went always gay and well attired, and had a hawk's eye after a pretty wench."

"Our Michael," replied the host, "had the look of a dog with a bottle at its tail, and wore a coat every rag of which was bidding good-day to the rest."

"O, men pick up good apparel in the wars," replied the guest.

"Our Mike," answered the landlord, "was more like to pick it up in a frippery warehouse, while the broker was looking another way; and, for the hawk's eye you talk of, his was always after my stray spoons. He was tapster's boy here in this blessed house for a quarter of a year; and between misreckonings, miscarriages, mistakes, and misdemeanours, had he dwelt with me for three months longer, I might have pulled down sign, shut up house, and given the devil the key to keep."

"You would be sorry, after all," continued the traveller, "were I to tell you poor Mike Lambourne was shot at the head of his regiment at the taking in of a sconce near Maestricht."

"Sorry!—it would be the blithest news I ever heard of him, since it would ensure me he was not hanged. But let him pass—I doubt his end will never do such credit to his friends; were it so, I should say—(taking another cup of sack)—Here's God rest him, with all my heart."

"Tush, man," replied the traveller, "never fear but you will have credit by your nephew yet, especially if he be the Michael Lambourne whom I knew, and loved very nearly, or altogether, as well as myself. Can you tell me no mark by which I could judge whether they be the same?"

"Faith, none that I can think of," answered Giles Gosling, "unless that our Mike had the gallows branded on his left shoulder for stealing a silver caudle-cup from Dame Snort of Hogsditch."

"Nay, there you lie like a knave, uncle," said the stranger, slipping aside his ruff, and turning down the sleeve of his doublet from his neck and shoulder; "by this good day, my shoulder is as unscarred as thine own."

"What, Mike, boy—Mike!" exclaimed the host, "and is it thou, in good earnest?—nay, I have judged so for this half hour; for I knew no other person would have ta'en half the interest in thee. But, Mike, an thy shoulder be unscathed as thou sayest, thou must own that Goodman Thong, the hangman, was merciful in his office, and stamped thee with a cold iron."

"Tush, uncle—truce with your jests—keep them to season your sour ale, and let us see what hearty welcome thou wilt give a kinsman who has rolled the world around for eighteen years; who has seen the sun set where it rises, and travelled till the west has become the east."

"Thou hast brought back one traveller's gift with thee, Mike, as I well see, and that was what thou least didst need, for I remember well, among thine other qualities, there was no believing a word which came from thy mouth."

"Here's an unbelieving Pagan for you, gentlemen!" said Michael

Lambourne, turning to those who witnessed this strange interview betwixt uncle and nephew, some of whom, being natives of the village, were no strangers to his juvenile wildness. "This may be called slaying a Cumnor fatted calf for me with a vengeance—but, uncle, I come not from the husks and the swine-trough, and I care not for thy welcome or no welcome; I carry that with me will make me welcome, wend where I will."

So saying, he pulled out a purse of gold, indifferently well filled, the sight of which produced a visible effect upon the company. Some shook their heads, and whispered to each other, while one or two of the less scrupulous speedily began to recollect him as a school-companion, a townsman, or so forth. On the other hand, two or three grave sedate-looking persons shook their head, and left the inn, hinting, that, if Giles Gosling wished to continue to thrive, he should turn his thriftless godless nephew adrift again, as soon as he could. Gosling demeaned himself as if he were much of the same opinion; for even the sight of the gold made less impression on the honest gentleman, than it usually doth upon one of his calling.

"Kinsman Michael," he said, "put up thy purse. My sister's son shall be called to no reckoning in my house for supper or lodging; and I reckon thou wilt hardly wish to stay longer, where thou art e'en but too well known."

"For that matter, uncle," replied the traveller, "I shall consult my own needs and conveniences. Meantime I wish to give the supper and sleeping cup to those good townsmen, who are not too proud to remember Mike Lambourne, the tapster's boy. If you will let me have entertainment for my money, so—if not, it is but a short two minutes walk to the Hare and Tabor, and I trust our neighbours will not grudge going thus far with me."

"Nay, Mike," replied his uncle, "as eighteen years have gone over thy head, and I trust thou art somewhat amended in thy conditions, thou shalt not leave my house at this hour, and shalt e'en have whatever in reason you list to call for. But I would I knew that that purse of thine, which thou vapourest of, were as well come by as it seems well filled."

"Here is an infidel for you, my good neighbours," said Lambourne, again appealing to the audience. "Here's a fellow will rip up his kinsman's follies of a good score of years standing—And for the gold, why, sirs, I have been where it grew, and was to be had for the gathering. In the New World have I been, man—in the Eldorado, where urchins play at cherry-pit with diamonds, and country-wenches thread rubies for necklaces, instead of rowan-tree berries; where the pan-tiles are made of pure gold, and the paving-stones of virgin-silver."

"By my credit, friend Mike," said young Laurence Goldthread, the cutting mercer of Abingdon, "that were a likely coast to trade to. And what may lawns, cypresses, and ribands fetch, where gold is so plenty?"

"O, the profit were unutterable," replied Lambourne, "especially when a handsome young merchant bears the pack himself; for the ladies of that clime are bona-robas, and being themselves somewhat sun-burnt, they will catch fire like tinder at a fresh complexion like thine, with a head of hair inclining to be red."

"I would I might trade thither," said the mercer, chuckling.

"Why, and so thou mayest," said Michael; "that is, if thou art the same brisk boy, who was partner with me at robbing the Abbot's orchard—'tis but a little touch of alchemy to decoct thy house and land into ready money, and that ready money into a tall ship, with sails, anchors, cordage, and all things conforming; then clap thy warehouse of goods under hatches, put fifty good fellows on deck, with myself to command them, and so hoise top-sails, and hey for the New World."

"Thou hast taught him a secret, kinsman," said Giles Gosling, "to decoct, an' that be the word, his pound into a penny, and his webs into a thread.—Take a fool's advice, neighbour Goldthread—tempt not the sea, for she is a devourer. Let cards and cockatrices do their worst, thy father's bales may bide a banging for a year or two, ere thou comest to the Spittal; but the sea hath a bottomless appetite, she would swallow the wealth of Lombard Street in a morning, as easily as I would a poached egg and a cup of clary—and for my kinsman's Eldorado, never trust me if I do not believe he has found it in the pouches of some such gull as thyself.—But take no snuff in the nose about it; fall to and welcome, for here comes the supper, and I heartily bestow it on all that will take share, in honour of my hopeful nephew's return, always trusting that he has come home another man.—In faith, kinsman, thou art as like my poor sister as ever was son to mother."

"Not quite so like old Benedict Lambourne her husband, though," said the mercer, nodding and winking. "Doest thou remember, Mike, what thou saidst when the ferule was over thee for striking up thy father's crutches?—it is a wise child, saidst thou, that knows its own father. Dr Bricham laughed till he cried again, and his crying saved yours."

"Well, he made it up to me many a day after," said Lambourne; "and how is the worthy pedagogue?"

"Dead," said Giles Gosling, "this many a day since."

"That he is," said the clerk of the parish; "I sat by his bed the whilst —He passed away in a blessed frame, '*Morior—mortuus sum vel fui—*

mori'—these were his latest words, and he just added, 'My last verb is conjugated.'"

"Well, peace be with him," said Mike, "he owes me nothing."

"No, truly," replied Goldthread; "and every lash which he laid on he always was wont to say spared the hangman a labour."

"One would have thought he left him little to do then," said the clerk. "And yet Goodman Thong had no sinecure of it with our friend, after all."

"*Voto a dios!*" exclaimed Lambourne, his patience appearing to fail him, as he snatched his broad slouched hat from the table and placed it on his head, so that the shadow gave the sinister expression of a Spanish bravo, to eyes and features which naturally boded nothing pleasant. "Harkee, my masters—All is fair among friends, and under the rose; and I have already permitted my worthy uncle here, and all of you, to use your pleasure with the frolics of my nonage. But I carry sword and dagger, my good friends, and can use them lightly too upon occasion—I have learned to be dangerous upon point of honour ever since I served the Spaniard, and I would not have you provoke me to the degree of falling foul."

"Why, what would you do?" said the clerk.

"Ay, sir, what would you do?" said the mercer, bustling up on the other side of the table.

"Slit your throat, and spoil your Sunday's quavering, Sir Clerk," said Lambourne, fiercely; "Cudgel you, my worshipful dealer in flimsy sarsenets, into one of your own bales."

"Come, come," said the host, interposing, "I will have no swaggering here.—Nephew, it will become you best to shew no haste to take offence; and you, gentlemen, will do well to remember, that if you are in an inn, still you are the innkeeper's guests, and should spare the honour of his family.—I protest your silly broils make me as oblivious as yourself; for yonder sits my silent guest as I call him, who hath been my two days inmate, and hath never spoken a word, save to ask for his food and his reckoning—gives no more trouble than a very peasant—pays his shot like a prince royal—looks but at the sum total of the reckoning, and does not know what day he shall go away. O, 'tis a jewel of a guest! And yet, hang-dog that I am, I have suffered him to sit by himself like a castaway in yonder obscure nook, without so much as asking him to take bite or sup alongst with us. It were but the right guerdon of my incivility, were he to set off to the Hare and Tabor before the night grows older."

With his white napkin gracefully arranged over his left arm, his velvet cap laid aside for the moment, and his best silver flagon in his right hand, mine host walked up to the solitary guest whom he mentioned, and thereby turned upon him the eyes of the assembled company.

He was a man aged betwixt twenty-five and thirty, rather above the middle size, dressed with plainness and decency, yet bearing an air of ease, which almost amounted to dignity, and seemed to infer that his habit was rather beneath his rank. His countenance was reserved and thoughtful, with dark hair and dark eyes—the last, upon any momentary excitement, sparkled with uncommon lustre, but on other occasions had the same meditative and tranquil cast which was exhibited by his features. The busy curiosity of the little village had been employed to discover his name and quality, as well as his business at Cumnor; but nothing had transpired on either subject which could lead to its gratification. Giles Gosling, headborough of the place, and a steady friend to Queen Elizabeth and the Protestant religion, was at one time inclined to suspect his guest of being a Jesuit, or seminary priest, of whom Rome and Spain sent at this time so many to grace the gallows in England. But it was scarce possible to retain such a prepossession against a guest who gave so little trouble, paid his reckoning so regularly, and who proposed, as it seemed, to make a considerable stay in the Bonny Black Bear.

"Papists," argued Giles Gosling, "are a pinching, close-fisted race, and this man would have found a lodging with the wealthy squire at Bessellsley, or with the old knight at Wootton, or in some other of their Roman dens, instead of living in a house of public entertainment, as every honest man and good Christian should. Besides, on Friday, he stuck by the powdered beef and carrot, though there were as good spitchcock'd eels on the board as ere were ta'en out of the Isis."

Honest Giles, therefore, satisfied himself that his guest was no Roman, and with all comely courtesy besought the stranger to pledge him in a draught of the cool tankard, and honour with his attention a small collation which he was giving to his nephew, in honour of his return, and, as he verily hoped, of his reformation. The stranger at first shook his head, as if declining the courtesy; but mine host proceeded to urge him with arguments founded on the credit of his house, and the construction which the good people of Cumnor might put upon such an unsocial humour.

"By my faith, sir," he said, "it touches my reputation that men should be merry in my house, and we have ill tongues amongst us at Cumnor, (as where be there not?) who put an evil mark on men who pull their hat over their brows as if they were looking back to the days that are gone, instead of enjoying the blithe sunshiny weather which God has sent us in the rarest looks of our sovereign mistress, Queen Elizabeth, whom Heaven long bless and preserve."

"Why, mine host," answered the stranger, "there is no treason, sure, in a man enjoying his own thoughts, under the shadow of his own bonnet. You have lived in the world twice as long as I have, and you must know there are thoughts that will haunt us in spite of ourselves, and to which it is in vain to say, begone, and let me be merry."

"By my sooth," answered Giles Gosling, "if such troublesome guests haunt your mind, and will not get them gone for plain English, we will have one of Father Bacon's pupils from Oxford, to conjure them away with logic and with Hebrew—Or, what say you to laying them in a glorious red sea of claret, my noble guest? Come, sir, excuse my freedom. I am an old host, and must have my talk. This peevish humour of melancholy sits ill upon you—it suits not with a sleek boot, a hat of a trim block, a fresh cloak, and a full purse—A pize on it, send it off to those who have their legs swathed with a hay-wisp, their heads thatched with a felt bonnet, their jerkin as thin as a cobweb, and their pouch without ever a cross to keep the fiend Melancholy from dancing in it. Cheer up, sir! or by this good liquor we will banish thee from the joys of blithesome company, into the mists of melancholy and the land of little-ease. Here be a set of good fellows willing to be merry; do not you scowl on them like the Devil looking over Lincoln."

"You say well, my worthy host," said the guest, with a melancholy smile, which, melancholy as it was, gave a very pleasant expression to his countenance—"You say well, my jovial friend; and they that are moody like myself, should not disturb the mirth of those who are happy—I will drink a round with your guests with all my heart, rather than be termed a mar-feast."

So saying, he arose and joined the company, which, encouraged by the precept and example of Michael Lambourne, and consisting chiefly of persons much disposed to profit by the opportunity of a merry meal at the expense of their landlord, had already made some inroads upon the limits of temperance; as was evident from the tone in which Michael inquired after his old acquaintances in the town, and the bursts of laughter with which each answer was received. Giles Gosling himself was somewhat scandalized at the obstreperous nature of their mirth, especially as he involuntarily felt some respect for his unknown guest. He paused, therefore, at some distance from the table occupied by these noisy revellers, and began to make a sort of apology for their license.

"You would think," he said, "to hear these fellows talk, that there was not one of them who had not been bred to live by Stand and Deliver; and yet to-morrow you will find them a set of as pains-taking mechanics and so forth, as ever cut an inch short of measure, or paid a letter of change in light crowns over a counter. The mercer there wears his hat awry, over a shagged head of hair that looks like a curly water-dog's back, goes unbraced, wears his cloak on one side, and affects a ruffianly vapouring humour,—when in his shop at Abingdon, he is, from his flat cap to his glistening shoes, as precise in his apparel as if he was named for mayor. He talks of breaking parks, and taking the high-way, in such fashion that you would think he haunted every night betwixt Hounslow and London; when indeed he may be found sound asleep in his feather-bed, with a candle placed beside him on one side, and a Bible on the other, to fright away the goblins."

"And your nephew, mine host, this same Michael Lambourne, who is lord of the feast? is he, too, such an would-be ruffler as the rest of them?"

"Why there you push me hard," said the host; "my nephew is my nephew, and though he was a desperate Dick of yore, yet Mike may have mended like other folks, you wot—And I would not have you think all I said of him, even now, was strict gospel—I knew the wag all the while, and wished to pluck his plumes from him—And now, sir, by what name shall I present my worshipful guest to these gallants?"

"Marry, mine host," replied the stranger, "you may call me Tressilian."

"Tressilian?" answered my host of the Bear, "a worthy name; and, as I think, of Cornish lineage; for what says the sooth proverb—

> By Pol, Tre, and Pen,
> You may know the Cornish men.

Shall I say the worthy Mr Tressilian of Cornwall?"

"Say no more than I have given you warrant for, mine host, and so shall you be sure you speak no more than is true. A man may have one of these honourable prefixes to his name, yet be born far from Saint Michael's Mount."

Mine host pushed his curiosity no further, but presented Mr Tressilian to his nephew's company, who, after exchange of salutations, and drinking to the health of their new companion, pursued the conversation in which he found them engaged, seasoning it with many an intervening pledge.

Chapter Two

Talk you of young Master Lancelot?
Merchant of Venice

AFTER some brief interval, Master Goldthread, at the earnest instigation of mine host, and the joyous concurrence of his guests, indulged the company with the following morsel of melody:

> Of all the birds in bush or tree,
>   Commend me to the owl,
> Since he may best ensample be
>   To those the cup that trowl.
>   For when the sun hath left the west,
>   He chuses the tree that he loves the best,
>   And he whoops out his song, and he laughs at his jest;
>   Then though hours be late, and weather foul,
>   We'll drink to the health of the bonny, bonny owl.
>
> The lark is but a bumpkin fowl,
>   He sleeps in his nest till morn;
> But my blessing upon the jolly owl,
>   That all night blows his horn.
>   Then up with your cup till you stagger in speech,
>   And match me this catch, though you swagger and screech,
>   And drink till you wink, my merry men each;
>   For though hours be late, and weather be foul,
>   We'll drink to the health of the bonny, bonny owl.

"There is savour in this, my hearts," said Michael, when the mercer had finished his song, "and some goodness seems left among you yet —But what a beadroll you have read me of old comrades, and to every man's name tacked some ill-omened motto! And so Swashing Will of Wallingford hath bid us good night?"

"He died the death of a fat buck," said one of the party, "being shot with a cross-bow bolt, by old Thatcham, the Duke's stout park-keeper at Donnington Castle."

"Ay, he always loved venison well," replied Michael, "and a cup of claret to it to boot—and so here's to his memory. Do me right, my masters."

When the health of this departed worthy had been duly honoured, Lambourne proceeded to enquire after Prance of Padworth.

"Pranced off—made immortal ten years since," said the mercer; "marry, sir, Oxford Castle and Goodman Thong, and a tenpenny-worth of cord, best know how."

"What, so they hung poor Prance high and dry? so much for loving to walk by moonlight—a cup to his memory my masters—All merry fellows like moonlight. What has become of Hal with the plume?—he who lived near Yattenden, and wore the long feather—I forget his name."

"What, Hal Hempseed?" replied the mercer, "why, you may remember he was a sort of a gentleman, and would meddle in state matters, and so he got into the mire about the Duke of Norfolk's matter these two or three years since, fled the country with a pursuivant's warrant at his heels, and has never since been heard of."

"Nay, after these baulks," said Michael Lambourne, "I need hardly enquire after Tony Forster; for when ropes and cross-bow shafts, and pursuivant's warrants, and such like gear were so rife, Tony could hardly 'scape them."

"Which Tony Forster mean you?" said the inn-keeper.

"Why, he they call Tony Fire-the-Faggot, because he brought a light to kindle the faggots round Latimer and Ridley, when the wind blew out Jack Thong's torch, and no man else would give him light for love or money."

"Tony Forster lives and thrives," said the host, "but, kinsman, I would not have you call him Tony Fire-the-Faggot, if you would not brook the stab."

"How! is he grown ashamed on't?" said Lambourne; "why, he was wont to boast of it, and say he liked as well to see a roasted heretic, as a roasted ox."

"Ay, but, kinsman, that was in Mary's time," replied the landlord, "when Tony's father was Reeve here to the Abbot of Abingdon. But since that, Tony married a pure precisian, and is as good a Protestant, I warrant you, as the best."

"And looks grave, and holds his head high, and scorns his old companions," said the mercer.

"Then he hath prospered, I warrant him," said Lambourne; "for ever when a man hath got nobles of his own, he keeps out of the way of those whose exchequers lie in other men's purpose."

"Prospered, quotha!" said the mercer, "why, you remember Cumnor-Place, the old mansion-house beside the church-yard?"

"By the same token, I robbed the orchard three times—what of that?—it was the old Abbot's residence when there was plague or sickness at Abingdon."

"Ay," said the host, "but that has been long over; and Anthony Forster hath a right in it, and lives there by some grant from a great courtier, who had the church-lands from the crown; and there he dwells, and has as little to do with any poor wight in Cumnor, as if he were himself a belted knight."

"Nay," said the mercer, "it is not altogether pride in Tony neither —there is a fair lady in the case, and Tony will scarce let the light of day look on her."

"How," said Tressilian, who now for the first time interfered in their conversation, "did ye not say this Forster was married, and to a precisian?"

"Married he was, and to as bitter a precisian as ever eat flesh in Lent; and a cat-and-dog life she led with Tony, as men said. But she is dead, rest be with her, and Tony hath but a slip of a daughter; so it is thought he means to wed this stranger, that folks keep such a coil about."

"And why so?—I mean, why do they keep a coil about her?" said Tressilian.

"Why, I wot not," answered the host, "except that men say she is as beautiful as an angel, and no one knows whence she comes, and every one wishes to know why she is kept so closely mewed up. For my part, I never saw her—You have, I think, Master Goldthread?"

"That I have, old boy," said the mercer. "Look you, I was riding hither from Abingdon—I passed under the east oriel window of the old mansion, where all the old saints and histories and such like are painted—it was not the common path I took, but one through the Park; for the postern-door was upon the latch, and I thought I might take the privilege of an old comrade to ride across through the trees, both for shading, as the day was somewhat hot, and for avoiding of dust, because I had on my peach-coloured doublet, pinked out with cloth of gold."

"Which garment," said Michael Lambourne, "thou would'st willingly make twinkle in the eyes of a fair dame—ah! villain, thou wilt never leave thy old tricks."

"Not so—not so," said the mercer, with a smirking laugh; "not altogether so—but curiosity, thou knowest, and a strain of compassion withal,—for the poor young lady sees nothing from morn to even but Tony Forster, with his scowling black brows, his bull's head, and his bandy legs."

"And thou would'st willingly shew her a dapper body, in a silken jerkin—a limb like a short-legged hen's, in a cordovan boot, and a round, simpering, 'What d'ye lack' sort of countenance, set off with a velvet bonnet, a turkey feather, and a gilded brooch. Ah! jolly mercer, they who have good wares are fond to shew them.—Come, gentles, let not the cup stand—here's to long spurs, short boots, full bonnets, and empty skulls!"

"Nay, now, you are jealous of me, Mike," said Goldthread; "and yet my luck was but what might have happened to thee, or any man."

"Marry confound thine impudence," retorted Lambourne; "thou would'st not compare thy pudding face, and thy sarsenet manners, to a gentleman and a soldier!"

"Nay, nay, good sir," said Tressilian, "let me beseech you will not interrupt the gallant citizen; methinks he tells his tale so well, I could hearken to him till midnight."

"It's more of your favour than of my desert," answered Master Goldthread; "but since I give you pleasure, worthy Master Tressilian, I shall proceed, maugre all the jibes and quips of this valiant soldier, who, peradventure, hath had more cuffs than crowns in the Low Countries.—And so, sir, as I passed under the great painted window, leaving my rein loose on my ambling palfrey's neck, partly for mine ease and partly that I might have the more leisure to peer about, I hears me the lattice open; and never credit me, sir, if there did not stand there the person of as fair a woman as ever crossed mine eyes, and I think I have looked on as many pretty wenches, and with as much judgment, as other folks."

"May I ask her appearance, sir?" said Tressilian.

"O sir," replied Master Goldthread, "I promise you, she was in gentlewoman's attire—a very quaint and pleasing dress, that might have served the Queen herself; for she had a forepart with body and sleeves, of ginger-coloured satin, which, in my judgment, must have cost by the yard some thirty shillings, lined with murrey taffeta, and laid down and guarded with two broad laces of gold and silver. And her hat, sir, was truly the best-fashioned thing that I have seen in these parts, being of tawney taffeta, embroidered with scorpions of Venice gold, and having a border garnished with gold fringe;—I promise you, sir, an absolute and all surpassing device. Touching her skirts, they were in the old pass-devant fashion."

"I did not ask you of her attire, sir," said Tressilian, who had shewn some impatience during this minute description, "but of her complexion—the colour of her hair, her features."

"Touching her complexion," answered the mercer, "I am not so special certain; but I marked that her fan had an ivory handle, curiously inlaid;—and then again, as to the colour of her hair, why, I can warrant, be its hue what it might, that she wore above it a net of green silk, parcel twisted with gold."

"A most mercer-like memory," said Lambourne; "the gentleman asks him of the lady's beauty, and he talks of her fine clothes!"

"I tell thee," said the mercer, somewhat disconcerted, "I had little time to look at her; for just as I was about to give her the good time of day, and for that purpose had puckered my features with a smile"——

"Like those of a jackanape, simpering at a chesnut," said Michael Lambourne.

"—Upstarted of a sudden," continued Goldthread, without heeding the interruption, "Tony Forster himself, with a cudgel in his hand"——

"And broke thy head across, I hope, for thine impertinence," said his entertainer.

"That were more easily said than done," answered Goldthread indignantly; "no, no—there was no breaking of heads—it's true, he advanced his cudgel, and spoke of laying on, and asked why I did not keep the public road, and such like; and I would have knocked him over the pate handsomely for his pains, only for the lady's presence, who might have swooned, for what I know."

"Now, out upon thee for a faint-spirited slave!" said Lambourne. "What adventurous knight ever thought of the lady's terror, when he went to thwack giant, dragon, or magician, in her presence, and for her deliverance? But why talk to thee of dragons, who would be driven back by a dragon-fly. There thou hast missed the fairest opportunity!"

"Take it thyself, then, bully Mike," answered Goldthread.— "Yonder is the enchanted manor, and the dragon and the lady all at thy service, if thou darest venture on them."

"Why, so I would for a quartern of sack," said the soldier—"Or stay —I am foully out of linen—wilt thou bet a piece of Hollands against these five angels, that I go not up to the Hall to-morrow, and force Tony Forster to introduce me to his fair guest?"

"I accept your wager," said the mercer; "and I think, though thou hadst ever the impudence of the devil, I shall gain on thee this bout. Our landlord here shall hold stakes, and I will stake down gold till I send the linen."

"I will hold stakes on no such matter," said Gosling. "Good now, my kinsman, drink your wine in quiet, and let such ventures alone. I promise you, Master Forster hath interest enough to lay you up in lavender in the Castle at Oxford, or to get your legs made acquainted with the town-stocks."

"That would be but renewing an old intimacy; for Mike's shins and the town's wooden pinfold have been well known to each other ere now," said the mercer; "but he shall not budge from his wager, unless he means to pay forfeit."

"Forfeit?" said Lambourne; "I scorn it. I value Tony Forster's wrath no more than a shelled pea-cod, and I will visit his Lindabrides, by Saint George, be he willing or no."

"I would gladly pay your halves of the risk, sir," said Tressilian, "to be permitted to accompany you on the adventure."

"In what would that advantage you, sir?" answered Lambourne.

"In nothing, sir," said Tressilian, "unless to mark the skill and valour with which you conduct yourself. I am a traveller, who seeks for strange rencounters and uncommon passages, as the knights of yore did after adventures and feats of arms."

"Nay, if it pleasures you to see a trout tickled," answered Lambourne, "I care not how many witness my skill. And so here I drink success to my enterprize; and he that will not pledge me on his knees is a rascal, and I will cut his legs off by the garters."

The draught which Michael Lambourne took upon this occasion, had been preceded by so many others, that reason tottered on her throne. He swore one or two incoherent oaths at the mercer, who refused, reasonably enough, to pledge a sentiment, which inferred the loss of his own wager.

"Wilt thou chop logic with me," said Lambourne, "thou knave, with no more brains than are in a skein of ravelled silk? by Heaven, I will cut thee into fifty yards of galloon lace!"

But as he attempted to draw his sword for this doughty purpose, Michael Lambourne was seized upon by the tapster and the chamberlain, and conveyed to his own apartment, there to sleep himself sober at his leisure.

The party then broke up, and the guests took their leave; much more to the contentment of mine host than of some of themselves, who were unwilling to quit good liquor, when it was to be had for free cost, so long as they were able to sit by it. They were, however, compelled to remove; and go at length they did, leaving Gosling and Tressilian in the empty apartment.

"By my faith," said the former, "I wonder where our great folks find pleasure, when they spend their means in entertainments, and in playing mine host without sending in a reckoning. It is what I but rarely practise; and, by Saint Julian, it grieves me beyond measure. Each of these empty stoups now, which my nephew and his drunken comrades have swilled off, should have been a matter of profit to one in my line, and I must set them down a dead loss. I cannot, for my heart, conceive the pleasure of noise, and nonsense, and drunken freaks, and drunken quarrels, and smut, and blasphemy, and so forth, when a man loses money instead of gaining by it. And yet many a fair estate is lost in upholding such an useless course, and that greatly contributes to the decay of publicans; for who the devil do you think would pay for drink at the Black Bear, when he can have it for nothing at my Lord's or the Squire's?"

Tressilian perceived that the wine had made some impression even upon the seasoned brain of mine host, which was chiefly to be inferred from his declaiming against drunkenness. As he himself had carefully avoided the bowl, he would have availed himself of the frankness of the moment, to extract from Gosling some further information upon the subject of Anthony Forster, and the lady whom the mercer had seen in his mansion-house; but his inquiries only set the host upon a new theme of declamation against the wiles of the fair sex, in which he brought, at full length, the whole wisdom of Solomon to reinforce his own. Finally, he turned his admonitions, mixed with much objurgation, upon his tapsters and drawers, who were employed in removing the relics of the entertainment, and restoring order to the apartment; and at length, joining example to precept, though with no good success, he demolished a salver with half a score of glasses, in attempting to shew how such service was done at the Three Cranes in the Vintry, then the most topping tavern in London. This last accident so far recalled him to his better self, that he retired to his bed, slept sound, and awaked a new man in the morning.

Chapter Three

Nay, I'll hold touch—the game shall be play'd out,
It ne'er shall stop for me, this merry wager;
That which I say when gamesome, I'll avouch
In my most sober mood, ne'er trust me else.
The Hazard-table

"AND HOW doth your kinsman, good mine host?" said Tressilian, when Giles Gosling first appeared in the public room on the morning following the revel which we described in the last chapter. "Is he well, and will he abide by his wager?"

"For well, sir, he started two hours since, and hath visited I know not what purlieus of his old companions; hath but now returned, and is at this instant breakfasting on new-laid eggs and muscadine; and for his wager, I caution you as a friend to have little to do with that, or indeed with aught that Mike proposes. Wherefore, I counsel you to a warm breakfast upon a culiss, which shall restore the tone of the stomach; and let my nephew and Master Goldthread swagger about their wager as they list."

"It seems to me, mine host," said Tressilian, "that you know not well what to say about this kinsman of yours; and that you can neither blame nor commend him without some twinge of conscience."

"You have spoken truly, Master Tressilian," replied Giles Gosling. "Here is Natural Affection whimpering into one ear, 'Giles, Giles, why wilt thou take away the good name of thy own nephew? Wilt thou defame thy sister's son, Giles Gosling? wilt thou defoul thine own nest, dishonour thine own blood?' And then, again, comes Justice, and says, 'Here is a worthy guest as ever came to the Bonny Black Bear; one who never challenged a reckoning, (as I say to your face you never did, Master Tressilian—not that you have had cause,) one who knows not why he came, so far as I can see, or when he is going away; and wilt thou, being a publican, having paid scot and lot these thirty years in this town of Cumnor, and being at this instant headborough, wilt thou suffer this guest of guests, this man of men, this six-hooped pot (as I would say) of a traveller, to fall into the meshes of thy nephew, who is known for a swasher and a desperate Dick, a carder and a dicer, a professor of the seven damnable sciences, if ever man took degrees in them?'—No, by Heaven! I might wink, and let him catch such a small butterfly as Goldthread; but thou, my guest, shalt be forewarned, forearmed, sobeit thou wilt listen to thy trusty host."

"Why, mine host, thy counsel shall not be cast away," replied Tressilian; "however, I must uphold my share in this wager, having once passed my word to that effect. But lend me, I pray, some of thy counsel.—This Forster, who or what is he, and why makes he such mystery of his female inmate?"

"Troth," replied Gosling, "I can add but little to what you heard last night. He was one of Queen Mary's Papists, and now he is one of Queen Elizabeth's Protestants; he was an on-hanger of the Abbot of Abingdon, and now he lives as master of the manor-house. Above all, he was poor and is rich. Folks talk of private apartments in his old waste mansion-house, bedizened fine enough to serve the Queen, God bless her. Some men think he found a treasure in the orchard, some that he sold himself to the devil for treasure, and some say that he cheated the Abbot out of the church plate, which was hidden in the old Manor-house at the Reformation. Rich, however, he is, and God and his conscience, with the devil perhaps besides, only know how he came by it. He has had sulky ways too, breaking off intercourse with all that are of the place, as if he had either some strange secret to keep, or held himself to be made of another clay than we are. I think it like my kinsman and he will quarrel, if Mike thrusts his acquaintance on him; and I am sorry that you, my worthy Master Tressilian, will still think of going in my nephew's company."

Tressilian again assured him, that he would proceed with great caution, and that he should have no fears on his account; in short, bestowed on him all the customary assurances with which those who are determined on a rash action, are wont to parry the advice of their friends.

Meantime, the traveller accepted the landlord's invitation, and had just finished the excellent breakfast which was served to him and Gosling by pretty Cicely, the beauty of the bar, when the hero of the preceding night, Michael Lambourne, entered the apartment. His toilette had apparently cost him some labour, for his clothes, which differed from those he wore on his journey, were of the newest fashion, and put on with great attention to the display of his person.

"By my faith, uncle," said the gallant, "you made a wet night of it, and I feel it followed by a dry morning. I will pledge you willingly in a cup of bastard.—How, my pretty coz, Cicely! why, I left thee but a child in the cradle, and there thou stand'st in thy velvet waistcoat, as tight a girl as England's sun shines on. Know thy friends and kindred,

Cicely, and come hither, child, that I may kiss thee, and give thee my blessing."

"Cumber not yourself about Cicely, kinsman," said Giles Gosling, "but e'en let her go her way, a' God's name; for although your mother were her father's sister, yet that shall not make you and her cater-cousins."

"Why, uncle," replied Lambourne, "think'st thou I am infidel, and would harm those of mine own house?"

"It is for no harm that I speak, Mike," answered his uncle, "but a simple humour of precaution which I have—true, thou art as well gilded as a snake when he casts his old slough in the spring-time; but for all that, thou creepest not into my Eden—I will look after mine Eve, Mike, and so content thee. But how brave thou be'est, lad! To look on thee now, and compare thee with Master Tressilian here, in his sad-coloured riding-suit, who would not say that thou wert the real gentleman, and he the tapster's boy?"

"Troth, uncle," replied Lambourne, "no one would say so but one of your country-breeding, that knows no better. I will say, and I care not who hears me, there is something about the real gentry that few men come up to that are not born and bred to the mystery. I wot not where the trick lies; but although I can enter an ordinary with as much audacity, rebuke the waiters and drawers as loudly, drink as deep a health, swear as round an oath, and fling my gold as freely about as any of the jingling spurs and white feathers that are around me,—yet, hang me if I can ever catch the true grace of it, though I have practised for an hundred times—the man of the house sets me lowest at the board, and carves to me the last; and the drawer says,—'Coming, friend,' without any more reverend or regardful addition. But, hang it, let it pass—Care killed a cat. I have gentry enough to pass the career on Tony Fire-the-Faggot, and that will do for the matter in hand."

"You hold your purpose, then, of visiting your old acquaintance?" said Tressilian to the adventurer.

"Ay, sir," replied Lambourne; "when stakes are made, the game must be played; that is gamester's law, all over the world. You, sir, unless my memory fails me, (for I did steep it somewhat too deeply in the sack-butt) took some share in my hazard."

"I propose to accompany you on your adventure," said Tressilian, "if you will do me so much grace as to permit me; and I have staked my share of the forfeit in the hands of our worthy host."

"That he hath," answered Giles Gosling, "in as fair Harry-nobles as ever were melted into sack by a good fellow. So, luck to your enterprize, since you will needs venture on Tony Forster; but, by my credit, you were better take another draught before you depart, for your welcome at the Hall, yonder, will be somewhat of the driest. And if you do get into peril, beware of taking to cold steel; but send for me, Giles Gosling the headborough, and I may be able to make something out of Tony yet, for as proud as he is."

The nephew dutifully obeyed his uncle's hint, by taking a second and deeper pull at the tankard, observing, that his wit never served him so well as when he had washed his temples with a deep morning's draught; and they set forth together for the habitation of Anthony Forster.

The village of Cumnor is pleasantly situated on a hill, and in a wooded park closely adjacent, was situated the ancient mansion occupied at this time by Anthony Forster, of which the ruins may be still extant. The park was then full of large trees, and, in particular, of ancient and mighty oaks, which stretched their giant arms over the high wall surrounding the demesne, thus giving it a melancholy, secluded, and monastic appearance. The entrance to the park lay through an old-fashioned gateway in the outer wall, the door of which was closed by two huge oaken leaves, thickly studded with nails, like the gate of an old town.

"We shall be finely holped up here," said Michael Lambourne, looking at the gateway, "if this fellow's suspicious humour should refuse us admission altogether, as it is like he may, in case this linsey-wolsey fellow of a mercer's visit to his premises has disquieted him. But, no," he added, pushing the huge gate, which gave way, "the door stands invitingly open; and here we are within the forbidden ground, without other impediment than the passive resistance of a heavy oak door, moving on rusty hinges."

They stood now in an avenue overshadowed by such old trees as we have described, and which had been bordered at one time by high hedges of yew and holly. But these having been untrimmed for many years, had run up into great bushes, or rather dwarf-trees, and now encroached, with their dark and melancholy boughs, upon the road which they once had screened. The avenue itself was grown up with grass, and, in one or two places, interrupted by piles of withered brushwood, which had been lopped from trees cut down in the neighbouring park, and was here stacked for drying. Formal walks and avenues, which, at different points, crossed this principal approach, were, in like manner, choked up and interrupted by piles of brushwood and billets, and in other places, by underwood and brambles. Besides the general effect of desolation which is so strongly impressed, whenever we behold the contrivances of man wasted and obliterated by neglect, and witness the marks of social life effaced gradually by the influence of vegetation, the size of the trees, and the outspreading extent of their boughs, diffused a gloom over the scene, even when the sun was at highest, and made a proportional impression on the mind of those who visited it. This was felt even by Michael Lambourne, however alien his habits were to receiving any impressions, excepting from things which addressed themselves immediately to his passions.

"This wood is as dark as a wolf's mouth," said he to Tressilian, as they walked together slowly along the solitary and broken approach, and were just come in sight of the monastic front of the old mansion, with its shafted windows, brick walls, overgrown with ivy and creeping shrubs, and twisted stalks of chimneys, of heavy stone-work. "And yet," continued Lambourne, "it is fairly done on the part of Forster too; for since he chuses not visitors, it is right to keep his place in a fashion that will invite few to trespass upon his privacy. But had he been the Anthony I once knew him, these sturdy oaks had long since become the property of some honest woodmonger, and the manor-close here had looked lighter at midnight than it now does at noon, while Forster played fast and loose with the price, in some cunning corner in the purlieus of White-friars."

"Was he then such an unthrift," asked Tressilian.

"He was," answered Lambourne, "like the rest of us, no saint, and no saver. But what I liked worst of Tony was, that he loved to take his pleasure by himself, and grudged, as men say, every drop of water that went past his own mill. I have known him deal with such measures of wine when he was alone, as I would not have ventured on with aid of the best toper in Berkshire;—that, and some sway towards superstition, which he had by temperament, rendered him unworthy the company of a good fellow and gallant picaroon, such as I have ever shewn myself. And now he has earthed himself here, in a den just befitting such a sly fox as himself."

"May I ask you, Master Lambourne," said Tressilian, "since your old companion's humour jumps so little with your own, wherefore you are so desirous to renew acquaintance with him?"

"And may I ask you, in return, Master Tressilian," answered Lambourne, "wherefore you have shewn yourself so desirous to accompany me on this party?"

"I told you my motive," said Tressilian, "when I took share in your wager,—it was simple curiosity."

"Law you there now!" answered Lambourne: "See how you civil and discreet gentlemen think to use us who live by the free exercise of our wits! Had I answered your question, by saying that it was simple curiosity which led me to visit my old comrade Anthony Forster, I warrant you had set it down for an evasion, and a turn of my trade. But any answer, I suppose, must serve my turn."

"And wherefore should not bare curiosity," said Tressilian, "be a sufficient reason for my taking this walk with you?"

"O, content yourself, sir," replied Lambourne; "you cannot put the change on me so easy as you think, for I have lived among the quick-stirring spirits of the age too long, to swallow chaff for grain. You are a gentleman of birth and breeding—your bearing makes it good;—of civil habits and fair reputation—your manners declare it, and my uncle avouches it—And yet you associate yourself with a sort of scant-of-grace, as men call me; and, knowing me to be such, you make yourself my companion in a visit to a man whom you are a stranger to, and all out of mere curiosity forsooth—the excuse, if curiously balanced, would be found to want some scruples of just weight, or so."

"If your suspicions were just," said Tressilian, "you have shown no confidence in me to invite or deserve mine."

"O, if that be all," said Lambourne, "my motives lie above water. While this gold of mine lasts,"—taking out his purse, chucking it into the air, and catching it as it fell,—"I will make it buy pleasure, and when it is out, I must have more. Now, if this mysterious Lady of the Manor—this fair Lindabrides of Tony Fire-the-Faggot, be so admirable a piece as men say, why there is a chance she may aid me to melt my nobles into groats; and, again, if Anthony be so wealthy a chuff as report speaks him, he may prove the philosopher's stone to me, and convert my groats into fair rose-nobles again."

"A comfortable proposal truly," said Tressilian; "but I see not what chance there is of accomplishing it."

"Not to-day, or perchance to-morrow," answered Lambourne; "I expect not to catch the old Jack till I have disposed my ground-baits handsomely. But I know something more of his affairs this morning than I did last night, and I will so use my knowledge that he shall think it more perfect than it is.—Nay, without expecting either pleasure or profit, or both, I had not stepped a stride within this manor, I can tell you; for I promise you I hold our visit not altogether without risk. But here we are, and we must make the best on't."

While he thus spoke, they had entered a large orchard which surrounded the house on two sides, though the trees, abandoned by the care of man, were overgrown and mossy, and seemed to bear little fruit. Those which had been formerly trained as espaliers, had now resumed their natural mode of growing, and exhibited grotesque forms, partaking of the original training which they had received. The greater part of the ground, which had once been parterres and flower-gardens, was suffered in like manner to run to waste, excepting a few patches which had been dug up, and planted with ordinary pot-herbs.

Some statues, which had ornamented the garden in its days of splendour, were now thrown down from their pedestals and broken in pieces, and a large summer-house, having a heavy stone front, decorated with carving, representing the life and actions of Sampson, was in the same dilapidated condition.

They had just traversed this garden of the sluggard, and were within a few steps of the door of the mansion when Lambourne had ceased speaking; a circumstance very agreeable to Tressilian, as it saved him the embarrassment of either commenting upon or replying to the frank avowal which his companion had just made of the sentiments and views which induced him to come hither. Lambourne knocked roundly and boldly at the huge door of the mansion, observing at the same time, he had seen a less strong one upon a county jail. It was not until they had knocked more than once, that an aged sour-visaged domestic reconnoitred them through a small square hole in the door, well-secured with bars of iron, and demanded what they wanted.

"To speak with Master Forster instantly, on pressing business of the state," was the ready reply of Michael Lambourne.

"Methinks you will find difficulty to make that good," said Tressilian in a whisper to his companion, while the servant went to carry the message to his master.

"Tush," replied the adventurer; "no soldier would go on were he always to consider when and how he should come off. Let us once obtain entrance, and all will go well enough."

In a short time the servant returned, and drawing with a careful hand both bolt and bar, opened the gate, which admitted them through an archway into a square court, surrounded by buildings. Opposite to the arch was another door, which the serving-man in like manner unlocked, and thus introduced them into a stone-paved parlour, where there was but little furniture, and that of the rudest and most ancient fashion. The windows were tall and ample, reaching almost to the roof of the room, which was composed of black oak; those opening to the quadrangle, were obscured by the height of the surrounding buildings, and, as they were traversed with massive shafts of solid stone-work, and thickly painted with religious devices, and scenes taken from scripture history, by no means admitted light in proportion to their size; and what did penetrate through them, partook of the dark and gloomy tinge of the stained glass.

Tressilian and his guide had time enough to observe all these particulars, for they waited some space in the apartment ere the present master of the mansion at length made his appearance. Prepared as he was to see an inauspicious and ill-looking person, the ugliness of Anthony Forster considerably exceeded what Tressilian had anticipated. He was of middle stature, built strongly, but so clumsily, as to border on deformity, and to give all his motions the ungainly awkwardness of a left-legged and left-handed man. His hair, in arranging which men at that time, as at present, were very nice and curious, instead of being carefully cleaned and disposed into short curls, or else set up on end, as is represented in old paintings, in a manner resembling that used by fine gentlemen of our own day, escaped in sable negligence from under a furred bonnet, and hung in elf-locks, which seemed strangers to the comb, over his rugged brows, and around his very singular and unprepossessing countenance. His keen dark eyes were deep set beneath broad and shaggy eye-brows, and, as they were usually bent on the ground, seemed as if they were themselves ashamed of the expression natural to them, and were desirous to conceal it from the observation of men. At times, however, when, more intent on observing others, he suddenly raised them, and fixed them keenly on those with whom he conversed, they seemed to express both the fiercer passions, and the power of mind which could at will suppress or disguise the intensity of inward feeling. The features which corresponded with these eyes and this form were irregular, and marked so as to be fixed forever on the mind of him who had once seen them. Upon the whole, as Tressilian could not help acknowledging to himself, the Anthony Forster who now stood before them, was the last person, judging from personal appearance, upon whom one would have chosen to intrude an unexpected and undesired visit. His attire was a doublet of russet leather, like those worn by the better sort of country folks, girt with a buff belt, in which was stuck on the right side, a long knife or dudgeon dagger, and on the other a cutlass. He raised his eyes as he entered the room, and fixed a keenly penetrating glance upon his two visitors, then cast them down as if counting his steps, while he advanced slowly into the middle of the room, and said, in a low and smothered tone of voice, "Let me pray you, gentlemen, to tell me the cause of this visit."

He looked as if he expected the answer from Tressilian; so true was Lambourne's observation, that the superior air of breeding and dignity shone through the disguise of an inferior dress. But it was Michael who replied to him, with the easy familiarity of an old friend, and a tone which seemed unembarrassed by any doubt of the most cordial reception.

"Ha! my dear friend and ingle, Tony Forster!" he exclaimed, seizing upon his unwilling hand, and shaking it with such emphasis as almost to stagger the sturdy frame of the person whom he addressed; "how fares it with you for many a long year?—What! have you altogether forgotten your friend, gossip, and play-fellow, Michael Lambourne?"

"Michael Lambourne!" said Forster, looking at him a moment, then dropping his eyes, and with little ceremony extricating his hand from the friendly grasp of the person by whom he was addressed, "are you Michael Lambourne?"

"Ay; sure as you are Anthony Forster," replied Lambourne.

"Tis well!" answered his sullen host; "and what may Michael Lambourne expect for his visit hither?"

"*Voto a Dios*," answered Lambourne, "I expected a better welcome than I am like to meet, I think."

"Why, thou gallows-bird—thou jail-rat—thou friend for the hangman and his customers," replied Forster, "hast thou the assurance to expect countenance from any one whose neck is beyond the compass of a Tyburn tippet?"

"It may be with me as you say," replied Lambourne; "and suppose I grant it to be so for argument's sake, I were still good enough society for mine ancient friend Anthony Fire-the-Faggot, though he be, for the present, by some indescribable title, the master of Cumnor-Place."

"Hark you, Michael Lambourne," said Forster; "you are a gambler now, and live by the counting of chances. Compute me the odds that I do not, on this instant, throw you out of that window into the ditch there."

"Twenty to one that you do not," answered the sturdy visitor.

"And wherefore, I pray you?" demanded Anthony Forster, setting his teeth and compressing his lips, like one who endeavours to suppress some violent internal emotion.

"Because," said Lambourne, coolly, "you dare not for your life lay a finger on me. I am younger and stronger than you, and have a double portion of the fighting devil, though not, it may be, quite so much of the undermining fiend, that finds an under-ground way to his purpose —who hides halters under folk's pillows and puts ratsbane into their porridge, as the play says."

Forster looked at him earnestly, then turned away and paced the room twice, with the same steady and considerate pace with which he had entered; then suddenly came back and extended his hand to Michael Lambourne, saying, "Be not wroth with me, good Mike; I did but try whether thou hadst parted with aught of thine old and honourable frankness, which your enviers and backbiters called saucy impudence."

"Let them call it what they will," said Michael Lambourne, "it is the commodity we must carry through the world with us.—Uds daggers! I tell thee, man, my own stock of assurance was too small to trade upon, I was fain to take in a ton or two more brass at every port I stopped at in the voyage of life; and I started overboard what modesty and scruples I had remaining, in order to make room for the stowage."

"Nay, nay," replied Forster, "touching scruples and modesty, you sailed hence in ballast.—But who is this gallant, honest Mike?—is he a Corinthian—a cutter like thyself?"

"I prithee, know Master Tressilian, bully Forster," replied Lambourne, presenting his friend in answer to his friend's question, "know him and honour him, for he is a gentleman of many admirable qualities; and though he traffics not in my line of business, at least so far as I know, he has, nevertheless, a just respect and admiration for artists of our class. He will come to in time, as seldom fails; but as yet he is only a Neophyte, only a Proselyte, and frequents the company of cocks of the game, as a puny fencer does the schools of the masters, to see how a foil is handled by the teachers of defence."

"If such be his quality, I will pray your company in another chamber, honest Mike, for what I have to say to thee is for thy private ear.— Meanwhile, I pray you, sir, to abide us in this apartment, and without leaving it—there be those in this house who would be alarmed by the sight of a stranger."

Tressilian acquiesced, and the two worthies left the apartment together, in which he remained alone to await their return.

Chapter Four

Not serve two masters?—Here's a youth will try it—
Would fain serve God, yet give the devil his due;
Says grace before he doth a deed of villainy,
And returns thanks devoutly when 'tis acted.
Old Play

THE ROOM into which the Master of Cumnor Hall conducted his worthy visitant, was of yet greater extent than that in which they had at first conversed, and had yet more the appearance of dilapidation. Large oaken presses, filled with shelves of the same, surrounded the room, and had, at one time, served for the arrangement of a numerous collection of books, many of which yet remained, but torn and defaced, covered with dust, deprived of their costly clasps and bindings, and tossed together in heaps upon the shelves, as things altogether disregarded, and abandoned to the pleasure of every spoiler. The very presses themselves seemed to have incurred the displeasure of those enemies of learning, who had destroyed the volumes with which they had been heretofore filled. They were, in several places, dismantled of their shelves, and otherwise broken and damaged, and were, moreover, mantled with cobwebs, and covered with dust.

"The men who wrote these books," said Lambourne, looking round him, "little thought whose keeping they were to fall into."

"Nor what yeoman's service they were to do me," quoth Anthony Forster—"the cook hath used them for scouring his pewter, and the groom hath had nought else to clean my boots with this many a month past."

"And yet," said Lambourne, "I have been in cities where such commodities would have been deemed too good for such offices."

"Pshaw, pshaw," answered Forster, "they are Popish trash, every one of them,—private studies of the mumping old Abbot of Abingdon. The nineteenthly of a pure gospel sermon were worth a cart-load of such rakings of the kennel of Rome."

"God-a-mercy, Master Tony Fire-the-Faggot!" said Lambourne, by way of reply.

Forster scowled darkly at him, as he replied, "Hark ye, friend Mike; forget that name, and the passage which it relates to, if you would not have our newly-revived comradeship die a sudden and a violent death."

"Why," said Michael Lambourne, "you were wont to glory in the share you had in the death of the two old heretical bishops."

"That," said his comrade, "was while I was in the gall of bitterness and bond of iniquity, and applies not to my walk or my ways, now that I am called forth into the lists. Mr Melchisidec Maultext compared my misfortune in that matter to that of the Apostle Paul, who kept the clothes of the witnesses who stoned Saint Stephen. He held forth on the matter three Sabbaths past, and illustrated the use of the same by the conduct of an honourable person present, meaning me."

"I prithee peace, Forster," said Lambourne, "for I know not how it is, I have a sort of creeping comes over my skin when I hear the devil quote Scripture. And besides, man, how couldst thou have the heart to quit that convenient old religion, which you could slip off or on as easily as your glove? Do I not remember how you were wont to carry your conscience to confession, as duly as the month came round? and when thou hadst had it scoured, and burnished, and white-washed by the priest, thou wert ever ready for the worst villainy which could be devised, like a child who is always readiest to rush into the mire when he has got his Sunday's clean jerkin on."

"Trouble not thyself about my conscience," said Forster, "it is a thing thou canst not understand, having never had one of thine own; but let us rather to the point, and say to me, in one word, what is thy business with me, and what hopes have drawn thee hither?"

"The hope of bettering myself, to be sure," answered Lambourne, "as the old woman said, when she leapt over the bridge at Kingston. Look you, this purse has all that is left of as round a sum as a man would wish to carry in his slop-pouch. You are here well established, it would seem, and, as I think, well befriended, for men talk of thy being under some special protection; thou canst not dance in a net and they not see thee. Now I know such protection is not purchased for nought; you have services to render for it, and in these I propose to help thee."

"But how if I lack no assistance from thee, Mike? I think thy modesty might suppose that were a case possible."

"That is to say," retorted Lambourne, "that you would engross the whole work, rather than divide the reward—but be not over-greedy, Anthony. Covetousness bursts the sack and spills the grain. Look you, when the huntsman goes to kill a stag, he takes with him more dogs than one—He has the staunch lyme-hound to track the wounded buck over hill and dale, but he hath also the fleet gaze-hound to kill him at view. Thou art the lyme-hound, I am the gaze-hound, and thy patron will need the aid of both, and can well afford to requite it. Thou hast deep sagacity—an unrelenting purpose—a steady long-breathed malignity of nature, that surpasses mine. But then, I am the bolder, the quicker, the more ready, both at action and expedient. Separate, our properties are not so perfect; but unite them, and we drive the world before us. How say'st thou—shall we hunt in couples?"

"It is a currish proposal in thee thus to thrust thyself upon my private matters," replied Forster; "but thou wert ever an ill-nurtured whelp."

"You shall have no cause to say so, unless you spurn my courtesy," said Michael Lambourne; "but if so, keep thee well from me, Sir Knight, as the romance has it. I will either share your counsels or traverse them; for I have come here to be busy, either with thee or against thee."

"Well," said Anthony Forster, "since thou dost leave me so fair a choice, I will rather be thy friend than thine enemy. Thou art right, I can prefer thee to the service of a patron, who has enough of means to make us both, and an hundred more. And, to say truth, thou art well qualified for his service. Boldness and dexterity he demands—the justice-books bear witness in thy favour—no starting at scruples in his service—why, who ever suspected thee of a conscience?—an assurance he must have, who would follow a courtier—and thy brow is as impenetrable as a Milan visor. There is but one thing I would fain see amended in thee."

"And what is that, my most precious friend Anthony?" replied

Lambourne; "for I swear by the pillow of the Seven Sleepers, I will not be slothful in mending it."

"Why, you gave a sample of it even now," said Forster. "Your speech twangs too much of the old stamp, and you garnish it ever and anon with singular oaths, that savour of Papistrie. Besides your exterior man is altogether too deboshed and irregular to become one of his lordship's followers, since he has a reputation to keep up in the eye of the world. You must somewhat reform your dress, upon a more grave and composed fashion; wear your cloak on both shoulders, and your falling band unruffled and well starched—You must enlarge the brim of your beaver, and diminish the superfluity of your trunk-hose —go to church, or, which will be better, to meeting, at least once a month—protest only upon your faith and conscience—lay aside your swashing look, and never touch the hilt of your sword, but when you would draw the carnal weapon in good earnest."

"By this light, Anthony, thou art mad," answered Lambourne, "and describest rather the gentleman-usher to a puritan's wife, than the follower of an ambitious courtier! Yes, such a thing as thou would'st make of me, should wear a book at his girdle instead of a poniard, and might just be suspected of manhood enough to squire a proud dame-citizen to the lecture at Saint Antoline's, and quarrel in her cause with any flat-cap'd thread-maker that would take the wall of her. He must ruffle it in another sort that would walk to court in a nobleman's train."

"O, content you, sir," replied Forster, "there is a change since you knew the English; and there are those who can hold their way through the boldest courses, and the most secret, and yet never a swaggering word, or an oath, or a profane word in their conversation."

"That is to say," replied Lambourne, "they are in a trading copartnery, to do the devil's business without mentioning his name in the firm—well, I will do my best to counterfeit, rather than lose ground in this new world, since thou sayest it is so precise. But, Anthony, what is the name of this nobleman, in whose service I am to turn hypocrite?"

"Aha! Master Michael, are you there with your bears?" said Forster, with a grim smile; "and is this the knowledge you pretend of my concernments?—How know you now there is such a patron in *rerum natura*, and that I have not been putting a jape upon you all this time?"

"Thou put a jape on me, thou sodden-brained gull!" answered Lambourne, nothing daunted; "why, dark and muddy as thou think'st thyself, I would engage in a day's space to see as clear through thee and thy concernments, as thou call'st them, as through the filthy horn of an old stable lantern."

At this moment their conversation was interrupted by a scream from the next apartment.

"By the holy Cross of Abingdon!" said Anthony Forster, forgetting his protestantism in his alarm, "I am a ruined man."

So saying, he rushed into the apartment whence the sound issued, followed by Michael Lambourne. But to account for the sounds which interrupted their conversation, it is necessary to recede a little way in our narrative.

It has been already observed, that when Lambourne accompanied Forster into the library, they left Tressilian alone in the ancient parlour. His dark eye followed them forth of the apartment with a glance of contempt, a part of which his mind instantly transferred to himself, for having stooped to be even for a moment their familiar companion. "These are the associates, Amy,"—it was thus he communed with himself,—"to which thy cruel levity—thine unthinking and most unmerited falsehood, has condemned him, of whom his friends once hoped far other things, and who now scorns himself as he will be scorned by others, for the baseness he stoops to for the love of thee! But I will not leave the pursuit of thee, once the object of my purest and most devoted affection, though to me thou canst henceforth be nothing but a thing to weep over—I will save thee from thy betrayer, and from thyself—I will restore thee to thy parent—to thy God. I cannot bid the bright star again sparkle in the sphere it has shot from, but"——

A slight noise in the apartment interrupted his reverie; he looked round, and in the beautiful and richly-attired female who entered at that instant by a side-door, he recognized the object of his search. The first impulse arising from this discovery, urged him to conceal his own face with the collar of his cloak, until he should find a favourable moment of making himself known. But his purpose was disconcerted by the young lady, (she was not above eighteen years old) who ran joyfully towards him, and, pulling him by the cloak, said playfully, "Nay, my sweet friend, after I have waited for you so long, you come not to my bower to play the masquer—You are arraigned of treason to true love and fond affection; and you must stand up at the bar, and answer it with face uncovered—how say you, Guilty or not?"

"Alas, Amy!" said Tressilian, in a low and melancholy tone, as he suffered her to draw the mantle from his face. The sound of his voice, and still more the unexpected sight of his face, changed in an instant the lady's playful mood—She staggered back, turned as pale as death, and put her hands before her face. Tressilian was himself for a moment much overcome, but seeming suddenly to remember the necessity of using an opportunity which might not again occur, he said in a low tone, "Amy, fear me not."

"Why should I fear you?" said the lady, withdrawing her hands from her beautiful face, which was now covered with crimson,—"why should I fear you, Mr Tressilian?—or wherefore have you intruded yourself into my dwelling, uninvited, sir, and unwished for?"

"Your dwelling, Amy!" said Tressilian. "Alas! is a prison your dwelling?—a prison, guarded by one of the most sordid of men, but not a greater wretch than his employer."

"This house is mine," said Amy, "mine while I chuse to inhabit it— If it is my pleasure to live in seclusion, who shall gainsay me?"

"Your father, maiden," answered Tressilian, "your broken-hearted father; who dispatches me in quest of you with that authority which he cannot exert in person. Here is his letter, written while he blessed the pain of body which somewhat stunned the agony of his mind."

"The pain!—is my father then ill?" said the lady.

"So ill," answered Tressilian, "that even your utmost haste may not find him alive; but all shall be instantly prepared for your departure, the instant you yourself will give consent."

"Tressilian," answered the lady, "I cannot, I must not, I dare not leave this place—go back to my father—tell him I will obtain leave to see him within twelve hours from hence—go back, Tressilian—tell him I am well—I am happy—happy could I think he was so—tell him not to fear that I will come, and in such manner that all the grief Amy has given him shall be forgotten—the poor Amy is now greater than she dare name.—Go, good Tressilian—I have injured thee too, but believe me I have power to heal the wounds I have caused—I robbed you of a childish heart, which was not worthy of you, and I can repay it with honours and advancement."

"Do you say this to me, Amy?—do you offer me pageants of idle ambition, for the quiet peace you have robbed me of?—But be it so—I came not to upbraid, but to serve and to free you.—You cannot disguise it from me; you are a prisoner—otherwise your kind heart— for it was once a kind heart—would have been already at your father's bed-side.—Come—poor, deceived, unhappy girl—all shall be forgot —all shall be forgiven—fear not my importunity for what regarded our contract—it was a dream, and I have awaked—But come—your father yet lives—come, and one word of affection—one tear of penitence, will efface the memory of all that has passed."

"Have I not already said, Tressilian," replied she, "that I will surely come to my father, and that without more delay than is necessary to discharge other—and equally binding duties?—Go, carry him the news—I come as sure as there is light in Heaven—that is, when I obtain permission."

"Permission?—permission to visit your father on his sick-bed, perhaps on his death-bed!" repeated Tressilian, impatiently; "and permission from whom?—From the villain, who, under disguise of friendship, abused every duty of hospitality, and stole thee from thy father's roof!"

"Do him no slander, Tressilian!—he whom thou speakest of wears a sword as sharp as thine—sharper, vain man—for the best deeds thou hast ever done in peace or war, were as unworthy to be named with his, as thy obscure rank to match itself with the sphere he moves in.—Leave me!—go, do mine errand to my father, and when he next sends to me, let him chuse a more welcome messenger."

"Amy," replied Tressilian, calmly, "thou canst not move me by thy reproaches.—Tell me one thing, that I may bear at least one ray of comfort to my aged friend—This rank of his which thou doest boast—doest thou share it with him, Amy?—Does he claim a husband's right to controul thy motions?"

"Stop thy base unmannered tongue!" said the lady; "to no question that derogates from my honour, do I deign an answer."

"You have said enough in refusing to reply," answered Tressilian; "and mark me, unhappy as thou art, I am armed with thy father's full authority to command thy obedience, and I will save thee from the slavery of sin and of sorrow, even despite of thyself, Amy."

"Menace no violence here!" exclaimed the lady, drawing back from him, and alarmed at the determination expressed in his look and manner; "threaten me not, Tressilian, for I have means to repel force."

"But not, I trust, the wish to use them in so evil a cause," said Tressilian. "With thy will—thine uninfluenced, free, and natural will, Amy, thou canst not chuse this state of slavery and dishonour—thou hast been bound by some spell—entrapped by some art—art now detained by some compelled vow.—But thus I break the charm—Amy, in the name of thine excellent, thy broken-hearted father, I command thee to follow me."

As he spoke, he advanced and extended his arm, as with the purpose of laying hold upon her. But she shrunk back from his grasp, and uttered the scream, which, as we before noticed, brought into the apartment Lambourne and Forster.

The latter exclaimed, so soon as he entered, "Fire and faggot! what have we here!" Then addressing the lady in a tone betwixt entreaty and command, he added, "Uds precious! Madam, what make you here out of bounds?—retire—retire—there is life and death in this matter.—And you, friend, whoever you may be, leave this house—out with you, before my dagger's hilt and your costard become acquainted—Draw, Mike, and rid us of the knave."

"Not I, on my soul," replied Lambourne; "he came hither in my company, and he is safe from me by cutter's law, at least till we meet again.—But hark ye, my Cornish comrade, you have brought a Cornish flaw with you hither, a hurricanoe as they call it in the Indies—make yourself scarce—depart—vanish—or we'll have you summoned before the Mayor of Halgaver, and that before Dudman and Ramhead meet."*

"Away, base groom!" said Tressilian—"And you, madam, fare you well—What life is left in your father's bosom will depart, at the news I have to tell him."

He departed, the lady saying faintly as he left the room, "Tressilian—be not rash—say no scandal of me."

"Here is proper gear," said Forster. "I pray you go to your chamber, my lady, and let us consider how this is to be answered—nay, tarry not."

"I move not at your command, sir," answered the lady.

"Nay, but you must, fair lady," replied Forster; "excuse my freedom, but, by blood and nails, this is no time to strain courtesies—You must go to your chamber.—Mike, follow that meddling coxcomb, and as you desire to thrive, see him safely clear of the premises, while I bring this headstrong lady to reason—draw thy tool, man, and after him."

"I'll follow him," said Michael Lambourne, "and see him fairly out of Flanders—But for hurting a man I have drunk my morning's draught withal, 'tis clean against my conscience." So saying, he left the apartment.

Tressilian, meanwhile, pursued with hasty steps the first path which promised to conduct him through the wild and over-grown park in which the mansion of Forster was situated. Haste and distress of mind led his steps astray, and instead of taking the avenue which led towards the village, he chose another, which, after he had pursued it for some time with a hasty and reckless step, conducted him to the other side of the demesne, where a postern-door opened through the wall, and led into the open country.

Tressilian paused an instant. It was indifferent to him by what road he left a spot now so odious to his recollection; but it was probable that the postern-door was locked, and his retreat by that pass rendered impossible.

"I must make the attempt, however," he said to himself; "the only means of reclaiming this lost—this miserable—this still most lovely and most unhappy girl—must rest on her father's appeal to the broken laws of the country—I must haste to apprize him of this heart-breaking intelligence."

*Two headlands on the Cornish coast.

As Tressilian, thus conversing with himself, approached to try some means of opening the door, or climbing over it, he perceived there was a key put into the lock from the outside. It turned round, the bolt revolved, and a cavalier, who entered, muffled in his riding-cloak, and wearing a slouched hat with a drooping feather, stood at once within four yards of him who was desirous of going out. They exclaimed at once, in tones of resentment and surprise, the one "Varney!" the other "Tressilian!"

"What make you here?" was the stern question put by the stranger to Tressilian, when the moment of surprise was past,—"What make you where your presence is neither expected nor desired?"

"Nay, Varney," replied Tressilian, "what make *you* here? Are you come to triumph over the innocence you have destroyed, as the vulture or carrion-crow comes to batten on the lamb, whose eyes it has first plucked out?—Or are you come to encounter the merited vengeance of an honest man?—Draw, dog, and defend thyself."

Tressilian drew his sword as he spoke, but Varney only laid hand on the hilt of his own, as he replied, "Thou art mad, Tressilian—I own appearances are against me, but by every oath a priest can make, or a man can swear, Mistress Amy Robsart hath had no injury from me, and in truth I were somewhat loath to hurt you in this cause—Thou know'st I can fight."

"I have heard thee say so, Varney," replied Tressilian; "but now, methinks, I would fain have some better evidence than thine own word."

"That shall not be lacking, if blade and hilt be but true to me," answered Varney; and drawing his sword with the right hand, he threw his cloak around his left, and attacked Tressilian with a vigour which, for a moment, seemed to give him the advantage of the combat. But this advantage lasted not long. Tressilian added to a spirit determined on revenge, a hand and eye admirably well adapted to the use of the rapier; so that Varney, finding himself hard pressed in his turn, endeavoured to avail himself of his superior strength, by closing with his adversary. For this purpose, he hazarded the receiving one of Tressilian's passes in his cloak, wrapt as it was around his arm, and ere his adversary could extricate his rapier thus entangled, he closed with him, shortening his own sword at the same time, with the purpose of dispatching him. But Tressilian was on his guard, and unsheathing his poniard, parried with the blade of that weapon the home-thrust, which would otherwise have finished the combat, and in the close which followed, displayed so much address, as might have confirmed the opinion that he drew his origin from Cornwall, whose natives are such masters in the art of wrestling, as, were the games of antiquity revived, might enable them to challenge all Europe to the ring. Varney, in his ill-advised attempt, received a fall so sudden and violent, that his sword flew several paces from his hand, and ere he could recover his feet, that of his antagonist was pointed to his throat.

"Give me the instant means of relieving the victim of thy treachery," said Tressilian, "or take your last look of thy Creator's blessed sun."

And while Varney, too confused or too sullen to reply, made a sudden effort to arise, his adversary drew back his arm, and would have executed his threat, but that the blow was arrested by the grasp of Michael Lambourne, who, directed by the clashing of swords, had come up just in time to save the life of Varney.

"Come, come, comrade," said Lambourne, "here is enough done, and more than enough—put up your fox, and let us be jogging—The Black Bear growls for us."

"Off, abject!" said Tressilian, shaking himself free of Lambourne's grasp; "darest thou come betwixt me and mine enemy?"

"Abject? Abject?" repeated Lambourne; "that shall be answered with cold steel whenever a bowl of sack has washed out memory of the morning's draught that we had together. In the meanwhile, do you see—shog—tramp—begone—we are two to one."

He spoke truth, for Varney had taken the opportunity to regain his weapon, and Tressilian perceived it was madness to press the quarrel farther against such odds. He took his purse from his side, and taking out two gold nobles, flung them to Lambourne; "There, caitiff, is thy morning wage—thou shalt not say thou hast been my guide unhired. —Varney, farewell—we shall meet where there are none to come betwixt us." So saying, he turned round and departed through the postern-door.

Varney seemed to want the inclination, or perhaps the power (for his fall had been a severe one) to follow his retreating enemy. But he glared darkly as he disappeared, and then addressed Lambourne; "Art thou a comrade of Forster's, good fellow?"

"Sworn friends, as the haft is to the knife," replied Michael Lambourne.

"Here is a broad piece for thee—follow yonder fellow, and see where he takes earth, and bring me word up to the mansion-house here. Cautious and silent, thou knave, as thou valuest thy throat."

"Enough said," replied Lambourne; "I can draw on a scent as well as a sleuth-hound."

"Begone then," said Varney, sheathing his rapier; and, turning his back on Michael Lambourne, he walked slowly towards the house. Lambourne stopped but an instant to gather the nobles which his late companion had flung towards him so unceremoniously, and muttered to himself, while he put them up in his purse, along with the gratuity of Varney, "I spoke to yonder gulls of Eldorado. By Saint Anthony, there is no Eldorado for men of our stamp equal to bonny old England. It rains nobles, by heaven—they lie on the grass as thick as dew-drops— you may have them for gathering. And if I have not my share of such glittering dew-drops, may my sword melt like an icicle!"

Chapter Five

——He was a man
Versed in the world as pilot in his compass.
The needle pointed ever to that interest
Which was his load-star, and he spread his sails
With vantage to the gale of others' passion.
The Deceiver—a Tragedy

ANTHONY FORSTER was still engaged in debate with his fair guest, who treated with scorn every entreaty and request that she would retire to her own apartment, when a whistle was heard at the entrance-door of the mansion.

"We are fairly sped now," said Forster; "yonder is thy lord's signal, and what to say about the disorder which has happened in this house-hold, by my conscience, I know not. Some evil fortune dogs the heels of that unhanged rogue Lambourne, and he has 'scaped the gallows against every chance, to come back and be the ruin of me!"

"Peace, sir," said the lady, "and undo the gate to your master.—My lord! my dear lord!" she then exclaimed, hastening to the entrance of the apartment, then added, with a voice expressive of disappointment, —"Pooh! it is but Richard Varney."

"Ay, madam," said Varney, entering and saluting the lady with a respectful obeisance, which she returned with a careless mixture of negligence and of displeasure, "it is but Richard Varney; but even the first grey cloud should be acceptable, when it lightens in the east, because it announces the approach of the blessed sun."

"How! comes my lord hither to-night?" said the lady, in joyful, yet startled agitation, and Anthony Forster caught up the word, and echoed the question. Varney replied to the lady, that his lord purposed to attend her, and would have proceeded with some compliment, when, running to the door of the parlour, she called aloud, "Janet— Janet—come to my tiring-room instantly." Then returning to Varney, she asked if her lord sent any farther commendations to her.

"This letter, honoured madam," said he, taking from his bosom a small parcel wrapt in scarlet silk, "and with it a token to the Queen of his Affections." With eager speed the lady hastened to undo the silken string which surrounded the little packet, and failing to unloose readily the knot with which it was secured, she again called loudly on Janet, "Bring me a knife—scissars—aught that may undo this envious knot."

"May not my poor poniard serve, honoured madam," said Varney, presenting a small dagger of exquisite workmanship, which hung in his Turkey-leather sword-belt.

"No, sir," replied the lady, rejecting the instrument which he offered—"Steel poniard shall cut no true-love knot of mine."

"It has cut a many, however," said Anthony Forster, half aside, and looking at Varney. By this time the knot was disentangled without any other help than the neat and nimble fingers of Janet, a simply-attired pretty maiden, the daughter of Anthony Forster, who came running at the repeated call of her mistress. A necklace of orient pearl, the companion of a perfumed billet, was now hastily produced from the packet. The lady gave the one after a slight glance to the charge of her attendant, while she read, or rather devoured, the contents of the other.

"Surely, lady," said Janet, gazing with admiration at the rich string of pearls, "the daughters of Tyre wore no fairer neck-jewels than these—and then the posey, 'For a neck that is fairer,'—each pearl is worth a freehold."

"Each word in this dear paper is worth the whole string, my girl—but come to my tiring-room, girl; we must be brave—My lord comes hither to-night.—He bids me grace you, Master Varney, and to me his wish is a law—I bid you to a collation in my bower this afternoon, and you too, Master Forster. Give orders that all is fitting, and that suitable preparations be made for my lord's reception to-night."—With these words she left the apartment.

"She takes state on her already," said Varney, "and distributes the favour of her presence, as if she were already the partner of his dignity —well—it is wise to practise beforehand, the part which fortune prepares us to play—the young eagle must gaze at the sun, ere he soars on strong wing to meet it."

"If holding her head aloft," said Forster, "will keep her eyes from dazzling, I warrant you the dame will not stoop her crest. She will presently soar beyond reach of my whistle, Master Varney. I promise you, she holds me already in slight regard."

"It is thine own fault, thou sullen uninventive companion," answered Varney, "who know'st no mode of controul, save downright brute force—canst thou not make home pleasant to her, with music and toys? canst thou not make the out-of-doors frightful to her, with tales of goblins?—thou livest here by the church-yard, and hast not even wit enough to raise a ghost, to scare thy females into good discipline."

"Speak not thus, Master Varney," said Forster; "the living I fear not, but I trifle not nor toy with my dead neighbours of the church-yard. I promise you, it requires a good heart to live so near it; worthy Master Holdforth, the afternoon's lecturer of Saint Antholine's, had a sore fright there the last time he came to visit me."

"Hold thy superstitious tongue!" answered Varney; "and while thou talk'st of visiting, answer me, thou paltering knave, how came Tressilian to be at the postern-door?"

"Tressilian!" answered Forster, "what know I of Tressilian?—I never heard his name."

"Why, villain, it was the very Cornish chough, to whom old Sir Hugh Robsart destined his pretty Amy, and hither the hot-brained fool has come to look after his fair run-away; there must be some order taken with him, for he thinks he hath wrong, and is not the mean hind that will sit down with it. Luckily he knows nought of my lord, but thinks he has only me to deal with. But how, in the fiend's name, came he hither?"

"Why, with Mike Lambourne, an you must know," answered Forster.

"And who is Mike Lambourne?" demanded Varney. "By Heaven! thou wert best set up a bush over thy door, and invite every stroller who passes by, to see what thou should'st keep secret even from the sun and air."

"Ay! ay! this is a court-like requital of my service to you, Master Richard Varney," replied Forster. "Did'st thou not charge me to seek out for thee a fellow who had a good sword, and an unscrupulous conscience? and was I not cumbering myself to find a fit man—for, thank Heaven, my acquaintance lies not amongst such companions—when, as Heaven would have it, this tall fellow, who is in all his quali-ties the very flashing knave thou didst wish, came hither to fix acquaintance upon me in the plenitude of his impudence, and I admitted his claim, thinking to do you a pleasure—and now see what thanks I get for disgracing myself by converse with him!"

"And did he," said Varney, "being such a fellow as thyself, only lacking, I suppose, thy present humour of hypocrisy, which lies as thin over thy hard ruffianly heart, as gold lacquer upon rusty iron—did he, I say, bring the saintly, sighing Tressilian in his train?"

"They came together, by Heaven!" said Forster; "and Tressilian—to speak Heaven's truth—obtained a moment's interview with our pretty moppet, while I was talking apart with Lambourne."

"Improvident villain! we are both undone," said Varney. "She has

of late been casting many a backward look to her father's halls, whenever her lordly lover leaves her alone. Should this preaching fool
whistle her back to her old perch, we were but lost men."

"No fear of that, my master," replied Anthony Forster; "she is in no
mood to stoop to his lure, for she yelled out on seeing him as if an
adder had stung her."

"That is good—can'st thou not get from thy daughter any inkling of
what passed between them, good Forster?"

"I tell you plain, Master Varney," said Forster, "my daughter shall
not enter our purposes, or walk in our paths. They may suit me well
enough, who know how to repent of my misdoings; but I will not have
my child's soul committed either for your pleasure or my lord's. I may
walk among snares and pitfalls myself, because I have discretion, but I
will not trust the poor child among them."

"Why, thou suspicious fool, I were as averse as thou art that thy
baby-faced girl should enter into my plans, or walk to hell at her
father's elbow. But indirectly thou might'st gain some intelligence of
her."

"And so I did, Master Varney," answered Forster; "and she said
her lady called out upon the sickness of her father."

"Good!" replied Varney; "that is a hint worth catching, and I will
work upon it. But the country must be rid of this Tressilian—I would
have cumbered no man about the matter, for I hate him like strong
poison—his presence is hemlock to me—and this day I had been rid
of him, but that my foot slipped, when, to speak truth, had not thy
comrade yonder come to my aid, and held his hand, I should have
known by this time whether you and I have been treading the path to
heaven or hell."

"And you can speak thus of such a risk!" said Forster; "you keep a
stout heart, Master Varney—for me, if I did not hope to live many
years, and to have time for the great work of repentance, I would not
go forward with you."

"O! thou shalt live as long as Methuselah," said Varney, "and
amass as much wealth as Solomon; and thou shalt repent so devoutly,
that thy repentance shall be more famous than thy villainy,—and that is
a bold word. But for all this, Tressilian must be looked after. Thy
ruffian yonder is gone to dog him. It concerns our fortunes, Anthony."

"Ay, ay," said Forster, sullenly, "this it is to be leagued with one
who knows not even so much of Scripture, as that the labourer is
worthy of his hire. I must, as usual, take all the trouble and risk."

"Risk! and what is the mighty risk, I pray you? This fellow will come
prowling again about your demesne or into your house, and if you take
him for a house-breaker or a park-breaker, is it not most natural you

should welcome him with cold steel or hot lead? Even a mastiff will pull down those who come near his kennel; and who shall blame him?"

"Ay, I have a mastiff's work and a mastiff's wages among you," said Forster. "Here have you, Master Varney, secured a good freehold estate out of this old superstitious foundation; and I have but a poor lease of this mansion under you, voidable at your honour's pleasure."

"Ay, and thou would'st fain convert thy leasehold into a copyhold— the thing may chance to happen, Anthony Forster, if thou doest good service for it.—But softly, good Anthony—it is not the lending a room or two of this old house for keeping my lord's pretty paroquet—nay, it is not the shutting thy doors and windows to keep her from flying off, that may deserve—remember the manor and tithes are rated at the clear annual value of seventy-nine pounds five shillings and fivepence halfpenny, besides the value of the wood. Come, come, thou must be conscionable; great and secret service may deserve both this and a better thing.—And now let thy knave come and pluck off my boots— get us some dinner, and a cup of thy best wine.—I must visit this mavis, brave in apparel, unruffled in aspect, and gay in temper. I trust by skilful teaching she may learn to whistle that to our good lord shall advantage both thee, and me."

They parted, and at the hour of noon, which was then that of dinner, they again met at their meal, Varney gaily dressed like a courtier of the time, and even Anthony Forster improved in appearance, as far as dress could amend an exterior so unfavourable.

This alteration did not escape Varney. When the meal was finished, the cloth removed, and they left to their private discourse—"Thou art gay as a goldfinch, Anthony," said Varney, looking at his host; "methinks thou wilt whistle a jigg anon—but I crave your pardon, that would secure your ejection from the congregation of the zealous botchers, the pure-hearted weavers, and the sanctified bakers of Abingdon, who let their ovens cool while their brains get heated."

"To answer you in the spirit, Master Varney," said Forster, "were —excuse the parable—to fling sacred and precious things before swine. So I will speak to thee in the language of the world, which he, who is King of the World, hath taught thee to understand and profit by in no common measure."

"Say what thou wilt, honest Tony," replied Varney; "for be it according to thine absurd faith, or according to thy most villainous practice, it cannot chuse but be rare matter to qualify this cup of Alicant. Thy conversation is relishing and poignant, and beats caviar, dried neats-tongue, and all other provocatives that give savour to good liquor."

"Well, then, tell me," said Anthony Forster, "is not our good lord and master's turn better served, and his anti-chamber more suitably filled, with decent, God-fearing men, who will work his will and their own profit quietly, and without worldly scandal, than that he should be manned, and attended, and followed by such open debauchees and ruffianly swordsmen as Tider, Killigrew, this fellow Lambourne, whom you have put me to seek out for you, and other such, who bear the gallows in their face and murther in their right hand—who are a terror to peaceable men, and a scandal to my lord's service?"

"Oh, content you, good Master Anthony Forster," answered Varney; "he that flies at all manner of game must keep all kinds of hawks, both short and long-winged. The course my lord holds is no easy one, and he must stand provided at all points with trusty retainers to meet all sorts of service. He must have his gay courtier, like myself, to ruffle it in the presence-chamber, and to lay hand on hilt when any speaks in disparagement of my lord's honour—"

"Ay," said Forster, "and to whisper a word for him into a fair lady's ear, when he may not approach her himself."

"Then," said Varney, going on without appearing to notice the interruption, "he must have his lawyers—deep subtile pioneers—to draw his contracts—his pre-contracts, and his post-contracts, and to find the way to make the most of grants of church-lands, and commons, and licenses for monopoly—And he must have physicians who can spice a cup or a caudle—And he must have his cabalists, like Dee and Allan, for conjuring up the devil—And he must have ruffling swordsmen, who would fight the devil when he is raised and at the wildest—And above all, but without prejudice to the others, he must have such godly, innocent, puritanic souls as thou, honest Anthony, who defy Satan, and do his work at the same time."

"You would not say, Master Varney," said Forster, "that our good lord and master, whom I hold to be fulfilled in all nobleness, would use such base and sinful means to rise, as thy speech points at?"

"Tush, man," said Varney, "never look at me with so sad a brow—you trap me not—nor am I in your power, as your weak brain may imagine, because I name to you freely the engines, the springs, the screws, the tackle, and braces, by which great men rise in stirring times.—Sayest thou our good lord is fulfilled of all nobleness?—Amen, and so be it—he has the more need to have those about him who are unscrupulous in his service, and who, because they know that his fall will overwhelm and crush them, must wager both blood and brain, soul and body, in order to keep him aloft; and this I tell thee, because I care not who knows it."

"You speak truth, Master Varney," said Anthony Forster; "he that is head of a party, is but a boat on a wave, that raises not itself, but is moved upward by the billow which it floats upon."

"Thou art metaphorical, honest Anthony," replied Varney; "that velvet doublet hath made an oracle of thee—we will have thee to Oxford to take thy degrees in the arts.—And, in the meantime, hast thou arranged all the matters which were sent from London, and put the western chambers in such sort as may answer my lord's humour?"

"They may serve a king on his bridal-day," said Anthony; "and I promise you that Dame Amy sits in them yonder, as proud and gay as if she were the Queen of Sheba."

"'Tis the better, good Anthony," answered Varney; "we must found our future fortunes on her good liking."

"We build on sand then," said Anthony Forster; "for supposing that she sails away to court in all her lord's dignity and authority, how is she like to look back upon me, who am her jailor as it were, to detain her here against her will, keeping her a caterpillar on an old wall, when she would fain be a painted butterfly in a court garden?"

"Fear not her displeasure, man," said Varney. "I will shew her that all thou hast done in this matter was good service, both to my lord and her; and when she chips the egg-shell and walks alone, she shall own we have hatched her greatness."

"Look to yourself, Master Varney," said Forster, "you may mis-reckon foully in this matter—She gave you but a frosty reception this morning, and, I think, looks on you, as well as me, with an evil eye."

"You mistake her, Forster—you mistake her utterly—To me she is bound by all the ties which can secure her to one who has been the means of gratifying both her love and ambition. Who was it that took the obscure Amy Robsart, the daughter of an impoverished and dotard knight—the destined bride of a moonstruck, moping enthusi-ast, like Edmund Tressilian, from her lowly fates, and held out to her in prospect, the brightest fortune in England, or perchance in Europe? Why, man, it was I—as I have often told thee—that found opportunity for their secret meetings—It was I who watched the wood while he beat for the deer—It was I who, to this day, am blamed by her family as companion of her flight, and were I in their neighbourhood, would be fain to wear a shirt of better stuff than Holland linen, lest my ribs should be acquainted with Milan steel. Who carried their letters? —I. Who amused the old knight and Tressilian?—I. Who planned her escape?—it was I. It was I, in short, who pulled this pretty little daisy from its lowly nook, and placed it in the proudest bonnet in Britain."

"Ay, Master Varney," said Forster, "but it may be, she thinks that had the matter remained with you, the flower had been stuck so slightly into the cap, that the first breath of a changeable breeze of passion, had blown the poor daisy to the common."

"She should consider," said Varney, smiling, "the true faith I owed my lord and master prevented me at first from counselling marriage— and yet I did counsel marriage when I saw she would not be satisfied without the—the sacrament or the ceremony callest thou it, Anthony?"

"Still she has you at feud on another score," said Forster; "and I tell it you that you may look to yourself in time—She would not hide her splendour in this dark lantern of an old monastic house, but would fain shine a countess amongst countesses."

"Very natural, very right," answered Varney; "but what have I to do with that?—she may shine through horn or through crystal at my lord's pleasure, I have nought to say against it."

"She deems that you have an oar upon that side of the boat, Master Varney," replied Forster, "and that you can pull it or no, at your good pleasure. In a word, she ascribes the secrecy and obscurity in which she is kept, to your secret counsel to my lord, and to my strict agency; and so she loves us both as a sentenced man loves his judge and his jailor."

"She must love us better ere she leave this place, Anthony," answered Varney. "If I have counselled for weighty reasons that she remain here for a season, I can also advise her being brought forth in the full blow of her dignity. But I were mad to do so, holding so near a place to my lord's person, were she mine enemy. Bear this truth in upon her as occasion offers, Anthony, and let me alone for extolling you in her ear, and exalting you in her opinion—Ka me, ka thee—it is a proverb all over the world—the lady must know her friends, and be made to judge of the power they have of being her enemies—mean-while, watch her strictly, but with all outward observance that thy rough nature will permit. 'Tis an excellent thing that sullen look and bull-dog humour of thine; thou shouldst thank God for it, and so should my lord; for when there is aught harsh or hard-natured to be done, thou doest it as if it flowed from thine own natural doggedness, and not from orders, and so my lord escapes the scandal.—But hark— some one knocks at the gate—Look out at window—let no one enter —this were an ill night to be interrupted."

"It is he whom we spoke of before dinner," said Forster, as he looked through the casement; "it is Michael Lambourne."

"Oh, admit him, by all means," said the courtier, "he comes to give some account of his guest—it imports us much to know the move-ments of Edmund Tressilian—admit him, I say, but bring him not hither—I will come to you presently in the Abbot's library."

Forster left the room, and the courtier, who remained behind, paced the parlour more than once in deep thought, his arms folded on his bosom, until at length he gave vent to his meditations in broken words, which we have somewhat enlarged and connected, that the soliloquy may be intelligible to the reader.

"Tis true," he said, suddenly stopping, and resting his right hand on the table at which they had been sitting, "this base churl hath fathomed the very depth of my fear, and I have been unable to disguise it from him—She loves me not—I would it were as true that I loved not her—Idiot that I was, to move her in my own behalf, when wisdom bade me be a true broker to my lord!—and this fatal error has placed me more at her discretion than a wise man would willingly be at that of the best piece of painted Eve's flesh of them all. Since the hour that my policy made so perilous a slip, I cannot look at her without fear, and hate, and fondness, so strangely mingled, that I know not whether, were it at my choice, I would rather possess or ruin her. But she must not leave this retreat until I am assured on what terms we are to stand. My lord's interest—and so far it is mine own—for if he sinks, I fall in his train—demands concealment of this obscure marriage—and I will not lend her my arm to climb to her chair of state, that she may set her foot on my neck when she is fairly seated. I must work an interest in her, either through love or through fear—and who knows but I may yet reap the sweetest and best revenge for her former scorn?—that were indeed a masterpiece of courtlike art!—Let me but once be her counsel-keeper—let her confide to me a secret, did it but concern the robbery of a linnet's nest, and, fair Countess, thou art mine own." He again paced the room in silence, stopped, filled and drank a cup of wine, as if to compose the agitation of his mind, and muttering, "Now for a close heart, and an open and unruffled brow," he left the apartment.

Chapter Six

The dews of summer night did fall,
    The moon, sweet regent of the sky,
Silver'd the walls of Cumnor-hall,
    And many an oak that grew thereby.
                                    MICKLE

FOUR APARTMENTS, which occupied the western side of the old quadrangle at Cumnor-Place, had been fitted up with extraordinary splendour. This had been the work of several days prior to that on which our story opened. Workmen sent from London, and not permitted to leave the premises until the work was finished, had converted the apartments in that whole side of the building, from the dilapidated appearance of a dissolved monastic house, into the semblance of a royal palace. A mystery was observed in all these arrangements; the workmen came thither and returned by night, and all measures were taken to prevent the prying curiosity of the villagers to observe or speculate upon the changes which were taking place in the mansion of their once indigent, but now wealthy neighbour, Anthony Forster. Accordingly, the secrecy desired was so far preserved, that nothing got abroad but vague and uncertain reports, which were received and repeated, but without attaching much credit to them.

On the evening of which we treat, the new and highly decorated suite of rooms were, for the first time, illuminated, and that with a brilliancy which might have been visible half-a-dozen miles off, had not oaken shutters, carefully secured with bolt and padlock, and mantled with long curtains of silk and of velvet, deeply fringed with gold, prevented the radiance from being seen without.

The principal apartments, as we have seen, were four in number, each opening into the other. Access was given to them by a large scale staircase, as they were then called, of unusual length and height, which had its landing-place at the door of an antichamber, shaped somewhat like a gallery. This apartment the Abbot had used as an occasional council-room, but it was now beautifully wainscotted with dark foreign wood of a brown colour, and bearing a high polish, said to have been brought from the Western Indies, and to have been wrought in London with infinite difficulty, and much damage to the tools of the workmen. The dark colour of this finishing was relieved by the number of lights in silver sconces, which hung against the walls, and by six large and richly-framed pictures, by the first masters of the age. A massy oaken table, placed at the lower end of the apartment, served to accommodate such as chose to play at the then fashionable game of shovel-board; and there was at the other end, an elevated gallery for the musicians or minstrels, who might be summoned to increase the festivity of the evening.

From this antichamber opened a banquetting room of moderate size, but brilliant enough to dazzle the eyes of the spectator with the richness of its furnitures. The walls, lately so bare and ghastly, were now clothed with hangings of sky-blue velvet and silver; the chairs were of ebony, richly carved, with cushions corresponding to the hangings, and the place of the silver sconces which enlightened the antichamber, was supplied by a huge chandelier of the same precious metal. The floor was covered with a Spanish foot-cloth, or carpet, on which flowers and fruits were represented in such glowing and natural colours, that you hesitated to place the foot on such exquisite workmanship. The table, of old English oak, stood ready covered with the finest linen, and a large portable court-cupboard was placed with the leaves of its embossed folding-doors displayed, shewing the shelves within, decorated with a full display of plate and porcelain. In the midst of the table stood a salt-cellar of Italian workmanship, a beautiful and splendid piece of plate about two feet high, moulded into a representation of the giant Briareus, whose hundred hands of silver presented to the guest various sorts of spices, or condiments, to season their food withal.

The third apartment was called the withdrawing room. It was hung with the fairest tapestry, representing the fall of Phaeton; for the looms of Flanders were now much occupied on classical subjects. The principal seat of this apartment was a chair of state, raised a step from the floor, and large enough to contain two persons. It was surmounted by a canopy, which, as well as the cushions, side-curtains, and the very foot-cloth, was composed of crimson-velvet, embroidered with seed-pearl. On the top of the canopy were two coronets, resembling those of an earl and countess. Stools covered with velvet, and some cushions disposed in the Moorish fashion, and ornamented with Arabesque needle-work, supplied the place of chairs in this apartment, which contained musical instruments, embroidery frames, and other articles for ladies' pastime. Besides lesser lights, the withdrawing-room was illuminated by four tall torches of virgin wax, each of which was placed in the grasp of a statue, representing an armed Moor, who held on his left arm a round buckler of silver, highly polished, interposed betwixt his breast and the light, which was thus brilliantly reflected as from a crystal mirror.

The sleeping chamber belonging to this splendid suite of apartments, was decorated in a taste less showy, but not less rich, than had been displayed in the others. Two silver lamps, fed with perfumed oil, diffused at once a delicious odour and a trembling twilight-seeming shimmer through the quiet apartment. It was carpeted so thick, that the heaviest step could not have been heard, and the bed, richly heaped with down, was spread with an ample coverlet of silk and gold; from under which peeped forth cambric sheets, and blankets as white as the lambs which yielded the fleece that made them. The curtains were of blue velvet, lined with crimson silk, deeply festooned with gold, and embroidered with the loves of Cupid and Psyche. On the toilet was a beautiful Venetian mirror, in a frame of silver fillagree, and beside it stood a gold posset-dish to contain the night-draught. A pair of pistols and a dagger, mounted with gold, were displayed near the head of the bed, being the arms for the night, which were presented to honoured guests, rather, it may be supposed, in the way of ceremony, than from any apprehension of danger. We must not omit to mention, what was more to the credit of the manners of the time, that in a small recess, illuminated by a taper, were disposed two hassocks of velvet and gold, corresponding with the bed furniture, before a desk of carved ebony. This recess had formerly been the private oratory of the Abbot, but the crucifix was removed, and instead, there were placed on the desk two Books of Common Prayer, richly bound, and embossed with silver. With this enviable sleeping apartment, which was so far removed from every sound save that of the wind sighing among the oaks of the park, that Morpheus might have coveted it for his own proper repose, corresponded two wardrobes, or dressing-rooms as they are now termed, suitably furnished, and in a style of the same magnificence which we have already described. It ought to be added, that a part of the building in the adjoining wing was occupied by the kitchen and its offices, and served to accommodate the personal attendants of the great and wealthy nobleman, for whose use these magnificent preparations had been made.

The divinity, for whose sake this temple had been decorated, was well worthy the cost and pains which had been bestowed. She was seated in the withdrawing-room which we have described, surveying with the pleased eye of natural and innocent vanity, the splendour which had been so suddenly created, as it were in her honour. For, as her own residence at Cumnor-Place formed the cause of the mystery observed in all the preparations for opening these apartments, it was sedulously arranged, that until she took possession of them, she should have no means of knowing what was going forward in that part of the ancient building, or of exposing herself to be seen by the workmen engaged in the decorations. She had been, therefore, introduced upon that evening to a part of the mansion which she had never yet seen, so different from all the rest, that it appeared, in comparison, like an enchanted palace. And when she first examined and occupied these splendid rooms, it was with the wild and unrestrained joy of a rustic beauty, who finds herself suddenly invested with a splendour which her most extravagant wishes had never shaped for her, and at the same time with the keen feeling of an affectionate heart, which knows that all the enchantment which surrounds her, is the work of the great Magician Love.

The Countess Amy, therefore,—for to that rank she was exalted by her private but solemn union with England's proudest Earl,—had for a time flitted hastily from room to room, admiring each new proof of her lover and her bridegroom's taste, and feeling that admiration enhanced. as she recollected that all she gazed upon was one continued proof of his ardent and devoted affection.—"How beautiful are these hangings!—how natural these paintings, which seem to contend with life!—how richly wrought is that plate, which looks as if all the galleons of Spain had been intercepted on the broad seas to furnish it forth!—And oh, Janet!" she exclaimed repeatedly to the daughter of Anthony Forster, the close attendant, who, with equal curiosity, but somewhat less ecstatic joy, followed on her mistress's footsteps—"O, Janet! how much more delightful to think, that all these fair things have been assembled by his love, for the love of me! and that this evening—this very evening, which wears darker and darker every instant, I shall thank him more for the love that has created such an unimaginable paradise, than for all the wonders it contains."

"The Lord is to be thanked first," said the pretty puritan, "who gave thee, lady, the kind and courteous husband, whose love has done so much for thee. I, too, have done my poor share. But if you thus run wildly from room to room, the toil of my crisping and my curling pins will vanish like the frost-work on the window when the sun is high."

"Thou sayest true, Janet," said the young and beautiful Countess, stopping suddenly from her tripping race of enraptured delight, and looking at herself from head to foot in a large mirror, such as she had never before seen, and which, indeed, had few to match it even in the Queen's palace—"Thou sayest true, Janet," she answered, as she saw, with pardonable self-applause, the noble mirror reflect such charms as were seldom presented to its fair and polished surface; "I have more of the milk-maid than the countess, with these cheeks flushed with haste, and all these brown curls, which you laboured to bring to order, straying as wild as the tendrils of an unpruned vine— my falling ruff is chafed too, and shews the neck and bosom more than is modest and seemly—Come, Janet—we will practise state—we will go to the withdrawing-room, my good girl, and thou shalt put these rebel locks in order, and imprison within lace and cambric the breast that beats too high."

They went to the withdrawing apartment accordingly, where the Countess playfully stretched her upon the pile of Moorish cushions, half sitting, half reclining, half wrapt in her own thoughts, half listening to the prattle of her attendant.

While she was in this attitude, and with a corresponding expression betwixt listlessness and expectation on her fine and expressive features, you might have searched sea and land without finding any thing half so expressive or half so lovely. The wreath of brilliants which mixed with her dark brown hair, did not match in lustre the hazel eye which a light brown eye-brow, pencilled with exquisite delicacy, and long eye-lashes of the same colour, relieved and shaded. The exercise she had just taken, her excited expectation and gratified vanity, spread a glow over her fine features, which were sometimes censured for being rather too pale. The necklace of milk-white pearls which she wore, the same which she had just received as a true-love token from her husband, were excelled in purity by her teeth, and by the colour of her skin, saving where the blush of pleasure and self-satisfaction had somewhat stained the neck with a shade of light crimson.—"Now have done with these busy fingers, Janet," she said to her busy hand-maiden, who was still officiously employed in bringing her hair and her dress into order—"Have done, I say—I must see your father ere my lord arrives, and also Master Richard Varney, whom my lord has highly in his esteem—but I could tell that of him would lose him favour."

"O do not do so, good my lady!" replied Janet; "leave him to God, who punishes the wicked in his own time; but do not you cross Varney's path, for so thoroughly hath he my lord's ear, that few have thriven who have thwarted his courses."

"And from whom had you this, my most righteous Janet?" said the Countess; "or why should I keep terms with so mean a gentleman as Varney, being, as I am, wife to his master and his patron?"

"Nay, madam," replied Janet Forster, "your ladyship knows better than I—but I have heard my father say, he would rather cross a hungry wolf, than thwart Richard Varney in his courses—and he has oft charged me to have a care of holding commerce with him."

"Thy father said well, girl, for thee," replied the lady, "and I dare swear meant well—it is a pity, though, his face and manner do little match his true purpose—for I think his purpose may be true."

"Doubt it not, my lady," answered Janet—"Doubt not that my father purposes well, though he is a plain man, and his blunt looks may belie his heart."

"I will not doubt it, girl, were it only for thy sake; and yet he has one of those faces which makes men tremble when they look on it. I think even thy mother, Janet—nay, have done with that poking-iron—could hardly look upon him without quaking."

"If it were so, madam," answered Janet Forster, "my mother had those who could keep her in honourable countenance. Why, even you, my lady, both trembled and blushed when Varney brought the letter from my lord."

"You are bold, damsel," said the Countess, rising from the cushions on which she sate half reclined in the arms of her attendant —"Know, that there are causes of trembling which have nothing to do with fear.—But, Janet," she added, immediately relapsing into the good-natured and familiar tone which was natural to her, "believe me I will do what credit I can to your father, and the rather that you, sweetheart, are his child.—Alas! alas!" she added, a sudden sadness passing over her fine features, and her eyes filling with tears, "I ought the rather to hold sympathy with thy kind heart, that my own poor father is uncertain of my fate, and they say lies sick and sorrowful for my worthless sake—But I will soon cheer him—the news of my happiness and advancement will make him young again.—And that I may cheer him the sooner"—she wiped her eyes as she spoke—"I must be cheerful myself—My lord must not find me insensible to his kindness, or sorrowful when he snatches a visit to his recluse, after so long an absence.—Be merry, Janet—the night wears on, and my lord must soon arrive.—Call thy father hither, and call Varney also—I cherish resentment against neither; and though I may have some room to complain of both, it shall be their own fault if ever a complaint against them reaches the Earl through my means.—Call them hither, Janet."

Janet Forster obeyed her mistress; and in a few minutes afterwards, Varney entered the withdrawing-room with the graceful ease and unclouded front of an accomplished courtier, skilled, under the veil of external politeness, to disguise his own feelings, and to penetrate into those of others. Anthony Forster plodded into the apartment after him, his natural gloomy vulgarity of aspect seeming to become yet more remarkable, from his clumsy attempt to conceal the anxious mixture of anxiety and dislike with which he looked on her, over whom he had hitherto exercised so severe a controul, now so splendidly attired, and decked with so many pledges of the interest which she possessed in her husband's affections. The blundering reverence which he made, rather *at* than *to* the Countess, had confession in it—it was like the reverence which the criminal makes to the judge, when he at once confesses his guilt and implores mercy,—which is at the same time an impudent and embarrassed attempt at defence or extenuation, a confession of a fault, and an entreaty for lenity.

Varney, who, in right of his gentle blood, had pressed into the room before Anthony Forster, knew better what to say than he, and said it with more assurance and a better grace.

The Countess greeted him indeed with an appearance of cordiality, which seemed a complete amnesty for whatever she might have to complain of. She rose from her seat, and advanced two steps towards him, holding forth her hand as she said, "Master Richard Varney, you brought me this morning such welcome tidings, that I fear surprise and joy made me neglect my lord and husband's charge to receive you with distinction. We offer you our hand, sir, in reconciliation."

"I am unworthy to touch it," said Varney, dropping on one knee, "save as a subject honours that of a prince."

He touched with his lips those fair and slender fingers, so richly loaded with rings and jewels; then rising, with graceful gallantry, was about to hand her to the chair of state, when she said, "No, good Master Richard Varney, I take not my place there until my lord himself conducts me. I am for the present but a disguised Countess, and will not take dignity on me until authorized by him whom I derive it from."

"I trust, my lady," said Forster, "that in doing the commands of my lord your husband, in your restraint and so forth, I have not incurred your displeasure, seeing that I did but my duty towards your lord and mine; for Heaven, as holy writ saith, hath given the husband supremacy and dominion over the wife—I think it runs so, or something like it."

"I receive at this moment so pleasant a surprise, Master Forster," answered the Countess, "that I cannot but excuse the rigid fidelity which secluded me from these apartments, until they had assumed an appearance so new and so splendid."

"Ay, lady," said Forster, "it hath cost many a fair crown, and that more need not be wasted than is absolutely necessary——I leave you till my lord's arrival with good Master Richard Varney, who, as I think, hath somewhat to say to you from your most noble lord and husband. —Janet, follow me, to see that all be in order."

"No, Master Forster," said the Countess, "we will your daughter remains here in our apartment—Out of earshot, however, if Varney hath aught to say to me from my lord."

Forster made his clumsy reverence, and departed, with an aspect that seemed to grudge the profuse expense, which had been wasted upon changing his house from a bare and ruinous grange to an Asiatic palace. When he was gone, his daughter took her embroidering frame, and went to establish herself at the bottom of the apartment, while Richard Varney, with a profoundly humble courtesy, took the lowest stool he could light upon, and placing it by the side of the cushions on which the Countess had now again seated herself, sat with his eyes for a time fixed on the ground, and in profound silence. "I thought, Master Varney," said the Countess, when she saw he was not likely to open the conversation, "that you had something to communicate from my lord and husband—so at least I understood Master Forster, and therefore I removed my waiting-maid. If I am mistaken, I will recal her to my side; for her needle is not so absolutely perfect in tent and cross-stitch, but what my superintendance is advisable."

"Lady," said Varney, "Forster was partly mistaken in my purpose—it was not *from*, but *of*, your noble husband, and my approved and most honoured patron, that I am led, and indeed bound to speak."

"The theme is most welcome, sir," said the Countess, "whether it be of or from my noble husband. But be brief, for I expect his hasty approach."

"Briefly then, madam," replied Varney, "and boldly, for my argument requires both haste and courage—You have this day seen Tressilian."

"I have, sir, and what of that?"

"Nothing that concerns me, lady. But think you, honoured madam, that your lord will hear it with equal equanimity?"

"And wherefore should he not?—to me alone was Tressilian's visit embarrassing and painful, for he brought news of my good father's illness."

"Of your father's illness, madam!" answered Varney. "It must have been sudden then—very sudden—for the messenger whom I dispatched, at my lord's instance, found the good knight on the hunting-field, cheering his beagles with his wonted jovial field-cry. I trust, Tressilian has but forged this news—he hath his reasons, madam, as well you know, for disquieting your present happiness."

"You do him injustice, Master Varney," replied the Countess with animation—"You do him much injustice. He is the freest, the most open, the most gentle heart that breathes—my honourable lord ever excepted, I know not one to whom falsehood is more odious than to Tressilian."

"I crave your pardon, madam," said Varney, "I meant the gentleman no injustice—I knew not how nearly his cause affected you. A man may, in some circumstances, disguise the truth for fair and honest purpose; for were it to be forever spoken, and upon all occasions, this were no world to live in."

"You have a courtly conscience, Master Varney," said the Countess, "and your veracity will not, I think, interrupt your preferment in this world, such as it is.—But Tressilian—I must do him justice, for I have done him wrong, as none knows better than thou—Tressilian's conscience is of other mold—The world thou speakest of has not that which could bribe him from the way of truth and honour; and for living in it with a soiled fame, the ermine would as soon seek to lodge in the den of the foul pole-cat. For this my father loved him—for this I would have loved him—if I could.—And yet in this case he had what seemed to him, unknowing alike of my marriage, and to whom I was united, such powerful reasons to withdraw me from this place, that I well trust he exaggerated much my father's indisposition, and that thy better news may be the truer."

"Believe me they are, madam," answered Varney; "I pretend not to be a champion of that same naked virtue called Truth, to the very outrance. I can consent that her charms be hidden with a veil, were it but for decency's sake. But you must think lower of my head and heart, than is due to one whom my noble lord calls his friend, if you suppose I could wilfully and unnecessarily palm upon you a falsehood so soon detected, in a matter which concerns your happiness."

"Master Varney," said the Countess, "I know that my lord esteems you, and holds you a faithful and a good pilot in those seas in which he has spread so high and so venturous a sail. Do not suppose, therefore, I meant hardly by you, when I spoke the truth in Tressilian's vindication—I am, as you well know, country-bred, and like plain rustic truth better than courtly compliment; but I must change my fashions with my sphere, I presume."

"True, madam," said Varney, smiling, "and though you speak now in jest, it will not be amiss that in earnest your present speech had some connection with your real purpose.—A court-dame—take the most noble—the most virtuous—the most unimpeachable that stands around our Queen's throne—would, for example, have shunned to speak the truth, or what she thought such, in praise of a discarded suitor, before the dependant and confidant of her noble husband."

"And wherefore," said the Countess, colouring impatiently, "should I not do justice to Tressilian's worth, before my husband's friend—before my husband himself—before the whole world?"

"And with the same openness your ladyship," said Varney, "will this night tell my noble lord your husband, that Tressilian has discovered your place of residence, so anxiously concealed from the world—that he has had an interview with you."

"Unquestionably it will be the first thing I tell him, together with every word that he said, and that I answered. I shall speak my own shame in this, for Tressilian's reproaches, less just than he esteemed them, were not altogether unmerited—I will speak, therefore, with pain, but I will speak, and speak all."

"Your ladyship will do your pleasure," answered Varney; "but methinks it were as well, since nothing calls for so frank a disclosure, to spare yourself this pain, and my noble lord the disquiet, and Master Tressilian, since belike he must be thought of in the matter, the danger which is like to ensue."

"I can see nought of all these terrible consequences," said the lady, composedly, "unless by imputing to my noble lord unworthy thoughts, which I am sure never harboured in his generous heart."

"Far be it from me to do so," said Varney—and then, after a moment's silence, he added, with a real or affected plainness of manner, very different from his usual smooth courtesy—"Come, madam, I will shew you that a courtier dare speak truth as well as another, when it concerns the weal of those whom he honours and regards, ay, and although it may infer his own danger."—He waited as if to receive commands, or at least permission to go on, but as the lady remained silent, he proceeded, but obviously with caution.—"Look around you," he said, "noble lady, and observe the barriers with which this place is surrounded, the studious mystery with which the brightest jewel that England possesses is secluded from the admiring gaze— See with what rigour your walks are circumscribed, and your movements restrained, at the beck of yonder churlish Forster—consider all this, and judge for yourself what can be the cause."

"My lord's pleasure," answered the Countess; "and I am bound to seek no other motive."

"His pleasure it is indeed," said Varney; "and his pleasure arises out of a love worthy of the object which inspires it—but he who possesses a treasure, and who values it, is oft anxious, in proportion to the value he puts upon it, to secure it from the depredations of others."

"What needs all this talk, Master Varney?" said the lady, in reply; "you would have me believe that my noble lord is jealous—suppose it true, I know a cure for jealousy."

"Indeed, madam!" said Varney.

"It is," replied the lady, "to speak the truth to my lord at all times, to hold up my mind and my thoughts before him as pure as that polished mirror; so that when he looks into my heart, he shall only see his own features reflected there."

"I am mute, madam," answered Varney; "and as I have no reason to grieve for Tressilian, who would have my heart's blood were he able, I shall reconcile myself easily to what may befall the gentleman, in consequence of your frank disclosure of his having presumed to intrude upon your solitude.—You, who know my lord so much better than I, will judge if he be like to bear the insult unavenged."

"Nay, if I could think myself the cause of Tressilian's ruin," said the Countess,—"I who have already occasioned him so much distress, I might be brought to be silent.—And yet what will it avail, since he was seen by Forster, and I think by some one else?—No, no, Varney, urge it no more, I will tell the whole matter to my lord; and with such pleading for Tressilian's folly, as shall dispose my lord's generous heart rather to serve than to punish him."

"Your judgment, madam," said Varney, "is far superior to mine, especially as you may, if you will, prove the ice before you step on it, by mentioning Tressilian's name to my lord, and observing how he bears it. For Forster and his attendant, they know not Tressilian by sight, and I can easily give them some reasonable excuse for the appearance of an unknown stranger."

The lady paused for an instant, and then replied, "If, Varney, it be indeed true that Forster knows not as yet that the man he saw was Tressilian, I own I were unwilling he should learn what no ways concerns him. He bears himself already with austerity enough, and I wish him not be judge or privy-councillor in my affairs."

"Tush," said Varney; "what has the surly groom to do with your ladyship's concerns?—no more, surely, than the ban-dog which watches his court-yard. If he is in aught distasteful to your ladyship, I have interest enough to have him exchanged for a seneschal that shall be more agreeable to you."

"Master Varney," said the Countess, "let us drop this theme— when I complain of the attendants whom my lord has placed around me, it must be to my lord himself.—Hark! I hear the trampling of horse—He comes! he comes!" she exclaimed, jumping up in ecstacy.

"I cannot think it is he," said Varney; "or that you can hear the tread of his horse through these closely mantled casements."

"Stop me not, Varney—my ears are keener than thine—it is he!"

"But madam!—but madam!" exclaimed Varney, anxiously, and still placing himself in her way—"I trust that what I have spoken in humble duty and service, will not be turned to my ruin—I hope that my faithful advice will not be bewrayed to my prejudice—I implore that"——

"Content thee, man—content thee!" said the Countess, "and quit my skirt—you are too bold to detain me—content thyself, I think not of thee."

At this moment the folding-doors flew wide open, and a man of majestic mien, muffled in the folds of a long dark riding-cloak, entered the apartment.

Chapter Seben

——This is He
Who rides on the court-gale; controuls its tides;
Knows all their secret shoals and fatal eddies;
Whose frown abases, and whose smile exalts.
He shines like any rainbow—and, perchance,
His colours are as transient.
Old Play

THERE WAS some little displeasure and confusion on the Countess's brow, owing to her struggle with Varney's pertinacity; but it was exchanged for an expression of the purest joy and affection, as she threw herself into the arms of the noble stranger who entered, and clasping him to her bosom, exclaimed, "At length—at length thou art come!"

Varney discreetly withdrew as his lord entered, and Janet was about to do the same, when her mistress signed to her to remain. She took her place at the farther end of the apartment, and remained standing, as if ready for attendance.

Meanwhile, the Earl, for he was of no inferior rank, returned his lady's caress with the most affectionate ardour, but affected to resist when she strove to take his cloak from him.

"Nay," she said, "but I will unmantle you—I must see if you have kept your word to me, and come as the Great Earl men call thee, and not as heretofore like a private cavalier."

"Thou art like the rest of the world, Amy," said the Earl, suffering her to prevail in the playful contest; "the jewels, and feathers, and silk, are more to them than the man whom they adorn—many a poor blade looks gay in a velvet scabbard."

"But so cannot men say of thee, thou noble Earl," said his lady, as the cloak dropped on the floor, and shewed him dressed as princes when they ride abroad; "thou art the good and well-tried steel, whose inly worth deserves, yet disdains, its outward ornament. Do not think Amy can love thee better in this glorious garb, than she did when she gave her heart to him who wore the russet brown cloak in the woods of Devon."

"And thou too," said the Earl, as gracefully and majestically he led his beautiful Countess towards the chair of state which was prepared for them both,—"thou too, my love, hast donned a dress which becomes thy rank, though it cannot improve thy beauty. What think'st thou of our court taste?"

The lady cast a sidelong glance upon the great mirror as they passed it by, and then said, "I know not how it is, but I think not of my own seeming, while I look at the reflection of thine. Sit thou there," she said, as they approached the state, "like a thing for men to worship and to wonder at."

"Ay, love," said the Earl. "If thou wilt share my state with me."

"Not so," said the Countess; "I will sit on this footstool at thy feet, that I may spell over thy splendour, and learn, for the first time, how princes are attired."

And with a childish wonder, which her youth and rustic education rendered not only excusable but becoming, mixed as it was with a delicate shew of the most tender conjugal affection, she examined and admired from head to foot the noble form and princely attire of him, who formed the proudest ornament of the court of England's Maiden Queen, renowned as it was for splendid courtiers, as well as for wise counsellors. Regarding affectionately his lovely bride, and gratified by her unrepressed admiration, the dark eye and noble features of the

Earl expressed passions more gentle than the commanding and aspiring look, which usually sate upon his broad forehead, and in the piercing brilliancy of his dark eye, and he smiled at the simplicity which dictated the questions she put to him concerning the various ornaments with which he was decorated.

"The embroidered strap, as thou callest it, around my knee," he said, "is the English Garter, an ornament which kings are proud to wear. See, here is the star which belongs to it, and here the Diamond George, the jewel of the Order. You have heard how King Edward and the Countess of Salisbury"——

"O, I know all that tale," said the Countess, slightly blushing, "and how a lady's garter became the proudest badge of English chivalry."

"Even so," said the Earl; "and this most honourable Order I had the good hap to receive at the same time with three most noble associates, the Duke of Norfolk, the Marquis of Northampton, and the Earl of Rutland. I was the lowest of the four in rank—but what then? —he that climbs a ladder must begin at the first round."

"But this other fair collar, so richly wrought, with some jewel like a sheep hung by the middle attached to it, what," said the young Countess, "does that emblem signify?"

"This collar," said the Earl, "with its double fusilles interchanged with these knobs, which are supposed to present flint-stones, sparkling with fire, and sustaining the jewel you inquire after, is the badge of the noble Order of the Golden Fleece, once appertaining to the House of Burgundy. It hath high privileges, my Amy, belonging to it, this most noble Order; for even the King of Spain himself, who hath now succeeded to the honours and demesnes of Burgundy, may not sit in judgment upon a knight of the Golden Fleece, unless by assistance and consent of the Great Chapter of the Order."

"And is this an Order belonging to the cruel King of Spain?" said the Countess. "Alas! my noble lord, that you will defile your noble English breast by bearing such an emblem! Bethink you of the most unhappy Queen Mary's days, when this same Philip held sway with her in England, and of the piles which were built for our noblest, and our wisest, and our most truly sanctified prelates and divines—And will you, whom men call the standard-bearer of the true Protestant faith, be contented to wear the emblem and mark of such a Romish tyrant as He of Spain?"

"O, content you, my love," answered the Earl; "we who spread our sails to court gales of favour, cannot always display the ensigns we love the best, or at all times refuse sailing under colours which we like not. Believe me, I am not the less good Protestant, that for policy I must accept the honour offered me by Spain, in admitting me to this his highest order of knighthood. Besides, it belongs properly to Flanders; and Egmont, Orange, and others, have pride in seeing it displayed on an English bosom."

"Nay, my lord, you know your own path best," replied the Countess.—"And this other collar, to what country does this fair jewel belong?"

"To a very poor one, my love," replied the Earl; "this is the Order of Saint Andrew, revived by the last James of Scotland. It was bestowed on me when it was thought the young widow of France and Scotland would gladly have wedded an English baron; but a free coronet of England is worth a crown matrimonial held at the humour of a woman, and owing only the poor rocks and bogs of the north."

The Countess paused, as if what he last said had excited some painful but interesting train of thought; and, as she still remained silent, the Earl proceeded.

"And now, loveliest, your wish is gratified, and you have seen your vassal in such of his trim array as accords with riding vestments. For robes of state and coronets are only for princely halls."

"Well, then," said the Countess, "my gratified wish has, as usual, given rise to a new one."

"And what is it thou can'st ask that I can deny?" said the fond husband.

"I wished to see my Earl visit this obscure and secret bower," said the Countess, "in all his princely array, and now, methinks, I long to sit in one of his princely halls, and see him enter dressed in sober russet, as when he won poor Amy Robsart's heart."

"That is a wish easily granted," said the Earl—"the sober russet shall be donned to-morrow if you will."

"But shall I," said the lady, "go with you to one of your castles, to see how the richness of your dwelling will correspond with your peasant habit."

"Why, Amy," said the Earl, looking around, "are not these apartments decorated with sufficient splendour? I gave the most unbounded orders, and, methinks, they have been indifferently well obeyed—but if thou canst tell me aught which remains to be done, I will instantly give direction."

"Nay, my lord, now you mock me," replied the Countess; "the gaiety of this rich lodging exceeds my imagination as much as it does my desert—but shall not your wife, my love—at least one day soon—be surrounded with the honour, which arises not from the toils of the mechanic who decks her apartment, nor from the silks and jewels with which your generosity adorns her, but by her place among the matronage, as the avowed wife of England's noblest Earl?"

"One day—" said her husband, "yes, Amy, my love, one day this shall surely happen; and, believe me, thou canst not wish for that day more fondly than I. With what rapture could I retire from labours of state, and cares and toils of ambition, to spend my life in dignity and honour on my own broad domains, with thee, my lovely Amy, for my friend and companion! But, Amy, this cannot yet be; and these dear but stolen interviews, are all I can give to the loveliest and the best beloved of her sex."

"But *why* can it not be?" urged the Countess, in the softest tones of persuasion,—"why can it not immediately take place—this more perfect, this uninterrupted union, for which you say you wish, and which the laws of God and man alike command?—Ah! did you but desire it half so much as you say, mighty and favoured as you are, who, or what, should bar your attaining your wish?"

The Earl's brow was overcast.

"Amy," he said, "you speak of what you understand not. We that toil in courts are like those who climb a mountain of loose sand—we dare make no halt until some projecting rock afford us a secure stance and resting place—if we pause, soon we slide down by our own weight, an object of universal derision. I stand high, but I stand not secure enough to follow my own inclination. To declare my marriage, were to be the artificer of my own ruin—but, believe me, I will reach a point, and that speedily, when I can do justice to thee and to myself. Meantime, poison not the bliss of the present moment, by desiring that which cannot at present be. Let me rather know whether all here is managed to thy liking. How does Forster bear himself to you?—in all things respectful I trust, else the fellow shall dearly rue it."

"He reminds me sometimes of the necessity of this privacy," answered the lady with a sigh; "but that is reminding me of your wishes, and therefore, I am rather bound to him than disposed to blame him for it."

"I have told you the stern necessity which is upon us," replied the Earl. "Forster is, I note, somewhat sullen of mood, but Varney warrants to me his fidelity and devotion to my service. If thou hast aught, however, to complain of the mode in which he discharges his duty, he shall abye it."

"O, I have nought to complain of," answered the lady, "so he discharges his task with fidelity to you. And his daughter Janet is the kindest and best companion of my solitude—her little air of precision sits so well upon her."

"Is she indeed?" said the Earl. "She who gives you pleasure, must not pass unrewarded—come hither, damsel."

"Janet," said the lady, "come hither to my lord."

Janet, who, as we already noticed, had discreetly retired to some distance, that her presence might be no check upon the private conversation of her lord and lady, now came forwards; and as she made her reverential courtesy, the Earl could not help smiling at the contrast which the extreme simplicity of her dress, and the prim demureness of her looks made, with a very pretty countenance and a pair of black eyes, that laughed in spite of their mistress's desire to look grave.

"I am bound to you, pretty damsel," said the Earl, "for the contentment which your service hath given to this lady." As he said this, he took from his finger a ring of some price, and offered it to Janet Forster, adding, "Wear this, for her sake and for mine."

"I am well pleased, my lord," answered Janet, demurely, "that my poor service hath gratified my lady, whom no one can draw nigh to without desiring to please; but we of the precious Mr Holdforth's congregation, seek not, like the gay daughters of this world, to twine gold around our fingers, or wear stones upon our necks, like the vain women of Tyre and of Sidon."

"O, what! you are a grave professor of the precise sisterhood, pretty Mrs Janet," said the Earl, "and so I think is your father. In sincerity I like you both the better for it; for I have been prayed for, and wished well to in your congregations. And you may the better afford the lack of ornaments, Mrs Janet, because your fingers are slender, and your neck white. But here is what neither papist nor puritan, latitudinarian nor precisian, ever boggles or makes mouths at—e'en take it, my girl, and employ it as you list."

So saying, he put into her hand five broad gold pieces of Philip and Mary.

"I would not accept this gold neither," said Janet, "but that I hope to find a use for it, will bring a blessing on us all."

"Even please thyself, pretty Janet," said the Earl, "and I will be well satisfied—And I prithee let them hasten the evening collation."

"I have bidden Master Varney and Master Forster to sup with us, my lord," said the Countess, as Janet retired to obey the Earl's commands, "has it your approbation?"

"What you do ever must have so, my sweet Amy," replied her husband; "and I am the better pleased thou hast done them this grace, because Richard Varney is my sworn man, and a close brother of my secret counsel; and for the present, I must needs repose much trust in this Anthony Forster."

"I had a boon to beg of thee, and a secret to tell thee, my dear lord," said the Countess with a faultering accent.

"Let both be for to-morrow, my love," replied the Earl. "I see they open the folding-doors into the banquetting parlour, and as I have ridden far and fast, a cup of wine will not be unacceptable."

So saying, he led his lovely wife into the next apartment, where Varney and Forster received them with the deepest reverences, which the first paid after the fashion of the court, and the second after that of the congregation. The Earl returned their salutation with the negligent courtesy of one long used to such homage; while the Countess repaid it with a punctilious solicitude, which shewed it was not quite so familiar to her.

The banquet, at which they seated themselves, corresponded in magnificence with the splendour of the apartment in which it was served up, but no domestic gave his attendance. Janet alone stood ready to wait upon the company; and, indeed, the board was so well supplied with all that could be desired, that little or no assistance was necessary. The Earl and his lady occupied the upper end of the table, and Varney and Forster sat beneath the salt, as was the custom with inferiors. The latter, overawed perhaps by society to which he was altogether unused, did not utter a single syllable during the repast; while Varney, with great tact and discernment, sustained just so much of the conversation, as, without the appearance of intrusion on his part, prevented it from languishing, and maintained the good humour of the Earl at the highest pitch. This man was indeed highly qualified by nature to discharge the part in which he found himself placed, being discreet and cautious on the one hand, and on the other, quick, keen-witted, and imaginative; so that even the Countess, prejudiced as she was against him on many accounts, felt and enjoyed his powers of conversation, and was more disposed than she had ever hitherto found herself, to join in the praises which the Earl lavished on his favourite. The hour of rest at length arrived, the Earl and Countess retired to their apartment, and all was silent in the castle for the rest of the night.

Early on the ensuing morning, Varney acted as the Earl's chamberlain as well as his master of horse, though the latter was his proper office in that magnificent household, where knights and gentlemen of good descent were well contented to hold such menial situations, as nobles themselves held in that of the sovereign. The duties of each of these charges were familiar to Varney, who, sprung from an ancient but somewhat decayed family, had been the Earl's page during his earlier and more obscure fortunes, and, faithful to him in adversity, had afterwards contrived to render himself no less useful to him in his rapid and splendid advance to fortune; thus establishing in him an interest resting both on present and past services, which rendered him an almost indispensable sharer of his confidence.

"Help me to do on a plainer riding-suit, Varney," said the Earl, as he laid aside his morning-gown, flowered with silk, and lined with sables, "and put these chains and fetters there (pointing to the collars of the various Orders which lay on the table) into their place of security—my neck last night was well nigh broke with the weight of them. I am half resolved they shall gall me no more. They are bonds which knaves have invented to fetter fools. How think'st thou, Varney?"

"Faith, my good lord," said his attendant, "I think fetters of gold are like no other fetters—they are ever the weightier the welcomer."

"For all that, Varney," replied his master, "I am half resolved they shall bind me to the court no longer. What can further service and higher favour give me, beyond the high rank and large estate which I have already secured?—What brought my father to the block, but that he could not bound his wishes within right and reason?—I have, you know, had mine own ventures and mine own escapes; I am well nigh resolved to tempt the sea no farther, but sit me in quiet down on the shore."

"And gather cockle-shells, with Dan Cupid to aid you," said Varney.

"How mean you by that, Varney?" said the Earl, somewhat hastily.

"Nay, my lord," said Varney, "be not angry with me. If your lordship is happy in a lady so rarely lovely, that to enjoy her company with somewhat more freedom, you are willing to part with all you have hitherto lived for, some of your poor servants may be sufferers; but your bounty hath placed me so high, that I shall ever have enough to maintain a poor gentleman in the rank befitting the high office he has held in your lordship's family."

"Yet you seem discontented when I propose throwing up a dangerous game, which may end in the ruin of both of us."

"I, my lord?" said Varney; "surely I have no cause to regret your lordship's retreat?—it will not be Richard Varney who will incur the displeasure of majesty, and the ridicule of the court, when the stateliest fabric that ever was founded upon a prince's favour, melts away like a morning frost-work.—I would only have you yourself be assured, my lord, ere you take a step which cannot be retracted, that you consult your fame and happiness in the course you propose."

"Speak on then, Varney," said the Earl; "I tell thee I have determined nothing, and will weigh all considerations on either side."

"Well then, my lord," replied Varney, "we will suppose the step taken, the frown frowned, the laugh laughed, and the moan moaned. You are retired, we will say, to some of your most distant castles, so far from court that you hear neither the sorrow of your friends, nor the glee of your enemies. We will suppose, too, that your successful rival will be satisfied (a thing greatly to be doubted) with abridging and cutting away the branches of the great tree, which so long kept the sun from him, and that he does not insist upon tearing you up by the roots. Well, the late prime favourite of England, who wielded her general's staff and controuled her parliaments, is now a rural baron, hunting, hawking, and drinking fat ale with country esquires, and mustering his men at the command of the High Sheriff"——

"Varney, forbear!" said the Earl.

"Nay, my lord, you must give me leave to conclude my picture.— Sussex governs England—the Queen's health fails—the succession is to be settled—A road is opened to ambition more splendid than ambition ever dreamed.—You hear all this as you sit by the hob, under the shade of your hall-chimney—you then begin to think what hopes you have fallen from, and what insignificance you have embraced— and all that you might look babies in the eyes of your fair wife oftener than once a fortnight."

"I say, Varney," said the Earl, "no more of this. I said not that the step, which my own ease and comfort would urge me to, was to be taken hastily, or without due consideration to the public safety. Bear witness to me, Varney, I subdue my wishes of retirement, not because I am moved by the call of private ambition, but that I may preserve the position in which I may best serve my country at the hour of need.— Order our horses presently—I will wear, as formerly, one of the livery cloaks, and ride before the portmantle.—Thou shalt be master for the day, Varney—neglect nothing that can blind suspicion. We will to horse ere men are stirring. I will but take leave of my lady, and be ready. I impose a restraint on my own poor heart, and wound one yet more dear to me; but the patriot must subdue the husband."

Having said this in a melancholy but firm accent, he left the dressing apartment.

"I am glad thou art gone," thought Varney, "or, practised as I am in the follies of mankind, I had laughed in the very face of thee! Thou mayst tire if thou wilt of thy new bauble, thy pretty piece of painted Eve's flesh there, I will not be thy hindrance. But of thine old bauble, Ambition, thou shalt not tire, for as you climb the hill, my lord, you must drag Richard Varney up with you; and if he can urge you to the ascent he means to profit by, believe me he will spare neither whip nor spur.—And for you, my pretty lady, that would be Countess outright, you were best not thwart my courses, lest you are called to an old reckoning on a new score. 'Thou shalt be master,' did he say—By my faith, he may find that he spoke truer than he is aware of—And thus he, who in the estimation of so many wise-judging men can match Burleigh and Walsingham in policy, and Sussex in war, becomes pupil to his own menial; and all for a hazel eye and a little cunning red and white, and so falls Ambition. And yet if the charms of mortal woman could excuse a man's politic pate for becoming bewildered, my lord had the excuse at his right hand this blessed evening that has last passed over us. Well—let things roll as they may, he shall make me great, or I will make myself happy; and for that softer piece of creation, if she speak not out her interview with Tressilian, as well I think she dare not, she also must traffic with me for concealment and mutual support in spite of all this scorn.—I must to the stables.— Well, my lord, I order your retinue now; the time may soon come that *my* master of the horse shall order mine own."

So saying, he left the apartment.

In the meanwhile the Earl had re-entered the bed-chamber, bent on taking a hasty farewell of the lovely Countess, and scarce daring to trust himself in private with her, to hear requests again urged, which he found it difficult to parry, yet which his recent conversation with his master of horse had determined him not to grant.

He found her in a white cymar of silk lined with furs, her little feet unstocking'd and hastily thrust into slippers; her unbraided hair escaping from under her midnight coif, with little array but her own loveliness, rather augmented than diminished by the grief which she felt at the approaching moment of separation.

"Now, God be with thee, my dearest and loveliest!" said the Earl, scarce tearing himself from her embrace, yet again returning to fold her again and again in his arms, and again bidding farewell, and again returning to kiss and bid adieu once more. "The sun is on the verge of the blue horizon—I dare not stay.—Ere this I should have been ten miles from hence."

Such were the words, with which at length he strove to cut short their parting interview.

"You will not grant my request then," said the Countess. "Ah, false knight! did ever lady, with bare foot in slipper, seek boon of a brave knight, yet return with denial?"

"Any thing, Amy, any thing thou canst ask I will grant," answered the Earl—"always excepting," he said, "that which might ruin us both."

"Nay," said the Countess, "I urge not my wish to be acknowledged in the character which would make me the envy of England—as the wife, that is, of my brave and noble lord, the first as the most fondly beloved of English nobles.—Let me but share the secret with my dear father!—Let me but end his misery on my unworthy account—they say he is ill, the good old kind-hearted man."

"*They* say?" asked the Earl, hastily; "who says? Did not Varney convey to Sir Hugh all we dare at present tell him concerning your happiness and welfare? and has he not told you that the good old knight was following, with good heart and health, his favourite and wonted exercise? Who has dared put other thoughts into your head?"

"O, no one, my lord, no one," said the Countess, something alarmed at the tone in which the question was put; "but yet, my lord, I would fain be assured by mine own eye-sight that my father is well."

"Be contented, Amy—thou canst not now have communication with thy father or his house. Were it not a deep course of policy to commit no secret unnecessarily to the custody of more than must needs be, it were sufficient reason for secrecy that yonder Cornish man, yonder Trevanion, or Tressilian, or whatsoever his name is, haunts the old knight's house, and must necessarily know whatever is communicated there."

"My lord," answered the Countess, "I do not think it so. My father has been long noted a worthy and honourable man; and for Tressilian, if we can pardon ourselves the ill we have wrought him, I will wager the coronet I am to share with you one day, that he is incapable of returning injury for injury."

"I will not trust him, however, Amy," said her husband; "by my honour I will not trust him—I would rather the foul fiend intermingled in our secret than this Tressilian!"

"And why, my lord?" said the Countess, though she shuddered slightly at the tone of determination in which he spoke; "let me but know why you think thus hardly of Tressilian?"

"Madam," replied the Earl, "my will ought to be a sufficient reason —if you desire more, consider how this Tressilian is leagued, and with whom—He stands high in the opinion of this Radcliffe, this Sussex, against whom I am barely able to maintain my ground in the opinion of our suspicious mistress; and if he had me at such advantage, Amy, as to become acquainted with the tale of our marriage, before Elizabeth were fitly prepared, I were an outcast from her grace forever—a bankrupt at once in favour and in fortune, perhaps, for she hath in her a touch of her father Henry,—a victim, a very victim, to her offended and jealous resentment."

"But why, my lord," again replied his lady, "should you deem thus injuriously of a man whom you know so little? What you do know of Tressilian is through me, and it is I who assure you that in no circumstances will he betray your secret. If I did him wrong in your behalf, my lord, I am now the more concerned you should do him justice.—You are offended at my speaking of him, what would you say had I actually myself seen him?"

"If you had," replied the Earl, "you would do well to keep that interview as secret as that which is spoken in a confessional. I seek no one's ruin; but he who thrusts himself on my secret privacy, and meddles with that which it concerns me to keep private, were better look well to his future walk. The Bear brooks no one to cross his awful path."

"Awful, indeed!" said the Countess, turning very pale.

"You are ill, my love," said the Earl, supporting her in his arms; "stretch yourself on your couch again, it is but early days for you to leave it. Have you aught else, involving less than my fame, my fortune, and my life, to ask of me?"

"Nothing, my lord and love," answered the Countess, faintly; "something there was that I would have told you, but your anger has driven it from my recollection."

"Reserve it till our next meeting, my love," said the Earl fondly, and again embracing her; "and barring only those requests which I cannot and dare not now grant, thy wish must be more than England and all its dependancies can fulfil, if it is not gratified to the letter."

Thus saying, he took a final farewell. At the bottom of the staircase he received from Varney an ample livery cloak and slouched hat, in which he wrapped himself so as to disguise his person, and completely conceal his features. Horses were ready in the court-yard for himself and Varney; for one or two of his train, entrusted with the secret so far as to know or guess that the Earl intrigued with a beautiful lady at that mansion, though her name and quality were unknown to them, had been already dismissed over night.

Anthony Forster himself held the rein of the Earl's palfrey, a stout and able nag for the road; while his old serving-man held the bridle of the more shewy and gallant steed which Richard Varney was to occupy in the character of master.

As the Earl approached, however, Varney advanced to hold his master's bridle, and to prevent Forster from paying that duty to the Earl, which he probably considered as belonging to his own office. Forster scowled at an interference which seemed intended to prevent his paying his court to his patron, but gave place to Varney; and the Earl, mounting without farther observation, and forgetting that his assumed character of a domestic threw him into the rear of his supposed master, rode pensively out of the quadrangle, not without waving his hand repeatedly in answer to the signals which were made by the Countess with her kerchief, from the windows of the apartment.

While his stately form vanished under the dark archway which led out of the quadrangle, Varney muttered, "There goes fine policy—the servant before the master;" then as he disappeared, seized the moment to speak a word with Forster. "Thou look'st dark on me,

Anthony," he said, "as if I had deprived thee of a parting nod of my
lord; but I have moved him to leave thee a better remembrance for thy
faithful service. See here! a purse of as good gold as ever chinked
under a miser's thumb and forefinger. Ay, count them, lad," said he,
as Forster received the gold with a grim smile, "and add to them the
goodly remembrance he gave last night to Janet."

"How's this! how's this!" said Anthony Forster, hastily; "gave he
gold to Janet?"

"Ay, man, wherefore not?—does not her service to his fair lady
require guerdon?"

"She shall have none on't," said Forster; "she shall return it. I know
him—his dotage on one face is as brief as it is deep—his affections are
as fickle as the moon."

"Why, Forster, thou art mad—thou doest not hope for such good
fortune, as that my lord should cast an eye on Janet?—who, in the
fiend's name, would listen to the thrush when the nightingale is
singing?"

"Thrush or nightingale, all is one to the fowler; and, Master Varney,
you can sound the quailpipe most daintily for him to wile wantons into
his nets. I desire no such devil's preferment for Janet as you have
brought many a poor maiden to—Doest thou laugh?—I will keep one
limb of my family, at least, from Satan's clutches, that thou may'st rely
on—She shall restore the gold."

"Ay, or give it to thy keeping, Tony, which will serve as well,"
answered Varney; "but I have that to say which is more serious.—Our
lord is returning to court in an evil humour for us."

"How meanest thou? is he tired already of his pretty toy—his play-
thing yonder? He has purchased her at a monarch's ransom, and I
warrant me he rues his bargain."

"Not a whit, Tony; he doats on her, and will forsake the court for
her—then down go hopes, possessions, and safety—church-lands
are resumed, Tony, and well if the holders be not called to accompt in
Exchequer."

"That were ruin," said Forster, his brow darkening with apprehension; "and all this for a woman!—had it been for his soul's sake, it
were something; and I sometimes wish I myself could fling away the
world that cleaves to me, and be as one of the poorest of our church."

"Thou art like enough to be so, Tony," answered Varney; "but I
think the devil will give thee little credit for thy compelled poverty, and
so thou losest on all hands. But follow my counsel, and Cumnor-Place
shall be thy copyhold yet—Say nothing of this Tressilian's visit—not a
word until I give thee notice."

"And wherefore, I pray you?" said Forster, suspiciously.

"Dull beast!" replied Varney; "in my lord's present humour it were the ready way to confirm him in his resolution of retirement, should he know that his lady was haunted with such a spectre in his absence. He would be for playing the dragon himself over his golden fruit, and then, Tony, thy occupation is ended. A word to the wise—farewell—I must follow him."

He turned his horse, struck him with the spurs, and rode off under the archway in pursuit of his master.

"Would thy occupation were ended, or thy neck broken, damned pander!" said Anthony Forster. "But I must follow his beck, for his interest and mine are the same, and he can wind the proud Earl to his will. Janet shall give me these pieces though—they shall be laid out in some way for God's service, and I will keep them separate in my strong chest, till I can fall upon a fitting employment for them. No contagious vapour shall breathe on Janet—she shall remain pure as a blessed spirit, were it but to pray God for her father. I need her prayers, for I am at a hard pass—Strange reports are abroad concerning my way of life—the congregation look cold on me, and when Master Holdforth spoke of hypocrites being like a whited sepulchre, which within was full of dead men's bones, methought he looked full at me. The Romish was a comfortable faith; Lambourne spoke true in that. A man had but to follow his thrift by such ways as offered—tell his beads —hear a mass—confess, and be absolved. These puritans tread a harder and a rougher path; but I will try—I will read my Bible for an hour, ere I again open mine iron chest."

Varney, meantime, spurred after his lord, whom he found waiting for him at the postern-gate of the park.

"You waste time, Varney," said the Earl; "and it presses. I must be at Woodstock before I can safely lay aside my disguise; and till then, I journey in some peril."

"It is but two hours brisk riding, my lord," said Varney; "for me, I only stopped to enforce your commands of care and secrecy on yonder Forster, and to enquire about the abode of the gentleman whom I would promote to your lordship's train, in the room of Trevors."

"Is he fit for the meridian of the antichamber, think'st thou?" said the Earl.

"He promises well, my lord," replied Varney; "but if your lordship were pleased to ride on, I could go back to Cumnor, and bring him to your lordship at Woodstock before you are out of bed."

"Why, I am asleep there, thou know'st, at this moment," said the Earl; "and I pray you not to spare horse-flesh, that you may be with me at my levee."

So saying, he gave his horse the spur, and proceeded on his journey, while Varney rode back to Cumnor by the public road, avoiding the park, and, alighting at the door of the Bonny Black Bear, desired to speak with Master Michael Lambourne. That respectable character was not long of appearing before his new patron, but it was with downcast looks.

"Thou hast lost the scent," said Varney, "of thy comrade Tressilian.—I know it by thy hang-dog visage. Is this thy alacrity, thou impudent knave?"

"Cogswounds!" said Lambourne, "there was never a trail more finely hunted. I ran him to earth at mine uncle's here—stuck to him like bees-wax—saw him at supper—watched him to his chamber, and presto—he is gone next morning, the very hostler knows not how."

"This sounds like practice upon me, sir," replied Varney; "and if it prove so, by my soul you shall abye it."

"Sir, the best hound will be sometimes at fault," answered Lambourne; "how should it serve me that this fellow should have thus evanished? You may ask mine host, Giles Gosling—ask the tapster and hostler—ask Cicely, and the whole household, how I kept eyes on Tressilian while he was on foot—On my soul, I could not be expected to watch him like a sick nurse, when I had seen him fairly a-bed in his chamber. That will be allowed me, surely."

Varney did, in fact, make some enquiry among the household, which confirmed the truth of Lambourne's statement. Tressilian, it was unanimously agreed, had departed suddenly and unexpectedly, betwixt night and morning.

"But I will wrong no one," said mine host; "he left on the table in his lodging the full value of his reckoning, with some allowance to the servants of the house, which was the less necessary, that he saddled his own gelding, as it seems, without the hostler's assistance."

Thus satisfied of the rectitude of Lambourne's conduct, Varney began to talk to him upon his future prospects and the mode in which he meant to bestow himself, intimating that he understood from Forster, he was not disinclined to enter into the household of a nobleman.

"Have you," said he, "ever been at court?"

"No," replied Lambourne; "but ever since I was ten years old, I have dreamt once a-week that I was there, and made my fortune."

"It may be your own fault if your dream comes not true," said Varney; "are you needy?"

"Um!" replied Lambourne; "I love pleasure."

"That is a sufficient answer, and an honest one," said Varney. "Know you aught of the requisites expected from the retainer of a rising courtier?"

"I have imagined them to myself, sir," answered Lambourne; "as for example, a quick eye—a close mouth—a ready and bold hand—a sharp wit, and a blunt conscience."

"And thine, I suppose," said Varney, "has had its edge blunted long since."

"I cannot remember, sir, that its edge was ever over keen," replied Lambourne. "When I was a youth, I had some few whimsies, but I ground them partly out of my recollection on the rough grindstone of the wars, and what remained, I washed out in the broad waves of the Atlantic."

"Thou hast served, then, in the Indies?"

"In both East and West," answered the candidate for court-service, "by both sea and land; I have served both the Portugal and the Spaniard—both the Dutchman and the Frenchman, and have made war on our own account with a crew of jolly fellows, who held there was no peace beyond the Line."

"Thou may'st do me, and my lord, and thyself, good service," said Varney, after a pause. "But observe, I know the world—and, answer me truly, canst thou be faithful?"

"Did you not know the world," answered Lambourne, "it were my cue to say ay, without further circumstance, and to swear to it with life, honour, and so forth.—But as it seems to me that your worship is one who desires rather honest truth than politic falsehood—I reply to you, that I can be faithful to the gallow's foot, ay, to the loop that dangles from it, if I am well used and well recompensed;—not otherwise."

"To thy other virtues thou canst add, no doubt," said Varney, in a jeering tone, "the knack of seeming serious and religious, when the moment demands it."

"It would cost me nothing," said Lambourne, "to say yes—but to speak on the square, I must needs say no. If you want a hypocrite, you may take Anthony Forster, who, from his childhood, had some sort of phantom haunting him, which he called religion, though it was that sort of godliness which always ended in being great gain. But I have no such knack of it."

"Well," replied Varney, "if thou hast no hypocrisy, hast thou not a nag here in the stable?"

"Ay, sir," said Lambourne, "that shall take hedge and ditch with my Lord Duke's best hunters. When I made a little mistake on Shooter's Hill, and stopped an ancient grazier, whose pouches were better lined than his brain-pan, the bonny bay nag carried me sheer off, in spite of the whole hue and cry."

"Saddle him then, instantly, and attend me," said Varney. "Leave thy clothes and baggage under charge of mine honest host, and I will conduct thee to a service, in which, if thou do not better thyself, the fault shall not be fortune's, but thine own."

"Brave and hearty!" said Lambourne, "and I am mounted in an instant.—Knave, hostler, saddle my nag without the loss of one instant, as dost value the safety of thine noddle.—Pretty Cicely, take half this purse to comfort thee for my sudden departure."

"Gogsnouns!" replied the father, "Cicely wants no such token from thee—go away, Mike, and gather grace if thou canst, though I think thou goest not to the land where it grows."

"Let me look at this Cicely of thine, mine host," said Varney; "I have heard much talk of her beauty."

"It is a sun-burnt beauty," said mine host, "well qualified to stand out rain and wind, but little calculated to converse such gallants as you. She keeps her chamber, and cannot encounter the glance of such sunny-day courtiers as yourself, my noble guest."

"Well, peace be with her, my good host," answered Varney; "our horses are impatient—We bid you good day."

"Does my nephew go with you, so please you?" said Gosling.

"Ay, such is his purpose," answered Richard Varney.

"You are right—fully right," replied mine host. "You are, I say, fully right, my kinsman. Thou hast got a gay horse, see thou light not unaware upon a halter—or if thou wilt needs be made immortal by means of a rope, which thy purpose of following this gentleman renders not unlikely, I charge thee to find a gallows as far from Cumnor as thou conveniently may'st; and so I commend you to your saddle."

The master of horse and his new retainer took horse accordingly, leaving the landlord to conclude his ill-omened farewell, to himself and at leisure; and set off together at a rapid pace, which precluded conversation until the ascent of a steep sandy hill permitted them to resume it.

"You are contented then," said Varney, to his companion, "to take court-service?"

"Ay, worshipful sir, if you like my terms as well as I like yours."

"And what are your terms?" demanded Varney.

"If I am to have a quick eye for patron's interest, he must have a dull one towards my faults," said Lambourne.

"Ay," said Varney, "so they lie not so grossly open that he must needs break his shins over them."

"Agreed," said Lambourne. "Next, if I run down game, I must have the picking of the bones."

"That is but reason," replied Varney, "so that your betters are served before you."

"Good!" said Lambourne; "and it only remains to be said, that if the law and I quarrel, my patron must bear me out, for that is a chief point."

"Reason again," said Varney, "if the quarrel hath happened in your master's service."

"For the wage and so forth, I say nothing," replied Lambourne; "it is the secret guerdon that I must live by."

"Never fear," said Varney; "thou shalt have clothes and spending-money to ruffle it with the best of thy degree, for thou goest to a household where you have gold, as they say, by the eye."

"That jumps all well with my humour," replied Michael Lambourne; "and it only remains that you tell me my master's name."

"My name is Master Richard Varney," answered his companion.

"But I mean," said Lambourne, "the name of the noble lord to whose service you are to prefer me."

"How, knave, art thou too good to call *me* master?" said Varney, hastily; "I would have thee bold to others, but not saucy with me."

"I crave your worship's pardon," said Lambourne; "but you seemed familiar with Anthony Forster, now I am familiar with Anthony myself."

"Thou art a shrewd knave, I see," replied Varney. "Mark me—I do indeed propose to introduce thee into a nobleman's household; but it is upon my person thou wilt chiefly wait, and upon my countenance that you will depend. I am his master of horse—thou wilt soon know his name—it is one which shakes the council and wields the state."

"By this light, a brave spell to conjure with," said Lambourne, "if a man would discover hidden treasures!"

"Used with discretion, it may prove so," replied Varney; "but mark —if thou conjure with it at thine own hand, it will raise a devil who will tear thee in fragments."

"Enough said," answered Lambourne; "I will not exceed my limits."

The travellers then resumed the rapid rate of travelling, which their discourse had interrupted, and soon arrived at the Royal Park of Woodstock. This ancient possession of the crown of England was very different from what it had been when it was the residence of the fair Rosamond, and the scene of Henry the Second's secret and illicit amours; and yet more unlike to the scene which it exhibits in the present day, when Blenheim-House commemorates the victory of Marlborough, and no less the genius of Vanburgh, though decried in his own time by men of taste far inferior to his own. It was, in Elizabeth's time, an ancient mansion in bad repair, which had long ceased to be honoured with the royal residence, to the great impoverishment of the adjacent village. The inhabitants, however, had made several

petitions to the Queen to have the favour of the sovereign's countenance occasionally bestowed upon them; and upon this very business,
ostensibly at least, was the noble lord we have already introduced to
our readers a visitor at Woodstock.

Varney and Lambourne galloped without ceremony into the court-
yard of the ancient and dilapidated mansion, which presented on that
morning a scene of bustle which it had not exhibited for two reigns.
Officers of the Earl's household, livery-men and retainers, went and
came with all the insolent fracas which attaches to their profession.
The neigh of horses and the baying of hounds were heard; for my
lord, in his occupation of inspecting and surveying the manor and
demesne, was, of course, provided with the means of following his
pleasure in the chase or park, said to have been the earliest that was
enclosed in England, and which was well stocked with deer which had
long roamed there unmolested. Several of the inhabitants of the village, in anxious hope of a favourable result from this unwonted visit,
loitered about the court-yard, and awaited the great man's coming
forth. Their attention was excited by the hasty arrival of Varney, and a
murmur ran amongst them, "The Earl's master of the horse!" while
they hastened to bespeak favour by hastily unbonneting, and proffer-
ing to hold the bridle and stirrup of the favoured retainer and his
attendant.

"Stand somewhat aloof, my masters!" said Varney, haughtily, "and
let the domestics do their office."

The mortified peasants fell back at the signal; while Lambourne,
who had his eye upon his superior's deportment, repelled the services
of those who offered to assist him, with yet more discourtesy—"Stand
back, Jack peasant, with a murrain to you, and let these knave footmen
do their duty!"

While they gave their nags to the attendants of the household, and
walked into the mansion with an air of superiority which long practice
and consciousness of birth rendered natural to Varney, and which
Lambourne endeavoured to imitate as well as he could, the poor
inhabitants of Woodstock whispered to each other, "Well-a-day—
God save us from all such misproud princoxes!—an the master be like
the men, why the fiend may take all, and yet have no more than his
due."

"Silence, good neighbours!" said the Bailiff, "keep tongue betwixt
teeth—we shall know more by and bye.—But never will a lord come
to Woodstock so welcome as bluff old King Harry!—he would horse-
whip a fellow one day with his own royal hand, and then fling him an
handful of silver groats, with his own broad face on them, to 'noint the
sore withal."

"Ay, rest be with him!" echoed the auditors; "it will be long ere this Lady Elizabeth horsewhip any of us."

"There is no saying," answered the Bailiff. "Meanwhile, patience, good neighbours, and let us comfort ourselves by thinking that we deserve such notice at her grace's hands."

Meanwhile, Varney, closely followed by his new dependant, made his way to the hall, where men of more note and consequence than those left in the court-yard awaited the appearance of the Earl, who as yet kept his chamber. All paid court to Varney, with more or less deference, as suited their own rank, or the urgency of the business which brought them to his lord's levee. To the general question of, "When comes my lord forth, Master Varney?" he gave brief answers, as, "See you not my boots? I am but just returned from Oxford, and know nothing of it," and the like, until the same query was put in a higher tone by a personage of more importance. "I will inquire at the chamberlain, Sir Thomas Copely," was the reply. The chamberlain, distinguished by his silver key, answered, that the Earl only awaited Master Varney's return to come down, but that he would first speak with him in his private chamber. Varney, therefore, bowed to the company, and took leave, to enter his lord's apartment.

There was a murmur of expectation which lasted a few minutes, and was at length hushed by the opening of the folding-doors at the upper end of the apartment, through which the Earl made his entrance, marshalled by his chamberlain and the steward of his family, and followed by Richard Varney. In his noble mien and princely features, men read nothing of that insolence which was practised by his dependants. His courtesies were indeed measured by the rank of those to whom they were addressed, but even the meanest person present had a share of his gracious notice. The inquiries which he made respecting the condition of the manor, of the Queen's rights there, and of the advantages and disadvantages which might attend her occasional residence at the royal seat of Woodstock, seemed to shew that he had most earnestly investigated the matter of their petition, and with a desire to forward the interest of the place.

"Now the Lord love his noble countenance," said the Bailiff, who had thrust himself into the presence-chamber; "he looks something pale. I warrant him he hath spent the whole night in perusing our memorial. Master Toughyarn, who took six months to draw it up, said it would take a week to understand it; and see if the Earl hath not knocked the marrow out of it in twenty-four hours!"

The Earl then acquainted them that he should move their sovereign to honour Woodstock occasionally with her residence during her royal progresses, that the town and its vicinity might derive, from her countenance and favour, the same advantages as from those of her predecessors. Meanwhile, he rejoiced to be the expounder of her gracious pleasure, in assuring them that, for the increase of trade and encouragement of the worthy burgesses of Woodstock, her majesty was minded to erect the town into a Staple for wool.

This joyful intelligence was received with the acclamations not only of the better sort who were admitted to the audience-chamber, but of the commons who waited without.

The freedom of the corporation was presented to the Earl upon knee by the magistrates of the place, together with a purse of gold pieces, which the Earl handed to Varney, who, on his part, gave a share to Lambourne, as the most acceptable earnest of his new service.

The Earl and his retinue took horse soon after, to return to court, accompanied by the shouts of the inhabitants of Woodstock, who made the old oaks ring with re-echoing, "Long live Queen Elizabeth, and the noble Earl of Leicester!" The urbanity and courtesy of the Earl even threw a gleam of popularity over his attendants, as their haughty deportment had formerly obscured that of their master; and men shouted, "Long life to the Earl, and to his gallant followers!" as Varney and Lambourne, each in his rank, rode proudly through the streets of Woodstock.

Chapter Eight

Host. I will hear you, Master Fenton;
And I will, at least, keep your counsel.
Merry Wives of Windsor

IT BECOMES necessary to return to the detail of those circumstances which accompanied, and indeed occasioned, the sudden disappearance of Tressilian from the sign of the Black Bear at Cumnor. It will be recollected that this gentleman, after his rencounter with Varney, had returned to Giles Gosling's caravansary, where he shut himself up in his own chamber, demanded pen, ink, and paper, and announced his purpose to remain private for the day; in the evening he appeared again in the public room, where Michael Lambourne, who had been on the watch for him, agreeably to his engagement to Varney, endeavoured to renew his acquaintance with him, and hoped he retained no unfriendly recollection of the part he had taken in the morning's scuffle.

But Tressilian repelled his advances firmly, though with civility—"Master Lambourne," said he, "I trust I have recompensed to your pleasure the time you have wasted on me. Under the shew of wild

bluntness which you exhibit, I know you have sense enough to understand me, when I say frankly, that the object of our temporary
acquaintance having been accomplished, we must be strangers to
each other in future."

"*Voto!*" said Lambourne, twirling his whiskers with one hand, and
grasping the hilt of his weapon with the other; "if I thought that this
usage was meant to insult me"——

"You would bear it with discretion, doubtless," replied Tressilian,
"as you must do at any rate. You know too well the distance that is
betwixt us, to require me to explain myself farther—Good evening."

So saying, he turned his back upon his former companion, and
entered into discourse with the landlord. Michael Lambourne felt
strongly disposed to bully; but his wrath died away in a few incoherent
oaths and ejaculations, and he sank unresistingly under the ascendancy which superior spirits possess over persons of his habits and
description. He remained moody and silent in a corner of the apartment, paying the most marked attention to every motion of his late
companion, against whom he began now to nourish a quarrel on his
own account, which he trusted to avenge by the execution of Varney's
directions. The hour of supper arrived, and was followed by that of
repose, when Tressilian, like others, retired to his sleeping apartment.

He had not been in bed long, when the train of sad reveries, which
supplied the place of rest in his disturbed mind, was suddenly interrupted by the jar of a door on its hinges, and a light was seen to
glimmer in the apartment. Tressilian, who was as brave as steel,
sprang from his bed at this alarm, and had laid hand upon his sword,
when he was prevented from drawing it by a voice which said, "Be not
too rash with your rapier, Master Tressilian—It is I, your host Giles
Gosling."

At the same time, unshrouding the dark lantern, which had hitherto
only emitted an indistinct glimmer, the goodly aspect and figure of the
landlord of the Black Bear was visibly presented to his astonished
guest.

"What mummery is this, mine host?" said Tressilian; "have you
supped as jollily as last night, and so mistaken your chamber? or is
midnight a time for masquerading it in your guest's lodging?"

"Master Tressilian," replied mine host, "I know my place and my
time as well as e'er a merry landlord in England. But here has been my
hang-dog kinsman watching you as close as ever cat watched a
mouse; and here have you, on the other hand, quarrelled and fought,
either with him or with some other person, and I fear that danger will
come of it."

"Go to, thou art but a fool, man," said Tressilian; "thy kinsman is beneath my resentment; and besides, why should'st thou think I had quarrelled with any one whomsoever?"

"Oh! sir," replied the inn-keeper, "there was a red spot on thy very cheek-bone, which boded of a late brawl, as sure as the conjunction of Mars and Saturn threatens misfortune—and when you returned, the buckles of your girdle were brought forward, and your step was quick and hasty, and all things shewed your hand and your hilt had been lately acquainted."

"Well, good mine host, if I have been obliged to draw my sword," said Tressilian, "why should such a circumstance fetch thee out of thy warm bed at this time of night? Thou seest the mischief is all over."

"Under favour, that is what I doubt. Anthony Forster is a dangerous man, defended by strong court patronage, which hath borne him out in matters of very deep concernment. And then, my kinsman—why, I have told you what he is, and if these two old cronies have made up their old acquaintance, I would not, my worshipful guest, that it should be at thy cost. I promise you, Mike Lambourne has been making very particular enquiries at mine hostler, when and which way you ride. Now, I would have you think, whether you may not have done or said something for which you may be way-laid, and taken at disadvantage."

"Thou art an honest man, mine host," said Tressilian, after a moment's consideration, "and I will deal frankly with thee. If these men's malice is directed against me—as I deny not but it may—it is because they are the agents of a more powerful villain than themselves."

"You mean Master Richard Varney, do you not?" said the landlord; "he was at Cumnor-Place yesterday, and came not thither so private but what he was espied by one who told me."

"I mean the same, mine host."

"Then, for God's sake, worshipful Master Tressilian," said honest Gosling, "look well to yourself. This Varney is the protector and patron of Anthony Forster, who holds under him, and by his favour, some lease of yonder mansion and the park. Varney got a large grant of the lands of the Abbacy of Abingdon, and Cumnor-Place amongst others, from his master, the Earl of Leicester. Men say he can do every thing with him, though I hold the Earl too good a nobleman to employ him as some men talk of.—And then the Earl can do any thing (that is any thing right or fitting) with the Queen, God bless her; so you see what an enemy you have made yourself."

"Well—it is done, and I cannot help it," answered Tressilian.

"Uds precious, but it must be helped in some manner!" said the host. "Richard Varney—why, what between his influence with my

lord, and his pretending to so many old and vexatious claims in right of
the Abbot here, men fear almost to mention his name, much more to
set themselves against his practices. You may judge by our discourses
the last night. Men said their pleasure of Tony Forster, but not a word
of Richard Varney, though all men judge him to be at the bottom of
yonder mystery about the pretty wench. But perhaps you know more
of that matter than I do, for women, though they wear not swords, are
occasion for many a blade's exchanging a sheath of neat's leather for
one of flesh and blood."

"I do indeed know more of that poor unfortunate lady than thou
doest, my friendly host; and so bankrupt am I, at this moment, of
friends and advice, that I will willingly make a counsellor of thee, and
tell thee the whole history, the rather that I have a favour to ask when
my tale is ended."

"Good Master Tressilian," said the landlord, "I am but a poor
innkeeper, little able to adjust or counsel such a guest as yourself. But
as sure as I have risen decently above the world, by giving good
measure and reasonable charges, I am an honest man; and as such, if I
may not be able to assist you, I am not, at least, capable to abuse your
confidence. Say away, therefore, as confidently as if you spoke to your
father; and thus far at least be certain, that my curiosity, for I will not
deny that which belongs to my calling, is joined to a reasonable degree
of discretion."

"I doubt it not, mine host," answered Tressilian; and while his
auditor remained in anxious expectation, he meditated for an instant
how he should commence his narrative. "My tale," he at length said,
"to be quite intelligible, must begin at some distance back.—You have
heard of the battle of Stoke, my good host, and perhaps of old Sir
Roger Robsart, who, in that battle, valiantly took part with Henry VII.,
the Queen's grandfather, and routed the Earl of Lincoln, Lord
Geraldin and his wild Irish, and the Flemings, whom the Duchess of
Burgundy had sent over, in the quarrel of Lambert Simnel?"

"I remember both one and the other," said Giles Gosling, "it is
sung of a dozen times a-week on my ale-bench below.—Sir Roger
Robsart of Devon—O, ay,—'tis him of whom minstrels sing to this
hour,—

> He was the flower of Stoke's red field,
>   When Martin Swart on ground lay slain;
> In raging rout he never reel'd,
>   But like a rock did firm remain.

Ay, and then there was Martin Swart I have heard my grandfather talk
of, and of the jolly Almains whom he commanded, with their slashed

doublets and quaint hose, all frounced with ribbons above the nether stocks. Here's a song goes of Martin Swart, too, an I had but memory for it:—

> Martin Swart and his men,
> Saddle them, saddle them,
> Martin Swart and his men,
> Saddle them well."

"True, good mine host—the day was long talked of; but if you sing so loud, you will awake more listeners than I care to commit my confidence unto."

"I crave pardon, my worshipful guest," said mine host, "I was oblivious. When an old song comes across us merry old knights of the spiggot, it runs away with discretion."

"Well, mine host, my grandfather, like some other Cornish-men, kept a warm affection to the House of York, and espoused the quarrel of this Simnel, assuming the title of Earl of Warwick, as the county afterwards, in great numbers, countenanced the cause of Perkin Warbeck, calling himself the Duke of York. My grandsire joined Simnel's standard, and was taken fighting desperately at Stoke, where most of the leaders of that unhappy army were slain in their harness. The good knight, to whom he rendered himself, Sir Roger Robsart, protected him from the immediate vengeance of the King, and dismissed him without ransom. But he was unable to guard him from other penalties of his rashness, being the heavy fines by which he was impoverished, according to Henry's mode of weakening his enemies. The good knight did what he might to mitigate the distresses of my ancestor; and their friendship became so strict, that my father was bred up as the sworn brother and intimate of the present Sir Hugh Robsart, the only son of Sir Roger, and the heir of his honest, and generous, and hospitable temper, though not equal to him in martial achievements."

"I have heard of good Sir Hugh Robsart," interrupted the host, "many a time and oft. His huntsman and sworn servant, Will Badger, hath spoke of him an hundred times in this very house—a jovial knight he is, and hath loved hospitality and open house-keeping more than the present fashion, which lays as much gold-lace on the seams of a doublet as would feed a dozen of tall fellows with beef and ale for a twelvemonth, and let them have their evening at the ale-house once a-week, to do good to the publican."

"If you have seen Will Badger, mine host," said Tressilian, "you have heard enough of Sir Hugh Robsart; and, therefore, I will but say, that the hospitality you boast of hath proved somewhat detrimental to the estate of his family, which is perhaps of the less consequence, as he has but one daughter to whom to bequeath it. And here begins my share in the tale. Upon my father's death, now several years since, the good Sir Hugh would willingly have made me his constant companion. There was a time, however, at which I felt the kind knight's excessive love for field-sports detained me from studies, by which I might have profited more; but I ceased to regret the leisure which gratitude and hereditary friendship compelled me to bestow on these rural avocations. The exquisite beauty of Mistress Amy Robsart, as she grew up from childhood to woman, could not escape one whom circumstances obliged to be so constantly in her company—I loved her, in short, my host, and her father saw it."

"And crossed your true loves, no doubt?" said mine host; "it is the way in all such cases, and I judge it must have been so in your instance, from the heavy sigh you uttered even now."

"The cause was different, mine host. My suit was highly approved by the generous Sir Hugh Robsart—it was his daughter who was cold to my passion."

"She was the more dangerous enemy of the two," said the innkeeper. "I fear your suit proved a cold one."

"She yielded me her esteem," said Tressilian, "and seemed not unwilling that I should hope it might ripen into a warmer passion. There was a contract of future marriage executed betwixt us, upon her father's intercession; but to comply with her anxious request, the execution was deferred for a twelvemonth. During this period, Richard Varney appeared in the country, and, availing himself of some distant family connexion with Sir Hugh Robsart, spent much of his time in his company, until, at length, he almost lived in the family."

"That could bode no good to the place he honoured with his residence," said Gosling.

"No, by the rood!" replied Tressilian. "Misunderstanding and misery followed his presence, yet so strangely, that I am at this moment at a loss to trace the gradations of their encroachment upon a family, which had, till then, been so happy. For a time Amy Robsart received the attentions of this man Varney with the indifference attached to common courtesies; then followed a period in which she seemed to regard him with dislike, and even with disgust; and then an extraordinary species of connection appeared to grow up betwixt them. Varney dropped those airs of pretension and gallantry, which had marked his former approaches; and Amy, on the other hand, seemed to renounce the ill-disguised disgust with which she had regarded them. They seemed to have more of privacy and confidence together, than I fully liked; and I suspected that they met in private, where there was less restraint than in our presence. Many circumstances, which I noticed but little at the time—for I deemed her heart as open as her angelic countenance—have since arisen on my memory, to convince me of their private understanding. But I need not detail them—the fact speaks for itself. She vanished from her father's house—Varney disappeared at the same time—and this very day I have seen her in the character of his paramour, living in the house of his sordid dependant Forster, and visited by him, muffled, and by a secret entrance."

"And this, then, is the cause of your quarrel? Methinks, you should have been sure that the fair lady either desired or deserved your interference."

"Mine host," answered Tressilian, "my father, such I must ever consider Sir Hugh Robsart, sits at home struggling with his grief, or if so far recovered, vainly attempting to drown, in the practice of his field-sports, the recollection that he had once a daughter—a recollection which ever and anon breaks from him under circumstances the most pathetic. I could not brook the idea that he should live in misery, and Amy in guilt; and I endeavoured to seek her out, with the hope of inducing her to return to her family. I have found her, and when I have either succeeded in my attempt, or have found it altogether unavailing, it is my purpose to embark for the Virginia voyage."

"Be not so rash, good sir," replied Giles Gosling; "and cast not yourself away because a woman—to be brief—*is* a woman, and changes her lovers like her suit of ribbands, with no better reason than mere phantasy. And ere we probe this matter further, let me ask you what circumstances of suspicion directed you so truly to this lady's residence, or rather to her place of concealment?"

"The last is the better chosen word, mine host," answered Tressilian; "and touching your question, the knowledge that Varney held large grants of the demesnes formerly belonging to the Monks of Abingdon, directed me to this neighbourhood; and your nephew's visit to his old comrade Forster, gave me the means of conviction on the subject."

"And what is now your purpose, worthy sir?—excuse my freedom in asking the question so broadly."

"I purpose, mine host," said Tressilian, "to renew my visit to the place of her residence to-morrow, and to seek a more detailed communication with her than I have had to-day. She must indeed be widely changed from what she once was, if my words make no impression upon her."

"Under your favour, Master Tressilian," said the landlord, "you can follow no such course. The lady, if I understand you, has already rejected your interference in the matter."

"It is but too true," said Tressilian; "I cannot deny it."

"Then, marry, by what right or interest do you process a compulsory interference with her inclination, disgraceful as it may be to herself and to her parents? Unless my judgment gulls me, those under whose protection she has thrown herself, would have small hesitation to reject your interference, even if it were that of a father or brother; but as a discarded lover, you expose yourself to be repelled with the strong hand, as well as with scorn. You can apply to no magistrate for aid or countenance; and you are hunting, therefore, a shadow in water, and will only, (excuse my plainness,) come by ducking and danger in attempting to catch it."

"I will appeal to the Earl of Leicester," said Tressilian, "against the infamy of his favourite—he courts the severe and strict sect of puritans—he dare not, for sake of his own character, refuse my appeal, even although he were destitute of the principles of honour and nobleness with which fame invests him. Or I will appeal to the Queen herself."

"Should Leicester," said the landlord, "be disposed to protect his dependent (as indeed Varney is said to be very confident with him,) the appeal to the Queen may bring them both to reason. Her Majesty is strict in such matters, and (if it be not treason to speak it) will rather, it is said, pardon a dozen of courtiers for falling in love with herself, than one for giving preference to another woman. Coragio then, my brave guest! for if thou layest a petition from Sir Hugh at the foot of the throne, bucklered by the story of thine own wrongs, the favourite Earl dared as soon leap into the Thames at the fullest and deepest, as offer to protect Varney in a cause of this nature. But to do this with any chance of success, you must go formally to work; and without staying here to tilt with the master of horse to a privy councillor, and expose yourself to the dagger of his cameradoes, you should hie you to Devonshire, get a petition drawn up for Sir Hugh Robsart, and make as many friends as you can to forward your interest at court."

"You have spoken well, mine host," said Tressilian, "and I will profit by your advice, and leave you to-morrow early."

"Nay, leave me to-night, sir, before to-morrow comes," said the landlord. "I never prayed for a guest's arrival more eagerly than I do to have you safely gone. My kinsman's destiny is most like to be hanged for something, but I would not that the cause were the murder of an honoured guest of mine. 'Better ride safe in the dark,' says the proverb, 'than in day-light with a murderer at your elbow.' Come, sir, I move you for your own safety. Your horse and all is ready, and here is your score."

"It is somewhat under a noble," said Tressilian, giving one to the host; "give the balance to pretty Cicely, your daughter, and the servants of the house."

"They shall taste of your bounty, sir," said Gosling, "and you should taste of my daughter's lips in grateful acknowledgment, but that at this hour she cannot grace the porch to greet your departure."

"Do not trust your daughter too far with your guests, mine good landlord," said Tressilian.

"O, sir, we will keep measure; but I wonder not that you are jealous of them all.—May I crave to know with what aspect the fair lady at the Place yesterday received you?"

"I own," said Tressilian, "it was angry as well as confused, and affords me little hope that she is yet awakened from her unhappy delusion."

"In that case, sir, I see not why you should play the champion of a wench that will none of you, and incur the resentment of a favourite's favourite, as dangerous a monster as ever a knight-adventurer encountered in the old story books."

"You do me wrong—gross wrong," said Tressilian; "I do not desire that Amy should ever turn thought upon me more—let me but see her restored to her father, and all that I have to do in Europe—perhaps in the world—is over and ended."

"A wiser resolution were to drink a cup of sack, and forget her," said the landlord. "But five-and-twenty and fifty look on those matters with other eyes, especially when one case of peepers is set in the skull of a young gallant, and the other in that of an old publican. I pity you, Master Tressilian, but I see not how I can aid you in the matter."

"Only thus far, mine host," replied Tressilian—"Keep a watch on the motions of those at the Place, which thou canst easily learn without suspicion, as all men's news fly to the ale bench; and be pleased to communicate the tidings in writing to such person, and to no other, who shall bring you this ring as a special token—look at it—it is of value, and I will freely bestow it on you."

"Nay, sir," said the landlord, "I desire no recompence—but it seems an unadvised course in me, being in a public line, to connect myself with a matter of this dark and perilous nature.—I have no interest in it."

"You, and every father in the land, who would have his daughter released from the snares of shame, and sin, and misery, have an interest deeper than aught concerning earth only could create."

"Well, sir," said the host, "these are brave words; and I do pity in my soul the frank-hearted old gentleman, who has minished his estate in good house-keeping for the honour of his county, and now has his daughter, who should be the stay of his age, and so forth, whisked up by such a kite as Varney is. And though your part in the matter is somewhat of the wildest, yet I will e'en be a madcap for company, and help you in your honest attempt to get back the good man's child, so far as being your faithful intelligencer can serve. And as I shall be true to you, I pray you to be trusty to me, and keep my secret; for it were bad for the custom of the Black Bear, should it be said his keeper interfered in such matters. Varney has interest enough with the justices to dismount my noble emblem from the post on which he swings so gallantly, to call in my license, and ruin me from garret to cellar."

"Do not doubt my secrecy, mine host," said Tressilian; "I will retain, besides, the deepest sense of thy service, and of the risk thou doest run—remember the ring is my sure token—and now, farewell—for it was thy wise advice that I should tarry here as short time as may be."

"Follow me, then, Sir Guest," said the landlord, "and tread as gently as if eggs were under your foot, instead of deal boards—no one must know when or how you departed."

By the aid of his dark lantern he conducted Tressilian, as soon as he had made himself ready for his journey, through a long intricacy of passages, which opened to an outer court, and from thence to a remote stable, where he had already placed his guest's horse. He then aided him to fasten on the saddle the small portmantle which contained his necessaries, opened a postern-door, and with a hearty shake of the hand, and a reiteration of his promise to attend to what went on at Cumnor-Place, he dismissed his guest to his solitary journey.

Chapter Nine

Far in the lane a lonely hut he found,
No tenant ventured on the unwholesome ground;
Here smokes his forge, he bares his sinewy arm,
And early strokes the sounding anvil warm;
Around his shop the steely sparkles flew,
As for the steed he shaped the bending shoe.
                                GAY'S *Trivia*

AS IT WAS deemed proper by the traveller himself, as well as by Giles Gosling, that Tressilian should avoid being seen in the neighbourhood of Cumnor by those whom accident might make early stirrers, the landlord had given him a route, consisting of various bye-ways and lanes, which he was to follow in succession, and which, all the turns and short-cuts duly observed, was to conduct him to the public road to Marlborough.

But, like counsel of every other kind, this species of direction is much more easily given than followed; and what betwixt the intricacy of the way, the darkness of the night, Tressilian's ignorance of the country, and the sad and perplexing thoughts with which he had to contend, his journey proceeded so slowly, that morning found him only in the vale of Whitehorse, memorable for the defeat of the Danes in former days, with his horse tired and deprived of a fore-foot shoe, an accident which threatened to put a stop to his journey, by laming the animal. The residence of a smith was his first object of inquiry, in which he received little satisfaction from the dulness or sullenness of one or two peasants, early bound for their labour, who gave brief and indifferent answers to his questions on the subject. Anxious at length, that the partner of his journey should suffer as little as possible from the unfortunate accident, Tressilian dismounted, and led his horse in the direction of a little hamlet, where he hoped either to find or hear tidings of such an artificer as he now wanted. Through a deep and muddy lane, he at length waded on to the place, which proved only an assemblage of five or six miserable huts, about the doors of which one or two people, whose appearance seemed as rude as that of their dwellings, were beginning the toils of the day. One cottage, however, seemed of rather superior aspect, and the old dame, who was sweeping her threshold, appeared something less rude than her neighbours. To her, Tressilian addressed the oft-repeated question, whether there was a smith in this neighbourhood, or any place where he could refresh himself and his horse. The dame looked him in the face with peculiar expression, as she replied, "Smith! ay, truly, is there a smith —what would'st ha' wi' un, mon?"

"To shoe my horse, good dame," answered Tressilian; "you may see that he has thrown a fore-foot shoe."

"Master Holiday!" exclaimed the dame, without returning any direct answer—"Master Herasmus Holiday, come and speak to mon, and please you."

"*Favete linguis*," answered a voice from within; "I cannot now come forth, Gammer Sludge, being in the very sweetest bit of my morning studies."

"Nay, but, good now Master Holiday, come ye out, do ye—Here's a mon would to Wayland Smith, and I care not to shew him way to devil —His horse hath cast shoe."

"*Quid mihi cum caballo*," replied the man of learning from within; "I think there is but one wise man in the Hundred, and they cannot shoe a horse without him!"

And forth came the honest pedagogue, for such his dress bespoke him. A long, lean, shambling, stooping figure, was surmounted by a head thatched with lank black hair somewhat inclining to grey. His features had the cast of habitual authority, which I suppose Dionysius carried with him from the throne to the schoolmaster's pulpit, and bequeathed as a legacy to all of the same profession. A black buckram cassock was gathered at his middle with a belt, at which hung, instead of knife or weapon, a goodly leathern pen-and-ink-case. His ferula stuck on the other side, like Harlequin's wooden sword; and he carried in his hand the tattered volume which he had been busily perusing.

On seeing a person of Tressilian's appearance, which he was better able to estimate than the country-folks had been, the schoolmaster unbonneted, and accosted him with, *"Salve, domine. Intelligisne linguam latinam?"*

Tressilian mustered his learning to reply, *"Linguæ latinæ haud penitus ignarus, venia tua, domine eruditissime, vernaculam libentius loquor."*

The Latin reply had upon the schoolmaster the effect which the mason's sign is said to produce on the brethren of the trowel. He was at once interested in the learned traveller, listened with gravity to his story of a tired horse and a lost shoe, and then replied with solemnity, "It may appear a simple thing, most worshipful, to reply to you that there dwells, within a brief mile of these *tuguria*, the best *faber ferrarius*, the most accomplished blacksmith that ever nailed iron upon horse. Now, were I to say so, I warrant me you would think yourself *compos voti*, or, as the vulgar have it, a made man."

"I should at least," said Tressilian, "have a direct answer to a plain question, which seems difficult to be obtained in this country."

"It is a mere sending of a sinful soul to the evil un," said the old woman, "the sending a living creature to Wayland Smith."

"Peace, Gammer Sludge!" said the pedagogue; *"pauca verba,* Gammer Sludge; look to the furmity, Gammer Sludge; *curetur jentaculum,* Gammer Sludge, this gentleman is none of thy gossips." Then turning to Tressilian, he resumed his lofty tone, "And so, most worshipful, you would really think yourself *felix bis terque,* should I point out to you the dwelling of this same smith."

"Sir," replied Tressilian, "I should in that case have all that I want at present—a horse fit to carry me—out of hearing of your learning" —the last words he muttered to himself.

"O cæca mens mortalium!" said the learned man; "well was it sung by Junius Juvenalis, *'numinibus vota exaudita malignis.'"*

"Learned Magister," said Tressilian, "your erudition so greatly exceeds my poor intellectual capacity, that you must excuse my seeking elsewhere for information which I can better understand."

"There again now," replied the pedagogue, "how fondly you fly from him that would instruct you! Truly says Quinctilian"——

"I pray, sir, let Quinctilian be for the present, and answer, at a word and in English, if your learning can condescend so far, whether there is any place here where I can have opportunity to refresh my horse, until I can have him shod?"

"Thus much courtesy, sir," said the schoolmaster, "I can readily render you, that although there be in this poor hamlet (*nostra paupera regna,*) no regular hospitium, as my namesake Erasmus calleth it, yet forasmuch as you are somewhat embued, or at least tinged as it were, with good letters, I will use mine interest with the good woman of the house to accommodate you with a platter of furmity—an wholesome food, for which I have found no Latin phrase—your horse shall have a share of the cow-house, with a bottle of sweet hay, in which the good woman Sludge so much abounds, that it may be said of her cow, *fœnum habet in cornu;* oats shall also be forthcoming, and if it please you to bestow on me the pleasure of your company, the banquet shall cost *ne semissem quidem*, so much is Gammer Sludge bound to me for the pains I have bestowed on the top and bottom of her hopeful heir Dickie, whom I have painfully made to travel through the accidens."

"Now, God yield ye for it, Mr Herasmus," said the good Gammer, "and grant that little Dickie may be the better for his accident!—and for the rest, if the gentleman list to stay, breakfast shall be on the board in the wringing of a dish-clout; and for horse-meat, and man's-meat, I bear no such base mind as to ask a penny."

Considering the state of his horse, Tressilian, upon the whole, saw no better course than to accept the invitation thus learnedly made and hospitably confirmed, and take chance that when the good pedagogue had exhausted every species of conversation, he might possibly condescend to tell him where he could find the smith they spoke of. He entered the hut accordingly, and sat down with learned Magister Erasmus Holiday, partook of his furmity, and listened to his learned account of himself for a good half hour, ere he could get him to talk upon any other topic. The reader will readily excuse our accompanying this man of learning into all the details with which he favoured Tressilian, of which the following sketch may suffice.

He was born at Hogsnorton, where, according to popular saying, the pigs play upon the organ, a proverb which he interpreted allegorically, as having reference to the herd of Epicurus, of which Horace confessed himself a porker. His name of Erasmus, he derived partly from his father having been the son of a renowned washer-woman, who had held that great scholar in clean linen all the while he was at Oxford; a task of some difficulty, as he was only possessed of two shirts, "the one," as she expressed herself, "to wash the other." The vestiges of one of these *camiciæ*, as Master Holiday boasted, were still in his possession, having fortunately been detained by his grandmother to cover the balance of her bill. But he thought there was a still higher and over-ruling cause for his having had the name of Erasmus conferred on him, namely, the secret presentiment of his mother's mind, that, in the babe to be christened, was a hidden genius, which should one day lead him to rival the fame of the great scholar of Amsterdam. The schoolmaster's surname led him as far into dissertation as his Christian appellative. He was inclined to think that he bore the name of Holiday *quasi lucus a non lucendo*, because he gave such few holidays to his school; "Hence," said he, "the schoolmaster is termed, classically, *Ludi Magister*, because he deprives boys of their play." And yet, on the other hand, he thought it might bear a very different interpretation, and refer to his own exquisite art in arranging pageants, morris-dances, May-day festivities, and such like holiday delights, for which he assured Tressilian he had positively the purest and the most inventive brain in England; insomuch, that his cunning in framing such pleasures had made him known to many honourable persons, both in country and court, and especially to the noble Earl of Leicester—"And although he may now seem to forget me," he said, "in the multitude of state affairs, yet I am well assured, that had he some pretty pastime to array for entertainment of the Queen's Grace, horse and man would be seeking the humble cottage of poor Erasmus Holiday. *Parvo contentus*, in the meanwhile, I hear my pupils parse, and construe, worshipful sir, and drive away my time with the aid of the Muses. And I have at all times, when in correspondence with foreign scholars, subscribed myself Erasmus ab Die Fausto, and have enjoyed the distinction due to the learned under that title; witness the erudite Diedrichus Buikerschochius, who dedicated to me under that title his treatise on the letter *Tau*. In fine, sir, I have been a happy and distinguished man."

"May it long be so, sir," said the traveller; "but permit me to ask, in your own learned phrase, *Quid hoc ad Iphycli boves*, what has all this to do with the shoeing of my poor nag?"

"*Festina lente*," said the man of learning, "we will presently come to that point. You must know that some two or three years past, there came to these parts one who called him Doctor Doboobie, although it may be he never wrote even *Magister artium*, save in right of his hungry belly. Or it may be that if he had any degrees, they were of the devil's giving, for he was what the vulgar call a white witch—a cunning man, and such like.—Now, good sir, I perceive you are impatient; but if a man tell not his tale his own way, how have you warrant that he can tell it yours?"

"Well, then, learned sir, take your way," answered Tressilian; "only let us travel at a sharper pace, for my time is somewhat of the shortest."

"Well, sir," resumed Erasmus Holiday, with the most provoking perseverance, "I will not say that this same Demetrius Doboobius, for so he wrote himself when in foreign parts, was an actual conjuror, but certain it is, that he professed to be a brother of the mystical Order of the Rosy Cross, a disciple of Geber (*ex nomine cujus venit verbum vernaculum*, gibberish.) He cured wounds by salving the weapon instead of the sore—told fortunes by palmistry—discovered stolen goods by the sieve and shears—gathered the right maddow and the male fern seed, through use of which men walk invisible—pretended some advances towards the panacea, or universal elixir, and affected to convert good lead into sorry silver."

"In other words," said Tressilian, "he was a quack salver and common cheat; but what has all this to do with my nag, and the shoe which he has lost?"

"With your worshipful patience," replied the diffusive man of letters, "you shall understand that presently—*patientia* then, right worshipful, which word, according to our Marcus Tullius, is '*difficilium rerum diurna perpessio.*' This same Demetrius Doboobie, after dealing with the country, as I have told you, began to acquire fame *inter magnates*, among the prime men of the land, and there is likelihood he might have aspired to great matters, had not, according to vulgar fame, (for I aver not the thing as concording with my certain knowledge,) the devil claimed his right one dark night, and flown off with Demetrius, who was never seen or heard of afterwards. Now here comes the *medulla*, the very marrow of my tale. This Doctor Doboobie had a servant, a poor snake, whom he employed in trimming his furnace, regulating it by just measure—compounding his drugs—tracing his circles—cajoling his patients, *et sic de cæteris.*—Well, right worshipful, the Doctor being removed thus strangely, and in a way which struck the whole country with terror, this poor Zany thinks to himself, in the words of Maro, '*Uno avulso non deficit alter;*' and, even as a tradesman's apprentice sets himself up in his master's shop when he is dead, or hath retired from business, so doth this Wayland assume the dangerous trade of his defunct master. But although, most worshipful sir, the world is ever prone to listen to the pretensions of such unworthy men, who are, indeed, mere *saltim banqui* and *charlatani*, though usurping the style and skill of doctors of medicine, yet the pretensions of this poor Zany, this Wayland, were too gross to pass on them, nor was there a mere rustic, a villager, who was not ready to accost him in the sense of Persius, though in their own rugged words,—

Diluis helleborum, certo compescere puncto
Nescius examen? vetat hoc natura medendi.

which I have thus rendered in a poor paraphrase of mine own,—

Wilt thou mix hellebore, who doest not know
How many grains doth to the mixture go?
The art of medicine this forbids, I trow.

Moreover, the evil reputation of the master, and his strange and doubtful end, or at least, sudden disappearance, prevented any, excepting the most desperate of men, to seek any advice or opinion from the servant; wherefore, the poor vermin was likely at first to clem for very hunger. But the devil that serves him, since the death of Demetrius Doboobie, put him on a fresh device. This knave, whether from the inspiration of the devil, or from early education, shoes horses better than e'er a man betwixt us and Iceland; and so he gives up his practice on the bipeds, the two-legged and unfledged species, called mankind, and betakes him entirely to shoeing of horses."

"Indeed! and where does he lodge all this time?" said Tressilian. "And does he shoe horses well?—shew me his dwelling presently."

"O, cæca mens hominum! though by the way I used that quotation before. But I would the classics could afford me any sentiment, of power to stop those who are so willing to rush upon their own destruction. Hear but, I pray you, the conditions of this man," said he, in continuation, "ere you are so willing to place yourself within his danger"——

"A takes no money for a's work," said the dame, who stood by, enraptured as it were with the fine words and learned apothegms, which glided so fluently from her erudite inmate, Master Holiday. But the interruption pleased not the magister.

"Peace," said he, "Gammer Sludge; know your place, if it be your will. Sufflamina, Gammer Sludge, and allow me to expound this matter to our worshipful guest.—Sir," said he, again addressing Tressilian, "this old woman speaks true, though in her own rude style; for certainly this faber ferrarius, or blacksmith, takes money of no one."

"And that is a sure sign he deals with Satan," said Dame Sludge; "since no good Christian would ever refuse the wages of his labour."

"The old woman hath touched it again," said the pedagogue; "rem acu tetigit—she hath pricked it with her needle's point.—This Wayland takes no money, indeed, nor doth he shew himself to any one."

"And can this madman, for such I hold him," said the traveller, "aught like good skill of his trade?"

"O, sir, in that let us give the devil his due—Mulciber himself, with all his Cyclops, could hardly amend him. But assuredly there is little wisdom in taking counsel or receiving aid from one, who is but too plainly in league with the author of evil."

"I must take my chance of that, good Master Holiday," said Tressilian, rising; "and as my horse must now have eaten his provender, I must needs thank you for your good cheer, and pray you to shew me this man's residence, that I may have the means of proceeding on my journey."

"Ay, ay, do ye shew him, Master Herasmus," said the old dame, who was, perhaps, desirous to get her house freed of her guest. "A' must needs go, when the devil drives."

"*Do manus*," said the magister, "I submit—taking the world to witness, that I have possessed this honourable gentleman with the full injustice which he has done and shall do to his own soul, if he becomes thus a trinketer with Satan. Neither will I go furth with our guest myself, but rather send my pupil. *Heus Ricarde! Adsis, nebulo.*"

"Under your favour, not so," answered the old woman; "you may peril your own soul, if you list, but my son shall budge on no such errand; and I wonder at you, Domine Doctor, to propose such a piece of service for little Dickie."

"Nay, my good Gammer Sludge," answered the preceptor, "Ricardus shall but go to the top of the hill, and indicate with his digit to the stranger, the dwelling of Wayland Smith. Believe not that any evil can come to him, he having read this morning, fasting, a chapter of the Septuagint, and, moreover, having had his lesson in the Greek Testament."

"Ay," said his mother, "and I have sown a sprig of witch's elm in the neck of un's doublet, ever since that foul thief has begun his practices on man and beast in these parts."

"And as he goes oft (as I hugely suspect) to this conjuror for his own pastime, he may for once go thither, or near it, to pleasure us, and to assist this stranger. *Ergo, heus Ricarde! adsis quæso, mi didascule.*"

The pupil, thus affectionately invoked, at length came tumbling into the room; a queer, shambling, ill-made urchin, who, by his stunted growth, seemed about twelve or thirteen years old, though he was probably, in reality, a year or two older, with a carroty pate in huge disorder, a freckled sun-burnt visage, with a snub nose, a long chin, and two peery grey eyes, which had a droll obliquity of vision, approaching to a squint, though perhaps not a decided one. It was impossible to look at the little man without some disposition to laugh, especially when Gammer Sludge, seizing upon and kissing him, in spite of his struggling and kicking in reply to her caresses, termed him her own precious pearl of beauty.

"*Ricarde*," said the preceptor, "you must forthwith (which is *profecto*) set forth so far as the top of the hill, and shew this man of worship Wayland Smith's work-shop."

"A proper errand of a morning," said the boy, in better language than Tressilian expected; "and who knows but the devil may fly away with me before I come back?"

"Ay, marry may un," said Dame Sludge. "And ye might have thought twice, Master Domine, ere you send my dainty darling on arrow such errand. It is not for such doings I feed your belly and clothe your back, I warrant you."

"Pshaw—*nugæ*, good Gammer Sludge," answered the preceptor; "I ensure you that Satan, if there be Satan in the case, shall not touch a thread of his garment; for Dickie can say his *pater* with the best, and may defend the foul fiends—*Eumenides Stygiumque nefas.*"

"Ay, and I have sewed a sprig of the mountain-ash into his collar," said the good woman, "which will avail more than your clerkship, I wus; but for all that, it is ill to seek the devil or his mates either."

"My good boy," said Tressilian, who saw, from a grotesque sneer on Dickie's face, that he was more like to act upon his own bottom, than by the instruction of his elders, "I will give thee a silver groat, my pretty fellow, if you will but guide me to this man's forge."

The boy gave him a knowing side-look, which seemed to promise acquiescence, while at the same time he exclaimed, "I be your guide to Wayland Smith's! Why, man, did I not say that the devil might fly off with me, just as the kite there (looking to the window) is flying off with one of grandame's chicks."

"The kite! the kite!" exclaimed the old woman in return, and forgetting all other matters in her alarm, hastened to the rescue as fast as her old legs could carry her.

"Now for it," said the urchin to Tressilian; "snatch your beaver, get out your horse, and have at the silver groat you spoke of."

"Nay, but tarry, tarry," said the preceptor, "*Sufflamina, Ricarde.*"

"Tarry yourself," said Dickie, "and think what answer you are to make to grannie for sending me post to the devil."

The teacher, aware of the responsibility he was incurring, bustled up in great haste to lay hold of the urchin and prevent his departure; but Dickie slipped through his fingers, bolted from the cottage, and sped him to the top of a neighbouring rising ground; while the preceptor, despairing, by well-taught experience, of recovering his pupil by speed of foot, had recourse to the most honied epithets the Latin vocabulary affords, to persuade his return. But to *mi anime, corculum meum,* and all such classical endearments, the truant turned a deaf ear, and kept frisking on the top of the rising ground like a goblin by moonlight, making signs to his new acquaintance, Tressilian, to follow him.

The traveller lost no time in getting out his horse, and departing to join his elvish guide, after half-forcing on the poor deserted teacher a recompense for the entertainment he had received, which partly allayed the terror he had for facing the return of the old lady of the mansion. Apparently this took place soon afterwards, for ere Tressilian and his guide had proceeded far on their journey, they heard the screams of a cracked female voice, intermingled with the classical objurgations of Master Erasmus Holiday. But Dickie Sludge, equally deaf to the voice of maternal tenderness and of magisterial authority, skipped on unconcernedly before Tressilian, only observing, that "if they cried themselves hoarse, they might go lick the honey-pot, for he had eaten up all the honey-comb himself on yesterday even."

Chapter Ten

> There entering in, they found the goodman selfe
> Full busylie unto his work ybent,
> Who was to weet a wretched wearish elf,
> With hollow eyes and rawbone cheeks forspent,
> As if he had been long in prison pent.
> *The Faerie Queene*

"ARE WE FAR from the dwelling of this smith, my pretty lad?" said Tressilian to his young guide.

"How is it you call me?" said the boy, looking askew at him with his sharp grey eyes.

"I call you my pretty lad—is there any offence in that, my boy?"

"No—but were you with my grandame and Domine Holiday, you might sing chorus to the old song of

> We three
> Tom-fools be."

"And why so, my little man?" said Tressilian.

"Because," answered the ugly urchin, "you are the only three ever called me pretty lad—now my grandame does it because she is parcel blind by age, and whole blind by kindred—and my master, the poor Domine, does it to curry favour, and have the fullest platter of furmity, and the warmest seat by the fire. But what you call me pretty lad for, you know best yourself."

"Thou art a sharp wag at least, if not a pretty one. But what do thy play-fellows call thee?"

"Hobgoblin," answered the boy, readily; "but for all that, I would rather have my own ugly viznomy than any of their jolterheads, that have no more brains in them than a brick-bat."

"Then you fear not this smith, whom we are going to see."

"Me fear him!" answered the boy; "if he were the devil folks think him, I would not fear him; but though there is something queer about him, he's no more a devil than you are. And that's what I would not tell to every one."

"And why do you tell it to me then, my boy?" said Tressilian.

"Because you are another guess gentleman than those we see here every day," replied Dickie; "and though I am as ugly as sin, I would not have you think me an ass, especially as I may have a boon to ask of you one day."

"And what is that, my lad, whom I must not call pretty?" replied Tressilian.

"O, if I were to ask it just now," said the boy, "you would deny it me. But I will wait till we meet at court."

"At court, Richard! are you bound for court?" said Tressilian.

"Ay, ay, that's just like the rest of them," replied the boy; "I warrant me you think, what should such an ill-favoured, scrambling urchin do at court? But let Richard Sludge alone; I have not been cock of the hen-roost here for nothing. I will make sharp wit mend foul feature."

"But what will your grandame say, and your tutor, Domine Holiday?"

"E'en what they like," replied Dickie; "the one has her chickens to reckon, and the other his boys to whip; I would have given them the candle to hold long since, and shewn this trumpery hamlet a fair pair of heels, but that Domine promises I should go with him to bear share in the next pageant he is to set forth, and they say there are to be great revels shortly."

"And whereabouts are they to be held, my little friend?" said Tressilian.

"O, at some castle far in the north," answered his guide—"a world's breadth from Berkshire. But our old Domine holds that they cannot go forward without him; and it may be he is right, for he has put in order many a fair pageant. He is not half the fool you would take him for, when he gets to work he understands; and so he can spout verses like a play-actor, when, God wot, if you set him to steal a goose's eggs, he would be drubbed by the gander."

"And you are to play a part in his next show?" said Tressilian, somewhat interested by the boy's boldness of conversation, and shrewd estimate of character.

"In faith," said Richard Sludge, in answer, "he has so promised me; and if he break his word, it will be the worse for him; for let me take the bit between my teeth, and turn my head down hill, and I will shake him off with a fall that may harm his bones—And I should not like much to hurt him neither," said he, "for the tiresome old fool has painfully laboured to teach me all he could.—But enough of that— here are we at Wayland Smith's forge-door."

"You jest, my little friend," said Tressilian; "here is nothing but a bare moor, and that ring of stones, with the great one in the midst, like a Cornish barrow."

"Ay, and that great flat stone in the midst, which lies across the top of these uprights," said the boy, "is Wayland Smith's counter, that you must tell down your money upon."

"What do you mean by such folly?" said the traveller, beginning to be angry with the boy, and vexed with himself for having trusted such a hare-brained guide.

"Why," said Dickie, with a grin, "you must tie your horse to that upright stone that has the ring in't, and then you must whistle three times, and lay me down your silver groat on that flat stone, walk out of the circle, sit down on the west side of that little thicket of bushes, and take heed you look neither to right nor to left for ten minutes, or so long as you shall hear the hammer clink, and whenever it ceases, say your prayers for the space you could tell a hundred,—or count over a hundred, which will do as well,—and then come into the circle, you will find your money gone and your horse shod."

"My money gone to a certainty!" said Tressilian; "but as for the rest—hark ye, my lad, I am not your schoolmaster, but if you play off your waggery on me, I will take a part of his task off his hands, and punish you to purpose."

"Ay, when you can catch me!" said the boy, and presently took to his heels across the heath, with a velocity which baffled every attempt of Tressilian to overtake him, loaded as he was with his heavy boots. Nor was it the least provoking part of the urchin's conduct, that he did not exert his utmost speed, like one who finds himself in danger or who is frightened, but preserved just such a rate as to encourage Tressilian to continue the chase, and then darted away from him with the swiftness of the wind, when his pursuer supposed he had nearly run him down, doubling, at the same time, and winding so as always to keep near the place from which he started.

This lasted until Tressilian, from very weariness, stood still, and was about to abandon the pursuit entirely with a hearty curse on the

ill-favoured urchin, who had engaged him in an exercise so ridiculous. But the boy, who had planted himself on the top of a hillock
close in front, began to clap his long thin hands, point with his skinny
fingers, and twist his wild and ugly features into such extravagant
expression of laughter and derision, that Tressilian began half to
doubt whether he had not in view an actual hobgoblin.

Provoked extremely, yet at the same time feeling an irresistible
desire to laugh, so very odd were the boy's grimaces and gesticula-
tions, he returned to his horse, and mounted him with the purpose of
having Dickie at more advantage.

The boy no sooner saw him mount his horse, than he hollo'd out
to him, that rather than he should spoil his white-footed nag, he
would come to him, on condition he would keep his fingers to himself.

"I will make no condition with thee, thou naughty varlet!" said
Tressilian; "I will have thee at my mercy in a moment."

"Aha, Master Traveller," said the boy, "there is a marsh hard by,
would swallow all the horses of the Queen's Guard—I will into it, and
see where you will go then.—You shall hear the bittern bump, and the
wild drake quack, ere you get hold of me, I promise you."

Tressilian looked out, and from the appearance of the ground
behind the hillock, believed it might be as the boy said, and accordingly determined to strike up a peace with so light-footed and ready-
witted an enemy—"Come down," he said, "thou mischievous brat!—
Leave thy mopping and mowing, and come hither; I will do thee no
harm, as I am a gentleman."

The boy answered his invitation with the utmost confidence, and
danced down from his stance in a galliard sort of step, keeping his eye
at the same time fixed on Tressilian's, who, once more dismounted,
stood with his horse's bridle in his hand, breathless, and half
exhausted with his fruitless exercise, though not one drop of moisture
appeared on the freckled forehead of the urchin, which looked like a
piece of dry and discoloured parchment, drawn tight across the brow
of a fleshless skull.

"And tell me," said Tressilian, "why you use me thus, thou mischievous imp? or what your meaning is by telling me so absurd a
legend as you wished but now to put on me? Or rather shew me, in
good earnest, this smith's forge, and I will give thee what will buy thee
apples through the whole winter."

"Were you to give me an orchard of pippins," said Dickie Sludge, "I
can guide thee no better than I have done. Lay down thy silver token
on the flat stone—Whistle three times—then come sit down on the
western side of the thicket of gorse; I will sit by you, and I give you free

leave to wring my head off, unless you hear the smith at work within two minutes after we are seated."

"I will be tempted to take thee at thy word," said Tressilian, "if you make me do aught half so ridiculous for your own mischievous sport—however, I will prove your spell.—Here, then, I tie my horse to this upright stone—I must lay my silver groat here, and whistle three times, sayest thou?"

"Ay, but you must whistle louder than an unfledged owzle," said the boy, as Tressilian, having laid down his money, and half ashamed of the folly he practised, made a careless whistle—"You must whistle louder than that, for who knows where the smith is that you call for?—He may be in the King of France's stables for what I know."

"Why, you said but now he was no devil," replied Tressilian.

"Man or devil," said Dickie, "I see that I must summon him for you;" and therewithal he whistled sharp and shrill, with an acuteness of sound that almost thrilled through Tressilian's brain—"That is what I call whistling," said he, after he had repeated the signal thrice; "and now to cover, to cover, or Whitefoot will not be shod this day."

Tressilian, musing what the upshot of this mummery was to be, yet satisfied there was to be some serious result, by the confidence with which the boy had put himself in his power, suffered himself to be conducted to that side of the little thicket of gorse and brushwood which was farthest from the circle of stones, and there sat down: and as it occurred to him that, after all, this might be a trick for stealing his horse, he kept his hand on the boy's collar, determined to make him hostage for its safety.

"Now, hush and listen," said Dickie, in a low whisper; "you will soon hear the tack of a hammer that was never forged of earthly iron, for the stone it was made of was shot from the moon." And in effect Tressilian did immediately hear the light stroke of a hammer, as when a farrier is at work. The singularity of such a sound, in so very lonely a place, made him involuntarily shudder; but looking at the boy, and discovering, by the arch malicious expression of his countenance, that the urchin saw and enjoyed his slight tremor, he became convinced that the whole was a concerted stratagem, and determined to know by whom, or for what purpose, the trick was played off.

Accordingly, he remained perfectly quiet all the while that the hammer continued to sound, being about the time usually employed in fixing a horse-shoe. But the instant the sound ceased, Tressilian, instead of interposing the space which his guide had requested, started up with his sword in his hand, ran round the thicket, and confronted a man in a farrier's leathern apron, but otherwise fantastically attired in a bear-skin dressed with the fur on, and a cap of the

same, which almost hid the sooty and begrimed features of the wearer
—"Come back, come back!" cried the boy to Tressilian, "or you will
be torn to pieces—no man lives that looks on him."—In fact, the
invisible smith (now fully visible) heaved up his hammer, and shewed
symptoms of doing battle.

But when the boy observed that neither his own entreaties, nor the
menaces of the farrier appeared to change Tressilian's purpose, but
that, on the contrary, he confronted the hammer with his drawn
sword, he exclaimed to the smith in turn, "Wayland, touch him not, or
you will come by the worse!—the gentleman is a true gentleman, and
a bold."

"So thou hast betrayed me, Flibbertigibbet," said the smith; "it
shall be the worse for thee."

"Be who thou wilt," said Tressilian, "thou art in no danger from
me, so thou tell me the meaning of this practice, and why thou drivest
thy trade in this mysterious fashion."

The smith, however, turning to Tressilian, exclaimed, in a threatening tone, "Who questions the Keeper of the Crystal Castle of Light,
the Lord of the Green Lion, the Rider of the Red Dragon?—Hence!
—avoid thee, ere I summon Talpack with his fiery lance, to quell,
crush, and consume!" These words he uttered with violent gesticulation, mouthing and flourishing his hammer.

"Peace, thou vile cozener, with thy gipsey cant!" replied Tressilian,
scornfully, "and follow to the next magistrate, or I will cut thee over
the pate."

"Peace, I pray thee, good Wayland!" said the boy; "credit me the
swaggering vein will not pass here. You must cut boon whids."*

"I think, worshipful sir," said the smith, sinking his hammer, and
assuming a more gentle and submissive tone of voice, "that so a
poor man does his day's job, he might be permitted to work it out
after his own fashion. Your horse is shod, and your farrier paid—
What need you cumber yourself further, than to mount and pursue
your journey?"

"Nay, friend, you are mistaken," replied Tressilian; "every man has
a right to take the mask from the face of a cheat and a juggler; and your
mode of living raises suspicion that you are both."

"If you are so determined, sir," said the smith, "I cannot help myself
save by force, which I were unwilling to use towards you, Master
Tressilian;—not that I fear your weapon, but because I know you to
be a worthy, kind, and well-accomplished gentleman, who will rather
help than harm a poor man that is in a strait."

"Well said, Wayland," said the boy, who had anxiously awaited the

* "Give good words."—*Slang dialect.*

issue of their conference. "But let us to thy den, man, for it is ill for thy health to stand here talking in the open air."

"Thou art right, Hobgoblin," replied the smith; and going to the little thicket of gorse on the side nearest to the circle, and opposite to that at which his customer had so lately couched, he discovered a trap-door curiously covered with bushes, raised it, and, descending into the earth, vanished from their eyes. Notwithstanding Tressilian's curiosity, he had some hesitation at following the fellow into what might be a den of robbers, especially when he heard the smith's voice, as if issuing from the bowels of the earth, call out, "Flibbertigibbet, do you come last, and be sure to fasten the trap!"

"Have you seen enough of Wayland Smith now?" whispered the urchin to Tressilian, with an arch sneer, as if marking his companion's uncertainty.

"Not yet," said Tressilian firmly, and shaking off his momentary irresolution, he descended into the narrow stair-case to which the entrance led, and was followed by Dickie Sludge, who made fast the trap-door behind him, and thus excluded every glimmer of day-light. The descent, however, was only a few steps, and led to a level passage of a few yards length, at the end of which appeared the reflection of a lurid and red light. Arrived at this point, with his sword drawn in his hand, Tressilian found that a turn to the left admitted him and Hobgoblin, who followed closely, into a small square vault, containing a smith's forge glowing with charcoal, the vapour of which filled the apartment with an oppressive smell, which would have been altogether suffocating, but that by some concealed vent the vault communicated with the upper air. The light afforded by the red fuel, and by a lamp suspended in an iron chain, served to shew that, besides an anvil, bellows, tongs, hammers, a quantity of ready-made horse-shoes, and other articles proper to the profession of a farrier, there were also stoves, alembics, crucibles, retorts, and other instruments of alchemy. The grotesque figure of the smith, and the ugly but whimsical features of the boy, seen by the gloomy and imperfect light of the charcoal-fire and the dying lamp, accorded very well with all this mystical apparatus, and in that age of superstition would have made some impression on the courage of most men.

But nature had endowed Tressilian with firm nerves, and his education, originally good, had been too sedulously improved by subsequent study to give way to any imaginary terrors; and after giving a glance around him, he again demanded of the artist who he was, and by what accident he came to know and to address him by his name.

"Your worship cannot but remember," said the smith, "that about three years hence, upon Saint Lucy's Eve, there came a travelling juggler to a certain hall in Devonshire, and exhibited his skill before a worshipful knight and a fair company—I see from your worship's countenance, dark as this place is, that my memory has not done me wrong."

"Thou hast said enough," said Tressilian, turning away, as wishing to hide from the speaker the painful train of recollections which his discourse had unconsciously awakened.

"The juggler," said the smith, "played his part so bravely, that the clowns and clown-like squires in the company held his art to be little less than magical; but there was one maiden of fifteen, or thereby, with the fairest face I ever looked upon, whose rosy cheek grew pale, and her bright eyes dim, at the sight of the wonders exhibited."

"Peace, I command thee, peace!" said Tressilian.

"I mean your worship no offence," said the fellow; "but I have cause to remember how, to relieve the young maiden's fears, you condescended to point out the mode in which these deceptions were practised, and to baffle the poor juggler by laying bare the mysteries of his art, as ably as if you had been a brother of his order.—She was indeed so fair a maiden, that, to win a smile of her, a man might well"——

"Not a word more of her, I charge thee!" said Tressilian; "I do well remember the night you speak of—one of the few happy evenings my life has known."

"She is gone, then," said the smith, interpreting after his own fashion the sigh with which Tressilian uttered these words—"She is gone, young, beautiful, and beloved as she was!—I crave your worship's pardon—I would have hammered on another theme—I see I have unwarily driven the nail to the quick."

This speech was made with a mixture of rude feeling, which inclined Tressilian favourably to the poor artizan, of whom before he was inclined to judge very harshly. But nothing can so soon attract the unfortunate, as real or seeming sympathy with their sorrows.

"I think," pursued Tressilian, after a minute's silence, "thou wert in those days a jovial fellow, who could keep a company merry by song, and tale, and rebeck, as well as by thy juggling tricks—why do I find thee a laborious handicraftsman, plying thy trade in so melancholy a dwelling, and under such extraordinary circumstances?"

"My story is not long," said the artist; "but your honour had better sit while you listen to it." So saying, he approached to the fire a three-footed stool, and took another himself, while Dickie Sludge, or Flibbertigibbet, as he called the boy, drew a cricket to the smith's feet, and looked up in his face with features which, as illumined by the glow of the forge, seemed convulsed with intense curiosity—"Thou too," said the smith to him, "shalt learn, as thou well deservest at my hand, the brief history of my life; and, in troth, it were as well tell it thee as leave thee to ferret it out, since Nature never packed a shrewder wit into a more ungainly casket.—Well, sir, if my poor story may pleasure you, it is at your command—But will you not taste a stoup of liquor, which I promise you that even in this poor cell I have in store?"

"Speak not of it," said Tressilian, "but go on with thy story, for my leisure is brief."

"You shall have no cause to rue the delay," said the smith, "for your horse shall be better fed in the meantime, than he hath been this morning, and made fitter for travel."

With that the artist left the vault, and returned after a few minutes interval. Here, also, we pause, that the narrative may commence in another chapter.

Chapter Eleven

> I say, my lord can such a subtilty
> (But all his craft ye must not wot of me,
> And somewhat help I yet to his working)
> That all the ground on which we ben riding,
> Till that we come to Canterbury town,
> He can all clean turnen so up so down,
> And pave it all of silver and of gold.
> *The Canon's Yeoman's Prologue—Canterbury Tales*

THE ARTIST resumed in the following terms:—

"I was bred a blacksmith, and knew my art as well as e'er a black-thumb'd, leathern-apron'd, swart-faced knave of that noble mystery. But I tired of ringing hammer-tunes on iron stithies, and went out into the world, where I became acquainted with a celebrated juggler, whose fingers had become rather too stiff for legerdemain, and who wished to have the aid of an apprentice in his noble mystery. I served him for six years, until I was master of my trade—I refer myself to your worship, whose judgment cannot be disputed, whether I did not learn to ply the craft indifferently well?"

"Excellently," said Tressilian; "but be brief."

"It was not long after I had performed at Sir Hugh Robsart's, in your worship's presence," said the artist, "that I took myself to the stage, and have swaggered with the bravest of them all, both at the Black Bull, the Globe, the Fortune, and elsewhere; but I know not how—apples were so plenty that year, that the lads in the two-penny gallery never took more than one bite out of them, and threw the rest of the pippin at whatever actor chanced to be on the stage. So I tired of it—renounced my half share in the company—gave my foil to my comrade—my buskins to the wardrobe, and shewed the theatre a clean pair of heels."

"Well, friend, and what," said Tressilian, "was your next shift?"

"I became," said the smith, "half partner, half domestic, to a man of much skill and little substance, who practised the trade of a physicianer."

"In other words," said Tressilian, "you were Jack Pudding to a quack salver."

"Something beyond that, let me hope, my good Master Tressilian," replied the artist; "and yet, to say truth, our practice was of an adventurous description, and the pharmacy which I had acquired in my first studies for the benefit of horses, was frequently applied to our human patients. But the seeds of all maladies are the same; and if turpentine, tar, pitch, and beef-suet, mingled with turmerick, gum-mastick, and one head of garlick, can cure the horse that hath been grieved with a nail, I see not but what it may benefit the man that hath been pricked with a sword. But my master's practice, as well as his skill, went far beyond mine, and dealt in more dangerous concerns. He was not only a bold adventurous practitioner in physic, but also, if your pleasure so chanced to be, an adept, who read the stars and expounded the fortunes of mankind, genethliacally, as he called it, or otherwise. He was a learned distiller of simples, and a profound chemist—made several efforts to fix mercury, and judged himself to have made a fair hit at the philosopher's stone. I have yet a program of his on that subject, which, if your honour understandeth, I believe you have the better, not only of all who read, but also of him who wrote it."

He gave Tressilian a scroll of parchment, bearing at top and bottom, and down the margin, the signs of the seven planets, curiously intermingled with talismanical characters and scraps of Greek and Hebrew. In the midst were some Latin verses from a cabalistical author, written out so fairly, that even the gloom of the place did not prevent Tressilian from reading them. The tenor of the original ran as follows:—

> Si fixum solvas, faciasque volare solutum,
> Et volucrem figas, facient te vivere tutum,
> Si pariat ventum, valet auri pondere centum
> Ventus ubi vult spirat—Capiat qui capere potest.

"I protest to you," said Tressilian, "all I understand of this jargon is, that the last words seem to mean 'Catch as catch can.'"

"That," said the smith, "is the very principle that my worthy friend and master, Doctor Doboobie, always acted upon; until, being besotted with his own imaginations, and conceited of his high chemical skill, he began to spend in cheating himself the money which he had acquired in cheating others, and either discovered or built for himself, I could never know which, this secret elaboratory, in which he used to seclude himself both from patients and disciples, who doubtless thought his long and mysterious absences from his ordinary residence in the town of Farringdon were occasioned by his progress in the mystic sciences, and facilitated by his intercourse with the invisible world. Me also he tried to deceive; but though I contradicted him not, he saw that I knew too much of his secrets to be any longer a safe companion. Meanwhile, his name waxed famous, or rather infamous, for many of those who resorted to him did so under persuasion that he was a sorcerer. And yet his supposed advance in the occult sciences, drew to him the secret resort of men too powerful to be named, for purposes too dangerous to be mentioned. Men cursed and threatened him, and bestowed on me, the innocent assistant of his studies, the nickname of the Devil's foot-post, which procured a volley of stones as soon as ever I ventured to shew my face in the street of the village. At length, my master suddenly disappeared, pretending to me that he was about to visit his elaboratory in this place, and discharging me to disturb him till two days were past. When this period had elapsed, I became anxious, and resorted to this vault, where I found the fires extinguished and the utensils in confusion, with a note from the learned Doboobius, as he was wont to style himself, acquainting me that we would never meet again, bequeathing me his chemical apparatus, and the parchment which I have just put into your hands, advising me strongly to prosecute the secret which it contained, which would infallibly lead me to the discovery of the grand magisterium."

"And didst thou follow this sage advice?" said Tressilian.

"Worshipful sir, no," replied the smith; "for being by nature cautious and suspicious, from knowing with whom I had ado, I made so many perquisitions before I ventured even to light a fire, that I at length discovered a small barrel of gunpowder, carefully hid beneath the furnace, with the purpose, no doubt, that as soon as I should commence the grand work of the transmutation of metals, the explosion should transmute the vault and all in it into a heap of ruins, which might serve at once for my slaughter-house and my grave. This cured me of alchemy, and fain would I have returned to the honest hammer and anvil; but who would carry a horse to be shoed by the Devil's post? Meantime, I had won the regard of my honest Flibbertigibbet here, he being then at Faringdon with his master, the sage Erasmus Holiday, by teaching him a few secrets, such as please youth at his age; and after much counsel together, we agreed, that since I could get no practice in the ordinary way, I should try how I could work out business amongst these ignorant boors, by practising upon their silly fears. And thanks to Flibbertigibbet who hath spread my renown, I have not wanted custom. But it is won at too great risk, and I fear I shall be at length taken up for a wizard; so that I seek but an opportunity to leave this vault when I can have the protection of some worshipful person against the fury of the populace, in case they chance to recognize me."

"And art thou," said Tressilian, "perfectly acquainted with the roads in this country?"

"I could ride them every inch by midnight," answered Wayland Smith, which was the name this adept had adopted.

"Thou hast no horse to ride upon," said Tressilian.

"Pardon me," replied Wayland; "I have as good a tit as ever yeoman bestrode; and I forgot to say it was the best part of the mediciner's legacy to me, excepting one or two of his medical secrets, which I picked up without his knowledge and against his will."

"Get thyself washed and shaved then," said Tressilian; "reform thy dress as well as thou canst, and fling away these grotesque trappings; and, so thou wilt be secret and faithful, thou shalt follow me for a short time, till thy pranks here are forgotten. Thou hast, I think, both address and courage, and I have matter to do that may require both."

Wayland Smith eagerly embraced the proposal, and protested his devotion to his new master. In a very few minutes he had made so great a change in his original appearance, by change of dress, trimming his beard and hair and so forth, that Tressilian could not help remarking, that he thought he would stand little need of a protector, since none of his old acquaintance was like to recognize him.

"My debtors would not pay me money perhaps," said Wayland, shaking his head; "but my creditors of every kind would be less easily blinded—and, in truth, I hold myself not safe, unless under the protection of a gentleman of birth and character, as that of your worship."

So saying, he led the way out of the cavern. He then called loudly for Hobgoblin, who, after lingering an instant, appeared with the horse furniture, when Wayland closed, and sedulously covered up the trap-door, observing, it might again serve him at his need, besides the tools were worth somewhat. A whistle from the owner brought to his side his nag that fed quietly on the common, and was accustomed to the signal. While he accoutred him for the journey, Tressilian drew his own girths faster, and in a few minutes both were ready to mount.

At this moment Sludge approached to bid them farewell.

"You are going to leave me then, my old play-fellow," said the boy;

"and there is an end of all our game at bo-peep with the cowardly lubbards whom I brought hither to have their broad-footed nags shod by the devil and his imps."

"It is even so," said Wayland Smith; "the best friends must part, Flibbertigibbet; but thou, my boy, art the only thing in the Vale of White Horse which I shall regret to leave behind me."

"Well, I bid thee not farewell," said Dickie Sludge, "for you will be at these revels, I judge, and so shall I; for if Domine Holiday take me not thither, by the light of day, which we see not in yonder dark hole, I will take myself there!"

"In good time," said Wayland; "but I pray you to do nought rashly."

"Nay, now ye would make a child—a common child of me, and tell me of the risk of walking without leading strings. But before you are a mile from these stones, you shall know, by a sure token, that I have more of the hobgoblin about me than you credit; and I will so manage, that, if you take advantage, you may profit by my prank."

"What doest thou mean, boy?" said Tressilian; but Flibbertigibbet only answered with a grin and a caper, and bidding both of them farewell, and at the same time exhorting them to make the best of their way from the place, he set them the example by running homeward with the same uncommon velocity with which he had baffled Tressilian's former attempts to get hold of him.

"It is in vain to chase him," said Wayland Smith; "for unless your worship is expert in lark-hunting, we should never catch hold of him —and besides what would it avail? Better make the best of our way from hence, as he advises."

They mounted their horses accordingly, and began to proceed at a round pace, as soon as Tressilian had explained to his guide the road in which he desired to travel.

After they had trotted nearly a mile, Tressilian could not help observing to his companion, that his horse felt more lively under him than even when he mounted in the morning.

"Are you avised of that?" said Wayland Smith, smiling. "That is owing to a little secret of mine. I mixed that with an handful of oats which shall save your worship's heels the trouble of spurring these six hours at least. Nay, I have not studied medicine and pharmacy for nought."

"I trust," said Tressilian, "your drugs will do my horse no harm."

"No more than the mare's milk which foaled him," answered the artist; and was proceeding to dilate on the excellence of his recipe, when he was interrupted by an explosion as loud and tremendous as the mine which blows up the rampart of a beleaguered city. The horses started, and the riders were equally surprised. They turned to gaze in the direction from which the thunder-clap was heard, and beheld, just over the spot they had left so recently, a huge pillar of dark smoke rising high into the clear blue atmosphere. "My habitation is gone to wrack," said Wayland, immediately conjecturing the cause of the explosion—"I was a fool to mention the doctor's kind intentions towards my mansion before that limb of mischief Flibbertigibbet—I might have guessed he would long to put so rare a frolic into execution. But let us hasten on, for the sound will collect the country to the spot."

So saying, he spurred his horse, and Tressilian also quickening his speed, they rode briskly forward.

"This, then, was the meaning of the little imp's token which he promised us," said Tressilian; "had we lingered near the spot we had found it a love-token with a vengeance."

"He would have given us warning," said the smith; "I saw him look back more than once to see if we were off—'tis a very devil for mischief, yet not an ill-natured devil either. It were long to tell your honour how I became first acquainted with him, and how many tricks he played me. Many a good turn he did me too, especially in bringing me customers; for his great delight was to see them sit shivering behind the bushes when they heard the click of my hammer. I think Dame Nature, when she lodged a double quantity of brains in that mishapen head of his, gave him the power of enjoying other people's distresses, as she gave them the pleasure of laughing at his ugliness."

"It may be so," said Tressilian; "those who find themselves severed from society by peculiarities of form, if they do not hate the common bulk of mankind, are at least not altogether indisposed to enjoy their mishaps and calamities."

"But Flibbertigibbet," answered Wayland, "hath that about him which may redeem his turn for mischievous frolic; for he is as faithful when attached, as he is tricky and malignant to strangers; and, as I said before, I have cause to say so."

Tressilian pursued the conversation no farther; and they continued their journey towards Devonshire without farther adventure, until they alighted at an inn in the town of Marlborough, since celebrated for having given title to the greatest general (excepting one) whom Britain ever produced. Here the travellers received, in the same breath, an example of the truth of two old proverbs, namely, that Ill news fly fast, and that Listeners seldom hear a good tale of themselves.

The inn-yard was in a sort of combustion when they alighted; insomuch, that they could scarce get man or boy to take care of their horses, so full were the whole household of some news which flew from tongue to tongue, yet the import of which they were for some time unable to discover. At length, indeed, they found it respected matters which touched them nearly.

"What is the matter, say you, master?" answered, at length, the head hostler, in reply to Tressilian's repeated questions—"Why, truly, I scarce know mysell. But here was a rider but now, who says that the devil hath flown away with him they called Wayland Smith, that wonn'd about three miles from the White Horse of Berkshire, this very blessed morning, in a flash of fire and a pillar of smoke, and rooted up the place he dwelt in, near that old cock-pit of upright stones, as cleanly as if it had all been delved up for a cropping."

"Why, then," said an old farmer, "the more is the pity—for that Wayland Smith (whether he was the devil's crony or no I skill not,) had a good notion of horse diseases, and it's to be thought the bots will spread in the country far and near, an Satan has not gi'en un time to leave his secret behind un."

"You may say that, Gaffer Grimesby," said the hostler in return; "I have carried a horse to Wayland Smith myself, for he passed all farriers in this country."

"Did you see him?" said Dame Alison Crane, mistress of the inn bearing that sign, and deigning to term husband the owner thereof, an insignificant hop-o'-my-thumb sort of person, whose halting gait, and long neck, and meddling hen-pecked insignificance, are supposed to have given origin to the celebrated old English tune of "My Dame hath a lame tame Crane."

On this occasion he chirp'd out a repetition of his wife's question, "Did'st see the devil, Jack Hostler, I say?"

"And what if I did see un, Master Crane?" replied Jack Hostler,—for, like all the rest of the household, he paid as little respect to his master as his mistress herself did.

"Nay, nought, Jack Hostler," replied the pacific Master Crane, "only if you saw the devil, methinks I would like to know what un's like?"

"You will know that one day, Master Crane," said his helpmate, "an' ye mend not your manners, and mind your business, leaving off such idle palabras—But truly, Jack Hostler, I should be glad to know myself what like the fellow was."

"Why, Dame," said the hostler, more respectfully, "as for what he was like I cannot tell, nor no man else, for why I never saw un."

"And how didst get thine errand done," said Gaffer Grimesby, "if thou seed'st him not?"

"Why, I had schoolmaster to write down ailment o' nag," said Jack Hostler; "and I went wi' the ugliest slip of a boy for my guide as ever man cut out o' lime-tree root to please a child withal. So I laid my bit of a scroll on a flat stean, wi' a good harry groat to keep it firm, and I waited my time aneath some bit pickle of gorse, when lo ye, the earth shook and trembled—and after a while I was wished by the slip of a boy to venture to the place—And lo ye, gone was my groat, and in its place was my packet which I was to cure nag's ailment withal."

"And what was it?—and did it cure your nag?" was uttered and echoed by all who stood around.

"Why, how can I tell you what it was?" said the hostler. "Simply it smelled and tasted—for I did make bold to put a pea's substance into my mouth—like hartshorn and savin mixed with vinegar—But then no hartshorn and savin ever wrought so speedy a cure—And I am dreading that if Wayland Smith be gone, the bots will have more power over horse and cattle."

The pride of art, which is certainly not inferior in its influence to any other pride whatsoever, here so far operated on Wayland Smith, that, notwithstanding the obvious danger of his being recognized, he could not help winking to Tressilian, and smiling mysteriously, as if triumphing in this undoubted evidence of his veterinary skill. In the meanwhile, the discourse continued.

"E'en let it be so," said a grave man in black, the companion of Gaffer Grimesby; "e'en let us perish under the evil God sends us, rather than the Devil be our doctor."

"Very true," said Dame Crane; "and I marvel at Jack Hostler that he would peril his own soul to cure the bowels of a nag."

"Very true, mistress," said Jack Hostler, "but the nag was my master's; and had it been your's, I think you would ha' held me cheap enow an I had feared the Devil when the poor beast was in such a taking—For the rest, let the clergy look to it. Every man to his craft, says the proverb; the parson to the prayer-book, and the groom to his curry-comb."

"I vow," said Dame Crane, "I think Jack Hostler speaks like a good Christian and a faithful servant, who will spare neither body nor soul in his master's service. However, the devil has lifted him in time, for a Constable of the Hundred came hither this morning to get old Gaffer Pinniewinks, the trier of witches, to go with him to the Vale of White-horse to comprehend Wayland Smith, and put him to his probation. I helped Pinniewinks to sharpen his pincers and his poking-awl, and I saw the warrant from Justice Blindas."

"Pooh—pooh—the devil would laugh both at Blindas and his war-rant, constable, and witch-finder to boot," said old Dame Crank, the papist laundress; "Wayland Smith's flesh would mind Pinniewinks's awl no more than a cambric ruff minds a hot piccadilloe-needle. But tell me, gentle-folks, if the devil ever had such a hand among ye, as to snatch away your smiths and your artists from under your nose, when the good Abbots of Abingdon had their own. By Our Lady, no!—they had their hallowed tapers, and their holy water, and their relics and what not, could send the foulest fiends a-packing.—Go ask a heretic parson to do the like—But ours were a comfortable people."

"Very true, Dame Crank," said the hostler; "so said Simpkins of Simonburn when the curate kissed his wife,—'They are a comfortable people,' said he."

"Silence, thou foul-mouthed vermin," said Dame Crank; "is it fit for a heretic horse-boy like thee, to handle a text like the Catholic clergy?"

"In troth no, dame," replied the man of oats; "and as you yourself are now no text for their handling, dame, whatever may have been the case in your day, I think we had e'en better leave them alone."

At this last exchange of sarcasm, Dame Crank set up her throat, and began a horrible exclamation against Jack Hostler, under cover of which Tressilian and his attendant escaped into the house.

They had no sooner entered a private chamber, to which Goodman Crane himself had condescended to usher them, and dispatched their worthy and obsequious host on the errand of procuring wine and refreshment, than Wayland began to give vent to his self-importance.

"You see, sir," said he, addressing Tressilian, "that I nothing fabled in asserting that I possessed fully the mighty mystery of a farrier, or mareschal, as the French more honourably term us. These dog-hostlers, who, after all, are the better judges in such a case, know what credit they should attach to my medicaments. I call you to witness, worshipful Master Tressilian, that nought, save the voice of calumny and the hand of malicious violence, hath driven me forth from a station in which I held a place alike useful and honoured."

"I bear witness, my friend, but will reserve my listening," answered Tressilian, "for a safer time; unless, indeed, you deem it essential to your reputation, to be translated, like your late dwelling, by the assistance of a flash of fire. For you see your best friends reckon you no better than a mere sorcerer."

"Now, heaven forgive them," said the artist, "who confound learned skill with unlawful magic! I trust a man may be as skilful, or more so, than the best chirurgeon ever meddled with horse-flesh, and yet may be upon the matter little more than other ordinary men, or at the worst no conjuror."

"God forbid else!" said Tressilian. "But be silent just for the present, since here comes mine host with an assistant, who seems something of the least."

Every body about the inn, Dame Crane herself included, had been indeed so interested and agitated by the story they had heard of Wayland Smith, and by the new, varying, and more marvellous editions of the incident, which arrived from various quarters, that mine host, in his righteous determination to accommodate his guests, had been able to obtain the assistance of none of the household, saving that of a little boy, a junior tapster, of about twelve years old, who was called Sampson.

"I wish," he said, apologizing to his guests, as he set down a flagon of sack, and promised some food immediately,—"I wish that the devil had flown away with my wife and my whole family instead of this same Wayland Smith, who, I dare say, after all said and done, was much less worthy of the distinction Satan has done him."

"I hold opinion with you, good fellow," replied Wayland Smith; "and I will drink to you upon that argument."

"Not that I would justify any man who deals with the devil," said mine host, after having pledged Wayland in a rousing draught of sack, "but that—Saw ye ever better sack, my masters?—but that, I say, a man had better deal with a dozen cheats and scoundrel fellows, such as this Wayland Smith, rather than with a devil incarnate, that takes possession of house and home, bed and board."

The poor fellow's detail of grievances was here interrupted by the shrill voice of his helpmate, screaming from the kitchen, to which he instantly hobbled, craving pardon of his guests. He was no sooner gone, than Wayland Smith expressed, by every contemptuous epithet in the language, his utter scorn for a nincompoop, who stuck his head under his wife's apron-string; and intimated, that, but for the sake of the horses, which required both rest and food, he would advise his worship Master Tressilian to push on a stage farther, rather than pay a reckoning to such a mean-spirited, crow-trodden, hen-pecked, cox-comb, as Gaffer Crane.

The arrival of a large dish of good cow-heel and bacon, something soothed the asperity of the artist, which wholly vanished before a choice capon, so delicately roasted, that the lard frothed on it, said Wayland, like May-dew on a lily; and both Gaffer Crane and his good dame became, in his eyes, very pains-taking, accommodating, obliging persons.

According to the manners of the times, the master and his attendant ate at the same table, and the latter observed with regret, how little attention Tressilian paid to his meal. He recollected, indeed, the pain he had given by mentioning the maiden in whose company he had first seen him; but, fearful of touching upon a topic too tender to be tampered with, he chose to ascribe his abstinence to another cause.

"This fare is perhaps too coarse for your worship," said Wayland, as the limbs of the capon disappeared before his own exertions; "but had you dwelt as long as I have done in yonder dungeon, which Flibberti- gibbet has translated to the upper element, a place where I dared hardly broil my food, lest the smoke should be seen without, you would think a fair capon a more welcome dainty."

"If you are pleased, friend," said Tressilian, "it is well. Neverthe- less, hasten thy meal if thou canst, for this place is unfriendly to thy safety, and my concerns crave hasty travelling."

Allowing, therefore, their horses no more rest than was absolutely necessary for them, they pursued their journey by a forced march as far as Bradford, where they reposed themselves for the night.

The next morning found them early travellers. And, not to fatigue the reader with unnecessary particulars, they traversed without adventure the counties of Wiltshire and Somerset, and about noon of the third day after Tressilian's leaving Cumnor, arrived at Sir Hugh Robsart's seat, called Lidcote Hall, on the frontiers of Devonshire.

Chapter Twelve

Ah me! the flower and blossom of your house,
The wind hath blown away to other towers.
JOANNA BAILLIE'S *Family Legend*

THE ANCIENT SEAT of Lidcote Hall was situated near the village of the same name, and adjoined to the wild and extensive forest of Exmoor, plentifully stocked with game, in which some ancient rights belonging to the Robsart family, entitled Sir Hugh to pursue his favourite amusement of the chase. The old mansion was a low, vener- able building, occupying a considerable space of ground, which was surrounded by a deep moat. The approach and drawbridge were defended by an octagonal tower, of ancient brick-work, but so clothed with ivy and other creepers, that it was difficult to discover of what materials it was constructed. The angles of this tower were each decorated with a turret, whimsically various in form and in size, and, therefore, very unlike the monotonous stone pepper-boxes, which, in modern Gothic architecture, are employed for the same purpose. One of these turrets was square, and occupied as a clock-house. But the clock was now standing still; a circumstance peculiarly striking to Tressilian, because the good old knight, among other harmless pecul- iarities, had a fidgetty anxiety about the exact measurement of time, very common to those who have a great deal of that commodity to dispose of, and find it lie heavy upon their hands,—just as we see shopkeepers amuse themselves with taking an exact account of their stock at the time there is least demand for it.

The entrance to the court-yard of the old mansion lay through an arch-way, surmounted by the foresaid tower, but the draw-bridge was down, and one leaf of the iron-studded folding-doors stood carelessly open. Tressilian hastily rode over the draw-bridge, entered the court, and began to call loudly on the domestics by their names. For some time he was only answered by the echoes and the howling of the hounds, whose kennel lay at no great distance from the mansion, and was surrounded by the same moat. At length Will Badger, the old and favourite attendant of the knight, who acted alike as squire of his body, and superintendant of his sports, made his appearance. The stout, weather-beaten forester shewed great signs of joy when he recognized Tressilian.

"Lord love you," he said, "Master Edmund, be it thou in flesh and fell?—Then thou mayst do some good on Sir Hugh, for it passes the wit of man, that is of mine own, and the Curate's, and Master Mumblazon's, to do aught wi' un."

"Is Sir Hugh then worse since I went away, Will?" demanded Tressilian.

"For worse in body—no—he is much better," replied the domestic; "but he is clean mazed as it were—eats and drinks as he is wont —but sleeps not, or rather wakes not, for he is ever in a sort of twilight, that is neither sleeping nor waking. Dame Swineford thought it was like the dead palsy.—But no, no, dame, said I, it is the heart, it is the heart."

"Can ye not stir his mind to any pastimes?" said Tressilian.

"He is clean and quite off his sports," said Will Badger; "hath neither touched backgammon or shovel-board—nor looked on the big book of harrotry wi' Master Mumblazon. I let the clock run down, thinking the missing the bell might somewhat move him, for you know, Master Edmund, he was particular in counting time. But he never said a word on't, so I may e'en set the old chime a trowling again. I made bold to tread on Bungay's tail too, and you know what a round rating that would ha' cost me once a-day—But he minded his whine no more than a madge howlet whooping down the chimney—so the case is beyond me."

"Thou shalt tell me the rest within doors, Will.—Meanwhile, let this person be ta'en to the buttery, and used with respect—He is a man of art."

"White art or black art, I would," said Will Badger, "that he had any art which could help us.—Here, Tom Butler, look to the man of art— And see as he steals none of thy spoons, lad," he added, in a whisper to the butler, who shewed himself at a low window, "I have known as honest a faced fellow have art enough to do that."

He then ushered Tressilian into a low parlour, and went, at his desire, to see in what state his master was, lest the sudden return of his darling pupil, and proposed son-in-law, should affect him too strongly. He returned immediately, and said that Sir Hugh was dozing in his elbow chair, but that Master Mumblazon would acquaint Master Tressilian the instant he awaked.

"But it is a chance if he knows you," said the huntsman, "for he has forgotten the name of every hound in the pack. I thought about a week since, he had gotten a favourable turn:—'Saddle me old Sorrel,' said he, suddenly, after he had taken his usual night-draught out of the great silver grace-cup, 'and take the hounds to Mount Hazelhurst to-morrow.' Glad men were we all, and out we had him in the morning, and he rode to cover as usual, with never a word but that the wind was south, and the scent would lie. But ere we had uncoupled the hounds, he began to stare round him, like a man that wakes suddenly out of a dream—turns bridle and walks back to Hall again, and leaves us to hunt at leisure by ourselves, if we listed."

"You tell a heavy tale, Will," replied Tressilian; "but God must help us—there is no aid in man."

"Then you bring us no news of young Mistress Amy?—But what need I ask—your brow tells the story. Ever I hoped, that if any man could or would track her, it must be you. All's over and lost now. But if ever I have that Varney within reach of a flight-shot, I will bestow a forked shaft on him; and that I swear by salt and bread."

As he spoke, the door opened, and Master Mumblazon appeared; a withered, thin, elderly gentleman, with a cheek like a winter apple, and his grey hair partly concealed by a small high hat, shaped like a cone, or rather like such a strawberry-basket as London fruiterers exhibit at their windows. He was too sententious a person to waste words on mere salutation; so, having welcomed Tressilian with a nod and a shake of the hand, he beckoned him to follow to Sir Hugh's great chamber, which the good knight usually inhabited. Will Badger followed, unasked, anxious to see whether his master would be relieved from his state of apathy by the arrival of Tressilian.

In a long low parlour, amply furnished with implements of the chase, and with sylvan trophies, by a massive stone chimney, over which hung a sword and suit of armour, somewhat obscured by neglect, sat Sir Hugh Robsart of Lidcote, a man of large size, which had been only kept within moderate compass by the most constant use of violent exercise. It seemed to Tressilian that the lethargy, under which his old friend appeared to labour, had, even during his few weeks absence, added bulk to his person; at least it had obviously diminished the vivacity of his eye, which, as they entered, first followed Master Mumblazon slowly to a large oaken desk, on which a ponderous volume lay open, and then rested, as if in uncertainty, on the stranger who had entered along with him. The Curate, a grey-headed clergyman, who had been a confessor in the days of Queen Mary, sat with a book in his hand in another recess in the apartment. He, too, signed a mournful greeting to Tressilian, and laid his book aside, to watch the effect his appearance should produce on the afflicted old man.

As Tressilian, his own eyes filling fast with tears, approached more and more nearly to the father of his betrothed bride, Sir Hugh's intelligence seemed to revive. He sighed heavily, as one who awakens from a state of stupor, a slight convulsion passed over his features, he opened his arms without speaking a word, and as Tressilian threw himself into them, he folded him to his bosom.

"There is something left to live for yet," were the first words he uttered; and while he spoke, he gave vent to his feelings in a paroxysm of weeping, the tears chasing each other down his sun-burnt cheeks and long white beard.

"I ne'er thought to have thanked God to see my master weep," said Will Badger; "but now I do, though I am like to weep for company."

"I will ask thee no questions," said the old Knight; "no questions— none, Edmund—thou hast not found her, or so found her, that she were better lost."

Tressilian was unable to reply, otherwise than by putting his hands before his face.

"It is enough—it is enough—but do not thou weep for her, Edmund. I have cause to weep, for she was my daughter,—thou hast cause to rejoice, that she did not become thy wife.—Great God! thou knowest best what is good for us—it was my nightly prayer that I should see Amy and Edmund wedded,—had it been granted, it had now been gall added to bitterness."

"Be comforted, my friend," said the Curate, addressing Sir Hugh. "It cannot be that the daughter of all our hopes and affections is the vile creature you would bespeak her."

"O, no," replied Sir Hugh, impatiently, "I were wrong to name broadly the base thing she is become—there is some new court name for it, I warrant me—it is honour enough for the daughter of an old De'nshire clown to be the lemman of a gay courtier,—of Varney too, —of Varney, whose grandsire was relieved by my father, when his fortune was broken, at the battle of—the battle of—where Richard was slain—Out on my memory—And I warrant none of you will help me"——

"The battle of Bosworth," said Master Mumblazon, "stricken

between Richard Crookback and Henry Tudor, grandsire of the Queen that now is, primo Henrici Septimi; and in the year one thousand four hundred and eighty five, *post Christum natum.*"

"Ay, even so," said the good Knight, "every child knows it—but my poor head forgets all it should remember, and remembers only what it would most willingly forget. My brain has been at fault, Tressilian, almost ever since thou hast been away, and even yet it hunts counter."

"Your worship," said the good clergyman, "had better retire to your apartment, and try to sleep for a little space,—the physician left a composing draught,—and our Great Physician has commanded us to use earthly means, that we may be strengthened to sustain the trials he sends us."

"True, true, old friend," said Sir Hugh, "and we will bear our trials manfully—we have lost but a woman.—See, Tressilian,"—he drew from his bosom a long ringlet of fair hair,—"see this lock!—I tell thee, Edmund, the very night she disappeared, when she bid me good even, as she was wont, she hung about my neck, and fondled me more than usual; and I, like an old fool, held her by this lock, until she took her scissars, severed it, and left it in my hand,—as all I was ever to see more of her!"

Tressilian was unable to reply, well judging what a complication of feelings must have crossed the bosom of the unhappy fugitive at that cruel moment. The clergyman was about to speak, but Sir Hugh interrupted him.

"I know what you would say, Master Curate,—after all, it is but a lock of woman's tresses,—and by woman, shame, and sin, and death, came into an innocent world—and learned Master Mumblazon, too, can say scholarly things of their inferiority."

"*C'est l'homme,*" said Master Mumblazon, "*qui se bast et qui conseille.*"

"True," said Sir Hugh, "and we will bear us, therefore, like men who have both mettle and wisdom in us.—Tressilian, thou art as welcome as if thou hadst brought better news. But we have spoken too long dry-lipped.—Amy, fill a cup of wine to Edmund, and another to me." Then instantly recollecting that he called upon her who could not hear, he shook his head, and said to the clergyman, "This grief is to my bewildered mind what the Church of Lidcote is to our south wood; we may lose ourselves among the briars and thickets, for a little space, but from the end of each avenue we see the old grey steeple and the grave of my forefathers. I would I were to travel that road tomorrow."

Tressilian and the Curate joined in urging the exhausted old man to lay himself to rest, and at length prevailed. Tressilian remained by his pillow till he saw that slumber at length sunk down on him, and then returned to consult with the Curate what steps should be adopted in these unhappy circumstances.

They could not exclude from their deliberations Master Michael Mumblazon; and they admitted him the more readily, that besides what hopes they entertained from his sagacity, they knew him to be so great a friend to taciturnity, that there was no doubt of his keeping counsel. He was an old bachelor, of good family, but small fortune, and distantly related to the House of Robsart; in virtue of which connection, Lidcote Hall had been honoured with his residence for the last twenty years. His company was agreeable to Sir Hugh, chiefly on account of his profound learning, which, though it only related to heraldry and genealogy, with such scraps of history as connected themselves with these subjects, was precisely of a kind to captivate the good old knight; besides the convenience which he found in having a friend to appeal to, when his own memory, as frequently happened, proved infirm, and played him false concerning names and dates, which, and all similar deficiencies, Master Michael Mumblazon supplied with due brevity and discretion. And, indeed, in matters concerning the modern world, he often gave, in his enigmatical and heraldric phrase, advice which was well worth attending to, or, in Will Badger's language, started the game while others beat the bush.

"We have had an unhappy time of it with the good Knight, Master Edmund," said the Curate. "I have not suffered so much since I was torn away from my beloved flock, and compelled to abandon them to the Romish wolves."

"That was in tertio Mariæ," said Master Mumblazon.

"In the name of heaven," continued the Curate, "tell us, has your time been better spent than ours, or have you any news of that unhappy maiden, who, being for so many years the principal joy of this broken down house, is now proved our greatest unhappiness? Have you not at least discovered her place of residence?"

"I have," replied Tressilian. "Know you Cumnor-Place, near Oxford?"

"Surely," said the clergyman; "it was a cell of removal for the monks of Abingdon."

"Whose arms," said Master Michael, "I have seen over a stone chimney in the hall,—a cross patonce betwixt four martlets."

"There," said Tressilian, "this unhappy maiden resides, in company with the villain Varney. But for a strange mishap, my sword had revenged all our injuries, as well as hers, on his worthless head."

"Thank God, that kept thine hand from blood-guiltiness, rash young man," answered the Curate. "Vengeance is mine, saith the

Lord, and I will repay it. It were better study to free her from the villain's nets of infamy."

"They are called, in heraldry, *laquei amoris*, or *lacs d'amour*," said Mumblazon.

"It is in that I require your aid, my friends," said Tressilian; "I am resolved to accuse this villain, at the very foot of the throne, of false-hood, seduction, and breach of hospitable laws. The Queen shall hear me, though the Earl of Leicester, the villain's patron, stood at her right hand."

"Her Grace," said the Curate, "hath set a comely example of con-tinence to her subjects, and will doubtless do justice on this inhospit-able robber. But wert thou not better apply to the Earl of Leicester, in the first place, for justice on his servant? If he grants it, thou dost save the risk of making thyself a powerful adversary, which will certainly chance, if, in the first instance, you accuse his master of the horse, and prime favourite, before the Queen."

"My mind revolts from your counsel," said Tressilian. "I cannot brook to plead my noble patron's cause—the unhappy Amy's cause—before any one save my lawful Sovereign. Leicester, thou wilt say, is noble—be it so—he is but a subject like ourselves, and I will not carry my plaint to him, if I can do better. Still, I will think on what thou hast said—But I must have your assistance to persuade the good Sir Hugh to make me his commissioner and fiduciary in this matter, for it is in his name I must speak, and not in mine own. Since she is so far changed as to doat upon this empty profligate courtier, he shall at least do her the justice which is yet in his power."

"Better she died *cælebs* and *sine prole*," said Mumblazon, with more animation than he usually expressed, "than part, *per pale*, the noble coat of Robsart with that of such a miscreant."

"If it be your object, as I cannot question," said the clergyman, "to save, as much as is yet possible, the credit of this unhappy young woman, I repeat, you should apply, in the first instance, to the Earl of Leicester. He is as absolute in his household as the Queen in her kingdom, and if he expresses to Varney that such is his pleasure, her honour will not stand so publicly committed."

"You are right, you are right," said Tressilian eagerly, "and I thank you for pointing out what I overlooked in my haste. I little thought ever to have besought grace of Leicester. But I could kneel to the proud Dudley, if doing so could remove one shade of shame from this unhappy damsel. You will assist me then to procure the necessary powers from Sir Hugh Robsart?"

The Curate assured him of his assistance, and the herald nodded assent.

"You must hold yourselves also in readiness to testify, in case you are called upon, the open-hearted hospitality which our good patron exercised towards this deceitful traitor, and the solicitude with which he laboured to seduce his unhappy daughter."

"At first," said the clergyman, "she did not, as it seemed to me, much affect his company. But latterly I saw them often together."

"*Seiant* in the parlour," said Michael Mumblazon, "and *passant* in the garden."

"I once came on them by chance," said the priest, "in the south wood, in a spring evening—Varney was muffled in a russet cloak, so that I saw not his face. They separated hastily, as they heard my step rustle amongst the leaves, and I observed she turned her head and looked long after him."

"With neck *reguardant*," said the herald—"And on the day of her flight, and that was on Saint Austen's eve, I saw Varney's groom, attired in his liveries, hold his master's horse and Mistress Amy's palfrey, bridled and saddled *proper* behind the wall of the church-yard."

"And now is she found mewed up in his secret place of retirement," said Tressilian. "The villain is taken in the manner, and I well wish he may deny his crime, that I may thrust conviction down his false throat. But I must prepare for my journey. Do you, gentlemen, dispose my patron to grant me such powers as are needful to act in his name."

So saying, Tressilian left the room.

"He is too hot," said the Curate; "and I pray to God that he may grant him the patience to deal with Varney as is fitting."

"Patience and Varney," said Mumblazon, "is worse heraldry than metal upon metal. He is more false than a syren, more rapacious than a griffin, more poisonous than a wyvern, and more cruel than a lion rampant."

"Yet I doubt much," said the Curate, "whether we can with all right ask from Sir Hugh Robsart, being in his present condition, any deed deputing his paternal right in Mistress Amy to whomsoever"——

"Your reverence need not doubt that," said Will Badger, who entered as he spoke, "for I will lay my life he is another man when he wakes, than he has been these thirty days past."

"Ay, Will," said the Curate, "hast then so much confidence in Doctor Diddleum's draught?"

"Not a whit," said Will, "because master ne'er tasted a drop on't, seeing it was emptied out by the housemaid. But here's a gentleman, who came attending on Master Tressilian, has given Sir Hugh a draught that is worth twenty of yon un. I have spoken cunningly with him, and a better farrier, or one who hath a more just notion of horse and dog ailments, I have never seen; and such a one would never be unjust to a Christian man."

"A farrier! you saucy groom—and by whose authority, pray?" said the Curate, rising in surprise and indignation; "or who will be warrant for this new physician?"

"For authority, an it like your reverence, he had mine; and for warrant, I trust, I have not been five-and-twenty years in this house, without having right to warrant the giving of a draught to beast or body —I who can gie a drench, and a ball, and bleed, or blister, if need, to my very self."

The counsellors of the House of Robsart thought it meet to carry this information instantly to Tressilian, who as speedily summoned before him Wayland Smith, and demanded of him, (in private however,) by what authority he had ventured to administer any medicine to Sir Hugh Robsart?

"Why," replied the artist, "your worship cannot but remember that I told you I had made more progress into my master's—I mean the learned Doctor Doboobie's—mystery than he was willing to own; and indeed half of his quarrel and malice against me was, that, besides I got something too deep into his secrets, several discerning persons, and particularly a buxom young widow of Abingdon, preferred my prescription to his."

"None of thy buffoonery, sir," said Tressilian, sternly. "If thou hast trifled with us—much more, if thou hast done aught that may prejudice Sir Hugh Robsart's health, thou shalt find thy grave at the bottom of a tin-mine."

"I know too little of the great *arcanum* to convert the ore to gold," said Wayland, firmly. "But truce to your apprehensions, Master Tressilian—I understood the good Knight's case, from what Master William Badger told me; and I hope I am able enough to administer a poor dose of mandragorn, which, with the sleep that must needs follow, is all that Sir Hugh Robsart requires to settle his distraught brains."

"I trust thou dealest fairly with me, Wayland?" said Tressilian.

"Most fairly and honestly, as the event shall shew," replied the artist. "What would it avail me to harm the poor old man for whom you are interested? you, to whom I owe it, that Gaffer Pinniewinks is not even now rending my flesh and sinews with his accursed pincers, and probing every mole in my body with his sharpened awl, (a murrain on the hands which forged it!) in order to find out the witch's mark!—I trust to yoke myself as a humble follower to your worship's train, and I only wish to have my faith judged of by the result of the good Knight's slumbers."

Wayland Smith was right in his prognostication. The sedative draught which his skill had prepared, and Will Badger's confidence had administered, was attended with the most beneficial effects. The patient's sleep was long and healthful, and the poor old Knight awoke, humbled indeed in thought, and weak in frame, yet a much better judge of whatever was subjected to his intellect than he had been for some time past. He resisted for a while the proposal made by his friends, that Tressilian should undertake a journey to court, to attempt the recovery of his daughter, and the redress of her wrongs, in so far as they might yet be repaired. "Let her go," he said; "she is but a hawk that goes down the wind; I would not bestow even a whistle to reclaim her." But though he for some time maintained this argument, he was at length convinced it was his duty to take the part to which natural affection inclined him, and consent that such efforts as could yet be made should be used by Tressilian in behalf of his daughter. He subscribed, therefore, a warrant of attorney, such as the Curate's skill enabled him to draw up; for in these simple days the clergy were often the advisers of their flock in law, as well as in gospel.

All matters were prepared for Tressilian's second departure, within twenty-four hours after he had returned to Lidcote Hall; but one material circumstance had been forgotten, which was first called to the remembrance of Tressilian by Master Mumblazon. "You are going to court, Master Tressilian," said he; "you will please remember, that your blazonry must be *argent*, and *or*—no other tinctures will pass current." The remark was equally just and embarrassing. To prosecute a suit at court, ready money was as indispensable even in the golden days of Elizabeth as at any succeeding period; and it was a commodity little at the command of the inhabitants of Lidcote Hall. Tressilian was himself poor; the revenues of good Sir Hugh Robsart were consumed, and even anticipated, in his hospitable mode of living; and it was finally necessary that the herald who started the doubt should himself solve it. Master Michael Mumblazon did so by producing a bag of money, containing nearly three hundred pounds in gold and silver of various coinage, the savings of twenty years; which he now, without speaking a syllable upon the subject, dedicated to the service of the patron whose shelter and protection had given him the means of making this little hoard. Tressilian accepted it without affecting a moment's hesitation, and a mutual grasp of the hand was all that passed betwixt them, to express the pleasure which the one felt in dedicating his all to such a purpose, and that which the other received from finding so material an obstacle to the success of his journey so suddenly removed, and in a manner so unexpected.

While Tressilian was making preparations for his departure early the ensuing morning, Wayland Smith desired to speak with him; and, expressing his hope that he had been pleased with the operation of his medicine in behalf of Sir Hugh Robsart, added his desire to accompany him to court. This was indeed what Tressilian himself had several times thought of; for the shrewdness, alertness of understanding, and variety of resource, which this fellow had exhibited during the time they had travelled together, had made him sensible that his assistance might be of importance. But then Wayland was in danger from the grasp of law; and of this Tressilian reminded him, mentioning something, at the same time, of the pincers of Pinniewinks, and the warrant of Master Justice Blindas. Wayland Smith laughed both to scorn.

"See you, sir!" said he, "I have changed my garb from that of a farrier to a serving-man; but were it still as it was, look at my moustaches—they now hang down—I will but turn them up and dye them with a tincture that I know of, and the devil would scarce know me again."

He accompanied these words with the appropriate action; and in less than a minute, by setting up his moustaches and his hair, he seemed a different person from him that had but now entered the room. Still, however, Tressilian hesitated to accept his services, and the artist became proportionally urgent.

"I owe you life and limb," he said, "and I would fain pay a part of the debt, especially as I know from Will Badger on what dangerous service your worship is bound. I do not indeed pretend to be what is called a man of mettle, one of those ruffling tear-cats, who maintain their master's quarrel with sword and buckler. Nay, I am even one of those who hold the end of a feast better than the beginning of a fray. But I know that I can serve your worship better in such quest as yours, than any of these sword-and-dagger-men, and that my head will be worth an hundred of their hands."

Tressilian still hesitated. He knew not much of this strange fellow, and was doubtful how far he could repose in him the confidence necessary to render him an useful attendant upon the present emergency. Ere he had come to a determination, the trampling of a horse was heard in the court-yard, and Master Mumblazon and Will Badger both entered hastily into Tressilian's chamber, speaking almost at the same moment.

"Here is a serving-man on the bonniest grey tit I ever see'd in my life," said Will Badger, who got the start;——"having on his arm a silver cognisance, being a fire-drake holding in his mouth a brick-bat, under a coronet of an Earl's degree," said Master Mumblazon, "and bearing a letter sealed of the same."

Tressilian took the letter, which was addressed "To the worshipful

Master Edmund Tressilian our loving kinsman—These—Ride, ride, ride,—for thy life, for thy life, for thy life." He then opened it, and found the following contents:—

"MASTER TRESSILIAN, OUR GOOD FRIEND AND COUSIN,

"We are at present so ill at ease, and otherwise so unhappily circumstanced, that we are desirous to have around us those of our friends, on whose loving kindness we can most especially repose confidence; amongst whom we hold our good Master Tressilian one of the foremost and nearest, both in good will and good ability. We therefore pray you, with your most convenient speed, to repair to our poor lodging, at Say's Court, near Deptford, where we will treat farther with you of matters which we deem it not fit to commit unto writing. And so we bid you heartily farewell, being your loving kinsman to command,

"RATCLIFFE, EARL OF SUSSEX."

"Send up the messenger instantly, Will Badger," said Tressilian; and as the man entered the room, he exclaimed, "Aha, Stevens, is it you? how does my good lord?"

"Ill, Master Tressilian," was the messenger's reply, "and having therefore the more need of good friends around him."

"But what is my lord's malady?" said Tressilian anxiously, "I heard nothing of his being ill?"

"I know not, sir," replied the man, "he is very ill at ease. The leeches are at a stand, and many of his household suspect foul practice; witchcraft, or worse."

"What are the symptoms?" said Wayland Smith, stepping hastily forward.

"Anan?" said the messenger, not comprehending his meaning.

"What does he ail?" said Wayland; "where lies his disease?"

The man looked at Tressilian, as if to know whether he should answer these inquiries from a stranger, and receiving a sign in the affirmative, he hastily enumerated gradual loss of strength, nocturnal perspirations, loss of appetite, faintness, &c.

"Joined," said Wayland, "to a gnawing pain in the stomach, and a low fever."

"Even so," said the messenger, somewhat surprised.

"I know how the disease is caused," said the artist, "and I know the cause. Your master has eaten of the manna of Saint Nicholas. I know the cure too—My master shall not say I studied in his laboratory for nothing."

"How mean you?" said Tressilian frowning. "We speak of one of the first nobles of England. Bethink you, this is no subject for buf-foonery."

"God forbid!" said Wayland Smith. "I say that I know his disease, and can cure him. Remember what I did for Sir Hugh Robsart."

"We will set forth instantly," said Tressilian. "God calls us."

Accordingly, hastily mentioning this new motive for his instant departure, though without mentioning either the suspicions of Stevens, or the assurances of Wayland Smith, he took the kindest leave of Sir Hugh and the family at Lidcote-Hall, who accompanied him with prayers and blessings, and, attended by Wayland and the Earl of Sussex's domestic, travelled with the utmost speed towards London.

END OF VOLUME FIRST

KENILWORTH

VOLUME II

Chapter One

——Ay, I know you have arsenick,
Vitriol, sal-tartre, argaile, alkaly,
Cinoper: I know all. This fellow, Captain,
Will come in time to be a great distiller,
And give a say (I will not say directly,
But very near) at the philosopher's stone.

The Alchemist

TRESSILIAN and his attendants pressed their route with all dispatch. He had asked the smith, indeed, when their departure was resolved on, whether he would not rather chuse to avoid Berkshire, in which he had played a part so suspicious. But Wayland returned a confident answer. He had employed the short interval they passed at Lidcote Hall in transforming himself in a wonderful manner. His wild and overgrown thicket of beard was now restrained to two small moustachios on the upper lip, turned up in a military fashion. A tailor from the village of Lidcote (well paid) had exerted his skill, under his customer's directions, so as completely to alter Wayland's outward man, and take off from his appearance almost twenty years of age. Formerly, besmirched with soot and charcoal—overgrown with hair, and bent double with the nature of his labour—disfigured too by his odd and fantastic dress, he seemed a man of fifty years old. But now, in a handsome suit of Tressilian's livery, with a sword by his side, and a buckler on his shoulder, he looked like a gay ruffling serving-man, whose age might be betwixt thirty and thirty-five, the very prime of human life. His loutish savage-looking demeanour seemed equally changed, into a forward, sharp, and impudent alertness of look and action.

When challenged by Tressilian, who desired to know the cause of a metamorphosis so singular and so absolute, Wayland only answered by singing a stave from a comedy, which was then new, and was supposed, among the more favourable judges, to augur some genius on the part of the author. We are happy to preserve the couplet, which ran exactly thus,—

> "Ban, ban, ca Caliban—
> Get a new master—Be a new man."

Although Tressilian did not recollect the verses, yet they reminded him that Wayland had once been a stage-player, a circumstance which, of itself, accounted indifferently well for the readiness with which he could assume so total a change of personal appearance. The artist himself was so confident of his disguise being completely changed, or of his having completely changed his disguise, which may be the more correct mode of speaking, that he regretted they were not to pass near his old place of retreat.

"I could venture," he said, "in my present dress, and with your worship's backing, to face Master Justice Blindas, even on a day of Quarter Sessions; and I would like to know what is become of Hobgoblin, who is like to play the devil in the world, if he can once slip the string, and leave his grannie and his Domine.—Ay, and the scathed vault!" he said, "I would willingly have seen what havoc the explosion of so much gunpowder has made among Doctor Demetrius Doboobie's retorts and phials. I warrant me, my fame haunts the Vale of the White Horse long after my body is rotten; and that many a lout ties up his horse, lays down his silver groat, and pipes like a sailor whistling in a calm, for Wayland Smith to come and shoe his tit for him. But the horse will catch the founders ere I answer the call."

In this particular, indeed, Wayland proved a true prophet; and so easily do fables rise, that an obscure tradition of his extraordinary practice in farriery prevails in the Vale of White Horse even unto this day;* and neither the tradition of Alfred's victory, nor of the celebrated Pusey Horn, are better preserved in Berkshire than the wild legend of Wayland Smith.

The haste of the travellers admitted their making no stay upon their journey, save what the refreshment of the horses required; and as many of the places through which they passed were under the influence of the Earl of Leicester, or persons immediately dependent on him, they thought it prudent to disguise their names, and the purpose of their journey. On such occasions the agency of Wayland Smith (by which name we will continue to distinguish the artist, though his real name was Lancelot Wayland) was extremely serviceable. He seemed, indeed, to have a pleasure in displaying the unusual alertness with

* See Camden's Britannia.—GOUGH'S *Edition*, vol. I. p.221.

which he could baffle investigation, and amuse himself by putting the
curiosity of tapsters and innkeepers on a false scent. During the
course of their brief journey, three different, and inconsistent reports
were circulated by him on their account; namely, first, that Tressilian
was the Lord Deputy of Ireland, come over in disguise to take the
Queen's pleasure concerning the great rebel Rory Oge MacCarthy
MacMahon; secondly, that the said Tressilian was an agent of Monsieur, coming to urge his suit to the hand of Elizabeth; thirdly, that he
was the Duke of Medina, come over, incognito, to adjust the quarrel
betwixt Philip and that princess.

Tressilian was angry, and expostulated with the artist on the various
inconveniences, and, in particular, the unnecessary degree of attention to which they were subjected, by the figments he thus circulated;
but he was pacified, (for who could be proof against such an argument?) by Wayland's assuring him that a general importance was
attached to his own (Tressilian's) striking presence, which rendered
it necessary to give an extraordinary reason for the secrecy and
rapidity of his journey.

At length they approached the metropolis, where, owing to the
more general recourse of strangers, their appearance excited neither
observation nor inquiry, and finally they entered London itself.

It was Tressilian's purpose to go down directly to Deptford, where
Lord Sussex resided, in order to be near the court, then held at
Greenwich, the favourite residence of Elizabeth, and honoured as her
birth-place. Still a brief halt in London was necessary; and it was
somewhat prolonged by the earnest entreaties of Wayland Smith, who
desired permission to take a walk through the City.

"Take thy sword and buckler, and follow me, then," said Tressilian; "I am about to walk myself, and we will go in company."

This he said, because he was not altogether so secure of the fidelity
of his new retainer to leave sight of him, at this interesting moment,
when rival factions at the court of Elizabeth were running so high.
Wayland Smith willingly acquiesced in the precaution, of which he
probably conjectured the motive, but only stipulated, that his master
should enter such chemists' or apothecaries' shops as he should
point out, in walking through Fleet Street, and permit him to make
some necessary purchases. Tressilian agreed, and obeying the signal
of his attendant, walked into more than four or five shops, where
he observed that Wayland purchased in each only one single drug,
in various quantities. The medicines which he first asked for, were
readily furnished, each in succession, but those which he afterwards required were less easily supplied—and Tressilian observed,
that he more than once, to the surprise of the shop-keeper, returned

the gum or herb that was offered to him, and compelled him to exchange it for the right sort, or else went on to seek it elsewhere. But one ingredient, in particular, seemed almost impossible to be found. Some chemists plainly admitted they had never seen it,—others denied that such a drug existed, excepting in the imagination of the unlearned,—and most of them attempted to satisfy their customer, by producing some substitute, which, when rejected by Wayland, as not being what he had asked for, they maintained possessed, in a superior degree, the self same qualities. In general, they all displayed some curiosity concerning the purpose for which he wanted it. One old meagre chemist, to whom the artist put the usual question, in terms which Tressilian neither understood, nor could recollect, answered frankly, there was none of the drug in London, unless Yoglan the Jew chanced to have some of it upon hand.

"I thought as much," said Wayland. And as soon as they left the shop, he said to Tressilian, "I crave your pardon, sir, but no artist can work without his tools. I must needs go to this Yoglan's; and I promise you, that if this detains you longer than your leisure seems to permit, you shall, nevertheless, be well apaid, by the use I will make of this rare drug. Permit me," he added, "to walk before you, for we are now to quit the broad street, and we will make double speed if I lead the way."

Tressilian acquiesced, and, following the smith down a lane which turned to the left hand towards the river, he found that his guide walked on with great speed, and apparently perfect knowledge of the town, through a labyrinth of bye-streets, courts, and blind alleys, until at length Wayland paused in the midst of a very narrow lane, the termination of which shewed a peep of the Thames looking misty and muddy, which back-ground was crossed by the masts of two lighters that lay waiting for the tide. The shop under which he halted had not, as in modern days, a glazed window; a paltry canvas screen sur-rounded such a stall as a cobler now occupies, having the front open, much in the manner of a fishmonger's booth of the present day. A little old smock-faced man, the very reverse of a Jew in complexion, for he was very soft-haired as well as beardless, appeared, and with many courtesies, asked Wayland what he pleased to want. He had no sooner named the drug, than the Jew started and looked surprised. "And vat might your vorship vant vith that drug which is not named, mein god, in forty years I have been chemist here?"

"These questions it is no part of my commission to answer," said Wayland; "I only wish to know if you have what I want, and having it, are willing to sell it?"

"Ay, mein god, for having it that I have, and for selling it I am chemist, and sell every drug." So saying, he exhibited a powder, and then continued, "But it will cost much monies—Vat I ave cost its weight in gold—ay, gold well-refined I vill say six times—it comes from Mount Sinai, where we had our blessed Law given forth, and the plant blossoms but once in one hundred year."

"I do not know how often it is gathered on Mount Sinai," said Wayland, after looking at the drug offered him with great disdain, "but I will wager my sword and buckler against your gaberdine, that this trash you offer me instead of what I asked for, may be had for gathering on the castle-ditch at Aleppo."

"You are a rude man," said the Jew; "and, besides, I ave no better than that—or if I ave, I will not sell it without order of a physician—or without you tell me vat you make of it."

The artist made brief answer in a language of which Tressilian could not understand a word, and which seemed to strike the Jew with the utmost astonishment. He stared upon Wayland like one who has suddenly recognized some mighty hero or dreaded potentate, in the person of an unknown and unmarked stranger. "Holy Elias!" he exclaimed, when he had recovered the first stunning effects of his surprise; and then passing from his former suspicious and surly manner to the very extremity of obsequiousness, he cringed low to the artist, and besought him to enter his poor house, to bless his miserable threshold by crossing it.

"Vill you not taste a cup with the poor Jew, Zacharias Yoglan?—Vill you Tokay ave?—vill you Lachrymæ taste?—vill you"——

"You offend in your proffers," said Wayland; "minister to me in what I require of you, and forbear further discourse."

The rebuked Israelite took his bunch of keys, and opening with circumspection a cabinet which seemed more strongly secured than the other cases of drugs and medicines amongst which it stood, he drew out a little secret drawer, having a glass lid, and containing a small portion of a black powder. This he offered to Wayland, his manner conveying the deepest devotion towards him, though an avaricious and jealous expression which seemed to grudge every grain of which his customer was about to possess himself, disputed ground in his countenance, with the obsequious deference which he desired it should exhibit.

"Have you scales?" said Wayland.

The Jew pointed to those which lay ready for common use in the shop, but he did so with a puzzled expression of doubt and fear, which did not escape the artist.

"They must be other than these," said Wayland sternly; "know you not that holy things lose their virtue if weighed in an unjust balance?"

The Jew hung his head, took from a steel-plated casket a pair of scales beautifully mounted, and said, as he adjusted them for the artist's use,—"With these I do mine own experiment—one hair of the high-priest's beard would turn them."

"It suffices," said the artist; and weighed out two drachms for himself of the black powder, which he very carefully folded up, and put into his pouch with the other drugs. He then demanded the price of the Jew, who returned, shaking his head and bowing,—

"No price—no, noting at all from such as you—but you will see the poor Jew again? you will look into his laboratory, where, God help him, he hath dried himself to the substance of the withered gourd of Jonah the holy prophet—you vill have pity on him, and shew him one little step on the great road?"

"Hush!" said Wayland, laying his finger mysteriously on his mouth, "it may be we shall meet again—thou hast already the *Schah-majm*, as thine own Rabbis call it—the general creation; watch therefore, and pray, for thou must attain the knowledge of Alchahest Elixir, Samech, ere I may commune further with thee." Then returning with a slight nod the reverential congés of the Jew, he walked gravely up the lane, followed by his master, whose first observation on the scene he had just witnessed, was, that Wayland ought to have paid the man for his drug, whatever it was.

"I pay him?" said the artist; "may the foul fiend pay me if I do!—had it not been that I thought it might displease your worship, I would have had an ounce or two of gold out of him, in exchange of the same just weight of brick-dust."

"I advise you to practise no such knavery while waiting upon me," said Tressilian.

"Did I not say," answered the artist, "that for that reason alone, I forbore him for the present.—Knavery, call you it?—why, yonder wretched skeleton hath wealth sufficient to pave the whole lane he lives in with dollars, yet scarce miss them out of his own iron chest; yet he goes mad after the philosopher's stone—and besides he would have cheated a poor serving-man, as he thought me at first, with trash that was not worth a penny—Match for match, quoth the devil to the collier; if his false medicine was worth my good crowns, my true brick-dust is as well worth his good gold."

"It may be so for aught I know," said Tressilian, "in dealings amongst Jews and apothecaries; but understand, that to have such tricks of legerdemain practised by one attending on me, diminishes my honour, and that I will not permit them. I trust thou hast now made up thy purchases?"

"I have, sir," replied Wayland; "and with these drugs will I, this very day, compound the true orvietan, that noble medicine which is so seldom found genuine and effective within these realms of Europe, for want of that most rare and precious drug which I got but now from Yoglan."

"But why not have made all your purchases at one shop?" said his master; "we have lost nearly an hour in running from one pounder of simples to another."

"Content you, sir," said Wayland. "No man shall learn my secret; and it would not be mine long, were I to buy all my materials from one chemist."

They now returned to their inn, (the famous Bell-Savage) and while the Lord Sussex's servant prepared the horses for their journey, Wayland, obtaining from the cook the service of a mortar, shut himself up in a private chamber, where he mixed, pounded, and amalgamated the drugs which he had bought, each in its due proportion, with a readiness and address that plainly shewed him well practised in all the manual operations of pharmacy.

By the time Wayland's electuary was prepared the horses were ready, and a short hour's riding brought them to the present habitation of Lord Sussex, an ancient house, called Say's Court, near Deptford, which had long pertained to a family of that name, but had, for upwards of a century, been possessed by the ancient and honourable family of Evelyn. The present representative of that ancient house took a deep interest in the Earl of Sussex, and had willingly accommodated both him and his numerous retinue in his hospitable mansion. Say's Court was afterwards the residence of the celebrated Mr Evelyn, whose "Silva" is still the manual of British planters; and whose life, manners, and principles, as illustrated in his Memoirs, ought equally to be the manual of English gentlemen.

Chapter Two

This is rare news thou tell'st me, my good fellow;
There are two bulls fierce battling on the green
For one fair heifer—if the one goes down
The dale will be more peaceful, and the herd,
Which have small interest in their brulziement,
May pasture there in peace.

Old Play

SAY'S COURT was watched like a beleaguered city; and so high rose the suspicions of the time, that Tressilian and his attendants were stopped and questioned repeatedly by centinels, both on foot and horseback, as they approached the abode of the sick Earl. In truth, the high rank which Sussex held in Queen Elizabeth's favour, and his known and avowed rivalry of the Earl of Leicester, caused the utmost importance to be attached to his welfare; for, at the period we treat of, all men doubted whether he or the Earl of Leicester might ultimately have the higher rank in her regard.

Elizabeth, like many of her sex, was fond of governing by factions, so as to balance two opposing interests, and reserve in her own hand the power of making either predominate, as the interest of state, or perhaps her own female caprice, (for to that foible even she was not superior,) might finally determine. To finesse—to hold the cards—to oppose one interest to another—to bridle him who thought himself highest in her esteem, by the fears he must entertain of another equally trusted, if not equally beloved, were arts which she used through her reign, and which enabled her, though frequently giving way to the weakness of favouritism, to prevent most of its evil effects on her kingdom and government.

The two nobles, who at present stood as rivals in her favour, possessed very different pretensions to share it; but it might be in general said, that the Earl of Sussex had been most serviceable to the queen, while Leicester was most dear to the woman. Sussex was, according to the phrase of the times, a martialist; had done good service in Ireland, and in Scotland, and especially in the great northern rebellion, in 1569, which was quelled, in a great measure, by his military talents. He was, therefore, naturally surrounded and looked up to by those who wished to make arms their road to distinction. The Earl of Sussex, moreover, was of more ancient and honourable descent than his rival, uniting in his person the representation of the Fitz Walters, as well as of the Ratcliffes, while the scutcheon of Leicester was stained by the degradation of his grandfather, the oppressive minister of Henry VII., and scarce improved by that of his father, the unhappy Dudley, Duke of Northumberland, executed on Tower-Hill in 1553. But in person, features, and address, weapons so formidable in the court of a female sovereign, Leicester had advantage more than sufficient to counterbalance the military services, high blood, and frank bearing of the Earl of Sussex; and he bore in the eye of the court and kingdom, the higher share in Elizabeth's favour, though (for such was her uniform policy) by no means so decidedly expressed as to warrant him against the final preponderance of his rival's pretensions. The illness of Sussex therefore happened so opportunely for Leicester, as to give rise to strange surmises among the public; while the followers of the one Earl were filled with the deepest apprehensions, and those of the other with the highest hopes of its probable issue. Meanwhile, —for in that old time men never forgot the probability that the matter might be determined by length of sword,—the retainers of each noble flocked around their patron, appeared well armed in the vicinity of the court itself, and disturbed the ear of the sovereign by their frequent and alarming debates, held even within the precincts of her palace. This preliminary statement is necessary, to render what follows intelligible to the reader.

On Tressilian's arrival at Say's Court, he found the place filled with the retainers of the Earl of Sussex, and of the gentlemen who came to attend their patron in his illness. Arms were in every hand, and a deep gloom on every countenance, as if they had apprehended an immediate and violent assault from the opposite faction. In the hall, however, to which Tressilian was ushered by one of the Earl's attendants, while another went to inform Sussex of his arrival, he found only two gentlemen in waiting. There was a remarkable contrast betwixt their dress, appearance, and manners. The attire of the elder gentleman, a person as it seemed of quality and in the prime of life, was very plain and soldier-like, his stature low, and his features of that kind which express sound common sense, without a grain of vivacity or imagination. The younger, who seemed about twenty, or upwards, was clad in the gayest habit used by persons of quality at the period, wearing a crimson velvet cloak richly ornamented with lace and embroidery, with a bonnet of the same, encircled with a gold chain turned three times round it, and secured by a medal. His hair was adjusted very nearly like that of some fine gentlemen of our own time, that is, it was combed upwards, and made to stand as it were on end, and in his ears he wore a pair of silver ear-rings, having each a pearl of considerable size. The countenance of this youth, besides being regularly handsome and accompanied by a fine person, was animated and striking in a degree that seemed to speak at once the firmness of a decided and the fire of an enterprizing character, the power of reflection, and the promptitude of determination.

Both these gentlemen reclined in the same posture on benches near each other; but each seeming engaged in his own meditations, looked straight upon the wall which was opposite to them, without speaking to his companion. The looks of the elder were of that sort, which convinced the beholder, that, in looking on the wall, he saw no more than the side of an old hall hung around with cloaks, antlers, bucklers, old pieces of armour, partizans, and such similar articles as were usually the furniture of such a place. The look of the younger gallant had in it something imaginative; he was sunk in reverie, and it seemed as if the empty space of air betwixt him and the wall, were the stage of a theatre on which his fancy was mustering her own dramatis personæ, and treating him with sights far different from those which his awakened and earthly vision could have offered.

At the entrance of Tressilian both started from their musing, and bade him welcome; the younger, in particular, with great appearance of animation and cordiality.

"Thou art welcome, Tressilian," said the youth; "thy philosophy stole thee from us when the household had objects of ambition to offer —it is an honest philosophy, since it returns thee to us, when there are only dangers to be shared."

"Is my lord, then, so dangerously indisposed?" said Tressilian.

"We fear the very worst," answered the elder gentleman, "and by the worst practice."

"Fye," replied Tressilian, "my Lord of Leicester is honourable."

"What doth he with such attendants, then, as he hath about him?" said the younger gallant. "The man who raises the devil may be honest, but he is answerable for the mischief he does, for all that."

"And is this all that are of you, my mates," said Tressilian, "that are about my lord in his utmost straits?"

"No, no," replied the elder gentleman, "there are Tracy, Markham, and several more; but we keep watch here by two at once, and some are weary and are sleeping in the gallery above."

"And some," said the young man, "are gone down to the dock yonder at Deptford, to look out such a hulk as they may purchase by clubbing their broken fortunes; and so soon as all is over, we will lay our noble lord in a noble green grave, have a blow at those who have hurried him thither, if opportunity suits, and then sail for the Indies with hearts as light as our purses."

"It may be," said Tressilian, "an I will embrace the same purpose, so soon as I have settled some business at court."

"Thou business at court!" they both exclaimed at once; "and thou make the Indian voyage!"

"Why, Tressilian," said the younger man, "art thou not wedded, and beyond these flaws of fortune, that drive folks out to sea when their bark bears fairest for the haven?—What has become of the lovely Indamira that was to match my Amoret for truth and beauty?"

"Speak not of her!" said Tressilian, averting his face.

"Ay, stands it so with you?" said the youth, taking his hand very affectionately; "then, fear not I will again touch the green wound— But it is strange as well as sad news—are none of our fair and merry fellowship to escape shipwreck of fortune and happiness in this sudden tempest? I had hoped thou wert in harbour, at least, my dear Edmund—But truly says another dear friend of thy name,

> What man that sees the ever whirling wheel
> Of Chance, the which all mortal things doth sway,
> But that thereby doth find and plainly feel,

> How Mutability in them doth play
> Her cruel sports to many men's decay."

The elder gentleman had risen from his bench, and was pacing the hall in some impatience, while the youth, with much earnestness and feeling, recited these lines. When he had done, the other wrapped himself in his cloak, and again stretched himself down, saying, "I marvel, Tressilian, you will feed the lad in this silly humour. If there were aught to draw a judgment upon a virtuous and honourable household like my lord's, renounce me if I think not it were this piping, whining, childish trick of poetry that came among us with Master Walter Wittypate here and his comrades, twisting into all manner of uncouth and incomprehensible forms of speech the honest plain English phrase which God gave us to express our meaning withal."

"Blount believes," said his comrade, laughing, "that the devil woo'd Eve in rhime, and that the mystic meaning of the Tree of Knowledge, refers solely to the art of clashing rhymes and meting out hexameters."

At this moment the Earl's chamberlain entered, and informed Tressilian that his lord required to speak with him.

He found Lord Sussex dressed, but unbraced and lying on his couch, and was shocked at the alteration disease had made in his person. The Earl received him with the most friendly cordiality, and inquired into the state of his courtship. Tressilian evaded his inquiries for the moment, and turning his discourse on the Earl's own health, he discovered, to his surprise, that the symptoms of his disorder corresponded minutely with those which Wayland had predicated concerning it. He hesitated not, therefore, to communicate to Sussex the whole history of his attendant, and the pretensions he set up to cure the disorder under which he laboured. The Earl listened with incredulous attention until the name of Demetrius was mentioned, and then suddenly called to his secretary to bring him a certain casket which contained papers of importance. "Take out from thence," he said, "the declaration of the rascal cook whom we had under examination, and look heedfully if the name of Demetrius be not there mentioned."

The secretary turned to the passage at once, and read, "And said declarant, being examined, saith, that he remembers having made the sauce to the said sturgeon-fish, after eating of which, the said noble Lord was taken ill; and he put the usual ingredients and condiments therein, namely"——

"Pass his trash," said the Earl, "and see whether he had not been supplied with his materials by a herbalist called Demetrius."

"It is even so," answered the secretary, "and he adds, he has not since seen the said Demetrius."

"This accords with thy fellow's story, Tressilian," said the Earl; "call him hither."

On being summoned to the Earl's presence, Wayland Smith told his former tale with firmness and consistency.

"It may be," said the Earl, "thou art sent by those who have begun this work, to end it for them; but bethink, if I miscarry under thy medicine, it may go hard with thee."

"That were severe measure," said Wayland, "since the issue of medicine, and the end of life, are in God's disposal. But I will stand the risk. I have not lived so long under ground, to be afraid of a grave."

"Nay, if thou be'st so confident," said the Earl of Sussex, "I will take the risk too, for the learned can do nothing for me. Tell me how this medicine is to be taken."

"That will I do presently," said Wayland; "but allow me to condition that, since I incur all the risk of this treatment, no other physician shall be permitted to interfere with it."

"That is but fair," replied the Earl; "and now prepare your drug."

While Wayland obeyed the Earl's commands, his servants, by the artist's direction, undressed their master, and placed him in bed.

"I warn you," he said, "that the first operation of this medicine will be to produce a heavy sleep, during which time the chamber must be kept undisturbed; as the consequences may otherwise be fatal. I myself will watch by the Earl, with any of the gentlemen of his chamber."

"Let all leave the room, save Stanley and this good fellow," said the Earl.

"And saving me also," said Tressilian. "I too am deeply interested in the effects of this potion."

"Be it so, good friend," said the Earl; "and now for our experiment —But first call in my secretary and chamberlain."

"Bear witness," he continued, when these officers arrived, "bear witness for me, gentlemen, that our honourable friend Tressilian is in no way responsible for the effects which this medicine may produce upon me, the taking it being my own free action and choice, believing it to be a remedy which God has furnished me by unexpected means, to recover me of my present malady. Commend me to my noble and princely Mistress; and say that I live and die her true servant, and wish to all about her throne the same singleness of heart and will to serve her, with more ability to do so than hath been assigned to poor Thomas Ratcliffe."

He then folded his hands, and seemed for a second or two absorbed in mental devotion, then took the potion in his hand, and, pausing, regarded Wayland with a look that seemed designed to penetrate his

very soul, but which caused no anxiety or hesitation in the countenance or manner of the artist.

"Here is nothing to be feared," said Sussex to Tressilian; and
swallowed the medicine without farther hesitation.

"I am now to pray your lordship," said Wayland, "to dispose yourself to rest as commodiously as you can; and of you, gentlemen, to
remain as still and mute as if you waited at your mother's death-bed."

The chamberlain and secretary then withdrew, giving orders that
all doors be bolted, and all noise in the house strictly prohibited.
Several gentlemen were voluntary watchers in the hall, but none
remained in the chamber of the sick Earl, save his groom of the
chamber, Stanley, the artist, and Tressilian.—Wayland Smith's predictions were speedily accomplished, and a sleep fell upon the Earl, so
deep and sound, that they who watched his bed-side began to fear,
that, in his weakened state, he might pass away without awakening
from his lethargy. Wayland Smith himself appeared anxious, and felt
the temples of the Earl slightly, from time to time, attending also
particularly to the state of respiration, which was full and deep, but at
the same time easy and uninterrupted.

Chapter Three

You logger-headed and unpolish'd grooms,
What, no attendance, no regard, no duty?
Where is the foolish knave I sent before?
Taming of the Shrew

THERE IS NO PERIOD at which men look worse in the eyes of each
other, or feel more uncomfortable, than when the first dawn of day-
light finds them watchers. Even Beauty of the first order, after the
vigils of a ball are interrupted by the dawn, would do wisely to withdraw herself from the gaze of her fondest and most partial admirers.
Such was the pale, inauspicious, and ungrateful light, which began to
beam upon those who had kept watch all night, in the hall at Say's
Court, and mingled its cold pale blue diffusion with the red, yellow,
and smoky beams of expiring lamps and torches. The young gallant,
whom we noticed in our last Chapter, had left the room for a few
minutes, to learn the cause of a knocking at the outward gate, and on
his return, was so struck with the forlorn and ghastly aspects of his
companions of the watch, that he exclaimed, "Pity of my heart, my
masters, how like owls you look! Methinks, when the sun rises, I shall
see you flutter off with your eyes dazzled, to stick yourselves into the
next ivy-tod or ruined steeple."

"Hold thy peace, thou gibing fool," said Blount, "hold thy peace. Is this a time for jeering, when the manhood of England is perchance dying within a wall's breadth of thee?"

"There thou liest," replied the gallant.

"How, lie!" exclaimed Blount, starting up, "lie, and to me?"

"Why, so thou didst, thou peevish fool," answered the youth; "thou didst lie on that bench even now, didst thou not? But art thou not a hasty coxcomb, to pick up a wry word so wrathfully? Nevertheless, loving and honouring my lord as truly as thou, or any one, I do say, that should Heaven take him from us, all England's manhood dies not with him."

"Ay," replied Blount, "a good portion will survive with thee, doubtless."

"And a good portion with thyself, Blount, and with stout Markham here, and Tracy, and all of us. But I am he will best employ the talent heaven has given to us all."

"As how, I prithee?" said Blount; "tell us your mystery of multiplying it."

"Why, sirs," answered the youth, "ye are like goodly land, which bears no crop because it is not quickened by manure; but I have that rising spirit in me, which will make my poor faculties labour to keep pace with it. My ambition will keep my brain at work, I warrant thee."

"I pray to God it does not drive thee mad," said Blount; "for my part, if we lose our noble lord, I bid adieu to the court and to the camp both. I have five hundred foul acres in Norfolk, and thither will I, and change the court pantoufle for the country hobnail."

"O base transmutation!" exclaimed his antagonist; "thou hast already got the true rustic slouch—thy shoulders stoop, as if thine hands were on the stilts of the plough, and thou hast a kind of grassy smell about thee, instead of being perfumed with essence, as a gallant and courtier should. On my soul, thou hast stolen out to roll thyself on a hay mow. Thy only excuse will be to swear by thy hilts, that the farmer had a fair daughter."

"I pray thee, Walter," said another of the company, "cease this raillery, which suits neither time nor place, and tell us who was at the gate but now."

"Doctor Master, physician to her Grace in ordinary, sent by her especial orders to inquire after the Earl's health," answered Walter.

"Ha! what!" exclaimed Tracy, "that was no slight mark of favour; if the Earl can but come through, he will match with Leicester yet. Is Master with my lord at present?"

"Nay," replied Walter, "he is half way back to Greenwich by this time, and in high dudgeon."

"Thou didst not refuse him admittance?" exclaimed Tracy.

"Thou wert not surely so mad?" ejaculated Blount.

"I refused him admittance as flatly, Blount, as you would refuse a penny to a blind beggar; as obstinately, Tracy, as thou didst ever deny access to a dun."

"Why, in the fiend's name, did you trust him to go to the gate?" said Blount to Tracy.

"It suited his years better than mine," answered Tracy; "but he has undone us all now thoroughly. My lord may live or die, he will never have a look of favour from her Majesty again."

"Nor the means of making fortunes for his followers," said the young gallant, smiling contemptuously;—"there lies the sore point, that will brook no handling. My good sirs, I sounded my lamentations for my lord somewhat less loudly than some of you; but when the point comes of doing him service, I will yield to none of you. Had this learned leech entered, thinkst thou not there had been such a coil betwixt him and Tressilian's mediciner, that not the sleeper only, but the very dead might have awakened? I know what 'larum belongs to the discord of doctors."

"And who is to take the blame of opposing the Queen's orders?" said Tracy; "for undeniably, Master came with her Grace's positive commands to cure the Earl."

"I, who have done the wrong, will bear the blame," said Walter.

"Then off flies the dreams of court favour thou hast nourished," said Blount; "and despite all thy boasted art and ambition, Devonshire will see thee shine a true younger, fit to sit low at the board, carve turn about with the chaplain, look that the hounds be fed, and see the squire's girths drawn when he goes a hunting."

"Not so," said the young man, colouring. "Not while Ireland and the Netherlands have wars, and not while the sea hath pathless waves —the rich West hath lands undreamed of, and Britain bold hearts to venture on the quest of them.—Adieu for a space, my masters. I go to walk in the court and look to the centinels."

"The lad hath quicksilver in his veins, that is certain," said Blount, looking at Markham.

"He hath that both in brain and blood," said Markham, "which may both make and mar him. But, in closing the door against Master, he hath done a daring and loving piece of service; for Tressilian's fellow hath ever averred, that to wake the Earl were death, and Master would wake the Seven Sleepers themselves, if he thought they slept not by the regular ordinance of medicine."

Morning was well advanced, when Tressilian, fatigued and overwatched, came down to the hall with the joyful intelligence, that the

Earl had awakened of himself, that he found his internal complaints much mitigated, and spoke with a cheerfulness, and looked around with a vivacity, which of themselves shewed a material and favourable change had taken place. Tressilian at the same time commanded the attendance of one or two of his followers, to report what had passed during the night, and to relieve the watchers in the Earl's chamber.

When the message of the Queen was communicated to the Earl of Sussex, he at first smiled at the repulse which the physician had received from his zealous young follower, but instantly recollecting himself, he bade Blount, his master of the horse, instantly take boat, and go down the river to the Palace of Greenwich, taking young Walter with him, and make a suitable compliment, expressing his grateful thanks to his Sovereign, and mentioning the cause why he had not been enabled to profit by the assistance of the wise and learned Doctor Master.

"A plague on it," said Blount, as he descended the stairs, "had he sent me with a cartel to Leicester, I think I should have done his errand indifferently well. But to go to our gracious Sovereign, before whom all words must be lackered over either with gilding or with sugar, is such a confectionary matter as clean baffles my poor old English brain.—Come with me, Master Walter Wittypate, that art the cause of our having all this ado. Let us see if thy neat brain, that frames so many flashy fireworks, can help out a plain fellow at need with some of thy shrewd devices."

"Never fear, never fear," exclaimed the youth, "it is I will help you through—Let me but fetch my cloak."

"Why, thou hast it on thy shoulders," said Blount—"the lad is mazed."

"No, this is Tracy's old mantle," answered Walter; "I go not with thee to court unless as a gentleman should."

"Why," said Blount, "thy braveries are like to dazzle the eyes of none but some poor groom or porter."

"I know that," said the youth; "but I am resolved I will have my own cloak, ay, and brush my doublet to boot, ere I stir forth with you."

"Well, well," said Blount, "here is a coil about a doublet and a cloak —get thyself ready, a God's name."

They were soon launched on the princely bosom of the broad Thames, upon which the sun now shone forth in all its splendour.

"There are two things scarce matched in the universe," said Walter to Blount,—"the sun in heaven, and the Thames on the earth."

"The one will light us to Greenwich well enough," said Blount, "and the other would take us there a little faster if it were ebb tide."

"And this is all thou think'st—all thou carest—all thou deem'st the use of the King of Elements, and the King of Rivers, to guide two such poor caitiffs as thyself and me upon an idle journey of courtly ceremony!"

"It is no errand of my seeking, faith," replied Blount, "and I could excuse both the sun and the Thames, the trouble of carrying me where I have no great mind to go; and where I expect but dog's wages for my trouble—And by my honour," he added, looking out from the head of the boat, "it seems to me as if our message were a sort of labour in vain; for see, the Queen's barge lies at the stairs, as if her Majesty were about to take water."

It was even so. The royal barge, manned with the Queen's watermen, richly attired in the regal liveries, and having the banner of England displayed, did indeed lie at the great stairs which ascended from the river, with two or three other boats for transporting such part of her retinue as were not in immediate attendance on her person. The yeomen of the guard, the tallest and most handsome men whom England could produce, guarded with their halberts the passage from the palace-gate to the river side, and all seemed in readiness for the Queen's coming forth, although the day was yet so early.

"By my faith, this bodes us no good," said Blount; "it must be some perilous cause puts her Grace in motion thus early. By my counsel, we were best put back again, and tell the Earl what we have seen."

"Tell the Earl what we have seen!" said Walter, "why, what have we seen but a boat, and men with scarlet jerkins, and halberts in their hands? Let us do his errand, and tell him what the Queen says in reply."

So saying, he caused the boat pull towards a landing-place at some distance from the principal one, which it would not, at that moment, have been thought respectful to approach, and jumped on shore, followed, though reluctantly, by his cautious and timid companion, Blount. As they approached the gate of the palace, one of the serjeant porters told them they could not at present enter, as her Majesty was in the act of coming forth. They used the name of the Earl of Sussex; but it proved no charm to subdue the officer, who alleged in reply, that it was as much as his post was worth, to disobey in the least tittle the commands which he had received.

"Nay, I told you as much before," said Blount; "do, I pray you, my dear Walter, let us take boat and return."

"Not till I see the Queen come forth," returned the youth, composedly.

"Thou art mad, stark mad, by the mass," answered Blount.

"And thou," said Walter, "art turned coward of the sudden. I have seen thee face half a score of shag-headed Irish kernes to thy own share of them, and now thou would'st blink and go back to shun the frown of a fair lady!"

At this moment the gates opened, and ushers began to issue forth in array, preceded and flanked by the band of Gentlemen Pensioners. After these, amid a crowd of lords and ladies, yet so disposed around her that she could see and be seen on all sides, came Elizabeth herself, then in the prime of womanhood and full glow of what in a Sovereign was called beauty and would in the lowest rank of life have been a noble figure, joined to a striking and commanding physiognomy. She leant on the arm of Lord Hunsdon, whose relation to her by her mother's side often procured him such distinguishing marks of Elizabeth's intimacy.

The young cavalier we have so often mentioned had probably never yet approached so near the person of his Sovereign, and he pressed forward as far as the line of warders permitted, in order to avail himself of the present opportunity. His companion, on the contrary, cursing his imprudence, kept drawing him backwards, till Walter shook him off impatiently, and letting his rich cloak drop carelessly from one shoulder; a natural action, which served, however, to display to the best advantage his well-proportioned person. Unbonneting at the same time, he fixed his eager gaze on the Queen's approach, with a mixture of respectful curiosity, and modest yet ardent admiration, which suited so well with his fine features, that the warders, struck with his rich attire and noble countenance, suffered him to approach the ground over which the Queen was to pass, somewhat closer than was permitted to ordinary spectators. Thus the adventurous youth stood full in Elizabeth's eye,—an eye never indifferent to the admiration which she deservedly excited amongst her subjects, or to the fair proportions of external form which chanced to distinguish any of her courtiers. Accordingly, she fixed her keen glance on the youth, as she approached the place where he stood, with a look in which surprise at his boldness seemed to be unmingled with resentment, while a trifling accident happened which attracted her attention towards him yet more strongly. The night had been rainy, and just where the young gentleman stood, a small quantity of mud interrupted the Queen's passage. As she hesitated to pass on, the gallant, throwing his cloak from his shoulders, laid it on the miry spot, so as to ensure her stepping over it dry-shod. Elizabeth looked at the young man, who accompanied this act of devoted courtesy with a profound reverence, and a blush that overspread his whole countenance. The Queen was confused, and blushed in her turn, nodded her head, hastily passed on, and embarked in her barge without saying a word.

"Come along, Sir Coxcomb," said Blount; "your gay cloak shall need the brush to-day, I wot. Nay, if you had meant to make a foot-cloth of your mantle, better have kept Tracy's old drab-de-burée, which despises all colours."

"This cloak," said the youth, taking it up and folding it, "shall never be brushed while in my possession."

"And that will not be long, if you learn not a little more economy—we shall have you in *cuerpo* soon, as the Spaniard says."

Their discourse was here interrupted by one of the Band of Pensioners.

"I was sent," said he, after looking at them attentively, "to a gentleman who hath no cloak, or a muddy one.—You sir, I think," addressing the younger cavalier, "are the man; you will please to follow me."

"He is in attendance on me," said Blount, "on me, the noble Earl of Sussex's master of horse."

"I have nothing to say to that," answered the messenger; "my orders are directly from her Majesty, and concern this gentleman only."

So saying, he walked away, followed by Walter, leaving Blount behind, with his eyes almost starting from his head with the excess of his astonishment. At length he gave vent to it in an exclamation—"Who the good jere would have thought this!" And shaking his head with a mysterious air, he walked to his own boat, embarked, and returned to Deptford.

The young cavalier was, in the meanwhile, guided to the water-side by the Pensioner, who shewed him considerable respect; a circumstance which, to persons in his situation, may be considered as an augury of no small consequence. He ushered him into one of the wherries which lay ready to attend the Queen's barge, which was already proceeding up the river, with the advantage of that flood-tide, of which, in the course of their descent, Blount had complained to his associate.

The two rowers used their oars with such expedition at the signal of the Gentleman Pensioner, that they very soon brought their little skiff under the stern of the Queen's boat, where she sate beneath an awning, attended with two or three ladies, and the nobles of her household. She looked more than once at the wherry in which the young adventurer was seated, spoke to those around her, and seemed to laugh. At length one of her attendants, by the Queen's order apparently, made a sign for the wherry to come along-side, and the young man was desired to step from his own skiff into the Queen's barge, which he performed with graceful agility at the fore part of the boat, and was brought aft to the Queen's presence, the wherry at the same time dropping into the rear. The youth underwent the gaze of majesty, not the less gracefully that his self-possession was mingled with embarrassment. The muddied cloak still hung upon his arm, and formed the natural topic with which the Queen introduced the conversation.

"You have this day spoiled a gay mantle in our service, young man. We thank you for your service, though the manner of offering it was both unusual, and something bold."

"In a sovereign's need," answered the youth, "it is each liege-man's duty to be bold."

"God's pity! that was well said, my lord," said the Queen, turning to a grave person who sate by her, and answered with a grave inclination of the head, and something of a mumbled assent. "Well, young man— Your gallantry shall not go unrewarded. Go to the wardrobe keeper, and he shall have orders to supply the suit which you have cast away in our service. Thou shalt have a suit, and that of the newest cut, I promise thee, on the word of a princess."

"May it please your grace," said Walter, hesitating. "It is not for so humble a servant of your majesty to measure out your bounties; but if it became me to chuse"——

"Thou would'st have gold, I warrant me," said the Queen, interrupting him; "fie, young man! We shame to say, that, in our capital, such and so various are the means of thriftless folly, that to give gold to youth is giving fuel to fire, and furnishing them with the means of self-destruction. If I live and reign, these means of unchristian excess shall be abridged. Yet thou may'st be poor," she added, "or thy parents may be—it shall be gold, if thou wilt, but thou shalt answer to me for the use on't."

Walter waited patiently until the Queen had done, and then modestly assured her, that gold was still less in his wish than the raiment her majesty had before offered.

"How, boy!" said the Queen, "neither gold nor garments? what is it thou would'st have of me, then?"

"Only permission, Madam—if it is not asking too high an honour— permission to wear the cloak which did you this trifling service."

"Permission to wear thine own cloak, thou silly boy!" said the Queen.

"It is no longer mine," answered Walter; "when your Majesty's foot touched it, it became a fit mantle for a prince, but far too rich a one for its former owner."

The Queen again blushed; and endeavoured to cover, by laughing, a slight degree of not unpleasing surprise and confusion.

"Heard you ever the like, my lords?—the youth's head is turned with reading romances—I must know something of him, that I may send him safe to his friends.—What art thou?"

"A gentleman of the household of the Earl of Sussex, so please your grace, sent hither with his Master of Horse, upon a message to your Majesty."

In a moment the gracious expression which Elizabeth's face had hitherto maintained, gave way to an expression of haughtiness and severity.

"My Lord of Sussex," she said, "has taught us how to regard his messages, by the value he places upon ours. We sent but this morning the physician in ordinary of our chamber, and that at no usual time, understanding his lordship's illness to be more dangerous than we had before apprehended. There is at no court in Europe a man more skilled in his holy and most useful science than Doctor Master, and he came from Us to our subject. Nevertheless, he found the gate of Say's Court defended by men with culvers, as if it had been on the Borders of Scotland, not in the vicinity of our court; and when he demanded admittance in our name, it was stubbornly refused. For this slight of a kindness, which had but too much of condescension in it, we will receive, at present at least, no excuse; and such we suppose to have been the purport of my Lord of Sussex's message."

This was uttered in a tone, and with a gesture, which made Lord Sussex's friends who were within hearing tremble. He whom the speech was addressed to, however, trembled not; but with great deference and humility, as soon as the Queen's passion gave him an opportunity, he replied:—"So please your most gracious Majesty, I was charged with no apology from the Earl of Sussex."

"With what were you then charged, sir?" said the Queen, with the impetuosity, which, amid nobler qualities, strongly marked her character; "was it with a justification?—or, God's death! with a defiance?"

"Madam," said the young man, "my Lord of Sussex knew the offence approached towards treason, and could think of nothing save of securing the offender, and placing him in your Majesty's hands, and at your mercy. He was fast asleep when your most gracious message reached him, a potion having been administered to that purpose by his physician; and he knew not of the ungracious repulse your Majesty's royal and most comfortable message had received, until this morning."

"And which of his domestics then, in the name of heaven, presumed to reject my message, without even admitting my own physician to the presence of him whom I sent him to attend?" said the Queen, much surprised.

"The offender, Madam, is before you," replied Walter, bowing very low; "the full and sole blame is mine; and my lord has most justly sent me to abye the consequences of a fault, of which he is as innocent as a sleeping man's dreams can be of a waking man's actions."

"What, was it thou?—thou thyself, that repelled my messenger and my physician from Say's Court?" said the Queen. "What could occasion such boldness in one who seems devoted—that is, whose exterior bearing shews devotion—to his Sovereign?"

"Madam," said the youth,—who, notwithstanding an assumed appearance of severity, thought that he saw something in the Queen's face that resembled not implacability,—"we say in our country, that the physician is for the time the liege sovereign of his patient. Now, my noble master was then under dominion of a leech, by whose advice he hath greatly profited, who had issued his commands that his patient should not that night be disturbed, on the very peril of his life."

"Thy master hath trusted some false varlet of an empiric," said the Queen.

"I know not, Madam, but by the fact, that he is now—this very morning—awaked much refreshed and strengthened, from the only sound sleep he hath had for many hours."

The nobles looked at each other, but more with the purpose to see what each thought of these news, than to exchange any remarks on what had happened. The Queen answered hastily, and without affecting to disguise her satisfaction, "By my word, I am glad he is better. But thou wert over bold to deny the access of my Doctor Master. Know'st thou not that Holy Writ saith, 'In the multitude of counsel there is safety'?"

"Ay, Madam," said Walter, "but I have heard learned men say, that the safety spoken of is for the physicians, not for the patient."

"By my faith, child, thou hast pushed me home," said the Queen, laughing; "for my Hebrew learning does not come quite at a call.— How say you, my Lord of Lincoln? hath the lad given a just interpretation of the text?"

"The word *safety*, most gracious Madam," said the Bishop of Lincoln, "for so hath been translated, it may be somewhat hastily, the Hebrew word"——

"My lord," said the Queen, interrupting him, "we said we had forgotten our Hebrew.—But for thee, young man, what is thy name and birth?"

"Raleigh is my name, most gracious Queen, the youngest son of a large but honourable family of Devonshire."

"Raleigh?" said Elizabeth, after a moment's recollection, "have we not heard of your service in Ireland?"

"I have been so fortunate as to do some service there, Madam," replied Raleigh, "scarce, however, of consequence sufficient to reach your Grace's ears."

"They hear farther than you think of," said the Queen graciously, "and have heard of a youth who defended a ford in Shannon against a whole band of wild Irish rebels, until the stream ran purple with their blood and his own."

"Some blood I may have lost," said the youth, looking down, "but it was where my best was due; and that is in your Majesty's service."

The Queen paused, and then said hastily, "You are very young, to have fought so well, and to speak so well. But you must not escape your penance for turning back Master—the poor man hath caught cold on the river; for our order reached him when he was just returned from certain visits in London, and he held it matter of loyalty and conscience instantly to set forth again. So hark ye, Master Raleigh, see thou fail not to wear thy muddy cloak, in token of penitence, till our pleasure be farther known—and here," she added, giving him a jewel of gold, in the form of a chess-man, "I give thee this to wear at the collar."

Raleigh, to whom nature had taught intuitively, as it were, those courtly arts which many scarce acquire from long experience, knelt, and, as he took from her hand the jewel, kissed the fingers which gave it. He knew, perhaps, better than almost any of the courtiers who surrounded her, to mingle the devotion claimed by the Queen, with the gallantry due to the personal beauty—and in this, his first attempt to unite them, he succeeded so well, as at once to gratify Elizabeth's personal vanity, and her love of power.

His master, the Earl of Sussex, had the full advantage of the satisfaction which Raleigh had afforded Elizabeth, on their first interview.

"My lords and ladies," said the Queen, looking around to the retinue by whom she was attended, "methinks, since we are upon the river, it were well to renounce our present purpose of going to the City, and surprise this poor Earl of Sussex with a visit. He is ill, and suffering doubtless under the fear of our displeasure, from which he hath been honestly cleared by the frank avowal of this malapert boy. What think ye? were it not an act of charity to give him such consolation as the thanks of a Queen, much bound to him for his loyal service, may perchance best minister?"

It may be readily supposed, that none to whom this speech was addressed, ventured to oppose its purport. "Your Grace," said the Bishop of Lincoln, "is the breath of our nostrils." The men of war averred, that the face of the Sovereign was a whetstone to the soldier's sword; while the men of state were not less of opinion, that the light of the Queen's countenance was a lamp to the paths of her councillors.

And the ladies agreed, with one voice, that no noble in England so well deserved the regard of England's Royal Mistress as the Earl of Sussex —the Earl of Leicester's right being received entire; so some of the more politic worded their assent—an exception to which Elizabeth paid no apparent attention. The barge had, therefore, orders to deposit its royal freight at Deptford, at the nearest and most convenient point of communication with Say's Court, in order that the Queen might satisfy her royal and maternal solicitude, by making personal inquiries after the health of the Earl of Sussex.

Raleigh, whose acute spirit foresaw and anticipated important consequences from the most trifling events, hastened to ask the Queen's permission to go before in the skiff, and announce the royal visit to his master; ingeniously suggesting, that the joyful surprise might prove prejudicial to his health, since the richest and most generous cordials may sometimes be fatal to those who have been long in a languishing state.

But whether the Queen deemed it too presumptuous in so young a courtier to interpose his opinion unasked, or whether she was moved by a recurrence of the feeling of jealousy, which had been instilled into her by reports that the Earl kept armed men about his person, she desired Raleigh, sharply, to reserve his counsel till it was required of him, and repeated her former orders, to be landed at Deptford, adding, "We will ourselves see what sort of household my Lord of Sussex keeps about him."

"Now the Lord have pity on us!" said the young courtier to himself. "Good hearts, the Earl hath many a one round him; but good heads are scarcer with us—and he himself is too ill to give direction. And Blount will be at his morning meal of Yarmouth herrings and ale; and Tracy will have his beastly black puddings and Rhenish—those thorough-paced Welchmen, Thomas ap Rice and Evan Evans, will be at work on their leek porridge and toasted cheese—and she detests, they say, all coarse meat, evil smells, and strong wines. Could they but think of burning some rosemary in the great hall—But *vogue la galère*, all must now be trusted to chance. Luck hath done indifferent well for me this morning, for I trust I have spoiled a cloak, and made a court fortune—may she do as much for my gallant patron!"

The royal barge soon stopped at Deptford, and, amidst the loud shouts of the populace, which her presence never failed to excite, the Queen, with a canopy borne over her head, walked, accompanied by her retinue, towards Say's Court, where the distant acclamations of the people gave the first notice of her arrival. Sussex, who was in the act of advising with Tressilian how he should make up the supposed breach in the Queen's favour, was infinitely surprised at learning her immediate approach—not that the custom of visiting her more distinguished nobility, whether in health or sickness, could be unknown to him; but the suddenness of the communication left no time for those preparations with which he well knew Elizabeth loved to be greeted, and the rudeness and confusion of his military household, much encreased by his late illness, rendered him altogether unprepared for her reception.

Cursing internally the chance which thus brought her gracious visitation on him unaware, he hastened down with Tressilian, to whose eventful and interesting story he had just given an attentive ear.

"My worthy friend," he said, "such support as I can give your accusation of Varney, you have a right to expect, alike from justice and gratitude. Chance will presently shew whether I can do aught with our Sovereign, or whether, in very deed, my meddling in your affair may not rather prejudice than serve you."

Thus spoke Sussex, while hastily casting around him a loose robe of sables, and adjusting his person in the best manner he could to meet the eye of his sovereign. But no hurried attention bestowed on his apparel could remove the ghastly effects of long illness on a countenance which nature had marked with features rather strong than pleasing. Besides, he was low of stature, and though broad-shouldered, athletic, and fit for martial achievement, his presence in a peaceful hall was not such as ladies love to look upon; a personal disadvantage, which was supposed to give Sussex, though esteemed and honoured by his Sovereign, considerable disadvantage when compared with Leicester, who was alike remarkable for elegance of manners, and for beauty of person.

The Earl's utmost dispatch only enabled him to meet the Queen as she entered the great hall, and he at once perceived there was a cloud on her brow. Her jealous eye had noticed the martial array of armed gentlemen and retainers with which the mansion-house was filled, and her first words expressed her disapprobation—"Is this a royal garrison, my Lord of Sussex? or have we by accident overshot Say's Court, and landed at our Tower of London?"

Lord Sussex hastened to offer some apology.

"It needs not," she said. "My lord, we intend speedily to take up a certain quarrel between your lordship and another great lord of our household, and at the same time to reprehend this uncivilized and dangerous practice of surrounding yourselves with armed, and even with ruffianly followers, as if, in the neighbourhood of our capital, nay in the very verge of our royal residence, you were preparing to wage civil war with each other. We are glad to see you so well recovered, my lord, though without the assistance of the learned physician whom we sent to you—Urge no further excuse—we know how that matter fell out, and we have corrected for it the wild slip, young Raleigh.—By the way, my lord, we will relieve your household of him, and take him into our own—something there is about him which merits to be better nurtured than he is like to be amongst your very military followers."

To this proposal Sussex, though scarce understanding how the Queen came to make it, could only bow and express his obedience. He then entreated her to remain till refreshment could be offered, but in this he could not prevail. And, after a few compliments of a much colder and more common-place character than might have been expected from a step so decidedly favourable as a personal visit, the Queen took her leave of Say's Court, having brought confusion thither along with her, and leaving doubt and apprehension behind her.

Chapter Four

> Then call them to our presence. Face to face,
> And frowning brow to brow, ourselves will hear
> The accuser and accused freely speak;—
> High-stomach'd are they both and full of ire,
> In rage deaf as the sea, hasty as fire.
>
> *Richard II*

"I AM ORDERED to attend at court to-morrow," said Leicester, speaking to Varney, "to meet, as they surmise, my Lord of Sussex. The Queen intends to take up matters betwixt us—this comes of her visit to Say's Court, of which you must needs speak so lightly."

"I maintain it was nothing," said Varney; "nay, I know from a sure intelligencer, who was within ear-shot of much that was said, that Sussex has lost rather than gained by that visit. The Queen said, when she stepped into the boat, that Say's Court looked like a guard-house, and smelt like an hospital. 'Like a cook's shop rather in Ram's Alley, Madam,' said the Countess of Rutland, who is ever your lordship's good friend. And then my Lord of Lincoln must needs put in his holy oar, and say, that my Lord of Sussex must be excused for his rude and old-world housekeeping, since he had as yet no wife."

"And what said the Queen?" said Leicester, hastily.

"She took him up roundly," said Varney, "and asked what my Lord Sussex had to do with a wife, or my Lord Bishop to speak on such a subject. If marriage is permitted, she said, I no where read that it is enjoined."

"She likes not marriages, or speech of marriage, among church-men," said Leicester.

"Nor among courtiers neither," said Varney; but, observing that

Leicester changed countenance, he instantly added, "that all the ladies who were present had joined in ridiculing Lord Sussex's housekeeping, and in contrasting it with the reception her Grace would have assuredly received at my Lord of Leicester's."

"You have gathered much tidings," said Leicester, "but you have forgotten or omitted the most important of all. She hath added another to those dangling satellites, whom it is her pleasure to keep revolving around her."

"Your lordship meaneth that Raleigh, the Devonshire youth," said Varney, "the Knight of the Cloak, as they call him at the court?"

"He may be Knight of the Garter one day, for aught I know," said Leicester, "for he advances rapidly—she hath chimed verses with him, and all such fooleries. I would gladly abandon, of my own free will, the part I have in her fickle favour, but I will not be elbowed out on it by the clown Sussex, or this new upstart. I hear Tressilian is with Sussex also, and high in his favour—I would spare him for considerations, but he will thrust himself on his fate—Sussex, too, is almost as well as ever in his health."

"My lord," replied Varney, "there will be rubs in the smoothest road, specially when it leads up hill. Sussex's illness was to us a godsend, from which I hoped much. He has recovered indeed, but he is not now more formidable than ere he fell ill, when he received more than one foil in wrestling with your lordship. Let not your heart fail you, my lord, and all shall be well."

"My heart never failed me, sir," replied Leicester.

"No, my lord," said Varney; "but it has betrayed you right often. He that would climb a tree, my lord, must grasp by the branches, not by the blossom."

"Well, well, well!" said Leicester, impatiently; "I understand thy meaning—My heart shall neither fail me nor seduce me. Have my retinue in order—see that their array be so splendid as to put down not only the rude companions of Ratcliffe, but the retainers of every other nobleman and courtier. Let them be well armed withal, but without any outward display of their weapons, wearing them as if more for fashion's sake than for use. Do thou thyself keep close to me, I may have business for you."——

The preparations of Sussex and his party were not less anxious than those of Leicester.

"Thy placet, impeaching Varney of seduction," said the Earl to Tressilian, "is by this time in the Queen's hand—I have sent it through a sure channel—methinks your suit should succeed, being, as it is, founded in justice and honour, and Elizabeth being the very muster of both. But I wot not how—the gipsey (so Sussex was wont to

call his rival on account of his dark complexion) hath much to say with
her in these holiday times of peace—Were war at the gates, I should
be one of her white boys; but soldiers, like their bucklers and bilboa
blades, get out of fashion in peace time, and satin sleeves and walking
rapiers bear the bell. Well, we must be gay since such is the fashion.—
Blount, hast thou seen our household put into their new braveries?—
But thou know'st as little of these toys as I do—thou wouldst be ready
enow at disposing a stand of pikes."

"My good lord," answered Blount, "Raleigh hath been here and
taken that charge upon him—Your train will glitter like a May morning.—Marry, the cost is another question. One might keep an hospital
of old soldiers at the charge of ten modern lacqueys."

"We must not count cost to-day, Nicholas," said the Earl, in reply;
"I am beholden to Raleigh for his care—I trust, though, he has
remembered that I am an old soldier, and would have no more of these
follies than needs must."

"Nay, I understand nought about it; but here are your honourable
lordship's brave kinsmen and friends coming in by scores to wait upon
you to court, where methinks we shall bear as brave a front as Leicester, let him ruffle it as he will."

"Give them the strictest charges," said Sussex, "that they suffer no
provocation short of actual violence to provoke them into quarrels—
they have hot bloods, and I would not give Leicester the advantage
over me by any imprudence of theirs."

The Earl of Sussex ran so hastily through these directions, that it
was with difficulty Tressilian at length found opportunity to express
his surprise that he should have proceeded so far in the affair of Sir
Hugh Robsart as to lay his petition at once before the Queen—"It was
the opinion of the young lady's friends," he said, "that Leicester's
sense of justice should be first appealed to, as the offence had been
committed by his officer, and so he had expressly told to Sussex."

"This could have been done without applying to me," said Sussex,
somewhat haughtily. "*I*, at least, ought not to have been a counsellor
when the object was a humiliating reference to Leicester; and I am
surprised that you, Tressilian, a man of honour, and my friend, would
assume such a mean course. If you said so, I certainly understood you
not in a matter which sounded so unlike yourself."

"My lord," said Tressilian, "the course I would prefer, for my own
sake, is that you have adopted; but the friends of this most unhappy
lady"——

"O, the friends—the friends," said Sussex, interrupting him; "they
must let us manage this cause in the way which seems best. This is the
time and the hour to accumulate every charge against Leicester and

his household, and your's the Queen will hold a heavy one. But at all events she hath the complaint before her."

Tressilian could not help suspecting that, in his eagerness to strengthen himself against his rival, Sussex had purposely adopted the course most likely to throw odium on Leicester, without considering minutely whether it were the mode of proceeding most like to be attended with success. But the step was irrevocable, and Sussex escaped from farther discussing it by dismissing his company, with the command, "Let all be in order at eleven o'clock; I must be at court and in the presence by high noon precisely."

While the rival statesmen were thus anxiously preparing for their approaching meeting in the Queen's presence, even Elizabeth herself was not without apprehensions of what might chance from the collision of two such fiery spirits, each backed by a strong and numerous body of followers, and dividing betwixt them, either openly or in secret, the hopes and wishes of most of her court. The band of Gentlemen Pensioners were all under arms, and a reinforcement of the yeomen of the guard was brought down the Thames from London. A royal proclamation was sent forth, strictly prohibiting nobles, of whatsoever degree, to approach the Palace with retainers or followers, armed with shot or long weapons; and it was even whispered, that the High Sheriff of Kent had secret instructions to have a part of the array of the county ready on the shortest notice.

The eventful hour, thus anxiously prepared for on all sides, at length approached, and, each followed by his long and glittering train of friends and followers, the rival Earls entered the Palace-yard of Greenwich at noon precisely.

As if by previous arrangement, or perhaps by intimation that such was the Queen's pleasure, Sussex and his retinue came to the Palace from Deptford by water, while Leicester arrived by land; and thus they entered the court-yard from opposite sides. This trifling circumstance gave Leicester a certain ascendency in the opinion of the vulgar, the appearance of his cavalcade of mounted followers shewing more numerous and more imposing than those of Sussex's party, who were necessarily upon foot. No shew or sign of greeting passed between the Earls, though each looked full at the other, both expecting perhaps an exchange of courtesies, which neither was willing to commence. Almost on the minute of their arrival the castle-bell tolled, the gates of the Palace were opened, and the Earls entered, each numerously attended by the gentlemen of their train whose rank gave them that privilege. The yeomen and inferior attendants remained in the court-yard, where the opposite parties eyed each other with looks of eager hatred and scorn, as if waiting with impatience for some cause of tumult, or some apology for mutual aggression. But they were restrained by the strict commands of their leaders, and overawed, perhaps, by the presence of an armed guard of unusual strength.

In the meanwhile, the more distinguished persons of each train followed their patrons into the lordly halls and anti-chambers of the royal Palace, flowing on in the same current, like two streams which are compelled into the same channel, yet shun to mix their waters. The parties arranged themselves, as it were instinctively, on the different sides of the lofty apartments, and seemed eager to escape from the transient union which the narrowness of the crowded entrance had for an instant compelled them to submit to. The folding doors at the upper end of the long gallery were immediately afterwards opened, and it was announced in a whisper that the Queen was in her presence-chamber, to which these gave access. Both Earls moved slow and stately towards the entrance; Sussex followed by Tressilian, Blount, and Raleigh, and Leicester by Varney. The pride of Leicester was obliged to give way to court-forms, and with a grave and formal inclination of the head, he paused until his rival, a peer of older creation than his own, passed before him. Sussex returned the reverence with the same formal civility, and entered the presence-room. Tressilian and Blount offered to follow him, but were not permitted, the Usher of the Black Rod alleging in excuse, that he had precise orders to look to all admissions that day. To Raleigh, who stood back on the repulse of his companions, he said, "You, sir, may enter," and he entered accordingly.

"Follow me close, Varney," said the Earl of Leicester, who had stood aloof for a moment to mark the reception of Sussex; and, advancing to the entrance, he was about to pass on, when Varney, who was close behind him, dressed out in the utmost bravery of the day, was stopped by the usher, as Tressilian and Blount had been before him. "How is this, Master Bowyer?" said the Earl of Leicester; "Know you who I am, and that this is my friend and follower?"

"Your lordship will pardon me," replied Bowyer, stoutly, "my orders are precise, and limit me to a strict discharge of my duty."

"Thou art a partial knave," said Leicester, the blood mounting to his face, "to do me this dishonour, when you but now admitted a follower of my Lord of Sussex."

"My lord," said Bowyer, "Master Raleigh is newly a sworn servant of her Grace, and to him my orders do not apply."

"Thou art a knave—an ungrateful knave," said Leicester; "but he that hath done, can undo—thou shalt not prank thee in thy authority long!"

His threat he uttered aloud, with less than his usual policy and discretion, and having done so, he entered the presence-chamber, and made his reverence to the Queen, who, attired with even more than her usual splendour, and surrounded by those nobles and statesmen whose courage and wisdom have rendered her reign immortal, stood ready to receive the homage of her subjects. She graciously returned the obeisance of the favourite Earl, and looked alternately at him and at Sussex, as if about to speak, when Bowyer, a man whose spirit could not brook the insult he had so openly received from Leicester, in the discharge of his office, advanced with his black rod in his hand, and knelt down before her.

"Why, how now, Bowyer," said Elizabeth, "thy courtesy seems strangely timed!"

"My Liege Sovereign," he said, while every courtier around trembled at his audacity, "I come but to ask, whether, in the discharge of mine office, I am to obey your Highness's commands, or those of the Earl of Leicester, who has publicly menaced me with his displeasure, and treated me with disparaging terms, because I denied entry to one of his followers, in obedience to your Grace's precise orders."

The spirit of Henry VIII. was instantly aroused in the bosom of his daughter, and she turned on Leicester with a severity which appalled him, as well as all his followers.

"God's death, my lord," such was her emphatic phrase, "what means this? We have thought well of you, and brought you near to our person; but it was not that you might hide the sun from our other faithful subjects. Who gave you license to contradict our orders, or controul our officers? I will have in this court, ay, and in this realm, but one mistress, and no master. Look to it that Master Bowyer sustains no harm for his duty to me faithfully discharged; for, as I am Christian woman and crowned Queen, I will hold you dearly answerable.—Go, Bowyer, you have done the part of an honest man and a true subject. We will brook no mayor of the palace here."

Bowyer kissed the hand which she extended towards him, and withdrew to his post, astonished at the success of his own audacity. A smile of triumph pervaded the faction of Sussex; that of Leicester seemed proportionally dismayed, and the favourite himself, assuming an aspect of the deepest humility, did not even attempt a word in his own exculpation.

He acted wisely; for it was the policy of Elizabeth to humble, not to disgrace him, and it was prudent to suffer her, without opposition or reply, to glory in the exertion of her authority. The dignity of the queen was gratified, and the woman began soon to feel for the mortification which she had imposed on her favourite. Her keen eye also observed the secret looks of congratulation exchanged amongst those who favoured Sussex, and it was no part of her policy to give either party a decisive triumph.

"What I say to my Lord of Leicester," she said, after a moment's pause, "I say also to you, my Lord of Sussex. You also must needs ruffle in the court of England, at the head of a faction of your own?"

"My followers, gracious Princess," said Sussex, "have indeed ruffled in your cause, in Ireland, in Scotland, and against yonder rebellious Earls in the north. I am ignorant that"——

"Do you bandy looks and words with me, my lord?" said the Queen, interrupting him; "methinks you might learn of my Lord of Leicester the modesty to be silent, at least, under our censure. I say, my lord, that my grandfather and my father, in their wisdom, debarred the nobles of this civilized land from travelling with such disorderly retinues; and think you, that because I wear a coif, their sceptre has in my hand been changed into a distaff? I tell you, no king in Christendom will less brook his court to be cumbered, his people oppressed, and his kingdom's peace disturbed by the arrogance of overgrown power, than she who now speaks with you.—My Lord of Leicester, and you, my Lord of Sussex, I command you both to be friends with each other; or by the crown I wear, you shall find an enemy who will be too strong for both of you."

"Madam," said the Earl of Leicester, "you who are yourself the fountain of honour, know best what is due to mine. I place it at your disposal, and only say, that the terms on which I have stood with my Lord of Sussex have not been of my seeking; nor had he cause to think me his enemy, until he had done me gross wrong."

"For me, Madam," said the Earl of Sussex, "I cannot appeal from your sovereign pleasure; but I were well content my Lord of Leicester should say in what I have, as he terms it, wronged him, since my tongue never spoke the word that I would not willingly justify either on foot or horseback."

"And for me," said Leicester, "always under my gracious Sovereign's pleasure, my hand shall be as ready to make good my words, as that of any man who ever wrote himself Ratcliffe."

"My lords," said the Queen, "these are no terms for this presence; and if you cannot keep your temper, we will find means to keep both that and you close enough. Let me see you join hands, my lords, and forget your idle animosities."

The two rivals looked at each other with reluctant eyes, each unwilling to make the first advance to execute the Queen's will.

"Sussex," said Elizabeth, "I entreat—Leicester, I command you." Yet, so were her words accented, that the entreaty sounded like command, and the command like entreaty. They remained still and stubborn, until she raised her voice to a height which argued at once impatience and absolute command.

"Sir Henry Lee," she said, to an officer in attendance, "have a guard in present readiness, and man a barge instantly.—My Lords of Sussex and Leicester, I bid you once more to join hands—and, God's death! he that refuses shall taste of our Tower fare ere he see our face again. I will lower your proud hearts ere we part, and that I promise, on the word of a Queen."

"The prison," said Leicester, "might be borne, but to lose your Grace's presence, were to lose light and life at once.—Here, Sussex, is my hand."

"And here," said Sussex," is mine, in truth and honesty; but"——

"Nay, under favour, you shall add no more," said the Queen. "Why, this is as it should be," she added, looking on them more favourably, "and when you, the shepherds of the people, unite to protect them, it shall be well with the flock we rule over. For, my lords, I tell you plainly, your follies and your brawls lead to strange disorders among your servants.—My Lord of Leicester, you have a gentleman in your household, called Varney?"

"Yes, gracious Madam," replied Leicester, "I presented him to kiss your royal hand when you were last at Nonsuch."

"His outside was well enough," said the Queen, "but scarce so fair, I should have thought, as to have caused a maiden of honourable birth and hopes to barter her fame for his good looks, and become his paramour. Yet so it is—this fellow of yours hath seduced the daughter of a good old Devonshire knight, Sir Hugh Robsart of Lidcote-hall, and she hath fled with him from her father's house like a cast-away.— My Lord of Leicester, are you ill, that you look so deadly pale?"

"No, gracious Madam," said Leicester; and it required every effort he could make to bring forth these few words.

"You are surely ill, my lord?" said Elizabeth, going towards him with hasty speech and hurried step, which indicated the deepest concern. "Call Master—call our surgeon in ordinary—Where be these loitering fools?—We lose the pride of our court through their negligence.—Or is it possible, Leicester," she continued, looking on him with a very gentle aspect, "can fear of my displeasure have wrought so deeply on thee? Doubt not for a moment, noble Dudley, that we could blame *thee* for the folly of thy retainer—thee, whose thoughts we know to be far otherwise employed? He that would climb the eagle's nest, my lord, cares not who are catching linnets at the foot of the precipice."

"Mark you that?" said Sussex, aside to Raleigh. "The devil aids him

surely! for all that would sink another ten fathom deep, seems but to
make him float the more easily. Had a follower of mine acted
thus"——

"Peace, my good lord," said Raleigh, "for God's sake, peace. Wait
the change of the tide; it is even now on the turn."

The acute observation of Raleigh, perhaps, did not deceive him; for
Leicester's confusion was so great, and, indeed, for the moment, so
irresistibly overwhelming, that Elizabeth, after looking at him with a
wondering eye, and receiving no intelligible answer to the unusual
expressions of grace and affection which had escaped from her, shot
her quick glance around the circle of courtiers, and reading, perhaps,
in their faces, something that accorded with her own awakened suspicions, she said suddenly, "Or is there more in this than we see—or
than you, my lord, wish that we should see? Where is this Varney?
Who saw him?"

"An it please your Grace," said Bowyer, "it is the same against
whom I this instant closed the door of the presence-room."

"An it please me?" repeated Elizabeth sharply, not at that
moment in the humour of being pleased with any thing, "It does
not please me that he should pass saucily into my presence, or that
you should exclude from it one who came to justify himself from an
accusation."

"May it please you," answered the perplexed usher, "if I knew, in
such case, how to bear myself, I would take heed"——

"You should have reported the fellow's desire to us, Master Usher,
and taken our directions. You think yourself a great man, because but
now we chid a nobleman on your account—but, after all, we hold you
but as the lead-weight that keeps the door fast. Call this Varney hither
instantly—there is one Tressilian also mentioned in this petition—let
them both come before us."

She was obeyed, and Tressilian and Varney appeared accordingly.
Varney's first glance was at Leicester, his second at the Queen. In the
looks of the latter, there appeared an approaching storm, and in the
downcast countenance of his patron, he could read no directions in
what way he was to trim his vessel for the encounter—he then saw
Tressilian, and at once perceived the peril of the situation in which he
was placed. But Varney was as bold-faced and ready-witted as he was
cunning and unscrupulous,—a skilful pilot in extremity, and fully
conscious of the advantages which he would obtain, could he extricate
Leicester from his present peril, and of the ruin that yawned for
himself, should he fail in doing so.

"Is it true, sirrah," said the Queen, with one of those searching
looks which few had the audacity to resist, "that you have seduced to

infamy a young lady of birth and breeding, the daughter of Sir Hugh Robsart of Lidcote-Hall?"

Varney kneeled down, and replied, with a look of the most profound contrition, "There had been some love passages betwixt him and Mistress Amy Robsart."

Leicester's flesh quivered with indignation as he heard his dependant make this avowal, and for one moment he manned himself to step forward, and, bidding farewell to the court and the royal favour, confess the whole mystery of the secret marriage. But he looked at Sussex, and the idea of the triumphant smile which would clothe his cheek upon hearing the avowal, sealed his lips. "Not now, at least," he thought, "or in this presence, will I afford him so rich a triumph." And pressing his lips close together, he stood firm and collected, attentive to each word which Varney uttered, and determined to hide to the last the secret on which his court-favour seemed to depend. Meanwhile, the Queen proceeded in her examination of Varney.

"Love passages!" said she, echoing his last words; "what passages, thou knave? and why not ask the wench's hand from her father, if thou hadst any honesty in thy love for her?"

"An it please your Grace," said Varney, still on his knees, "I dared not do so, for her father had promised her hand to a gentleman of birth and honour—I will do him justice, though I know he bears me ill will —one Master Edmund Tressilian, whom I now see in the presence."

"Soh!" replied the Queen; "and what was your right to make the simple fool break her worthy father's contract, through your love *passages*, as your conceit and assurance terms them?"

"Madam," replied Varney, "it is in vain to plead the cause of human frailty before a judge to whom it is unknown, or that of love, to one who never yields to the passion"—He paused an instant, and then added, in a very low and timid tone, "which she inflicts upon all others."

Elizabeth tried to frown, but smiled in her own despite, as she answered, "Thou art a marvellously impudent knave—Art thou married to the girl?"

Leicester's feelings became so complicated and so painfully intense, that it seemed to him as if his life was to depend on the answer made by Varney, who, after a moment's real hesitation, answered, "Yes."

"Thou false villain!" said Leicester, bursting forth into rage, yet unable to add another word to the sentence, which he had begun with such emphatic passion.

"Nay, my lord," said the Queen, "we will, by your leave, stand between this fellow and your anger. We have not yet done with him.— Knew your master, my Lord of Leicester, of this fair work of yours?

Speak truth, I command thee, and I will be thy warrant from danger on every quarter."

"Gracious Madam," said Varney, "to speak heaven's truth, my lord was the cause of the whole matter."

"Thou villain, would'st thou betray me?" said Leicester.

"Speak on," said the Queen hastily, her cheek colouring, and her eyes sparkling, as she addressed Varney; "speak on—here no commands are heard but mine."

"They are omnipotent, gracious Madam," replied Varney; "and to you there can be no secrets.—Yet I would not," he added, looking around him, "speak of my master's concerns to other ears."

"Fall back, my lords," said the Queen to those who surrounded her, "and do you speak on.—What hath the Earl to do with this guilty intrigue of thine?—See, fellow, that thou beliest him not."

"Far be it from me to traduce my noble patron," replied Varney; "yet I am compelled to own that some deep, overwhelming, yet secret feeling, hath of late dwelt in my lord's mind, hath abstracted him from the cares of the household, which he was wont to govern with such religious strictness, and hath left us opportunities to do follies, of which the shame, as in this case, partly falls upon our patron. Without this, I had not had means or leisure to commit the folly which has drawn on me his displeasure; the heaviest to endure by me, which I could by any means incur,—saving always the yet more dreaded resentment of your Grace."

"And in this sense, and no other, hath he been accessory to thy fault?" said Elizabeth.

"Surely, Madam, in no other," replied Varney; "but since somewhat hath chanced to him, he can scarce be called his own man. Look at him, Madam, how pale and trembling he stands—how unlike his usual majesty of manner—yet what has he to fear from aught I can say to your Highness? Ah! Madam, since he received that fatal packet!"

"What packet, and from whence?" said the Queen, eagerly.

"From whence, madam, I cannot guess; but I am so near to his person, that I know he has ever since worn, suspended around his neck, and next to his heart, that lock of hair which sustains a small golden jewel shaped like a heart—he speaks to it when alone—he parts not from it when he sleeps—no heathen ever worshipped an idol with such devotion."

"Thou art a prying knave to watch thy master so closely," said Elizabeth, blushing, but not with anger; "and a tattling knave to tell over again his fooleries.—What colour might the braid of hair be that thou pratest of?"

Varney replied, "A poet, Madam, might call it a thread from the golden web wrought by Minerva; but, to my thinking, it was paler than even the purest gold—more like the last parting sunbeam of the softest day of spring."

"Why, you are a poet yourself, Master Varney," said the Queen, smiling; "but I have not genius quick enough to follow your rare metaphors—Look round these ladies—is there—(she hesitated, and endeavoured to assume an air of great indifference)—Is there here, in this presence, any lady, the colour of whose hair reminds thee of that braid? Methinks, without prying into my Lord of Leicester's amorous secrets, I would fain know what kind of locks are like the thread of Minerva's web, or the—what was it?—the last rays of the May-day sun."

Varney looked round the presence-chamber, his eye travelling from one lady to another, until at length it rested upon the Queen herself, but with an aspect of the deepest veneration. "I see no tresses," he said, "in this presence worthy of such similies, unless where I dare not look on them."

"How, sir knave," said the Queen, "dare you intimate"——

"Nay, Madam," replied Varney, shading his eyes with his hand, "it was the beams of the May-day sun that dazzled my weak eyes."

"Go to—go to," said the Queen; "thou art a foolish fellow"—and turning quickly from him she walked up to Leicester.

Intense curiosity, mingled with all the various hopes, fears, and passions, which influence court-faction, had occupied the presence-chamber during the Queen's conference with Varney, as if with the strength of an eastern talisman. Men suspended every, even the slightest external motion, and would have ceased to breathe, had Nature permitted such an intermission of her functions. The atmosphere was contagious, and Leicester, who saw all around wishing or fearing his advancement or his fall, forgot all that love had previously dictated, and saw nothing for the instant but the favour or disgrace which depended on the nod of Elizabeth and the fidelity of Varney. He summoned himself hastily, and prepared to play his part in the scene which was like to ensue, when, as he judged from the glances which the Queen threw towards him, Varney's communications, be they what they might, were operating in his favour. Elizabeth did not long leave him in doubt; for the more than favour with which she accosted him decided his triumph in the eyes of his rival, and of the assembled court of England—"Thou hast a prating servant of this same Varney, my lord," she said; "it is lucky you trust him with nothing that can hurt you in our opinion, for believe me, he would keep no counsel."

"From your Highness," said Leicester, dropping gracefully on one knee, "it were treason he should. I would that my heart itself lay before you, barer than the tongue of any servant could strip it."

"What, my lord," said Elizabeth, looking kindly upon him, "is there no one little corner over which you would wish to spread a veil? Ah! I see you are confused at the question, and your Queen knows she should not look too deeply into her servants' motives for their faithful duty, lest she see what might, or at least ought to displease her."

Relieved by these last words, Leicester broke out into a torrent of expressions of deep and passionate attachment, which perhaps, at that moment, were not altogether fictitious. The mingled emotions which had at first overcome him, had now given way to the energetic vigour with which he had determined to support his place in the Queen's favour; and never did he seem to Elizabeth more eloquent, more handsome, more interesting, than while, kneeling at her feet, he conjured her to strip him of all his power, but to leave him the name of her servant—"Take from the poor Dudley," he exclaimed, "all that your bounty has made him, and bid him be the poor gentleman he was when your grace first shone on him; leave him no more than his cloak and his sword, but let him still boast he has—what in word or deed he never forfeited—the regard of his adored Queen and mistress!"

"No, Dudley!" said Elizabeth, raising him with one hand, while she extended the other that he might kiss it; "Elizabeth hath not forgotten that, whilst you were a poor gentleman, despoiled of your hereditary rank, she was as poor a princess, and that in her cause you then ventured all that oppression had left you—your life and honour.— Rise, my lord, and let my hand go!—Rise, and be what you have ever been, the grace of our court, and the support of our throne. Your mistress may be forced to chide your misdemeanours, but never without owning your merits.—And so help me God," she added, turning to the audience, who, with various feelings, witnessed this interesting scene,—"So help me God, gentlemen, as I think never sovereign had a truer servant than I have in this noble Earl."

A murmur of assent rose from the Leicestrian faction, which the friends of Sussex dared not oppose. They remained with their eyes fixed on the ground, dismayed as well as mortified by the public and absolute triumph of their opponents. Leicester's first use of the familiarity to which the Queen had so publicly restored him, was to ask her commands concerning Varney's offence. "Although," he said, "the fellow deserves nothing from me but displeasure, yet, might I presume to intercede"——

"In truth, we had forgotten his matter," said the Queen; "and it was ill done of us, who owe justice to our meanest, as well as to our highest subject. We are pleased, my lord, that you were the first to recall the matter to our memory.—Where is Tressilian, the accuser?—let him come before us."

Tressilian appeared, and made a low and beseeming reverence. His person, as we have elsewhere observed, had an air of grace and even of nobleness, which did not escape Queen Elizabeth's critical observation. She looked at him with attention as he stood before her unabashed, but with an air of the deepest dejection.

"I cannot but grieve for this gentleman," she said to Leicester. "I have inquired concerning him, and his presence confirms what I heard, that he is a scholar and a soldier, well accomplished both in arts and arms. We women, my lord, are fanciful in our choice—I had said now, to judge by the eye, there was no comparison to be held betwixt your follower and this gentleman. But Varney is a well spoken fellow, and to speak truth, that goes far with us of the weaker sex.—Look you, Master Tressilian, a bolt lost is not a bow broken. Your true affection, as I will hold it to be, hath been, it seems, but ill requited; but you have scholarship, and you know there have been false Cressidas to be found, from the Trojan war downwards. Forget, good sir, this Lady Light a' Love—teach your affection to see with a wiser eye. This we say to you, more from the writings of learned men, than our own knowledge, being, as we are, far removed by station and will, from the enlargement of experience in such idle toys of humorous passion. For this dame's father, we can make his grief the less, by advancing his son-in-law to such station as may enable him to give an honourable support to his bride. Thou shalt not be forgotten thyself, Tressilian—follow our court, and thou shalt see that a true Troilus hath some claim on our grace. Think of what that arch-knave Shakespeare says—a plague on him, his toys come into my head when I should think of other matter—Stay, how goes it?—

> Cressid was your's, tied with the bonds of heaven;
> These bonds of heaven are slipt, dissolved, and loosed,
> And with another knot five fingers tied,
> The fragments of her faith are bound to Diomed.

You smile, my Lord of Southampton—perchance I make your player's verse halt through my bad memory—but let it suffice—let there be no more of this mad matter."

And as Tressilian kept the posture of one who would willingly be heard, though, at the same time, expressive of the deepest reverence, the Queen added with some impatience,—"What would the man have? The wench cannot wed both of you?—She has made her election—not a wise one perchance—but she is Varney's wedded wife."

"My suit should sleep there, most gracious Sovereign," said

Tressilian, "and with my suit my revenge. But I hold this Varney's word no good warrant for the truth."

"Had that doubt been elsewhere urged," answered Varney, "my sword"——

"*Thy* sword!" interrupted Tressilian, scornfully; "with her Grace's leave, my sword shall shew"——

"Peace, you knaves both," said the Queen; "know you where you are?—This comes of your feuds, my lords," she added, looking towards Leicester and Sussex; "your followers catch your own humour, and must bandy and brawl in my court, and in my very presence, like so many Matamoros.—Look you, sirs, he that speaks of drawing swords in any other quarrel than mine or England's, by mine honour, I'll bracelet him with iron both on wrist and ancle!" She then paused a minute, and resumed in a milder tone, "I must do justice betwixt the bold and mutinous knaves notwithstanding.—My Lord of Leicester, will you warrant with your honour,—that is, to the best of your belief,—that your servant speaks truth in saying he hath married this Amy Robsart?"

This was a home-thrust, and had nearly staggered Leicester. But he had now gone too far to recede, and answered, after a moment's hesitation, "To the best of my belief—indeed on my certain knowledge—she is a wedded wife."

"Gracious Madam," said Tressilian, "may I yet request to know, when and under what circumstances this alleged marriage"——

"Out, sirrah," answered the Queen; "*alleged* marriage!—have you not the word of this illustrious Earl to warrant the truth of what his servant says? But thou art a loser—think'st thyself such at least—and thou shalt have indulgence—we will look into the matter ourselves more at leisure.—My Lord of Leicester, I trust you remember we mean to taste the good cheer of your Castle of Kenilworth on this week ensuing—we will pray you to bid our good and valued friend the Earl of Sussex to hold company with us there."

"If the noble Earl of Sussex," said Leicester, bowing to his rival with the easiest and with the most graceful courtesy, "will so far honour my poor house, I will hold it an additional proof of the amicable regard it is your Grace's desire we should entertain towards each other."

Sussex was more embarrassed—"I should," said he, "Madam, be but a clog on your gayer hours since my late severe illness."

"And have you been indeed so very ill?" said Elizabeth, looking on him with more attention than before; "you are in faith strangely altered, and deeply am I grieved to see it. But be of good cheer—we will ourselves look after the health of so valued a servant, and to whom we owe so much. Master shall order your diet; and that we ourselves may see that he is obeyed, you must attend us in this progress to Kenilworth."

This was said so peremptorily and at the same time with so much kindness, that Sussex, however unwilling to become the guest of his rival, had no resource but to bow low to the Queen in obedience to her commands, and to express to Leicester, with blunt courtesy, though mingled with embarrassment, his acceptance of his invitation. As the Earls exchanged compliments on the occasion, the Queen said to her High Treasurer, "Methinks, my lord, the countenances of these our two noble peers resemble that of the two famed classic streams, the one so dark and sad, the other so fair and noble—My old Master Ascham would have chid me for forgetting the author—It is Cæsar, as I think.—See what majestic calmness sits on the brow of the noble Leicester, while Sussex seems to greet him as if he did our will indeed, but not willingly."

"The doubt of your Majesty's favour," answered the Lord Treasurer, "may perchance occasion the difference, which does not—as what does?—escape your Grace's eye."

"Such doubt were injurious to us, my lord," replied the Queen. "We hold both to be near and dear to us, and will with impartiality employ both in honourable service for the weal of our kingdom. But we will break their farther conference at present.—My Lords of Sussex and Leicester, we have a word more with you. Tressilian and Varney are near your persons—you will see that they attend you at Kenilworth—And as we will then have both Paris and Menelaus within our call, so we will have this same fair Helen also, whose fickleness has caused this broil.—Varney, thy wife must be at Kenilworth, and forthcoming at my order.—My Lord of Leicester, we expect you will look to this."

The Earl and his follower bowed low, and raised their heads slowly, without daring to look at the Queen, or at each other; for both felt at the instant as if the nets and toils which their own falsehood had woven, were in the act of closing around them. The Queen, however, observed not their confusion, but proceeded to say, "My Lords of Sussex and Leicester, we require your presence at the privy-council to be presently held, where matters of importance are to be debated. We will then take the water for our divertisement, and you, my lords, will attend us.—And that reminds us of a circumstance—Do you, Sir Squire of the Soiled Cassock, (distinguishing Raleigh by a smile) fail not to observe that you are to attend us on our progress. You shall be supplied with suitable means to reform your wardrobe."

And so terminated this celebrated audience, in which, as

throughout her life, Elizabeth united the occasional caprice of her sex, with that sense and sound policy, in which neither man nor woman ever excelled her.

Chapter Five

Well, then—our course is chosen—spread the sail—
Heave oft the lead, and mark the soundings well—
Look to the helm, good master—many a shoal
Marks this stern coast, and rocks, where sits the syren,
Who, like Ambition, lures men to their ruin.
The Shipwreck

DURING the brief interval that intervened betwixt the dismissal of the audience and the sitting of the privy council, Leicester had time to reflect that he had that morning sealed his own fate. It was impossible for him now, he thought, after having, in the face of all that was honourable in England, pledged his truth (though in ambiguous phrase) for the statement of Varney, to contradict or disavow it, without exposing himself, not merely to the loss of court-favour, but to the highest displeasure of the Queen, his deceived mistress, and to the scorn and contempt at once of his rival and of all his compeers. This certainty rushed at once on his mind, together with all the difficulties which he would necessarily be exposed to in maintaining a secret, which seemed now equally essential to his safety, to his power, and to his honour. He was situated like one who walks upon ice, ready to give way around him, and whose only safety consists in moving onwards, by firm and unvacillating steps. The Queen's favour, to preserve which he had made such sacrifices, must now be secured by all means and at all hazards—it was the only plank which he could cling to in the tempest. He must settle himself, therefore, to the task of not only preserving, but augmenting the Queen's partiality—he must be the favourite of Elizabeth, or a man utterly shipwrecked in fortune and in honour. All other considerations must be laid aside for the moment, and he repelled the intrusive thoughts which forced on his mind the image of Amy, by saying to himself, there would be time to think hereafter how he was to escape from the labyrinth ultimately, since the pilot, who sees a Scylla under his bows, must not for the time think of the more distant dangers of Charybdis.

In this mood, the Earl of Leicester that day assumed his chair at the council table of Elizabeth; and when the hours of business were over, in this same mood did he occupy an honoured place near to her, during her pleasure excursion on the Thames. And never did he display to more advantage his powers as a politician of the first rank, or his parts as an accomplished courtier.

It chanced that on that day in council matters were agitated touching the affairs of the unfortunate Mary, the seventh year of whose captivity in England was now in doleful currency. There had been opinions in favour of this unhappy princess laid before Elizabeth's council, and supported with much strength of argument by Sussex and others, who dwelt more upon the law of nations and the breach of hospitality, than, however softened or qualified, was agreeable to the Queen's ear. Leicester adopted the contrary opinion with great animation and eloquence, and described the necessity of continuing the severe restraint of the Queen of Scots, as a measure essential to the safety of the kingdom, and particularly of Elizabeth's sacred person, the lightest hair of whose head, he maintained, ought, in their lordships' estimation, to be matter of more deep and anxious concern, than the life and fortunes of a rival, who, after setting up a vain and unjust pretence to the throne of England, was now, even while in the bosom of her country, the constant hope and theme of all enemies to Elizabeth, whether at home or abroad. He ended by craving pardon of their lordships, if in the zeal of speech he had given any offence; but the Queen's safety was a theme which hurried him beyond his usual moderation of debate.

Elizabeth chid him, but not severely, for the weight which he attached unduly to her personal interests; yet she owned, that since it had been the pleasure of heaven to combine those interests with the weal of her subjects, she did only her duty when she adopted such measures for self-preservation as circumstances forced upon her; and if the council in their wisdom should be of opinion, that it was needful to continue some restraint on the person of her unhappy sister of Scotland, she trusted they would not blame her if she requested of the Countess of Shrewsbury to use her with as much kindness as might be consistent with her safe keeping. And with this intimation of her pleasure, the council was dismissed.

Never was more anxious and ready way made for "my Lord of Leicester," than as he passed through the crowded anti-rooms to go towards the river-side, in order to attend her Majesty to her barge— Never was the voice of the ushers louder, to "make room—make room for the noble Earl"—Never were these signals more promptly and reverentially obeyed—Never were more anxious eyes turned on him to obtain a glance of favour, or even of mere recognition, while the heart of many a humble follower of his fortunes throbbed betwixt desire to offer his congratulations, and fear of intruding himself on the notice of one so infinitely above him. The whole court considered the issue of this day's audience, expected with so much doubt and anxiety, as a decisive triumph on the part of Leicester, and felt assured that the orb of his rival satellite, if not altogether obscured by his lustre, must revolve hereafter in a dimmer and more distant sphere. So thought the court; and courtiers, from high to low, acted accordingly.

On the other hand, never did Leicester return with such ready and condescending courtesy, or endeavour more successfully to gather (in the words of one, who at that moment stood at no great distance from him) "golden opinions from all sorts of men." For all he had a bow, a smile at least, and often a kind word. Most of these were addressed to courtiers, whose names have long gone down the tide of oblivion; but some, to such as sound strangely in our ears, when connected with the ordinary matters of human life, above which the gratitude of posterity has long elevated them. A few of Leicester's interlocutory sentences ran as follows:

"Poynings, good morrow, and how does your wife and fair daughter?—why come they not to court?—Adams, your suit is naught—the Queen will grant no more monopolies—but I may serve you in another matter.—My good Alderman Aylford, the suit of the City, affecting Queenhithe, shall be forwarded as far as my poor interest can serve.—Master Edmund Spencer, touching your Irish petition, I would willingly aid you, from my love to the Muses; but thou hast nettled the Lord Treasurer."

"My lord," said the poet, "were I permitted to explain"——

"Come to my lodging, Edmund," answered the Earl—"not tomorrow, or next day, but soon.—Ha, Will Shakespeare—wild Will!—thou hast given my nephew, Philip Sidney, love-powder—he cannot sleep without thy Venus and Adonis under his pillow!—we will have thee hanged for the veriest wizard in Europe. Heark thee, mad wag, I have not forgotten thy matter of the patent, and of the bears."

The Player bowed, and the Earl nodded and passed on—so that age would have told the tale—in ours, perhaps, we might say the immortal had done homage to the mortal. The next whom the favourite accosted, was one of his own zealous dependants.

"How now, Sir Francis Denning," he whispered, in answer to his exulting salutation, "that smile hath made thy face shorter by one-third than when I first saw it this morning.—What, Master Bowyer, stand you back, and think you I bear malice? You did but your duty this morning; and, if I remember aught of the passage betwixt us, it shall be in thy favour."

Then the Earl was approached, with several fantastic congees, by a person quaintly dressed in a doublet of black velvet, curiously slashed and pinked with crimson satin. A long cock's feather in the velvet bonnet, which he held in his hand, and an enormous ruff, stiffened to the extremity of the absurd taste of the times, joined with a sharp, lively, conceited expression of countenance, seemed to body forth a vain, hair-brained coxcomb, and small wit; while the rod he held, and an assumption of formal authority, appeared to express some sense of official consequence, which qualified the natural pertness of his manner. A perpetual blush, which occupied rather the sharp nose than the thin cheeks of this personage, seemed to speak more of "good life," as it was called, than of modesty; and the manner in which he addressed himself to the Earl, confirmed that suspicion.

"Good even to you, Master Robert Laneham," said Leicester, and seemed desirous to pass forward, without farther speech.

"I have a suit to your noble lordship," said the figure, boldly following him.

"And what is it, good master keeper of the council-chamber door?"

"*Clerk* of the council-chamber door," said Master Robert Laneham, with emphasis, by way of reply, and of correction.

"Well, qualify thine office as thou wilt, man," replied the Earl; "what would'st thou have with me?"

"Simply," answered Laneham, "that your lordship would be, as heretofore, my good lord, and procure me licence to attend the Summer Progress unto your lordship's most beautiful, and all-to-be unmatched Castle of Kenilworth."

"To what purpose, good Master Laneham," replied the Earl; "bethink you my guests must needs be many."

"Not so many," replied the petitioner, "but that your nobleness will willingly spare your old servitor his crib and his mess. Bethink you, my lord, how necessary is this rod of mine, to fright away all those listeners, who else would play at bo-peep with the honourable council, and be searching for key-holes and crannies in the door of the chamber, so as to render my staff as needful as a fly-flap in a butcher's shop."

"Methinks you have found out a fly-blown comparison for the honourable council, Master Laneham," said the Earl; "but seek not about to justify it. Come to Kenilworth, if you list; there will be store of fools there beside, and so you will be fitted."

"Nay, an there be fools, my lord," replied Laneham, with much glee, "I warrant I will make sport among them; for no greyhound loves to cote a hare, as I to turn and course a fool. But I have another singular favour to beseech of your honour."

"Speak it, and let me go," said the Earl; "I think the Queen comes forth instantly."

"My lord, I would fain bring a bed-fellow with me."

"How, you irreverend rascal!" said Leicester.

"Nay, my lord, my meaning is within the canons," answered his unblushing, or rather his ever-blushing petitioner. "I have a wife as curious as her grandmother, who eat the apple. Now, take her with me I may not, her Highness's orders being so strict against the officers bringing with them their wives in a progress, and so lumbering the court with womankind. But what I would crave of your lordship, is, to find room for her in some mummery, or pretty pageant, in disguise, as it were; so that, not being known for my wife, there may be no offence."

"The foul fiend seize ye both!" said Leicester, stung into uncontroulable passion by the recollections which this speech excited— "Why stop you me with such follies?"

The terrified clerk of the chamber-door, astonished at the burst of resentment he had so unconsciously produced, dropped his staff of office from his hand, and gazed on the incensed Earl with a foolish face of wonder and terror, which instantly recalled Leicester to himself.

"I meant but to try if thou hadst the audacity which befits thine office," said he hastily—"come to Kenilworth, and bring the devil with thee, if thou wilt."

"My wife, sir, hath played the devil ere now, in a Mystery, in Queen Mary's time—but we shall want a trifle for properties."

"Here is a crown for thee," said the Earl,—"make me rid of thee— the great bell rings."

Master Robert Laneham stared a moment at the agitation which he had excited, and then said to himself, as he stooped to pick up his staff, "The noble Earl runs wild humours to-day; but they who give crowns, expect us witty fellows to wink at their unsettled starts; and, by my faith, if they paid not for mercy, we would finger them tightly."

Leicester moved hastily on, neglecting the courtesies he had hitherto dispersed so liberally, and hurrying through the courtly crowd, until he paused in a small withdrawing room, into which he plunged to draw a moment's breath unobserved, and in seclusion.

"What am I now," he said to himself, "that am just jaded by the words of a mean, weather-beaten, goose-brained gull!—Conscience, thou art a blood-hound, whose growl wakes as readily at the paltry stir of a rat or mouse, as at the step of a lion.—Can I not quit myself by one bold stroke of a state so irksome, so unhonoured? What if I kneel to Elizabeth, and, owning the whole, throw myself on her mercy?"—

As he pursued this train of thought, the door of the apartment opened, and Varney rushed in.

"Thank God, my lord, that I have found you," was his exclamation.

"Thank the devil, whose agent thou art," was the Earl's reply.

"Thank whom you will, my lord," replied Varney; "but hasten to the water-side. The Queen is on board, and asks for you."

"Go, say I am taken suddenly ill," replied Leicester; "for, by heaven, my brain can sustain this no longer."

"I will say so," said Varney, with bitterness of expression; "for your place, ay, and mine, who, as your master of the horse was to have attended your lordship, is already filled up in the Queen's barge. The new minion, Walter Raleigh, and our old acquaintance, Tressilian, were called for to fill our places just as I hastened away to seek you."

"Thou art a devil, Varney," said Leicester hastily; "but thou hast the mastery for the present—I follow thee."

Varney replied not, but led the way out of the palace, and towards the river, while his master followed him, as if mechanically; until, looking back, he said in a tone which savoured of familiarity at least, if not of authority, "How is this, my lord?—your cloak hangs on one side,—your hose are unbraced—permit me"——

"Thou art a fool, Varney, as well as a knave," said Leicester, shaking him off and rejecting his officious assistance; "we are best thus, sir —when we require you to order our person, it is well, but now we want you not."

So saying, the Earl resumed at once his air of command, and with it his self-possession—shook his dress into yet wilder disorder—passed before Varney with the air of a superior and master, and in his turn led the way to the river-side.

The Queen's barge was on the very point of putting off; the seat allotted to Leicester in the stern, and that to his master of the horse in the bow of the boat, being already filled up. But on Leicester's approach, there was a pause, as if the bargemen anticipated some alteration in their company. The angry spot was, however, on the Queen's cheek, as, in that cold tone with which superiors endeavour to veil their internal agitation, while speaking to one to whom it would be derogation to express it, she pronounced the chilling words—"We have waited, my Lord of Leicester."

"Madam, and most gracious Princess," said Leicester, "you, who can pardon so many weaknesses which your own heart never knows, can best bestow your commiseration on those agitations of the bosom, which, for a moment, affect both head and limbs.—I came to your presence, a doubting and an accused subject; your goodness penetrated the clouds of defamation, and restored me to my own honour, and, what is yet dearer, to your favour—is it wonderful, though for me it is most unhappy, that my master of the horse should have found me in a state which scarce permitted me to make the exertion necessary to follow him to this place, when one glance of your Highness, although, alas! an angry one, has had power to do that for me, in which Esculapius might have failed?"

"How is this?" said Elizabeth hastily, looking at Varney; "hath your lord been ill?"

"Something of a fainting fit," answered the ready-witted Varney, "as your Grace may observe from his present condition. My lord's haste would not permit me leisure even to bring his dress into order."

"It matters not," said Elizabeth, as she gazed on the noble face and form of Leicester, to which even the strange mixture of passions by which his bosom had been so lately agitated, gave additional interest, "make room for my noble lord—Your place, Master Varney, has been filled up; you must find a seat in another barge."

Varney bowed, and withdrew.

"And you too, our young Squire of the Cloak," added she, looking at Raleigh, "must, for the time, go to the barge of our ladies of honour —for Tressilian, he hath already suffered too much by the caprice of women, that I should aggrieve him by mine."

Leicester seated himself in his place in the barge, and close to the Sovereign; Raleigh rose to retire, and Tressilian would have been so ill-timed in his courtesy as to offer to relinquish his own place to his friend, had not the acute glance of Raleigh himself, who seemed now in his native element, made him sensible, that so ready a disclamation of the royal favour might be misinterpreted. He sate silent, therefore, whilst Raleigh, with a profound bow, and a look of the deepest humiliation, was about to quit his place.

A noble courtier, the gallant Lord Willoughby, read, as he thought, something in the Queen's face, which seemed to pity Raleigh's real or assumed semblance of mortification.

"It is not for us old courtiers," he said, "to hide the sunshine from the young ones. I will, with her Majesty's leave, relinquish for an hour, that which all her subjects hold dearest, the delight of her Highness's presence, and mortify myself by walking in star-light, while I forsake for a brief season, the glory of Diana's own beams. I will take place in the boat which the ladies occupy, and permit this young cavalier his hour of promised felicity."

The Queen replied with an expression betwixt mirth and earnest, "If you are so willing to leave us, my lord, we cannot help the mortification. But, under favour, we do not trust you—old and experienced as you may deem yourself—with the care of our young ladies of honour. Your venerable age, my lord," she continued, smiling, "may be better assorted with that of my Lord Treasurer, who follows in the third boat, and whose experience even my Lord Willoughby's may be improved by."

Lord Willoughby hid his disappointment under a smile—laughed, was confused, bowed, and left the Queen's barge to go on board of my Lord Burleigh's. Leicester, who endeavoured to divert his thoughts from all internal reflection, by fixing them on what was passing around, watched this circumstance among others. But when the boat put off from the shore—when the music sounded from a barge which accompanied them—when the shouts of the populace were heard from the shore, and all reminded him of the situation in which he was placed, he abstracted his thoughts and feelings by a strong effort from every thing but the necessity of maintaining himself in the favour of his patroness, and exerted his talents of pleasing captivation with such success, that the Queen, alternately delighted with his conversation, and alarmed for his health, at length imposed a temporary silence on him, with playful yet anxious care, lest his flow of spirits should exhaust him.

"My lords," she said, "having passed for a time our edict of silence upon our good Leicester, we will call you to counsel on a gamesome matter, more fitted to be now treated of, amidst mirth and music, than in the gravity of our ordinary deliberations.—Which of you, my lords," said she, smiling, "know aught of a petition from Orson Pinnit, the keeper, as he qualifies himself, of our royal bears? Who stands god-father to his request?"

"Marry, with your Grace's good permission, that do I," said the Earl of Sussex.—"Orson Pinnit was a stout soldier before he was so mangled by the skenes of the Irish clan MacDonough, and I trust your Grace will be, as you always have been, good mistress to your good and trusty servants."

"Surely," said the Queen, "it is our purpose to be so, and in especial to our poor soldiers and sailors, who hazard their lives for little pay. We would give," she said, with her eyes sparkling, "yonder royal palace of ours to be an hospital for their use, rather than they should call their mistress ungrateful.—But this is not the question," she said, her tone, which had been awakened by her patriotic feelings, once more subsiding into the tone of gay and easy conversation; "for this Orson Pinnit's request goes something farther. He complains, that amidst the extreme delight with which men haunt the play-houses, and in especial their eager desire for seeing the exhibitions of one Will Shakespeare, (whom I think, my lords, we have all heard something of,) the manly amusement of bear-baiting is falling into comparative neglect; since men will rather throng to see these roguish players kill each other in jest, than to see our royal dogs and bears worry each other in bloody earnest—What say you to this, my Lord of Sussex?"

"Why, truly, gracious Madam," said Sussex, "you must expect little from an old soldier like me in favour of battles in sport, when they are compared with battles in earnest; and yet, by my faith, I wish Will Shakespeare no harm. He is a stout man at quarter-staff, and single falchion, as I am told, though a halting fellow; and stood, they say, a tough fight with the rangers of old Sir Thomas Lucy of Charlecot, when he broke his deer-park and kissed his keeper's daughter."

"I cry you mercy, my Lord of Sussex," said Queen Elizabeth, interrupting him; "that matter was heard in council, and we will not have this fellow's offence exaggerated—there was no kissing in the matter, and the defendant hath put the denial on record.—But what say you to his present practice, my lord, on the stage? for there lies the point, and not in any ways touching his former errors, in breaking parks, or the other follies you speak of."

"Why truly, Madam," replied Sussex, "as I said before, I wish the gamesome mad fellow no injury. Some of his whoreson poetry (I crave your Grace's pardon for such a phrase) has rung in mine ears as if they sounded to boot and saddle.—But then it is all froth and folly—no substance or seriousness in it, as your Grace has already well touched. —What are half a dozen knaves, with rusty foils and tattered targets, making but a mere mockery of a stout fight, to compare to the royal game of bear-baiting, which hath been graced by your Highness's countenance, and that of your royal predecessors, in this your princely kingdom, famous for matchless mastiffs, and bold bearwards, over all Christendom? Greatly is it to be doubted that the race of both will decay, if men will rather throng to hear the lungs of an idle player belch forth nonsensical bombast, instead of bestowing their pence in encouraging the bravest image of war that can be shewn in peace, and that is the sports of the Parish-garden. There you may see the bear lying at guard with his red pinky eyes, watching the onset of the mastiff, like a wily captain, who maintains his defence that an assailant may be tempted to adventure within his danger. And then comes Sir Mastiff, like a worthy champion, in full career at the throat of his adversary—and then shall Sir Bruin teach him the reward for those who, in over-courage, neglect the policies of war, and, catching him in his arms, strain him to his breast like a lusty wrestler, until rib after rib crack like the shot of a pistolet. And then shall another mastiff, as bold, but with better aim and sounder judgment, catch Sir Bruin by the nether lip, and hang fast, while he tosses about his blood and slaver, and tries in vain to shake Sir Talbot from his hold. And then"——

"Nay, by my honour, my lord," said the Queen, laughing, "you have described the whole so admirably, that, had we never seen a bear-baiting, as we have beheld a many, and hope, with heaven's allowance, to see many more, your words were sufficient to put the whole Bear-garden before our eyes.—But come, who speaks next in this case?—My Lord of Leicester, what say you?"

"Am I then to consider myself as unmuzzled, please your Grace?" replied Leicester.

"Surely, my lord—that is, if you feel hearty enough to take part in our game," answered Elizabeth. "And yet, when I think of your cognizance of the bear and ragged staff, methinks we had better hear some less partial orator."

"Nay, on my word, gracious Princess," said the Earl, "though my brother Ambrose of Warwick and I do carry the ancient cognizance your Highness deigns to remember, I nevertheless desire nothing but fair play on all sides; or, as they say, 'fight dog, fight bear.' And in behalf of the players, I must needs say they are witty knaves whose rants and whose jests keep the minds of the commons from busying themselves with state affairs, and listening to traitorous speeches, idle rumours, and disloyal insinuations. When men are agape to see how Marlow, Shakespeare, and others, work out their fanciful plots as they call them, the mind of the spectators is withdrawn from the conduct of their rulers."

"We would not have the mind of our subjects withdrawn from the consideration of our own conduct, my lord," answered Elizabeth; "because the more closely it is examined, the true motives by which we are guided will appear the more manifest."

"I have heard, however, Madam," said the Dean of St Asaph's, an eminent Puritan, "that these players are wont, in their plays, not only to introduce profane and lewd expressions, tending to foster sin and harlotry, but even to bellow out such reflections on government, its origin and its object, as tend to render the subject discontented, and shake the solid foundations of civil society. And it seems to be, under your Grace's favour, far less than safe to permit these naughty foul-mouthed knaves to ridicule the godly for their decent gravity, and in blaspheming heaven, and slandering their earthly rulers, to set at defiance the laws both of God and man."

"If we could think this were true, my lord," said Elizabeth, "we should give sharp correction for such offences. But it is ill arguing against the use of any thing from its abuse. And touching this Shakespeare, we think there is that in his plays that is worth twenty Beargardens; and that this new undertaking of his Chronicles, as he calls them, may entertain, with honest mirth, mingled with useful instruction, not only our subjects, but even the generation which may succeed to us."

"Your Majesty's reign will need no such feeble aid to make it remembered to the latest posterity," said Leicester. "And yet, in his

way, Shakespeare hath so touched some incidents of your Majesty's
happy government, as may countervail what has been spoken by his
reverence the Dean of St Asaph's. There are some lines, for example
—I would my nephew, Philip Sidney, were here, they are scarce ever
out of his mouth—they are in a mad tale of fairies, love-charms, and I
wot not what besides; beautiful however they are, however short they
may and must fall of the subject to which they bear a bold relation—
and Philip murmurs them, I think, even in his dreams."

"You tantalize us, my lord," said the Queen—"Master Philip Sidney is, we know, a minion of the Muses, and we are pleased it should
be so. Valour never shows to more advantage than when united with
taste and love of letters—but surely there are some others among our
young courtiers who can recollect what your lordship has forgotten
amid weightier affairs.—Master Tressilian, you are described to me
as a worshipper of Minerva—remember you aught of these lines?"

Tressilian's heart was too heavy, his prospects in life too fatally
blighted, to profit by the opportunity which the Queen thus offered to
him of attracting her attention, but he determined to transfer the
advantage to his more ambitious young friend; and, excusing himself
on the score of want of recollection, he added, that he believed the
beautiful verses, of which my Lord of Leicester had spoken, were in
the remembrance of Master Walter Raleigh.

At the command of the Queen, that cavalier repeated, with accent
and manner which even added to their exquisite delicacy of tact and
beauty of description, the celebrated vision of Oberon.

> "That very time I saw, (but thou could'st not,)
> Flying between the cold moon and the earth,
> Cupid, all arm'd: a certain aim he took
> At a fair vestal, throned by the west;
> And loos'd his love-shaft smartly from his bow,
> As it should pierce a hundred thousand hearts:
> But I might see young Cupid's fiery shaft
> Quench'd in the chaste beams of the wat'ry moon;
> And the imperial vot'ress passed on,
> In maiden meditation, fancy free."

The voice of Raleigh, as he repeated the last lines, became a little
tremulous, as if diffident how the Sovereign to whom the homage was
addressed might receive it, exquisite as it was. If this diffidence was
affected, it was good policy; but if real, there was little occasion for it.
The verses were not probably new to the Queen, for when was ever
such elegant flattery so long in reaching the royal ear to which it was
addressed? But it was not the less welcome when recited by such a
speaker as Raleigh. Alike delighted with the matter, the manner, and
the graceful form and animated countenance of the gallant young

reciter, Elizabeth kept time to every cadence, with look and with finger. When the speaker had ceased, she murmured over the last lines as if scarce conscious that she was overheard, and as she uttered the words,

"In maiden meditation, fancy free,"

she dropt into the Thames the supplication of Orson Pinnit, keeper of the royal bears, to find more favourable acceptance at Sheerness, or wherever the tide might waft it.

Leicester was spurred to emulation by the success of the young courtier's exhibition, as the veteran racer is roused when a high-mettled colt passes him on the way. He turned the discourse on shows, banquets, pageants, and on the characters of those by whom these gay scenes were then frequented. He mixed acute observation with light satire, in that just proportion which was free alike from malignant slander and insipid praise. He mimicked with ready accent the manners of the affected or the clownish, and made his own graceful tone and manners seem doubly such when he resumed it. Foreign countries—their customs—their manners—the rules of their courts —the fashions, and even the dress of their ladies, were equally his theme; and seldom did he conclude without conveying some compliment, always couched with delicacy, and expressed with propriety, to the Virgin Queen, her court and her government. Thus passed the conversation during this pleasure voyage, seconded by the rest of the attendants upon the royal person, in gay discourse, varied by remarks upon ancient classics and modern authors, and enriched by maxims of deep policy and sound morality, by the statesmen and sages who sate around, and mixed wisdom with the lighter talk of a female court.

When they returned to the palace, Elizabeth accepted, or rather selected, the arm of Leicester to support her, from the stairs where they landed, to the grand gate. It even seemed to him, (though that might arise from the flattery of his own imagination,) that during this short passage, she leaned on him somewhat more than the slippiness of the way necessarily demanded. Certainly her actions and words combined to express a degree of favour, which, even in his proudest days, he had not till then attained. His rival, indeed, was repeatedly graced by the Queen's notice; but it was in a manner that seemed to flow less from spontaneous inclination, than as extorted by a sense of his merit. And, in the opinion of many experienced courtiers, all the favour she shewed him was over-balanced, by her whispering in the ear of the Lady Derby, that now she saw sickness was a better alchemist than she before wotted of, seeing it had changed my Lord of Sussex's copper nose into a golden one.

The jest transpired, and the Earl of Leicester enjoyed his triumph, as one to whom court favour had been both the primary and the ultimate motive of life, while he forgot, in the intoxication of the moment, the perplexities and dangers of his own situation. Indeed, strange as it may appear, he thought less at that moment of the perils arising from his secret union, than of the marks of grace which Elizabeth from time to time shewed to young Raleigh. They were indeed transient, but they were conferred on one accomplished in mind and body, with grace, gallantry, literature, and valour. An accident occurred in the course of the evening which rivetted Leicester's attention to this object.

The nobles and courtiers who had attended the Queen on her pleasure expedition, were invited, with royal hospitality, to a splendid banquet in the hall of the palace. The table was not, indeed, graced by the presence of the Sovereign; for, agreeable to her idea of what was at once modest and dignified, the Maiden Queen, on such occasions, was wont to take in private, or with one or two favourite ladies, her light and temperate meal. After a moderate interval, the court again met in the splendid gardens of the palace, and continued to amuse themselves with various conversation until the Queen gave the signal for departure. It was while thus engaged, that the Queen suddenly asked a lady, who was near to her both in place and favour, what had become of the young Squire Lack-Cloak.

The Lady Paget answered, "she had seen Master Raleigh but two or three minutes since, standing at the window of a pavilion or pleasure house, which looked out on the Thames, and writing on the glass with a diamond ring."

"That ring," said the Queen, "was a small token I gave him, to make amends for his spoiled mantle—come, Paget, let us see what use he has made of it, for I can see through him already. He is a marvellously sharp-witted spirit."

They went to the spot, within sight of which, but at some distance, the young cavalier still lingered, as the fowler watches the net which he has set. The Queen approached the window, on which Raleigh had used her gift, to inscribe the following line:—

Fain would I climb, but that I fear to fall.

The Queen smiled, read it twice over with deliberation, once to Lady Paget, and once again to herself. "It is a pretty beginning," she said, after the consideration of a moment or two; "but methinks the muse hath deserted the young wit, at the very outset of his task—It were good-natured—were it not, Lady Paget,—to complete it for him? Try your rhyming faculties."

Lady Paget, prosaic from her cradle upwards, as ever any lady of the bed-chamber before or after her, disclaimed all possibility of assisting the young poet.

"Nay, then, we must sacrifice to the Muses ourselves," said Elizabeth.

"The sacrifice of no one can be so acceptable," said Lady Paget; "and your highness will impose such obligation on the ladies of Parnassus"——

"Hush, Paget," said the Queen, "you speak sacrilege against the immortal Nine—Yet virgins themselves, they should be exorable to a Virgin Queen—and, therefore—let me see how runs his verse—

Fain would I climb, but that I fear to fall.

Might not the answer, (for fault of a better) run thus:

If thy mind fail thee, do not climb at all."

The dame of honour uttered an exclamation of joy and surprise at so happy a termination; and certainly a worse has been applauded, even when coming from a less distinguished author.

The Queen, thus encouraged, took off a diamond ring, and saying, "We will give this gallant some cause of marvel, when he finds his couplet perfected without his own interference," she wrote her own line beneath that of Raleigh.

The Queen left the pavilion—but retiring slowly, and often looking back, she could see the young cavalier steal, with the flight of a lapwing, towards the place where he had seen her make a pause;—"She staid but to observe," as she said, "that her train had taken;" and then, laughing at the circumstance with the Lady Paget, she took the way slowly toward the palace. Elizabeth, as they returned, cautioned her companion not to mention to any one the aid she had given to the young poet—and Lady Paget promised scrupulous secrecy. It is to be supposed, that she made a mental reservation in favour of Leicester, to whom her ladyship without delay transmitted an anecdote, so little calculated to give him pleasure.

Raleigh, in the meanwhile, stole back to the window, and read, with a feeling of intoxication, the encouragement thus given him by the Queen in person to follow out his ambitious career, and returned to Sussex and his retinue, then on the point of embarking to go up the river, his heart beating high with gratified pride, and with hope of future distinction.

The reverence due to the person of the Earl prevented any notice being taken of the reception he had met with at court, until they had landed, and the household were assembled in the great hall at Say's Court; while that Lord, exhausted by his late illness, and the fatigues of the day, had retired to his chamber, demanding the attendance of Wayland, his successful physician. Wayland, however, was no where to be found; and, while some of the party were, with military impatience, seeking him, and cursing his absence, the rest flocked around Raleigh, to congratulate him on his prospects of court favour.

He had the good taste and judgment to conceal the decisive circumstance of the couplet, to which Elizabeth had deigned to find a rhyme; but other circumstances had transpired, which plainly intimated he had made some progress in the Queen's favour. All hastened to wish him joy on the mended appearance of his fortune: some from real regard; some, perhaps, from hopes that his preferment might hasten their own; and most from a mixture of these motives, and a sense that countenance shewn to any one of Sussex's household, was, in fact, a triumph to the whole. Raleigh returned the kindest thanks to them all, disowning, with becoming modesty, that one day's fair reception made a favourite, any more than one swallow a summer. But he observed that Blount did not join in the general congratulation, and, somewhat hurt at his apparent unkindness, he plainly asked him the reason.

Blount replied with equal sincerity—"My good Walter, I wish thee as well as any of those chattering gulls, who are whistling and whooping gratulations in thine ear, because it seems fair weather with thee. But I fear for thee, Walter, (and he wiped his honest eye,) I fear for thee with all my heart. These court-tricks, and gambols, and flashes of fine women's favour, are the tricks and trinkets that bring fair fortunes to farthings, and fair faces and witty coxcombs to the acquaintance of dull blocks and sharp axes."

So saying, Blount arose and left the hall, while Raleigh looked after him with an expression that blanked for a moment his bold and animated countenance.

Stanley just then entered the hall, and said to Tressilian, "My lord is calling for your fellow Wayland, and your fellow Wayland has just come hither in a sculler, and is calling for you, nor will he go to my lord till he sees you. The fellow looks as he were mazed, methinks—I would you would see him immediately."

Tressilian instantly left the hall, and causing Wayland Smith to be shewn into a withdrawing apartment, and lights placed, he conducted the artist thither, and was surprised when he observed the deadly paleness of his countenance.

"What is the matter with you, Smith?" said Tressilian; "have you seen the devil?"

"Worse, sir, worse," replied Wayland, "I have seen a basilisk—

thank God, I saw him first, for being so seen, and seeing not me, he will do the less harm."

"In God's name, speak sense," said Tressilian, "and say what you mean."

"I have seen my old master," said the artist—"Last night, a friend, whom I had acquired, took me to see the palace clock, judging me to be curious in such works of art. At the window of a turret next to the clock-house I saw my old master."

"Thou must have needs been mistaken," said Tressilian.

"I was not mistaken," said Wayland—"He that once hath his features by heart would know him amongst a million. He was anticly habited; but he cannot disguise himself from me, God be praised, as I can from him. I will not, however, tempt Providence by remaining within his ken. Tarleton the player himself could not so disguise himself, but that, sooner or later, Doboobie would find him out. I must away to-morrow; for, as we stand together, it were death to me to remain within reach of him."

"But the Earl of Sussex?" said Tressilian.

"He is in little danger from what he has hitherto taken, providing he swallow the matter of a bean's size of the Orvietan, every morning fasting—but let him beware of a relapse."

"And how is that to be guarded against?" said Tressilian.

"Only by such caution as you would use against the devil," answered Wayland. "Let my lord's clerk of the kitchen kill his lord's meat himself, and dress it himself, using no spice but what he procures from the surest hands—let the sewer serve it up himself, and let the master of my lord's household see that both clerk and sewer taste the dishes which the one dresses and the other serves. Let my lord use no perfumes which come not from well accredited persons; no unguents—no pomades. Let him, on no account, drink with strangers, or eat fruit with them, either in the way of nooning or otherwise. Especially, let him observe such caution, if he goes to Kenilworth—the excuse of his illness, and his being under diet, will, and must, cover the strangeness of such practice."

"And thou," said Tressilian, "what doest thou think to make of thyself?"

"France, Spain, either India, East or West, shall be my refuge," said Wayland, "ere I venture my life by residing within ken of Doboobie, Demetrius, or whatever else he calls himself for the time."

"Well," said Tressilian, "this happens not inopportunely—I had business for you in Berkshire, but in the opposite extremity to the place where thou art known; and ere thou hadst found out this new reason for living private, I had settled to send thee thither upon a secret embassage."

The artist expressed himself willing to receive his commands, and Tressilian, knowing he was well acquainted with the outline of his business at court, frankly explained to him the whole, mentioned the agreement which subsisted betwixt Giles Gosling and him, and told what had that day been averred in the presence-chamber by Varney, and supported by Leicester.

"Thou seest," he added, "that, in the circumstances in which I am placed, it behoves me to keep a narrow watch on the motions of these unprincipled men, Varney and his complices, Forster and Lambourne, as well as on those of my Lord Leicester himself, who, I suspect, is partly a deceiver, and not altogether the deceived in that matter. Here is my ring, as a pledge to Giles Gosling—here is besides gold, which shall be trebled if thou serve me faithfully. Away down to Cumnor, and see what happens there."

"I go with double good will," said the artist, "first, because I serve your honour, who has been so kind to me, and then, that I may escape my old master, who, if not an absolute incarnation of the devil, has at least as much of a dæmon about him, in will, word, and action, as ever polluted humanity.—And yet let him take care of me. I fly him now, as heretofore; but if, like the Scotch wild cattle, I am vexed by frequent pursuit, I may turn on him in hate and desperation.—Will your honour command my nag to be saddled? I will but give the medicine to my lord, divided in its proper proportions, with a few instructions. His safety will then depend on the care of his friends and domestics—for the past he is guarded, but let him beware of the future."

Wayland Smith accordingly made his farewell visit to the Earl of Sussex, dictated instructions as to his regimen, and precautions concerning his diet, and left Say's Court without waiting for morning.

Chapter Six

——The moment comes—
It is already come—when thou must write
The absolute total of thy life's vast sum.
The constellations stand victorious o'er thee,
The planets shoot good fortune in fair junctions,
And tell thee, "Now's the time."
            SCHILLER'S *Wallenstein*, by Coleridge.

WHEN LEICESTER returned to his lodging, after a day so important and so harassing, in which, after riding out more than one gale, and touching on more than one shoal, his bark had finally gained the harbour with banner displayed, he seemed to experience as much fatigue as a mariner after a perilous storm. He spoke not a word while his chamberlain exchanged his rich court-mantle for a furred night-robe, and when this officer signified that Master Varney desired to speak with his lordship, he replied only by a sullen nod. Varney, however, entered, accepting this signal as a permission, and the chamberlain withdrew.

The Earl remained silent and almost motionless in his chair, his head reclined on his hand, and his elbow resting upon the table which stood beside him, without seeming to be conscious of the entrance, or of the presence of his confidant. Varney waited for some minutes until he should speak, desirous to know what was the finally predominant mood of a mind, through which so many powerful emotions had that day taken their course. But he waited in vain, for Leicester continued still silent, and he saw himself under the necessity of being the first to speak. "May I congratulate your lordship," he said, "on the deserved superiority you have this day attained over your most formidable rival?"

Leicester raised his head, and answered sadly, but without anger, "Thou, Varney, whose ready invention has involved me in a web of most mean and perilous falsehood, knowest best what reason there is for gratulation on the subject."

"Do you blame me, my lord," said Varney, "for not betraying, on the first push, the secret on which your fortunes depended, and which you have so oft and so earnestly recommended to my safe keeping? Your lordship was present in person, and might have contradicted me and ruined yourself by an open avowal of the truth; but surely it was no part of a faithful servant to have done so without your commands."

"I cannot deny it, Varney," said the Earl, rising and walking across the room; "my own ambition has been traitor to my love."

"Say rather, my lord, that your love has been traitor to your great-ness, and barred you from such a prospect of honour and power as the world cannot offer to any other. To make my honoured lady a Coun-tess, you have missed the chance of being yourself"——

He paused and seemed unwilling to complete the sentence.

"Of being myself what?" demanded Leicester; "speak out thy meaning, Varney."

"Of being yourself a King, my lord," replied Varney; "and King of England to boot!—it is no treason to our Queen to say so, since it would have chanced by her obtaining that which all true subjects wish her—a lusty, noble, and gallant husband."

"Thou ravest, Varney," answered Leicester. "Besides, our times have seen enough to make men loath the Crown Matrimonial which men take from their wives' lap. There was Darnley in Scotland."

"He!" said Varney; "a gull, a fool, a thrice sodden ass, who suffered himself to be fired off into the air like a rocket on a rejoicing day. Had Mary had the hap to have wedded the noble Earl, once destined to share her throne, she had found a husband of different metal; and her husband had found in her a wife as complying and loving as the mate of the meanest squire, who follows the hounds a horseback, and holds her lord's bridle as he mounts."

"It might have been as thou say'st, Varney," said Leicester, a brief smile of self-satisfaction passing over his anxious countenance. "Henry Darnley knew little of woman—with Mary, a man who knew her sex might have had some chance of holding his own. But not with Elizabeth, Varney—for I think God, when he gave her the heart of a woman, gave her the head of a man to controul its follies.—No, I know her—she will accept love-tokens, ay, and requite them with the like— put sugared sonnets in her bosom—ay, and answer them too—push gallantry to the very verge where it becomes exchange of affection— but she writes *nil ultra* to all which is to follow, and would not barter one iota of her own supreme power for all the alphabet of both Cupid and Hymen."

"The better for you, my lord," said Varney, "that is, in the case supposed, if such be her disposition; since you think you cannot aspire to become her husband—her favourite you are, and may remain, if the lady at Cumnor-Place remains in her present obscurity."

"Poor Amy!" said Leicester, with a deep sigh; "she desires so earnestly to be acknowledged in presence of God and man!"

"Ay, but, my lord," said Varney, "is her desire reasonable?—that is the question.—Her religious scruples are solved—she is an honoured and beloved wife—enjoying the society of her husband at such times as his weightier duties permit him to afford her his company—What would she more? I am right sure that a lady so gentle and so loving would consent to live her life through in a certain obscurity—which is, after all, not dimmer than when she was at Lidcote-Hall—rather than diminish the least jot of her lord's honours and greatness by a pre-mature attempt to share them."

"There is something in what thou say'st," said Leicester; "and her appearance here were fatal—Yet she must be seen at Kenilworth; Elizabeth will not forget that she has so appointed."

"Let me sleep on that hard point," said Varney; "I cannot else perfect the device I have on the stithy, which I trust will satisfy the Queen and please my honoured lady, yet leave this fatal secret where it is now buried.—Has your lordship further commands for the night?"

"I would be alone," said Leicester. "Leave me, and place my steel casket on the table.—Be within summons."

Varney retired—and the Earl, opening the window of his apartment, looked out long and anxiously upon the brilliant host of stars
which glimmered in the brilliance of a summer firmament. The words
burst from him as at unawares—"I had never more need than that the
heavenly bodies should befriend me, for my earthly path is darkened
and confused."

It is well known that the age reposed a deep confidence in the vain
predictions of judicial astrology, and Leicester, though exempt from
the general controul of superstition, was not in this respect superior to
his time; but, on the contrary, was remarkable for the encouragement
which he gave to the professors of this pretended science. Indeed, the
wish to pry into futurity, so general among the human race of every
description, is peculiarly to be found amongst those who trade in state
mysteries, and the dangerous intrigues and cabals of courts.

With heedful precaution to see that it had not been opened, or its
locks tampered with, Leicester applied a key to the steel casket, and
drew from it, first, a parcel of gold pieces, which he put into a silk
purse; then a parchment inscribed with planetary signs, and the lines
and calculations used in framing horoscopes, on which he gazed
intently for a few moments; and, lastly, took forth a large key, which,
lifting aside the tapestry, he applied to a little concealed door in the
corner of the apartment, and, opening it, disclosed a stair constructed
in the thickness of the wall.

"Alasco," said the Earl, with a voice raised, yet no higher raised
than to be heard by the inhabitant of the small turret to which the stair
conducted—"Alasco, I say, descend."

"I come, my lord," answered a voice from above. The foot of an
aged man was heard, slowly descending the narrow stair, and Alasco
entered the Earl's apartment. The astrologer was a little man, and
seemed much advanced in age, for his beard was long and white, and
reached over his black doublet down to his silken girdle. His hair was
of the same venerable hue. But his eye-brows were as dark as the keen
and piercing black eyes which they shaded, and this peculiarity gave a
wild and singular cast to the physiognomy of the old man. His cheek
was still fresh and ruddy, and the eyes we have mentioned resembled
those of a rat, in acuteness, and even fierceness of expression. His
manner was not without a sort of dignity; and the interpreter of the
stars, though respectful, seemed altogether at his ease, and even
assumed a tone of instruction and command, in conversing with the
prime favourite of Elizabeth.

"Your prognostications have failed, Alasco," said the Earl, when
they had exchanged salutations—"He is recovering."

"My son," replied the astrologer, "let me remind you, I warranted not his death—nor is there any prognostication that can be derived from the heavenly bodies, their aspects and their conjunctions, which is not liable to be controuled by the will of Heaven. *Astra regunt homines, sed regit astra Deus.*"

"Of what avail, then, is your mystery?" replied the Earl.

"Of much, my son," replied the old man, "since it can shew the natural and probable course of events, although that course moves in subordination to an Higher Power. Thus, in viewing the horoscope which your lordship subjected to my skill, you will observe that Saturn, being in the sixth House in opposition to Mars, retrograde in the House of Life, cannot but denote long and dangerous sickness, the issue whereof is in the will of Heaven, though death may probably be inferred—Yet if I knew the name of the party, I would erect another scheme."

"His name is a secret," said the Earl; "yet, I must own, thy prognostication hath not been unfaithful. He has been sick, and dangerously so, not however to death. But hast thou again cast my horoscope as Varney directed thee, and art thou prepared to say what the stars tell of my present fortune?"

"My art stands at your command," said the old man; "and here, my son, is the map of thy fortunes, brilliant in aspect as ever beamed from those blessed signs whereby our life is influenced, yet not unchequered with fears, difficulties, and dangers."

"My lot were more than mortal were it otherwise," said the Earl; "proceed, father, and believe you speak with one ready to undergo his destiny in action and in passion, as may beseem a noble of England."

"Thy courage to do and to suffer, must be wound up yet a strain higher," said the old man. "The stars intimate yet a prouder title, yet an higher rank. It is for thee to guess their meaning, not for me to name it."

"Name it, I conjure you—name it, I command you," said the Earl, his eyes brightening as he spoke.

"I may not, and I will not," replied the old man; "the ire of princes is as the wrath of the lion. But mark, and judge for thyself. Here Venus, ascendant in the House of Life, and conjoined with Sol, showers down that flood of silver light, blent with gold, which promises power, wealth, dignity, all that the proud heart of man desires, and in such abundance, that never the future Augustus of that old and mighty Rome heard from his *Haruspices* such a tale of glory, as from this rich text my lore might read to my favourite son."

"Thou doest but jest with me, father," said the Earl, astonished at the strain of enthusiasm in which the astrologer delivered his prediction.

"Is it for him to jest who hath his eye on heaven, who hath his foot on the grave?" returned the old man, solemnly.

The Earl made two or three strides through the apartment, with his hand outstretched, as one who follows the beckoning signal of some phantom, waving him on to deeds of high import. As he turned, however, he caught the eye of the astrologer fixed on him, while an observing glance of the most shrewd penetration shot from under the penthouse of his shaggy black eye-brows. Leicester's haughty and suspicious soul at once caught fire; he darted towards the old man from the further end of the lofty apartment, only standing still when his extended hand was within a foot of the astrologer's body.

"Wretch!" he said, "if you dare to palter with me, I will have your skin stripped from your living flesh!—Confess thou hast been hired to deceive and to betray me—that thou art a cheat, and I thy silly prey and booty!"

The old man exhibited some symptoms of emotion, but not more than the furious deportment of his patron might have extorted from innocence itself.

"What means this violence, my lord?" he answered, "or in what can I have deserved it at your hand?"

"Give me proof," said the Earl, vehemently, "that you have not tampered with mine enemies."

"My lord," replied the old man, with dignity. "You can have no better proof than that which you yourself elected. In that turret I have spent the last twenty-four hours, under the key which has been in your own custody. The hours of darkness I have spent in gazing on the heavenly bodies with these dim eyes, and during those of light I have toiled this aged brain to complete the calculations arising from their combinations. Earthly food I have not tasted—earthly voice I have not heard—You are yourself aware I had no means of doing so—And yet I tell you—I who have been thus shut up in solitude and study—that within these twenty-four hours your star has become predominant in the horizon, and either the bright book of heaven speaks false, or there must have been a proportionate revolution in your fortunes upon earth —if nothing has happened within that space to secure your power, or advance your favour, then am I indeed a cheat, and the divine art, which was first devised in the plains of Chaldæa, is a foul imposture."

"It is true," said Leicester, after a moment's reflection, "thou wert closely immured—and it is also true that the change has taken place in my situation which thou sayest the horoscope indicates."

"Wherefore this distrust then, my son," said the astrologer, assuming a tone of admonition; "the celestial intelligences brook not diffidence, even in their favourites."

"Peace, father," answered Leicester, "I erred—not to mortal man, nor to celestial intelligence—under that which is Supreme—will Dudley's lips say more in condescension or apology. Speak rather to the present purpose—Amid these bright promises thou hast said there was a threatening aspect—Can thy skill tell whence, or by whose means, such danger seems to impend?"

"Thus far only," answered the astrologer, "does my art enable me to answer your query. The infortune is threatened by the malignant and adverse aspect, through means of a youth,—and, as I think, a rival; but whether in love or in prince's favour, I know not; nor can I give farther indication respecting him, than that he comes from the western quarter."

"The western—ha!" replied Leicester, "it is enough—the tempest does indeed brew in that quarter!—Cornwall and Devon—Raleigh and Tressilian—one of them is indicated—I must beware of both.— Father, if I have done thy skill injustice, I will make thee a lordly recompense."

He took a purse of gold from the strong casket which stood before him—"Have thou double the recompense which Varney promised.— Be faithful—be secret—Obey the directions thou shalt receive from my master of the horse, and grudge not at a little seclusion or restraint in my cause—it shall be richly considered.—Here, Varney—conduct this venerable man to thine own lodging—tend him heedfully in all things, but see that he holds communication with no one."

Varney bowed, and the astrologer kissed the Earl's hand in token of adieu, and followed the master of the horse to another apartment, in which were placed wine and refreshments for his use.

The astrologer sat down to his repast, while Varney shut two doors with great precaution, examined the tapestry, lest any listener lurked behind it, and then sitting down opposite to the sage, began to question him.

"Saw you my signal from the court beneath?"

"I did," said Alasco, for by such name he was at present called, "and shaped the horoscope accordingly."

"And it passed upon the patron without challenge?" continued Varney.

"Not without challenge," replied the old man, "but it did pass; and I added, as before agreed, danger from a discovered secret, and a western youth."

"My lord's fear will stand sponsor to the one, and his conscience to the other, of these prognostications," replied Varney. "Sure never man chose to run such a race as his, yet continued to retain those silly scruples! I am fain to cheat him to his own profit. But touching your matters, sage interpreter of the stars, I can tell you more of your own fortune than plan or figure can shew. You must begone from hence forthwith."

"I will not," said Alasco, peevishly. "I have been too much hurried up and down of late—immured for day and night in a desolate turret-chamber—I must enjoy my liberty, and pursue my studies, which are of more import than the fate of fifty statesmen, and favourites, that rise and burst like bubbles in the atmosphere of a court."

"At your pleasure," said Varney, with a sneer that habit had rendered familiar to his features, and which forms the principal characteristic which painters have assigned to that of Satan—"At your pleasure," he said, "you may enjoy your liberty, and your studies, until the daggers of Sussex's followers are clashing within your doublet, and against your ribs." The old man turned pale, and Varney proceeded. "Wot you not he hath offered a reward for the arch-quack and poison-vender, Demetrius, who sold certain precious spices to his lordship's cook?—What! turn you pale, old friend? Does Hali already see an infortune in the House of Life?—Why, heark thee, we will have thee down to an old house of mine in the country, where thou shalt live with a hob-nailed slave, whom thy alchemy may convert into ducats, for to such conversion alone is thy art serviceable."

"It is false, thou foul-mouthed railer," said Alasco, shaking with impotent anger; "it is well known that I have approached more nearly to projection than any hermetic artist who now lives. There are not six chemists in the world who possess so near an approximation to the grand arcanum"——

"Come, come," said Varney, interrupting him, "what means this, in the name of heaven? Do we not know one another? I believe thee to be so perfect,—so very perfect, in the mystery of cheating, that, having imposed upon all mankind, thou hast at length, in some measure, imposed upon thyself; and without ceasing to dupe others, hast become a species of dupe to thine own imagination. Blush not for it, man—thou art learned, and shalt have classical comfort:

> Ne quisquam Ajacem possit superare nisi Ajax.

No one but thyself could have gulled thee—And thou hast gulled the whole brotherhood of the Rosy Cross beside—none so deep in the mystery as thou. But heark thee in thine ear;—had the seasoning which spiced Sussex's broth wrought more surely, I would have thought better of the chemical science thou dost boast so highly."

"Thou art an hardened villain, Varney," replied Alasco; "many will do those things, who dare not speak of them."

"And many speak of them, who dare not do them," answered Varney; "but be not wroth—I will not quarrel with thee—If I did, I were fain to live on eggs for a month, that I might feed without fear. Tell me at once, how came thine art to fail thee at this great emergency?"

"The Earl of Sussex's horoscope intimates," replied the astrologer, "that the sign of the ascendant being in combustion"——

"Away with your gibberish," replied Varney; "think'st thou it is the patron thou speak'st with?"

"I crave your pardon," said the old man, "and swear to you, I know but one medicine that could have saved the Earl's life; and as no man living in England knows that antidote save myself,—moreover, as the ingredients, one of them in particular, are scarce possible to be come by, I must needs suppose his escape was owing to such a constitution of lungs and vital parts, as was never before bound up in a body of clay."

"There was some talk of a quack who waited on him," said Varney, after a moment's reflection. "Are you sure there is no one in England who has this secret of thine?"

"One man there was," said the doctor, "once my servant, who might have stolen this of me, with one or two other secrets of art. But content you, Master Varney, it is no part of my policy to suffer such interlopers to interfere in my trade. He pries into no mysteries more, I warrant you; for, as I well believe, he hath been wafted to heaven on the wing of a fiery dragon—Peace be with him.—But in this retreat of mine, shall I have the use of mine elaboratory?"

"Of a whole workshop, man," said Varney; "for a reverend father Abbot, who was fain to give place to bluff King Hal, and some of his courtiers, a score of years since, had a chemist's complete apparatus, which he was fain to leave behind him to his successors. Thou shalt there occupy, and melt, and puff, and blaze, and multiply, until the Green Dragon become a golden-goose, or whatever the newer phrase of the brotherhood may testify."

"Thou art right, Master Varney," said the alchemist, setting his teeth close, and grinding them together—"thou art right even in thy very contempt of right and of reason. For what thou sayest in mockery, may in sober verity chance to happen ere we meet again. If the most venerable sages of ancient days have spoken the truth—if the most learned of our own have rightly received it, if I have been accepted wheresoever I have travelled in Germany, in Poland, in Italy, and into the farther Tartary, as one to whom nature has unveiled her darkest secrets—if I have acquired the most secret signs and pass-words of the Jewish Cabala, so that the greyest beard in the synagogue would brush the steps to make them clean for me—if all this is so, there remains but one step—one little step—betwixt my long, deep, and dark and subterranean progress, and that blaze of light which shall shew Nature watching her richest and her most glorious production in the very cradle—One step betwixt dependence and the power of sovereignty—one step betwixt poverty and such a sum of wealth as earth, without that noble secret, cannot minister from all her mines in the old or the new-found world—to this I dedicate my future life, secure, for a brief period of studious patience, to rise above the mean dependence upon favourites, and *their* favourites, by which I am now enthralled!"

"Now, bravo! bravo! my good father," said Varney, with the usual Sardonic expression of ridicule on his countenance. "Yet all this approximation to the philosopher's stone, wringeth not one single crown out of my Lord Leicester's pouch, and far less out of Richard Varney's—*We* must have earthly and substantial services, man, and care not whom else thou canst delude with thy philosophical charlatanerie."

"My son Varney," said the alchemist, "the unbelief, gathered around thee like a frost-fog, hath dimmed thine acute perception to that which is a stumbling block to the wise, and which yet, to him who seeketh knowledge with humility, extends a lesson so clear, that he who runs may read. Hath not, think'st thou, Art the means of completing Nature's imperfect concoctions in her attempts to form the precious metals, even as by art we can perfect those other operations, of incubation, distillation, fermentation, and similar processes of an ordinary description, by which we extract life itself out of a senseless egg, summon purity and vitality out of muddy dregs, or call into vivacity the inert substance of a sluggish liquid?"

"I have heard all this before," said Varney; "and my heart is proof against such cant ever since I sent twenty good gold pieces, (marry it was in the nonage of my wit,) to advance the grand magisterium, which all, God help the while, vanished *in fumo*. Since that moment, when I paid for my freedom, I defy chemistry, astrology, palmistry, and every other occult art, were it as secret as hell itself, to unloose the stricture of my purse-strings. Marry, I neither defy the manna of Saint Nicholas, nor can I dispense with it. Thy first task must be to prepare some when thou getst down to my little sequestered retreat yonder, and then make as much gold as thou wilt."

"I will make no more of that dose," said the Alchemist, resolutely.

"Then," said the master of the horse, "thou shalt be hanged for what thou hast made already, and so were the Great Secret forever lost to mankind—do not on humanity this injustice, good father, but e'en bend to thy destiny, and make us an ounce or two of this same stuff, which cannot prejudice above one or two individuals, in order to gain time to discover the universal medicine, which shall clear away all mortal diseases at once. But cheer up, thou grave, learned, and most melancholy jackanape!—hast thou not told me, that a moderate portion of thy drug hath mild effects, no ways dangerous to the human frame, but which produce depression of spirits, nausea, headache, an unwillingness to change of place—even such a state of temper as would keep a bird from flying out of a cage, were the door left open?"

"I have said so, and it is true," said the alchemist; "this effect will it produce, and the bird who partakes of it in such proportion, shall sit for a season drooping on her perch, without thinking either of the free blue sky, or of the fair green wood, though the one be lighted by the rays of the rising sun, and the other ringing with the newly awakened song of all the feathered inhabitants of the forest."

"And this without danger to life?" said Varney, somewhat anxiously.

"Ay, so that proportion and measure be not exceeded; and so that one who knows the nature of the manna be ever near to watch the symptoms, and succour in case of need."

"Thou shalt regulate the whole," said Varney; "thy reward shall be princely, if thou keep'st time and touch, and exceedest not the due proportion to the prejudice of her health—otherwise thy punishment shall be as signal."

"The prejudice of *her* health!" repeated Alasco; "it is, then, a woman I am to use my skill upon?"

"No, thou fool," replied Varney, "said I not it was a bird—a reclaimed linnet, whose pipe might sooth a hawk when in mid stoop? —I see thine eye sparkle, and I know thy beard is not altogether so white as art has made it—*that*, at least, thou hast been able to transmute to silver. But mark me, this is no mate for thee. This caged bird is dear to one who brooks no rivalry, and far less such rivalry as thine, and her health must over all things be cared for. But she is in the case of being commanded down to yonder Kenilworth revels; and it is most expedient—most needful—most necessary, that she fly not thither. Of these necessities and their causes, it is not needful that she should know aught, and it is to be thought that her own wish may lead her to combat all ordinary reasons which can be urged for her remaining a house-keeper."

"That is but natural," said the alchemist with a strange smile, which yet bore a greater reference to the human character, than the uninterested and abstracted gaze which his physiognomy had hitherto expressed, where all seemed to refer to some world distant from that which was existing around him.

"It is so," answered Varney; "you understand women well, though it may have been long since you were conversant among them.—Well then, she is not to be contradicted—yet she is not to be humoured. Understand me—a slight illness, sufficient to take away the desire of removing from hence, and to make such of your wise fraternity as may be called in to aid, recommend a quiet residence at home, will, in one word, be esteemed good service, and remunerated as such."

"I am not to be asked to affect the House of Life?" said the chemist.

"On the contrary, we will have thee hanged if thou doest," replied Varney.

"And I must," added Alasco, "have opportunity to do my turn, and all facilities for concealment or escape, should there be detection."

"All, all, and every thing, thou infidel in all but the impossibilities of alchemy—Why, man, for what dost thou take me?"

The old man rose, and taking a light, walked towards the end of the apartment, where was a door which led to the small sleeping room destined for his reception during that night.—At the door he turned round, and slowly repeated Varney's question ere he answered it. "For what do I take thee, Richard Varney?—why, for a worse devil than I have been myself. But I am in your toils, and I must serve you till my term be out."

"Well, well," answered Varney hastily, "be stirring with grey light. It may be we shall not need thy medicine—Do nought till I myself come down—Michael Lambourne shall guide you to the place of your destination."

When Varney heard the adept's door shut and carefully bolted within, he stepped towards it, and with similar precaution carefully locked it on the outside, and took the key from the lock, muttering to himself, "Worse than *thee*, thou poisoning quack-salver and witch-monger, who, if thou art not a bounden slave to the devil, it is only because he disdains such an apprentice! I am a mortal man, and seek by mortal means the gratification of my passions, and advancement of my prospects—Thou art a vassal of hell itself.—So ho, Lambourne!" he called at another door, and Michael made his appearance, with a flushed cheek and an unsteady step.

"Thou art drunk, thou villain!" said Varney to him.

"Doubtless, noble sir," replied the unabashed Michael. "We have been drinking all night to the glories of the day, and to my noble Lord of Leicester, and his valiant master of the horse.—Drunk! oddspitti-kins, he that would refuse to swallow a dozen healths in such an even-ing, is a base besognio, and a puckfist, and shall swallow six inches of my dagger!"

"Hark ye, scoundrel," said Varney, "be sober on the instant—I command thee. I know thou canst throw off thy drunken folly, like a fool's coat, at thy pleasure; and if not, it were the worse for thee."

Lambourne drooped his head, left the apartment, and returned in two or three minutes with his face composed, his hair adjusted, his dress in order, and as great a difference from his former self as if the whole man had been changed.

"Art thou sober now, and doest thou comprehend me?" said Varney, sternly.

Lambourne bowed in acquiescence.

"Thou must presently down to Cumnor Place with the reverend man of art, who sleeps yonder in the little vaulted chamber. Here is the key, that thou may'st call him by times—take another trusty fellow with you—use him well on the journey, but let him not escape you—pistol him if he attempt it, and I will be your warrant. I will give thee letters to Forster. The doctor is to occupy the lower apartments of the eastern quadrangle, with freedom to use the old elaboratory and its implements.—He is to have no access to the lady but such as I shall point out—only she may be amused to see his philosophical jugglery. Thou wilt remain at Cumnor Place my farther orders; and, as thou livest, beware of the ale-bench and the aquavitæ flask. Each breath drawn in Cumnor Place must be kept severed from common air."

"Enough, my lord—I mean my worshipful master—soon, I trust, to be my worshipful knightly master. You have given me my lesson and my license;—I will execute the one, and will not abuse the other. I will be in the saddle by day-break."

"Do so, and deserve favour.—Stay—ere thou goest fill me a cup of wine—not out of that flask, sirrah,"—as Lambourne was pouring out from that which Alasco had left half finished, "fetch me a fresh one."

Lambourne obeyed, and Varney, after rinsing his mouth with the liquor, drank a full cup, and said, as he took up a lamp to retreat to his sleeping apartment, "It is strange—I am as little the slave of fancy as any one, yet I never speak for a few minutes with this fellow Alasco, but my mouth and lungs feel as if soiled with the fumes of calcined arsenic—pah!"

So saying, he left the apartment. Lambourne lingered, to drink a cup of the freshly opened flask. "It is from Saint-John's-Berg," he said, as he paused on the draught to enjoy its flavour, "and has the true relish of the violet. But I must forbear it now, that I may one day drink it at my own pleasure." And he quaffed a goblet of water to quench the fumes of the Rhenish wine, retired slowly towards the door, made a pause, and then, finding the temptation irresistible, walked hastily back, and took another long pull at the wine flask, without the formality of a cup.

"Were it not for this accursed custom," he said, "I might climb as high as Varney himself. But who can climb, when the room turns round with him like a parish-top? I would the distance were greater, or the road rougher, betwixt my hand and mouth!—But I will drink nothing to-morrow, save water—nothing save fair water."

Chapter Seben

> *Pistol.* And tidings do I bring, and lucky joys,
> And happy news of price.
> *Falstaff.* I prythee now deliver them like to men of this world.
> *Pistol.* A foutra for the world, and worldlings base!
> I speak of Africa, and golden joys.
> *Henry IV. Part 2*

THE PUBLIC ROOM of the Black Bear at Cumnor, to which the scene of our story now returns, boasted, on the evening which we treat of, no ordinary assemblage of guests. There had been a fair in the neighbourhood, and the cutting mercer of Abingdon, with some of the other personages whom the reader has already been made acquainted with, as friends and customers of Giles Gosling, had already formed their wonted circle around the evening fire, and were talking over the news of the day.

A lively, bustling, arch fellow, whose pack and oaken *ell-wand*, studded duly with brass points, denoted him to be of Autolycus's profession, occupied a good deal of the attention, and furnished a good deal of the amusement, of the evening. The pedlars of these days, it must be remembered, were men of far greater importance than the degenerate and degraded hawkers of our modern times. It was by means of these peripatetic venders that the country-trade, in the finer manufactures used in female dress particularly, was almost entirely carried on; and if a merchant of this description arrived at the dignity of travelling with a pack-horse, he was a person of no small consequence, and company for the most substantial yeoman or franklin whom he might meet in his wanderings.

The pedlar of whom we speak bore, accordingly, an active and unrebuked share in the merriment to which the rafters of the Bonny Black Bear of Cumnor resounded. He had his smile with pretty Mistress Cicely, his broad laugh with mine host, and his jest upon dashing Master Goldthread, who, though indeed without any such benevolent intention on his own part, was the general butt of the evening. The pedlar and he were closely engaged in a dispute upon the preference

due to the Spanish nether stock over the black Gascoigne hose, and
mine host had just winked to the guests around him, as who should
say, "You will have mirth presently, my masters," when the trampling
of horses was heard in the court-yard, and the hostler was loudly
summoned, with a few of the newest oaths then in vogue to add force
to the invocation. Out tumbled Will Hostler, John Tapster, and all the
militia of the inn, who had slunk from their posts in order to collect
some scattered crumbs of the mirth which was flying about among the
customers. Out sallied my host himself also, to do fitting salutation to
his new guests; and presently ushered into the apartment his own
worthy nephew, Michael Lambourne, pretty tolerably drunk, and
having under his escort the astrologer. Alasco, though still a little old
man, had, by altering his gown to a riding-dress, trimming his beard
and eye-brows, and so forth, struck at least a score of years from his
apparent age, and might now seem an active man of sixty, or little
upwards. He appeared at present exceedingly anxious, and insisted
with Lambourne that they should not enter the inn, but go straight
forward to the place of their destination. But Lambourne would not be
controuled. "By Cancer and Capricorn," he vociferated, "and the
whole heavenly host—besides all the stars I saw in the southern
heavens, to which these northern blinkers are but farthing candles, I
will be unkindly for no one's humour—I will stay and salute my worthy
uncle here.—Chesu! that good blood should ever be forgotten betwixt friends!—A gallon of your best, uncle, and let it go round to the
health of the noble Earl of Leicester!—What! Shall we not collogue
together, and warm the cockles of our ancient kindness?—Shall we
not collogue, I say?"

"With all my heart, kinsman," said mine host, who obviously wished
to be rid of him; "but are you to stand shot to all this good liquor?"

This is a question has quelled many a jovial toper, but it moved not
the purpose of Lambourne's soul. "Question my means, nuncle?" he
said, producing a handful of mixed gold and silver pieces; "question
Mexico and Peru—question the Queen's Exchequer—God save her
Majesty!—She is my good Lord's good mistress."

"Well, kinsman," said mine host, "it is my business to sell wine to
those who can buy it—So, Jack Tapster, do me thine office.—But I
would I knew how to come by money as lightly as thou doest, Mike."

"Why, uncle," said Lambourne, "I will tell thee a secret—D'ye see
this little old fellow here? as old and withered a chip as ever the devil
put into his porridge—and yet, uncle, between you and me—he hath
Potosi in that brain of his—'Sblood! he can coin ducats faster than I
can vent oaths."

"I will have none of his coinage in my purse though, Michael," said mine host; "I know what belongs to falsifying the Queen's coin."

"Thou art an ass, uncle, for as old as thou art—Pull me not by the skirts, doctor, thou art an ass thyself to boot—So, being both asses, I tell ye I spoke but metaphorically."

"Are you mad?" said the old man; "is the devil in you?—can you not let us begone without drawing all men's eyes on us?"

"Say'st thou?" said Lambourne; "Thou art deceived now—no man shall see you an I give the word.—By heavens, masters, an any one dare to look on this old gentleman, I will slash the eyes out of his head with my poniard—So sit down, old friend, and be merry—these are mine ancient inmates, and will betray no man."

"Had you not better withdraw to a private apartment, nephew," said Giles Gosling; "you speak strange matter," he added, "and there be intelligencers every where."

"I care not for them," said the magnanimous Michael—"intelligencers, pshaw!—I serve the noble Earl of Leicester—Here comes the wine—Fill around, Master Skinker, a carouse to the health of the Flower of England, the Noble Earl of Leicester! I say, the Noble Earl of Leicester! He that does me not reason is a swine of Sussex, and I'll make him kneel to the pledge, if I should cut his hams and smoke them for bacon."

None disputed a pledge given under such formidable penalties; and Michael Lambourne, whose drunken humour was not of course diminished by this new potation, went on in the same wild way, renewing his acquaintance with such of the guests as he had formerly known, and experiencing a reception in which there was now something of deference, mingled with a good deal of fear; for the least servitor of the favourite Earl, especially such a man as Lambourne, was, for very sufficient reasons, an object both of the one and the other.

In the meanwhile, the old man, seeing his guide in this uncontroulable humour, ceased to remonstrate with him, and sitting down in the most obscure corner of the room, called for a small measure of sack, over which he seemed, as it were, to slumber, withdrawing himself as much as possible from general observation, and doing nothing which could recal his existence to the recollection of his fellow-traveller, who by this time had got into close intimacy with his ancient comrade, Goldthread of Abingdon.

"Never believe me, bully Mike," said the mercer, "if I am not as glad to see thee as ever I was to see a customer's money!—Why, thou canst give a friend a sly place at a mask or a revel now, Mike; ay, or, I warrant thee, thou canst say in my lord's ear, when my honourable lord is down in these parts, and wants a Spanish ruff or the like—thou canst say in his ear, there is mine old friend, young Laurence

Goldthread of Abingdon, hath as good wares, lawn, tiffany, cambric, and so forth—ay, and is a pretty piece of man's flesh too as is in Berkshire, and will ruffle it for your lordship with any man of his inches; and thou may'st say"——

"I can say a hundred damned lies besides, mercer," answered Lambourne; "what, one must not stand upon a good word for a friend!"

"Here is to thee, Mike, with all my heart," said the mercer; "and thou canst tell one the reality of the new fashions too—Here was a rogue pedlar but now, was crying up the old-fashioned Spanish nether stock over the Gascoigne hose, although thou seest how well the French hose set off the leg and knee, being adorned with particoloured garters and garniture in conformity."

"Excellent, excellent," replied Lambourne; "why, thy limber bit of a thigh, thrust through that bunch of slashed buckram and tiffany, shews like a huswife's distaff, when the flax is half spun off."

"Said I not so?" said the mercer, whose shallow brain was now overflowed in his turn; "where then, where be this rascal pedlar?—there was a pedlar here but now, methinks—Mine host, where the foul fiend is this pedlar?"

"Where a wise man should be, Master Goldthread," replied Giles Gosling; "even shut up in his private chamber, telling over the sales of to-day, and preparing for the custom of to-morrow."

"Hang him, a mechanical chuff," said the mercer; "but for shame, it were a good deed to ease him of his wares,—a set of peddling knaves, who stroll through the land, and hurt the established trader. There are good fellows in Berkshire yet, mine host—Your pedlar may be met withal on Maiden Castle."

"Ay," replied Mine host, laughing, "and the meeter may meet his match—the pedlar is a tall man."

"Is he?" said Goldthread.

"Is he?" replied the host; "ay, by cock and pye is he—the very pedlar he who swaddled Robin Hood so tightly, as the song says,—

> Now Robin Hood drew his sword so good,
>   The pedlar drew his brand,
> And he hath raddled him, Robin Hood,
>   Till he neither could see nor stand."

"Hang him, foul scroyle, let him pass," said the mercer; "if he be such a one, there were small worship to be won upon him.—And now tell me, Mike—my honest Mike, how wears the Hollands you won of me?"

"Why, well, as you may see, Master Goldthread," answered Mike; "I will bestow a pot on thee for the handsel.—Fill the flaggon, Master Tapster."

"Thou wilt win no more Hollands, I think, on such wager, friend Mike," said the mercer; "for the sulky swain, Tony Forster, rails at thee all to nought, and swears you shall ne'er darken his doors again, for that your oaths are enough to blow the roof off a Christian man's dwelling."

"Doth he say so, the mincing hypocritical miser?" vociferated Lambourne;—"Why then he shall come down and receive my commands here, this blessed night, under my uncle's roof, and I will ring him such a black sanctus, that he shall think the devil hath him by the skirts for a month to come, for barely hearing me."

"Nay, now the pottle-pot is uppermost, with a witness," said the mercer. "Tony Forster obey thy whistle!—Alas! good Mike, go sleep —go sleep."

"I tell thee what, thou thin-faced gull," said Michael Lambourne, in high chafe, "I will wager thee fifty angels against the first five shelves of thy shop, numbering upward from the false light, with all that is on them, that I make Tony Forster come down to this public house, before we have finished three rounds."

"I will lay no bet to that amount," said the mercer, something sobered by an offer which intimated rather too private a knowledge, on Lambourne's part, of the secret recesses of his shop, "I will lay no such wagers," he said; "but I will stake five angels against thy five, if thou wilt, that Tony Forster will not leave his own roof, or come to ale-house after prayer time, for thee, or any man."

"Content," said Lambourne.—"Here, uncle, hold stakes, and let one of your young bleed-barrels there—one of your infant tapsters, trip presently up to the place, and give this letter to Master Forster, and say that I, his ingle Michael Lambourne, pray to speak with him at mine uncle's castle here, upon business of grave import.—Away with thee, child, for it is now sun down, and the wretch goeth to bed with the birds, to save mutton-suet—faugh!"

Shortly after this messenger was dispatched—an interval which was spent in drinking and buffoonery,—he returned with the answer, that Master Forster was coming presently.

"Won, won!" said Lambourne, darting on the stake.

"Not till he comes, if you please," said the mercer, interfering.

"Why, 'sblood, he is at the threshold," replied Michael—"What said he, boy?"

"If it please your worship," answered the messenger, "he looked out of window, with a musquetoon in his hand, and when I delivered your errand, which I did with fear and trembling, he said, with a vinegar aspect, that your worship might be gone to the infernal regions."

"Or to hell, I suppose," said Lambourne—"it is there he disposes of all that are not of the congregation."

"Even so," said the boy; "I used the other phrase, as the more poetical."

"An ingenuous youth," said Michael; "shalt have a drop to whet thy poetical whistle—and what said Forster next?"

"He called me back," answered the boy, "and bid me say, you might come to him, if you had aught to say to him."

"And what next?" said Lambourne.

"He read the letter, and seemed in a fluster, and asked if your worship was in drink—and I said you were speaking a little Spanish, as one who had been in the Canaries."

"Out, you diminutive pint-pot, whelped of an overgrown reckoning!" replied Lambourne—"Out!—But what said he then?"

"Why, he muttered, that if he came not, your worship would bolt out what were better kept in; and so he took his old flat cap, and thread-bare blue cloak, and, as I said before, he will be here incontinent."

"There is truth in what he said," replied Lambourne, as if speaking to himself—"My brain has played me its old dog's trick—but couragio —let him approach!—I have not rolled about in the world, for many a day, to fear Tony Forster, be I drunk or sober.—Bring me a flagon of cold water, to christen my sack withal."

While Lambourne, whom the approach of Forster seemed to have recalled to a sense of his own condition, was busied in preparing to receive him, Giles Gosling stole up to the apartment of the pedlar, whom he found traversing the room in much agitation.

"You withdrew yourself suddenly from the company," said the landlord to the guest.

"It was time, when the devil became one among you," replied the pedlar.

"It is not courteous in you to term my nephew by such a name," said Gosling, "nor is it kindly in me to reply to it; and yet, in some sort, Mike may be considered as a limb of Satan."

"Pooh—I talk not of the swaggering ruffian," replied the pedlar, "it is of the other, who, for aught I know—But when go they? or wherefore come they?"

"Marry, these are questions I cannot answer," replied the host. "But, look you, sir, you have brought me a token from worthy Master Tressilian—a pretty stone it is." He took out the ring, and looked at it, adding, as he put it into his purse again, that it was too rich a guerdon for any thing he could do for the worthy donor. He was, he said, in the public line, and it ill became him to be too inquisitive into other folks concerns; he had already said, that he could hear nothing, but that the lady lived still at Cumnor Place, in the closest seclusion, and, to such as by chance had a view of her, seemed pensive and discontent with her solitude. "But here," he said, "if you are desirous to gratify your master, is the rarest chance that hath occurred for this many a day. Tony Forster is coming down hither, and it is but letting Mike Lambourne smell another wine-flask, and the Queen's command would not move him from the ale-bench. So they are fast for an hour or so— Now, if you will don your pack, which will be your best excuse, you may, perchance, win the ear of the old servant, being assured of the master's absence, to let you try to get some custom of the lady, and then you may learn more of her condition than I or any other can tell you."

"True—very true," answered Wayland, for he it was; "an excellent device, but methinks something dangerous—for say Forster should return?"

"Very possible indeed," replied the host.

"Or say," continued Wayland, "the lady should render me cold thanks for my exertions?"

"As is not unlikely," replied Giles Gosling. "I marle, Master Tressilian will take such heed of her that cares not for him."

"In either case I were foully sped," said Wayland; "and therefore I do not, on the whole, much relish your device."

"Nay, but take me with you, good master serving-man," replied mine host, "this is your master's business and not mine. You best know the risk to be incurred, or how far you are willing to brave it. But that which you will not yourself hazard, you cannot expect others to risk."

"Hold, hold," said Wayland; "tell me but one thing—Goes yonder old man up to Cumnor?"

"Surely, I think so," said the landlord; "their servant said he was to take the baggage thither, but the ale-tap has been as potent for him as the sack-spiggot has been for Michael."

"It is enough," said Wayland, assuming an air of resolution—"I will thwart that old villain's projects—my affright at his baleful aspect begins to abate, and my hatred to arise. Help me on with my pack, good mine host—And look to thyself, old Albumazar—there is a malignant influence in thy horoscope, and it gleams from the constellation Ursa Major."

So saying, he assumed his burthen, and, guided by the landlord through the postern gate of the Black Bear, took the most private way from thence up to Cumnor Place.

Chapter Eight

Clown. You have of these pedlars, that have more
in 'em than you'd think, sister.
Winter's Tale, Act IV., Scene 3

IN HIS ANXIETY to obey the Earl's repeated charges of secrecy, as
well as from his own unsocial and miserly habits, Anthony Forster was
more desirous, by his mode of housekeeping, to escape observation,
than to resist intrusive curiosity. Thus, instead of a numerous household, to secure his charge, and defend his house, he studied, as much
as possible, to elude notice, by diminishing his attendants; so that,
unless when there were attendants of the Earl, or of Varney, in the
mansion, one old male domestic, and two old crones, who assisted in
keeping the Countess's apartment in order, were the only servants of
the family. It was one of these old women who opened the door when
Wayland knocked, and answered his petition, to be admitted to exhibit
his wares to the ladies of the family, with a volley of vituperation,
couched in what is there called the *jouring* dialect. The pedlar found
the means of checking this vociferation, by slipping a silver groat into
her hand, and intimating the present of some stuff for a coif, if the lady
would buy of his wares.

"God ield thee, for moine is aw in littocks—Slocket with thy pack
into gharn, mon—Her walks in gharn." Into the garden she ushered
the pedlar accordingly, and pointing to an old ruinous garden-house,
said, "Yonder be's her, mon,—yonder be's her—Zhe will buy
changes an zhe loikes stuffs."

"She has left me to come off as I may," thought Wayland, as he
heard the hag shut the garden-door behind him. "But they shall not
beat me, and they dare not murder me, for so little trespass, and by this
fair twilight. Hang it, I will on—a brave general never thought of his
retreat till he was defeated. I see two females in the old garden-house
yonder—But how to address them?—stay—Will Shakespeare, be my
friend in need. I will give them a taste of Autolycus." He then sung,
with a good voice, and becoming audacity, the popular play-house
ditty,

> "Lawn as white as driven snow,
> Cyprus black as e'er was crow,
> Gloves as sweet as damask roses,
> Masks for faces and for noses."

"What hath fortune sent us here for an unwonted sight, Janet?" said
the lady.

"One of these merchants of vanity, called pedlars," answered Janet, demurely, "who utters his light wares in lighter measures—I marvel old Dorcas let him pass."

"It is a lucky chance, girl," said the Countess; "we lead a heavy life here, and this may while off a weary hour."

"Aye, my gracious lady," said Janet; "but my father?"

"He is not *my* father, Janet, nor I hope my master," answered the lady—"I say, call the man hither—I want some things."

"Nay," replied Janet, "your ladyship hath but to say so in the next packet, and if England can furnish them they will be sent.—There will come mischief on't—pray, dearest lady, let me bid the man begone!"

"I will have thee bid him come hither," said the Countess,—"or stay, thou terrified fool, I will bid him myself, and spare thee a chiding."

"Ah! well-a-day, dearest lady, if that were the worst," said Janet, sadly, while the lady called to the pedlar, "Good fellow, step forward —undo thy pack—if thou hast good wares, chance has sent thee hither for my convenience, and thy profit."

"What may your ladyship please to lack?" said Wayland, unstrapping his pack, and displaying its contents with as much dexterity as if he had been bred to the trade. Indeed he had occasionally pursued it in the course of his roving life, and now commended his wares with all the volubility of a trader, and shewed some skill in the main art of placing prices upon them.

"What do I please to lack?" said the lady; "why, considering I have not for six long months bought one yard of lawn or cambric, or one trinket, the most inconsiderable, for my own use, and at my own choice, the better question is, what hast thou got to sell? Lay aside for me that cambric partlet and pair of sleeves—and those roundells of gold fringe, drawn out with cyprus—and that short cloak of cherry-coloured fine cloth, garnished with gold buttons and loops—is it not of an absolute fancy, Janet?"

"Nay, my lady," replied Janet, "if you consult my poor judgment, it is, methinks, over gawdy for a graceful habit."

"Now, out upon thy judgment, if it be no brighter, wench," said the Countess; "thou shalt wear it thyself for penance sake; and I promise, the gold buttons being somewhat massive, will comfort thy father, and reconcile him to the cherry coloured body. See that he snap them not away, Janet, and send them to bear company with the imprisoned angels which he keeps captive in his strong-box."

"May I pray your ladyship to spare my poor father!" said Janet.

"Nay, but why should any one spare him that is so sparing of his own nature?" replied the lady.—"Well, but to our gear—that head

garniture for myself, and that silver bodkin, mounted with pearl;—
and take off two gowns of that russet cloth for Dorcas and Alison,
Janet, to keep the old wretches warm against winter comes—And stay,
hast thou no perfumes and sweet-bags, or any handsome casting
bottles of the newest mode?"

"Were I pedlar in earnest, I were a made merchant," thought Wayland, as he busied himself to answer the demands which she
thronged one on another, with the eagerness of a young lady who has
been long secluded from such a pleasing occupation, "but how to
bring her to a moment's serious reflection." Then as he exhibited his
choicest collection of essences and perfumes, he at once arrested her
attention by observing, that these articles had almost arisen to double
value, since the magnificent preparations made by the Earl of Leicester to entertain the Queen and court at his princely Castle of Kenilworth.

"Ha!" said the Countess, hastily; "that rumour then is true, Janet."

"Surely, madam," answered Wayland; "and I marvel it hath not
reached your noble ladyship's ears. The Queen of England feasts with
the noble Earl for a week during the Summer's Progress; and there
are many who will tell you England will have a king, and England's
Elizabeth, God save her, a husband, ere the Progress be over."

"They lie like villains!" said the Countess, bursting forth
impatiently.

"For God's sake, madam, consider," said Janet, trembling with
apprehension; "who cumbers themselves about pedlar's tidings?"

"Yes, Janet!" exclaimed the Countess; "right, thou hast corrected
me justly. Such reports, blighting the reputation of England's brightest and noblest peer, can only find currency amongst the mean, the
abject, and the infamous."

"May I perish, lady," said Wayland Smith, observing that her violence directed itself towards him, "if I have done any thing to merit this
strange passion!—I have said but what many men say."

By this the Countess had recovered her composure, and endeavoured, alarmed by the anxious hints of Janet, to suppress all appearance of displeasure. "I were loth," she said, "good fellow, that our
Queen should change the virgin style, so dear to us her people—think
not of it." And then, as if desirous to change the subject, she added,
"And what is this paste, so carefully put up in the silver box?" as she
examined the contents of a casket in which drugs and perfumes were
contained in separate drawers.

"It is a remedy, madam, for a disorder, of which I trust your ladyship will never have reason to complain. The amount of a small turkey-
bean, swallowed daily for a week, fortifies the heart against those black

vapours which arise from solitude, melancholy, unrequited affection, disappointed hope"——

"Are you a fool, friend?" said the Countess, sharply; "or do you think, because I have good-naturedly purchased your trumpery goods at your roguish prices, that you may put any gullery you will on me?— Who ever heard that affections of the heart were cured by medicines given to the body?"

"Under your honourable favour," said Wayland, "I am an honest man, and have sold my goods at an honest price—As to this most precious medicine, when I told its qualities, I asked you not to purchase it, so why should I lie to you? I say not it will cure a rooted affection of the mind, which only God and time can do; but I say, that this restorative relieves the black vapours which are engendered in the body of that melancholy which broodeth in the mind. I have relieved many with it, both in court and city, and of late one Master Edmund Tressilian, a worshipful gentleman in Cornwall, who, on some slight, received, it was told me, where he had set his affections, was brought into that state of melancholy which made his friends alarmed for his life."

He paused, and the lady remained silent for some time, and then asked, with a voice which she strove in vain to render firm and indifferent in its tone, "Is the gentleman you have mentioned perfectly recovered?"

"Passably, madam," answered Wayland; "he hath at least no bodily complaint."

"I will take some of this medicine, Janet," said the Countess. "I too have sometimes that dark melancholy which overclouds the brain."

"You shall not do so, madam," said Janet; "who shall answer that this fellow vends what is wholesome?"

"I will myself warrant my good faith," said Wayland; and, taking a part of the medicine, he swallowed it before them. The Countess now bought what remained, a step to which Janet, by farther objections, only determined her the more obstinately. She even took the first dose upon the instant, and professed to feel her heart lightened and her spirits augmented,—a consequence which, in all probability, existed only in her own imagination. She then cast the purchases she had made together, flung her purse to Janet, and desired her to compute the amount and to pay the pedlar; while she herself, as if tired of the amusement she at first found in conversing with him, wished him good evening, and walked carelessly into the house, thus depriving Wayland of every opportunity to speak with her in private. He hastened, however, to attempt an explanation with Janet.

"Maiden," he said, "thou hast the face of one who should love her mistress. She hath much need of faithful service."

"And well deserves it at my hands," replied Janet; "but what of that?"

"Maiden, I am not altogether what I seem," said the pedlar, lowering his voice.

"The less like to be an honest man," said Janet.

"The more so," answered Wayland, "since I am no pedlar."

"Get thee gone then instantly, or I will call for assistance," said Janet; "my father must ere this be returned."

"Do not be so rash," said Wayland; "you will do what you may repent of. I am one of your mistress's friends; and she had need of more, not that thou should'st ruin those she hath."

"How shall I know that?" said Janet.

"Look me in the face," said Wayland Smith, "and see if thou dost not read honesty in my looks."

And in truth, though by no means handsome, there was in his physiognomy the sharp, keen expression of inventive genius and prompt intellect, which, joined to quick and brilliant eyes, a well-formed mouth, and an intelligent smile, often gives grace and interest to features which are both homely and irregular. Janet looked at him with the sly simplicity of her sect, and replied, "Notwithstanding thy boasted honesty, friend, and although I am not accustomed to read and pass judgment on such volumes as thou hast submitted to my perusal, I think I see in thy countenance something of the pedlar—something of the picaroon."

"On a small scale, perhaps," said Wayland Smith, laughing. "But this evening, or to-morrow, will an old man come hither with thy father, who has the stealthy step of the cat, the shrewd and vindictive eye of the rat, the fawning wile of the spaniel, the determined grasp of the mastiff—of him beware, for your own sake and that of your mistress. See you, fair Janet, he brings the venom of the aspic under the assumed innocence of the dove. What precise mischief he meditates towards you I cannot guess, but death and disease have ever dogged his footsteps.—Say nought of this to thy mistress—my art suggests to me that in her state, the fear of evil may be as dangerous as its operation—But see that she take my specific, for—(he lowered his voice and spoke low but impressively in her ear,) it is an antidote against poison—Hark, they enter the garden!"

In effect, a sound of noisy mirth and loud talking approached the garden door, alarmed by which Wayland Smith sprung into the midst of a thicket of overgrown shrubs, while Janet withdrew to the garden-house that she might not incur observation, and that she might at the same time conceal, at least for the present, the purchases made from the supposed pedlar, which lay scattered on the floor of the summer-house.

Janet, however, had no occasion for anxiety. Her father, his old attendant, Lord Leicester's domestic, and the astrologer, entered the garden in tumult and in extreme perplexity, endeavouring to quiet Lambourne, whose brain had now become completely fired with liquor, and who was one of those unfortunate persons, who, being once stirred with the vinous stimulus, do not fall asleep like other drunkards, but remain partially influenced by it for many hours, until at length, by successive draughts, they are elevated into a state of uncontroulable frenzy. Like many men in this state also, Lambourne neither lost the power of motion, speech, or expression; but, on the contrary, spoke with unwonted emphasis and readiness, and told all that at another time he would have been most desirous to have kept secret.

"What!" ejaculated Michael, at the full extent of his voice, "am I to have no welcome—no carouse, when I have brought fortune to your old ruinous dog-house in the shape of a devil's ally, that can change slate-shivers into Spanish dollars?—Here, you Tony Fire-the-Faggot, papist, puritan, hypocrite, miser, profligate, devil, compounded of all men's sins, bow down and reverence him who has brought into thy house the very mammon thou worshippest."

"For God's sake," said Forster, "speak low—come into the house —thou shalt have wine, or what thou wilt."

"No, old puckfist, I will have it here," thundered the inebriated ruffian—"here *al fresco*, as the Italian hath it.—No, no, I will not drink with that poisoning devil within doors, to be choked with the fumes of arsenic and quick-silver; I learned from Villain Varney to beware of that."

"Fetch him wine, in the name of all the fiends," said the alchemist.

"Aha! and thou wouldst spice it for me, old Truepenny, wouldst thou not? Ay, I should have coperas, and hellebore, and vitriol, and aquafortis, and twenty devilish materials, bubbling in my brain-pan like a charm to raise the devil in a witch's cauldron. Hand me the flask thyself, old Tony Fire-the-Faggot—and let it be cool—I will have no wine mulled at the pile of the old burned bishops—Or stay, let Leicester be King if he will—good—and Varney, Villain Varney, grand Vizier—why, excellent,—And what shall I be then?—Why, Emperor —Emperor Lambourne.—I will have this choice piece of beauty that they have walled up here for their private pleasures—I will have her this very night to serve my wine-cup, and put on my night-cap. What should a fellow do with two wives, were he twenty times an Earl?— Answer me that, Tony boy. You old reprobate hypocritical dog, whom

God struck out of the book of life, but tormented with the constant wish to be restored to it—you old bishop-burning, blasphemous fanatic, answer me that."

"I will stick my knife to the haft in him," said Forster, in a low tone, which trembled with passion.

"For the love of heaven, no violence," said the astrologer—"it cannot but be looked closely into.—Here, honest Lambourne, wilt thou pledge me to the health of the noble Earl of Leicester and Master Richard Varney?"

"I will, mine old Albumazar—I will, my trusty vender of rat's-bane —I would kiss thee, mine honest infractor of the Lex Julia, (as they said at Leyden,) didst thou not flavour so damnably of sulphur, and such fiendish apothecaries stuff.—Here goes it, up seyes—to Varney and Leicester!—two more noble mounting spirits—and more dark-seeking, deep-diving, high-flying, malicious, ambitious miscreants— well, I say no more, but I will whet my dagger on his heart-spone, that refuses to pledge me!—and so, my masters"——

Thus speaking, Lambourne exhausted the cup which the astrologer had handed him, and which contained not wine, but distilled spirits. He swore half an oath, dropped the empty cup from his grasp, laid his hand on his sword without being able to draw it, reeled, and fell without sense or motion into the arms of the domestic, who dragged him off to his chamber and put him to bed.

In the general confusion, Janet regained her lady's chamber unobserved, trembling like an aspen leaf, but determined to keep secret from the Countess the dreadful surmises which she could not help entertaining from the drunken ravings of Lambourne. Her fears, however, though they assumed no certain shape, kept pace with the advice of the pedlar; and she confirmed her mistress in her purpose of taking the medicine which he had recommended, from which it is probable she would otherwise have dissuaded her.

Neither had these intimations escaped the ears of Wayland, who knew much better how to interpret them. He had felt much compassion at beholding so lovely a creature as the Countess, and whom he had first seen in the bosom of domestic happiness, exposed to the machinations of such a gang of villains. His passions, too, had been highly excited, by hearing the voice of his old master, against whom he nourished, in equal degree, the passions of hatred and fear. He nourished also a pride in his own art and resources; and, dangerous as the task was, he that night formed a determination to attain the bottom of the mystery, and to aid the distressed lady, if it were yet possible. From some words which Lambourne had dropped amongst his ravings, Wayland now, for the first time, felt inclined to doubt that Varney had

acted entirely on his own account, in wooing and winning the affections of this beautiful creature. Fame asserted of this zealous retainer,
that he had accommodated his lord in former love intrigues; and it
occurred to Wayland Smith, that Leicester himself might be the party
chiefly interested. Marriage he could not suspect; but even the discovery of such a passing intrigue with a lady of Mistress Amy Robsart's
rank, was a secret of the deepest importance to the stability of the
favourite Earl's power over Elizabeth. "If Leicester would hesitate to
stifle such a rumour by very strange means," said he to himself, "he
has those about him who would do him that favour without waiting for
his consent. If I would meddle in this business, it must be as my old
master uses to compound his manna of Satan, with a close mask on my
face. So I will quit Giles Gosling to-morrow, and change my course
and place of residence as often as a hunted fox. I should like to see this
little puritan, too, once more. She looks both pretty and intelligent, to
have come of such a caitiff as Anthony Fire-the-Faggot."

Giles Gosling received the adieus of Wayland rather joyfully than
otherwise. The honest publican saw so much peril in crossing the
course of the Earl of Leicester's favourite, that his virtue was scarce
able to support him in the task, and he was well pleased when it was
likely to be removed from his shoulders; still, however, professing his
good will, and readiness, in case of need, to do Mr Tressilian or his
emissary any service, in so far as consisted with his character of a
publican.

Chapter Nine

Vaulting ambition, that o'erleaps itself,
And falls on 'tother side.

Macbeth

THE SPLENDOUR of the approaching revels at Kenilworth was now
the conversation through all England; and every thing was collected at
home, or from abroad, which could add to the gaiety or glory of the
proposed reception of Elizabeth, at the house of her most distinguished favourite. Meantime, Leicester appeared daily to advance in
the Queen's favour. He was perpetually by her side in council, willingly listened to in the moments of courtly recreation—favoured with
approaches even to familiar intimacy—looked up to by all who had
aught to hope at court—courted by foreign ministers with the most
flattering testimonies of respect from their sovereigns—the *Alter Ego*,
as it seemed, of the stately Elizabeth, who was now very generally
supposed to be studying the time and opportunity for associating him,
by marriage, into her sovereign power.

Amid such a tide of prosperity, this minion of fortune, and of the Queen's favour, was probably the most unhappy man in the realm which seemed at his devotion. He had the Fairy King's superiority over his friends and dependants, and saw much which they could not. The character of his mistress was intimately known to him; it was his minute and studied acquaintance with her humours, as well as her noble qualities, which, joined to his powerful mental qualities, and his eminent external accomplishments, had raised him so high in her favour; and it was that very knowledge of her disposition which led him to apprehend momentarily some sudden and overwhelming disgrace. He was like a pilot possessed of a chart, which points out to him all the peculiarities of his navigation, but which exhibits so many shoals, breakers, and reefs of rocks, that his anxious eye reaps little more from observing them, than to be convinced that his final escape can be little else than miraculous.

In fact, Queen Elizabeth had a character strangely compounded of the strongest masculine sense, with those foibles which are chiefly supposed proper to the female sex. Her subjects had the full benefit of her virtues, which far predominated over her weaknesses; but her courtiers, and those about her person, had often to sustain sudden and embarrassing turns of caprice, and the sallies of a temper which was both jealous and despotic. She was the nursing-mother of her people, but she was also the true daughter of Henry VIII.; and though early sufferings and an excellent education had repressed and modified, they had not altogether destroyed, the hereditary temper of that "hard-ruled King."—"Her mind," says her witty god-son, Sir John Harrington, who had experienced both the smiles and the frowns which he describes, "was oftime like the gentle air, that cometh from the western point in a summer's morn—'twas sweet and refreshing to all around her. Her speech did win all affections. And again, she could put forth such alterations, when obedience was lacking, as left no doubting *whose* daughter she was. When she smiled, it was a pure sunshine, that every one did chuse to bask in, if they could; but anon came a storm, from a sudden gathering of clouds, and the thunder fell, in a wondrous manner, on all alike."*

This variability of disposition, as Leicester well knew, was chiefly formidable to those who had a share in the Queen's affections, and depended rather on her personal regard, than on the indispensable services which they could render to her councils and her crown. The favour of Burleigh, or of Walsingham, of a description far less striking than that by which he was himself upheld, was founded, as Leicester well knew, in her judgment, not in her partiality; and was, therefore,

*Nugæ Antiquæ, Vol. I. pp. 355-356, 362.

free from all those principles of change and decay, necessarily incident to that which chiefly arose from personal accomplishments and female predilections. These great and sage statesmen were judged of by the Queen, only with reference to the measures they suggested, and the reasons by which they supported their opinions in council; whereas the success of Leicester's course depended on all those light and changeable gales of caprice and humour, which thwart or favour the progress of a lover in the favour of his mistress, and she, too, a mistress who was ever and anon becoming fearful lest she should forget the dignity, or compromise the authority of the Queen, while she indulged the affections of the woman. Of the difficulties which surrounded his power, "too great to keep or to resign," Leicester was fully sensible; and, as he looked anxiously round for the means of maintaining himself in his precarious situation, and sometimes contemplated those of descending from it with safety, he saw but little hope of either. At such moments, his thoughts turned to dwell upon his secret marriage, and its consequences; and it was with bitterness against himself, if not against his unfortunate Countess, that he ascribed to that hasty measure, adopted in the ardour of what he now called inconsiderate passion, at once the impossibility of placing his power on a solid basis, and the imminent prospect of its precipitate downfall.

"Men say," thus ran his thoughts, in these anxious and repentant moments, "that I might marry Elizabeth, and become King of England—all suggest this. The match is carolled in ballads, while the rabble throw their caps up—It has been touched upon in the schools—whispered in the presence-chamber—recommended from the pulpit—prayed for in the Calvinistic churches abroad—touched on by statists in the very council at home—These bold insinuations have been rebutted by no rebuke, no resentment, no chiding, scarce even by the usual female protestation that she would live and die a virgin princess.—Her words have been more courteous than ever, though she knows such rumours are abroad—her actions more gracious—her looks more kind—nought seems wanting to make me King of England, and place me beyond the storms of court-favour, excepting the putting forth of mine own hand to take that crown imperial, which is the glory of the universe! and when I might stretch that hand out most boldly, it is fettered down by a secret and inextricable bond.—And here I have letters from Amy," he would say, catching them up with a movement of peevishness, "persecuting me to acknowledge her openly—to do justice to her and to myself—and I wot not what—methinks I have done less than justice to myself already. And she speaks as if

Elizabeth were to receive the knowledge of this matter, with the glee of a mother hearing of the happy marriage of a hopeful son!—She, the daughter of Henry, who spared neither man in his anger, nor woman in his desire,—She to find herself tricked, drawn on with toys of passion to the verge of acknowledging her love to a subject, and he a married man!—Elizabeth to learn that she had been dallied with in such fashion, as a gay courtier might trifle with a country wench—We should then learn *furens quid fœmina!*"

He would then pause, and call upon Varney, whose advice was now more frequently resorted to than ever, because the Earl remembered the remonstrances which he had made against his secret contract. And their consultation usually terminated in anxious deliberation, how, or in what manner, the Countess was to be produced at Kenilworth. These communings had for some time ended always in a resolution to delay the Progress from day to day. But at length a peremptory decision became necessary.

"Elizabeth will not be satisfied without her presence," said the Earl; "whether any suspicion hath entered her mind, as my own apprehensions suggest, or whether the petition of Tressilian is kept in her memory by Sussex, or some other secret enemy, I know not; but amongst all the favourable expressions which she uses to me, she often recurs to the story of Amy Robsart. I think that Amy is the slave in the chariot, who is placed there by my evil fortune to dash and to confound my triumph, even when at the highest. Shew me thy device, Varney, for solving the inextricable difficulty. I have thrown such impediments in the way of these accursed revels as I could even with a shade of decency, but to-day's interview has put all to a hazard. She said to me kindly, but peremptorily, 'We will give you no farther time for preparations, my lord, lest you should altogether ruin yourself— On Saturday, the 9th of July, we will be with you at Kenilworth—we pray you to forget none of our appointed guests and suitors, and in especial this light-o'-love, Amy Robsart—we would wish to see the woman who could postpone yonder poetical gentleman, Master Tressilian, to your man, Richard Varney.'—Now, Varney, ply thine invention, whose forge hath availed us so often; for sure as my name is Dudley, the danger menaced by my horoscope is now darkening around me."

"Can my lady be by no means persuaded to bear for a brief space the obscure character which circumstances impose on her?" said Varney, after some hesitation.

"How, sirrah! My Countess term herself *thy* wife!—that may neither stand with my honour nor with her's."

"Alas! my lord," answered Varney, "and yet such is the quality in which Elizabeth now holds her; and to contradict this opinion is to discover all."

"Think of something else, Varney," said the Earl, in great agitation; "this invention is naught—If I could give way to it, she would not; for I tell thee, Varney, if thou know'st it not, that not Elizabeth on the throne has more pride than the daughter of this obscure gentleman of Devon. She is flexible in many things, but where she holds her honour brought in question, she hath a spirit and temper as apprehensive as lightning, and as swift in execution."

"We have experienced that, my lord, else had we not been thus circumstanced," said Varney. "But what else to suggest I know not—methinks she who gives rise to the danger, should do somewhat towards parrying it."

"It is impossible," said the Earl, waving his hand; "I know neither authority nor entreaties would make her endure thy name for an hour."

"It is somewhat hard though," said Varney, in a dry tone; and, without pausing on that topic, he added, "Suppose some one were found to represent her?—such feats have been performed in the courts of as sharp-eyed monarchs as Queen Elizabeth."

"Utter madness, Varney," answered the Earl; "the counterfeit would be confronted with Tressilian, and discovery become inevitable."

"Tressilian might be removed from court," said the unhesitating Varney.

"And by what means?"

"There are many," said Varney, "by which a statesman in your situation, my lord, may remove from the scene one who pries into your affairs, and places himself in perilous opposition to you."

"Speak not to me of such policy, Varney," said the Earl, hastily; "which, besides, would avail nothing in the present case. Many others may be at court, to whom Amy may be known; and besides, on the absence of Tressilian, her father or some of her friends would be instantly summoned hither. Urge thine invention once more."

"My lord, I know not what to say," answered Varney; "but were I myself in such a perplexity, I would ride post down to Cumnor Place, and compel my wife to give her consent to such measures as her safety and mine required."

"Varney," said Leicester, "I cannot urge her to aught so repugnant to her noble nature, as a share in this stratagem—it would be a base requital to the love she bears me."

"Well, my lord," said Varney, "your lordship is a wise and an honourable man, and skilled in those high points of romantic scruple, which are current in Arcadia, perhaps, as your nephew, Philip Sidney, writes. I am your humble servitor—a man of this world, and only happy that my knowledge of it, and its ways, is such as your lordship has not scorned to avail yourself of. Now I would fain know, whether the obligation lies on my lady or on you, in this fortunate union; and which has most reason to shew complaisance to the other, and consider their wishes, conveniences, and safety?"

"I tell thee, Varney," said the Earl, "that all it was in my power to bestow upon her, was not merely deserved, but a thousand times overpaid, by her own virtue and beauty; for never did greatness descend upon a creature so formed by nature to grace and adorn it."

"It is well, my lord, you are so satisfied," answered Varney, with his usual Sardonic smile, which even respect to his patron could not at all times subdue—"you will have time enough to enjoy undisturbed the society of one so gracious and beautiful—that is, so soon as such a confinement in the Tower be over, as may correspond to the crime of deceiving the affections of Elizabeth Tudor—A cheaper penalty, I presume, you do not expect."

"Malicious fiend!" answered Leicester, "do you mock me in my misfortune?—Manage it as thou wilt."

"If you are serious, my lord," said Varney, "you must set forth instantly, and post to Cumnor Place."

"Do thou go thyself, Varney; the devil has given thee that sort of eloquence, which is most powerful in the worst cause. I should stand self-convicted of villainy, were I to urge such a deceit.—Begone, I tell thee—Must I entreat thee to mine own dishonour?"

"No, my lord," said Varney—"but if you are serious in entrusting me with the task of urging this most necessary measure, you must give me a letter to my lady, as my credentials, and trust to me for backing the advice it contains with all the force in my power. And such is my opinion of my lady's love for your lordship, and of her willingness to do that which is at once to contribute to your pleasure and your safety, that I am sure she will condescend to bear, for a few brief days, the name of so humble a man as myself, especially since it is not inferior in antiquity to that of her own paternal house."

Leicester seized on writing materials, and twice or thrice commenced a letter to the Countess, which he after tore into fragments. At length he finished a few distracted lines, in which he conjured her, for reasons nearly concerning his life and honour, to consent to bear the name of Varney for a few days, during the revels at Kenilworth. He added, that Varney would communicate all the reasons which rendered this deception indispensable; and having signed and sealed these credentials, he flung them over the table to Varney, with a motion that he should depart, which his adviser was not slow to comprehend and to obey.

Leicester remained like one stupified, till he heard the trampling of the horses, as Varney, who took no time even to change his dress, threw himself into the saddle, and, followed by a single servant, set off for Berkshire. At the sound, the Earl started from his seat, and ran to the window, with the momentary purpose of recalling the unworthy commission with which he had entrusted one, of whom he used to say, he knew no virtuous property save affection to his patron. But Varney was already beyond call—and the bright starry firmament, which the age considered as the Book of Fate, lying spread before him when he opened the casement, diverted him from his better and more manly purpose.

"There they roll, on their silent but potential course," said the Earl, looking around him, "without a voice which speaks to our ear, but with influences which affect, at every change, the indwellers of this vile earthly planet. This, if astrologers fable not, is the very crisis of my fate! the hour approaches, of which I was taught to beware—the hour, too, which I was encouraged to hope for.—A King was the word—but how?—the crown matrimonial—all hopes of that are gone—let them go—the rich Netherlands have demanded me for their leader, and, would Elizabeth consent, would yield to me *their* crown.—And have I not such a claim, even in this kingdom?—that of York, descending from George of Clarence to the House of Huntingdon, which, this lady failing, may have a fair chance—Huntingdon is of my house.— But I will plunge no deeper in these high mysteries. Let me hold my course in silence for a while, and in obscurity, like a subterranean river —the time shall come that I will burst forth in my strength, and bear all opposition before me."

While Leicester was thus stupifying the remonstrances of his own conscience, by appealing to political necessity for his apology, or losing himself amidst the wild dreams of ambition, his agent left town and tower behind him, on his hasty journey to Berkshire. *He* also nourished high hope. He had brought Lord Leicester to the point which he desired, of committing to him the most intimate recesses of his breast, and of using him as the channel of his most confidential intercourse with his lady. Henceforward it would, he foresaw, be difficult for his patron either to dispense with his services, or refuse his requests, however unreasonable. And if this disdainful dame, as he termed the Countess, should comply with the request of her husband, Varney, her pretended husband, must needs become so situated with respect to her, that there was no knowing where his audacity might be bounded, perhaps not till circumstances enabled him to obtain a triumph, which he thought of with a mixture of fiendish feelings, in which revenge for her previous scorn was foremost and predominant. Again he contemplated the possibility of her being totally intractable, and refusing obstinately to play the part assigned to her in the drama at Kenilworth.

"Alasco must then do his part," he said—"Sickness must serve her Majesty as an excuse for not receiving the homage of Mrs Varney—ay, and a sore and a wasting sickness it may prove, should Elizabeth continue to cast so favourable an eye on my Lord of Leicester. I will not forego the chance of being favourite of a monarch for want of determined measures, should these be necessary.—Forward, good horse, forward—ambition, and haughty hope of power, pleasure, and revenge, strike their stings as deep through my bosom as I plunge the rowels in thy flanks—On, good horse, on—the devil urges us both forward."

Chapter Ten

Say that my beauty was but small,
    Among court ladies all despised;
Why didst thou rend it from that hall,
    Where, scornful Earl, 'twas dearly prized?

No more thou comest with wonted speed,
    Thy once beloved bride to see;
But be she alive or be she dead,
    I fear, stern Earl, 's the same to thee.
      Cumnor-Hall, by WILLIAM JULIUS MICKLE

THE LADIES OF FASHION of the present, or of any other period, must have allowed, that the young and lovely Countess of Leicester had, besides her youth and beauty, two qualities which entitled her to a place amongst women of rank and distinction. She displayed, as we have seen in her interview with the pedlar, a liberal promptitude to make unnecessary purchases, solely for the pleasure of acquiring useless and showy trifles which ceased to please as soon as they were possessed; and she was, besides, apt to spend a considerable space of time every day in adorning her person, although the varied splendour of her attire could only attract the half satirical praise of the precise Janet, or an approving glance from the bright eyes which witnessed their own beams of triumph reflected from the mirror.

The Countess Amy had, indeed, to plead for indulgence in those frivolous tastes, that the education of the times had done little or nothing for a mind naturally gay and averse to study. If she had not loved to collect finery and to wear it, she might have woven tapestry or sewed embroidery, till her labours spread in gay profusion all over the walls and seats at Lidcote-Hall; or she might have varied Minerva's labours with the task of preparing a mighty pudding against the time that Sir Hugh Robsart returned from the greenwood. But Amy had no natural genius either for the loom, the needle, or the receipt-book. Her mother had died in infancy; her father contradicted her in nothing; and Tressilian, the only one who approached her, that was able or desirous to attend to the cultivation of her mind, had much hurt his interest with her, by assuming too eagerly the task of a preceptor; so that he was regarded by the lively, indulged, and idle girl, with some fear and much respect, but little or nothing of that softer emotion which it had been his hope and his ambition to inspire. And thus her heart lay readily open, and her fancy became easily captivated by the noble exterior and graceful deportment, and complacent flattery of Leicester, even before he was known to her as the dazzling minion of wealth and power.

The frequent visits of Leicester at Cumnor, during the earlier part of their union, had reconciled the Countess to the solitude and privacy to which she was condemned; but when these visits became rarer and more rare, and when the void was filled up with letters of excuse, not always very warmly expressed, and generally extremely brief, discontent and suspicion began to haunt almost constantly those splendid apartments which love had fitted up for beauty. Her answers to Leicester conveyed these feelings too bluntly, and pressed more naturally than prudently that she might be relieved from this obscure and secluded residence, by the Earl's acknowledgment of their marriage; and in arranging her arguments with all the skill she was mistress of, she trusted chiefly to the warmth of the entreaties with which she urged them. Sometimes she even ventured to mingle reproaches, of which Leicester conceived he had good reason to complain.

"I have made her Countess," he said to Varney, "surely she might wait till it consisted with my pleasure that she should put on a coronet."

The Countess Amy viewed the subject in directly an opposite light.

"What signifies," she said, "that I have rank and honour in reality, if I am to live an obscure prisoner, without either society or observance, and suffering in my character, as one of dubious or disgraced reputation? I care not for all those strings of pearl, which you fret me by warping into my tresses, Janet. I tell you, that at Lidcote-Hall, if I put but a fresh rose-bud among my hair, my good father would call me to him, that he might see it more closely; and the kind old curate would smile, and Master Mumblazon would say something about roses gules; and now I sit here, decked out like an image with gold and gems, and no one to see my finery but you, Janet. There was the poor Tressilian too—but it avails not speaking of him."

"It doth not, indeed, madam," said her prudent attendant; "and verily you make me sometimes wish you would not speak of him so often, or so rashly."

"It signifies nothing to warn me, Janet—I was born free, though I am now mewed up here like some fine foreign slave, rather than the wife of an English noble. I bore it all with pleasure while I was sure he loved me; but now, my tongue and heart shall be free, let them fetter my limbs as they will.—I tell thee, Janet, I love my husband—I will love him till my latest breath—I cannot cease to love him, even if I would, or if he—which, God knows, may chance—should cease to love me. But I will say, and loudly, I would have been happier to have remained in Lidcote-Hall; even although I must have married poor Tressilian, with his melancholy look, and his head full of learning, which I cared not for. He said if I would read his favourite volumes, there would come a time that I should be glad of it—I think it is come now."

"I bought you some books, madam," said Janet, "from a lame fellow who sold them in the Market-place yesterday—and who stared something boldly at me, I promise you."

"Let me see them, Janet," said the Countess; "but let them not be of your own precise cast.—How is this, most righteous damsel?—'A Pair of Snuffers for the Golden Candlestick'—'A Handful of Myrrh and Hissop to put a Sick Soul to its Purgation'—'A Draught of Water from the Valley of Baca'—'Foxes and Firebrands'—what gear call you this, maiden?"

"Nay, madam," said Janet, "it was but fitting and seemly to put grace in your ladyship's way; but an you will none of it, there are play-books, and poet-books, I trow."

The Countess proceeded carelessly in her examination, turning over such rare volumes as would now make the fortune of twenty retail booksellers. Here was a "Boke of Cookery, imprinted by Richard Lant," and "Skelton's Books"—"The Passtime of the People"—"The Castle of Knowledge," &c. But neither to this lore did the Countess's heart incline, and joyfully did she start up from the listless task of turning over the leaves of the pamphlets, and hastily did she scatter them through the floor, when the hasty clatter of horse's feet, heard in the court-yard, called her to the window, exclaiming, "It is Leicester!—it is my noble Earl!—it is my Dudley!—Every stroke of his horse's hoof sounds like a note of lordly music!"

There was a brief bustle in the castle, and Forster, with his down-ward look and sullen manner, entered the apartment to say, "that

Master Richard Varney was arrived from my lord, having ridden all night, and craved to speak with her ladyship instantly."

"Varney?—and to speak with me?—pshaw!—but he comes with news from Leicester—so admit him instantly."

Varney entered her dressing apartment, where she sat arrayed in her native loveliness, adorned with all that Janet's art, and a rich and tasteful undress, could bestow. But the most beautiful part of her attire was her beautiful and luxuriant light-brown locks, which floated in such rich abundance around a neck that resembled a swan's, and over a bosom heaving with an anxious expectation, which communicated a hurried tinge of red to her whole countenance.

Varney entered the room in the dress in which he had waited on his master that morning to court, and the splendour of which made a strange contrast with the disorder arising from hasty riding, during a dark night and foul ways. His brow bore an anxious and hurried expression, as one who has that to say of which he doubts the reception, and who yet hath posted on from the necessity of communicating the tidings. The Countess's anxious eye at once caught the alarm, as she exclaimed, "You bring news from my lord, Master Varney—Gracious Heaven, he is ill."

"No, madam, thank Heaven!" said Varney. "Compose yourself, and permit me to take breath ere I communicate my tidings."

"No breath, sir," replied the lady, impatiently; "I know your theatrical arts. Since your breath hath sufficed to bring you hither, it may suffice to tell your tale, at least briefly, and in the gross."

"Madam," answered Varney, "we are not alone, and my lord's message was for your ears only."

"Leave us, Janet, and Master Forster," said the lady; "but remain in the next apartment, and within call."

Forster and his daughter retired, agreeably to the Lady Leicester's commands, into the next apartment, which was the withdrawing-room. The door which led from the sleeping-chamber was then carefully shut and bolted, and the father and daughter remained both in a posture of anxious attention, the first with a stern, suspicious, anxious cast of countenance, and Janet with folded hands, and looks which seemed divided betwixt her desire to know the fortunes of her mistress, and her prayers to Heaven for her safety. Anthony Forster seemed himself to have some idea of what was passing through his daughter's mind, for he crossed the apartment and took her anxiously by the hand, saying, "That is right—pray, Janet, pray—we have all need of prayers, and some of us more than others—pray, Janet—I would pray myself, but I must listen to what goes on within—evil has been brewing, love—evil has been brewing—God forgive our sins, but

Varney's sudden and strange arrival bodes no good."

Janet had never before heard her father excite or even permit her attention to any thing which passed in their mysterious family, and now that he did so, his voice sounded in her ear—she knew not why— like that of a screech-owl denouncing some deed of terror and of woe. She turned her eyes fearfully towards the door, almost as if she expected some sounds of horror to be heard, or some sight of fear to display itself.

All, however, was as still as death, and the voices of those who spoke in the inner-chamber, were, if they spoke at all, carefully subdued to a tone which could not be heard in the next. At once, however, they were heard to speak fast, thick, and hastily; and presently after the voice of the Countess was heard exclaiming, at the highest pitch to which indignation could raise it, "Undo the door, sir, I command you! —undo the door!—I will have no other reply!" she continued, drowning with her vehement accents the low and muttered sounds which Varney was heard to utter betwixt whiles. "What ho! without there!" she persisted, accompanying her words with shrieks, "Janet, alarm the house!—Forster, break ope the door—I am detained here by a traitor!—use axe and lever, Master Forster—I will be your warrant!"

"It shall not need, madam," Varney was at length distinctly heard to say. "If you please to expose my lord's important concerns and your own to the general ear, I will not be your hindrance."

The door was unlocked and thrown open, and Janet and her father rushed in, anxious to learn the cause of these reiterated exclamations.

When they entered the apartment, Varney stood by the door grinding his teeth, with an expression in which rage, and shame, and fear, had each their share. The Countess stood in the midst of her apartment like a juvenile Pythoness, under the influence of the prophetic fury. The veins in her beautiful forehead started into swoln blue lines through the hurried impulse of the circulation—her cheek and neck glowed like scarlet—her eyes were like those of an imprisoned eagle, flashing red lightning on the foes whom it cannot reach with its talons. Were it possible for one of the Graces to have been animated by a Fury, the countenance could not have united so much beauty with so much hatred, scorn, defiance, and resentment. The gesture and attitude corresponded with the voice and looks, and altogether presented a spectacle which was at once beautiful and fearful; so much of the sublime had the energy of passion united with the Countess Amy's natural loveliness. Janet, as soon as the door was open, ran to her mistress; and more slowly, yet with more haste than he was wont, Anthony Forster went to Richard Varney.

"In the Truth's name, what ails your ladyship?" said the former.

"What, in the name of Satan, have you done to her?" said Forster to his friend.

"Who, I?—nothing," answered Varney, but with sunken head and sullen voice; "nothing but communicated to her her lord's commands, which, if the lady list not to obey, she knows better how to answer it than I may pretend to do."

"Now, by Heaven, Janet!" said the Countess, "the false traitor lies in his throat!—he must needs lie, for he speaks to the dishonour of my noble lord—he must needs lie doubly, for he speaks to gain ends of his own, equally execrable and unattainable."

"You have misapprehended me, lady," said Varney, with a sulky species of submission and apology; "let this matter rest till your passion be abated, and I will explain all."

"Thou shalt never have an opportunity to do so," said the Countess. —"Look at him, Janet—he is fairly dressed, hath the outside of a gentleman, and hither he came to persuade me it was my lord's pleasure—nay, more, my wedded lord's commands, that I should go with him to Kenilworth, and before the Queen and nobles, and in presence of my own wedded lord, that I should acknowledge him— *him* there—that very cloak-brushing, shoe-cleaning fellow—*him* there, my lord's lacquey, for my liege lord and husband; furnishing against myself, great God! whenever I was to claim my right and my rank, such weapons as would hew my just claims from the root, and destroy my character to be regarded as an honourable matron of the English nobility!"

"You hear her, Forster, and you, young maiden, hear this lady," answered Varney, taking advantage of the pause which the Countess had made in her charge, more for lack of breath than for lack of matter —"You hear that her heat only objects to me the course which our good lord, for the purpose to keep certain matters secret, suggests in the very letter which she holds in her hands."

Forster here attempted to interfere with a face of authority, which he thought became the charge entrusted to him, "Nay, lady, I must needs say you are hasty in this—Such deceit is not utterly to be condemned when practised for a righteous end; and thus even the patriarch Abraham feigned Sarah to be his sister when they went down to Egypt."

"Ay, sir," answered the Countess; "but God rebuked that deceit even in the father of his chosen people, by the mouth of the heathen Pharaoh. Out upon you, that will read Scripture only to copy those things, which are held out to us as warnings, not as examples!"

"But Sarah disputed not the will of her husband, an it be your pleasure," said Forster, in reply; "but did as Abraham commanded, calling herself his sister, that it might be well with her husband for her sake, and that his soul might live because of her beauty."

"Now, so Heaven pardon me my useless anger," answered the Countess, "thou art as daring a hypocrite as yonder fellow is an impudent deceiver. Never will I believe that the noble Dudley gave countenance to so dastardly, so dishonourable a plan—thus I tread on his infamy, if his indeed it be, and thus destroy its remembrance for ever!"

So saying, she tore to pieces Leicester's letter, and stamped, in the extremity of impatience, as if she would have annihilated the minute fragments into which she had rent it.

"Bear witness," said Varney, collecting himself, "she has torn my lord's letter, in order to burthen me with the scheme of his devising; and although it promises nought but danger and trouble to me, she would lay it to my charge, as if I had any purpose of mine own in it."

"Thou liest, thou treacherous slave!" said Countess Amy, in spite of Janet's attempts to keep her silent, in the sad foresight that her vehemence might only furnish arms against herself. "Thou liest," she continued—"Let me go, Janet—Were it the last word I have to speak, he lies—he had his own foul ends to seek; and broader he would have displayed them, had my passion permitted me to preserve the silence which at first encouraged him to unfold his vile projects."

"Madam," said Varney, overwhelmed in spite of his effrontery, "I entreat you to believe yourself mistaken."

"As soon will I believe light darkness—have I drank of oblivion?— do I not remember former passages, which, known to Leicester, had gained thee the preferment of a gallows, instead of the honour of his intimacy.—I would I were a man but for five minutes—it were space enough to make a craven like thee confess his villainy. But go— begone—tell thy master, that when I take the foul course to which such scandalous deceits as thou hast recommended on his behalf must necessarily lead me, I will give him a rival something worthy of the name. He shall not be supplanted by an ignominious lacquey, whose best fortune is to catch his master's last suit of clothes ere it is thread-bare, and who is only fit to seduce a suburb-wench by the bravery of new roses in his master's old pantofles. Go, begone, sir—I scorn thee so much, that I am ashamed to have been angry with thee."

Varney left the room with a mute expression of rage, and was followed by Forster, whose apprehension, naturally slow, was over-powered by the eager and abundant discharge of indignation, which, for the first time, he had heard burst from the lips of a being, who had seemed till that moment too languid, and too gentle, to nurse an angry thought, or utter an intemperate expression. Forster, therefore, pursued Varney from place to place, persecuting him with interrogatories, to which the other replied not, until they were in the opposite side of the quadrangle, and in the old library with which the reader has already been made acquainted. Here he turned round on his persevering follower, and thus addressed him, in a tone tolerably equal; that brief walk having been sufficient to give one so habituated to command his temper, time to rally and recover his presence of mind.

"Tony," he said, with his usual sneering laugh, "it avails not to deny the Woman and the Devil, who, as thine oracle Holdforth will confirm to thee, cheated man at the beginning, have this day proved more powerful than my discretion. Yon termagant looked so tempting, and had the art to preserve her countenance so naturally, while I communicated my lord's message, that, by my faith, I thought I might say some little thing for myself. She thinks she hath my head under her girdle now, but she is deceived.—Where is Doctor Alasco?"

"In his laboratory," answered Forster; "it is the hour he is not spoken withal—we must wait till noon is past, or spoil his important— What said I important?—I would say interrupt his divine studies."

"Ay, he studies the devil's divinity," said Varney,—"but when I want him, one hour must suffice as well as another—lead the way to his pandæmonium."

So spoke Varney, and with hasty and perturbed steps followed Forster, who conducted him through private passages, many of which were well nigh ruinous, to the opposite side of the quadrangle, where, in a subterranean apartment, now occupied by the chemist Alasco, one of the Abbots of Abingdon, who had a turn for the occult sciences, had, much to the scandal of his convent, established a laboratory, in which, like other fools of the time, he spent much precious time, and money besides, in pursuit of the grand arcanum.

Anthony Forster paused before the door, which was scrupulously secured within, and again shewed a marked hesitation to disturb the sage in his operations. But Varney, less scrupulous, roused him, by knocking and voice, until at length, slowly and reluctantly, the inmate of the apartment undid the door. The chemist appeared, with his eyes bleared with the heat and vapours of the stove or alembic over which he brooded, and the interior of his cell displayed the confused assemblage of heterogeneous substances, and extraordinary implements, belonging to his profession. The old man was muttering, with spiteful impatience, "Am I for ever to be recalled to the affairs of earth from those of heaven?"

"To the affairs of hell," answered Varney, "for that is thy proper element.—Forster, we need thee at our conference."

Forster slowly entered the room. Varney, following, barred the door, and they betook themselves to secret council.

In the meanwhile, the Countess traversed the apartment, with shame and anger contending on her lovely cheek.

"The villain," she said, "the cold-blooded calculating slave!—but I unmasked him, Janet—I made the snake uncoil all his folds before me, and crawl abroad in his naked deformity—I suspended my resentment, at the danger of suffocating under the effort, until he had let me see the very bottom of a heart more foul than hell's darkest corner.—And thou, Leicester, is it possible thou couldst bid me for a moment deny my wedded right in thee, or thyself yield it to another? But it is impossible—the villain has lied in all.—Janet, I will not remain here longer—I fear him—I fear thy father—I grieve to say it, Janet—but I fear thy father, and, worst of all, this odious Varney. I will escape from Cumnor."

"Alas! madam, whither would you fly, or by what means will you escape from these walls?"

"I know not, Janet," said the unfortunate young lady, looking upwards, and clasping her hands together, "I know not where I shall fly, or by what means; but I am certain the God I have served will not abandon me in this dreadful crisis, for I am in the hands of wicked men."

"Do not think so, dear lady," said Janet; "my father is stern and strict in his temper, and severely true to his trust—but yet"——

"Speak not of him, Janet," replied the lady; "for thy sake I have striven to fear him less—but it will not be."

At this moment, Anthony Forster entered the apartment, bearing in his hand a glass cup, and a small flask. His manner was singular; for, while approaching the Countess with the respect due to her rank, he had till this time suffered to become visible, or had been unable to suppress, the obdurate sulkiness of his natural disposition, which, as is usual with those of his unhappy temper, was chiefly exerted towards those over whom circumstances gave him controul. But at present he shewed nothing of that sullen consciousness of authority which he was wont to conceal under a clumsy affectation of civility and deference, as a ruffian hides his pistols and bludgeon under his ill-fashioned gaberdine. And yet it seemed as if his smile was more in fear than in courtesy, and as if, while he pressed the Countess to taste of the choice cordial, which should refresh her spirits after her late alarm, he was conscious of meditating some farther injury. His hand trembled also, his voice faultered, and his whole outward behaviour exhibited so much that was suspicious, that his daughter Janet, after she had stood looking at him in astonishment for some seconds, seemed at once to collect herself to execute some hardy resolution, raised her head, assumed an attitude and gait of determination and authority, and walking slowly betwixt her father and her mistress, took the salver from the hand of the former, and said in a low, but marked and decided tone, "Father, I will fill for my noble mistress, when such is her pleasure."

"Thou, my child?" said Forster, eagerly and apprehensively; "no, my child—it is not thou shalt render the lady this service."

"And why, I pray you," said Janet, "if it be fitting that the noble lady should partake of the cup at all?"

"Why—why," said the seneschal, hesitating, and then bursting into passion, as the readiest mode of supplying the lack of all other reason —"Why, because it is my pleasure, minion, that you should not—get you gone to the evening lecture."

"Now, as I hope to hear lecture again," replied Janet, "I will not go thither this night, unless I am better assured of my mistress's safety. Give me that flask, father;"—and she took it from his reluctant hand, while he resigned it as if conscience-struck—"And now," she said, "father, that which shall benefit my mistress, cannot do *me* prejudice —father, I drink to you."

Forster, without speaking a word, rushed on his daughter and wrested the flask from her hand; then, as if embarrassed by what he had done, and totally unable to resolve what he should do next, he stood with it in his hand, one foot advanced and the other drawn back, glaring on his daughter with a countenance, in which rage, fear, and convicted villainy, formed a hideous combination.

"This is strange, my father," said Janet, keeping her eye fixed on his, in the manner in which those who have the charge of lunatics are said to overawe their unhappy patients; "will you neither let me serve my lady, nor drink to her myself?"

The courage of the Countess sustained her through this dreadful scene, of which the import was not the less obvious that it was not even hinted at. She preserved even the rash carelessness of her temper, and though her cheek had grown pale at the first alarm, her eye was calm and almost scornful. "Will *you* taste this rare cordial, Master Forster? perhaps you will not yourself refuse to pledge us, though you permit not Janet to do so—drink, sir, I pray you."

"I will not," answered Forster.

"And for whom, then, is the precious beverage reserved, sir?" said the Countess.

"For the devil, who brewed it," answered Forster; and, turning on his heel, he left the chamber.

Janet looked at her mistress with a countenance expressive in the highest degree of shame, dismay, and sorrow.

"Do not weep for me, Janet," said the Countess, kindly.

"No, madam," replied her attendant, in a voice broken by sobs, "it is not for you I weep, it is for myself—it is for that unhappy man. Those who are dishonoured before man—those who are condemned by God, have cause to mourn—not those who are innocent!—Farewell, madam!" she said, hastily assuming the mantle in which she was wont to go abroad.

"Do you leave me, Janet?" said her mistress—"desert me in such an evil strait?"

"Desert you, madam!" exclaimed Janet; and, running back to her mistress, she imprinted a thousand kisses on her hand—"desert you! —may the hope of my trust desert me when I do so!—No, madam; well you said the God you serve will open you a path for deliverance. There is a way of escape; I have prayed night and day for light, that I might see how to act betwixt my duty to yonder unhappy man, and that which I owe to you. Sternly and fearfully that light has now dawned, and I must not shut the door which God opens.—Ask me no more. I return in brief space."

So speaking, she wrapped herself in her mantle, and saying to the old woman whom she passed in the outer room, that she was going to evening prayer, she left the house.

Meanwhile her father had reached once more the laboratory, where he found the accomplices of his intended guilt.

"Has the sweet bird sipped?" said Varney, with half a smile; while the astrologer put the same question with his eyes, but spoke not a word.

"She has not, nor she shall not from my hands," replied Forster; "would you have me do murther in my daughter's presence?"

"Wert thou not told, thou sullen and yet faint-hearted slave," answered Varney with bitterness, "that no *murther*, as thou call'st it, with that staring look and stammering tone, is designed in the matter? —wert thou not told, that a brief illness, such as a woman puts on in very wantonness, that she may wear her night-gear at noon, and lie on a settle when she should mind her domestic business, is all here aimed at? Here is a learned man will swear it to thee by the key of the Castle of Wisdom."

"I swear it," said Alasco, "that the elixir thou hast there in the flask will not prejudice life! I swear it by that immortal and indestructible quintessence of gold, which pervades every substance in nature, though its secret existence can be traced by him only, to whom Tresmigistus renders the key of the Cabala."

"An oath of force," said Varney. "Forster, thou wert worse than a pagan to disbelieve it. Believe me, moreover, who swear by nothing but my own word, that if you be not conformable, there is no hope, no, not a glimpse of hope, that this thy leasehold may be transmewed into a copyhold. Thus, Alasco will leave your pewter artillery untransmigrated, and I, honest Anthony, will still have thee for my tenant."

"I know not, gentlemen," said Forster, "where your designs tend; but in one thing I am bound up,—that, fall back fall edge, I will have one in this place that may pray for me, and that one shall be my daughter. I have lived ill, and the world has been too weighty with me; but she is as innocent as ever she was when on her mother's lap, and she, at least, shall have her portion in that happy city, whose walls are of pure gold, and the foundations garnished with all manner of precious stones."

"Ay, Tony," said Varney, "that were a paradise to thy heart's contents.—Debate the matter with him, Doctor Alasco; I will be with you anon."

So speaking, Varney arose, and, taking the flask from the table, he left the room.

"I tell thee, my son," said Alasco to Forster, as soon as Varney had left them, "that whatever this bold and profligate railer may say of the mighty science, in which, by heaven's blessing, I have advanced so far, that I would not call the wisest of living artists my better or my teacher —I say, howsoever yonder reprobate may scoff at things too holy to be apprehended by men merely of carnal and evil thoughts, yet believe, that the city beheld by St John, in that bright vision of the Apocalypse, that New Jerusalem, of which all Christian men hope to partake, sets forth typically the discovery of the GRAND SECRET, whereby the most precious and perfect of Nature's works are elicited out of her basest and most crude productions; just as the light and gaudy butterfly, the most beautiful child of the summer breeze, breaks forth from the dungeon of a sordid chrysalis."

"Master Holdforth said nought of this exposition," said Forster, doubtfully—"And moreover, Doctor Alasco, the Holy Writt says, that the gold and precious stones of the Holy City are in no sort for those who work abomination or frame lies."

"Well, my son," said the Doctor, "and what is your inference from thence?"

"That those," said Forster, "who distil poisons, and administer them in secrecy, can have no portion in those unspeakable riches."

"You are to distinguish, my son," replied the alchemist, "betwixt that which is necessarily evil in its progress and in its end also, and that which being evil, is, nevertheless, capable of working forth good. If, by the death of one person, the happy period shall be approached nearer to us, in which all that is good shall be attained, by wishing its presence

—all that is evil escaped, by desiring its absence—in which sickness, and pain, and sorrow, shall be the obedient servants of human wisdom, and made to fly at the slightest signal of a sage,—in which that which is now richest and rarest shall be within the compass of every one who shall be obedient to the voice of wisdom,—when the art of healing shall be lost and absorbed in the one universal medicine,—when sages shall become monarchs of the earth, and death itself retreat before their crown,—if this blessed consummation of all things can be hastened by the slight circumstance, that a frail earthly body, which must needs partake corruption, shall be consigned to the grave a short space earlier than in the course of nature, what is such a sacrifice to the advancement of the holy Millenium?"

"Millenium is the reign of the Saints," said Forster, somewhat doubtfully.

"Say it is the reign of the Sages, my son," answered Alasco; "or rather the reign of Wisdom itself."

"I touched on the question with Master Holdforth last exercising night," said Forster; "but he says your doctrine is heterodox, and a damnable and false exposition."

"He is in the bonds of ignorance, my son," answered Alasco, "and as yet burning bricks in Egypt; or, at best, wandering in the dry desert of Sinai. You did ill to speak to such a man of such matters. I will, however, give thee proof, and that shortly, which I will defy that peevish divine to confute, though he should strive with me as the magicians strove with Moses before King Pharaoh. I will do projection in thy presence, my son,—in thy very presence,—and thine eyes shall witness the truth."

"Stick to that, learned sage," said Varney, who at this moment entered the apartment; "if he refuse the testimony of thy tongue, yet how shall he deny that of his own eyes?"

"Varney!" said the adept—"Varney already returned! Hast thou"——he stopped short.

"Have I done mine errand, thou wouldst say," replied Varney—"I have!—And thou," he added, shewing more symptoms of interest than he had hitherto exhibited, "art thou sure thou hast poured forth neither more nor less than the just measure?"

"Ay," replied the alchemist, "as sure as men can be in these nice proportions; for there is diversity of constitutions."

"Nay, then," said Varney, "I fear nothing. I know thou wilt not go a step farther to the devil than thou art justly considered for. Thou wert paid to create illness, and would esteem it thriftless prodigality to do murther at the same price. Come, let us each to our chamber—We shall see the event to-morrow."

"What didst thou do to make her swallow it?" said Forster, shuddering.

"Nothing," answered Varney, "but looked on her with that aspect which governs madmen, women, and children. They told me, in Saint Luke's Hospital, that I have the right look for overpowering a refractory patient—the keepers made me their compliments on't; so I know how to win bread, when my court-favour fails me."

"And art thou not afraid," said Forster, "lest the dose be disproportioned?"

"If so," replied Varney, "she will but sleep the sounder, and the fear of that shall not break my rest. Good night, my masters."

Anthony Forster groaned heavily, and lifted up his hands and eyes. The alchemist intimated his purpose to continue some experiment of high import during the greater part of the night, and the others separated to their places of repose.

Chapter Eleven

Now God be good to me in this wild pilgrimage!
All hope in human aid I cast behind me.
Oh, who would be a woman?—who that fool,
A weeping, pining, faithful, loving woman?
She hath hard measure still where she hopes kindest,
And all her bounties only make ingrates.
Love's Pilgrimage

THE SUMMER EVENING was closed, and Janet, just when her longer stay might have occasioned suspicion and inquiry in that jealous household, returned to Cumnor-Place, and hastened to the apartment in which she had left her lady. She found her with her head resting on her arms, which were crossed upon a table that stood before her. As Janet came in, she neither looked up nor stirred.

Her faithful attendant ran to her mistress with the speed of lightning, and rousing her at the same time with her hand, conjured the Countess in the most earnest manner to look up, and say what thus affected her. The unhappy lady raised her head accordingly, and looking on her attendant with a ghastly eye, and a cheek as pale as clay, "Janet," she said, "I have drank it."

"God be praised!" said Janet, hastily—"I mean God be praised that it is no worse—the potion will not harm you—rise, shake this lethargy from your limbs, and this despair from your mind."

"Janet," repeated the Countess again, "disturb me not—leave me at peace—let life pass quietly—I am poisoned."

"You are not, my dearest lady," answered the maiden eagerly—

"what you have swallowed cannot injure you, and I hastened hither to tell you that the means of escape are open to you."

"Escape!" exclaimed the lady, as she raised herself hastily in her chair, while light returned to her eye and life to her cheek; "but ah! Janet, it comes too late."

"Not so, dearest lady—rise, take mine arm, walk through the apartment—let not fancy do the work of poison—so—now feel you not that you are possessed of the full use of your limbs?"

"The torpor seems to diminish," said the Countess, as, supported by Janet, she walked to and fro in the apartment; "but is it then so, and have I not swallowed a deadly draught? Varney was here since thou wert gone, and commanded me, with eyes in which I read my fate, to swallow yon horrible drug. O, Janet! it must be fatal; never was harmless draught served by such a cup-bearer!"

"He did not deem it harmless, I fear," replied the maiden; "but God confounds the devices of the wicked—believe me, as I swear by the dear Gospel on which we trust, your life is safe from his practice. Did you not debate with him?"

"The house was silent," answered the lady—"thou gone—no other but he in the chamber—and he capable of every crime. I did but stipulate he would remove his hateful presence, and I drank whatever he offered.—But you spoke of escape, Janet; can I be so happy?"

"Are you strong enough to bear the tidings, and make the effort?"

"Strong!" answered the Countess—"Ask the hind, when the fangs of the deer-hound are stretched to gripe her, if she is strong enough to spring the chasm. I am equal to every effort that may relieve me from this place."

"Hear me then," said Janet. "One, whom I deem an assured friend of yours, has shewn himself to me in various disguises, and sought speech of me, which,—for my mind was not clear in the matter until this evening,—I have ever declined. He was the pedlar who brought you goods—the itinerant hawker who sold me books—whenever I stirred abroad I was sure to see him. The event of this night determined me to speak with him. He waits even now at the postern-gate of the park with means for your flight.—But have you strength of body? —have you courage of mind?—can you undertake the enterprize?"

"She that flies from death," said the lady, "finds strength of body— she that would escape from shame, lacks no strength of mind—the thoughts of leaving behind me the villain who menaces both my life and honour, would give me strength to rise from my death-bed."

"In God's name then, lady," said Janet, "I must bid you adieu, and to God's charge I must commit you."

"Will you not fly with me then, Janet?" said the Countess, anxiously

—"Am I to lose thee? Is this your faithful service?"

"Lady, I would fly with you as willingly as bird ever fled from cage, but my doing so would occasion instant discovery and pursuit. I must remain, and use means to disguise the truth for some time—may heaven pardon the falsehood, because of the necessity!"

"And am I then to travel alone with this stranger?" said the lady— "Bethink thee, Janet, may not this prove some deeper and darker scheme to separate me perhaps from you, who are my only friend?"

"No, madam, do not suppose it," answered Janet, readily; "the youth is an honest youth in his purpose to you; and a friend of Master Tressilian, under whose direction he has come hither."

"If he be a friend of Tressilian," said the Countess, "I will commit myself to his charge, as to that of an angel sent from heaven; for than Tressilian, never breathed mortal man more free of whatever was base, false, or selfish. He forgot himself whenever he could be of use to others—Alas! and how was he requited!"

With eager haste they collected the few necessaries which it was thought proper the Countess should take with her, and which Janet, with speed and dexterity, formed into a small bundle, not forgetting to add such ornaments of intrinsic value as came most readily in her way, and particularly a casket with jewels which she wisely judged might prove of service in some emergency. The Countess of Leicester next changed her own dress for one which Janet usually wore upon any brief journey, for they judged it necessary to avoid every external distinction which might attract attention. Ere these preparations were fully made, the moon had arisen in the summer heaven, and all in the retired mansion had betaken themselves to rest, or at least to the silence and retirement of their chambers.

There was no difficulty anticipated in escaping, whether from the house or garden, providing only they could elude observation. Anthony Forster had accustomed himself to consider his daughter as a conscious sinner might regard a visible guardian angel, which, notwithstanding his guilt, continued to hover around him, and therefore his trust in her knew no bounds. Janet commanded her own motions during the day-time, and had a master-key which opened the postern-door of the park, so that she could go to the village at pleasure, either upon the household affairs, which were entirely confided to her management, or to attend her devotions at the meeting-house of her sect. It is true, she was thus liberally entrusted, under the solemn condition that she would not avail herself of these privileges, to do anything inconsistent with the safe-keeping of the Countess; for so her residence at Cumnor-Place had been termed, since she began of late to exhibit impatience of the restrictions to which she was subjected. Nor is there reason to suppose, that any thing short of the dreadful suspicions which the scene of that evening had excited, could have induced Janet to have violated her word, or deceived her father's confidence. But from what she had witnessed, she now conceived herself not only justified, but imperatively called upon to make her lady's safety the principal object of her care, setting all other considerations aside.

The fugitive Countess with her guide were traversing with hasty steps the broken and interrupted path, which had once been an avenue, now totally darkened by the boughs of spreading trees which met above their head, and now receiving a doubtful and deceiving light from the beams of the moon, which penetrated where the axe had made openings in the wood. Their path was repeatedly interrupted by felled trees, or the large boughs which had been left on the ground till time served to make them into faggots and billets. The inconvenience and difficulty attending these interruptions, the breathless haste of the first part of their route, the exhausting sensations of hope and fear, so much affected the Countess's strength, that Janet was forced to propose that they should pause for a few minutes to recover breath and spirits. Both therefore stood still beneath the shadow of a huge old gnarled oak-tree, and both naturally looked back to the mansion which they had left behind them, whose long dark front was seen in the gloomy distance, with its huge stalks of chimneys, turrets, and clock-house, rising above the line of the roof, and definedly visible against the pure azure blue of the summer sky. One light only twinkled from the extended and shadowy mass, and it was placed so low that it rather seemed to glimmer from the ground in front of the mansion, than from one of the windows. The Countess's terror was awakened. —"They follow us!" she said, pointing out to Janet the light which thus alarmed her.

Less agitated than her mistress, Janet perceived that the gleam was stationary, and informed the Countess in a whisper, that the light proceeded from the solitary cell in which the alchemist pursued his occult experiments.—"He is of those," she added, "who sit up and watch by night that they may commit iniquity. Evil was the chance which sent hither a man, whose mixed speech of earthly wealth and unearthly or superhuman knowledge, has in it what does so especially captivate my poor father. Well spoke the good Master Holdforth— and, methought, not without meaning that those of our household should find therein a practical use. 'There be those,' he said, 'and their number is legion, who will rather, like the wicked Ahab, listen to the dreams of the false prophet Zedechias, than to the words of him by whom the Lord has spoken.' And he further insisted—'Ah, my brethren, there be many Zedechiases among you—men that promise you the light of their carnal knowledge, so you will surrender to them that of your heavenly understanding. What are they better than the tyrant Naas, who demanded the right eye of those who were subjected unto him?' And farther he insisted"——

It is uncertain how long the fair puritan's memory might have supported her in the recapitulation of Master Holdforth's discourse, for the Countess now interrupted her, and assured her she was so much recovered that she could now reach the postern without the necessity of a second delay.

They set out accordingly, and performed the second part of their journey with more deliberation, and of course more easily, than their first hasty commencement. This gave them leisure for reflection; and Janet now, for the first time, ventured to ask her lady, which way she proposed to direct her flight. Receiving no immediate answer,—for perhaps, in the confusion of her mind, this very obvious subject of deliberation had not occurred to the Countess,—Janet ventured to add, "Probably to your father's house, where you are sure of safety and protection?"

"No, Janet," said the lady, mournfully, "I left Lidcote-Hall while my heart was light and my name was honourable, and I will not return thither till my lord's permission and public acknowledgment of our marriage restores me to my native home, with all the rank and honour which he has bestowed on me."

"And whither will you then, madam?" said Janet.

"To Kenilworth, girl," said the Countess, boldly and freely. "I will see these revels—these princely pleasures—the preparation for which makes the land ring from side to side. Methinks, when the Queen of England feasts within my husband's halls, the Countess of Leicester should be no unbeseeming guest."

"I pray God you may be a welcome one," said Janet hastily.

"You abuse my situation, Janet," said the Countess angrily, "and you forget your own."

"I do neither, dearest madam," said the sorrowful maiden; "but have you forgotten that the noble Earl has given such strict charges to keep your marriage secret, that he may preserve his court-favour? and can you think that your sudden appearance at his castle, at such a juncture, and in such a presence, will be acceptable to him?"

"Thou thinkest I would disgrace him," said the Countess;—"nay, let go my arm, I can walk without aid, and work without counsel."

"Be not angry with me, lady," said Janet meekly, "and let me still support you; the road is rough, and you are little accustomed to walk in darkness."

"If you deem me not so mean as may disgrace my husband," said the Countess in the same resentful tone, "you suppose my Lord of Leicester capable of abetting, perhaps of giving aim and authority to the base proceedings of your father and Varney, whose errand I will do to the good Earl."

"For God's sake, madam, spare my father in your report," said Janet; "let my services, however poor, be some atonement for his errors."

"I were most unjust, dearest Janet, were it otherwise," said the Countess, resuming at once the fondness and confidence of her manner towards her faithful attendant. "Yes, Janet, not a word of mine shall do your father prejudice. But thou seest, my love, I have no desire but to throw myself on my husband's protection. I have left the abode he assigned me, because of the villainy of the persons by whom I was surrounded—but I will disobey his commands in no other particular. I will appeal to him alone—I will be protected by him alone—to no other, than at his pleasure, have I or will I communicate the secret union which combines our hearts and our destinies. I will see him, and receive from his own lips the directions for my future conduct. Do not argue against my resolution, Janet; you will only confirm me in it— and to own the truth, I am resolved to know my fate at once, and from my husband's own mouth, and to seek him at Kenilworth is the surest way to attain my purpose."

While Janet hastily revolved in her mind the difficulties and uncertainties attendant on the unfortunate lady's situation, she was inclined to alter her first opinion, and to think, upon the whole, that since the Countess had withdrawn herself from the retreat in which she had been placed by her husband, it was her first duty to repair to his presence, and possess him with the reasons of such conduct. She knew what importance the Earl attached to the concealment of their marriage, and could not but own, that by taking any step to make it public without his permission, the Countess would incur, in a high degree, the indignation of her husband. If she retired to her father's house without an explicit avowal of her rank, her situation was likely greatly to prejudice her character, and if she made such an avowal, it might occasion an irreconcileable breach with her husband. At Kenilworth, again, she might plead her cause with her husband himself, whom Janet, though distrusting him more than the Countess did, believed incapable of being accessary to the base and desperate means which his dependants, from whose power the lady was now escaping, might resort to, in order to stifle her complaints of the treatment she had received at their hands. But at the worst, and were the Earl himself to deny her justice and protection, still at Kenilworth, if she chose to make her wrongs public, the Countess might have Tressilian for her advocate, and the Queen for her judge, for so much Janet had learned in her short conference with Wayland. She was, therefore, on the whole, reconciled to her lady's proposal of going towards Kenilworth, and so expressed herself; recommending, however, to the Countess the utmost caution in making her arrival known to her husband.

"Hast thou thyself been cautious, Janet?" said the Countess; "this guide, in whom I must put my confidence, hast thou not entrusted to him the secret of my condition?"

"From me he has learned nothing," said Janet, "nor do I believe that he knows more than what the public in general believe of your situation."

"And what is that?" said the lady.

"That you left your father's house—but I shall offend you again if I go on," said Janet, interrupting herself.

"Nay, go on," said the Countess; "I must learn to endure the evil report which my folly has brought upon me—they think, I suppose, that I have left my father's house to follow lawless pleasure—it is an error which will soon be removed,—indeed it shall, for I will live with spotless fame, or I will cease to live.—I am accounted, then, the paramour of my Leicester?"

"Most men say of Varney," said Janet; "yet some call him only the convenient cloak of his master's pleasures; for reports of the profuse expence in garnishing yonder apartments have secretly gone abroad, and such doings far surpass the means of Varney. But this latter opinion is little prevalent; for men dare hardly even hint suspicion when so high a name is concerned, lest the Star-chamber should punish them for scandal of the nobility."

"They do well to speak low," said the Countess, "who would mention the illustrious Dudley as the accomplice of such a wretch as Varney.—We have reached the postern—Ah! Janet, I must bid thee farewell!—Weep not, my good girl," said she, endeavouring to cover her own reluctance to part with her faithful attendant under an attempt at playfulness, "and against we meet again, reform me, Janet, that precise ruff of thine for an open rabatine of lace and cut work, that will let men see thou hast a fair neck; and that kirtle of Philippine cheney, with that bugle lace which befits only a chamber-maid, into three-piled velvet and cloth of gold—thou wilt find plenty of stuffs in my chamber, and I freely bestow them on you. Thou must be brave, Janet; for though thou art now but the attendant of a distressed and errant lady, who is both nameless and fameless, yet, when we meet again, thou must be dressed as beseems the gentlewoman nearest in love and in service to the first Countess in England."

"Now, may God grant it, dear lady!—not that I may go with gayer apparel, but that we may both wear our kirtles over lighter hearts."

By this time the lock of the postern-door had, after some hard wrenching, yielded to the master-key; and the Countess, not without internal shuddering, saw herself beyond the walls which her husband's strict commands had assigned to her as the boundary of her walks. Waiting with much anxiety for their appearance, Wayland Smith stood at some distance, shrouding himself behind a hedge which bordered the high-road.

"Is all safe?" said Janet to him, anxiously, as he approached them with caution.

"All," he replied; "but I have been unable to procure a horse for the lady. Giles Gosling, the cowardly hilding, refused me one on any terms; lest, forsooth, he should suffer—but no matter. She must ride on my palfrey, and I must walk by her side until I come by another horse. There will be no pursuit, if you, pretty Mistress Janet, forget not thy lesson."

"No more than the wise widow of Tekoa forgot the words which Joab put into her mouth," answered Janet. "To-morrow, I say that my lady is unable to rise."

"Ay, and that she hath aching and heaviness of the head—a throbbing at the heart, and lists not to be disturbed—fear not, they will take the hint, and trouble thee with few questions—they understand the disease."

"But," said the lady, "my absence must be soon discovered, and they will murther her in revenge.—I will rather return than expose her to such danger."

"Be at ease on my account, madam," said Janet; "I would you were as sure of receiving the favour you desire from those to whom you must make appeal, as I am that my father, however angry, will suffer no harm to befal me."

The Countess was now placed by Wayland upon his horse, around the saddle of which he had placed his cloak, so folded as to make her a commodious seat.

"Adieu, and may the blessing of God wend with you!" said Janet, again kissing her mistress's hand, who returned her benediction with a mute caress. They then tore themselves asunder, and Janet, addressing Wayland, exclaimed, "May Heaven deal with you at your need, as you are true or false to this most injured and most helpless lady!"

"Amen! pretty Janet," replied Wayland;—"and believe me, I will so acquit myself of my trust, as may tempt even your pretty eyes, saint-like as they are, to look less scornfully on me when we next meet."

The latter part of this adieu was whispered into Janet's ear; and, although she made no reply to it directly, yet her manner, influenced no doubt by her desire to leave every motive in force which could operate towards her mistress's safety, did not discourage the hope which Wayland's words expressed. She re-entered the postern-door, and locked it behind her, while, Wayland taking the horse's bridle in his hand and walking close by its head, they began in silence their dubious and moonlight journey.

Although Wayland Smith used the utmost dispatch which he could make, yet this mode of travelling was so slow, that when morning began to dawn through the eastern mists, he found himself not farther than about ten miles distant from Cumnor. "Now, a plague upon all smooth-spoken hosts!" said Wayland, unable longer to suppress his mortification and uneasiness. "Had the false loon, Giles Gosling, but told me plainly two days since, that I was to reckon nought upon him, I had shifted better for myself. But they have such a custom of promising whatever is called for, that it is not till the steed is to be shod you find they are out of iron. Had I but known, I could have made twenty shifts; nay, for that matter, and in so good a cause, I would have thought little to have prigged a prancer from the next common—it had but been sending back the brute to the Headborough. The farcy and the founders confound every horse in the stables of the Black Bear!"

The lady endeavoured to comfort her guide, observing the dawn would enable him to make more speed.

"True, madam," replied he; "but then it will enable other folks to take note of us, and that may prove an ill beginning of our journey. I had not cared a spark from my anvil about the matter, had we been farther advanced. But this Berkshire has been notoriously haunted e'er since I knew the country, with that sort of malicious elves, who sit up late and rise early, for no other purpose than to pry into other folks' affairs. I have been endangered by them ere now. But do not fear," he added, "good madam; for wit, meeting with opportunity, will not miss to find a salve for every sore."

The alarms of her guide made more impression on the Countess's mind than the comfort which he judged fit to administer along with it. She looked anxiously around her, and as the shadows withdrew from the landscape, and the heightening glow of the eastern sky promised the speedy rise of the sun, expected at every turn that the increasing light would expose them to the view of the vengeful pursuers, or present some dangerous and unsurmountable obstacle to the prosecution of their journey. Wayland Smith perceived her uneasiness, and, displeased with himself for having given her cause of alarm, strode on with affected alacrity, now talking to the horse as one expert in the language of the stable, now whistling to himself low and interrupted snatches of tunes, and now assuring the lady there was no danger, while at the same time he looked sharply around to see that there was nothing in sight, which might give the lie to his words while they were issuing from his mouth. Thus did they journey on, until an unexpected incident gave them the means of continuing their pilgrimage with more speed and convenience.

Chapter Twelve

Richard. A horse!—a horse!—my kingdom for a horse!
Catesby.——My lord, I'll help you to a horse.
                                                    Richard III

OUR TRAVELLERS were in the act of passing a small thicket of trees close by the road-side, when the first living being presented himself whom they had seen since their departure from Cumnor-Place. This was a stupid lout of a farmer's boy, in a grey jerkin, with his head bare, his hose about his heels, and huge startups upon his feet. He held by the bridle what of all things they most wanted, a palfrey, namely, with a side-saddle, and all other garniture for a woman's mounting; and he hailed Wayland Smith with, "Zur, be ye zure the party?"

"Ay, that I be, my lad," answered Wayland, without an instant's hesitation; and it must be owned that consciences, trained in a stricter school of morality, might have given way to an occasion so tempting. While he spoke he caught the rein out of the boy's hand, and almost at the same time helped down the Countess from his own horse, and aided her to mount on that which chance had thus presented for her acceptance. Indeed, so naturally did the whole take place, that the Countess, as it afterwards appeared, never suspected but what the horse had been placed there to meet them by the precaution of the guide or some of his friends.

The lad, however, who was thus hastily dispossessed of his charge, began to stare hard, and scratch his head, as if seized with some qualms of conscience for delivering up the animal on such brief explanation.—"I be right zure thou be'st the party," said he, muttering to himself, "but thou shouldst ha zaid *Beans*, thou knaw'st."

"Ay, ay," said Wayland, speaking at a venture; "and thou *Bacon*, thou know'st."

"Noa, noa," said the lad; "boide ye—boide ye—it was *Pease* ye should ha said."

"Well, well," answered Wayland, "pease be it, a' God's name, though bacon were the better password."

And, being by this time mounted on his own horse, he caught the rein of the palfrey from the uncertain hold of the hesitating young boor, flung him a small piece of money, and made amends for lost time by riding briskly off without farther parley. The lad was still visible from the hill up which they were riding, and Wayland, as he looked back, beheld him standing with his fingers in his hair as immoveable as a guide-post, and his head turned in the direction in which they were escaping from him. At length, just as they topped the hill, he saw the clown stoop to lift up the silver groat which his benevolence had imparted.—"Now this is what I call a Godsend," said Wayland; "this is a bonny well-ridden bit of a going thing, and it will carry us so far till we get you as well mounted, and then we will send it back to satisfy the Hue and Cry."

But he was deceived in his expectations; and fate, which seemed at first to promise so fairly, soon threatened to turn the incident, which he thus gloried in, into the cause of their utter ruin.

They had not ridden a short mile from the place where they left the lad, before they heard a man's voice shouting on the wind behind them, "Robbery! Robbery!—Stop thief!" and similar exclamations, which Wayland's conscience readily assured him must arise out of the transaction to which he had been just accessary.

"I had better have gone barefoot all my life," he said; "it is the Hue and Cry, and I am a lost man. Ah! Wayland, Wayland, many a time thy father said horse-flesh would be the death of thee. Were I once safe among the horse-coursers in Smithfield, or Turnball Street, they should have leave to hang me as high as Paul's, if I e'er meddled more with nobles, knights, or gentlewomen."

Amidst these dismal reflections, he turned his head repeatedly to see by whom he was chased, and was much comforted when he could only discover a single rider, who was, however, well mounted, and came after them at a speed which left them no chance of escaping, even had the lady's strength permitted her to ride as fast as her palfrey might have been able to gallop.

"There may be fair play betwixt us sure," thought Wayland, "where there is but one man on each side, and yonder fellow sits on his horse more like a monkey than a cavalier. Pshaw! if it come to the worst, it will be easy unhorsing him. Nay, 'snails! I think his horse will take the matter in his own hand, for he has the bridle betwixt his teeth. Oons, what care I for him?" said he, as the pursuer drew yet nearer; "it is but the little animal of a mercer from Abingdon, when all is over."

Even so it was, as the experienced eye of Wayland had descried at a distance. For the valiant mercer's horse, which was a beast of mettle, feeling himself put to his speed, and discerning a couple of horses riding fast, at some hundred yards distance before him, betook himself to the road with such alacrity, as totally deranged the seat of his rider, who not only came up with, but passed, at full gallop, those whom he had been pursuing, pulling the reins with all his might, and ejaculating "Stop! stop!", an interjection which seemed however rather to regard his own palfrey, than what seamen call "the chase." With the same involuntary speed, he shot a-head, (to use another nautical phrase) about a furlong, ere he was able to stop and turn his horse, and then rode back towards our travellers, adjusting, as well as he could, his disordered dress, resettling himself in the saddle, and endeavouring to substitute a bold and martial frown, for the confusion and dismay which sate upon his visage during his involuntary career.

Wayland had just time to caution the lady not to be alarmed, adding, "this fellow is a gull, and I will use him as such," when the mercer recovered breath and audacity enough to confront them and order him, in a menacing tone, to deliver up his palfrey.

"How?" said the smith, in King Cambyses' vein, "are we commanded to stand and deliver on the King's high-way? Then out, Excalibar, and tell this knight of prowess, that dire blows must decide between us."

"Haro and help, and hue and cry, every true man!" said the mercer, "I am withstood in seeking to recover mine own."

"Thou swearest thy Gods in vain, foul paynim," said Wayland, "for I will through with my purpose, were death at the end on't. Nevertheless, know, thou false man of frail cambric and ferrateen, that I am he, even the pedlar, whom thou didst boast to meet on Maiden-castle-moor, and spoil of his pack; wherefore betake thee to thy weapons presently."

"I spoke but in jest, man," said Goldthread; "I am an honest shop-keeper and citizen, who scorn to leap on any man from behind a hedge."

"Then, by my faith, most puissant mercer, I am sorry for my vow, which was, that wherever I met thee, I would despoil thee of thy palfrey, and bestow it upon my leman, unless thou couldst defend it by blows of force. But the vow is passed and registered—and all I can do for thee, is to leave the horse at Doddington, in the nearest hostelrie."

"But I tell thee, friend," said the mercer, "it is the very horse on which I was this day to carry Jane Thackham, of Shottesbrook, as far as the parish-church yonder, to become Dame Goldthread. She hath jumped out of the shot-window of old Gaffer Thackham's grange; and lo ye, yonder she stands, at the place where she should have met the palfrey, with her camlet riding-cloak, and ivory-handled whip, like a picture of Lot's wife. I pray you, in good terms, let me have back the palfrey."

"Grieved am I," said Wayland, "as much for the fair damsel, as for thee, most noble imp of muslin. But vows must have their course—thou wilt find the palfrey at the Angel yonder at Doddington. It is all I may do for thee, with a safe conscience."

"To the devil with thy conscience!" said the dismayed mercer—"Would'st thou have a bride walk to church on foot?"

"Thou may'st take her on thy crupper, Sir Goldthread," answered Wayland; "it will take down thy steed's mettle."

"And how if you—if you forget to leave my horse, as you propose?" said Goldthread, not without hesitation, for his soul was afraid within him.

"My pack shall be pledged for it—yonder it lies with Giles Gosling, in his chamber with the damask'd leathern hangings, stuffed full with velvet, single, double, treble-piled—rash, taffeta, and paropa—shag, damask, and mockado, plush, and grogram"——

"Hold! hold!" exclaimed the mercer; "nay, if there be, in truth and sincerity, but the half of these wares—but if ever I trust bumpkin with bonny bayard again!"

"As you list for that, good Master Goldthread, and so good morrow to you—and well parted," he added, riding on cheerfully with the lady, while the discountenanced mercer rode back much slower than he came, pondering what excuse he should make to the disappointed bride, who stood waiting for her gallant groom in the midst of the king's high-way.

"Methought," said the lady, as they rode on, "yonder fool stared at me, as if he had some remembrance of me; yet I kept my muffler as high as I might."

"If I thought so," said Wayland, "I would ride back, and cut him over the pate—there would be no fear of harming his brains, for he never had so much as would make pap to a sucking gosling. We must now push on, however, and at Doddington we will leave the oaf's horse, that he may have no farther temptation to pursue us, and endeavour to assume such a change of shape as may baffle his pursuit, if he should persevere in it."

The travellers reached Doddington without farther alarm, where it became matter of necessity that the Countess should enjoy two or three hours repose, during which Wayland disposed himself, with equal address and alacrity, to carry through those measures on which the safety of their future journey seemed to depend.

Exchanging his pedlar's gaberdine for a smock-frock, he carried the palfrey of Master Goldthread to the Angel Inn, which was at the other end of the village from that where our travellers had taken up their quarters. In the progress of the morning, as he travelled about his other business, he saw the steed brought forth, and delivered to the cutting mercer himself, who, at the head of a valorous posse of the Hue and Cry, came to rescue by force of arms what was delivered to him without any other ransom than the price of a huge quantity of ale, drunk out by his assistants, thirsty, it would seem, with their walk, and concerning the price of which Master Goldthread had a fierce dispute with the Headborough, whom he had summoned to aid him in raising the country.

Having made this act of prudent, as well as just restitution, Wayland procured such change of apparel for the lady, as well as himself, as gave them both the appearance of country people of the better class; it being farther resolved, that, in order to attract the less observation, she should pass upon the road for the sister of her guide. A good, but not a gay horse, fit to keep pace with his own, and gentle enough for a lady's use, completed the preparations for the journey; for making which, he had been furnished with sufficient funds by Tressilian. And thus, about noon, after the Countess had been refreshed by the sound repose of several hours, they resumed their journey, with the purpose of making the best of their way to Kenilworth, by Coventry and Warwick. They were not, however, destined to travel far, without meeting some cause of apprehension.

It is necessary to premise, that the landlord of the inn had informed them, a jovial party, intended, as he understood, to present some of the masques or mummeries, which made a part of the entertainment with which the Queen was usually welcomed on the royal Progresses, had left the village of Doddington an hour or two before them, in order to proceed to Kenilworth. Now it had occurred to Wayland, that, by attaching themselves in some sort to this groupe, as soon as they should overtake them on the road, they would be less likely to attract notice, than if they continued to travel entirely by themselves. He communicated his idea to the Countess, who, only anxious to arrive at Kenilworth without interruption, left him free to chuse the manner in which this was to be accomplished. They pressed forward their horses, therefore, with the purpose of overtaking the party of intended revellers, and making the journey in their company; and had just seen the little company, consisting partly of riders, partly of people on foot, crossing the summit of a gentle hill, at about half a mile's distance, and disappearing on the other side, when Wayland, who maintained the most circumspect observation of all that met his eye in every direction, was aware that a rider was coming up behind them on a horse of uncommon action, accompanied by a serving man, whose utmost efforts were unable to keep up with his master's trotting hackney, and who, therefore, was fain to follow him at a hand gallop. Wayland looked anxiously back at these horsemen, became considerably disturbed in his manner, looked back again, and became pale, as he said to the lady—"That is Richard Varney's trotting gelding—I would know him among a thousand nags—this is a worse business than meeting the mercer."

"Draw your sword," answered the lady, "and pierce my bosom with it, rather than I should fall into his hands."

"I would rather by a thousand times," answered Wayland, "pass it through his body, or even mine own. But to say truth, fighting is not my best point, though I can look on cold iron like another, when needs must be. And indeed, as for my sword—(put on I pray you)—it is a poor provant rapier, and I warrant you he has a special Toledo. He has a serving man too, and I think it is the drunken ruffian Lambourne, upon the horse on which men say—(I pray you heartily to put on)—he did the great robbery of the west-country grazier. It is not that I fear either Varney or Lambourne in a good cause—(your palfrey will go yet faster if you urge him)—But yet—(nay, I pray you let him not break off into the gallop, lest they should see we fear them, and give chace—keep him only at the full trot,)—But yet, though I fear them not, I would we were well rid of them, and that rather by policy than by violence. Could we once reach the party before us, we may herd among them, and pass unobserved, unless Varney be really come in express pursuit of us, and then, happy man be his dole."

While he thus spoke, he alternately urged and restrained his horse, desirous to maintain the fleetest pace that was consistent with the idea of an ordinary journey on the road, but to avoid such rapidity of movement as might give rise to suspicion that they were flying.

At such a pace, they ascended the gentle hill we have mentioned, and, looking from the top, had the pleasure to see that the party which had left Doddington before them, were in the little valley or bottom on the other side, where the road was traversed by a rivulet, beside which was a cottage or two. In this place they seemed to have made a pause, which gave Wayland hopes of joining with them, and becoming a part of their company, ere Varney should overtake them. He was the more anxious, as his companion, though she made no complaints, and expressed no fear, began to look deadly pale, so that he was afraid she might drop from her horse. Notwithstanding this symptom of decaying strength, she pushed on her palfrey so briskly, that they joined the party in the bottom of the valley, ere Varney appeared on the top of the gentle eminence which they descended.

They found the company to which they meant to associate themselves in great disorder; the women with dishevelled locks, and looks
of great importance, ran in and out of one of the cottages, and the men
stood around holding the horses, and looking silly enough, as is usual
in cases where their assistance is not wanted.

Wayland and his charge paused, as if out of curiosity, and then
gradually, without making any inquiries, or being asked any questions,
they mingled with the groupe, as if they had always made part of it.

They had not stood there above five minutes, anxiously keeping as
much to the side of the road as possible, so as to place the other
travellers betwixt them and Varney, when Lord Leicester's master of
the horse, followed by Lambourne, came riding fiercely down the hill,
their horses' flanks and the rowels of their spurs shewing bloody
tokens of the rate at which they travelled. The appearance of the
stationary groupe around the cottages, wearing their buckram suits in
order to protect their masquing dresses, having their light cart for
transporting their scenery, and carrying various fantastic properties in
their hands for the more easy conveyance, let the riders at once into
the character and purpose of the company.

"You are revellers," said Varney, "designing for Kenilworth?"

"*Recte quidem, Domine spectatissime,*" answered one of the party.

"And why the devil stand you here," said Varney, "when your
utmost dispatch will but bring you to Kenilworth in time? The Queen
dines at Warwick to-morrow, and you loiter here, ye knaves."

"In very truth, sir," said a little diminutive urchin, wearing a vizard
with a couple of sprouting horns of an elegant scarlet hue, having
moreover a black serge jerkin drawn close to his body by lacing,
garnished with red stockings, and shoes so shaped as to resemble
cloven feet,—"in very truth, sir, and you are in the right on't. It is my
father the Devil, who, being taken in labour, has delayed our present
purpose, by increasing our company with an imp too many."

"The devil he has!" answered Varney, whose laugh, however, never
exceeded a sarcastic smile.

"It is even as the juvenal hath said," added the masquer who spoke
first; "our major devil, for this is but our minor one, is even now at
Lucina fer opem, within that very *tugurium.*"

"By Saint George, or rather by the Dragon, who may be a kinsman
of the fiend in the straw, a most comical chance!" said Varney. "How
sayest thou, Lambourne, wilt thou stand godfather for the nonce?—if
the devil were to chuse a gossip, I know no one more fit for the office."

"Saving always when my betters are in presence," said Lambourne,
with the civil impudence of a servant who knows his services to be so
indispensable, that his jest will be permitted to pass muster.

"And what is the name of this devil or devil's dam, who has timed her turns so strangely?" said Varney. "We can ill afford to spare any of our actors."

"*Gaudet nomine Sybillæ*," said the first speaker. "She is called Sybill Laneham, wife of Master Robert Laneham"——

"Clerk to the Council-chamber door," said Varney; "why she is inexcusable, having had experience how to have ordered her matters better. But who were those, a man and woman I think, who rode so hastily up the hill before me even now?—do they belong to your company?"

Wayland was about to hazard a reply to this alarming inquiry, when the little diablotin again thrust in his oar.

"So please you," he said, coming close up to Varney, and speaking so as not to be overheard by his companions, "the man was our devil major, who has tricks enough to supply the lack of a hundred such as Dame Laneham; and the woman—if you please—is the sage person whose assistance is most particularly necessary to our distressed comrade."

"Oh, what, you have got the wise woman then?" said Varney. "Why truly, she rode like one bound to a place where she was needed—and you have a spare limb of Satan, besides, to supply the place of Mistress Laneham?"

"Ay, sir," said the boy, "they are not so scarce in this world as your honour's virtuous eminence would suppose—This master-fiend shall spit a few flashes of fire, and eruct a volume or two of smoke on the spot, if it will do you pleasure—you would think he had Ætna in his abdomen."

"I lack time just now, most hopeful imp of darkness, to witness his performance," said Varney; "but here is something for you all to drink the lucky hour—and so, as the play says, 'God be with your labour!'"

Thus speaking, he struck his horse with the spurs, and rode on his way.

Lambourne tarried a moment or two behind his master, and rummaged his pouch for a piece of silver, which he bestowed on the communicative imp, as he said, for his encouragement on his path to the infernal regions, some sparks of whose fire, he said, he could discover flashing from him already. Then having received the boy's thanks for his generosity, he also spurred his horse, and rode after his master as fast as the fire flashes from flint.

"And now," said the wily imp, sideling close up to Wayland's horse, and cutting a gambol in the air, which seemed to vindicate his title to relationship with the prince of that element, "I have told them who *you* are, do you in return tell me who *I* am?"

"Either Flibbertigibbet," answered Wayland Smith, "or else an imp of the devil in good earnest."

"Thou hast hit," answered Dickie Sludge; "I am thine own Flibbertigibbet, man; and I have broken forth with my learned preceptor, as I told thee I would do, whether he would or not.—But what lady hast thou got with thee? I saw thou wert at fault the first question was asked, and so I drew up for thy assistance. But I must know all who she is, dear Wayland."

"Thou shalt know fifty finer things, my dear ingle," said Wayland; "but a truce to thine inquiries just now; and since you are bound for Kenilworth, thither will I too, even for the love of thy sweet face and waggish company."

"Thou should'st have said my waggish face and sweet company," said Dickie; "but how wilt thou travel with us—I mean in what character?"

"E'en in that thou hast assigned me, to be sure—as a juggler; thou know'st I am used to the craft," answered Wayland.

"Ay, but the lady?" answered Flibbertigibbet; "credit me, I think she *is* one, and thou art in a sea of troubles about her at this moment, as I can perceive by thy fidgetting."

"O, she, man!—she is a poor sister of mine," said Wayland—"she can sing and play o' the lute, would win the fish out o' the stream."

"Let me hear her instantly," said the boy; "I love the lute rarely; I love it of all things, though I never heard it."

"Then how canst thou love it, Flibbertigibbet?" said Wayland.

"As knights do ladies in old tales," answered Dickie—"on hearsay."

"Then love it on hearsay a little longer, till my sister is recovered from the fatigue of her journey," said Wayland;—muttering afterwards betwixt his teeth, "The devil take the imp's curiosity!—I must keep fair weather with him, or we shall fare the worse."

He then proceeded to state to Master Holiday his own talents as a juggler, with those of his sister as a musician. Some proof of his dexterity was demanded, which he readily gave in such a style of excellence, that, delighted at obtaining such an accession to their party, they readily acquiesced in the apology which he offered, when a display of his sister's talents was required. The new-comers were invited to partake of the refreshments with which the party were provided; and it was with some difficulty that Wayland Smith obtained an opportunity of being apart with his supposed sister during the meal, of which interval he availed himself to entreat her to forget for the present both her rank and her sorrows, and condescend, as the most probable chance of remaining concealed, to mix in the society of those with whom she was to travel.

The Countess allowed the necessity of the case, and when they resumed their journey, endeavoured to comply with her guide's advice, by addressing herself to a female near her, and expressing her concern for the woman whom they were thus obliged to leave behind them.

"O, she is well tended, madam," replied the dame whom she addressed, who, from her jolly and laughter-loving demeanour, might have been the very emblem of the Wife of Bath; "and my gossip Laneham thinks as little of these matters as any one. By the ninth day, an the revels last so long, we shall have her with us at Kenilworth, even if she should travel with her bantling on her back."

There was something in this speech which took away all desire in the Countess of Leicester to continue the conversation; but having broken the charm by speaking to her fellow-traveller first, the good dame, who was to play Rare Gillian of Croydon, in one of the interludes, took care that silence did not again settle on the journey, but entertained her silent companion with a thousand anecdotes of revels, from the days of King Harry down, with the reception given them by the great folks, and all the names of those who played the principal characters; but ever concluding with "they would be nothing to the princely pleasures of Kenilworth."

"And when shall we reach Kenilworth?" said the Countess, with an agitation which she in vain attempted to conceal.

"We that have horses may, with late riding, get to Warwick to-night, and Kenilworth may be distant some four or five miles—But then we must wait till the foot-people come up—although it is like my good Lord of Leicester will have horses or light carriage to meet them, and bring them up without being travel-toiled, which is no good preparation, as you may suppose, for dancing before your betters—And yet, Lord help me, I have seen the day I would have tramped five leagues of lea-land, and turned on my toe the whole evening after, as a juggler spins a pewter platter on the point of a needle. But age has clawed me somewhat in his clutch, as the song says; though, if I like the tune and like my partner, I'll dance the heys yet with any merry lass in Warwickshire, that writes that unhappy figure four with a round O after it."

If the Countess was overwhelmed with the garrulity of this good dame, Wayland Smith, on his part, had enough to do to sustain and parry the constant attacks made upon him by the indefatigable curiosity of his old acquaintance Richard Sludge. Nature had given that arch youngster a prying cast of disposition, which matched admirably with his sharp wit; the former inducing him to plant himself as a spy on other people's affairs, and the latter quality leading him perpetually to interfere, after he had made himself master of that which concerned him not. He spent the live-long day in attempting to peer under the Countess's muffler, and apparently what he could there discern greatly sharpened his curiosity.

"That sister of thine, Wayland," he said, "has a fair neck to have been born in a smithy, and a pretty taper hand to have been used for twirling a spindle—faith, I'll believe in your relationship when the crow's egg is hatched into a cygnet."

"Go to," said Wayland, "thou art a prating boy, and shouldst be breeched for thine assurance."

"Well," said the imp, drawing off, "all I say is,—remember you have kept a secret from me! and if I give thee not a Rowland for thine Oliver, say my name is not Dickon Sludge."

This threat, and the distance at which Hobgoblin kept from him for the rest of the way, alarmed Wayland very much, and he suggested to his pretended sister, that, on the pretext of weariness, she should express a desire to stop two or three miles short of the fair town of Warwick, promising to rejoin the troop in the morning. A small village inn afforded them a resting-place; and it was with secret pleasure that Wayland saw the whole party, including Dickon, pass on, after a courteous farewell, and leave them behind.

"To-morrow, madam," he said to his charge, "we will, with your leave, again start early, and reach Kenilworth before the rout which are to assemble there."

The Countess gave assent to the proposal of her faithful guide; but, somewhat to his surprise, said nothing farther on the subject, which left Wayland under the disagreeable uncertainty whether or no she had formed any plan for her own future proceedings, as he knew her situation demanded circumspection, although he was but imperfectly acquainted with all its peculiarities. Concluding, however, that she must have friends within the castle, to whose advice and assistance she could safely trust, he supposed his task would be best accomplished by conducting her thither in safety, agreeably to her repeated commands.

Chapter Thirteen

Hark, the bells summon, and the bugle calls,
But she the fairest answers not—the tide
Of nobles and of ladies throngs the halls,
But she the loveliest must in secret hide.
What eyes were thine, proud Prince, which in the gleam
Of yon gay meteors lost that better sense,
That o'er the glow-worm doth the star esteem,
And merit's modest blush o'er courtly insolence?
The Glass Slipper

THE UNFORTUNATE COUNTESS of Leicester had, from her infancy upward, been treated by those around her with indulgence as unbounded as injudicious. The natural sweetness of her disposition had saved her from becoming insolent and ill-humoured; but the caprice which preferred the handsome and insinuating Leicester before Tressilian, of whose high honour and unalterable affection she herself entertained so firm an opinion—that fatal error, which ruined the happiness of her life, had its origin in the mistaken kindness that had spared her childhood the painful, but most necessary lesson, of submission and self-command. From the same indulgence, it followed that she had ever been accustomed to express her wishes, leaving to others the task of fulfilling them; and thus, at the most momentous period of her life, she was alike destitute of experience and presence of mind, and utterly unable to form for herself any reasonable or prudent plan of conduct.

These difficulties pressed on the unfortunate lady with overwhelming force, on the morning which seemed to be the crisis of her fate. Overlooking every intermediate consideration, she had only desired to be at Kenilworth, and to approach her husband's presence; and now, when she was in the vicinity of both, a thousand considerations arose at once upon her mind, startling her with accumulated doubts and dangers, some real, some imaginary, and all exalted and exaggerated by a situation alike helpless, and destitute of aid and counsel.

A sleepless night rendered her so weak in the morning, that she was altogether unable to attend Wayland's early summons. The trusty guide became extremely distressed on the lady's account, and somewhat alarmed on his own, and was on the point of going alone to Kenilworth, in the hope of discovering Tressilian, and intimating to him the lady's approach, when about nine in the morning he was summoned to attend her. He found her dressed, and ready for resuming her journey, but with a paleness of countenance which alarmed him for her health. She intimated her desire that the horses might be got instantly, and resisted with impatience her guide's request, that she would take some refreshment before setting forward. "I have had," she said, "a cup of water—the wretch who is dragged to execution needs no stronger cordial, and that may serve me which suffices for him—do as I command you." Wayland Smith still hesitated. "What would you have?" she said—"Have I not spoken plainly?"

"Yes, madam," answered Wayland; "but may I ask what is your farther purpose?—I only wish to know, that I may guide myself by your wishes—the whole country is afloat, and streaming towards the Castle of Kenilworth—it will be difficult travelling thither, even if we had the necessary passports for safe-conduct and free-admittance— unknown and unfriended, we may come by mishap.—Your ladyship will forgive my speaking my poor mind—Were we not better try to find out the masquers, and again join ourselves with them?"—The Countess shook her head, and her guide proceeded, "Then I see but one other remedy."

"Speak out, then," said the lady, not displeased, perhaps, that he should thus offer the advice which she was ashamed to ask; "I believe thee faithful—what wouldst thou counsel?"

"That I should warn Master Tressilian," said Wayland, "that you are in this place. I am right certain he would get to horse with a few of Lord Sussex's followers, and assure your personal safety."

"And is it *me* you advise," said the Countess, "to put myself under the protection of Sussex, the unworthy rival of the noble Leicester?" Then, seeing the surprise with which Wayland stared upon her, and afraid of having too strongly intimated her interest in Leicester, she added, "And for Tressilian, it must not be—mention not to him, I charge you, my unhappy name; it would but double *my* misfortunes, and involve *him* in dangers beyond the power of rescue." She paused; but when she observed that Wayland continued to look on her with that anxious and uncertain gaze, which indicated a doubt whether her brain was settled, she assumed an air of composure, and added, "Do thou but guide me to Kenilworth Castle, good fellow, and thy task is ended, since I will then judge what farther is to be done—thou hast yet been true to me—here is something that will make thee rich amends."

She offered the artist a ring, containing a valuable stone. Wayland looked at it, hesitated a moment, and then returned it. "Not," he said, "that I am above your kindness, madam, being but a poor fellow, who have been forced, God help me! to live by worse shifts than the bounty of such a person as you. But as my old master the farrier used to say to his customers, 'No cure no pay.' We are not yet in Kenilworth Castle, and it is time enough to discharge your guide, as they say, when you take your boots off. I trust in God your ladyship is as well assured of fitting reception when you arrive, as you may hold yourself certain of my best endeavours to conduct you thither safely. I go to get the horses; meantime let me pray you once more, as your poor physician as well as guide, to take some sustenance."

"I will—I will," said the lady, hastily. "Begone, begone instantly!— It is in vain I assume audacity," said she when he left the room; "even this poor groom sees through my affectation of courage, and fathoms the very ground of my fears."

She then attempted to follow her guide's advice by taking some food, but was compelled to desist, as the effort to swallow even a single morsel gave her so much uneasiness as amounted well nigh to suffocation. A moment afterwards the horses appeared at the latticed window—the lady mounted, and found that relief from the free air and change of place, which is frequently experienced in similar circumstances.

It chanced well for the Countess's purpose that Wayland Smith, whose previous wandering and unsettled life had made him acquainted with almost all England, was intimate with all the bye-roads, as well as the direct communications, through the beautiful county of Warwick. For such was the throng which flocked in all directions towards Kenilworth, to see the entry of Elizabeth into that splendid mansion of her prime favourite, that the principal roads were actually blockaded and interrupted, and it was only by circuitous bye-paths that the travellers could proceed on their journey.

The Queen's purveyors had been abroad, sweeping the farms and villages of those articles usually exacted during a royal Progress, and for which the owners were afterwards to obtain a tardy payment from the Board of Green Cloth. The Earl of Leicester's household officers had been scouring the country for the same purpose; and many of his friends and allies, both near and remote, took this opportunity of ingratiating themselves, by sending in large quantities of provisions and delicacies of all kinds, with game in huge quantities, and whole tons of the best liquors, foreign and domestic. Thus the high roads were filled with droves of bullocks, sheep, and calves and hogs, and choked with loaded wains, whose axle-trees cracked under their burdens of wine-casks and hogsheads of ale, and huge hampers of grocery goods, and slaughtered game, and salted provisions, and sacks of flour. Perpetual stoppages took place as these wains became entangled; and their rude drivers, swearing and brawling till their wild passions were fully raised, began to debate precedence with their waggon-whips and quarter-staves, which occasional riots were usually quieted by a purveyor, deputy-marshal's-man, or some other person in authority, breaking the head of both parties.

There were, besides, players and mummers, jugglers and showmen of every description, traversing in joyous bands the paths which led to the Palace of Princely Pleasure; for so the travelling minstrels had termed Kenilworth in the songs which already had come forth in anticipation of the revels which were there expected. In the midst of this motley show, mendicants were exhibiting their real or pretended miseries, forming a strange, though common, contrast betwixt the vanities and the sorrows of human existence. All these floated along with the immense tide of population, whom mere curiosity had drawn together; and where the mechanic, in his leathern apron, elbowed the dink and dainty dame, his city mistress; where clowns, with hob-nailed shoes, were treading on the kibes of substantial burghers and gentlemen of worship; and where Joan of the dairy, with robust pace, and red sturdy arms, rowed her way onward, amongst those prim and pretty moppets, whose sires were knights and squires.

The throng and confusion was, however, of a gay and cheerful character. All came forth to see and to enjoy, and all laughed at the trifling inconveniences which at another time might have chafed their temper. Excepting the occasional brawls which we have mentioned amongst that irritable race the carmen, the mingled sounds which arose from the multitude were those of light-hearted mirth, and tiptoe jollity; the musicians preluded on their instruments—the minstrels hummed their songs—the licensed jester whooped betwixt mirth and madness, as he brandished his bauble—the morrice-dancers jangled their bells—the rustics halloo'd and whistled—men laughed loud, and maidens giggled shrill; while many a broad jest flew like a shuttle-cock from one party to be caught in the air and returned from the opposite side of the road by another, at which it was aimed.

No infliction can be so distressing to a mind absorbed in melan-choly, as being plunged into a scene of mirth and revelry, forming an accompaniment so dissonant from its own feelings. Yet, in the case of the Countess of Leicester, the noise and tumult of this giddy scene distracted her thoughts, and rendered her this sad service, that it became impossible for her to brood on her own misery, or to form terrible anticipations of her approaching fate. She travelled on, like one in a dream, following implicitly the guidance of Wayland, who, with great address, now threaded his way through the general throng of passengers, now stood still until a favourable opportunity occurred of again moving forward, and frequently turning altogether out of the direct road, followed some circuitous by-path, which brought them into it again, after having given them the opportunity of traversing a considerable way with greater ease and rapidity.

It was thus he avoided Warwick, within whose Castle (that fairest monument of ancient and chivalrous splendour which yet remains uninjured by time) Elizabeth had passed the previous night, and where she was to tarry until past noon, at that time the general hour of dinner throughout England, after which repast she was to proceed to Kenilworth. In the meanwhile, each passing groupe had something to say in the Sovereign's praise, though not absolutely without the usual intermixture of satire which qualifies more or less our estimate of our neighbours, especially if they chance to be also our betters.

"Heard you," said one, "how graciously she spoke to Master Bailiff and the Recorder, and to good Master Griffin the preacher, as they kneeled down at her coach-window?"

"Ay, and how she said to Aglionby, 'Little Master Recorder, men would have persuaded me that you were afraid of me, but truly I think, so well did you reckon up to me the virtues of a sovereign, that I have more reason to be afraid of you'—and then with what a grace she took the fair-wrought purse with the twenty gold sovereigns, seeming as though she would not willingly handle it, and yet taking it withal."

"Ay, ay," said another, "her fingers closed on it pretty willingly methought, when all was done; and methought, too, she weighed them for a second in her hand, as who should say, I hope they be avoirdupois."

"She needed not, neighbour," said a third; "it is only when the corporation pay the accounts of a poor handicraft like me, that they put him off with clipt coin.—Well, there is a God above all—Little Master Recorder, since that is the word, will be greater now than ever."

"Come, good neighbour," said the first speaker, "be not envious— she is a good Queen, and a generous—she gave the purse to the Earl of Leicester."

"I envious?—beshrew thy heart for the word!" replied the handi- craft—"But she will give all to the Earl of Leicester anon, methinks."

"You are turning ill, lady," said Wayland Smith to the Countess of Leicester, and proposed that she should draw off from the road, and halt till she recovered. But, subduing her feelings at this, and different speeches to the same purpose, which caught her ear as they passed on, she insisted that her guide should proceed to Kenilworth with all the haste which the numerous impediments of their journey permitted. Meantime, Wayland's anxiety at her repeated fits of indisposition, and her obvious distraction of mind, was hourly increasing, and he became extremely desirous, that, according to her reiterated requests, she should be safely introduced into the Castle, where, he doubted not, she was secure of a kind reception, though she seemed unwilling to reveal on whom she reposed her hopes.

"An I were once rid of this peril," thought he, "and if any man shall find me playing squire of the body to a damosel-errant, he shall have leave to beat my brains out with my own sledge-hammer."

At length the princely Castle appeared, upon improving which, and the domains around, the Earl of Leicester had, it is said, expended sixty thousand pounds sterling, a sum equal to half a million of our present money.

The outer wall of this splendid and gigantic structure enclosed seven acres, a part of which was occupied by extensive stables, and by a pleasure garden, with its trim arbours and parterres, and the rest formed the large base-court, or outer yard, of the noble Castle. The lordly structure itself, which rose near the centre of this spacious enclosure, was composed of a huge pile of magnificent castellated buildings, apparently of different ages, surrounding an inner court, and bearing in the names attached to each portion of the magnificent mass, and in the armorial bearings which were there blazoned, the emblems of mighty chiefs who had long passed away, and whose history, could Ambition have lent ear to it, might have read a lesson to the haughty favourite, who had now acquired and was augmenting the fair domain. A large and massive Keep, which formed the citadel of the Castle, was of uncertain though great antiquity. It bore the name of Cæsar, perhaps from its resemblance to that in the Tower of London so called. Some antiquaries ascribed its foundation to the time of Kenelph, from whom the Castle had its name, a Saxon King of Mercia, and others to an early æra after the Norman Conquest. On the exterior walls frowned the scutcheon of the Clintons, by whom they were founded in the reign of Henry I., and of the yet more redoubted Simon de Montfort, by whom, during the Barons' Wars, Kenilworth was long held out against Henry III. Here Mortimer, Earl of March, famous alike for his rise and his fall, had once gaily revelled, while his dethroned sovereign, Edward II., languished in its dungeons. Old John of Gaunt, "time-honoured Lancaster," had widely extended the Castle, erecting that noble and massive pile which yet bears the name of Lancaster's Buildings; and Leicester himself had outdone the former possessors, princes and powerful as they were, by erecting another immense structure, which now lies crushed under its own ruins, the monument of its owner's ambition. The external wall of this royal Castle was, on the south and west sides, adorned and defended by a lake partly artificial, across which Leicester had constructed a stately bridge, that Elizabeth might enter the Castle by a path hitherto untrodden, instead of the usual entrance to the northward, over which he had erected a gate-house or barbican, which still exists, and is equal in extent and superior in architecture, to the baronial castle of many a northern chief.

Beyond the lake lay an extensive chase, full of red deer, fallow deer, roes, and every species of game, and abounding with lofty trees, from amongst which the extended front and massive towers of the castle were seen to rise in majesty and beauty. We cannot but add, that of this lordly palace, where princes feasted and heroes fought, now in the bloody earnest of storm and siege, and now in the games of chivalry, where beauty dealt the prize which valour won, all is now desolate. The bed of the lake is but a rushy swamp; and the massive ruins of the Castle only serve to shew what their splendour once was, and to impress on the musing visitor the transitory value of human possessions, and the happiness of those who can enjoy a humble lot in virtuous contentment.

It was with far different feelings that the unfortunate Countess of Leicester viewed those grey and massive towers, when she first beheld them rise above the embowering and richly shaded woods, over which they seemed to preside. She, the undoubted wife of the great Earl, of Elizabeth's minion, and England's mighty favourite, was approaching the presence of her husband, and that husband's sovereign, under the protection, rather than the guidance, of a poor juggler; and though unquestioned Mistress of that proud Castle, whose lightest word ought to have had force sufficient to make its gates leap from their massive hinges to receive her, yet she could not conceal from herself the difficulty and peril which she must experience in gaining admission into her own halls.

The risk and difficulty, indeed, seemed to increase every moment, and at length threatened altogether to put a stop to her farther progress, at the great gate leading to a broad and fair road, which, traversing the breadth of the Chase for the space of two miles, and commanding several most beautiful views of the Castle and lake, terminated at the newly constructed bridge, to which it was an appendage, and which was destined to form the Queen's approach to the Castle on that memorable occasion.

Here the Countess and Wayland found the gate at the end of this avenue, which opened on the Warwick road, guarded by a body of the Queen's mounted yeomen of the guard, armed in corslets richly carved and gilded, and wearing morions instead of bonnets, having their carabines resting with the butt-end on their thighs. These guards, who did duty wherever the Queen went in person, were here stationed under direction of a pursuivant, graced with the Bear and Ragged Staff on his arm, as belonging to the Earl of Leicester, and peremptorily refused all admittance, excepting to such as were guests invited to the festival, or persons who were to perform some part in the mirthful exhibitions which were proposed.

The press was of consequence great around the entrance, and persons of all kinds presented every sort of plea for admittance; to which the guards turned an inexorable ear, pleading, in return to fair words and even to fair offers, the strictness of their orders, founded on the Queen's well-known dislike to the rude pressing of a multitude. With those whom such reasons did not serve, they dealt more rudely, repelling them without ceremony by the pressure of their powerful barbed horses, and good round blows from the stock of their carabines. These last manœuvres produced undulations amongst the crowd, which rendered Wayland much afraid that he might perforce be separated from his charge in the throng. Neither did he know what excuse to make in order to obtain admittance, and he was debating the matter in his head with great uncertainty, when the Earl's pursuivant having cast an eye upon him, exclaimed, to his no small surprise, "Yeomen, make room for the fellow in the orange-tawny cloak— Come forward, Sir Coxcomb, and make haste. What, in the fiend's name, has kept you waiting?—come forward with your bale of woman's gear."

While the pursuivant gave Wayland this pressing yet uncourteous invitation, which, for a minute or two, he could not imagine was applied to him, the yeomen speedily made a free passage for him, and, only cautioning his companion to keep the muffler close around her face, he entered the gate leading her palfrey, but with such a drooping crest, and such a look of conscious fear and anxiety, that the crowd, not greatly pleased at any rate with the preference bestowed upon them, accompanied their entrance with hooting, and a loud laugh of derision.

Admitted thus within the chace, though with no very flattering notice in distinction, Wayland and his charge rode forward, musing what difficulties it would be next their lot to encounter, through the broad avenue, which was centinelled on either side by a long line of retainers, armed with swords and partizans, richly dressed in the Earl of Leicester's liveries, and bearing his cognizance of the Bear and Ragged Staff, each placed within three paces of each other, so as to line the whole road from the entrance into the park to the bridge. And, indeed, when the lady obtained the first commanding view of the Castle, with its stately towers rising from within a long sweeping line of outward walls, ornamented with battlements, and turrets, and platforms, at every point of defence, with many a banner streaming from its walls, and such a bustle of gay crests, and waving plumes, disposed on the terraces and battlements, and all the gay and gorgeous scene, poor Amy's heart, unaccustomed to such splendour, sank as if it died within, and for a moment she asked herself, what she had offered up to Leicester to deserve to become the partner of this princely splendour. But her pride and generous spirit resisted the whisper which bade her despair.

"I have given him," she said, "all that woman has to give—name and fame, heart and hand, have I given the lord of all this magnificence at the altar, and England's Queen could give him no more. He is my husband—I am his wife—Whom God hath joined, man cannot sunder. I will be bold in claiming my right; even the bolder, that I come thus unexpected, and thus forlorn. I know my noble Dudley well—he will be something impatient at my disobeying him, but Amy will weep, and Dudley will forgive her."

These meditations were interrupted by a cry of surprise from her guide Wayland, who suddenly felt himself grasped firmly round the body by a pair of long thin black arms, belonging to some one who had dropped himself out of an oak tree, upon the croupe of his horse, amidst the shouts of laughter which burst from the centinels.

"This must be the devil, or Flibbertigibbet again!" said Wayland, after a vain struggle to disengage himself, and unhorse the urchin who clung to him; "do Kenilworth oaks bear such acorns?"

"In sooth do they, Master Wayland," said his unexpected adjunct, "and many others, too hard for you to crack, for as old as you are, without my teaching you. How would you have passed the pursuivant at the upper gate yonder, had not I warned him our principal juggler was to follow us? and here have I waited for you, having clambered up into the tree from the top of our wain, and I suppose they are all mad for want of me by this time."

"Nay, then, thou art a limb of the devil in good earnest," said Wayland. "I give thee way, good imp, and will walk by thy counsel; only as thou art powerful be merciful."

As he spoke, they approached a strong tower, at the south extremity of the long bridge we have mentioned, which served to protect the outer gateway of the castle of Kenilworth.

Under such disastrous circumstances, and in such singular company, did the unfortunate Countess of Leicester approach, for the first time, the magnificent abode of her almost princely husband.

END OF VOLUME SECOND

KENILWORTH

VOLUME III

Chapter One

Snug. Have you the lion's part written? pray, if it be,
    give it me, for I am slow of study.
Quince. You may do it extempore, for it is nothing but roaring.
                                    Midsummer-Night's Dream

WHEN THE COUNTESS of Leicester arrived at the outer gate of
the Castle of Kenilworth, she found the tower, beneath which its
ample portal arch opened, guarded in a singular manner. Upon the
battlements were placed gigantic warders, with clubs, battle-axes,
and other implements of ancient warfare, designed to represent the
soldiers of King Arthur; those primitive Britons, by whom, according to romantic tradition, the Castle had been first tenanted, though
history carried back its antiquity only to the times of the Heptarchy.
Some of these tremendous figures were real men, dressed up with
vizards and buskins; others were mere pageants composed of
paste-board and buckram, which, viewed from beneath, formed a
sufficiently striking representation of what was intended. But the
gigantic porter who waited at the gate beneath, and actually discharged the duties of warder, owed none of his terrors to fictitious
means. He was a man whose huge stature, thewes, sinews, and bulk
in proportion, would have enabled him to enact Colbrand, Ascapart, or any other giant of romance, without raising himself nearer
to heaven even by the altitude of a chopin. The legs and knees of
this son of Anak were bare, as were his arms from a span below the
shoulder; but his feet were defended with sandals, fastened with
cross straps of scarlet leather, studded with brazen knobs. A close
jerkin of scarlet velvet, looped with gold, with short breeches of the
same, covered his body and a part of his limbs; and he wore on his
shoulders, instead of a cloak, the skin of a black bear. The head of

259

this formidable person was uncovered, excepting by his shaggy black hair, which descended on either side around features of that huge, lumpish, and heavy cast, which are often annexed to men of very uncommon size, and which, notwithstanding some distinguished exceptions, have created a general prejudice against giants, as being a dull and sullen kind of persons. This tremendous warder was appropriately armed with a heavy club, spiked with steel. In fine, he represented excellently one of those giants of popular romance, who figure in every fairy tale, or legend of knight-errantry.

The demeanour of this modern Titan, when Wayland Smith bent his attention to him, had in it something arguing much mental embarrassment and vexation; for sometimes he sat down for an instant on a massive stone bench, which seemed placed for his accommodation beside the gate-way, and then ever and anon he started up, scratching his huge head, and striding to and fro on his post, like one under a fit of impatience and anxiety. It was while the porter was pacing before the gate in this agitated manner, that Wayland, modestly, yet as a matter of course, (not however without some mental misgiving,) was about to pass him, and enter the portal arch. The porter, however, stopped his progress, bidding him, in a thundering voice, "Stand back!" and enforcing his injunction by heaving up his steel-shod mace, and dashing it on the ground before Wayland's horse's nose with such vehemence, that the pavement flashed fire, and the archway rang to the clamour. Wayland, availing himself of Dickie's hint, began to state that he belonged to a band of performers to which his presence was indispensible, that he had been accidentally detained behind, and much to the same purpose. But the warder was inexorable, and kept muttering and murmuring something betwixt his teeth, which Wayland could make little of; and addressing betwixt whiles a refusal of admittance, couched in language which was but too intelligible. A specimen of his speech might run thus.—"What, how now, my masters? (to himself)—Here's a stir—here's a coil.—(Then to Wayland)—You are a loitering knave, and shall have no entrance—(Again to himself,)—Here's a throng—here's a thrusting.—I shall ne'er get through with it—Here's a—humph—ha—(To Wayland)—Back from the gate, or I'll break the pate of thee—(Once more to himself)—Here's a—no—I shall never get through it."

"Stand still," whispered Flibbertigibbet into Wayland's ear, "I know where the shoe pinches, and will tame him in an instant."

He dropped down from the horse, and skipping up to the porter, plucked him by the tail of the bear-skin, so as to induce him to decline his huge head, and whispered something in his ear. Not at the command of the lord of some eastern talisman did ever Afrite change his horrid frown into a look of smooth submission, more suddenly than the gigantic porter of Kenilworth relaxed the terrors of his look, at the instant Flibbertigibbet's whisper reached his ears. He flung his club upon the ground, and caught up Dickie Sludge, raising him to such a distance from the earth, as might have proved perilous had he chanced to let him slip.

"It is even so," he said, with a thundering sound of exultation—"it is even so, my little dandieprat—But who the devil could teach it thee?"

"Do not thou care about that," said Flibbertigibbet; "but"——he looked at Wayland and the lady, and then sunk what he had to say in a whisper, which needed not be a loud one, as the giant held him for his convenience close to his ear. The porter then gave Dickie a warm caress, and set him on the ground with the same care which a careful housewife uses in replacing a cracked china cup upon her mantle-piece, calling out at the same time to Wayland and the lady, "In with you—in with you—and take heed how you come too late another day when I chance to be porter."

"Ay, ay, in with you," added Flibbertigibbet; "I must stay a short space with mine honest Philistine, my Goliath of Gath here; but I will be with you anon, and at the bottom of all your secrets, were they as deep and dark as the Castle dungeon."

"I do believe thou would'st," said Wayland; "but I trust the secret will be soon out of my keeping, and then I shall care the less whether thou or any one knows it."

They now crossed the entrance tower, which obtained the name of the Gallery-tower, from the following circumstance:—The whole bridge, extending from the entrance to another tower on the opposite side of the lake, called Mortimer's Tower, was so disposed as to make a spacious tilt-yard, about one hundred and thirty yards in length, and ten in breadth, strewed with the finest sand, and defended on either side by strong and high palisades. The broad and fair gallery, destined for the ladies who were to witness the feats of chivalry presented on this area, was erected on the northern side of the outer tower, to which it gave name. Our travellers passed slowly along the bridge or tilt-yard, and arrived at Mortimer's Tower, at its farthest extremity, through which the approach led into the outer, or base court of the Castle. Mortimer's Tower bore on its front the scutcheon of the Earl of March, whose daring ambition overthrew the throne of Edward II. and aspired to share his power with the "She-wolf of France," to whom the unhappy monarch was wedded. The gate, which opened under this ominous memorial, was guarded by many warders in rich liveries; but they offered no opposition to the entrance of the Countess and her guide, who, having passed by license of the principal porter at the Gallery-tower, were not, it may be supposed, liable to interruption from his deputies. They entered accordingly, in silence, the great outward court of the Castle, having then full before them that vast and lordly pile, with all its stately towers, each gate open, as if in sign of unlimited hospitality, and the apartments filled with noble guests of every degree, besides dependants, retainers, domestics of every description, and all the appendages and promoters of mirth and revelry.

Amid this stately and busy scene, Wayland halted his horse, and looked upon the lady, as if waiting her commands what was next to be done, since they had safely reached the place of destination. As she remained silent, Wayland, after waiting a minute or two, ventured to ask her in direct terms, what were her next commands. She raised her hand to her forehead, as if in the act of collecting her thoughts and resolution, while she answered him in a low and suppressed voice, like the murmurs of one who speaks in a dream—"Commands? I may indeed claim right to command, but who is there will obey me."

Then suddenly raising her head like one who has formed a decisive resolution, she addressed a gaily dressed domestic, who was crossing the court with importance and bustle in his countenance.—"Stop, sir," she said, "I desire to speak with the Earl of Leicester."

"With whom, an it please you?" said the man, surprised at the demand; and then looking upon the mean equipage of her who used towards him such a tone of authority, he added with insolence, "Why, what Bess of Bedlam is this, would ask to see my lord on such a day as the present?"

"Friend," said the Countess, "be not insolent—my business with the Earl is most urgent."

"You must get some one else to do it, were it thrice as urgent," said the fellow.—"I should summon my lord from the Queen's royal presence to do *your* business, should I?—I were like to be thanked with a horse-whip. I marvel our old porter took not measure of such ware with his club, instead of giving them passage; but his brain is addled with getting his speech by heart."

Two or three persons stopped, attracted by the fleering way in which the serving-man expressed himself; and Wayland, alarmed both for himself and the lady, hastily addressed himself to one who appeared the most civil, and thrusting a piece of money into his hand, held a moment's counsel with him, on the subject of finding a place of temporary retreat for the lady. The person to whom he spoke, being one in some authority, rebuked the others for their incivility, and commanding one fellow to take care of the strangers' horses, he desired them to follow him. The Countess retained presence of mind sufficient to see that it was absolutely necessary she should comply with his request; and, leaving the rude lacqueys and grooms to crack their brutal jests about light heads, light heels, and so forth, Wayland and she followed in silence the deputy usher, who undertook to be their conductor.

They entered the inner court of the Castle by the great gateway, which extended betwixt the principal Keep or Donjon, called Cæsar's Tower, and a stately building which passed by the name of King Henry's Lodging, and were thus placed in the centre of the noble pile, which presented on its different fronts magnificent specimens of every species of castellated architecture, from the Conquest to the reign of Elizabeth, with the appropriate style and ornaments of each.

Across this inner court also they were conducted by their guide to a small but strong tower, occupying the north-west angle of the building, adjacent to the great hall, and filling up a space betwixt the immense range of kitchens and the end of the great hall itself. The lower part of this tower was occupied by some of the household officers of Leicester, owing to its convenient vicinity to the places where their duty lay; but in the upper storey, which was reached by a narrow winding stair, was a small chamber, which, in the great demand for lodgings, had been on the present occasion fitted up for the reception of guests, though generally said to have been used as a place of confinement for some unhappy person who had been there murdered. Tradition called this prisoner Mervyn, and transferred his name to the tower. That it had been used as a prison was not improbable; for the floor of each storey was arched, the walls of tremendous thickness, while the space of the chamber did not exceed fifteen feet square. The window, however, was pleasant, though narrow, and commanded a delightful view of what was called the *Pleasance;* a space of ground enclosed and decorated with arches, trophies, statues, fountains, and other architectural monuments, which formed one access from the castle itself to the garden. There was a bed in the apartment, and other preparations for the reception of a guest, to which the Countess paid but slight attention, her notice being instantly arrested by the sight of writing materials placed on the table, (not very commonly to be found in the bed-rooms of these days) which instantly suggested the idea of writing to Leicester, and remaining private until she had received his answer.

The deputy-usher having introduced them into this commodious apartment, courteously asked Wayland, whose generosity he had experienced, whether he could do any thing farther for his service. Upon receiving a gentle hint, that some refreshment would not be unacceptable, he presently conveyed the smith to the buttery-hatch, where dressed provisions of all sorts were distributed, with hospitable profusion, to all who asked for them. Wayland was readily supplied with some light provisions, such as he thought would best suit the faded appetite of the lady, and did not omit the opportunity of himself making a hasty but hearty meal on more substantial fare. He then returned to the apartment in the turret, where he found the Countess, who had finished her letter to Leicester; and, in lieu of a seal and silken thread, had secured it with a braid of her own beautiful tresses.

"Good friend," said she to Wayland, "whom God hath sent to aid me at my utmost need, I do beseech thee, as the last trouble you shall take for an unfortunate lady, to deliver this letter to the noble Earl of Leicester. Be it received as it may," she said, with features agitated betwixt hope and fear, "thou, good fellow, shalt have no more cumber with me—but I hope the best; and if ever lady made a poor man rich, thou hast surely deserved it at my hand, should my happy days ever come round again. Give it, I pray you, into Lord Leicester's own hand, and mark how he looks on receiving it."

Wayland, on his part, readily undertook the commission, but anxiously prayed the lady, in his turn, to partake of some refreshment; in which he at length prevailed, more through importunity, and her desire to see him begone on his errand, than from any inclination the Countess felt to comply with his request. He then left her, advising her to lock her door on the inside, and not to stir from her little apartment—and went to seek an opportunity of discharging her errand, as well as of carrying into effect a purpose of his own, which circumstances had induced him to form.

In fact, from the conduct of the lady during the journal—her long fits of profound silence—the irresolution and uncertainty which seemed to pervade all her movements, and the obvious incapacity of thinking and acting for herself, under which she seemed to labour, Wayland had formed the not improbable opinion, that the difficulties of her situation had in some degree affected her understanding.

When she had escaped from the seclusion of Cumnor Place, and the dangers to which she was there exposed, it would have seemed her most rational course to retire to her father's, or elsewhere, at a distance from the power of those by whom these dangers had been created. When, instead of doing so, she demanded to be conveyed to Kenilworth, Wayland had been only able to account for her conduct, by supposing that she meant to put herself under the tutelage of Tressilian, and to appeal to the protection of the Queen. But now, instead of following this natural course, she entrusted him with a letter to Leicester, the patron of Varney, and within whose jurisdiction at least, if not under his express authority, all the evils she had already suffered were inflicted upon her. This seemed an unsafe, and even a desperate measure, and Wayland felt anxiety for his own safety, as well as that of the lady, should he execute her commission, before he had secured the advice and countenance of a protector. He therefore resolved, before delivering the letter to Leicester, that he would seek out Tressilian, and communicate to him the arrival of the lady at Kenilworth, and thus at once rid himself of all further responsibility, and devolve the task of guiding and protecting this unfortunate lady upon the patron who had first employed him in her service.

"He will be a better judge than I can," said Wayland, "whether she is to be gratified in this humour of appeal to Leicester, which seems like an act of insanity; and, therefore, I will turn the matter over on his hands, deliver him the letter, receive what they list to give me by way of guerdon, and then shew the Castle of Kenilworth a pair of light heels; for, after the work I have been engaged in, it will be, I fear, neither a safe nor wholesome place of residence; and I would rather shoe colts on the coldest common in England, than share in its gayest revels."

Chapter Two

In my time I have seen a boy do wonders.
Robin, the red tinker, had a boy
Would ha' run through a cat-hole.
                                        The Coxcomb

AMID the universal bustle which filled the Castle and its environs, it was no easy matter to find any individual; and Wayland was still less likely to light upon Tressilian, whom he sought so anxiously, because, sensible of the danger of attracting attention, in the circumstances in which he was placed, he dared not make general inquiries among the retainers or domestics of Leicester. He learned, however, by indirect questions, that, in all probability, Tressilian must have been one of a large party of gentlemen in attendance on the Earl of Sussex, who had accompanied their patron that morning to Kenilworth, where Leicester had received them with marks of the most formal respect and distinction. He farther learned, that both Earls, with their followers, and many other nobles, knights, and gentlemen, had taken horse, and gone towards Warwick several hours since, for the purpose of escorting the Queen to Kenilworth.

Her Majesty's arrival, like other great events, was delayed from hour to hour; and it was now announced by a breathless post, that her Majesty being detained by her gracious desire, to receive the homage of her lieges who had thronged to wait upon her at Warwick, it would be the hour of twilight ere she entered the Castle. The intelligence released for a time those who were upon duty, in the immediate expectation of the Queen's appearance, and ready to play their part in the solemnities with which it was to be accompanied; and Wayland, seeing several horsemen enter the Castle, was not without hopes that Tressilian might be of the number. That he might not lose an opportunity of meeting his patron in case this should be the case, Wayland placed himself in the base-court of the Castle, near Mortimer's Tower, and watched every one who went or came by the bridge, the extremity of which was protected by that building. Thus stationed, nobody could enter or leave the Castle without his observation, and most anxiously did he study the garb and countenance of every horseman, as, passing from under the opposite Gallery-tower, they paced slowly, or curvetted, along the tilt-yard, and approached the entrance of the base-court.

But while Wayland gazed thus eagerly to discover him whom he saw not, he was pulled by the sleeve by one by whom he himself would not willingly have been seen.

This was Dickie Sludge, or Flibbertigibbet, who, like the imp whose name he bore, and whom he had been accoutred so as to resemble, seemed to be ever at the ear of those who thought least of him. Whatever were Wayland's internal feelings, he judged it necessary to express pleasure at their unexpected meeting.

"Ha! is it thou, my minikin—my miller's thumb—my prince of caco-dæmons—my little mouse?"

"Ay," said Dickie, "the mouse which gnawed asunder the toils, just when the lion who was caught in them began to look wonderfully like an ass."

"Why, thou little hop-the-gutter, thou art as sharp as vinegar this afternoon. But tell me, how did'st thou come off with yonder jolter-headed giant, whom I left thee with?—I was afraid he would have stripped thy clothes, and so swallowed thee as men peel and eat a roasted chesnut."

"Had he done so," replied the boy, "he would have had more brains in his guts than ever he had in his noddle. But the giant is a courteous monster, and more grateful than many other folks whom I have helped at a pinch, Master Wayland Smith."

"Beshrew me, Flibbertigibbet," replied Wayland, "but thou art sharper than a Sheffield whittle! I would I knew by what charm you muzzled yonder old bear."

"Ay, that is in your own manner," answered Dickie; "you think fine speeches will pass muster instead of good will—however, as to this honest porter, you must know, that when we presented ourselves at the gate yonder, his brain was overburthened with a speech which had been penned for him, and withal proved rather an overmatch for his gigantic faculties. Now this same pithy oration had been indited, like sundry others, by my learned magister, Erasmus Holiday, so I had heard it often enough to remember every line. As soon as I heard him blundering, and floundering like a fish upon dry land, through the first verse, and perceived him at a stand, I knew where the shoe pinched, and helped him to the next word, when he caught me up in an ecstacy, even as you saw but now. I promised, as the price of your admission, to hide me under his bearish gaberdine, and prompt him in the hour of need. I have just now been getting some food in the Castle, and am about to return to him."

"That's right—that's right, my dear Dickie," replied Wayland; "haste thee, for Heaven's sake! else the poor giant will be utterly disconsolate for want of his dwarfish auxiliary—Away with thee, Dickie."

"Ay, ay!" answered the boy—"Away with Dickie, when we have got what good of him we can.—You will not let me know the story of this lady, then, who is as much sister of thine as I am?"

"Why, what good would it do thee, thou silly elf?" said Wayland.

"O, stand ye on these terms?" said the boy; "well, I care not greatly about the matter,—only, I never smell out a secret, but I try to be either at the right or the wrong end of it, and so good evening to you."

"Nay, but Dickie," said Wayland, who knew the boy's restless and intriguing disposition too well not to fear his enmity—"stay, my dear Dickie—part not with old friends so shortly!—Thou shalt know all I know of the lady one day."

"Ay!" said Dickie; "and that day may prove a nigh one—fare thee well, Wayland—I will to my large-limbed friend, who, if he have not so sharp a wit as some folks, is at least more grateful for the service which other folks render him. And so again, good evening to ye."

So saying, he cast a somerset through the gateway, and, lighting on the bridge, ran with the extraordinary agility, which was one of his distinguished attributes, towards the Gallery-tower, and was out of sight in an instant.

"I would to God I were safe out of this Castle again!" prayed Wayland, internally; "for now that this mischievous imp has put his finger in the pye, it cannot but prove a mess fit for the devil's eating. I would to Heaven Master Tressilian would appear!"

Tressilian, whom he was thus anxiously expecting in one direction, had returned to Kenilworth by another access. It was indeed true, as Wayland had conjectured, that, in the earlier part of the day, he had accompanied the Earls on their cavalcade towards Warwick, not without hope that he might in that town hear some tidings of his emissary. Being disappointed in this expectation, and observing Varney amongst Leicester's attendants, seeming as if he had some purpose of advancing to and addressing him, he conceived, in the present circumstances, it was wisest to avoid the interview. He, therefore, left the presence-chamber where the High-Sheriff of the county was in the very midst of his dutiful address to her Majesty; and, mounting his horse, rode back to Kenilworth by a remote and circuitous road, and entered the Castle by a small sally-port in the western wall, at which he was readily admitted as one of the followers of the Earl of Sussex, toward whom Leicester had commanded the utmost courtesy to be exercised. It was thus that he met not Wayland, who was impatiently watching his arrival, and whom he himself would have been, at least, equally desirous to have seen.

Having delivered his horse to the charge of his attendant, he walked for a space in the Pleasance and in the garden, rather to indulge in comparative solitude his own reflections, than to admire those singular beauties of nature and art which the magnificence of Leicester had there assembled. The greater part of the persons of condition had left the Castle for the present, to form part of the Earl's cavalcade; others, who remained behind, were on the battlements, outer walls, and towers, eager to view the splendid spectacle of the royal entry. The garden, therefore, while every other part of the Castle resounded with the human voice, was silent, but for the whispering of the leaves, the emulous warbling of the tenants of a large aviary, with their happier companions who remained denizens of the free air, and the plashing of the fountains, which, forced into the air from sculptures of fantastic and grotesque forms, fell down with ceaseless sound into the great basins of Italian marble.

The melancholy thoughts of Tressilian cast a gloomy shade on all the objects with which he was surrounded. He compared the magnificent scenes which he here traversed, with the deep woodland and wild moorlands which surrounded Lidcote-Hall, and the image of Amy Robsart glided like a phantom through every landscape which his imagination summoned up. Nothing is perhaps more dangerous to the future happiness of men of deep thought and retired habits, than the entertaining an early, long, and unfortunate attachment. It frequently sinks so deep into the mind, that it becomes their dream by night and their vision by day—mixes itself with every source of interest and enjoyment; and when blighted and withered by final disappointment, it seems as if the springs of the heart were dried up along with it. This aching of the heart, this languishing after a shadow which has lost all the gaiety of its colouring, this dwelling on the remembrance of a dream from which we have been long roughly awakened, is the weakness of a gentle and generous heart, and it was that of Tressilian.

He himself at length became sensible of the necessity of forcing other objects upon his mind; and for this purpose he left the Pleasance, in order to mingle with the noisy crowd upon the walls, and view the preparation for the pageants. But as he left the garden, and heard the busy hum mixed with music and laughter, which floated around him, he felt an uncontroulable reluctance to mix with society, whose feelings were in a tone so different from his own, and resolved, instead of doing so, to retire to the chamber assigned him, and employ himself in study until the tolling of the great castle-bell should announce the arrival of Elizabeth.

Tressilian crossed accordingly by the passage betwixt the immense range of kitchens and the great hall, and ascended to the third storey of Mervyn's Tower, and applying himself to the door of the small apartment which had been allotted to him, was surprised to find it was locked. He then recollected that the deputy-chamberlain had given him a master-key, advising him, in the present confused state of the Castle, to keep his door as much shut as possible. He applied this key to the lock, the bolt revolved, he entered, and in the same instant saw a female form seated in the apartment, and recognized that form to be Amy Robsart. His first idea was, that a heated imagination had raised the image on which it doated into visible existence; his second, that he beheld an apparition—the third and abiding conviction, that it was Amy herself, paler, indeed, and thinner than in the days of heedless happiness, when she possessed the form and hue of a wood-nymph, with the beauty of a sylph; but still Amy, unequalled in loveliness by aught which had ever visited his eyes.

The astonishment of the Countess was scarce less than that of Tressilian, although it was of shorter duration, because she had heard from Wayland that he was in the Castle. She had started up at his first entrance, and now stood facing him, the paleness of her cheeks having given way to a deep blush.

"Tressilian," she said, at length, "why come you here?"

"Nay, why come *you* here, Amy," returned Tressilian, "unless it is at length to claim that aid, which, as far as one man's heart and arm can extend, shall instantly be rendered to you?"

She was silent a moment, and then answered in a sorrowful, rather than an angry tone,—"I require no aid, Master Tressilian, and would rather be injured than benefited by any which your kindness can offer me. Believe me, I am near one whom law and love oblige to protect me."

"The villain then hath done you the poor justice which remained in his power," said Tressilian; "and I behold before me the wife of Varney!"

"The wife of Varney!" she replied, with all the emphasis of scorn; "with what base name, sir, does your boldness stigmatize the—the—the"—She hesitated, dropped her tone of scorn, looked down, and was confused and silent, for she recollected what fatal consequence might attend her completing the sentence with "the Countess of Leicester," which were the words that naturally suggested themselves. It would have been a betrayal of the secret, on which her husband had assured her that his fortunes depended, to Tressilian, to Sussex, to the Queen, and to the whole assembled court. "Never," she thought, "will I break my promised silence. I will submit to every suspicion rather than that."

The tears rose to her eyes, as she stood silent before Tressilian; while, looking on her with mingled grief and pity, he said, "Alas! Amy, your eyes contradict your tongue. That speaks of a protector, willing and able to watch over you; but these tell me you are ruined and deserted by the wretch to whom you have attached yourself."

She looked on him, with eyes in which anger sparkled through her tears, but only repeated the word "wretch!" with a scornful emphasis.

"Yes, *wretch!*" said Tressilian; "for were he aught better, why are you here, and alone in my apartment? why was not fitting provision made for your honourable reception?"

"In your apartment?" repeated Amy; "in *your* apartment?—it shall instantly be relieved of my presence." She hastened towards the door; but the sad recollection of her deserted state at once pressed on her mind, and, pausing on the threshold, she added, in a voice unutterably pathetic, "Alas! I had forgot—I know not where to go"——

"I see—I see it all," said Tressilian, springing to her side, and leading her back to the seat, on which she sunk down—"You do need aid—you do need protection, though you will not own it; and you shall not need it in vain. Leaning on my arm, as the representative of your excellent and broken-hearted father, on the very threshold of this Castle-gate, you shall meet Elizabeth; and the first deed she shall do in the towers of Kenilworth, shall be an act of justice to her sex and her subjects. Strong in my good cause, and in the Queen's justice, the power of her minion shall not shake my resolution. I will instantly seek Sussex."

"Not for all that is under heaven!" said the Countess, much alarmed, and feeling the absolute necessity of obtaining time, at least, for consideration. "Tressilian, you were wont to be generous. Grant me one request, and believe, if it be your wish to save me from misery, and from madness, you will do more by making me the promise I ask of you, than Elizabeth can do with all her power."

"Ask me any thing for which you can allege reason," said Tressilian; "but demand not of me"——

"O, limit not your boon, dear Edmund!" exclaimed the Countess—"you once loved that I should call you so—limit not your boon to reason! for my case is all madness, and phrenzy must guide the counsels which alone can aid me."

"If you speak thus wildly," said Tressilian, astonishment again overpowering both his grief and his resolution, "I must believe you indeed incapable of thinking or acting for yourself."

"Oh no!" she exclaimed, sinking on one knee before him, "I am not mad—I am but a creature unutterably miserable, and, from circumstances the most singular, dragged on to a precipice by the arm of him who thinks he is keeping me from it—even by yours, Tressilian—by yours, whom I have honoured, respected—all but loved—And yet loved too—loved too, Tressilian—though not as you wished me."

There was an energy—a self-possession—an abandonment in her voice and manner—a total resignation of herself to his generosity, which, together with the kindness of her expressions to himself, moved him deeply. He raised her, and, in broken accents, entreated her to be comforted.

"I cannot," she said, "I will not be comforted, till you grant me my request! I will speak as plainly as I dare—I am now awaiting the commands of one who has a right to issue them—The interference of a third person—of you in especial, Tressilian, will be ruin—utter ruin to me. Wait but four-and-twenty hours, and it may be that the poor Amy may have the means to shew that she values, and can reward, your disinterested friendship—that she is happy herself, and has the means to make you so—It is surely worth your patience, for so short a space?"

Tressilian paused, and weighing in his mind the various probabilities which might render a violent interference more prejudicial than advantageous, both to the happiness and reputation of Amy; considering also that she was within the walls of Kenilworth, and could suffer no injury in a castle honoured with the Queen's residence, and filled with her guards and attendants,—he conceived, upon the whole, that he might render her more evil than good service, by intruding upon her his appeal to Elizabeth on her behalf. He expressed his resolution cautiously however, doubting naturally whether Amy's hopes of extricating herself from her difficulties rested on any thing stronger than a blinded attachment to Varney, whom he supposed to be her seducer.

"Amy," he said, while he fixed his sad and expressive eyes on her's, which, in her ecstacy of doubt, terror, and perplexity, she cast up towards him, "I have ever remarked, that when others called thee girlish and wilful, there lay under that external semblance of youthful and self-willed folly, deep feeling and strong sense. In this I will confide, trusting your own fate in your own hands for the space of twenty-four hours, without my interference by word or act."

"Do you promise me this, Tressilian?" said the Countess. "Is it possible you can yet repose so much confidence in me?—do you promise, as you are a gentleman and man of honour, to intrude in my matters, neither by speech or action, whatever you may see or hear that seems to you to demand your interference?—will you so far trust me?"

"I will, upon my honour," said Tressilian; "but when that space is expired"——

"When that space is expired," she said, interrupting him, "you are free to act as your judgment shall determine."

"Is there nought besides which I can do for you, Amy?" said Tressilian.

"Nothing," said she, "save to leave me—that is, if—I blush to acknowledge my helplessness by asking it—if you can spare me the use of this apartment for the twenty-four hours."

"This is most wonderful!" said Tressilian; "what hope or interest can you have in a Castle, where you cannot command even an apartment?"

"Argue not, but leave me," she said; and added, as he slowly and unwillingly retired, "Generous Edmund! the time may come, when Amy may shew she deserved thy noble attachment."

Chapter Three

What, man, ne'er lack a draught, when the full can
Stands at thine elbow, and craves emptying!—
Nay, fear not me, for I have no delight
To watch men's vices, since I have myself
Of virtue nought to boast of.—I'm a striker,
Would have the world strike with me, pell-mell, all.
Pandæmonium

TRESSILIAN, in strange agitation of mind, had hardly stepped down the first two or three steps of the winding stair-case, when, greatly to his surprise and displeasure, he met Michael Lambourne, wearing an impudent familiarity of visage, for which Tressilian felt much disposed to throw him down stairs; until he remembered the prejudice which Amy, the only object of his solicitude, was likely to receive from his engaging in any act of violence at that time, and in that place.

He therefore contented himself with looking sternly upon Lambourne, as upon one whom he deemed unworthy of notice, and attempted to pass him in his way down stairs, without any symptom of recognition. But Lambourne, who, amidst the profusion of that day's hospitality, had not failed to take a deep, though not an overpowering cup of sack, was not in the humour of humbling himself before any man's looks. He stopped Tressilian upon the stair-case without the least bashfulness or embarrassment, and addressed him as if he had been on kind and intimate terms:—"What, no grudge between us I hope upon old scores, Master Tressilian?—nay, I am one who remember former kindness rather than later feud—I'll convince you that I mean honestly and kindly, ay, and comfortably by thee."

"I desire none of your intimacy," said Tressilian—"keep company with your mates."

"Now see how hasty he is!" said Lambourne; "and how these gentles, that are made questionless out of the porcelain clay of the earth, look down upon poor Michael Lambourne! You would take Master Tressilian now for the most maid-like, modest, simpering squire of dames, that ever made love when candles were long i' the stuff—snuff—call you it?—Why you would play the saint on us, Master Tressilian, and forget that even now thou hast a commodity in thy very bed-chamber, to the shame of my lord's Castle, ha! ha! ha! have I touched you, Master Tressilian?"

"I know not what you mean," said Tressilian, inferring, however, too surely, that this licentious ruffian must have been sensible of Amy's presence in his apartment; "but if," he continued, "thou art varlet of the chambers, and lackest a fee, there is one to leave mine unmolested."

Lambourne looked at the piece of gold, and put it in his pocket, saying—"Now, I know not but you might have done more with me by a kind word, than by this chiming rogue. But after all he pays well that pays with gold—and Mike Lambourne was never a make-bate, or a spoil-sport, or the like. E'en live and let others live, that is my motto—Only, I would not let some folks cock their beaver at me neither, as if they were made of silver ore, and I of Dutch pewter. So if I keep your secret, Master Tressilian, you may look sweet on me at least; and were I to want a little backing or countenance, being caught, as you see the best of us may be, in a sort of peccadillo—why, you owe it me—and so e'en make your chamber serve you and some bird in bower beside—it's all one to Mike Lambourne."

"Make way, sir," said Tressilian, unable to bridle his indignation, "you have had your fee."

"Um!" said Lambourne, giving place, however, while he sulkily muttered between his teeth, repeating Tressilian's words—"Make way—and you have had your fee—but it matters not, I will spoil no sport, as I said before; I am no dog in the manger—mind that." He spoke louder and louder, as Tressilian, by whom he felt himself over-awed, got farther and farther out of hearing. "I am no dog in the manger—but I will not carry coals neither—mind that, Master Tres-silian; and I will have a peep at this wench, whom you have quartered so commodiously in our old haunted room—afraid of ghosts belike, and not too willing to sleep alone. If *I* had done this now in a strange lord's castle, the word had been,—The porter's lodge for the knave! and,—Have him flogged—trundle him down stairs like a turnip!—Ay but your virtuous gentlemen take strange privileges over us, who are downright servants of our senses. Well—I have my Master Tressi-lian's head under my belt by this lucky discovery, that is one thing certain; and I will try to get a sight of this Lindabrides of his, that is another."

Chapter Four

Now fare thee well, my master—if true service
Be guerdon'd with hard looks, e'en cut the tow-line,
And let our barks across the pathless flood
Hold several courses——

Shipwreck

TRESSILIAN walked into the outer yard of the Castle, scarce know-ing what to think of his late strange and most unexpected interview with Amy Robsart, and dubious if he had done well, being intrusted with the delegated authority of her father, to pass his word so solemnly to leave her to her own guidance for so many hours. Yet how could he have denied her request. Dependant as she had too probably ren-dered herself upon Varney, such was his natural reasoning, the happi-ness of her future life might depend upon her not driving him to extremities, and since no power of Tressilian's could extricate her from the power of that man, supposing he was to acknowledge Amy to be his wife, what title had he to destroy the hope of domestic peace, which might yet remain to her, by setting enmity betwixt them? Tres-silian resolved, therefore, scrupulously to observe his word pledged to Amy, both because it had been given, and because, as he still thought, while he considered and reconsidered that extraordinary interview, it could not with justice or propriety have been refused.

In one respect, he had gained much towards securing effectual protection for this unhappy and still beloved object of his early affection. Amy was no longer mewed up in a distant and solitary retreat, under the charge of persons of doubtful reputation. She was in the Castle of Kenilworth, within the verge of the Royal Court for the time, free from all risk of violence, and liable to be produced before Elizabeth on the first summons. These were circumstances which could not but assist greatly the efforts which he might have occasion to use in her behalf.

While he was thus balancing the advantages and perils which attended her unexpected presence in Kenilworth, Tressilian was hastily and anxiously accosted by Wayland, who, after hastily ejaculating, "Thank God, your worship is found at last!" proceeded with breathless caution to pour into his ear the intelligence, that the lady had escaped from Cumnor Place.

"And is at present in this Castle," said Tressilian; "I know it, and I have seen her—Was it by her own choice she found refuge in my apartment?"

"No," answered Wayland; "but I could think of no other way of safely bestowing her, and was but too happy to find a deputy-usher who knew where you were quartered;—in jolly society truly, the hall on the one hand, and the kitchen on the other!"

"Peace, this is no time for jesting," answered Tressilian, sternly.

"I wot that but too well," said the artist, "for I have felt this three days as if I had an halter round my neck. This lady knows not her own mind—she will have none of your aid—commands you not to be named to her—and is about to put herself into the hands of Leicester. I had never got her safe into your chamber, had she known the owner of it."

"Is it possible?" said Tressilian. "But she may have hopes the Earl will exert his influence in her favour over his villainous dependant."

"I know nothing of that," said Wayland—"but I believe, if she is to reconcile herself with either Leicester or Varney, the side of the Castle of Kenilworth, which will be safest for us, will be the outside from which we can fastest fly away. It is not my purpose to abide an instant after delivery of the letter to Leicester, which waits but your commands to find its way to him. See, here it is—but no—a plague on it—I must have left it in my dog-hole, in the hay-loft yonder, where I am to sleep."

"Death and fury!" said Tressilian, transported beyond his usual patience; "thou hast not lost that on which may depend a stake more important than a thousand such lives as thine?"

"Lost it!" answered Wayland, readily; "that were a jest indeed!—no, sir, I have it carefully put up with my night-sack, and some matters

I have occasion to use—I will fetch it in an instant."

"Do so," said Tressilian; "be faithful, and thou shalt be well rewarded. But if I have reason to suspect thee, a dead dog were in better case than thou."

Wayland bowed, and took his leave with seeming confidence and alacrity; but, in fact, filled with the utmost dread and confusion. The letter was lost, that was certain, notwithstanding the apology which he had made to appease the impatient displeasure of Tressilian. It was lost—it might fall into wrong hands—it would then, certainly, occasion a discovery of the whole intrigue in which he had been engaged; nor, indeed, did he see much prospect of its remaining concealed, in any event. He felt much hurt, besides, at Tressilian's burst of impatience.

"Nay, if I am to be paid in this coin, for services where my neck is concerned, it is time I should look to myself. Here have I offended, for aught I know, to the death, the lord of this immense Castle, whose word were as powerful to take away my life, as the breath which speaks it to blow out a farthing candle. And all this for a mad lady, and a melancholy gallant; who, on the loss of a four-nooked bit of paper, has his hand on his poignado, and swears death and fury!—then there is the Doctor and Varney—I will save myself from the whole mess of them—Life is dearer than gold—I will fly this instant, though I leave my reward behind me."

These reflections naturally enough occurred to a mind like Wayland's, who found himself engaged far deeper than he had expected in a train of mysterious and unintelligible intrigues, in which the actors seemed hardly to know their own course. And yet, to do him justice, his personal fears were, in some degree, counterbalanced by his compassion for the deserted state of the lady.

"I care not a groat for Master Tressilian," he said; "I have done more than bargain by him, and I have brought his errant-damozel within his reach, so that he may look after her himself; but I fear the poor thing is in much danger amongst those stormy spirits. I will to her chamber, and tell her the fate which has befallen her letter, that she may write another if she list. She cannot lack a messenger, I trow, where there are so many lacqueys that can carry a letter to their lord. And I will tell her also that I leave the Castle, trusting her to God, her own guidance, and Master Tressilian's care and looking after—perhaps she may remember the ring she offered me—it was well earned, I trow—But she is a lovely creature, and—marry hang the ring! I will not bear a base mind for the matter. If I fare ill in this world for my good nature, I will have better chance in the next.—So now for the lady, and then for the road—via!"

With the stealthy step and jealous eye of the cat that steals on her prey, Wayland resumed the way to the Countess's chamber, sliding along by the side of the courts and passages, alike observant of all around him, and studious himself to escape observation. In this manner he crossed the outward and inward castle-yard, and the great arched passage, which, running betwixt the range of kitchen offices and the hall, led to the bottom of the little winding-stair that gave access to the chambers of Mervyn's Tower.

The artist congratulated himself on having escaped the various perils of his journey, and was in the act of ascending by two steps at once, when he observed that the shadow of a man, thrown from a door which stood a-jar, darkened the opposite wall of the stair-case. Wayland drew back cautiously, went down to the inner court-yard, spent about a quarter of an hour, which seemed at least quadruple its usual duration, in walking from place to place, and then returned to the tower, in hopes to find that the lurker had disappeared. He ascended as high as the suspicious spot—there was no shadow on the wall—He ascended a few steps farther—the door was still ajar, and he was doubtful whether to advance or retreat, when it was suddenly thrown wide, and Michael Lambourne bolted out upon the astonished Wayland. "Who the devil art thou? and what seek'st thou in this part of the Castle?—march into that chamber, and be hanged to thee!"

"I am no dog, to go at every man's whistle," said the artist, affecting a confidence which was belied by a certain shake in his voice.

"Say'st thou me so?—Come hither, Laurence Staples."

A huge ill-made and ill-looked fellow, upwards of six feet high, appeared at the door, and Lambourne proceeded: "If thou be'st so fond of this tower, my friend, thou shalt see its foundations, good twelve feet below the bed of the lake, and tenanted by certain jolly toads, snakes, and so forth, which thou wilt find mighty good company. Therefore, once more I ask you in fair play, who thou art, and what thou seek'st here?"

If the dungeon-grate once clashes behind me, thought Wayland, I am a gone man.—He therefore answered submissively, "He was the poor juggler whom his honour had met yesterday in Weatherly-bottom."

"And what juggling trick wert thou playing in this tower?—thy gang," said Lambourne, "lie over against Clinton's buildings."

"I came here to see my sister," said the juggler, "who is in Master Tressilian's chamber, just above."

"Aha!" said Lambourne, smiling, "here be truths—Upon my honour, for a stranger, this same Master Tressilian makes himself at home amongst us, and furnishes out his cell handsomely, with all sort of commodities—this will be a precious tale of the sainted Master Tressilian, and will be welcome to some folks, as a purse of broad pieces to me—Hark ye, fellow," he continued, addressing Wayland, "thou shalt not give Puss a hint to steal away—we must catch her on her form. So, back with that pitiful sheep-biting visage of thine, or I will fling thee from the window of the tower, and try if your juggling skill can save your bones."

"Your worship will not be so hard-hearted, I trust," said Wayland; "poor folks must live. I trust your honour will allow me to speak with my sister?"

"Sister on Adam's side, I warrant," said Lambourne; "or, if otherwise, the more knave thou. But sister or no sister, thou diest on point of fox, if thou comest a prying to this tower once more. And now I think of it, uds daggers and death! I will see thee out of the Castle, for this is a more main concern than thy jugglery."

"But, please your worship," said Wayland, "I am to enact Arion in the pageant upon the lake this very evening."

"I will act it myself, by Saint Christopher," said Lambourne—"Orion, call'st thou him?—I will act Orion, his belt and his seven stars to boot. Come along, for a rascal knave as thou art—follow me!—Or stay—Laurence, do thou bring him along."

Laurence seized by the collar of the cloak the unresisting juggler, while Lambourne, with hasty steps, led the way to that same sally-port, or secret postern, by which Tressilian had returned to the Castle, and which opened in the western wall, at no great distance from Mervyn's Tower.

While traversing with a rapid foot the space betwixt the tower and the sally-port, Wayland in vain racked his brain for some device which might avail the poor lady, for whom, notwithstanding his own imminent danger, he felt a deep interest. But when he was thrust out of the Castle, and informed by Lambourne, with a tremendous oath, that instant death would be the consequence of his again approaching it, he cast up his hands and eyes to heaven, as if to call God to witness he had stood to the uttermost in defence of the oppressed; then turned his back on the proud towers of Kenilworth, and went his way to seek a humbler and safer place of refuge.

Laurence and Lambourne gazed a little while after Wayland, and then turned to go back to their tower, when the former thus addressed his companion: "Never credit me, Master Lambourne, if I can guess why thou hast driven this poor caitiff from the Castle, just when he was to bear a part in the show that was beginning, and all this about a wench."

"Ah, Laurence," replied Lambourne, "thou art thinking of Black

Joan Jugges of Slingdon, and hast sympathy with human frailty. But couragio, most noble Duke of the Dungeon and Lord of Limbo, for thou art as dark in this matter as thine own dominions of Little-ease, my most reverend Seignor of the Low Countries of Kenilworth. Know that our most notable master, Richard Varney, would give as much to have a hole in this same Tressilian's coat, as would make us some fifty midnight carousals, with the full leave of bidding the steward go snick up, if he come to startle us too soon from our goblets."

"Nay, an that be the case, thou hast right," said Laurence Staples, the upper-warder, or in common phrase, the first jailor of Kenilworth Castle, and of the Liberty and Honour belonging thereto; "but how will you manage when you are absent at the Queen's entrance, Master Lambourne; for methinks thou must attend thy master there?"

"Why thou, mine honest prince of prisons, must keep ward in my absence—let Tressilian enter if he will, but see thou let no one come out—if the damsel herself would make a break, as 'tis not unlike she may, scare her back with rough words—she is but a paltry player's wench after all."

"Nay, for that matter," said Laurence, "I might shut the iron wicket upon her, that stands without the double door, and so force per force she will be bound to her hearing without more trouble."

"Then Tressilian will not get access to her," said Lambourne, reflecting a moment. "But 'tis no matter—she will be detected in his chamber, and that is all one.—But confess, thou old bat's-eyed dungeon-keeper, that you fear to keep awake by yourself in that Mervyn's Tower of thine?"

"Why, as to fear, Master Lambourne," said the fellow, "I mind it not the turning of a key; but strange things have been heard and seen in that tower.—Ye have heard, for as short time as you have been in Kenilworth, that it is haunted by the spirit of Arthur ap Mervyn, a wild chief taken by fierce Lord Mortimer, when he was one of the Lords Marchers of Wales, and murthered, as they say, in that same tower which bears his name?"

"O, I have heard the tale five hundred times," said Lambourne, "and how the ghost is always most vociferous when they boil leeks and stirabout, or fry toasted cheese in the culinary regions. Santo Diavolo, man, hold thy tongue, I know all about it."

"Ay, but thou dost not though," said the turnkey, "for as wise as thou wouldst make thyself. Ah, it is an awful thing to murther a prisoner in his ward!—you, that may have given a man a stab in a dark street, know nothing of it. To give a mutinous fellow a knock on the head with the keys, and bid him be quiet, that's what I call keeping order in the ward; but to draw weapon and slay him, as was done to this Welsh lord, *that* raises you a ghost that will render your prison-house untenable by any decent captive for some hundred years—and I have that regard for my prisoners, poor things, that I have put good squires and men of worship, that have taken a ride on the highway, or slandered my Lord of Leicester, or the like, fifty feet under ground, rather than I would put them into that upper chamber yonder that they call Mervyn's Bower. Indeed, by good Saint Peter of the Fetters, I marvel my noble lord, or Master Varney, would think of lodging guests there; and if this Master Tressilian could get any one to keep him company, and in especial a pretty wench, why truly I think he was in the right on't."

"I tell thee," said Lambourne, leading the way into the turnkey's apartment, "thou art an ass—go bolt the wicket on the stair, and trouble not thy noddle about ghosts.—Give me the wine-stoup, man; I am somewhat heated with chafing with yonder rascal."

While Lambourne drew a long draught from a pitcher of claret, which he made use of without any cup, the warder went on, vindicating his own belief in the supernatural, "Thou hast been few hours in this Castle, and hast been for the whole space so drunk, Lambourne, that thou art deaf, dumb, and blind. But we should hear less of your bragging, were you to pass a night with us at full moon, for then the ghost is busiest; and more especially when a rattling wind sets you in from the north-west, with some sprinkling of rain, and now and then a growl of thunder. Body o' me, what crackings and clashings, what groanings and what howlings will there be at such times in Mervyn's Bower, right as it were over our heads, till the matter of two quarts of distilled waters has not been enough to keep my lads and me together."

"Pshaw, man!" replied Lambourne, on whom his last draught, joined to repeated visitation of the pitcher upon former occasions, began to make some innovation, "thou speak'st thou know'st not what about spirits. No one knows justly what to say about them; and—in short—least said may in that matter be soonest amended. Some men believe in one thing, some in another—it is all matter of fancy. I have known them of all sorts, my dear Laurence Lock-the-Door, and sensible men too. There's a great lord—we'll pass his name, Laurence—he believes in the stars and moon, the planets and their courses, and so forth, and that they twinkle exclusively for his benefit; when in sober, or rather in drunken truth, Laurence, they are only shining to keep honest fellows like me out of the kennel. Well, sir, let his humour pass, he is great enough to indulge it.—Then look ye, there is another—a very learned man, I promise you, and can vent Greek and Hebrew as I can Thieves'-latin—he has an humour of sympathies and antipathies—of changing lead into gold and the like—why, via, let that pass too, and let him pay those in transmigrated coin, who are fools enough to let it be current with them.—Then here comest thou thyself, another great man, though neither learned nor noble, yet full six feet high, and thou, like a purblind mole, must needs believe in ghosts and goblins, and such like.—Now, there is, besides, a great man—that is, a great little man, or a little great man, my dear Laurence—and his name begins with V—and what believes he? Why nothing, honest Laurence—nothing in earth, heaven, or hell—And for my part, if I believe there is a devil, it is only because I think there must be some one to catch our friend by the back 'when soul and body sever,' as the ballad says—for your antecedent will have a consequent —*raro antecedentem,* as Doctor Bricham was wont to say—But this is Greek to you now, honest Laurence, and in sooth learning is dry work —hand me the pitcher once more."

"In faith, if you drink more, Michael," said the Warder, "you will be in sorry case either to play Arion or to wait on your master on such a solemn night; and I expect each moment to hear the great bell toll for the muster at Mortimer's Tower, to receive the Queen."

While Staples remonstrated, Lambourne drank; and then setting down the pitcher, which was nearly emptied, with a deep sigh, he said, in an under tone, which soon rose to a high one as his speech proceeded, "Never mind, Laurence—if I be drunk, I know that shall make Varney uphold me sober. But, as I said, never mind, I can carry my drink discreetly. Moreover, I am to go on the water as Orion, and shall take cold unless I take something comfortable before-hand. Not play Orion! Let us see the best roarer that ever strained his lungs for twelve pence out-mouth me. What if they see me a little disguised?— Wherefore should any man be sober to-night? answer me that—it is matter of loyalty to be merry—and I tell thee, there are those in the castle, who if they are not merry when drunk, have little chance to be merry when sober—I name no names, Laurence, but your pottle of sack is a fine shoeing-horn to pull on a loyal humour, and a merry one. Huzza for Queen Elizabeth!—for the noble Leicester!—for the worshipful Master Varney!—and for Michael Lambourne, that can turn them all round his finger!"

So saying, he walked down stairs, and across the inner court.

The Warder looked after him, shook his head, and, while he drew close and locked a wicket, which, crossing the stair-case, rendered it impossible for any one to ascend higher than the storey immediately beneath Mervyn's Bower, as Tressilian's chamber was named, he thus soliloquized with himself—"It's a good thing to be a favourite—I well nigh lost mine office, because one frosty morning Master Varney thought I smelled of aquavitæ; and this fellow can appear before him drunk as a wine-skin, and yet meet no rebuke. But then he is a pestilent clever fellow withal, and no one can understand above one half of what he says."

Chapter Five

Now bid the steeple rock—she comes, she comes!—
Speak for us, bells—speak for us, shrill-tongued tuckets.
Stand to thy linstock, gunner; let thy cannon
Play such a peal, as if a paynim foe
Came stretch'd in turban'd ranks to storm the ramparts.
We will have pageants too—but that craves wit,
And I'm a rough-hewn soldier.
The Virgin Queen—a Tragi-Comedy

TRESSILIAN, when Wayland had left him, as mentioned in the last chapter, remained uncertain what he ought next to do, when Raleigh and Blount came up to him arm in arm, yet, according to their wont, very eagerly disputing together. Tressilian had no great desire for their society in the present state of his feelings, but there was no possibility of avoiding them; and indeed he felt that, bound by his promise not to approach Amy, or take any step in her behalf, it would be his best course at once to mix with general society, and to exhibit on his brow as little as he could of the anguish and uncertainty which sat heavy at his heart. He therefore made a virtue of necessity, and hailed his comrades with, "All mirth to you, gentlemen—whence come ye?"

"From Warwick, to be sure," said Blount; "we must needs home to change our habits, like poor players, who must multiply their persons to outward appearance by change of suits—And you had better do the like, Tressilian."

"Blount is right," said Raleigh; "the Queen loves such marks of deference, and notices, as wanting in respect, those who, not arriving in her immediate attendance, may appear in their soiled and ruffled riding dress. But look at Blount himself, Tressilian, for the love of laughter, and see how his villainous tailor hath apparelled him—in blue, green, and crimson, with carnation ribbons, and yellow roses in his shoes!"

"Why, what would'st thou have?" said Blount. "I told the cross-legged thief to do his best, and spare no cost; and methinks these things are gay enough—gayer than thine own—I'll be judged by Tressilian."

"I agree—I agree," said Walter Raleigh. "Judge betwixt us, Tressilian, for the love of heaven!"

Tressilian, thus appealed to, looked on them both, and was immediately sensible at a single glance, that honest Blount had taken upon the tailor's warrant the pied garments which he had chosen to make, and was as much embarrassed by the quantity of points and ribands which garnished his dress, as a clown is in a holiday suit; while the dress of Raleigh was a well-fancied and rich suit, which the wearer bore as a garb too well adapted to his elegant person to attract particular attention. He said, therefore, "That Blount's dress was finest, but Raleigh's the best fancied."

Blount was satisfied with his decision. "I knew mine was finest," he said; "if that knave Doublestitch had brought me home such a simple doublet as that of Raleigh's, I would have beat his brains out with his own pressing-iron. Nay, if we must be fools, ever let us be fools of the first head, say I."

"But why gettest thou not on thy braveries, Tressilian?" said Raleigh.

"I am excluded from my apartment by a silly mistake," said Tressilian, "and separated for the time from my baggage. I was about to seek thee, to beseech a share of thy lodging."

"And welcome," said Raleigh; "it is a noble one. My Lord of Leicester has done us that kindness, and lodged us in princely fashion. If his courtesy be extorted reluctantly, it is at least extended far. I would advise you to tell your streight to the Earl's chamberlain—you will have instant redress."

"Nay, it is not worth while, since you can spare me room," replied Tressilian—"I would not be troublesome.—Has any one come hither with you?"

"O, ay," said Blount; "Varney and a whole tribe of Leicestrians, besides about a score of us honest Sussex folks.—We are all, it seems, to receive the Queen at what they call the Gallery-tower, and witness some fooleries there; and then we're to remain in attendance upon the Queen in the Great Hall, God bless the mark, while those who are now waiting upon her Grace get rid of their slough, and doff their riding-suits. Heaven help me, if her Grace should speak to me, I shall never know what to answer!"

"And what has detained them so long at Warwick?" said Tressilian, unwilling that their conversation should return to his own affairs.

"Such a succession of fooleries," said Blount, "as were never seen at Bartholomew-fair—we have had speeches and players, and dogs and bears, and men making monkies, and women making moppets of themselves—I marvel the Queen could endure it. But ever and anon came in something of 'the lovely light of her gracious countenance,' or some such trash. Ah! vanity makes a fool of the wisest. But, come, let

us on to this same Gallery-tower,—though I see not what thou, Tressilian, canst do with thy riding-dress and boots."

"I will take my station behind thee, Blount," said Tressilian, who
saw that his friend's unusual finery had taken a strong hold of his
imagination; "thy goodly size and gay dress will cover my defects."

"And so thou shalt, Edmund," said Blount. "In faith I am glad thou
think'st my garb well-fancied, for all Master Wittypate here; for when
one does a foolish thing, it is right to do it handsomely."

So saying, Blount cocked his beaver, threw out his leg, and
marched manfully forwards, as if at the head of his brigade of
pikemen, ever and anon looking with complaisance on his crimson
stockings, and the huge yellow roses which blossomed on his shoes.
Tressilian followed, wrapped in his own sad thoughts, and scarce
minding Raleigh, whose quick fancy, amused by the awkward vanity of
his respectable friend, vented itself in jests, which he whispered into
Tressilian's ear.

In this manner they crossed the long bridge, or tilt-yard, and took
their station, with other gentlemen of quality, before the outer gate of
the Gallery or Entrance-tower. The whole amounted to about forty
persons, all selected as of the first rank under that of knighthood, and
were disposed in double rows on either side of the gate, like a guard of
honour, within the close hedge of pikes and partizans, which was
formed by Leicester's retainers, wearing his liveries. The gentlemen
carried no arms, save their swords and daggers. These gallants were
as gaily dressed as imagination could devise; and as the garb of the
time permitted a great display of expensive magnificence, nought was
to be seen but velvet and cloth of gold and silver, ribands, feathers,
gems, and golden chains. In spite of his more serious subjects of
distress, Tressilian could not help feeling, that he, with his riding-
suit, however handsome it might be, made rather an unworthy figure
amongst these "fierce vanities," and the rather because he saw that his
dishabille was the subject of wonder among his own friends, and of
scorn amongst the partizans of Leicester.

We could not suppress this fact, though it may seem something at
variance with the gravity of Tressilian's character; but the truth is, that
a regard for personal appearance is a species of self-love, from which
the wisest are not exempt, and to which the mind clings so instinctively, that not only the soldier advancing to almost inevitable death,
but even the doomed criminal who goes to certain execution, shews an
anxiety to array his person to the best advantage. But this is a
digression.

It was the twilight of a summer night, (9th July, 1575,) the sun
having for some time set, and all were in anxious expectation of the

Queen's immediate approach. The multitude had remained assembled for many hours, and their numbers were still rather upon the increase. A profuse distribution of refreshments, together with roasted oxen, and barrels of ale set a-broach in different places of the road, had kept the populace in perfect love and loyalty towards the Queen and her favourite, which might have somewhat abated had fasting been added to watching. They passed away the time, therefore, with the usual popular amusements of whooping, hallooing, shrieking, and playing rude tricks upon each other, forming the chorus of discordant sounds usual on such occasions. These prevailed all through the crowded roads and fields, and especially beyond the gate of the Chace, where the greater number of the common sort were stationed; when, all of a sudden, a single rocket was seen to shoot into the atmosphere, and, at the instant, far-heard over flood and field, the great bell of the Castle tolled.

Immediately there was a pause of dead silence, succeeded by a deep hum of expectation, the united voice of many thousands, none of whom spoke above their breath; or, to use a singular expression, the whisper of an immense multitude.

"They come now, for certain," said Raleigh. "Tressilian, that sound is grand. We hear it from this distance, as mariners, after a long voyage, hear, upon their night-watch, the tide rush upon some distant and unknown shore."

"Mass!" answered Blount; "I hear it rather as I used to hear mine own kine lowing from the close at Wittens-westlowe."

"He will assuredly graze presently," said Raleigh to Tressilian; "his thought is all of fat oxen and fertile meadows—he grows little better than one of his own beeves, and only becomes grand when he is provoked to pushing and goring."

"We shall have him at that presently," said Tressilian, "if you spare not your wit."

"Tush, I care not," answered Raleigh; "but thou too, Tressilian, hast turned a kind of owl, that flies only by night; hast exchanged thy songs for screechings, and good company for an ivy-tod."

"But what manner of animal art thou thyself, Raleigh," said Tressilian, "that thou holdest us all so lightly?"

"Who, I?" replied Raleigh. "An eagle am I, that never will think of dull earth, while there is a heaven to soar in, and a sun to gaze upon."

"Well bragged, by Saint Barnaby!" said Blount; "but, good Master Eagle, beware the cage, and beware the fowler. Many birds have flown as high, that I have seen stuffed with straw, and hung up to scare kites. —But hark, what a dead silence hath fallen on them at once!"

"The procession pauses," said Raleigh, "at the gate of the Chace, where a sybil, one of the *fatidicæ*, meets the Queen, to tell her fortune. I saw the verses; there is little savour in them, and her Grace has been already crammed full with such poetical compliments. She whispered to me during the Recorder's speech yonder, at Ford-mill, as she entered the liberties of Warwick, how she was '*pertæsa barbaræ loquelæ.*'"

"The Queen whispered to *him!*" said Blount, in a kind of soliloquy; "Good God, to what this world will come!"

His farther meditations were interrupted by a shout of applause from the multitude, so tremendously vociferous, that the country echoed for miles around. The guards, thickly stationed upon the road by which the Queen was to advance, caught up the acclamation, which ran like wild-fire to the Castle, and announced to all within it that Queen Elizabeth had entered the Royal Chace of Kenilworth. The whole music of the Castle sounded at once, and a round of artillery, with a salvo of small arms, was discharged from the battlements; but the noise of drums and trumpets, and even of the cannon themselves, was but faintly heard, amidst the roaring and reiterated welcomes of the multitude.

As the noise began to abate, a broad glare of light was seen to appear from the gate of the Park, and, broadening and brightening as it came nearer, advanced along the open and fair avenue that led towards the Gallery-tower; and which, as we have already noticed, was lined on either hand by the retainers of the Earl of Leicester. The word was passed along the line, "The Queen! The Queen! Silence, and stand fast!"

Onward came the cavalcade, illuminated by two hundred thick waxen torches, in the hands of as many horsemen, which cast a light like that of broad day all around the procession, but especially on the principal groupe, of which the Queen herself, arrayed in the most splendid manner, and blazing with jewels, formed the central figure. She was mounted on a milk-white horse, which she reined with peculiar grace and dignity; and in the whole of her stately and noble carriage, you saw the daughter of an hundred kings.

The ladies of the court, who rode beside her Majesty, had taken especial care that their own external appearance should not be more glorious than their rank and the occasion altogether demanded, so that no inferior luminary might appear to approach the orbit of royalty. But their personal charms, and the magnificence by which, under every prudential restraint, they were necessarily distinguished, exhibited them as the very flower of a realm so far famed for splendour and beauty. The magnificence of the courtiers, free from such restraints as prudence imposed on the ladies, was yet more unbounded.

Leicester, who glittered like a golden image with jewels and cloth of gold, rode on her Majesty's right hand, as well in quality of her host, as of her Master of the Horse. The black steed which he mounted had not a single white hair on his body, and was one of the most renowned chargers in Europe, having been purchased by the Earl at large expence for this royal occasion. As the noble steed chafed at the slow pace of the procession, and, arching his stately neck, champed on the silver bits which restrained him, the foam flew from his mouth, and specked his well-formed limbs as if with spots of snow. The rider well became the high place which he held, and the proud animal which he bestrode; for no man in England, or perhaps in Europe, was more perfect than Dudley in horsemanship, and all other exercises belonging to his quality. He was bare-headed, as were all the courtiers in the train; and the red torch-light shone upon his long curled tresses of dark hair, and on his noble features, to the beauty of which even the severest criticism could only object the lordly fault, as it may be termed, of a forehead somewhat too high. On that proud evening, these features wore all the grateful solicitude of a subject, to shew himself sensible of the high honour which the Queen was conferring on him, and all the pride and satisfaction which became so glorious a moment. Yet, though neither eye nor feature betrayed aught but the feelings which suited the occasion, some of the Earl's personal attendants remarked, that he was unusually pale, and expressed to each other their fear that he was taking more fatigue than consisted with his health.

Varney followed close behind his master, as the principal esquire in waiting, and had charge of his lordship's black velvet bonnet, garnished with a clasp of diamonds, and surmounted by a white plume. He kept his eye constantly on his master; and, for reasons with which the reader is not unacquainted, was, amongst Leicester's numerous dependants, he who was most anxious that his lord's strength and resolution should carry him successfully through a day so agitating. For although Varney was one of the few—the very few—moral monsters, who contrive to lull to sleep the remorse of their own bosoms, and are drugged into moral insensibility by atheism, as men in extreme agony are lulled by opium, yet he knew that in the breast of his patron there was already awakened the fire that is never quenched, and that he felt, amid all the pomp and magnificence we have described, the gnawing of the worm that dieth not. Still, however, assured as Lord Leicester stood, by Varney's own intelligence, that his Countess laboured under an indisposition which formed an

unanswerable apology to the Queen for her not appearing at Kenilworth, there was little danger, his wily retainer thought, that a man so
ambitious would betray himself by giving way to any external weakness.

The train, male and female, who attended immediately upon the
Queen's person, were of course of the bravest and the fairest,—the
highest born nobles, and the wisest counsellors, of that distinguished
reign, to repeat whose names were but to weary the reader. Behind
came a long crowd of knights and gentlemen, whose rank and birth,
however distinguished, were thrown into shade, as their persons into
the rear of a procession, whose front was of such august majesty.

Thus marshalled, the cavalcade approached the Gallery-tower,
which formed, as we have often observed, the extreme barrier of the
Castle.

It was now the part of the huge porter to step forward; but the
lubbard was so overwhelmed with confusion of spirit,—the contents
of one immense black jack of double ale, which he had just drank to
quicken his memory, having at the same time treacherously confused
the brain it was intended to clear,—that he only groaned piteously,
and remained sitting on his stone seat; and the Queen would have
passed on without greeting, had not his secret ally, Flibbertigibbet,
who lay perdue behind him, thrust a pin into the rear of the short
femoral garment which we elsewhere described.

The porter uttered a sort of a yell, which came not amiss into his
part, started up with his club, and dealt a sound douse or two on each
side of him; and then, like a coach-horse pricked by the spur, started
off at once into the full career of his address, and by dint of active
prompting on the part of Dickie Sludge, delivered, in sounds of gigantic intonation, a speech which may be thus abridged;—the reader
being to suppose that the first lines were addressed to the throng who
approached the gateway; the conclusion, at the approach of the
Queen, upon sight of whom, as struck by some heavenly vision, the
gigantic warder dropped his club, resigned his keys, and gave open
way to the Goddess of the night, and all her magnificent train.

> "What stir, what turmoil, have we for the nones?
> Stand back, my masters, or beware your bones!
> Sirs, I'm a warder, and no man of straw,
> My voice keeps order, and my club gives law.
> Yet soft—nay stay—what vision have we here?
> What dainty darling's this—what peerless peer?
> What loveliest face, that loving ranks enfold,
> Like brightest diamond chased in purest gold?
> Dazzled and blind, mine office I forsake,
> My club, my keys, my knee, my homage take.

Bright paragon, pass on in joy and bliss;—
Beshrew the gate that opes not wide at such a sight as this!"

Elizabeth received most graciously the homage of the herculean
porter, and, bending her head to him in requital, passed through his
guarded tower, from the top of which was poured a clamorous blast of
warlike music, which was replied to by other bands of minstrelsy
placed at different points on the Castle walls, and by others again
stationed in the Chace; while the tones of the one, as they yet vibrated
on the echoes, were caught up and answered by new harmony from
different quarters.

Amidst these bursts of music, which, as if the work of enchantment,
seemed now close at hand, now softened by distant space, now wailing
so low and sweet as if that distance was gradually prolonged until only
the last lingering strains alone could reach the ear, Queen Elizabeth
crossed the Gallery-tower, and came upon the long bridge, which
extended from thence to Mortimer's Tower, and which was already as
light as day, so many torches had been fastened to the palisades on
either side. Most of the nobles here alighted, and sent their horses to
the neighbouring village of Kenilworth, following the Queen on foot,
as did the gentlemen who had stood in array to receive her at the
Gallery-tower.

On this occasion, as at different times during the evening, Raleigh
addressed himself to Tressilian, and was not a little surprised at his
vague and unsatisfactory answers; which, joined to his leaving his
apartment without any assigned reason, appearing in an undress when
it was likely to be offensive to the Queen, and some other symptoms of
irregularity which he thought he discovered, led him to doubt whether
his friend did not labour under some temporary derangement.

Meanwhile, the Queen had no sooner stepped on the bridge than a
new spectacle was provided; for as soon as the music gave signal that
she was so far advanced, a raft, so disposed as to resemble a small
floating island, illuminated by a great variety of torches, and surrounded by floating pageants formed to represent sea-horses, on
which sat Tritons, Nereids, and other fabulous deities of the seas and
rivers, made its appearance upon the lake, and issuing from behind a
small heronry where it had been concealed, floated gently towards the
farther end of the bridge.

On the islet appeared a beautiful woman, clad in a watchet-
coloured silken mantle, bound with a broad girdle, inscribed with
characters like the phylacteries of the Hebrews. Her feet and arms
were bare, but her wrists and ancles were adorned with gold bracelets
of uncommon size. Amidst her long silky black hair, she wore a crown
or chaplet of artificial misletoe, and bore in her hand a rod of ebony

tipped with silver. Two Nymphs attended on her, dressed in the same antique and mystical guise.

The pageant was so well managed, that this Lady of the Floating Island, having performed her voyage with much picturesque effect, landed at Mortimer's Tower with her two attendants, just as Elizabeth presented herself before that outwork. The stranger then, in a well-penned speech, announced herself as that famous Lady of the Lake, renowned in the stories of King Arthur, who had nursed the youth of the redoubted Sir Lancelot, and whose beauty had proved too powerful both for the wisdom and the spells of the mighty Merlin. Since that early period she had remained possessed of her crystal dominions, she said, despite the various men of fame and might by whom Kenilworth had been successively tenanted. The Saxons, the Danes, the Normans, the Saintlowes, the Clintons, the Mountforts, the Mortimers, and the Plantagenets, great though they were in arms and magnificence, had never, she said, caused her to raise her head from the waters which hid her crystal palace. But a greater than all these great names had now appeared, and she came in homage and duty to welcome the peerless Elizabeth to all sport, which the Castle and its environs, which lake or land could afford.

The Queen received this address also with great courtesy, and made answer in raillery, "We thought this lake had belonged to our own dominions, fair dame; but since so famed a lady claims it for hers, we will be glad at some other time to have further communing with you touching our joint interests."

With this gracious answer the Lady of the Lake vanished, and Arion, who was amongst the maritime deities, appeared upon his dolphin. But Lambourne, who had taken upon him the part in the absence of Wayland, being chilled with remaining immersed in an element to which he was not friendly, having never got his speech by heart, and not having, like the porter, the advantage of a prompter, paid it off with impudence, tearing off his vizard, and swearing, "Cogs bones! he was none of Arion or Orion either, but honest Mike Lambourne, that had been drinking her Majesty's health from morning till midnight, and was come to bid her heartily welcome to Kenilworth Castle."

This unpremeditated buffoonery answered the purpose probably better than the set speech would have done. The Queen laughed heartily, and swore (in her turn) that he had made the best speech she had heard that day. Lambourne, who instantly saw his jest had saved his bones, jumped on shore, gave his dolphin a kick, and declared he would never meddle with fish again, except at dinner.

At the same time that the Queen was about to enter the Castle, that

memorable discharge of fireworks by water and land took place, which
Master Laneham, formerly introduced to the reader, has strained all
his eloquence to describe.

"Such," says the Clerk of the Council-chamber door, "was the
blaze of burning darts, the gleams of stars coruscant, the streams and
hail of fiery sparks, lightnings of wild-fire, and flight and shot of
thunder-bolts, with continuance, terror, and vehemency, that the
heavens thundered, the waters surged, and the earth shook; and for
my part, hardy as I am, it made me very vengeably afraid." *

Chapter Six

Nay, this is matter for the month of March,
When hares are maddest. Either speak in reason,
Giving cold argument the wall of passion,
Or I break up the court.
BEAUMONT AND FLETCHER

IT IS by no means our purpose to describe minutely all the princely
festivities of Kenilworth, after the fashion of Master Robert
Laneham, whom we quoted in the conclusion of the last Chapter. It is
sufficient to say, that under the discharge of the splendid fire-works,
which we have borrowed Laneham's eloquence to describe, the
Queen entered the base-court of Kenilworth, through Mortimer's
Tower, and moving on through pageants of heathen gods and heroes
of antiquity, who offered gifts and compliments on the bended knee,
at length found her way to the great hall of the Castle, gorgeously hung
for her reception with the richest silken tapestry, blazing with torches,
misty with perfumes, and sounding to strains of soft and delicious
music. At the upper end of this splendid apartment, was a state canopy, overshadowing a royal throne, and beside was a door, which
opened to a long suite of apartments, decorated with the utmost
magnificence for the Queen and her ladies, whenever it should be her
pleasure to be private.

The Earl of Leicester having handed the Queen up to the throne,
and seated her there, knelt down before her, and kissing the hand
which she held out, with an air in which romantic and respectful

*See Laneham's Account of the Queen's Entertainment at Killingworth Castle, in
1575, a very diverting tract, written by as great a coxcomb as ever blotted paper. The
original is extremely rare, but it has been twice reprinted; once in Mr Nicholas's very
curious and interesting collection of the Progresses and Public Processions of Queen
Elizabeth, vol. I.; and more lately in No. I. of a work termed *Kenilworth Illustrated*,
beautifully printed at Chiswick, for Meridew of Coventry, and Radclyff of Birmingham,
and which, if continued with the same good taste and execution, will be one of the finest
antiquarian publications that has lately appeared.

gallantry was happily mingled with loyal devotion, he thanked her, in terms of the deepest gratitude, for the highest honour which a sovereign could render to a subject. So handsome did he look when kneeling before her, that Elizabeth was tempted to prolong the scene a little longer than there was, strictly speaking, necessity for; and ere she raised him, she passed her hand over his head, so near, as almost to touch his long curled and perfumed hair, and with a movement of fondness, that seemed to intimate, she would, if she dared, have made the motion a slight caress.

She at length raised him, and, standing beside the throne, he explained to her the various preparations which had been made for her amusement and accommodation, all of which received her prompt and gracious approbation. The Earl then prayed her Majesty for permission, that he himself, and the nobles who had been in attendance upon her during the journey, might retire for a few minutes, and put themselves into a guise more fitting for dutiful attendance, during which space, those gentlemen of worship, (pointing to Varney, Blount, Tressilian, and others,) who had already put themselves into fresh attire, would have the honour of keeping her presence-chamber.

"Be it so, my lord," answered the Queen; "you could manage a theatre well, who can thus command a double set of actors. For ourselves, we will receive your courtesies this evening but clownishly, since it is not our purpose to change our riding attire, being in effect something fatigued with a journey, which the concourse of our good people hath rendered slow, though the love they have shewn our person hath, at the same time, made it delightful."

Leicester, having received this permission, retired accordingly, and was followed by those nobles who had attended the Queen to Kenilworth in person. The gentlemen who had preceded them, and were of course dressed for the solemnity, remained in attendance. But being most of them of rather inferior rank, they remained at an awful distance from the throne which Elizabeth occupied. The Queen's sharp eye soon distinguished Raleigh amongst them, with one or two others who were personally known to her, and she instantly made them a sign to approach, and accosted them very graciously. Raleigh, in particular, the adventure of whose cloak, as well as the incident of the verses, remained on her mind, was very graciously received; and to him she most frequently applied for information concerning the names and rank of those who were in presence. These he communicated concisely, and not without some traits of humorous satire, by which Elizabeth seemed much amused. "And who is yonder clownish fellow?" she said, looking at Tressilian, whose soiled dress on this occasion greatly obscured his good mien.

"A poet, if it please your Grace," replied Raleigh.

"I might have guessed that from his careless garb," said Elizabeth. "I have known some poets so thoughtless as to throw their cloaks into gutters."

"It must have been when the sun dazzled both their eyes and their judgment," answered Raleigh.

Elizabeth smiled and proceeded, "I asked that slovenly fellow's name, and you only told me his profession."

"Tressilian is his name," said Raleigh, with internal reluctance, for he foresaw nothing favourable to his friend from the manner in which she took notice of him.

"Tressilian!" answered Elizabeth. "O, the Menelaus of our romance. Why, he has dressed himself in a guise that will go far to exculpate his fair and false Helen. And where is Farnham, or whatever his name is—my Lord of Leicester's man, I mean—the Paris of this Devonshire tale?"

With still greater reluctance Raleigh named and pointed out to her Varney, for whom the tailor had done all that art could perform in making his exterior agreeable; and who, if he had not grace, had a sort of tact and habitual knowledge of breeding, which came in place of it.

The Queen turned her eye from the one to the other—"I doubt," she said, "this same poetical Master Tressilian, who is too learned, I warrant me, to remember what presence he is to appear in, may be one of those of whom Geoffrey Chaucer says wittily, the most learned clerks are not the wisest men. I remember that Varney is a smooth-tongued varlet. I doubt this fair runaway had reasons for breaking her faith."

To this Raleigh durst make no answer, aware how little he should benefit Tressilian by contradicting the Queen's sentiments, and not at all certain, on the whole, whether the best thing that could befall him, would not be that she should put an end at once by her authority to this affair, upon which it seemed to him Tressilian's thoughts were fixed with unavailing and distressing pertinacity. As these reflections passed through his active brain, the lower door of the hall opened, and Leicester, accompanied by several of his kinsmen, and of the nobles who had embraced his faction, re-entered the Castle-hall.

The favourite Earl was now apparelled all in white, his shoes being of white velvet; his under-stocks (or stockings) of knit silk; his upper stocks of white velvet, lined with cloth of silver, which was shewn at the slashed part of the middle thigh; his doublet of cloth of silver, the close jerkin of white velvet, embroidered with silver and seed-pearl; his girdle and the scabbard of his sword of white velvet with golden buckles; his poniard and sword hilted and mounted with gold; and over all, a rich loose robe of white satin, with a border of golden embroidery a foot in breadth. The collar of the Garter, and the azure Garter itself around his knee, completed the appointments of the Earl of Leicester; which were so well matched by his fair stature, graceful gesture, fine proportion of body, and handsome countenace, that at that moment he was admitted by all who saw him, as the goodliest person whom they had ever looked upon. Sussex and the other nobles were also richly attired, but in point of splendour and gracefulness Leicester far exceeded them all.

Elizabeth received him with great complacence. "We have one piece of royal justice," she said, "to attend to—it is a piece of justice, too, which interests us as a woman, as well as in the character of mother and guardian of the English people."

An involuntary shudder came over Leicester, as he bowed low, expressive of his readiness to receive her royal commands; and a similar cold fit came over Varney, whose eyes (seldom during that evening removed from his patron,) instantly perceived, from the change in his looks, slight as that was, of what the Queen was speaking. But Leicester had wrought his resolution up to the point which, in his crooked policy, he judged necessary; and when Elizabeth added— "It is of the matter of Varney and Tressilian we speak—is the lady here, my lord?" his answer was ready:—"Gracious madam, she is not."

Elizabeth bent her brows and compressed her lips. "Our orders were strict and positive, my lord," was her answer——

"And should have been obeyed, good my liege," answered Leicester, "had they been expressed in the form of the lightest wish. But— Varney, step forward—this gentleman will inform your Grace of the cause why the lady (he could not force his rebellious tongue to utter the words—*his wife*,) cannot attend on your royal presence."

Varney advanced, and pleaded with readiness, what indeed he firmly believed, the absolute incapacity of the party, (he dared not, in Leicester's presence, term her his wife,) to wait on her Grace.

"Here," said he, "are attestations from a most learned physician, whose skill and honour are well known to my good Lord of Leicester; and from an honest and devout Protestant, a man of credit and substance, one Anthony Forster, the gentleman in whose house she is at present bestowed, that she now labours under an illness which altogether unfits her for such a journey as betwixt this Castle and the neighbourhood of Oxford."

"This alters the matter," said the Queen, taking the certificates in her hand, and glancing at their contents—"Let Tressilian come forward.—Master Tressilian, we have much sympathy for your situation, the rather that you seem to have set your heart deeply on this same Amy Robsart, or Varney. Our power, thanks to God and the willing obedience of a loving people, is worth something, but there are some things which it cannot compass. We cannot, for example, command the affections of a giddy young girl, or make her love sense and learning better than a courtier's fine doublet; and we cannot controul sickness, with which it seems this lady is afflicted, who may not, by reason of such infirmity, attend our court here, as we had required her to do. Here are the testimonials of the physician who hath her under his charge, and the gentleman in whose house she resides, so setting forth."

"Under your Majesty's favour," said Tressilian hastily, and, in his alarm for the consequence of the imposition practised on the Queen, forgetting, in part at least, his own promise to Amy, "these certificates speak not the truth."

"How, sir!" said the Queen,—"Impeach my Lord of Leicester's veracity! But you shall have fair hearing. In our presence the meanest of our subjects shall be heard against the proudest, and the least known against the most favoured; therefore you shall be heard fairly, but beware you speak not without a warrant. Look at these certificates in your own hand, and say manfully if you impugn the truth of them, and upon what evidence."

As the Queen spoke, his promise and all its consequences rushed on the mind of the unfortunate Tressilian, and while they controuled his natural inclination to pronounce that a falsehood which he knew from the evidence of his senses to be untrue, gave an indecision and irresolution to his appearance and utterance, which made strongly against him in the mind of Elizabeth, as well as of all who beheld him. He turned the papers over and over, as if he had been an idiot, incapable of comprehending their contents. The Queen's impatience began to become visible.—"You are a scholar, sir," she said, "and of some note, as I have heard; yet you seem wondrous slow in reading text hand—How say you, are these certificates true or no?"

"Madam," said Tressilian, with obvious embarrassment and hesitation, desirous to avoid admitting evidence which he might afterwards have occasion to confute, yet equally desirous to keep his word to Amy, and to give her, as he had promised, space to plead her own cause in her own way—"Madam—Madam, your Grace calls on me to admit evidences which ought to be proved valid by those who found their defence upon them."

"Why, Tressilian, thou art critical as well as poetical," said the Queen, bending on him a brow of displeasure; "methinks, these writings, being produced in the presence of the noble Earl to whom this Castle pertains, and his honour being appealed to as the guarantee of their authenticity, might be evidence enough for thee. But since thou lists to be so formal—Varney, or rather my Lord of Leicester, for the affair becomes yours," (these words, though spoken at random, thrilled through the Earl's marrow and bones) "what evidence have you as touching these certificates?"

Varney hastened to reply, preventing Leicester,—"So please your Majesty, my young Lord of Oxford, who is here in presence, knows Master Anthony Forster's hand and his character."

The Earl of Oxford, a young unthrift, whom Forster had more than once accommodated with loans on usurious interest, acknowledged, on this appeal, that he knew him as a wealthy and independent franklin, supposed to be worth much money, and verified the certificate produced to be his hand-writing.

"And who speaks to the Doctor's certificate?" said the Queen. "Alasco, methinks, is his name."

Master, her Majesty's physician (not the less willingly that he remembered his repulse from Say's Court, and thought that his present testimony might gratify Leicester, and mortify the Earl of Sussex and his faction,) acknowledged he had more than once consulted with Doctor Alasco, and spoke of him as a man of extraordinary learning and hidden acquirements, though not altogether in the regular course of practice. The Earl of Huntingdon, Lord Leicester's brother-in-law, and the old Countess of Rutland, next sang his praises, and both remembered the thin beautiful Italian hand in which he was wont to write his receipts, and which corresponded to the certificate produced as his.

"And now, I trust, Master Tressilian, this matter is ended," said the Queen. "We will do something ere the night is older to reconcile old Sir Hugh Robsart to the match. You have done your duty something more than boldly; but we were no woman had we not compassion for the wounds which true love deals; so we forgive your audacity, and your uncleansed boots withal, which have well nigh overpowered my Lord of Leicester's perfumes."

So spoke Elizabeth, whose nicety of scent was one of the characteristics of her organization, as appeared long afterwards when she expelled Essex from her presence, on a charge against his boots, similar to that which she now expressed against those of Tressilian.

But Tressilian had by this time collected himself, astonished as he had at first been by the audacity of the falsehood so feasibly supported, and placed in array against the evidence of his own eyes. He rushed forwards, kneeled down, and caught the Queen by the skirt of the robe. "As you are Christian woman," he said, "Madam, as you are crowned Queen, to do equal justice among your subjects—as you hope yourself to have fair hearing (which God grant you) at that last bar at which we must all plead, grant me one small request!—decide not this matter so hastily—give me but twenty four hours interval, and I will, at the end of that brief space, produce evidence which will shew to a demonstration, that these certificates, which state this unhappy lady to be now ill at ease in Oxfordshire, are false as hell!"

"Let go my train, sir!" said Elizabeth, who was startled at his vehemence, though she had too much of lion in her to fear; "the fellow must be distraught—that witty knave, my godson Harrington, must have him into his rhimes of Orlando Furioso!—And yet, by this light, there is something strange in the vehemence of his demand.— Speak, Tressilian; what wilt thou do if, at the end of these four-and-twenty hours, thou canst not confute a fact so solemnly proved as this lady's illness?"

"I will lay down my head on the block," answered Tressilian.

"Pshaw!" replied the Queen. "God's light! thou speak'st like a fool —what head falls in England but by just sentence of English law?—I ask thee, man—if thou hast sense to understand me—wilt thou, if thou shalt fail in this improbable attempt of thine, render me a good and sufficient reason why thou doest undertake it?"

Tressilian paused, and again hesitated; because he felt convinced, that if, within the interval demanded, Amy should become reconciled to her husband, he would in that case do her the worst of offices, by again ripping up the whole circumstances before Elizabeth, and showing how that wise and jealous princess had been imposed upon by false testimonials. The consciousness of this dilemma renewed his extreme embarrassment of look, voice, and manner; he hesitated, looked down, and on the Queen repeating her question with a stern voice and flashing eye, he admitted with faultering words, "That it might be—he could not positively—that is, in certain events—explain the reasons and grounds on which he acted."

"Now, by the soul of King Henry," said the Queen, "this is either moonstruck madness, or very knavery!—Seest thou, Raleigh, thy friend is far too Pindaric for this presence. Have him away, and make us quit of him, or it shall be the worse; for his flights are too unbridled for aught but Parnassus, or Saint Luke's Hospital. But come back instantly thyself, when he is placed under fitting restraint. We wish we had seen the beauty which could make such havoc in a wise man's brain."

Tressilian was again endeavouring to address the Queen, when Raleigh, in obedience to the orders he had received, interfered, and, with Blount's assistance, half led half forced him out of the presence-chamber, where he himself indeed began to perceive his presence did his cause more harm than good.

When they had attained the anti-chamber, Raleigh entreated Blount to see Tressilian safely conducted into the apartments allotted to the Earl of Sussex's followers, and, if necessary, recommended that a guard should be mounted on him.

"This extravagant passion," he said, "and, as it would seem, the news of the lady's illness, has utterly wrecked his excellent judgment. But it will pass away if he be kept quiet—only let him break forth again at no rate; for he is already far in her Highness's displeasure, and should she be again provoked, she will find for him a worse place of confinement, and sterner keepers."

"I judged as much as that he was mad," said Nicholas Blount, looking down upon his own crimson stockings and yellow roses, "whenever I saw him with these damned boots, which stunk so in her nostrils.—I will but see him stowed, and be back with you presently. —But, Walter, did the Queen ask who I was?—methought she glanced an eye at me."

"Twenty—twenty eye-glances she sent, and I told her all how thou wert a brave soldier, and a——But for God's sake, get off Tressilian."

"I will—I will," said Blount; "but methinks this court-haunting is no such bad pastime, after all. We shall rise by it, Walter, my brave lad. Thou said'st I was a good soldier, and a—What besides, dearest Walter?"

"An all unutterable—codshead—for God's sake begone."

Tressilian, without farther resistance or expostulation, followed, or rather suffered himself to be conducted by Blount to Raleigh's lodging, where he was formally installed into a small truckle bed, placed in a wardrobe, and designed for a domestic. He saw but too plainly, that no remonstrances would avail to procure the help or sympathy of his friends, until the lapse of the time for which he had pledged himself to remain inactive, should enable him either to explain the whole circumstances to them, or remove from him every pretext or desire of farther interference with the fortunes of Amy, by her having found means to place herself in a state of reconciliation with her husband.

With great difficulty, and only by the most patient and mild remonstrances with Blount, he escaped the disgrace and mortification of having two of Sussex's stoutest yeomen quartered in his apartment. At last, however, when Nicholas had seen him fairly deposited in his truckle-bed, and had bestowed one or two hearty kicks, and as hearty curses, on the boots, which, in his lately acquired spirit of foppery, he considered as a strong symptom, if not the cause, of his friend's malady, he contented himself with the modified measure of locking the door on the unfortunate Tressilian; whose gallant and disinterested efforts to save a female who had treated him with ingratitude, thus terminated, for the present, in the displeasure of his Sovereign, and the conviction of his friends, that he was little better than a madman.

Chapter Seben

The wisest Sovereigns err like private men,
And royal hand has sometimes laid the sword
Of chivalry upon a worthless shoulder,
Which better had been branded by the hangman.
What then?—Kings do their best—and they and we
Must answer for the intent, and not the event.
Old Play

"IT IS a melancholy matter," said the Queen, when Tressilian was withdrawn, "to see a wise and learned man's wit thus pitifully unsettled. Yet this public display of his imperfection of brain plainly shews us that his supposed injury and accusation were fruitless; and therefore, my Lord of Leicester, we remember your suit formerly made to us in behalf of your faithful servant Varney, whose good gifts and fidelity, as they are useful to you, ought to have due reward from us, knowing well that your lordship, and all you have, are so earnestly devoted to our service. And we render Varney the honour more especially, that we are a guest, and we fear a chargeable and troublesome guest, under your lordship's roof; and also for the satisfaction of the good old Knight of Devon, Sir Hugh Robsart, whose daughter he hath married; and we trust the especial mark of grace which we are about to confer, will reconcile him to his son-in-law.—Your sword, my Lord of Leicester."

The Earl unbuckled his sword, and, taking it by the point, presented on bended knee the hilt to Elizabeth.

She took it slowly, drew it from the scabbard, and while the ladies who stood around turned away their eyes with real or affected shuddering, she noted with a curious eye the high polish and rich damasked ornaments upon the glittering blade.

"Had I been a man," she said, "methinks none of my ancestors would have loved a good sword better. As it is with me, I like to look on one, and could, like the *fata Morgana*, of whom I have read in some Italian rhimes—were my godson Harrington here, he could tell me the passage—even trim my hair, and arrange my head-gear, in such a steel mirror as this is.—Richard Varney, come forth and kneel down. In the name of God and Saint George, we dub thee knight! Be

Faithful, Brave, and Fortunate.—Arise, Sir Richard Varney."

Varney arose and retired, making a deep obeisance to the Sovereign who had done him so much honour.

"The buckling of the spur, and what other rites remain," said the Queen, "may be finished to-morrow in the chapel; for we intend Sir Richard Varney a companion in his honours. And as we must not be partial in conferring such distinction, we mean on this matter to confer with our cousin of Sussex."

That noble Earl, who since his arrival at Kenilworth, and indeed since the commencement of this Progress, had found himself in a subordinate situation to Leicester, was now wearing a heavy cloud on his brow—a circumstance which had not escaped the Queen, who hoped to appease his discontent, and to follow out her system of balancing policy by a mark of peculiar favour, the more gratifying as it was tendered at a moment when his rival's triumph appeared to be complete.

At the summons of Queen Elizabeth, Sussex hastily approached her person; and being asked on which of his followers, being a gentleman and of merit, he would wish the honour of knighthood to be conferred, he answered, with more sincerity than policy, that he would have ventured to speak for Tressilian, to whom he conceived he owed his own life, and who was a distinguished soldier and scholar, besides a man of unstained lineage—"Only," he said, "he feared the events of that night"——and then he stopped.

"I am glad your lordship is thus considerate," said Elizabeth; "the events of this night would make us, in the eyes of our subjects, as mad as this poor brain-sick gentleman himself—for we ascribe his conduct to no malice—should we chuse this moment to do him grace."

"In that case," said the Earl of Sussex, somewhat discountenanced, "your Majesty will allow me to name my master of the horse, Master Nicholas Blount, a gentleman of fair estate and ancient name, who has served your majesty both in Scotland and Ireland, and brought away bloody marks on his person, all honourably taken and requited."

The Queen could not help shrugging her shoulders slightly even at this second suggestion; and the Countess of Rutland, who read in the Queen's manner that she had expected Sussex to have named Raleigh, and thus to have enabled her to gratify her own wish while she honoured this recommendation, only waited till the Queen assented to what he had proposed, and then said, that she hoped, since these two high nobles had been each permitted to suggest a candidate for the honours of chivalry, she, in behalf of the ladies in presence, might have a similar indulgence.

"I were no woman to refuse you such a boon," said the Queen, smiling.

"Then," pursued the Countess, "in the name of these fair ladies present, I request your Majesty to confer the rank of knighthood on Walter Raleigh, whose birth, deeds of arms, and promptitude to serve our sex with sword or pen, deserve such distinction from us all."

"Gramercy, fair ladies," said Elizabeth, smiling, "your boon is granted; and the gentle squire Lack-Cloak shall become the good knight Lack-Cloak, at your desire. Let the two aspirants for the honour of chivalry step forward."

Blount was not as yet returned from seeing Tressilian, as he conceived, safely disposed of; but Raleigh came forth, and, kneeling down, received at the hand of the Virgin Queen that title of honour, which was never conferred on a more distinguished or more illustrious object.

Shortly afterwards Nicholas Blount entered, and, hastily apprized by Sussex, who met him at the door of the hall, with the Queen's gracious purpose towards him, he was desired to advance towards the throne. It is a sight sometimes seen, and it is both ludicrous and pitiable, when an honest man of plain common sense is surprised, by the coquetry of a pretty woman, or any other cause, into those frivolous fopperies which only sit well upon the youthful, the gay, and those to whom long practice has rendered them a second nature. Poor Blount was in this situation. His head was already giddy from a consciousness of unusual finery, and the supposed necessity of suiting his manners to the gaiety of his dress; and now this sudden view of promotion altogether completed the conquest of the newly inhaled spirit of foppery over his natural disposition, and converted a plain, honest, awkward man into a coxcomb of a new and most ridiculous kind.

The knight-expectant advanced up the hall, the whole length of which he had unfortunately to traverse, turning out his toes with so much zeal, that he presented his leg at every step with its broad side foremost, so that it greatly resembled an old-fashioned knife with a curved point, when seen sideways. The rest of his gait was in proportion to this unhappy amble, and, with a mixture of bashful fear, and self-satisfaction, was so unutterably ridiculous, that Leicester's friends did not suppress a titter, in which many of Sussex's partizans were unable to resist joining, though ready to eat their nails with mortification. Sussex himself lost all patience, and could not forbear whispering into the ear of his friend, "Curse thee! can'st thou not walk like a man and a soldier?" an interjection which only made honest Blount start and stop, until a glance at his yellow roses and crimson stockings restored his self-confidence, when on he went at the same pace as before.

The Queen conferred on poor Blount the honour of knighthood with a marked sense of reluctance. That wise Princess was fully aware of the propriety of using great circumspection and economy in bestowing those titles of honour, which the Stewarts, who succeeded to her throne, distributed with such imprudent liberality as greatly diminished their value. Blount had no sooner arisen and retired, than she turned to the Countess of Rutland. "Our woman wit," she said, "dear Rutland, is sharper than that of those proud things in doublet and hose. See'st thou, out of these three knights, thine is the only true metal to stamp chivalry's imprint upon?"

"Sir Richard Varney, surely—the friend of my Lord of Leicester— surely _he_ has merit," said the Countess.

"Varney has a sly countenance, and a smooth tongue," replied the Queen. "I fear me he will prove a knave—but the promise was of ancient standing. My Lord of Sussex must have lost his own wits, I think, to recommend to us first a madman like Tressilian, and then a clownish fool like this other fellow. I protest, Rutland, that while he sat on his knees before me, mopping and mowing as if he had scalding porridge in his mouth, I had much to forbear cutting him over the pate, instead of striking his shoulder."

"Your Majesty gave him a smart _accolade_," said the Countess; "we who stood behind heard the blade clatter on his collar-bone, and the poor man fidgetted too as if he felt it."

"I could not help it, wench," said the Queen, laughing; "but we will have this same Sir Nicholas sent to Ireland or Scotland, or somewhere, to rid our court of so antic a chevalier."

The discourse became then more general, and soon after there was a summons to the banquet.

In order to obey this signal, the company were under the necessity of crossing the inner court of the Castle, that they might reach the new buildings, containing the large banquetting room, in which preparations for supper were made upon a scale of profuse magnificence, corresponding to the occasion.

In the course of this passage, and especially in the court-yard, the new-made knights were assailed by the heralds, pursuivants, minstrels, &c. with the usual cry of _Largesse, largesse, chevaliers très hardis!_ an ancient invocation, intended to awaken the bounty of the acolytes of chivalry towards those whose business it was to register their armorial bearings, and celebrate the deeds by which they were illustrated. The call was of course liberally and courteously answered by those to whom it was addressed. Varney gave his largesse with an affectation of complaisance and humility. Raleigh bestowed his with the graceful ease peculiar to one who has attained his own place, and is familiar with its dignity. Honest Blount gave what his tailor had left him of his half-year's rent, dropping some pieces in his hurry, then stooping down to look for them, and then distributing them amongst the various claimants, with the anxious face and mien of the parish beadle dividing a dole among paupers.

These donations were accepted with the usual clamour and *vivats* of applause common on such occasions; but as the parties gratified were chiefly dependants of Lord Leicester, it was Varney whose name was repeated with the loudest acclamation. Lambourne, especially, distinguished himself by his vociferations of "Long life to Sir Richard Varney!—Health and honour to Sir Richard!—Never was a more worthy knight dubbed!"—then, suddenly sinking his voice, he added, —"since the valiant Sir Pandarus of Troy,"—a winding up of his clamorous applause, which set all men a laughing who were within hearing of it.

It is unnecessary to say any thing farther of the festivities of the evening, which were so brilliant in themselves, and received with such obvious and willing satisfaction by the Queen, that Leicester retired to his own apartment, with all the giddy raptures of successful ambition. Varney, who had changed his splendid attire, and now waited on his patron in a very modest and plain undress, attended to do the honours of the Earl's *coucher*.

"How! Sir Richard," said Leicester, smiling, "your new rank scarce suits the humility of this attendance."

"I would disown that rank, my lord," said Varney, "could I think it was to remove me to a distance from your lordship's person."

"Thou art a grateful fellow," said Leicester; "but I must not allow you to do what would abate you in the opinion of others."

While thus speaking, he still accepted, without hesitation, the offices about his person, which the new made knight seemed to render as eagerly as if he had really felt, in discharging the task, that pleasure which his words expressed.

"I am not afraid of men's misconstruction," he said, in answer to Leicester's remark, "since there is not—(permit me to undo the collar)—a man within the castle, who does not expect very soon to see persons of a rank far superior to that which, by your goodness, I now hold, rendering the duties of the bed-chamber to you, and accounting it an honour."

"It might, indeed, so have been," said the Earl, with an involuntary sigh; and then presently added, "My gown, Varney—I will look out on the night. Is not the moon near to the full?"

"I think so, my lord, according to the calendar," answered Varney.

There was an abutting window, which opened on a small projecting balcony of stone, battlemented as is usual in Gothic castles. The Earl undid the lattice, and stepped out into the open air. The station he had chosen commanded an extensive view of the lake, and woodlands beyond, where the clear moonlight rested on the clear blue waters, and the distant masses of oak and elm trees. The moon rode high in the heavens, attended by thousands and thousands of inferior lumin-aries. All seemed already to be hushed in the nether world, excepting occasionally the voice of the watch (for the yeomen of the guard performed that duty wherever the Queen was present in person,) and the distant baying of the hounds, disturbed by the preparations amongst the grooms and prickers for a magnificent hunt, which was to be the amusement of the next day.

Leicester looked out on the blue arch of heaven, with gestures and a countenance expressive of anxious exultation, while Varney, who remained within the darkened apartment, could (himself unnoticed) with a secret satisfaction, see his patron stretch his hands with earnest gesticulation towards the heavenly bodies.

"Ye distant orbs of living fire," so ran the muttered invocation of the ambitious Earl, "ye are silent while you wheel your mystic rounds, but wisdom has given to you a voice. Tell me, then, to what end is my high course destined. Shall the greatness to which I have aspired be bright, pre-eminent, and stable as your own; or am I but doomed to draw a brief and glittering train along the nightly darkness, and then to sink down to earth, like the base refuse of those artificial fires with which men emulate your rays?"

He looked on the heavens in profound silence for a minute or two longer, and then again stepped into the apartment, where Varney seemed to have been engaged in putting the Earl's jewels into a casket.

"What said Alasco of my horoscope?" demanded Leicester. "You already told me, but it has escaped me, for I think but lightly of that art."

"Many learned and great men have thought otherwise," said Var-ney; "and, not to flatter your lordship, my own opinion leans that way."

"Ay, Saul among the prophets?" said Leicester—"I thought thou wert sceptical in all such matters as thou could'st neither see, hear, smell, taste, or touch, and that thy belief was limited by thy senses."

"Perhaps, my lord," said Varney, "I may be misled by my wish to find the predictions of astrology true on the present occasion. Alasco says, that your favourite planet is culminating, and that the adverse influence—he would not use a plainer term—though not overcome, was evidently combust, I think he said, or retrograde."

"It is even so," said Leicester, looking at an abstract of astrological calculations which he had in his hand; "the stronger influence will prevail, and, as I think, the evil hour pass away.—Lend me your hand, Sir Richard, to doff my gown—and remain an instant, if it is not too burthensome to your knighthood, while I compose myself to sleep. I believe the bustle of this day has fevered my blood, for it streams through my veins like a current of molten lead—remain an instant, I pray you—I would fain feel my eyes heavy ere I closed them."

Varney officiously assisted his lord to bed, and placed a massive silver night-lamp, with a short sword, on a marble table which stood close by the head of the couch. Either in order to avoid the light of the lamp, or to hide his countenance from Varney, Leicester drew the curtain, heavy with entwined silk and gold, so as completely to shade his face. Varney took a seat near the bed, but with his back towards his master, as if to intimate that he was not watching him, and quietly waited till Leicester himself led the way to the topic by which his mind was engrossed.

"And so, Varney," said the Earl, after waiting in vain till his dependent should commence the conversation, "men talk of the Queen's favour towards me."

"Ay, my good lord," said Varney; "of what can they else, since it is so strongly manifested."

"She is indeed my good and gracious mistress," said Leicester, after another pause; "but it is written, 'Put not thy trust in Princes.'"

"A good sentence and a true," said Varney, "unless you can unite their interest with yours so absolutely, that they must needs sit on your wrist like hooded hawks."

"I know what thou meanest," said Leicester impatiently, "though thou art to-night so prudentially careful of what thou sayest to me—Thou would'st intimate, I might marry the Queen if I would."

"It is your speech, my lord, not mine," answered Varney; "but whose ever be the speech, it is the thought of ninety-nine out of an hundred men throughout broad England."

"Ay, but," said Leicester, turning himself in his bed, "the hundredth knows better. Thou, for example, knowest the obstacle that cannot be overleaped."

"It must, my lord, if the stars speak true," said Varney, composedly.

"What talk'st thou of them," said Leicester, "that believest not in them or in aught else?"

"You mistake, my lord, under your gracious pardon," said Varney; "I believe in many things that predict the future. I believe, if showers fall in April, that we shall have flowers in May; that if the sun shines, grain will ripen; and in much natural philosophy to the same effect, which, if the stars swear to me, I will say the stars speak the truth. And in like manner, I will not disbelieve that which I see wished for and expected on earth, solely because astrologers have read it in the heavens."

"Thou art right," said Leicester, again tossing himself on his couch —"Earth does wish for it. I have had advices from the reformed churches of Germany—from the Low Countries—from Switzerland, urging this as a point on which Europe's safety depends. France will not oppose it—The ruling party in Scotland look to it as their best security—Spain fears it, but cannot prevent it—And yet thou knowest it is impossible."

"I know not that, my lord," said Varney, "the Countess is indisposed."

"Villain!" said Leicester, starting up on his couch, and seizing the sword which lay on the table beside, "go thy thoughts that way?—thou wouldst not murther!"

"For whom, or what, do you hold me, my lord?" said Varney, assuming the superiority of an innocent man subjected to unjust suspicion. "I said nothing to deserve such a horrid imputation as your violence infers. I said but that the Countess was ill—and Countess, and lovely and beloved as she is, surely your lordship must hold her to be mortal. She may die, and your lordship's hand become once more your own."

"Away! Away!" said Leicester; "let me have no more of this."

"Good night, my lord," said Varney, seeming to understand this as a command to depart; but Leicester's voice interrupted his purpose.

"Thou scapest me not thus, sir Fool," said he; "I think thy knighthood has addled thy brain—Confess, thou hast talked of impossibilities, as of things which might come to pass."

"My lord, long live your fair Countess," said Varney; "but neither your love nor my good wishes can make her immortal. But, grant she live long to be happy herself, and to render you so, I see not but you may be King of England notwithstanding."

"Nay, now, Varney, thou art stark-mad," said Leicester.

"I would I were myself within the same nearness to a good estate of freehold," said Varney. "Have we not known in other countries, how a left-handed marriage might subsist betwixt persons of differing degree?—ay, and be no hindrance to the husband conjoining himself afterwards to a more suitable partner."

"I have heard of such things in Germany," said Leicester.

"Ay, and the most learned doctors in foreign universities justify the practice from the Old Testament," said Varney. "And after all, where is the harm? The beautiful partner, whom you have chosen for true love, has your secret hours of relaxation and affection. Her fame is safe—her conscience may slumber securely—You have wealth to provide royally for your issue, should Heaven bless you with offspring. Meanwhile you may give to Elizabeth ten times the leisure, and ten thousand times the affection, that ever Don Philip of Spain spared to her sister Mary; yet you know how she doated on him though so cold and neglectful. It requires but a close mouth and an open brow, and you keep your Eleanor and your fair Rosamond far enough separate. —Leave me to build you a bower to which no jealous Queen shall find a clew."

Leicester was silent for a moment, then sighed, and said, "It is impossible.—Good night, Sir Richard Varney—yet stay—Can you guess what meant Tressilian by shewing himself in such careless guise before the Queen to-day?—to strike her tender heart, I should guess, with all the sympathies due to a lover, abandoned by his mistress, and abandoning himself."

Varney, smothering a sneering laugh, answered, "He believed Master Tressilian had no such matter in his head."

"How!" said Leicester; "what mean'st thou?—there is ever knavery in that laugh of thine, Varney."

"I only meant, my lord," said Varney, "that Tressilian has taken the sure way to avoid heart-breaking. He hath had a companion—a female companion—a mistress—a sort of player's wife or sister, as I believe,—with him in Mervyn's Bower, where I quartered him for certain reasons of my own."

"A mistress!—mean'st thou a paramour?"

"Ay, my lord; who else waits for hours in a gentleman's chamber?"

"By my faith, time and space fitting, this were a good tale to tell," said Leicester. "I ever distrusted those bookish, hypocritical, seeming-virtuous scholars. Well—Master Tressilian makes somewhat familiar with my house—if I look it over, he is indebted to it for certain recollections. I would not harm him more than I can help. Keep eye on him, however, Varney."

"I lodged him for that reason," said Varney, "in Mervyn's Tower, where he is under the eye of my very vigilant, if he were not also my very drunken servant, Michael Lambourne, whom I have told your Grace of."

"Grace!" said Leicester; "what means thou by that epithet?"

"It came unawares, my lord; and yet it sounds so very natural, that I cannot recal it."

"'Tis thine own preferment that hath turned thy brain," said Leicester, laughing; "new honours are as heady as new wine."

"May your lordship soon have cause to say so from experience," said Varney; and, wishing his patron good night, he withdrew.

Chapter Eight

Here stands the victim—there the proud betrayer,
E'en as the hind pulled down by strangling dogs
Lies at the hunter's feet—who courteous proffers
To some high dame, the Dian of the chace,
To whom he looks for guerdon, his sharp blade,
To gash the sobbing throat.
The Woodsman

WE ARE now to return to Mervyn's Bower, the apartment, or rather the prison, of the unfortunate Countess of Leicester, who for some time kept within bounds her uncertainty and her impatience. She was aware that, in the tumult of the day, there might be some delay ere her letter could be safely conveyed to the hands of Leicester, and that some time more might elapse ere he could extricate himself from the necessary attendance on Elizabeth, to come and visit her in her secret bower.—"I will not expect him," she said, "till night—he cannot be absent from his royal guest, even to see me—he will, I know, come earlier if it be possible, but I will not expect him before night."—And yet all the while she did expect; and, while she tried to argue herself into a contrary belief, each hasty noise, of the hundred which she heard, sounded like the hurried step of Leicester on the staircase, hasting to fold her in his arms.

The fatigue of body which Amy had lately undergone, joined with the agitation of mind natural to so cruel a state of uncertainty, began by degrees strongly to affect her nerves, and she almost feared her total inability to maintain the necessary self-command through the scenes which might lie before. But, although spoiled by an over-indulgent system of education, Amy had naturally a mind of great power, united with a frame which her share in her father's woodland exercises had rendered uncommonly healthy. She summoned to her aid each mental and bodily resource; and not unconscious how much the issue of her fate might depend on her own self-possession, she prayed internally for strength of body and for mental fortitude, and resolved, at the same time, to yield to no nervous impulse which might weaken either.

Yet when the great bell of the Castle, which was placed in Cæsar's Tower, at no great distance from that called Mervyn's, began to send its pealing clamour abroad, in signal of the arrival of the royal procession, the din was so painfully acute to ears rendered nervously sensitive by anxiety, that she could hardly forbear shrieking with anguish, in answer to every stunning clash of the relentless peal.

Shortly afterwards, when the small apartment was at once enlightened by the shower of artificial fires with which the air was suddenly filled, and which crossed each other like fiery spirits, each bent on his own separate mission, or like salamanders executing a frolic dance in the region of the Sylphs, the Countess felt at first as if each rocket shot close by her eyes, and discharged its sparks and flashes so nigh that she could feel a sense of the heat. But she struggled against these fantastic terrors, and compelled herself to arise, stand by the window, look out, and gaze upon a sight, which at another time would have appeared to her at once captivating and fearful. The magnificent towers of the Castle were enveloped in garlands of artificial fire, or shrouded with tiaras of pale smoke. The surface of the lake glowed like molten iron, while many fire-works, (then thought extremely wonderful, though now common,) whose flame continued to exist in the opposing element, dived and rose, hissed and roared, and spouted fire, like so many dragons of enchantment sporting upon a burning lake.

Even Amy was for a moment interested by what was to her so new a scene. "I had thought it magical art," she said, "but poor Tressilian taught me to judge of such things as they are—Great God! And may not these idle splendours resemble my own hoped for happiness,—a single spark, which is instantly swallowed up by surrounding darkness,—a precarious glow, which rises but for a brief space into the air, that its fall may be the lower? O, Leicester! after all—all that thou hast said—hast sworn—that Amy was thy love, thy life—Can it be that thou art the Magician at whose nod these enchantments arise, and that she sees them, as an outcast, if not a captive?"

The sustained, prolonged, and repeated bursts of music, from so many different quarters, and at so many varying points of distance, which sounded as if not the Castle of Kenilworth only, but the whole country around, had been at once the scene of solemnizing some high national festival, carried the same oppressive thought still closer to her heart, while some notes wailed in distant and falling tones, as if in compassion for her sorrows, and some burst close and near upon her, as if mocking her misery, with all the insolence of unlimited mirth. "These sounds," she said, "are mine—mine, because they are HIS; but I cannot say,—Be still, these loud strains suit me not; and the voice of the meanest peasant that mingles in the dance, would have more power to modulate the music, than the command of her who is mistress of all."

By degrees the sounds of revelry died away, and the Countess withdrew from the window at which she had sate listening to it. It was night, but the moon afforded considerable light in the room, so that

Amy was able to make the arrangement which she judged necessary. There was hope that Leicester might come to her apartment as soon as the revel in the Castle had subsided; but there was also risk she might be disturbed by some unauthorized intruder. She had lost confidence in the key, since Tressilian had entered so easily, though the door was locked on the inside; yet all the additional security she could think of, was to place the table across the door, that she might be warned by the noise should any one attempt to enter. Having taken these necessary precautions, the unfortunate lady withdrew to her couch, stretched herself down on it, mused in anxious expectation, and counted more than one hour after midnight, till exhausted nature proved too strong for love, for grief, for fear, nay even for uncertainty, and she slept.

Yes, she slept. The Indian sleeps at the stake, in the intervals between his tortures; and mental torments, in like manner, exhaust by long continuance the sensibility of the sufferer, so that an interval of lethargic repose must necessarily ensue, ere the pangs which they inflict can again be renewed.

The Countess slept then for several hours, and dreamed that she was in the ancient house at Cumnor Place, listening for the low whistle with which Leicester often used to announce his presence in the court-yard, when arriving suddenly on one of his stolen visits. But on this occasion, instead of a whistle, she heard the peculiar blast of a bugle-horn, such as her father used to wind on the fall of the stag, and which huntsmen then called a *mort*. She ran, as she thought, to a window that looked into the court-yard, which she saw filled with men in mourning garments. The old Curate seemed about to read the funeral service. Mumblazon, tricked out in an antique dress, like an ancient herald, held aloft a scutcheon, with its usual decorations of skulls, cross-bones, and hour-glasses, surrounding a coat-of-arms, of which she could only distinguish that it was surmounted with an Earl's coronet. The old man looked at her with a ghastly smile, and said, "Amy, are they not rightly quartered?" Just as he spoke, the horns again poured on her ear the melancholy yet wild strain of the mort, or death-note, and she awoke.

The Countess awoke to hear a real bugle-note, or rather the combined breath of many bugles, sounding not the *mort*, but the jolly *reveillée*, to remind the inmates of the Castle of Kenilworth, that the pleasures of the day were to commence with a magnificent stag-hunting in the neighbouring Chase. Amy started up on her couch, listened to the sound, saw the first beams of the summer morning already twinkle through the lattice of her window, and recollected, with feelings of giddy agony, where she was, and how circumstanced.

"He thinks not of me," she said—"he will not come nigh me!—a Queen is his guest, and what cares he in what corner of his huge Castle a wretch like me pines in doubt, which is fast fading into despair?" At once a sound at the door, as of some one attempting to open it softly, filled her with an ineffable mixture of joy and fear; and, hasting to remove the obstacle she had placed against the door, and to unlock it, she had yet the precaution to ask, "Is it thou, my love?"

"Yes, my Countess," murmured a whisper in reply.

She threw open the door, and exclaiming, "Leicester!" flung her arms around the neck of the man who stood without, muffled in his cloak.

"No—not quite Leicester," answered Michael Lambourne, for he it was, returning the caress with vehemence,—"not quite Leicester, my lovely and most loving duchess, but as good a man."

With an exertion of force of which she would at another time have thought herself incapable, the Countess freed herself from the profane and profaning grasp of this drunken debauchee, and retreated into the midst of her apartment, where despair gave her courage to make a stand.

As Lambourne, on entering, dropped the lap of his cloak from his face, she knew Varney's profligate servant; the very last person, excepting his detested master, by whom she would have wished to be discovered. But she was still closely muffled in her travelling dress, and as Lambourne had scarce ever been admitted to her presence at Cumnor-Place, her person, she hoped, might not be so well known to him as his was to her, owing to Janet's pointing him frequently out as he crossed the court, and telling stories of his wickedness. She might have had still greater confidence in her disguise, had her experience enabled her to discover that he was much intoxicated; but this could scarce have consoled her for the risk which she might incur from such a character, in such a time, place, and circumstances.

Lambourne flung the door behind him as he entered, and folding his arms, as if mimicking the attitude of distraction into which Amy had thrown herself, he proceeded thus: "Hark ye, most fair Callipolis —or most lovely Countess of clouts, and divine Duchess of dark corners—if thou takest all that trouble of skewering thyself together, like a trussed fowl, that there may be more pleasure in the carving, even save thyself the labour. I like thy first frank manner the best—for rubs in the road of pleasure are—like (he made a step towards her, and staggered)—like a damned uneven floor as this is, where a gentleman may break his neck, if he does not walk as upright as a posture-master on the tight-rope."

"Stand back!" said the Countess; "do not approach nearer me, on thy peril."

"My peril!—and stand off—Why, how now, madam? Must you have a better mate than honest Mike Lambourne? I have been in America, girl, where the gold grows, and have brought off such a load on't"——

"Good friend," said the Countess, in great terror at the ruffian's determined and audacious manner, "I prithee begone, and leave me."

"And so I will, pretty one, when we are tired of each other's company—not a jot sooner."—He seized her by the arm, while, incapable of further defence, she uttered shriek upon shriek. "Nay, scream away if you like it," said he, still holding her fast; "I have heard the sea at the loudest, and I mind a squalling woman no more than a miauling kitten —damn me!—I have heard fifty or a hundred screaming at once, when there was a town stormed."

The cries of the Countess, however, brought unexpected aid, in the person of Laurence Staples, who had heard her exclamations from his apartment below, and entered in good time to save her from being discovered, if not from more atrocious violence. Laurence was drunk also, from the debauch of the preceding night; but fortunately his intoxication had taken a different turn from that of Lambourne.

"What devil's noise is this in the ward?" he said—"What! man and woman together in the same cell? that is against rule. I will have decency under my rule, by Saint Peter of the Fetters."

"Get thee down stairs, thou drunken beast," said Lambourne; "Seest thou not the lady and I would be private."

"Good sir, worthy sir!" said the Countess, addressing the jailor, "do but save me from him, for the sake of mercy!"

"She speaks fairly," said the jailor, "and I will take her part. I love my prisoners; and I have had as good under my key, as they have had in Newgate or the Compter. And so, being one of my lambkins, as I say, no one shall disturb her in her pen-fold. So, let go the woman, or I'll knock your brains out with my keys."

"I'll make a blood-pudding of thy midriff first," answered Lambourne, laying his left hand on his dagger, but still detaining the Countess by the arm with his right—"So have at thee, thou old ostrich, whose only living is upon a bunch of iron keys."

Laurence seized the arm of Michael, and prevented him from drawing his dagger; and as Lambourne struggled and strove to shake him off, the Countess made a sudden exertion on her side, and slipping her hand out of the glove on which the ruffian still kept hold, she gained her liberty, and escaping from the apartment, ran down stairs; while, at the same moment, she heard the two combatants fall on the floor with a noise which increased her terror. The outer wicket offered no impediment to her flight, having been opened for Lambourne's admittance; so that she succeeded in escaping down the stair, and fled into the Pleasance, which seemed to her hasty glance the direction in which she was most likely to avoid pursuit.

Meanwhile, Laurence and Lambourne rolled on the floor of the apartment, closely grappled together. Neither had, happily, opportunity to draw their daggers; but Laurence found space enough to dash his heavy keys across Michael's face, and Michael, in return, grasped the turnkey so felly by the throat, that the blood gushed from nose and mouth; so that they were both gory and obscene spectacles, when one of the other officers of the household, attracted by the noise of the fray, entered the room, and with some difficulty effected the separation of the combatants.

"A murrain on you both," said the charitable mediator, "and especially on you, Master Lambourne! What the fiend lie you here for, fighting on the floor like two butchers' curs in the kennel of the shambles?"

Lambourne arose, and, somewhat sobered by the interposition of a third party, looked with something less than his usual brazen impudence of visage; "We fought for a wench, an thou must know," was his reply.

"A wench! where is she?" said the officer.

"Why, vanished, I think," said Lambourne, looking around him; "unless Laurence hath swallowed her—that filthy paunch of his swallows as many distressed damsels and oppressed orphans, as e'er a giant in King Arthur's history: they are his prime food; he devours them body, soul, and substance."

"Ay, ay! it's no matter," said Laurence, gathering up his huge ungainly form from the floor; "but I have had your betters, Master Michael Lambourne, under the little turn of my forefinger and thumb; and I shall have thee, before all's done, under my hatches— the impudence of thy brow will not always save thy shin-bones from iron, and thy foul thirsty gullet from a hempen cord."—The words were no sooner out of his mouth, when Lambourne again made at him.

"Nay, go not to it again," said the sewer, "or I will call for him shall tame you both, and that is Master Varney—Sir Richard, I mean—he is stirring, I promise you—I saw him cross the court just now."

"Didst thou, by G—?" said Lambourne, seizing on the basin and ewer which stood in the apartment; "Nay, then, element do thy work —I thought I had enough of thee last night, when I floated about for Orion, like a cork on a cask of ale."

So saying, he fell to work to cleanse from his face and hands the signs of the fray, and to get his apparel into some order.

"What hast thou done to him?" said the sewer, speaking aside to the jailor; "his face is fearfully swelled."

"It is but the impress of the keys of my cabinet—too good an imprint for his gallows-face. No man shall abuse or insult my prisoners; they are my jewels, and I lock them in safe casket accordingly.— And so, mistress, leave off your wailing—Hey! why surely there was a woman here!"

"I think you are all mad this morning," said the sewer; "I saw no woman here, nor no man neither in a proper sense, but only two beasts rolling on the floor."

"Nay, then I am undone," said the jailor; "the prison's broken, that is all. Kenilworth prison is broken, which was the strongest jail betwixt this and the Welch marches—Ay, and a house that has had knights, and earls, and kings sleeping in it, as secure as if they had been in the Tower of London. It is broken, the prisoners fled, and the jailor in much danger of being hanged."

So saying, he retreated down to his own den to conclude his lamentation, or to sleep himself sober. Lambourne and the sewer followed him close, and it was well for them, since the jailor, out of mere habit, was about to lock the wicket after him; and had they not been within the reach of interfering, they would have had the pleasure of being shut up in the turret-chamber, from which the Countess had been just delivered.

That unhappy lady, as soon as she found herself at liberty, fled, as we have already mentioned, into the Pleasance. She had seen this richly ornamented space of ground from the window of Mervyn's Tower; and it occurred to her, at the moment of her escape, that, amongst its numerous arbours, bowers, fountains, statues, and grottoes, she might find some recess, in which she could be concealed until she had an opportunity of addressing herself to a protector, to whom she might communicate as much as she dared of her forlorn situation, and through whose means she might supplicate an interview with her husband.

"If I could see my guide," she thought, "I would learn if he had delivered my letter—even if I could see Tressilian, it were better to risk Dudley's anger, by confiding my whole situation to one who is the very soul of honour, than to run the hazard of farther insult among the insolent menials of this ill-ruled place. I will not again venture into an inclosed apartment. I will wait, I will watch—amidst so many human beings, there must be some kind heart which can judge and compassionate what mine endures."

In truth, more than one party entered and traversed the Pleasance. But they were in joyous groupes of four or five persons together, laughing and jesting in their own fullness of mirth and lightness of heart.

The retreat which she had chosen, gave her the easy alternative of avoiding observation. It was but stepping back to the farthest recess of a grotto, ornamented with rustic work and moss-seats, and terminated by a fountain, and she might easily remain concealed, or at her pleasure discover herself to any solitary wanderer, whose curiosity might lead him into that romantic retirement. Anticipating such an opportunity, she looked into the clear basin, which the silent fountain held up to her like a mirror, and felt shocked at her own appearance, and doubtful at the same time, muffled and disfigured as her disguise made her seem to herself, whether any female, (and it was from the compassion of her own sex that she chiefly expected sympathy,) would engage in conference with so suspicious an object. Reasoning thus like a woman, to whom external appearance is scarcely in any circumstances a matter of unimportance, and like a Beauty who had some confidence in the power of her own charms, she laid aside her travelling cloak and capotaine hat, and placed them beside her, so that she could assume them in an instant, ere one could penetrate from the entrance of the grotto to its extremity, in case the intrusion of Varney or of Lambourne should render such disguise necessary. The dress which she wore under these vestments was somewhat of a theatrical cast, so as to suit the assumed personage of one of the females who was to act in the pageant. Wayland had found the means of arranging it thus upon the second day of their journey, having experienced the service arising from the assumption of such a character on the preceding day. The fountain, acting both as a mirror and ewer, afforded Amy the means of a brief toilette, of which she availed herself as hastily as possible, then took in her hand her small casket of jewels in case she might find them useful intercessors, and retiring to the darkest and most sequestered nook, sat down on a seat of moss, and awaited till fate should give her some chance of rescue, or of propitiating an intercessor.

Chapter Nine

Have you not seen the partridge quake,
　　Viewing the hawk approaching nigh?
She cuddles close beneath the brake,
　　Afraid to sit, afraid to fly.
　　　　　　　　　　　PRIOR

IT CHANCED upon that memorable morning, that one of the earliest of the huntress train, who appeared from her chamber in full array for the Chase, was the Princess, for whom all these pleasures were instituted, England's Maiden Queen. I know not if it were by chance, or out of the befitting courtesy due to a mistress by whom he was so much honoured, that she had scarcely made one step beyond the threshold of her chamber, ere Leicester was by her side, and proposed to her, until the preparations for the Chase had been completed, to view the Pleasance, and the gardens which it connected with the Castle-yard.

To this new scene of pleasures they walked, the Earl's arm affording his Sovereign the occasional support which she required, where flights of steps, then a favourite ornament in a garden, conducted them from terrace to terrace, and from parterre to parterre. The ladies in attendance, gifted with prudence, or endowed perhaps with the amiable desire of acting as they would be done by, did not conceive their duty to the Queen's person required them, though they lost not sight of her, to approach so near as to share, or perhaps disturb, the conversation betwixt the Queen and the Earl, who was not only her host, but also her most trusted, esteemed, and favoured servant. They contented themselves with admiring the grace of this illustrious couple, whose robes of state were now exchanged for hunting suits, almost equally magnificent.

Elizabeth's sylvan dress, which was of a pale blue silk, with silver lace and *aiguillettes*, approached in form to that of the ancient Amazons; and was, therefore, well suited at once to her height, and to the dignity of her mien, which her conscious rank and long habit of authority had rendered in some degree too masculine to be seen to the best advantage in ordinary female weeds. Leicester's hunting suit of Lincoln-green, richly embroidered with gold, and crossed by the gay baldric, which sustained a bugle-horn, and a wood-knife instead of a sword, became its master, as did his other vestments of court or of war. For such were the perfections of his form and mien, that Leicester was always supposed to be seen to the greatest advantage in the character and dress which for the time he presented.

The conversation of Elizabeth with the favourite Earl has not reached us in detail. But those who watched at some distance, (and the eyes of courtiers and court ladies are right sharp,) were of opinion, that on no occasion did the dignity of Elizabeth, in gesture and motion, seem so decidedly to soften away into a mien expressive of indecision and tenderness. Her step was not only slow, but even unequal, a thing most unwonted in her carriage; her looks seemed bent on the ground, and there was a timid disposition to withdraw from her companion, which external gesture in females often indicates exactly the opposite tendency in the secret mind. The Countess of

Rutland, who ventured nearest, was even heard to aver, that she discerned a tear in Elizabeth's eye, and a blush on her cheek; and still farther, "She bent her looks on the ground to avoid mine," said the Countess; "she who, in her ordinary mood, could look down a lion." To what conclusions these symptoms led is sufficiently evident; nor were they probably entirely groundless. The progress of a private conversation betwixt two persons of different sexes, is often decisive of their fate, and gives it a turn very distinct perhaps from what they themselves anticipate. Gallantry becomes mingled with conversation, and affection and passion come gradually to mingle with gallantry. Nobles, as well as shepherd swains, will, in such a trying moment, say more than they intended; and Queens, like village maidens, will listen longer than they should.

Horses in the meanwhile neighed, and champed the bits with impatience in the base-court; hounds yelled in their couples, and yeomen, rangers, and prickers, lamented the exhaling of the dew, which would prevent the scent from lying. But Leicester had another chace in view, or, to speak more justly towards him, had become engaged in it without premeditation, as the high-spirited hunter which follows the cry of the hounds that have crossed his path by accident. The Queen—an accomplished and handsome woman—the pride of England, the hope of France and Holland, and the dread of Spain, had probably listened with more than usual favour to that mixture of romantic gallantry with which she always loved to be addressed; and the Earl had, in vanity, in ambition, or in both, thrown in more and more of that delicious ingredient, until his importunity became the language of love itself.

"No, Dudley," said Elizabeth, yet it was with broken accents—"No, I must be the mother of my people—other ties, that make the lowly maiden happy, are denied to her Sovereign—no, Leicester, urge it no more—were I as others, free to seek my own happiness—then, indeed—But it cannot—cannot be—delay the chace—delay it for half an hour—and leave me, my lord."

"How, leave you, Madam!" said Leicester,—"Has my madness offended you?"

"No, Leicester, not so!" answered the Queen hastily; "but it is madness, and must not be repeated—go—but go not far from hence —and meantime let no one intrude on my privacy."

While she spoke thus, Dudley bowed deeply, and retired with a slow and melancholy air. The Queen stood gazing after him, and murmured to herself—"Were it possible—Were it *but* possible!—But no—no—Elizabeth must be the wife and mother of England alone."

As she spoke thus, and in order to avoid some one whose step she heard approaching, the Queen turned into the grotto in which her hapless, and but yet too successful rival lay concealed.

The mind of England's Elizabeth, if somewhat shaken by the agitating interview to which she had just put a period, was of that firm and decided character which soon recovers its natural tone. It was like one of those ancient druidical monuments, called Rocking-stones. The finger of Cupid, boy as he is painted, could put her feelings in motion, but the power of Hercules could not have destroyed their equilibrium. As she advanced with a slow pace towards the inmost extremity of the grotto, her countenance, ere she had proceeded half the length, had recovered its dignity of look, and her mien its air of command.

It was then the Queen became aware, that a female figure was placed beside, or rather partly behind, an alabaster column, at the foot of which arose the pellucid fountain, which occupied the inmost recess of the twilight grotto. The classical mind of Elizabeth suggested the story of Numa and Egeria, and she doubted not that some Italian sculptor had here represented the Naiad, whose inspirations gave laws to Rome. As she advanced, she became doubtful whether she beheld a statue, or a form of flesh and blood. The unfortunate Amy, indeed, remained motionless, betwixt the desire which she had to make her condition known to one of her own sex, and her awe for the stately form which approached her, and which, though her eyes had never before beheld, her fears instantly suspected to be the personage she really was. Amy had arisen from her seat with the purpose of addressing the lady, who entered the grotto alone, and, as she at first thought, so opportunely. But when she recollected the alarm which Leicester had expressed at the Queen knowing aught of their union, and became more and more satisfied that the person whom she now beheld was Elizabeth herself, she stood with one foot advanced and one withdrawn, her arms, head, and hands perfectly motionless, and her cheek as pallid as the alabaster pedestal against which she leaned. Her dress was of pale sea-green silk, little distinguished in that imperfect light, and somewhat resembled the drapery of a Grecian Nymph, such an antique disguise having been thought the most secure, where so many masquers and revellers were assembled; so that the Queen's doubt of her being a living form was well justified by all contingent circumstances, as well as by the bloodless cheek and the fixed eye.

Elizabeth remained in doubt, even after she had approached within a few paces, whether she did not gaze on a statue so cunningly fashioned, that by that doubtful light it could not be distinguished from reality. She stopped, therefore, and fixed upon this interesting object her princely look with so much keenness, that the astonishment which had kept Amy immoveable, gave way to awe, and she gradually cast down her eyes, and drooped her head under the commanding gaze of the Sovereign. Still, however, she remained in all respects, saving this slow and profound inclination of the head, motionless and silent.

From her dress, and the casket which instinctively she held in her hand, Elizabeth naturally conjectured that the beautiful but mute figure which she beheld, was a performer in one of the various theatrical pageants which had been placed in different situations to surprise her with their homage, and that the poor player, overcome with awe at her presence, had either forgot the part assigned her, or lacked courage to go through it. It was natural and courteous to give her some encouragement; and Elizabeth accordingly said in a tone of condescending kindness,—"How now, fair Nymph of this lovely grotto— art thou spell-bound and struck with dumbness by the charms of the wicked Enchanter whom men term Fear?—We are his sworn enemy, maiden, and can reverse his charm. Speak, we command thee."

Instead of answering her by speech, the unfortunate Countess dropped on her knee before the Queen, let her casket fall from her hand, and clasping her palms together, looked up in the Queen's face with such a mixed agony of fear and supplication, that Elizabeth was considerably affected.

"What may this mean?" she said; "this is a stronger passion than befits the occasion. Stand up, damsel—What wouldst thou have with us?"

"Your protection, Madam," faultered forth the unhappy petitioner.

"Each daughter of England has it while she is worthy of it," replied the Queen; "but your distress seems to have a deeper root than a forgotten task. Why, and in what, do you crave our protection?"

Amy hastily endeavoured to recal what she were best to say, which might secure herself from the imminent dangers which surrounded her, without endangering her husband; and plunging from one thought to another, amidst the chaos which filled her mind, she could at length, in answer to the Queen's repeated enquiries, in what she sought protection, only faulter out, "Alas! I know not."

"This is folly, maiden," said Elizabeth impatiently; for there was something in the extreme confusion of the suppliant, which irritated her curiosity as well as interested her feelings. "The sick man must tell his malady to the physician, nor are WE accustomed to ask questions so oft, without receiving an answer."

"I request—I implore," stammered forth the unfortunate Countess,—"I beseech your gracious protection—against—against one Varney." She choaked well nigh as she uttered the fatal word, which was instantly caught up by the Queen.

"What, Varney—Sir Richard Varney—the servant of Lord Leicester!—What, damsel, are you to him, or he to you?"

"I—I—was his prisoner—and he practised on my life—and I broke forth to—to"——

"To throw thyself on my protection, doubtless," said Elizabeth. "Thou shalt have it—that is, if thou art worthy; for we will sift this matter to the uttermost.—Thou art," she said, bending on the Countess an eye which seemed designed to pierce her very inmost soul,—"thou art Amy, daughter of Sir Hugh Robsart of Lidcote-Hall?"

"Forgive me—forgive me—most gracious Princess!" said Amy, dropping once more on her knee, from which she had arisen.

"For what should I forgive thee, silly wench?" said Elizabeth; "for being the daughter of thine own father?—thou art brain-sick, surely. Well, I see I must wring thy story from thee by inches—thou did'st deceive thine old and honoured father—thy look confesses it—cheated Master Tressilian—thy blush avouches it—and married this same Varney."

Amy sprung on her feet, and interrupted the Queen eagerly, with, "No, Madam, no—as there is a God above us, I am not the sordid wretch you would make me! I am not the wife of that contemptible slave—of that most deliberate villain! I am not the wife of Varney! I would rather be the bride of Destruction!"

The Queen, overwhelmed in her turn by Amy's vehemence, stood silent for an instant, and then replied, "Why, God ha' mercy!—I see thou can'st talk fast enough when the theme likes thee. Nay, tell me, woman," she continued, for to the impulse of curiosity was now added that of an undefined jealousy that some deception had been practised on her,—"tell me, woman—for by God's day, I WILL know—whose wife, or whose paramour art thou? speak out, and be speedy—thou wert better dally with a lioness than with Elizabeth."

Urged to this extremity, dragged as it were by irresistible force to the verge of the precipice, which she saw but could not avoid,—permitted not a moment's respite by the eager words, and menacing gestures of the offended Queen, Amy at length uttered in despair, "The Earl of Leicester knows it all."

"The Earl of Leicester!" said Elizabeth, in utter astonishment—"The Earl of Leicester!" she repeated, with kindling anger,—"Woman, thou art set on to this—thou doest belie him—he takes no keep of such things as thou art. Thou art suborned to slander the noblest lord, and the truest-hearted gentleman, in England! But were he the right hand of our trust, or something yet dearer to us, thou shalt have thy hearing, and that in his presence. Come with me—come with me instantly!"

As Amy shrunk back with terror, which the incensed Queen interpreted as that of conscious guilt, Elizabeth hastily advanced, seized on her arm, and hastened with swift and long steps out of the grotto, and along the principal alley of the Pleasance, dragging with her the terrified Countess, whom she still held by the arm, and whose utmost exertions could but just keep pace with those of the indignant Queen.

Leicester was at this moment the centre of a splendid groupe of lords and ladies, assembled together under an arcade, or portico, which closed the alley. The company had drawn together in that place, to attend the commands of her Majesty that the hunting-party should go forward, and their astonishment may be imagined, when instead of seeing Elizabeth advance towards them with her usual measured dignity of motion, they beheld her walking so rapidly, that she was in the midst of them ere they were aware; and then observed, with fear and surprise, that her features were flushed betwixt anger and agitation, that her hair was loosened by her haste of motion, and that her eyes sparkled as they wont when the spirit of Henry VIII. mounted highest in his daughter. Nor were they less astonished at the appearance of the pale, extenuated, half-dead, yet still lovely female, whom the Queen upheld by main strength with one hand, while with the other she waved aside the ladies and nobles who pressed towards her, under the idea that she was taken suddenly ill. "Where is my Lord of Leicester?" she said, in a tone that thrilled with astonishment all the courtiers who stood around—"Stand forth, my Lord of Leicester!"

If, in the midst of the most serene day of summer, when all was light and laughing around, a thunderbolt was to fall from the clear blue vault of heaven, and rend the earth at the very feet of some careless traveller, he could not gaze upon the smouldering chasm, which so unexpectedly yawned before him, with half the astonishment and fear which Leicester felt at the sight that so suddenly presented itself. He had that instant been receiving, with a political affectation of disavowing and misunderstanding their meaning, the half uttered, half intimated congratulations of the courtiers upon the favour of the Queen, carried apparently to its highest pitch during the interview of that morning; from which most of them seemed to augur, that he might soon arise from their equal in rank to become their master. And now, while the subdued yet proud smile with which he disclaimed those inferences was yet curling his cheek, the Queen shot into the circle, her passions excited to the uttermost; and, supporting with one hand, and apparently without an effort, the pale and sinking form of his almost expiring wife, and pointing with the finger of the other to her half dead features, demanded in a voice that sounded to the ears of the astounded statesman like the last dread trumpet-call, that summons body and spirit to the judgment seat, "Knowest thou this woman?"

As at the blast of that last trumpet, the guilty shall call upon the mountains to cover them, Leicester's inward thoughts invoked the stately arch which he had built in his pride, to burst its strong conjunction, and overwhelm them in its ruins. But the cemented stones, architrave and battlement, stood fast; and it was the proud master himself, who, as if some actual pressure had bent him to the earth, kneeled down before Elizabeth, and prostrated his brow to the marble flagstones on which she stood.

"Leicester," said Elizabeth, in a voice which trembled with passion, "could I think thou hast practised on me—on me thy Sovereign—on me thy confiding, thy too partial mistress, the base and ungrateful deception which thy present confusion surmises—by all that is holy, false lord, that head of thine were in as great peril as ever was thy father's!"

Leicester had not conscious innocence, but he had pride to support him. He raised slowly his brow and features, which were black and swoln with contending emotions, and only replied, "My head cannot fall but by the censure of my peers—to them I will plead, and not to a princess who thus requites my faithful service."

"What! my lords," said Elizabeth, looking around. "We are defied, I think—defied in the Castle we have ourselves bestowed on this proud man!—My Lord Shrewsbury, you are Marshall of England—Attach him of high treason."

"Whom does your Grace mean?" said Shrewsbury, much surprised, for he had that instant joined the astonished circle.

"Whom should I mean, but that traitor, Dudley, Earl of Leicester!—Cousin of Hunsdon, order out your band of gentlemen pensioners, and take him into instant custody.—I say, villain, make haste!"

Hunsdon, a rough old noble, from his relationship to the Boleyns accustomed to use more freedom with the Queen than almost any others, replied bluntly, "And it is like your Grace might order me to the Tower to-morrow, for making too much haste. I do beseech you to be patient."

"Patient—God's life!" exclaimed the Queen,—"name not the word to me—thou know'st not of what he is guilty!"

Amy, who had by this time in some degree recovered herself, and who saw her husband, as she conceived, in the utmost danger from the rage of an offended Sovereign, instantly, (and, alas! how many women have done the same,) forgot her own wrongs, and her own danger, in her apprehensions for him, and throwing herself before the Queen, embraced her knees, while she exclaimed, "He is guiltless, Madam—he is guiltless—no one can lay aught to the charge of the noble Leicester."

"Why, minion," answered the Queen, "did'st not thou, thyself, say that the Earl of Leicester was privy to thy whole history?"

"Did I say so?" repeated the unhappy Amy, laying aside every consideration of consistency, and of self-interest; "O, if I did, I foully belied him. May God so judge me, as I believe he was never privy to a thought that would harm me!"

"Woman!" said Elizabeth, "I will know who has moved thee to this; or my wrath—and the wrath of kings is a flaming fire—shall wither and consume thee like a weed in the furnace."

As the Queen uttered this threat, Leicester's better angel called his pride to his aid, and reproached him with the utter extremity of meanness which would overwhelm him for ever, if he stooped to take shelter under the generous interposition of his wife, and abandoned her, in return for her kindness, to the resentment of the Queen. He had already raised his head, with the dignity of a man of honour, to avow his marriage, and proclaim himself the protector of his Countess, when Varney, born, as it appeared, to be his master's evil genius, rushed into the presence, with every mark of disorder on his face and apparel.

"What means this saucy intrusion?" said Elizabeth, while Varney, with the air of a man altogether overwhelmed with grief and confusion, prostrated himself before her feet, exclaiming, "Pardon, my Liege, pardon!—Or at least let your justice avenge itself on me, where it is due; but spare my noble, my generous, my innocent patron and master!"

Amy, who was yet kneeling, started up as she saw the man whom she deemed most odious place himself so near her, and was about to fly towards Leicester, when, checked at once by the uncertainty and even timidity which his looks had reassumed as soon as the appearance of his confidant seemed to open a new scene, she hung back, and, uttering a faint scream, besought of her Majesty to cause her to be imprisoned in the lowest dungeon of the castle—to deal with her as the worst of criminals—"but spare," she exclaimed, "my sight and hearing, what will destroy the little judgment I have left—the sight of that unutterable and most shameless villain!"

"And why, sweetheart?" said the Queen, moved by a new impulse; "what hath he, this false knight, since such thou accountest him, done to thee?"

"Oh, worse than sorrow, madam, and worse than injury—he has

sown dissention where most there should be peace. I shall go mad if I look longer on him."

"Beshrew me, but I think thou art distraught already," answered the Queen.—"My Lord Hunsdon, look to this poor distressed young woman, and let her be safely bestowed, and in honest keeping, till we require her to be forthcoming."

Two or three of the ladies in attendance, either moved by compassion for a creature so interesting, or by some other motive, offered their service to look after her; but the Queen briefly answered, "Ladies, under favour, no.—You have all (give God thanks) sharp ears and nimble tongues—our kinsman Hunsdon has ears of the dullest, and a tongue somewhat rough, but yet of the slowest.—Hunsdon, look to it that none have speech of her."

"By Our Lady!" said Hunsdon, taking in his strong sinewy arms the fading and almost swooning form of Amy, "she is a lovely child; and though a rough nurse, your Grace hath given her a kind one. She is safe with me as one of my own lady-birds of daughters."

So saying, he carried her off, unresistingly and almost unconsciously; his war-worn locks and long grey beard mingling with her light-brown tresses, as her head reclined on his strong square shoulder. The Queen followed him with her eye—she had already, with that self-command which forms so necessary a part of a Sovereign's accomplishments, suppressed every appearance of agitation, and seemed as if she desired to banish all traces of her burst of passion from the recollection of those who had witnessed it. "My Lord of Hunsdon," she said, "is but a rough nurse for so tender a babe."

"My Lord of Hunsdon," said the Dean of St Asaph, "I speak it not in defamation of his more noble qualities, hath a broad license in speech, and garnishes his discourse somewhat too freely with the cruel and superstitious oaths, which savour both of profaneness and of old papestrie."

"It is the fault of his blood, Mr Dean," said the Queen, turning sharply round upon the reverend dignitary as she spoke; "and you may blame mine with the same distemperature. The Boleyns were ever a hot and plain-spoken race, more hasty to speak their mind than careful to chuse their expressions. And by my word—I hope there is no sin in that affirmation—I question if it were much cooled by mixing with that of Tudor."

As she made this last observation she smiled graciously, and stole her eyes almost insensibly round to seek those of the Earl of Leicester, to whom she now began to think she had spoken with hasty harshness upon the unfounded suspicion of a moment.

The Queen's eye found the Earl in no mood to accept the implied offer of conciliation. His own looks had followed, with late and rueful repentance, the faded form whom Hunsdon had just borne from the presence; they now reposed gloomily on the ground, but more—so at least it seemed to Elizabeth—with the expression of one who has received an unjust affront, than of him who is conscious of guilt. She turned her face angrily from him, and said to Varney, "Speak, Sir Richard, and explain these riddles—thou hast sense, and the use of speech, at least, which elsewhere we look for in vain."

As she said this, she darted another resentful glance towards Leicester, while the wily Varney hastened to tell his own story.

"Your Majesty's piercing eye," he said, "has already detected the cruel malady of my beloved lady; which, unhappy that I am, I would not suffer to be expressed in the certificate of her physician, seeking to conceal what has now broken out with so much the more scandal."

"She is then distraught?" said the Queen—"indeed we doubted not of it—her whole demeanour bears it out. I found her moping in a corner of yonder grotto; and every word which she spoke—which indeed I dragged from her as by the rack—she instantly recalled and forswore. But how came she hither?—why had you her not in safe-keeping?"

"My gracious Liege," said Varney, "the worthy gentleman under whose charge I left her, Master Anthony Forster, has come hither but now, as fast as man and horse could travel, to shew me of her escape, which she managed with the art peculiar to many when afflicted with this malady—he is at hand for examination."

"Let it be for another time," said the Queen. "But, Sir Richard, we envy you not your domestic felicity; your lady railed on you bitterly, and seemed ready to swoon at beholding you."

"It is the nature of persons in her disorder, so please your Grace," answered Varney, "to be ever most inveterate in their spleen against those, whom, in their better moments, they hold nearest and dearest."

"We have heard so, indeed," said Elizabeth, "and give faith to the saying."

"May your Grace then be pleased," said Varney, "to command my unfortunate wife to be delivered into the custody of her friends?"

Leicester partly started; but, making a strong effort, he subdued his emotion, while Elizabeth answered sharply, "You are something too hasty, Master Varney; we will have first a report of the lady's health and state of mind from Master, our own physician, and then determine what shall be thought just. You shall have licence, however, to see her, that if there be any matrimonial quarrel betwixt you—such things we have heard do occur, even betwixt a loving couple—you may make it up, without further scandal to our court, or trouble to ourselves."

Varney bowed low, and made no other answer.

Elizabeth again looked towards Leicester, and said, with a degree of condescension which could only arise out of the most heartfelt interest, "Discord, as the Italian poet says, will find her way into peaceful convents, as well as into the privacy of families; and we fear our own guards and ushers will hardly exclude her from courts. My Lord of Leicester, you are offended with us, and we have right to be offended with you. We will take the lion's part upon us, and be the first to forgive."

Leicester smoothed his brow, as by an effort, but the trouble was too deep-seated that its placidity should at once return. He said, however, that which fitted the occasion, "that he could not have the happiness of forgiving, because she who commanded him to do so, could commit no injury towards him."

Elizabeth seemed content with this reply, and intimated her pleasure that the sports of the morning should proceed. The bugles sounded—the hounds bayed—the horses pranced—but the courtiers and ladies sought the amusement to which they were summoned with hearts very different from those which had leaped to the morning's *reveillée*. There was doubt, and fear, and expectation on every brow, and surmise and intrigue in every whisper.

Blount took an opportunity to whisper into Raleigh's ear, "This storm came like a levanter in the Mediterranean."

"*Varium et mutabile*"—answered Raleigh, in a similar tone.

"Nay, I know nought of your Latin," said Blount; "but I thank God Tressilian took not the sea during that hurricano. He could scarce have missed shipwreck, knowing as he does so little how to trim his sails to a court gale."

"Thou wouldst have instructed him?" said Raleigh.

"Why, I have profited by my time as well as thou, Sir Walter," replied honest Blount. "I am knight as well as thou, and of the earlier creation."

"Now, God further thy wit," said Raleigh; "but for Tressilian, I would I knew what were the matter with him. He told me this morning he would not leave his chamber for the space of twelve hours, or thereby, being bound by a promise. This lady's madness, when he shall learn it, will not, I fear, cure his infirmity. The moon is at the fullest, and men's brains are working like yeast. But hark! they sound to mount. Let us to horse, Blount; we young knights must deserve our spurs."

Chapter Ten

——Sincerity,
Thou first of virtues! let no mortal leave
The onward path, although the earth should gape,
And from the gulf of hell destruction cry,
To take dissimulation's winding way.

Douglas

IT WAS not till after a long and successful morning's sport, and a prolonged repast which followed the return of the Queen to the Castle, that Leicester at length found himself alone with Varney, from whom he now learned the whole particulars of the Countess's escape, as they had been brought to Kenilworth by Forster, who, in his terror for the consequences, had himself posted thither with the tidings. As Varney, in his narrative, took especial care to be silent concerning those practices on the Countess's health which had driven her to so desperate a resolution, Leicester, who could only suppose that she had adopted it out of jealous impatience, to attain the avowed state and appearance belonging to her rank, was not a little offended at the levity with which his wife had broken his strict commands, and exposed him to the resentment of Elizabeth.

"I have given," he said, "to this daughter of an obscure Devonshire gentleman, the proudest name in England. I have made her sharer of my bed and of my fortunes. I ask but of her a little patience, ere she launch out upon the full current of her grandeur, and the infatuated woman will rather hazard her own shipwreck and mine, will rather involve me in a thousand whirlpools, shoals, and quick-sands, and compel me to a thousand devices which shame me in mine own eyes, than tarry for a little space longer in the obscurity to which she was born.—So lovely, so delicate, so fond, so faithful—yet to lack in so grave a matter the patience which one might hope from the veriest fool —it puts me beyond my patience."

"We may post it over yet well enough," said Varney, "if my lady will be but ruled, and take on her the character which the time commands."

"It is but too true, Sir Richard," said Leicester, "there is now indeed no other remedy. I have heard her termed thy wife in my presence, without contradiction. She must bear the title until she is far from Kenilworth."

"And long afterwards, I trust," said Varney; then instantly added, "For I cannot but hope it will be long after ere she bear the title of Lady Leicester—I fear me it may scarce be with safety during the life of this Queen. But your lordship is best judge, you alone knowing what passages have taken place betwixt Elizabeth and you."

"You are right, Varney," said Leicester; "I have this morning been both fool and villain—And when Elizabeth hears of my unhappy marriage, she cannot but think herself treated with that premeditated slight which women never forgive. We have once this day stood upon terms little short of defiance; and to those, I fear, we must again return."

"Is her resentment, then, so implacable?" said Varney.

"Far from it," replied the Earl. "For, being what she is in spirit and in station, she has even this day been but too condescending, in giving me opportunities to repair what she thinks my faulty heat of temper."

"Ay," answered Varney, "the Italians say right—in lovers' quarrels, the party that loves most, is always most willing to acknowledge the greater fault.—So then, my lord, if this union with the lady could be concealed, you stand with Elizabeth as you did."

Leicester sighed, and was silent for a moment, ere he replied, "Varney, I think thou art true to me, and I will tell thee all. I do *not* stand where I did. I have spoken to Elizabeth—under what mad impulse I know not—on a theme which cannot be abandoned without touching every female feeling to the quick, and which yet I dare not and cannot prosecute. She can never, never forgive me, for having caused and witnessed those yieldings to human passion."

"We must do something, my lord," said Varney, "and that speedily."

"There is nought to be done," answered Leicester, despondingly; "I am like one that has long toiled up a dangerous precipice, and when he is within one perilous stride of the top, finds his progress arrested when retreat has become impossible. I see above me the pinnacle which I cannot reach—beneath me the abyss into which I must fall, as soon as my relaxing grasp and dizzy brain join to hurl me from my present precarious stance."

"Think better of your situation, my lord," said Varney—"let us try the experiment in which you have but now acquiesced. Keep we your marriage from Elizabeth's knowledge, and all may yet be well. I will instantly go to the lady myself—She hates me, because I have been earnest with your lordship, as she but truly suspects, in opposition to what she terms her rights. I care not for her prejudices—She shall listen to me; and I will shew her such reasons for yielding to the pressure of the times, that I doubt not to bring back her consent to whatever measures these exigencies may require."

"No, Varney," said Leicester; "I have thought upon what is to be done, and I will myself speak with Amy."

It was now Varney's turn to feel, upon his own account, the terrors which he affected to participate solely on account of his patron. "Your lordship will not yourself speak with the lady?"

"It is my fixed purpose," said Leicester; "fetch me one of thy livery-cloaks; I will pass the centinel as thy servant. Thou art to have free access to her."

"But, my lord"——

"I will have no *buts*," replied Leicester; "it shall be even thus, and not otherwise. Hunsdon sleeps, I think, in Saintlowe's Tower. We can go thither from these apartments by the private passage, without risk of meeting any one. Or what if I do meet Hunsdon? he is more my friend than enemy, and thick-witted enough to adopt any belief that is thrust on him—fetch me the cloak instantly."

Varney had no alternative save obedience. In a few minutes Leicester was muffled in the mantle, pulled his bonnet over his brows, and followed Varney along the secret passage of the Castle which communicated with Hunsdon's apartment, in which there was scarce a chance of meeting any inquisitive person, and hardly light enough for any such to have satisfied their curiosity. They emerged at a door where Lord Hunsdon had, with military precaution, placed a centinel, one of his own northern retainers as it fortuned, who readily admitted Sir Richard Varney and his attendant, saying only, in his northern dialect, "I would, man, thou could'st make the mad lady be still yonder; for her moans do sae dirl through my head, that I would rather keep watch in a snow-drift, in the wastes of Catlowdie."

They hastily entered, and shut the door behind them.

"Now, good devil, if there be one," said Varney within himself, "for once help a votary at a dead pinch, for my boat is amongst the breakers."

The Countess Amy, with her hair and her garments dishevelled, was seated upon a sort of couch, in an attitude of the deepest affliction, out of which she was startled by the opening of the door. She turned hastily round, and fixing her eye on Varney, exclaimed, "Wretch! art thou come to frame some new plan of villainy?"

Leicester cut short her reproaches by stepping forward, and dropping his cloak, while he said, in a voice rather of authority than of affection, "It is with me, madam, you have to commune, not with Sir Richard Varney."

The change effected in the Countess's look and manner was like magic. "Dudley!" she exclaimed, "Dudley! and art thou come at last?" And with the speed of lightning she flew to her husband, clung around his neck, and, unheeding the presence of Varney, overwhelmed him with caresses, while she bathed his face in a flood of tears; muttering, at the same time, but in broken and disjointed monosyllables, the fondest expressions which love teaches his votaries.

Leicester, as it seemed to him, had reason to be angry with his lady for transgressing his commands, and thus placing him in the perilous situation in which he had that morning stood. But what displeasure could keep its ground before those testimonies of affection from a being so lovely, that even the negligence of dress, and the withering effects of fear and grief, which would have impaired the beauty of others, rendered her's but the more interesting. He received and repaid her caresses with fondness, mingled with melancholy, the last of which she seemed scarcely to observe, until the first transport of her own joy was over; when, looking anxiously in his face, she asked if he was ill.

"Not in my body, Amy," was his answer.

"Then I will be well too.—O Dudley! I have been ill!—very ill, since we last met!—for I call not this morning's horrible vision a meeting. I have been in sickness, in grief, and in danger—But thou art come, and all is joy, and health, and safety."

"Alas! Amy," said Leicester, "thou hast undone me!"

"I, my lord," said Amy, her cheek at once losing its transient flush of joy—"how could I injure that which I love better than myself."

"I would not upbraid you, Amy," replied the Earl; "but are you not come hither contrary to my express commands—and does not your presence here endanger both yourself and me?"

"Does it, does it indeed!" she exclaimed eagerly; "then why am I here a moment longer? O if you knew by what fears I was urged to quit Cumnor Place!—but I will say nothing of myself—only that if it might be otherwise, I would not willingly return *thither;*—yet if it concern your safety"——

"We will think, Amy, of some other retreat," said Leicester; "and you shall go to one of my Northern castles, under the personage—it will be but needful, I trust, for a very few days—of Varney's wife."

"How, my Lord of Leicester!" said the lady, disengaging herself from his embraces; "is it to your wife you give the dishonourable counsel to acknowledge herself the bride of another—and of all men, the bride of that Varney?"

"Madam, I speak it earnest—Varney is my true and faithful servant, trusted in my deepest secrets. I had better lose my right hand than his service at this moment. You have no cause to scorn him as you do."

"I could assign a cause, my lord," replied the Countess; "and I see he shakes even under that assured look of his—but he that is necessary as your right hand to your safety, is free from any accusation of mine—may he be true to you; and that he may be true, trust him not too much or too far. But it is enough to say, that I will not go with him unless by violence, nor would I acknowledge him as my husband, were all"——

"It is a temporary deception, madam," said Leicester, irritated by her opposition, "necessary for both our safeties, endangered by you through female caprice, or the premature desire to seize on a rank to which I gave you title, only under condition that our marriage, for a time, should continue secret. If my proposal disgust you, it is yourself have brought it on both of us. There is no other remedy—you must do what your own impatient folly hath rendered necessary—I command you."

"I cannot put your commands, my lord," said Amy, "in balance with those of honour and conscience. I will NOT, in this instance, obey you —you may achieve your own dishonour, to which these crooked policies naturally tend, but I will do nought that can blemish mine. How could you again, my lord, acknowledge me as a pure and chaste matron, worthy to share your fortunes, when, holding that high character, I had strolled the country the acknowledged wife of such a profligate fellow as your servant Varney!"

"My lord," said Varney interposing, "my lady is too much prejudiced against me, unhappily, to listen to what I can offer; yet it may please her better than what she proposes. She has good interest with Master Edmund Tressilian, and could doubtless prevail on him to consent to be her companion to Lidcote-hall, and there she might remain in safety until time permitted the developement of this mystery."

Leicester was silent, but stood looking eagerly on Amy, with eyes which seemed suddenly to glow as much with suspicion as displeasure.

The Countess only said, "Would to God I were in my father's house!—when I left it, I little thought I was leaving peace of mind and honour behind me."

Varney proceeded with a tone of deliberation, "Doubtless this will make it necessary to take strangers into my Lord's counsels; but surely the Countess will be warrant for the honour of Master Tressilian, and such of her father's family"——

"Peace, Varney," said Leicester; "by Heaven I will strike my dagger into thee, if again thou namest Tressilian as a partner of my counsels!"

"And wherefore not?" said the Countess; "unless they be counsels fitter for such as Varney, than for a man of stainless honour and integrity.—My lord, my lord, bend no angry brows on me—it is the

truth, and it is I who speak it. I once did Tressilian wrong for your sake
—I will not do him the further injustice of being silent when his
honour is brought in question. I can forbear," she said, looking at
Varney, "to pull the mask off hypocrisy, but I will not permit virtue to
be slandered in my hearing."

There was a dead pause. Leicester stood displeased, yet undeter-
mined, and too conscious of the weakness of his cause; while Varney,
with a deep and hypocritical affectation of sorrow, mingled with humility, bent his eyes on the ground.

It was then that the Countess Amy displayed, in the midst of distress and difficulty, the natural energy of character, which would, had
fate allowed, have rendered her a distinguished ornament to the rank
which she held. She walked up to Leicester with a composed step, a
dignified air, and looks in which strong affection assayed in vain to
shake the firmness of conscious truth and rectitude of principle. "You
have spoke your mind, my lord," she said, "in these difficulties with
which, unhappily, I have found myself unable to comply—this gentleman—this person I would say—has hinted at another scheme, to
which I object not but as it displeases you. Will your lordship be
pleased to hear what a young and timid woman, but your most affectionate wife, can suggest in the present extremity?"

Leicester was silent, but bent his head towards the Countess, as an
intimation that she was at liberty to proceed.

"There hath been but one cause for all these evils, my lord," she
proceeded, "and it resolves itself into the mysterious duplicity with
which you have been induced to surround yourself. Extricate yourself
at once, my lord, from the tyranny of these disgraceful trammels. Be
like a true English gentleman, knight, and earl, who holds that truth is
the foundation of honour, and that honour is dear to him as the breath
of his nostrils. Take your ill-fated wife by the hand—lead her to the
footstool of Elizabeth's throne—say, that in a moment of infatuation,
moved by supposed beauty, of which none perhaps can now trace even
the remains, I gave my hand to this Amy Robsart.—You will then have
done justice to me, my lord, and to your own honour; and should law
or power require you to part from me, I will oppose no objection—
since I may then with honour hide a grieved and broken heart in those
shades from which your love withdrew me."

There was so much of dignity, so much of tenderness in the Countess's remonstrance, that it moved all that was noble and generous in
the soul of her husband. The scales seemed to fall from his eyes, and
the duplicity and tergiversation of which he had been guilty, stung him
at once with remorse and shame.

"I am not worthy of you, Amy," he said, "that could weigh aught which ambition has to give against such a heart as thine. I have a bitter penance to perform, in disentangling, before sneering foes and astounded friends, all the meshes of my own deceitful policy.—And the Queen—but let her take my head, as she has threatened."

"Your head, my lord!" said the Countess; "because you used the freedom and liberty of an English subject in chusing a wife?—for shame; it is this distrust of the Queen's justice, this apprehension of dangers which cannot but be imaginary, that, like so many scare-crows, have induced you to forsake the straight-forward path, which, as it is the best, is also the safest."

"Ah, Amy, thou little knowest!" said Dudley; but, instantly check-ing himself, he added, "Yet she shall not find in me a safe or easy victim of arbitrary vengeance.—I have friends—I have allies—I will not, like Norfolk, be dragged to the block, as a victim to sacrifice—fear not, Amy; thou shalt see Dudley bear himself worthy of his name. I must instantly communicate with some of those friends on whom I can best rely; for, as things stand, I may be made prisoner in my own Castle."

"O, my good lord," said Amy, "make no faction in a peaceful state! —there is no friend can help us so well as our own candid truth and honour. Bring but these to our assistance, and you are safe amidst a whole army of the envious and malignant. Leave these behind you, and all other defence will be fruitless—Truth, my noble lord, is well painted unarmed."

"But Wisdom, Amy," answered Leicester, "is arrayed in panoply of proof. Argue not with me on the means I shall use to render my confession—since it must be called so—as safe as may be; it will be fraught with enough of danger, do what we will.—Varney, we must hence.—Farewell, Amy, whom I am to vindicate as mine own, at an expence and risk of which thou alone could'st be worthy. You shall soon hear farther from me."

He embraced her fervently, muffled himself as before, and accom-panied Varney from the apartment. The latter, as he left the room, bowed low, and, as he raised his body, regarded Amy with a peculiar expression, as if he desired to know how far his own pardon was included in the reconciliation which had taken place betwixt her and her lord. The Countess looked upon him with a fixed eye, but seemed no more conscious of his presence, than if there had been nothing but vacant air on the spot where he stood.

"She has brought me to the crisis," he muttered—"She or I are lost. There was something—I wot not if it was fear or pity, that prompted me to avoid this fatal crisis. It is now decided—She or I must perish."

While he thus spoke, he observed, with surprise, that a boy, repulsed by the centinel, made up to Leicester, and spoke with him. Varney was one of those politicians, whom not the slightest appearances escape without inquiry. He asked the centinel what the lad wanted with him, and received for answer, that the boy had wished him to transmit a parcel to the mad lady, but that he cared not to take charge of it, such communication being beyond his commission. His curiosity satisfied in this particular, he approached his patron, and heard him say—"Well, boy, the packet shall be delivered."

"Thanks, good Master Serving-man," said the boy, and was out of sight in an instant.

Leicester and Varney returned with hasty steps to the Earl's private apartment, by the same passage which had conducted them to Saintlowe Tower.

Chapter Eleven

——I have said
She's an adultress—I have said with whom
More, she's a traitor, and Camillo is
A federary with her, and one that knows
What she should shame to know herself.
Winter's Tale

THEY WERE no sooner in the Earl's cabinet, than, taking his tablets from his pocket, he began to write, speaking partly to Varney, partly to himself:—"There are many of them close bounden to me, and especially those in good estate and high office; many who, if they look back towards my benefits, or forward towards the perils which may befal themselves, will not, I think, be disposed to see me stagger unsupported. Let me see—Knollis is sure, and through his means Guernsey and Jersey—Horsey commands in the Isle of Wight—My brother-in-law, Huntingdon, and Pembroke, command Wales— Through Bedford I command the Puritans, with their interest, so powerful in all the boroughs—My brother of Warwick is equal, well nigh, to myself, in wealth, following, and dependencies—Sir Owen Hopton is at my devotion; he commands the Tower of London, and the national treasure deposited there—My father and grandfather needed never to have stooped their heads to the block, had they thus forecast their enterprizes.—Why look you so sad, Varney? I tell thee, a tree so deep-rooted is not easily to be torn up by the tempest."

"Alas! my lord," said Varney, with well acted passion, and then assumed the same look of despondency which Leicester had before noted.

"Alas!" repeated Leicester, "and wherefore alas, Sir Richard?

Doth your new spirit of chivalry supply no more vigorous ejaculation, when a noble struggle is impending? Or, if *alas* means thou wilt flinch from the conflict, thou mayest leave the Castle, or go join mine enemies, whichsoever you think best."

"Not so, my lord," answered his confidant; "Varney will be found fighting or dying by your side. Forgive me, if, in love to you, I see more fully than your noble heart permits you to do, the inextricable difficulties with which you are surrounded. You are strong, my lord, and powerful; yet, let me say it without offence, you are so only by reflected light of the Queen's favour. While you are Elizabeth's favourite, you are all, save in name, like an actual sovereign. But let her call back the honours she has bestowed, and the Prophet's gourd did not wither more suddenly. Declare against the Queen, and I do not say that in the wide nation, or in this province alone, you would find yourself instantly deserted and outnumbered; but I will say, that even in this very Castle, and in the midst of your vassals, kinsmen, and dependants, you would be a captive, nay a sentenced captive, should she please to say the word. Think upon Norfolk, my lord,—upon the powerful Northumberland,—the splendid Westmoreland;—think on all who have made head against this sage Princess. They are dead, captive, or fugitive. This is not like other thrones, which can be over-turned by a combination of powerful nobles; the broad foundations which support it are in the extended love and affections of the people. You might share it with Elizabeth if you would; but neither yours, nor any other power, foreign or domestic, will avail to overthrow, or even to shake it."

He paused, and Leicester threw from his tablets with an air of reckless despite. "It may be as thou say'st," he said; "and, in sooth, I care not whether truth or cowardice dictate thy forebodings. But it shall not be said I fell without a struggle.—Give orders, that those of my retainers who served under me in Ireland be gradually drawn into the main Keep, and let our gentlemen and friends stand on their guard, and go armed, as if they expected an onset from the followers of Sussex. Possess the town's-people with some apprehension; let them take arms, and be ready, at a signal given, to master the Pensioners and Yeomen of the Guard."

"Let me remind you, my lord," said Varney, with the same appearance of deep and melancholy interest, "that you have given me orders to prepare for disarming the Queen's guard. It is an act of high treason. But you shall nevertheless be obeyed."

"I care not," answered Leicester, desperately;—"I care not. Shame is behind me, Ruin before me; I must on."

Here there was another pause, which Varney at length broke with the following words: "It is come to the point I have long dreaded. I must either witness, like an ungrateful beast, the downfal of the best and kindest of masters, or I must speak that which I would have buried in the deepest oblivion, or told by any other mouth than mine."

"What is that thou sayest, or would say?" replied the Earl; "we have no time to waste in words, when the times call us to action."

"My speech is soon made, my lord—would to God it were as soon answered. Your marriage is the sole cause of the threatened breach with your Sovereign, my lord, is it not?"

"Thou knowest it is!" replied Leicester. "What needs so fruitless a question?"

"Pardon me, my lord," said Varney; "the use lies here. Men will wager their lands and lives in defence of a rich diamond, my lord; but were it not first prudent to look if there is no flaw in it?"

"What means this?" said Leicester, with eyes sternly fixed on his dependant; "of whom doest thou dare to speak?"

"It is——of the Countess Amy, my lord, of whom I am unhappily bound to speak; and of whom I *will* speak, were your lordship to kill me for my zeal."

"Thou mayest happen to deserve it at my hand," said the Earl; "but speak on, I will hear thee."

"Nay, then, my lord, I will be bold. I speak for my own life as well as for your lordship's. I like not this lady's tampering and trickstering with this same Edmund Tressilian. You know him, my lord—you know he had formerly an interest in her, which it cost your lordship some pains to supersede. You know the eagerness with which he has pressed on the suit against me in behalf of this lady, the open object of which is to drive your lordship to an avowal of what I must ever call your most unhappy marriage, the point to which my lady also is willing, at any risk, to urge you."

Leicester smiled constrainedly. "Thou meanest well, good Sir Richard, and would, I think, sacrifice thine own honour, as well as that of any other person, to save me from what thou think'st a step so terrible. But, remember,"—he spoke these words with the most stern decision,—"you speak of the Countess of Leicester."

"I do, my lord," said Varney; "but it is for the welfare of the Earl of Leicester. My tale is but begun. I do most strongly believe that this Tressilian has, from the beginning of his moving in her cause, been in connivance with her ladyship the Countess."

"Thou speak'st wild madness, Varney, with the sober face of a preacher. Where, or how, could they communicate together?"

"My lord," said Varney, "unfortunately I can shew that but too well. It was just before the supplication was presented to the Queen, in

Tressilian's name, that I met him, to my utter astonishment, at the postern gate, which leads from the demesne at Cumnor-Place."

"Thou met'st him, villain! and why didst thou not strike him dead?" exclaimed Leicester.

"I drew on him, my lord, and he on me; and had not my foot slipped, he had not, perhaps, been again a stumbling-block in your lordship's path."

Leicester seemed struck mute with surprise. At length he answered, "What other evidence hast thou of this, Varney, save thine own assertion?—for, as I will punish deeply, I will examine coolly and warily. Sacred Heaven! but no—I will examine coldly and warily—coldly and warily." He repeated these words more than once to himself, as if in the very sound there was a sedative quality; and again compressing his lips, as if he feared some violent expression might escape from them, he asked again, "What farther proof?"

"Enough, my lord," said Varney, "and to spare. I would it had rested with me alone, for with me it might have been silenced for ever. But my servant, Michael Lambourne, witnessed the whole, and was, indeed, the means of first introducing Tressilian into the castle. And therefore I took him into my service, and retained him in it, though something of a debauched fellow, that I might have his tongue always under my own command." He then acquainted Lord Leicester with the circumstances attending Tressilian's visit at Cumnor Place, when he made use of the agency of Lambourne to make his way into the place of Amy's residence. He pointed out to the astounded Leicester how easy it was to prove the circumstance of their interview true, by evidence of Anthony Forster, with the corroborative testimonies of the various persons at Cumnor, who had heard the wager laid, and seen Lambourne and Tressilian set off together. In the whole narrative, Varney hazarded nothing fabulous, excepting that, not indeed by direct assertion, but by inference, he led his patron to suppose that the interview betwixt Amy and Tressilian had been longer than the few minutes to which it was in reality limited.

"And wherefore was I not told of all this?" said Leicester, sternly. "Why did all of ye—in particular thou, Varney—keep back from me such material information?"

"Because, my lord," replied Varney, "the Countess pretended to Forster and to me, that Tressilian had intruded himself upon her; and I concluded their interview had been in all honour, and that she would at her own time tell it to your lordship. Your lordship knows with what unwilling ears we listen to evil surmises against those whom we love; and I thank Heaven, I am no make-bate or informer, to be the first to sow them."

"Thou art but too ready to receive them, however, Sir Richard," replied his patron. "How know'st thou that this interview was not in all honour, as thou hast said? Methinks the wife of the Earl of Leicester might speak for a short time with such a person as Tressilian, without injury to me, or suspicion to herself."

"Questionless, my lord," answered Varney; "had I thought other-wise, I had been no keeper of the secret. But here lies the rub—Tressilian leaves not the place without establishing a correspondence with a poor man, the landlord of an inn in Cumnor, for the purpose of carrying off the lady. He sends down an emissary of his, whom I trust soon to have in right sure keeping under Mervyn's Tower. Killigrew and Lambsbey are scouring the country in quest of him. The host is rewarded with a ring for keeping counsel—your lordship may have noted it on Tressilian's hand—here it is. This fellow, this agent, makes his way to the Place as a pedlar, holds conference with the lady, and they make their escape together by night—rob a poor fellow of a horse by the way, such was their guilty haste; and at length reach this Castle, where the Countess of Leicester finds refuge—I dare not say in what place."

"Speak, I command thee," said Leicester; "speak, while I retain sense enough to hear thee."

"Since it must be so," answered Varney, "the lady resorted immed-iately to the apartment of Tressilian, where she remained many hours, partly in company with him, and partly alone. I told you Tressilian had a paramour in his chamber—I little dreamed that paramour was"——

"Amy, thou would'st say," answered Leicester; "but it is false, false as the smoke of hell! Ambitious she may be—fickle and impatient—'tis a woman's fault; but false to me!—never, never—the proof—the proof of this!" he exclaimed, hastily.

"Carrol, the Deputy Marshal, ushered her thither by her own desire, on yesterday afternoon—Lambourne and the Warder both found her there at an early hour this morning."

"Was Tressilian there with her?" said Leicester, in the same hurried tone.

"No, my lord—you may remember," answered Varney, "that he was that night placed with Sir Nicholas Blount, under arrest."

"Did Carrol, or the other fellows, know who she was?" demanded Leicester.

"No, my lord," replied Varney; "Carrol and the Warder had never seen the Countess, and Lambourne knew her not in her disguise. But, in seeking to prevent her leaving the cell, he obtained possession of one of her gloves, which, I think, your lordship may know."

He gave the glove, which had the Bear and Ragged Staff, the Earl's impress, embroidered upon it in seed-pearls.

"I do, I do recognize it," said Leicester. "They were my own gift. The fellow of it was on the arm which she threw this very day around my neck!"—He spoke this with violent agitation.

"Your lordship," said Varney, "might yet further inquire of the lady herself, respecting the truth of these passages."

"It needs not—it needs not," said the tortured Earl; "it is written in characters of burning light, as if they were branded on my very eye-balls! I see her infamy—I can see nought else; and,—gracious Heaven!—for this vile woman was I about to commit to danger the lives of so many noble friends—shake the foundation of a lawful throne—carry the sword and torch through the bosom of a peaceful land—wrong the kind mistress who made me what I am—and would, but for that hell-framed marriage, have made me all that man can be! All this I was ready to do for a wanton, who trinkets and traffics with my worst foes!—And thou, villain, why didst thou not speak sooner?"

"My lord," said Varney, "a tear from my lady would have blotted out all I could have said—besides, I had not these proofs until this very morning, when Anthony Forster's sudden arrival, with the examinations and declarations, which he had extorted from the inn-keeper Gosling, and others, explained the manner of her flight from Cumnor-Place, and my own researches discovered the steps which she had taken here."

"Now, may God be praised for the light he has given! so full, so satisfactory, that there breathes not a man in England who shall call my proceeding rash, or my revenge unjust.—And yet, Varney—So young, so fair, so fawning, and so false! Hence, then, her hatred to thee, my trusty and faithful servant, because you withstood her plots, and endangered her paramour's life."

"I never gave her any other cause of dislike, my lord," replied Varney; "but she knew that my councils went directly to diminish her influence with your lordship; and that I was, and have been, ever ready to peril my life against your enemies."

"It is too, too apparent," replied Leicester. "Yet, with what an air of magnanimity she exhorted me to commit my head to the Queen's mercy, rather than wear the veil of falsehood a moment longer! Methinks, the angel of truth himself has such tones of high-souled impulse. Can it be so, Varney?—Can falsehood use thus boldly the language of truth?—Can infamy thus assume the guise of purity?— Varney, thou has been my servant from a child—I have raised thee high—I can raise thee higher. Think, think for me!—Thy brain was ever shrewd and piercing—may she not be innocent?—prove her so, and all I have yet done for thee shall be as nothing—nothing—in comparison of thy recompence!"

The agony with which his master spoke, had some effect even on the hardened Varney, who, in the midst of his own wicked and ambitious designs, really loved his patron as well as such a wretch was capable of loving any thing; but he comforted himself, and subdued his self-reproaches with the reflection, that if he inflicted upon the Earl some immediate and transitory pain, it was in order to pave his way to the throne, which, were this marriage dissolved by death or otherwise, he deemed Elizabeth would willingly share with his benefactor. He, therefore, persevered in his diabolical policy; and, after a moment's consideration, answered the anxious queries of the Earl with a melancholy look, as if he had in vain sought some exculpation for the Countess; then suddenly raising his head, he said, with an expression of hope, which instantly communicated itself to the countenance of his patron,—"Yet, wherefore, if guilty, should she have perilled herself by coming hither? Why not rather have fled to her father's, or elsewhere?—though that, indeed, might have interfered with her desire to be acknowledged as Countess of Leicester."

"True, true, true!" exclaimed Leicester, his transient gleam of hope giving way to the utmost bitterness of feeling and expression; "thou art not fit to fathom a woman's depth of wit, Varney. I see it all. She would not quit the estate and title of the wittol who had wedded her. Ay, and if in my madness I had started into rebellion, or if the angry Queen had taken my head, as she this morning threatened, the wealthy dower, which law would have assigned to the Countess Dowager of Leicester, had been no bad wind-fall to the beggarly Tressilian. Well might she goad me on to danger, which could not end otherwise than profitable to her.—Speak not for her, Varney! I will have her blood!"

"My lord," replied Varney, "the wildness of your distress breaks forth in the wildness of your language."

"I say, speak not for her," replied Leicester; "she has dishonoured me—she would have murthered me—all ties are burst between us. She shall die the death of a traitress and adultress, well merited both by the laws of God and man! And—what is this casket," he said, "which was even now thrust into my hand by a boy, with the desire I would convey it to Tressilian, as he could not give it to the Countess? By Heaven! the words surprised me as he spoke them, though other matters chased them from my brain; but now they return with double fury.—It is her casket of jewels!—force it open, Varney; force the hinges open with thy poniard."

She refused the aid of my dagger once, thought Varney, as he unsheathed the weapon, to cut the string which bound a letter, but now it shall work a mightier ministry in her fortunes.

With this reflection, by using the three-cornered stiletto-blade as a wedge, he forced open the slender silver hinges of the casket. The Earl no sooner saw them give way, than he snatched the casket from Sir Richard's hand, wrenched off the cover, and tearing out the splendid contents, flung them on the floor in a transport of rage, while he eagerly searched for some letter or billet, which should make the fancied guilt of his innocent Countess yet more apparent. Then stamping furiously on the gems, he exclaimed, "Thus I annihilate the miserable toys for which thou hast sold thyself, body and soul, consigned thyself to an early and timeless death, and me to misery and remorse for ever!—Speak not for her, Varney—She dies!"

So saying, he left the room, and rushed into an adjacent closet, the door of which he locked and bolted.

Varney looked after him, while something of a more human feeling seemed to contend with his habitual sneer. "I am sorry for his weakness," he said, "but love has made him a child. He throws down and treads on those costly toys—with the same vehemence would he dash to pieces this frailest toy of all, of which he used to rave so fondly. But that taste also will be forgotten, when its object is no more. Well is he has an eye to value things as they deserve, and that nature has given to Varney. When Leicester shall be a sovereign, he will think as little of the gales of passion, through which he gained that royal port, as ever did sailor in harbour, of the perils of a voyage. But these tell-tale articles must not remain here—they are rather too rich vails for the drudges who dress the chamber."

While Varney was employed in gathering together and putting them into a secret drawer of a cabinet that chanced to be open, he saw the door of Leicester's closet open, the tapestry pushed aside, and the Earl's face thrust out, but with eyes so dead, and lips and cheeks so bloodless and pale, that he started at the sudden change. No sooner did his eyes encounter the Earl's than the latter withdrew his head, and shut the door of the closet. This manœuvre Leicester repeated twice, without speaking a word, so that Varney began to doubt whether his brain was not actually affected by his mental agony. The third time, however, he beckoned, and Varney obeyed the signal. When he entered, he soon found his patron's perturbation was not caused by insanity, but by the fellness of purpose which he entertained, contending with various contrary passions. They passed a full hour in close consultation; after which the Earl of Leicester, with an incredible exertion, dressed himself, and went to attend his royal guest.

Chapter Twelve

You have displaced the mirth, broke the good meeting
With most admired disorder.

Macbeth

IT WAS afterwards remembered, that during the banquets and revels
which occupied the remainder of this eventful day, the bearing of
Leicester and of Varney were different totally from their usual
demeanour. Sir Richard Varney had been held rather a man of council
and of action, than a votary of pleasure. Business, whether civil or
military, had seemed always to be his proper sphere; while in festivals
and revels, although he well understood how to trick them up and
present them, his own part was that of a mere spectator; or if he
exercised his wit, it was in a rough, caustic, and severe manner, rather
as if he scoffed at the exhibition and the guests, than shared the
common pleasure.

But upon the present day his character seemed changed. He mixed
among the younger courtiers and ladies, and appeared for the moment
to be actuated by a spirit of light-hearted gaiety, which rendered him a
match for the liveliest. Those who had looked upon him as a man
given up to graver and more ambitious pursuits, a bitter sneerer and
passer of sarcasms at the expense of those, who, taking life as they find
it, were disposed to snatch at each pastime it presents, now perceived
with astonishment that his wit could carry as smooth an edge as their
own, his laugh be as lively, and his brow as unclouded. By what art of
damnable hypocrisy he could draw this veil of gaiety over the black
thoughts of one of the worst of human bosoms, must remain unintelligible to all but his compeers, if any such ever existed; but he was a man
of extraordinary powers, and those powers were unhappily dedicated
in all their energy to the very worst of purposes.

It was entirely different with Leicester. However habituated his
mind usually was to play the part of a good courtier, and appear gay,
assiduous, and free from all care but that of enhancing the pleasure of
the moment, while his bosom internally throbbed with the pangs of
unsatisfied ambition, jealousy, or resentment, his heart had now a yet
more dreadful guest, whose workings could not be overshadowed or
suppressed; and you might read in his vacant eye and troubled brow,
that his thoughts were far absent from the scenes in which he was
compelling himself to play a part. He looked, moved, and spoke, as if
by a succession of continued efforts; and it seemed as if his will had in
some degree lost the promptitude of command over the acute mind

and goodly form of which it was the regent. His actions and gestures, instead of appearing the consequence of simple volition, seemed, like those of an automaton, to wait the revolution of some internal machinery ere they could be performed; and his words fell from him piece-meal, interruptedly, as if he had first to think what he was to say, then how it was to be said, and as if, after all, it was only by an effort of continued attention that he completed a sentence without forgetting both the one and the other.

The singular effects which these distractions of mind produced upon the behaviour and conversation of the most accomplished courtier of England, as they were visible to the lowest and dullest menial who approached his person, could not escape the notice of the most intelligent princess of the age. Nor is there the least doubt, that the alternate negligence and irregularity of his manner, would have called down Elizabeth's severe displeasure on the Earl of Leicester, had it not occurred to her to account for it, by supposing that the apprehension of that displeasure which she had expressed towards him with such vivacity that very morning, was dwelling upon the spirits of her favourite, and, spite of his efforts to the contrary, distracted the usual graceful tenor of his mien, and the charms of his conversation. When this idea, so flattering to female vanity, had once obtained possession of her mind, it proved a full and satisfactory apology for the numerous errors and mistakes of the Earl of Leicester; and the watchful circle around observed with astonishment, that instead of resenting his repeated negligence, and want of even ordinary attention, (although these were points on which she was usually extremely rigorous,) the Queen sought, on the contrary, to afford him time and means to recollect himself, and deigned to assist him in doing so, with an indulgence which seemed altogether inconsistent with her usual character. It was clear, however, that this could not last much longer, and that Elizabeth must finally put another and more severe construction on Leicester's uncourteous conduct, when the Earl was summoned by Varney to speak with him in a different apartment.

After having had the message twice delivered to him, he rose, and was about to withdraw, as it were, by instinct—then stopped, and turning round, entreated permission of the Queen to absent himself for a brief space upon matters of pressing importance.

"Go, my lord," said the Queen; "we are aware our presence must occasion sudden and unexpected occurrences, which require to be provided for on the instant. Yet, my lord, as you would have us believe ourselves your welcome and honoured guest, we entreat you to think less of our good cheer, and favour us with more of your good countenance than we have this day enjoyed; for whether prince or peasant be the guest, the welcome of the host will always be the better part of the entertainment. Go, my lord; and we trust to see you return with an unwrinkled brow, and those free thoughts which you are wont to have at the disposal of your friends."

Leicester only bowed low in answer to this rebuke, and retired. At the door of the apartment he was met by Varney, who eagerly drew him apart and whispered in his ear, "All is well!"

"Has Master seen her?" said the Earl.

"He has, my lord; and as she would neither answer his queries, nor allege any reason for her refusal, he will give full testimony that she labours under a mental disorder, and may be best committed to the charge of her friends. The opportunity is therefore free, to remove her as we proposed."

"But Tressilian?" said Leicester.

"He will not know of her departure for some time," replied Varney; "it shall take place this very evening. And to-morrow he shall be cared for."

"No, by my soul," answered Leicester; "I will take vengeance on him with mine own hand!"

"You, my lord, and on so inconsiderable a man as Tressilian!—no, my lord, he hath long wished to visit foreign parts. Let me care for him —I will take care he returns not hither to tell tales."

"Not so, by Heaven, Varney!" exclaimed Leicester.—"Inconsiderable do you call an enemy, that hath had power to wound me so deeply, that my whole after life must be one scene of remorse and misery?—No; rather than forego the right of doing myself justice with my own hand on that accursed villain, I will unfold the whole truth at Elizabeth's footstool, and let her vengeance descend at once on them and on myself."

Varney saw with great alarm that his lord was wrought up to such a pitch of agitation, that if he gave not way to him, he was perfectly capable of adopting the desperate resolution which he had announced, and which was instant ruin to all the schemes of ambition which Varney had formed for his patron and for himself. But the Earl's rage seemed at once incontroulable and deeply concentrated; and while he spoke, his eyes shot fire, his voice trembled with excess of passion, and the light foam stood on his lip.

His confidant made a bold and successful effort to obtain the mastery of him even in this hour of emotion.—"My lord," he said, leading him to a mirror, "behold your reflection in that glass, and think if these agitated features belong to one who, in a condition so extreme, is capable of forming a resolution for himself."

"What, then, would'st thou make me?" said Leicester, struck at the

change in his own physiognomy, though offended at the freedom with
which Varney made the appeal. "Am I to be thy ward, thy vassal,—the
property and subject of my servant?"

"No, my lord," said Varney, firmly, "but master of yourself, and of
your own passion. My lord, I, your born servant, shame to see how
poorly you bear yourself in the storm of fury. Go to Elizabeth's feet,
confess your marriage—impeach your wife and her paramour of adul-
tery—and avow yourself, amongst all your peers, the wittol who
married a country girl, and was cozened by her and her book-learned
gallant.—Go, my lord—But first take the farewell of Richard Varney,
with all the benefits you ever conferred on him. He served the noble,
the lofty, the high-minded Leicester, and was more proud of depending on him, than he would be of commanding thousands. But the
abject lord who stoops to every adverse circumstance, whose judicious
resolves are scattered like chaff before every wind of passion—Him
Richard Varney serves not. He is as much above him in constancy of
mind, as beneath him in rank and fortune."

Varney spoke this without hypocrisy, for, though the firmness of
mind which he boasted was hardness and impenetrability, yet he really
felt the ascendancy which he vaunted; while the interest which he
actually felt in the fortunes of Leicester, gave unusual emotion to his
voice and manner.

Leicester was overpowered by his assumed superiority; it seemed
to the unfortunate Earl as if his last friend was about to abandon him.
He stretched his hand towards Varney, as he uttered the words, "Do
not leave me—What would'st thou have me do?"

"Be thyself, my noble master," said Varney, touching the Earl's
hand with his lips, after having respectfully grasped it in his own; "be
yourself, superior to those storms of passion which wreck inferior
minds. Are you the first who has been cozened in love—the first
whom a vain and licentious woman has cheated into an affection,
which she has afterwards scorned and misused? and will you suffer
yourself to be driven frantic, because you have not been wiser than the
wisest men whom the world has seen? Let her be as if she had not
been—let her pass from your memory, as unworthy of having ever
held a place there. Let your strong resolve of this morning, which I
have both courage and zeal enough to execute, be like the *fiat* of a
superior Being, a passionless act of Justice. She hath deserved death
—let her die!"

While he was speaking, the Earl held his hand fast, compressed his
lips hard, and seemed as if he laboured to catch from Varney a portion
of the cold, ruthless, and dispassionate firmness which he recommended. When he was silent, the Earl still continued to grasp his

hand, until, with an effort at calm decision, he was able to articulate, "Be it so—she dies!—But one tear might be permitted."

"Not one, my lord," interrupted Varney, who saw by the quivering eye and convulsed cheek of his patron, that he was about to give way to a burst of emotion,—"Not a tear—the time permits it not—Tressilian must be thought of"——

"That indeed is a name," said the Earl, "to convert tears into blood. Varney, I have thought on this, and I have determined—neither entreaty nor argument shall move me—Tressilian shall be my own victim."

"It is madness, my lord; but you are too mighty for me to bar your way to your revenge. Yet resolve at least to chuse fitting time and opportunity, and to forbear him until those shall be devised."

"Thou shalt order me in what thou wilt," said Leicester, "only thwart me not in this."

"Then, my lord," said Varney, "I first request of you to lay aside the wild, suspected, and half-frenzied demeanour, which hath this day drawn the eyes of all the court upon you; and which, but for the Queen's partial indulgence, which she hath extended towards you in a degree far beyond her nature, she had never given you the opportunity to atone for."

"Have I indeed been so negligent?" said Leicester, as one who awakes from a dream; "I thought I had coloured it well; but fear nothing, my mind is now eased—I am calm. My horoscope shall be fulfilled; and that it may be fulfilled, I will tax to the highest every faculty of my mind. Fear me not, I say—I will to the Queen instantly—not thine own looks and language shall be more impenetrable than mine.—Hast thou aught else to say?"

"I must crave your signet-ring," said Varney, gravely, "in token to those of your servants whom I must employ, that I possess your full authority in commanding their aid."

Leicester drew off the signet-ring, which he commonly used, and gave it to Varney with a hagard and stern expression of countenance, adding only, in a low half-whispered tone, but with terrific emphasis, the words, "What thou doest, do quickly."

Some anxiety and wonder took place, meanwhile, in the Presence-hall, at the prolonged absence of the noble Lord of the Castle, and great was the delight of his friends, when they saw him enter as a man, from whose bosom, to all human seeming, a weight of care had been just removed. Amply did Leicester that day redeem the pledge he had given to Varney, who soon saw himself no longer under the necessity of maintaining a character so different from his own, as that which he had assumed in the earlier part of the day, and gradually relapsed into the same grave, shrewd, caustic observer of conversation and incident, which constituted his usual part in society.

With Elizabeth, Leicester played his game as one, to whom her natural strength of talent, and her weakness in one or two particular points, were well known. He was too wary to exchange on a sudden, the sullen personage which he had played before he retired with Varney; but on approaching her, it seemed softened into a melancholy, which had a touch of tenderness in it, and which, in the course of conversing with Elizabeth, and as she dropped in compassion one mark of favour after another to console him, passed into a flow of affectionate gallantry, the most assiduous, the most delicate, the most insinuating, yet at the same time the most respectful, with which a Queen was ever addressed by a subject. Elizabeth listened, as in a sort of enchantment; her jealousy of power was lulled asleep; her resolution to forsake all social or domestic ties, and dedicate herself exclusively to the care of her people, began to be shaken, and once more the star of Dudley culminated in the court-horizon.

But Leicester did not enjoy this triumph over nature, and over conscience, without its being embittered to him, not only by the internal rebellion of his feelings against the violence which he exercised over them, but by many accidental circumstances, which in the course of the banquet, and during the subsequent amusements of the evening, jarred upon that nerve, the least vibration of which was agony.

The courtiers were, for example, in the great hall, after having left the banquetting-room, awaiting the appearance of a splendid masque, which was the expected entertainment of the evening, when the Queen interrupted a wild career of wit, which the Earl of Leicester was running against Lord Willoughby, Raleigh, and some other courtiers, by saying—"We will impeach you of high treason, my lord, if you proceed in this attempt to slay us with laughter. And here comes a thing may make us all grave at his pleasure, our learned physician Master, with news belike of our poor suppliant, Lady Varney—nay, my lord, we will not have you leave us, for this being a dispute betwixt married persons, we do not hold our own experience deep enough to decide thereon, without good counsel.—How now, Master, what think'st thou of the run-away bride?"

The smile with which Leicester had been speaking, when the Queen interrupted him, remained arrested on his lips, as if it had been carved there by the chisel of Angelo, or of Chantrey; and he listened to the speech of the physician, with the same immoveable cast of countenance.

"The Lady Varney, gracious Sovereign," said Master, "is sullen, and would hold little conference with me touching the state of her health, talking wildly of being soon to plead her own cause before your own presence, and of answering no meaner person's inquiries."

"Now, the heavens forefend!" said the Queen; "we have already suffered from the misconstructions and broils which seem to follow this poor brain-sick lady wherever she comes.—Think you not so, my lord?" she added, appealing to Leicester, with something in her look that indicated regret, even tenderly expressed, for their disagreement of that morning. Leicester compelled himself to bow low. The utmost force he could exert, was inadequate to the farther effort of expressing in words his acquiescence in the Queen's sentiment.

"You are vindictive," she said, "my lord; but we will find time and place to punish you. But once more to this same trouble-mirth, this Lady Varney—What of her health, Master?"

"She is sullen, madam, as I already said," replied Master, "and refuses to answer interrogatories, or be amenable to the authority of the mediciner. I conceive her to be possessed with a delirium, which I incline to term rather *hypochondria* than *phrenesis;* and I think she were best cared for by her husband in his own house, and removed from all this bustle of pageants, which disturbs her weak brain with the most fantastic phantoms. She drops hints as if she were some great person in disguise—some Countess or Princess perchance. God help them, such are the hallucinations of these infirm persons."

"Nay, then," said the Queen, "away with her with all speed. Let Varney care for her with fitting humanity; but let him rid the Castle of her forthwith. She will think herself lady of all, I warrant you. It is pity so fair a form, however, should have an infirm understanding.—What think you, my lord?"

"It is a pity indeed," said the Earl, repeating the words like a task which was set him.

"But perhaps," said Elizabeth, "you do not join with us in our opinion of her beauty; and indeed we have known men prefer a statelier and more Juno-like form, to that drooping fragile shape, that hung its head like a broken lily. Ay, men are tyrants, my lord, who esteem the animation of the strife above the triumph of an unresisting conquest, and, like sturdy champions, love best those women who can wage contest with them.—I could think with you, Rutland, that give my Lord of Leicester such a piece of painted wax work for a bride, he would have wished her dead ere the end of the honey-moon."

As she said this, she looked on Leicester so expressively, that, while his heart revolted against the egregious falsehood, he did himself so much violence as to reply in a whisper, that Leicester's love was more lowly than her Majesty deemed, since it was settled where he could never command, but must ever obey.

The Queen blushed, and bid him be silent; yet looked as if she expected that he would not obey her commands. But at that moment the flourish of trumpets and kettle-drums from a high balcony which overlooked the hall, announced the entrance of the masquers, and relieved Leicester from the horrible state of constraint and dissimulation in which the result of his own duplicity had placed him.

The masque which entered consisted of four separate bands, which followed each other at brief intervals, each consisting of six principal persons and as many torch-bearers, and each representing one of the various nations by which England had at different times been occupied.

The aboriginal Britons, who first entered, were ushered in by two ancient Druids, whose hoary hair was crowned with a chaplet of oak, and who bore in their hands branches of misletoe. The masquers who followed these venerable figures were succeeded by two Bards, arrayed in white, and bearing harps, which they occasionally touched, singing at the same time certain stanzas of an ancient hymn to Belus, or the Sun. The aboriginal Britons had been selected from amongst the tallest and most robust young gentlemen in attendance on the court. Their masks were accommodated with long shaggy beards and hair; their vestments were of the hides of wolves and bears; while their legs, arms, and the upper part of their bodies, being sheathed in flesh-coloured silk, on which were traced in grotesque lines representations of the heavenly bodies, and of animals and other terrestrial objects, gave them the lively appearance of our painted ancestors, whose freedom was first entrenched upon by the Romans.

The sons of Rome, who came to civilize as well as to conquer, were next produced before the princely assembly; and the manager of the revels had correctly imitated the high crest and military habits of that celebrated people, accommodating them with the light yet strong buckler, and the short two-edged sword, the use of which had made them victors of the world. The Roman eagles were borne before them by two standard-bearers, who recited a hymn to Mars, and the classical warriors followed with the grave and haughty step of men who aspired at universal conquest.

The third quadrille represented the Saxons, clad in the bear-skins which they had brought with them from the German forests, and bearing in their hand the redoubtable battle-axes which made such havoc among the natives of Britain. They were preceded by two Scalds, who chaunted the praises of Odin.

Last came the knightly Normans, in their mail shirts and hoods of steel, with all the panoply of chivalry, and marshalled by two

Minstrels, who sung of war and ladies' love.

These four bands entered the spacious hall with the utmost order, a short pause being made, that the spectators might satisfy their curiosity as to each quadrille before the appearance of the next. They then marched completely round the hall, in order the more fully to display themselves, and at length ranging their torch-bearers behind them, drew up in their several ranks, on the two opposite sides of the hall, so that the Romans confronting the Britons, and the Saxons the Normans, seemed to look on each other with eyes of wonder, which presently appeared to kindle into anger, expressed by menacing gestures. At the burst of a strain of martial music from the galleries the masquers drew their swords on all sides, and advanced against each other in the measured steps of a sort of Pyrrhic or military dance, clashing their swords against their adversaries' shields, and clattering them against their blades as they past each other in the progress of the dance. It was a very pleasant spectacle to see how the various bands, preserving regularity amid motions which seemed to be totally irregular, mixed together, and then disengaging themselves, resumed each their own original rank as the music varied.

In this symbolical dance was represented the conflicts which had taken place amongst the various nations which had anciently inhabited Britain.

At length, after many mazy evolutions, which afforded great pleasure to the spectators, the sound of a loud-voiced trumpet was heard, as if it blew for instant battle, or for victory won. The masquers instantly ceased their mimic strife, and collecting themselves under their original leaders, or presenters, for such was the appropriate phrase, seemed to share the anxious expectation which the spectators experienced concerning what was next to appear.

The doors of the hall were thrown wide, and no less a person entered than the fiend-born Merlin, dressed in a strange and mystical attire, suited to his ambiguous birth and magical power. About him and behind him fluttered or gambolled many extraordinary forms, intended to represent the spirits who waited to do his powerful bidding; and so much did this part of the pageant interest the menials and others of the lower class then in the Castle, that many of them forgot even the reverence due to the Queen's presence, so far as to thrust into the lower part of the hall.

The Earl of Leicester, seeing his officers had some difficulty to repel these intruders, without more disturbance than was fitting where the Queen was in presence, arose and went himself to the bottom of the hall; Elizabeth at the same time, with her usual feeling for the common people, requesting that they might be permitted to remain undisturbed to witness the pageant. Leicester went under this pretext; but his real motive was to gain a moment to himself, and to relieve his mind, were it but for one instant, from the dreadful task of hiding, under the guise of gaiety and gallantry, the lacerating pangs of shame, anger, remorse, and thirst for vengeance. He imposed silence by his look and sign upon the vulgar crowd, at the lower end of the apartment; but, instead of instantly returning to wait on her Majesty, he wrapped his cloak around, and mixing with the crowd, stood in some degree an undistinguished spectator of the progress of the masque.

Merlin having entered and advanced into the midst of the hall, summoned the presenters of the contending bands around him by a wave of his magical rod, and announced to them, in a poetical speech, that the Isle of Britain was now commanded by a Royal Maiden, to whom it was the will of fate that they should all homage, and request of her to pronounce on the various pretensions which each set forth to be esteemed the pre-eminent stock, from which the present natives, the happy subjects of that angelical Princess, derived their lineage.

In obedience to this mandate, the bands, each moving to solemn music, passed in succession before Elizabeth; doing her as they passed, each after the fashion of the people whom they represented, the lowest and most devotional homage, which she returned with the same gracious courtesy that had marked her whole conduct since she came to Kenilworth.

The presenters of the several masques, or quadrilles, then alleged, each in behalf of his own troop, the reasons which they had for claiming pre-eminence over the rest; and when they had been all heard in turn, she returned them this gracious answer: "That she was sorry she was not better qualified to decide upon the doubtful question which had been propounded to her by direction of the famous Merlin, but that it seemed to her that no single one of these celebrated nations could claim pre-eminence over the others, as having most contributed to form the Englishman of her own time, who seemed to her to derive from each of them some worthy attribute of his character. Thus," she said, "the Englishman had from the ancient Briton his bold and tameless spirit of freedom,—from the Roman his disciplined courage in war, with his love of letters and civilization in time of peace, —from the Saxon his wise and equitable laws,—and from the chivalrous Norman his love of honour and courtesy, with his generous desire for glory."

Merlin answered with readiness, that it did indeed require that so many choice qualities should meet in the English, as might render them in some measure the muster of the perfections of other nations, since that alone could render them in some degree deserving of the blessings they enjoyed under the reign of England's Elizabeth.

The music then sounded, and the quadrilles, together with Merlin and his assistants, had begun to remove from the crowded hall, when Leicester, who was, as we have noticed, stationed for the moment near the bottom of the hall, and consequently engaged in some degree in the crowd, felt himself pulled by the cloak, while a voice whispered in his ear, "I do desire some instant conference with you."

Chapter Thirteen

How is't with me, when every noise appals me?
                              Macbeth

"I DESIRE some conference with you." The words were simple in themselves, but Lord Leicester was in that alarmed and feverish state of mind, when the most ordinary occurrences seem fraught with alarming import; and he turned hastily round to survey the person by whom they had been spoken. There was nothing remarkable in the speaker's appearance, which consisted of a black silk doublet and sheer mantle, with a black vizard on his face; for it appeared he had been among the crowd of masks who had thronged into the hall in the retinue of Merlin, though he did not wear any of the extravagant disguises by which most of them were distinguished.

"Who are you, or what do you want with me?" said Leicester, not without betraying, by his accents, the hurried state of his spirits.

"No evil, my lord," replied the mask, "but much good and honour, if you will rightly understand my purpose. But I must speak with you more privately."

"I can speak with no nameless stranger," answered Leicester, dreading he knew not precisely what from the request of the stranger; "and those who are known to me, must seek another and a fitter time to ask an interview."

He would have turned away, but the mask still detained him.

"Those who talk to your lordship of what your own honour demands, have a right over your time, whatever occupations you may lay aside in order to indulge them."

"How! my honour? Who dare impeach it?" said Leicester.

"Your own conduct alone can furnish grounds for accusing it, my lord, and it is that topic on which I would speak with you."

"You are insolent," said Leicester, "and abuse the hospitable licence of the time, which prevents me from having you punished. I demand your name?"

"Edmund Tressilian of Cornwall," answered the mask. "My tongue has been bound by a promise for four-and-twenty hours,—the space is passed,—I now speak, and do your lordship the justice to address myself first to you."

The thrill of astonishment which had penetrated to Leicester's very heart at hearing that name pronounced by the voice of the man he most detested, and by whom he conceived himself so deeply injured, at first rendered him immoveable, but instantly gave way to such a thirst for revenge as the pilgrim in the desart feels for the water-brooks. He had but sense and self-government enough left to prevent his stabbing to the heart the audacious villain, who, after the ruin he had brought upon him, dared, with such unmoved assurance, thus to practise upon him farther. Determined to suppress for the moment every symptom of agitation, in order to perceive the full scope of Tressilian's purpose, as well as to secure his own vengeance, he answered in a tone so altered by restrained passion as scarce to be intelligible,—"And what does Master Edmund Tressilian of Cornwall require at my hand?"

"Justice, my lord," answered Tressilian, calmly but firmly.

"Justice," said Leicester, "all men are entitled to—You, Master Tressilian, are peculiarly so, and be assured you shall have it."

"I expect nothing less from your nobleness," answered Tressilian; "but time presses, and I must speak with you to-night—may I wait on you in your chamber?"

"No," answered Leicester, sternly, "not under a roof, and that roof mine own. We will meet under the free cope of heaven."

"You are discomposed or displeased, my lord," replied Tressilian; "yet there is no occasion for distemperature—the place is equal to me, so you allow me one half hour of your time uninterrupted."

"A shorter period will, I trust, suffice," answered Leicester— "Meet me in the Pleasance, when the Queen has retired to her chamber."

"Enough," said Tressilian, and withdrew; while a sort of rapture seemed for the moment to occupy the mind of Leicester.

"Heaven," he said, "is at last favourable to me, and has put within my reach the wretch who has branded me with this deep ignominy— who has inflicted on me this cruel agony. I will blame fate no more, since I am afforded the means of tracing the wiles by which he means still farther to practise on me, and then of at once convicting and punishing his villainy. To my task—to my task!—I will not sink under it now, since midnight, at farthest, will bring me vengeance."

While these reflections thronged through Leicester's mind, he again made his way amid the obsequious crowd, which divided to give him passage, and resumed his place, envied and admired, beside the person of his Sovereign. But, could the bosom of him whom they universally envied, have been laid open before the inhabitants of that crowded hall, with all its dark thoughts of guilty ambition, blighted affection, deep vengeance, and conscious scenes of meditated cruelty, crossing each other like spectres in the circle of some foul enchantress; which of them, from the most ambitious noble in the courtly circle, down to the most wretched menial, who lived by shifting of trenchers, would have desired to change characters with the favourite of Elizabeth, and the Lord of Kenilworth!

New tortures awaited him as soon as he had rejoined Elizabeth.

"You come in time, my lord," she said, "to decide a dispute between us ladies. Here has Sir Richard Varney asked our permission to depart from the Castle with his infirm lady, having, as he tells us, your lordship's consent to his absence, so he can obtain ours. Certes, we have no will to withhold him from the affectionate charge of this poor young person—But you are to know, that Sir Richard Varney hath this day shewn himself so much captivated with these ladies of ours, that here is our Countess of Rutland says, he will carry his poor insane wife no farther than the lake, plunge her in, to tenant the crystal palaces that the enchanted nymph told us of, and return a jolly widower, to dry his tears, and to make up the loss among our train. How say you, my lord?—we have seen Varney under two or three different guises— you know what are his proper attributes—think you he is capable of playing his lady such a knave's trick?"

Leicester was confounded, but the danger was urgent, and a reply absolutely necessary. "The ladies," he said, "think too lightly of one of their own sex, in supposing she could deserve such a fate, or too ill of ours, to think it could be inflicted otherwise."

"Hear him, my ladies," said Elizabeth; "like all his sex he would excuse their cruelty by imputing fickleness to us."

"Say not us, madam," replied the Earl; "we say that meaner women, like the lesser lights of heaven, have revolutions and phases, but who shall impute mutability to the sun, or to Elizabeth?"

The discourse presently afterwards assumed a less perilous tendency, and Leicester continued to support his part in it with spirit, at whatever expense of mental agony. So pleasing did it seem to Elizabeth, that the castle-bell had sounded midnight ere she retired from the company, a circumstance unusual in her quiet and regular habits of disposing of time. Her departure was of course the signal for breaking up the company, who dispersed to their several places of repose, to dream over the pastimes of the day, or to anticipate those of the morrow.

The unfortunate Lord of the Castle, and founder of the proud festival, retired to far different thoughts. His direction to the valet who attended him, was to send Varney instantly to his apartment. The messenger returned after some delay, and informed him that an hour had elapsed since Sir Richard Varney had left the Castle, by the postern-gate, with three other persons, one of whom was transported in a horse-litter.

"How came he to leave the Castle after the watch was set?" said Leicester; "I thought he went not till day-break."

"He gave satisfactory reasons, as I understand," said the domestic, "to the guard, and, as I hear, shewed your lordship's signet"——

"True—true," said the Earl; "yet he has been hasty—do any of his attendants remain behind?"

"Michael Lambourne, my lord," said the valet, "was not to be found when Sir Richard departed, and his master was much incensed at his absence. I saw him but now saddling his horse to gallop after his master."

"Bid him come hither instantly," said Leicester; "I have a message to his master."

The servant left the apartment, and Leicester traversed it for some time in deep meditation—"Varney is over zealous," he said, "over pressing—he loves me, I think—but he hath his own ends to serve, and he is inexorable in pursuit of them—if I rise he rises, and he hath shewn himself already but too eager to rid this obstacle which seems to stand betwixt me and sovereignty. Yet I will not stoop to bear this disgrace. She shall be punished, but it shall be more advisedly. I already feel, even in anticipation, that over-haste would light the flames of hell in my bosom. No—one victim is enough at once, and that victim already waits me."

He seized up writing materials, and hastily traced these words:—
"Sir Richard Varney—We have resolved to defer the matter entrusted to your care, and strictly command you to proceed no farther in relation to our Countess, until our further order. We also command your instant return to Kenilworth, as soon as you have safely bestowed that with which you are entrusted. But if the safe-placing of your present charge shall detain you longer than we think for, we command you, in that case, to send back our signet-ring by a trusty and speedy messenger, we having present need of the same. And requiring your strict obedience in these things, and commending you to God's keeping, we rest your assured good friend and master,

"R. LEICESTER.

"Given at our Castle of Kenilworth, the tenth of July, in the year of Salvation one thousand five hundred and seventy-five."

As Leicester had finished and sealed this mandate, Michael Lambourne, booted up to mid thigh, having his riding-cloak girthed round him with a broad belt, and a felt-cap on his head, like that of a courier, entered his apartment, ushered in by the valet.

"What is thy capacity of service?" said the Earl.

"Equerry to your lordship's master of the horse," answered Lambourne, with his customary assurance.

"Tie up thy saucy tongue, sir," said Leicester; "the jests that may suit Richard Varney's presence, suit not mine. How soon wilt thou overtake thy master?"

"In one hour's riding, my lord, if man and horse hold good," said Lambourne, with an instant alteration of demeanour, from an approach to familiarity to the deepest respect. The Earl measured him with his eye from top to toe.

"I have heard of thee," he said; "men say thou art a prompt fellow in thy service, but too much given to brawling and to wassail to be trusted with things of moment."

"My lord," said Lambourne, "I have been soldier, sailor, traveller, and adventurer; and these are all trades where men enjoy to-day, because they have no surety of to-morrow. But though I may misuse mine own leisure, I have never neglected the duty I owe my master."

"See that it be so in this instance," said Leicester, "and it shall do thee good. Deliver this letter speedily and carefully into Sir Richard Varney's hands."

"Does my commission reach no farther?" said Lambourne.

"No," answered Leicester, "but it deeply concerns me that it be carefully as well as hastily executed."

"I will spare neither care nor horse-flesh," answered Lambourne, and immediately took his leave. "So, this is the end of my private audience, from which I hoped so much," he muttered to himself, as he went through the long gallery, and down the back stair-case. "Cogsbones! I thought the Earl had wanted a cast of mine office in some secret intrigue, and it all ends in carrying a letter! Well, his pleasure shall be done, however, and as his lordship well says, it may do me good another time. The child must creep ere he walk, and so must your infant courtier. I will have a look into this letter, however, which he hath sealed so sloven-like."—Having accomplished this, he clapped his hands together in ecstacy, exclaiming, "The Countess— the Countess!—I have the secret that shall make or mar me.—But come forth, Bayard," he added, leading his horse into the court-yard, "for your flanks and my spurs must be presently acquainted."

Lambourne mounted, accordingly, and left the Castle by the postern-gate, where his free passage was permitted, in consequence of a message to that effect left by Sir Richard Varney.

As soon as Lambourne and the valet had left the apartment, Leicester proceeded to change his dress for a very plain one, threw his mantle around him, and taking a lamp in his hand, went by the private passage of communication to a small postern-door which opened into the court-yard, near to the entrance of the Pleasance. His reflections were of a more calm and determined character than they had been at any late period, and he endeavoured to claim, even in his own eyes, the character of a man more sinned against than sinning.

"I have suffered the deepest injury," such was the tenor of his meditations, "yet I have restricted the instant revenge which was in my power, and have limited it to that which is manly and noble. But shall the union which this false woman has thus disgraced, remain an abiding fetter on me, to check me in the noble career to which my destinies invite me?—no—there are other means of disengaging such ties, without unloosing the cords of life—in the sight of God, I am no longer bound by the union she has broken—kingdoms shall divide us —oceans roll betwixt us, and their waves, whose abysses have swallowed whole navies, shall be the sole depositaries of the deadly mystery."

By such a train of argument did Leicester labour to reconcile his conscience to the prosecution of plans of vengeance, so hastily adopted, and of schemes of ambition, which had become so woven in with every purpose and action of his life, that he was incapable of the effort of relinquishing them; until his revenge appeared to him to wear a face of justice, and even of generous moderation.

In this mood, the vindictive and ambitious Earl entered the superb precincts of the Pleasance, then illumed by the full moon. The broad yellow light was reflected on all sides from the white freestone, of which the pavement, balustrades, and architectural ornaments of the place were constructed; and not a single fleecy cloud was visible in the azure sky, so that the scene was nearly as light as if the sun had but just left the horizon. The numerous statues of white marble glimmered in the pale light, like so many sheeted ghosts just arisen from their sepulchres, and the fountains threw their jets into the air, as if they sought that their waters should be silvered by the moon-beams, ere they fell down again upon their basins in showers of sparkling silver. The day had been sultry, and the gentle night-breeze, which sighed along the terrace of the Pleasance, raised not a deeper breath than the fan in the hand of youthful beauty. The bird of summer night had built many a nest in the bowers of the adjacent garden, and the tenants now indemnified themselves for silence during the day, by a full chorus of their own unrivalled warblings, now joyous, now pathetic, now united, now responsive to each other, as if to express their delight in the placid and delicious scene to which they poured their melody.

Musing on matters far different from the fall of waters, the gleam of moon-light, or the song of the nightingale, the stately Leicester walked slowly from the one end of the terrace to the other, his cloak wrapped around him, and his sword under his arm, without seeing any thing resembling the human form.

"I have been fooled by my own generosity," he said, "if I have suffered the villain to escape me—ay, and perhaps to go to the rescue of the Adultress, who is so poorly guarded."

These were his thoughts, which were instantly dispelled, when, turning to look back towards the entrance, he saw a human form advancing slowly from the portico, and darkening the various objects with its shadow, as passing them successively, in its approach towards him.

"Shall I strike, ere I again hear his detested voice?" was Leicester's thought, as he grasped the hilt of his sword. "But no! I will see which way his vile practice tends. I will watch, disgusting as it is, the coils and mazes of the loathsome snake, ere I put forth my strength and crush him."

His hand quitted the sword-hilt, and he advanced slowly towards Tressilian, collecting, for their meeting, all the self-possession he could command, until they came front to front with each other.

Tressilian made a profound reverence, to which the Earl replied with a haughty inclination of the head, and the words, "You sought secret conference of me, sir—I am here, and attentive."

"My lord," said Tressilian, "I am so earnest in that which I have to say, and so desirous to find a patient, nay a favourable hearing, that I will stoop to exculpate myself from whatever might prejudice your lordship against me. You think me your enemy?"

"Have I not some apparent cause?" answered Leicester, perceiving that Tressilian paused for a reply.

"You do me wrong, my lord. I am a friend, but neither a dependant nor partizan of the Earl of Sussex, whom courtiers call your rival; and it is some considerable time since I ceased to consider either courts, or court-intrigues, as suited to my temper or genius."

"No doubt, sir," answered Leicester; "there are other occupations more worthy a scholar, and for such the world holds Master Tressilian —Love has his intrigues as well as Ambition."

"I perceive, my lord," replied Tressilian, "you give much weight to my early attachment for the unfortunate young person of whom I am about to speak, and perhaps think I am prosecuting her cause out of rivalry, more than a sense of justice."

"No matter for my thoughts, sir," said the Earl; "proceed—you have as yet spoken of yourself only; an important and worthy subject doubtless, but which, perhaps, does not altogether so deeply concern me, that I should postpone my repose to hear it. Spare me farther prelude, sir, and speak to the purpose, if indeed you have aught to say that concerns me. When you have done, I, in my turn, have something to communicate."

"I will speak, then, without farther prelude, my lord," answered Tressilian; "having to say that which, as it concerns your lordship's honour, I am confident you will not think your time wasted in listening to. I have to request an account from your lordship of the unhappy Amy Robsart, whose history is too well known to you. I regret deeply that I did not at once take this course, and make yourself judge between me and the villain by whom she is injured. My lord, she extricated herself from an unlawful and most perilous state of confinement, trusting to the effects of her own remonstrance upon her unworthy husband, and extorted from me a promise, that I would not interfere in her behalf until she had used her own efforts to have her rights acknowledged by him."

"Ha!" said Leicester, "remember you to whom you speak?"

"I say her unworthy husband, my lord," repeated Tressilian, "and my respect can find no softer language. The unhappy young woman is withdrawn from my knowledge, and sequestered in some secret place of this Castle,—if she be not transferred to some place of seclusion better fitted for bad designs. This must be reformed, my lord,—I speak it as authorized by her father,—and this ill-fated marriage must be avouched and proved in the Queen's presence, and the lady placed without restraint, and at her own free disposal. And, permit me to say, it concerns no one's honour that these most just demands of mine should be complied with, so much as it does that of your lordship."

The Earl stood as if he had been petrified, at the extreme coolness with which the man, whom he considered as having injured him so deeply, pleaded the cause of his criminal paramour, as if she had been an innocent woman, and he a disinterested advocate; nor was his wonder lessened by the warmth with which Tressilian seemed to demand for her the rank and situation which she had disgraced, and the advantages of which she was doubtless to share with the lover who advocated her cause with such effrontery. Tressilian had been silent for more than a minute ere the Earl recovered from the excess of his astonishment; and, considering the prepossessions with which his mind was occupied, there is little wonder that his passion gained the mastery of every other consideration. "I have heard you, Master Tressilian," said he, "without interruption, and I bless God that my ears were never before made to tingle by the words of so frontless a villain. The task of chastising you is fitter for the hangman's scourge than the sword of a nobleman, but yet——villain, draw and defend thyself!"

As he spoke the last words, he dropped his mantle on the ground, struck Tressilian smartly with his sheathed sword, and instantly drawing his rapier, put himself into a posture of assault. The vehement fury of his language at first filled Tressilian, in his turn, with surprise equal to what Leicester had felt when he addressed him. But astonishment gave rise to resentment, when the unmerited insults of his language were followed by a blow, which immediately put to flight every thought save that of instant combat. Tressilian's sword was instantly drawn, and though perhaps somewhat inferior to Leicester in the use of the weapon, he understood it well enough to maintain the contest with great spirit, the rather that of the two he was for the time the more cool, since he could not help imputing Leicester's conduct either to actual frenzy, or to the influence of some strong delusion.

The rencontre had continued for several minutes, without either party receiving a wound, when of a sudden voices were heard beneath the portico, which formed the entrance of the terrace, mingled with the steps of men advancing hastily. "We are interrupted," said Leicester to his antagonist; "follow me."

At the same time a voice from the portico said, "The jackanape is right—they are tilting here."

Leicester, meanwhile, drew off Tressilian into a sort of recess behind one of the fountains, which served to conceal them, while six of the yeomen of the Queen's guard, with their halberds in their hands, passed along the middle walk of the Pleasance, and they could hear one say to the rest, "We will never find them to-night amongst all these squirting funnels, squirrel-cages, and rabbit-holes; but if we light not on them before we reach the farther end, we will return, and mount a guard at the entrance, and so secure them till morning."

"A proper matter," said another, "the drawing of swords so near the Queen's presence, ay, and in her very Palace as 'twere!—Hang it, they must be some poor drunken game-cocks fallen to sparring—'twere pity almost we should find them—the penalty is chopping off a hand, is it not?—'twere hard to lose hand for handling a bit of steel, that comes so natural to one's gripe."

"Thou art a brawler thyself, George," said another; "but take heed, for the law stands as thou say'st."

"Ay," said the first, "an the act be not mildly construed; for thou know'st 'tis not the Queen's Palace, but my Lord of Leicester's."

"Why, for that matter, the penalty may be as severe," said another; "for an our gracious Mistress be Queen, as she is, God save her, my

Lord of Leicester is as good as King."

"Hush! thou knave!" said a third; "how know'st thou who may be within hearing?"

They passed on, making a kind of careless search, but seemingly more intent on their own conversation than bent on discovering the persons who had created the nocturnal disturbance.

They had no sooner passed forward along the terrace, than Leicester, making a sign to Tressilian to follow him, glided away in an opposite direction, and escaped through the portico undiscovered. He conducted Tressilian to Mervyn's Tower, in which he was now again lodged; and then, ere parting with him, said these words, "If thou hast courage to continue and bring to end what is thus broken off, be near me when the court goes forth to-morrow—we shall find a time, and I will give you a signal when it is fitting."

"My lord," said Tressilian, "at another time I might have inquired the meaning of this strange and furious inveteracy against me. But you have laid that on my shoulder, which only blood can wash away; and were you as high as your proudest wishes ever carried you, I would have from you satisfaction for my wounded honour."

On these terms they parted, but the adventures of the night were not yet ended with Leicester. He was compelled to pass by Saintlowe's Tower, in order to gain the private passage which led to his own chamber, and in the entrance thereof he met Lord Hunsdon half-clothed, and with a naked sword under his arm.

"Are you awakened too, with this 'larum, my Lord of Leicester?" said the old soldier. "'Tis well—By gog's-nails, the nights are as noisy as the day in this Castle of yours—Some two hours since, I was waked by the screams of that poor brain-sick Lady Varney, whom her husband was forcing away—I promise you, it required both your warrant and the Queen's, to keep me from entering into the game, and cutting that Varney of your's over the head—And now there is a brawl down in the Pleasance, or what call you the stone terrace walk, where all yonder gimcracks stand?"

The first part of the old man's speech went through the Earl's heart like a knife; to the last he answered that he himself had heard the clash of swords, and had come down to take order with those who had been so insolent so near the Queen's presence.

"Nay then," said Hunsdon, "I will be glad of your lordship's company."

Leicester was thus compelled to turn back with the rough old Lord to the Pleasance, where Hunsdon heard from the yeomen of the guard, who were under his immediate command, the unsuccessful search they had made for the authors of the disturbance; and bestowed for their pains some round dozen of curses on them, as lazy knaves and blind whoresons. Leicester also thought it necessary to seem angry that no discovery had been effected; but at length suggested to Lord Hunsdon, that after all it could only be some foolish young men, who had been drinking healths pottle-deep, and who would be sufficiently scared by the search which had taken place after them. Hunsdon, who was himself attached to his cup, allowed that a pint-flagon might cover many of the follies which it had caused. "But," added he, "unless your lordship will be less liberal in your house-keeping, and restrain the overflow of ale, and wine, and wassail, I foresee it will end in my having some of those good fellows into the guard-house, and treating them to a doze of the strappadoe—And with this warning, good night to you."

Joyful at being rid of his company, Leicester took leave of him at the entrance of his lodging, where they had first met, and entering the private passage, took up the lamp which he had left there, and by its expiring light found the way to his own apartment.

Chapter Fourteen

> Room! room! for my horse will wince
> If he come within so many yards of a prince;
> For to tell you true, and in rhyme,
> He was foal'd in Queen Elizabeth's time;
> When the great Earl of Lester
> In this castle did feast her.
>
> *Masque of Owls.*—BEN JONSON

THE AMUSEMENT with which Elizabeth and her court were next day to be regaled, was an exhibition by the true-hearted men of Coventry, who were to represent the strife between the English and the Danes, agreeably to a custom long preserved in their ancient borough, and warranted for truth by old histories and chronicles. In this pageant, one party of the town's folks presented the Saxons and the other the Danes, and set forth both in rude rhymes and with hard blows the contentions of these two fierce nations, and the Amazonian courage of the English women, who, according to the story, were the principal agents in the general massacre of the Danes, which took place at Hock-tide, in the year of God 1002. This sport, which had been long a favourite pastime with the men of Coventry, had, it seems, been put down by the influence of some zealous clergymen, of the more precise cast, who chanced to have considerable interest with the magistrates. But the generality of the inhabitants had petitioned the Queen that they might have their play again, and be honoured with permission to represent it before her Highness. And when the matter was canvassed in the little council, which usually attended the Queen for dispatch of business, the proposal, although opposed by some of the stricter sort, found favour in the eyes of Elizabeth, who said that such toys occupied, without offence, the minds of many, who, lacking them, might find worse subjects of pastime; and that their pastors, however commendable for learning and godliness, were somewhat too sour in preaching against the pastime of their flocks, and so the pageant was permitted to proceed.

Accordingly, after a morning repast, which Master Laneham calls an ambrosial breakfast, the principal persons of the court, in attendance upon her Majesty, passed to the Gallery-tower, to witness the approach of the two contending parties of English and Danes; and after a signal had been given, the gate which opened in the circuit of the Chase was thrown wide, to admit them. On they came foot and horse; for some of the more ambitious burghers and yeomen had put themselves into fantastic dresses, to resemble the chivalry of the two different nations. However, to prevent fatal accidents, they were not permitted to appear on real horses, but had only license to accoutre themselves with those hobby-horses, as they are called, which anciently formed the chief delight of a morrice-dance, and which still are exhibited on the stage, in the grand battle fought at the conclusion of Mr Bayes's tragedy. The infantry followed in similar disguises. The whole exhibition was to be considered as a sort of anti-masque, or burlesque of the more stately pageants, in which the nobility and gentry bore part in the show, and, to the best of their knowledge, imitated with accuracy the personages whom they represented. The Hocktide play was of a different character, the actors being persons of inferior degree, and their habits the better fitted for the occasion, the more incongruous and ridiculous that they were in themselves. Accordingly their array, which the progress of our tale allows us no time to describe, was ludicrous enough, and their weapons, though formidable enough to deal sound blows, were long alder-poles instead of lances, and sound cudgels for swords; and for fence, both cavalry and infantry were well equipped with stout head-pieces, and targets of thick leather.

Captain Coxe, that celebrated humourist of Coventry, whose library of ballads, almanacks, and penny histories, fairly wrapped up in parchment, and tied round for security with a piece of whip-cord, remains still the envy of antiquaries, being himself the ingenious person under whose direction the pageant had been set forth, rode valiantly on his hobby-horse before the bands of English, high-trussed, saith Laneham, and brandishing his long sword, as became an experienced man of war, who had fought under the Queen's father, bluff King Henry, at the siege of Boulogne. This chieftain was, as right and reason craved, the first to enter the lists, and, passing the Gallery at the head of his myrmidons, kissed the hilt of his sword to the Queen, and executed at the same time a gambade, the like whereof had not been practised by two-legged hobby-horse. Then passing on with all his followers of cavaliers and infantry, he drew them up with martial skill at the opposite extremity of the bridge, or tilt-yard, until his antagonists could be fairly prepared for the onset.

This was no long interval; for the Danish cavalry and infantry, no way inferior to the English in number, valour, and equipment, instantly arrived, with the northern bag-pipe blowing before them in token of their country, and headed by a cunning master of defence, only inferior to the renowned Captain Coxe, if to him, in the discipline of war. The Danes, as invaders, took their station under the Gallery-tower, and opposite to that of Mortimer; and, when their arrangements were completely made, a signal was given for the encounter.

Their first charge upon each other was rather moderate, for either party had some dread of being forced into the lake. But as reinforcements came up on either side, the encounter grew from a skirmish into a blazing battle. They rushed upon one another, as Master Laneham testifies, like rams inflamed by jealousy, with such furious encounter, that both parties were often overthrown, and the clubs and targets made a most horrible clatter. In many instances, that happened which had been dreaded by the more experienced warriors, who began the day of strife. The rails which defended the ledges of the bridge, had been, perhaps of purpose, left but slightly fastened, and gave way under the pressure of those who thronged to the combat, so that the hot courage of many of the combatants received a sufficient cooling. These incidents might have occasioned more serious damage than became such an affray, for many of the champions who met with this mischance could not swim, and those who could, were encumbered with their suits of leathern and of paper armour; but the case had been provided for, and there were several boats in readiness to pick up the unfortunate warriors, and convey them to the dry land, where, dripping and dejected, they comforted themselves with the hot ale and strong waters which were liberally allowed to them, without shewing any desire to re-enter so desperate a conflict.

Captain Coxe alone, that paragon of Black-Letter Antiquaries, after twice experiencing, horse and man, the perilous leap from the bridge into the lake, equal to any extremity to which the favourite heroes of chivalry, whose exploits he studied in an abridged form, whether Amadis, Belianis, Bevis, or his own Guy of Warwick, had ever been subjected—Captain Coxe, we repeat, did alone, after two such mischances, rush again into the heat of conflict, his bases, and the foot-cloth of his hobby-horse dropping water, and twice reanimated by voice and example the drooping spirits of the English; so that at length their victory over the Danish invaders became, as was just and reasonable, complete and decisive. Worthy he was to be rendered immortal by the pen of Ben Jonson, who, fifty years after-wards, deemed that a masque, exhibited at Kenilworth, could be ushered in by none with so much propriety, as by the ghost of Captain Coxe, mounted upon his redoubted hobby-horse.

These rough rural gambols may not altogether agree with the readers' preconceived idea of an entertainment presented before Elizabeth, in whose reign letters revived with such brilliancy, and whose court, governed by a female, whose sense of propriety was equal to her strength of mind, was no less distinguished for delicacy and refinement, than her counsels for wisdom and fortitude. But whether from the political wish to seem interested in popular sports, or whether from a spark of old Henry's rough masculine spirit, which Elizabeth's sometimes displayed, it is certain the Queen laughed heartily at the rude imitation, or rather burlesque of chivalry, which was presented in the Coventry play. She called near her person the Earl of Sussex and Lord Hunsdon, partly perhaps to make amends to the former, for the long and private audiences with which she had indulged the Earl of Leicester, by engaging him in conversation upon a pastime, which better suited his taste than those pageants that were furnished forth from the stores of antiquity. The disposition which the Queen shewed to laugh and jest with her military leaders, gave the Earl of Leicester the opportunity he had been watching for of with-drawing from the royal presence, which to the court around, so well had he chosen his time, had the graceful appearance of leaving his rival free access to the Queen's person, instead of availing himself of his right as her landlord, to stand perpetually betwixt others, and the light of her countenance.

Leicester's thoughts, however, had a far different object from mere courtesy; for no sooner did he see the Queen fairly engaged in con-versation with Sussex and Hunsdon, behind whose back stood Sir Nicholas Blount, grinning from ear to ear at each word which was spoken, than, making a sign to Tressilian, who, according to appoint-ment, watched his motions at a little distance, he extricated himself from the press, and walking towards the Chase, made his way through the crowds of ordinary spectators, who, with open mouth, stood gazing on the battle of the English and the Danes. When he had accomplished this, which was a work of some difficulty, he shot another glance behind him to see that Tressilian had been equally successful, and as soon as he saw him also free from the crowd, he led the way to a small thicket, behind which stood a lackey, with two horses ready saddled. He flung himself on the one, and made signs to Tressilian to mount the other, who obeyed without speaking a single word.

Leicester then spurred his horse, and galloped without stopping until he reached a sequestered spot, environed by lofty oaks, about a mile's distance from the Castle, and in an opposite direction from the scene to which curiosity was drawing every spectator. He there dismounted, bound his horse to a tree, and only pronouncing the words, "Here there is no risk of interruption," laid his cloak across his saddle, and drew his sword.

Tressilian imitated his example punctually, yet could not forbear saying, as he drew his weapon, "My lord, as I have been known to many as one who does not fear death, when placed in balance with honour, methinks I may, without derogation, ask, wherefore, in the name of all that is honourable, your lordship dared to offer me such a mark of disgrace, as places us on these terms with respect to each other?"

"If you like not such marks of my scorn," replied the Earl, "betake yourself instantly to your weapon, lest I repeat the usage you complain of."

"It shall not need, my lord," said Tressilian. "God judge betwixt us! and your blood, if you fall, be on your own head."

He had scarce completed the sentence when they instantly closed in combat.

But Leicester, who was a perfect master of defence amongst all other exterior accomplishments of the time, had seen, on the preceding night, enough of Tressilian's strength and skill, to make him fight with more caution than heretofore, and prefer a secure revenge to a hasty one. For some minutes they fought with equal skill and fortune, till, in a desperate lounge which Leicester successfully put aside, Tressilian exposed himself at disadvantage; and, in a subsequent attempt to close, the Earl forced his sword from his hand, and stretched him on the ground. With a grim smile he held the point of his rapier within two inches of the throat of his fallen adversary, and placing his foot at the same time upon his breast, bade him confess his villainous wrongs towards him, and prepare for death.

"I have no villainy nor wrong towards thee to confess," answered Tressilian, "and am better prepared for death than thou. Use thine advantage as thou wilt, and may God forgive you. I have given you no cause for this."

"No cause!" exclaimed the Earl, "no cause!—but why parley with such a slave?—die a liar, as thou hast lived!"

He had withdrawn his arm for the purpose of striking the fatal blow, when it was suddenly seized from behind.

The Earl turned in wrath to shake off the unexpected obstacle, but was surprised to find that a strange-looking boy had hold of his sword-arm, and clung to it with such tenacity of grasp, that he could not shake him off without a considerable struggle, in the course of which Tressilian had opportunity to rise and possess himself once more of his weapon. Leicester again turned towards him with looks of unabated ferocity, and the combat would have recommenced with still more desperation on both parts, had not the boy clung to Lord Leicester's knees, and with a shrill tone implored him to listen one moment ere he prosecuted this quarrel.

"Stand up, and let me go," said Leicester, "or, by heaven, I will pierce thee with my rapier!—What hast thou to do to bar my way to revenge?"

"Much—much!" exclaimed the undaunted boy; "since my folly has been the cause of these bloody quarrels between you, and per-chance of worse evils. O, if you would ever again enjoy the peace of an innocent mind, if you hope again to sleep in peace and unhaunted by remorse, take so much leisure as to peruse this letter, and then do as you list."

While he spoke in this eager and earnest manner, to which his singular features and voice gave a goblin-like effect, he held up to Leicester a packet, secured with a long tress of woman's hair, of a beautiful light-brown colour. Enraged as he was, nay, almost blinded with fury to see his destined revenge so strangely frustrated, the Earl of Leicester could not resist this extraordinary supplicant. He snatched the letter from his hand—changed colour as he looked on the superscription—undid, with a faultering hand, the knot which secured it—glanced over the contents, and staggering back, would have fallen, had he not rested against the trunk of a tree, where he stood for an instant, his eyes bent on the letter, and his sword-point turned to the ground, without seeming to be conscious of the presence of an antagonist, towards whom he had shewn little mercy, and who might in turn have taken him at advantage. But for such revenge Tressilian was too noble-minded—he also stood still in surprise, waiting the issue of this strange fit of passion, but holding his weapon ready to defend himself in case of need, against some new and sudden attack on the part of Leicester, whom he again suspected to be under the influence of actual frenzy. The boy, indeed, he easily recognized as his old acquaintance Dickon, whose face, once seen, was scarcely to be forgotten; but how he came hither at so critical a moment, why his interference was so energetic, and above all how it came to produce so powerful an effect upon Leicester, were questions which he could not solve.

But the letter was of itself powerful enough to work effects yet more wonderful. It was that which the unfortunate Amy had written to her husband, in which she alleged the reasons and manner of her flight from Cumnor-Place, informed him of her having taken refuge at Kenilworth to enjoy his protection, and mentioned the circumstances which had compelled her to take refuge in Tressilian's apartment, earnestly requesting he would, without delay, assign her a more suitable asylum. The letter concluded with the most earnest expressions of devoted attachment, and submission to his will in all things, and particularly respecting her situation and place of residence, conjuring him only that she might not be placed under the guardianship or restraint of Varney.

The letter dropped from Leicester's hand when he had perused it. "Take my sword," he said, "Tressilian, and pierce my heart, as I would but now have pierced your's!"

"My lord," said Tressilian, "you have done me great wrong; but something within my breast ever whispered that it was through egregious error."

"Error, indeed!" said Leicester, and handed him the letter; "I have been made to believe a man of honour a villain, and the best and purest of creatures a false profligate.—Wretched boy! Why comes this letter now, and where has it lingered?"

"I dare not tell you, my lord," said the boy, withdrawing, as if to keep beyond his reach;—"but here comes one who was the bearer."

Wayland at the same moment came up; and, interrogated by Leicester, hastily detailed all the circumstances of his escape with Amy,— the fatal practices which had driven her to flight,— and her anxious desire to throw herself under the instant protection of her husband,— pointing out the evidence of the domestics of Kenilworth, "who could not," he observed, "but remember her eager inquiries after the Earl of Leicester on her first arrival."

"The villains!" exclaimed Leicester; "but O, that worst of villains, Varney!—And she is even now in his power!"

"But not, I trust in God," said Tressilian, "with any commands of fatal import?"

"No, no, no!" exclaimed the Earl hastily.—"I said something in madness—But it was recalled, fully recalled, by a hasty messenger; and she is now—she must now be safe."

"Yes," said Tressilian, "she must be safe, and I must be assured of her safety—my own quarrel with you is ended, my lord—But there is another to begin with the seducer of Amy Robsart, who has screened his guilt under the cloak of the infamous Varney."

"The *seducer* of Amy!" replied Leicester, with a voice like thunder; "say her husband!—her misguided, blinded, most unworthy husband!—She is as surely Countess of Leicester, as I am belted Earl. Nor can you, sir, point out that manner of justice which I will not render her at my own free will. I need scarce say, I fear not your compulsion."

The generous nature of Tressilian was instantly turned from consideration of any thing personal to himself, and centered at once upon Amy's welfare. He had by no means undoubting confidence in the fluctuating resolutions of Leicester, whose mind seemed to him agitated beyond the government of calm reason; neither did he, notwithstanding the assurances he had received, think Amy safe in the hands of his dependants. "My lord," he said, calmly, "I mean you no offence, and am far from seeking a quarrel. But my duty to Sir Hugh Robsart compels me to carry this matter instantly to the Queen, that the Countess's rank may be acknowledged, and her person."

"You shall not need, sir," replied the Earl, haughtily; "do not dare to interfere. No voice but Dudley's shall proclaim Dudley's infamy—To Elizabeth herself will I tell it, and then for Cumnor-Place with the speed of life and death!"

So saying, he unbound his horse from the tree, threw himself into the saddle, and rode at full gallop towards the Castle.

"Take me before you, Master Tressilian," said the page, seeing Tressilian mount in the same haste—"my tale is not all told out, and I need your protection."

Tressilian complied, and followed the Earl, though at a less furious rate. By the way the boy confessed, with much contrition, that in resentment at Wayland's evading all his inquiries concerning the lady, after Dickon conceived he had in various ways merited his confidence, he had purloined from him, in revenge, the letter with which Amy had entrusted him for the Earl of Leicester. His purpose was to have restored it to him that evening, as he reckoned himself sure of meeting with him, in consequence of Wayland's having to perform the part of Arion, in the pageant. He was indeed something alarmed when he saw to whom the letter was addressed; but he argued that, as Leicester did not return to Kenilworth until that evening, it would be again in the possession of the proper messenger as soon as, in the nature of things, it could possibly be delivered. But Wayland came not to the pageant, having been in the interim expelled by Lambourne from the Castle, and the boy, not being able to find him, or to get speech of Tressilian, and finding himself in possession of a letter addressed to no less a person than the Earl of Leicester, became much afraid of the consequences of his frolic. The caution, and indeed the alarm, which Wayland had expressed respecting Varney and Lambourne, led him to judge, that the letter must be designed for the Earl's own hand, and that he might prejudice the lady, by giving it to any of the domestics. He made an attempt or two to obtain an audience of Leicester, but the singularity of his features and meanness of his appearance, occasioned his being always repulsed by the insolent menials whom he applied to for that purpose. Once, indeed, he had nearly succeeded, when, in prowling about, he found in the grotto the casket, which he knew to belong to the unlucky Countess, having seen it on her journey; for nothing escaped his prying eye. Having strove in vain to restore it either to Tressilian or the Countess, he put it into the hands, as we have seen, of Leicester himself, but unfortunately did not recognize him in his disguise.

At length, the boy thought he was on the point of succeeding, when the Earl came down to the lower part of the hall; but just as he was about to accost him, he was prevented by Tressilian. As sharp in ear as in wit, the boy heard the appointment settled betwixt them, to take place in the Pleasance, and resolved to add a third to the party, in hopes that, either in coming or in returning, he might find an opportunity of delivering the letter to Leicester; for strange stories began to flit among the domestics, which alarmed him for the lady's safety. Accident, however, detained Dickon a little behind the Earl, and, as he reached the arcade, he saw them engaged in combat; in consequence of which he hastened to alarm the guard, having little doubt, that what bloodshed took place betwixt them, might arise out of his own frolic. Continuing to lurk in the portico, he heard the second appointment, which Leicester, at parting, assigned to Tressilian, and was keeping them in view during the encounter of the Coventry-men, when, to his surprise, he recognized Wayland in the crowd, much disguised, indeed, but not sufficiently so to escape the prying glance of his old comrade. They drew aside out of the crowd to explain their situation to each other. The boy confessed to Wayland what we have above told, and the artist, in return, informed him, that his deep anxiety for the fate of the unfortunate lady had brought him back to the neighbourhood of the Castle, upon his learning that morning at a village about ten miles distant, that Varney and Lambourne, whose violence he dreaded, had both left Kenilworth over-night.

While they spoke, they saw Leicester and Tressilian separate themselves from the crowd, dogged them until they mounted their horses, when the boy, whose speed of foot has been before mentioned, though he could not possibly keep up with them, yet arrived, as we have seen, soon enough to save Tressilian's life. The boy had just finished his tale when they arrived at the Gallery-Tower.

Chapter Fifteen

High o'er the eastern steep the sun is beaming,
And darkness flies with her deceitful shadows;—
So truth prevails o'er falsehood.
Old Play

AS TRESSILIAN rode over the bridge lately the scene of so much riotous sport, he could not but observe that men's countenances had singularly changed during the space of his brief absence. The mock fight was over, but the men, still in their masquing suits, stood together in groupes, like the inhabitants of a city who have been just startled by some strange and alarming news.

When he reached the base-court, appearances were the same—domestics, retainers, and under officers, stood together and whispered, bending their eyes towards the windows of the great hall, with looks which seemed at once alarmed and mysterious.

Sir Nicholas Blount was the first person of his own particular acquaintance Tressilian saw, who left him no time to make inquiries, but greeted him with, "God help thy heart, Tressilian, thou art fitter for a clown than a courtier—thou can'st not attend, as becomes one who follows her Majesty.—Here you are called for, wished for, waited for—no man but you will serve the turn; and here you come with this misbegotten brat on thy horse's neck, as if thou wert dry nurse to some sucking devil, and wert just returned from airing."

"Why, what is the matter?" said Tressilian, letting go the boy, who sprung to ground like a feather, and himself dismounting at the same time.

"Why, no one knows the matter," replied Blount; "I cannot smell it out myself, though I have a nose like other courtiers. Only, my Lord of Leicester has galloped along the bridge, as if he would have rode over all in his passage, demanded an audience of the Queen, and is closeted even now with her, and Burleigh and Walsingham—and you are called for—but whether the matter be treason or worse, no one knows."

"He speaks true, by heaven," said Raleigh, who that instant appeared; "you must come immediately to the Queen's presence."

"Be not rash, Raleigh," said Blount, "remember his boots—For heaven's sake, go to my chamber, dear Tressilian, and don my new bloom-coloured silken hose—I have worn them but twice."

"Pshaw!" answered Tressilian; "do thou take care of this boy, Blount; be kind to him, and look he escapes you not—much depends on him."

So saying, he followed Raleigh hastily, leaving honest Blount with the bridle of his horse in one hand, and the boy in the other. Blount gave a long look after him.

"Nobody," he said, "calls me to these mysteries,—and he leaves me here to play horse-keeper and child-keeper at once. I could excuse the one, for I love a good horse naturally; but to be plagued with a bratchet whelp.—Whence come ye, my fair-favoured little gossip?"

"From the Fens," answered the boy.

"And what didst learn there, forward imp?"

"To catch gulls, with their web-feet and yellow stockings," said the boy.

"Umph!" said Blount, looking down on his own immense roses,— "Nay, then the devil take him asks thee more questions."

Meantime Tressilian traversed the full length of the great hall, in which the astonished courtiers formed various groupes, and were whispering mysteriously together, while all kept their eyes fixed on the door, which led from the upper end of the hall into the Queen's withdrawing apartment. Raleigh pointed to the door—Tressilian knocked, and was instantly admitted. Many a neck was stretched to gain a view to the interior of the apartment; but the tapestry which covered the door on the inside, was dropped too suddenly to admit the slightest gratification of curiosity.

Upon entrance, Tressilian found himself, not without a strong palpitation of heart, in presence of Elizabeth, who was walking to and fro in a violent agitation, which she seemed to scorn to conceal, while two or three of her most sage and confidential counsellors exchanged anxious looks with each other, but seemed to delay speaking till her wrath had abated. Before the empty chair of state in which she had been seated, and which was half pushed aside by the violence with which she had started from it, knelt Leicester, his arms crossed, and his brows bent on the ground, still and motionless as the effigies upon a sepulchre. Beside him stood the Lord Shrewsbury, then Earl Marshal of England, holding his baton of office—the Earl's sword was unbuckled, and lay before him on the floor.

"Ho, sir!" said the Queen, coming close up to Tressilian, and stamping on the floor with the action and manner of Henry himself; "*you* knew of this fair work—*you* are an accomplice in this deception which has been practised on us—*you* have been a main cause of our doing injustice?" Tressilian dropped on his knee before the Queen, his good sense shewing him the risk of attempting any defence at that moment of irritation. "Art dumb, sirrah!" she continued; "thou know'st of this affair—doest thou not?"

"Not, gracious Madam, that this poor lady was Countess of Leicester."

"Nor shall any one know her for such," said Elizabeth. "Death of my life! Countess of Leicester!—I say Dame Amy Dudley—and well if she have not cause to write herself widow of the traitor Robert Dudley."

"Madam," said Leicester, "do with me what it may be your will to do—but work no injury on this gentleman—he hath in no way deserved it."

"And will he be the better for thy intercession," said the Queen, leaving Tressilian, who slowly arose, and rushing to Leicester, who continued kneeling,—"the better for thy intercession, thou doubly false—thou doubly forsworn?—of thy intercession, whose villainy hath made me ridiculous to my subjects, and odious to myself?—I could tear out mine own eyes for their blindness!"

Burleigh here ventured to interpose.

"Madam," he said, "remember that you are a Queen—Queen of England—mother of your people. Give not way to these wild storms of passion."

Elizabeth turned round to him, while a tear actually twinkled in her proud and angry eye. "Burleigh," she said, "thou art a statesman—thou doest not, thou canst not, comprehend half the scorn—half the misery, that man has poured on me."

With the utmost caution—with the deepest reverence, Burleigh took her hand at the moment he saw her heart was at the fullest, and led her aside to an oriel window, apart from the others.

"Madam," he said, "I am a statesman, but I am also a man—a man already grown old in your councils, who have not and cannot have a wish on earth but your glory and happiness—I pray you to be composed."

"Ah, Burleigh," said Elizabeth, "thou little knowest"—here her tears fell over her cheeks in despite of her.

"I do—I do know, my honoured Sovereign. O beware that you lead not others to guess that which they know not!"

"Ha!" said Elizabeth, pausing as if a new train of thought had suddenly shot across her brain. "Burleigh, thou art right—thou art right—any thing but disgrace—any thing but a confession of weakness—any thing but seem the cheated—slighted—'Sdeath! to think on it is distraction!"

"Be but yourself, my Queen," said Burleigh; "and soar far above a weakness which no Englishman will ever believe his Elizabeth could have entertained, unless the violence of her disappointment carries a sad conviction to his bosom."

"What weakness, my lord?" said Elizabeth, haughtily; "would you too insinuate that the favour in which I held yonder proud traitor, derived its source from aught"—But here she could no longer sustain the proud tone which she had assumed, and again softened as she said, "But why should I strive to deceive even thee, my good and wise servant!"

Burleigh stooped to kiss her hand with affection, and—rare in the annals of courts—a tear of true sympathy dropped from the eye of the minister on the hand of his Sovereign.

It is probable that the consciousness of possessing this sympathy, aided Elizabeth in supporting her mortification, and suppressing her extreme resentment; but she was still more moved by fear that her passion would betray to the public the affront and the disappointment, which, alike as a woman and a Queen, she was so anxious to conceal. She turned from Burleigh, and sternly paced the hall till her features had recovered their usual dignity, her mien its usual stateliness of regular motion.

"Our Sovereign is her noble self once more," whispered Burleigh to Walsingham; "mark what she does, and take heed you thwart her not."

She then approached Leicester, and said, with calmness, "My Lord Shrewsbury, we discharge you of your prisoner.—My Lord of Leicester, rise and take up your sword—A quarter of an hour's restraint, under the custody of our Marshal, my lord, is, we think, no high penance for months of falsehood practised upon us. We will now hear the progress of this affair."—She then seated herself in her chair, and said, "You, Tressilian, step forward, and say what you know."

Tressilian told his story generously, suppressing as much as he could what affected Leicester, and saying nothing of their having twice actually fought together. It is very probable that in doing so, he did the Earl good service; for had the Queen at that instant found any thing which she could visit upon him, without laying open sentiments of which she was ashamed, it might have fared hard with him. She paused when Tressilian had finished his tale.

"We will take that Wayland," she said, "into our own service, and place the boy in our Secretary-office for instruction, that he may in future use discretion towards letters. For you, Tressilian, you did wrong in not communicating the whole truth to us, and your promise not to do so was both imprudent and undutiful. Yet, having given your word to this unhappy lady, it was the part of a man and a gentleman to keep it; and on the whole, we esteem you for the character you have sustained in this matter.—My Lord of Leicester, it is now your turn to tell us the truth, an exercise to which you seem of late to have been too much a stranger."

Accordingly, she extorted by successive questions, the whole history of his first acquaintance with Amy Robsart—their marriage—his jealousy—the causes on which it was founded, and many particulars besides. Leicester's confession, for such it might be called, was extorted from him piece-meal, yet was upon the whole accurate, excepting that he totally omitted to mention that he had, by implication, or otherwise, assented to Varney's designs upon the life of his Countess. Yet the consciousness of this was what at that moment lay nearest to his heart; and although he trusted in great measure to the very positive counter-orders which he had sent by Lambourne, it was his purpose to set out for Cumnor-Place in person, as soon as he should be dismissed from the presence of the Queen, who, he concluded, would presently leave Kenilworth.

But the Earl reckoned without his guest. It is true, his presence and his communications were gall and wormwood to his once partial mistress. But, barred from every other and more direct mode of revenge, the Queen perceived that she gave her false suitor torture by these inquiries, and dwelt on them for that reason, no more regarding the pain which she herself experienced, than the savage cares for the searing of his own hands with the hot pincers with which he tears the flesh of his captive enemy.

At length, however, the haughty lord, like a deer that turns to bay, gave intimation that his patience was failing. "Madam," he said, "I have been much to blame—more than even your just resentment has expressed. Yet, Madam, let me say, that my guilt, if it be unpardonable, was not unprovoked; and that if beauty and condescending dignity could seduce the frail heart of a human being, I might plead both, as the causes of my concealing this secret from your Majesty."

The Queen was so much struck by this reply, which Leicester took care should be heard by no one but herself, that she was for the moment silenced, and the Earl had the temerity to pursue his advantage. "Your Grace, who has pardoned so much, will excuse my throwing myself on your royal mercy for those expressions, which were yester-morning accounted but a light offence."

The Queen fixed her eyes on him while she replied, "Now, by heaven, my lord, thy effrontery passes the bounds of belief, as well as patience! But it shall avail thee nothing.—What, ho! my lords, come all and hear the news—My Lord of Leicester's stolen marriage has cost me a husband, and England a King. His lordship is patriarchal in his tastes—one wife at a time was insufficient, and he designed US the honour of his left hand. Now, is not this too insolent,—that I could not grace him with a few marks of court-favour, but he must presume to think my hand and crown at his disposal?—You, however, think better of me; and I can pity this ambitious man, as I could a child, whose bubble of soap has burst between his hands. We go to the presence-chamber—My Lord of Leicester, we command your close attendance on us."

All was eager expectation in the hall, and what was the universal astonishment, when the Queen said to those next her, "The revels of Kenilworth are not yet exhausted, my lords and ladies—we are to solemnize the noble owner's marriage."

There was an universal expression of surprise.

"It is true, on our royal word," said the Queen; "he hath kept this secret even from us, that he might surprise with it at this very place and time. I see you are dying of curiosity to know the happy bride—It is Amy Robsart, the same who, to make up the May-game yesterday, figured in the pageant as the wife of his servant Varney."

"For God's sake, Madam," said the Earl, approaching her with a mixture of humility, vexation, and shame in his countenance, and speaking so low as to be heard by no one else, "take my head, as you threatened in your anger, and spare me these taunts! Urge not a falling man—tread not on a crushed worm."

"A worm, my lord?" said the Queen, in the same tone; "nay, a snake is the nobler reptile, and the more exact similitude—the frozen snake you wot of, which was warmed in a certain bosom"——

"For your own sake—for mine, madam," said the Earl—"while there is yet some reason left in me"——

"Speak aloud, my lord," said Elizabeth, "and at farther distance, so please you—your breath thaws our ruff. What have you to ask of us?"

"Permission," said the unfortunate Earl, humbly, "to travel to Cumnor-Place."

"To fetch home your bride belike?—Why, ay,—that is but right—for, as we have heard, she is indifferently cared for there. But, my lord, you go not in person—we have counted upon passing certain days in this Castle of Kenilworth, and it were slight courtesy to leave us without a landlord during our residence here. Under your favour, we cannot think to incur such disgrace in the eyes of our subjects. Tressilian shall go to Cumnor-Place instead of you, and with him some gentleman who hath been sworn of our chamber, lest my Lord of Leicester should be again jealous of his old rival.—Whom wouldst thou have to be in commission with thee, Tressilian?"

Tressilian, with humble deference, suggested the name of Raleigh.

"Why, ay," said the Queen; "so God ha' me, thou hast made a good choice. He is a young knight besides, and to deliver a lady from prison is an appropriate first adventure.—Cumnor-Place is little better than a prison, you are to know, my lords and ladies. Besides, there are certain faitours there whom we would willingly have in fast keeping. You will furnish them, Master Secretary, with the warrant necessary to secure the bodies of Richard Varney and the foreign Alasco, dead or alive. Take a sufficient force with you, gentlemen—bring the lady here in all honour—lose no time, and God be with you."

They bowed, and left the presence.

Who shall describe how the rest of that day was spent at Kenilworth? The Queen, who seemed to have remained there for the sole purpose of mortifying and taunting the Earl of Leicester, shewed herself as skilful in that female art of vengeance, as she was in the science of wisely governing her people. The train of state soon caught the signal, and, as he walked among his own splendid preparations, the Lord of Kenilworth, in his own Castle, already experienced the lot of a disgraced courtier, in the slight regard and cold manners of alienated friends, and the ill-concealed triumph of avowed and open enemies. Sussex, from his natural military frankness of disposition, Burleigh and Walsingham, from their penetrating and prospective sagacity, and some of the ladies, from the compassion of their sex, were the only persons in the crowded court who retained towards him the countenance they had borne in the morning.

So much had Leicester been accustomed to consider court-favour as the principal object of his life, that all other sensations were, for the time, lost in the agony which his haughty spirit felt at the succession of petty insults and studied neglects to which he had been subjected; but when he was retired to his own chamber for the night, that long fair tress of hair which had once secured Amy's letter, fell under his observation, and, with the influence of a counter-charm, awakened his heart to nobler and more natural feelings. He kissed it a thousand times; and while he recollected that he had it always in his power to shun the mortifications which he had that day undergone, by retiring into a dignified and even princelike seclusion, with the beautiful and beloved partner of his future life, he felt that he rose above the revenge which Elizabeth had condescended to take.

Accordingly, on the next day, the whole conduct of the Earl displayed so much dignified equanimity; he seemed so solicitous about the accommodations and amusement of his guests, yet so indifferent to their personal demeanour towards him; so respectfully distant to the Queen, yet so patient of her harassing displeasure, that Elizabeth changed her manner to him, and though cold and distant, ceased to offer him any direct affront. She intimated also with some sharpness to others around her, who thought they were consulting her pleasure shewing a neglectful conduct to the Earl, that while they remained at Kenilworth, they ought to shew the civility due from guests to the Lord of the Castle. In short, matters were so far changed in twenty-four hours, that some of the more experienced and sagacious courtiers foresaw a strong possibility of Leicester's restoration to favour, and regulated their demeanour towards him, as those who might one day claim merit for not having deserted him in adversity. It is time, however, to leave these intrigues and to follow Tressilian and Raleigh on their journey.

The troop consisted of six persons; for, besides Wayland, they had in company a royal pursuivant and two stout serving-men. All were well armed, and travelled as fast as it was possible with justice to their horses, which had a long journey before them. They endeavoured to procure some tidings as they rode along of Varney and his party, but could hear none, as they had travelled in the dark. At a small village about twelve miles from Kenilworth, where they gave some refreshment to their horses, a poor clergyman, the curate of the place, came out of his small cottage, and entreated any of the company who might know aught of surgery, to look in for an instant on a dying man.

The empiric Wayland undertook to do his best, and as the curate conducted him to the spot, he learned that the man had been found on the high-road about a mile from the village, by labourers, as they were going to their work on the preceding morning, and the curate had given him shelter in his house. He had received a gun-shot wound which seemed to be obviously mortal, but whether in a brawl or from robbers they could not learn, as he was in a fever, and spoke nothing connectedly. Wayland entered the dark and lowly apartment, and no sooner had the curate drawn aside the curtain, than he knew in the distorted features of the dying man the countenance of Michael Lambourne. Under pretence of seeking something which he wanted, Wayland hastily apprized his fellow-travellers of this extraordinary circumstance; and both Tressilian and Raleigh, full of boding apprehensions, hastened to the curate's house to see the dying man.

The wretch was by this time in the agonies of death, from which a much better surgeon than Wayland could not have rescued him, for the bullet had passed clear through his body. He was sensible, however, at least in part, for he knew Tressilian, and made signs that he wished him to stoop over his bed. Tressilian did so, and after some inarticulate murmurs, in which the names of Varney and Lady Leicester were alone distinguishable, Lambourne bade him "make haste, or he would come too late." It was in vain Tressilian urged the patient for farther information; he seemed to become in some degree delirious, and when he again made a signal to attract Tressilian's attention, it was only for the purpose of desiring to inform his uncle, Giles Gosling of the Black Bear, that "he had died without his shoes after all." A convulsion verified his words a few minutes after, and the travellers derived nothing from having met with him, saving the obscure fears concerning the fate of the Countess, which his dying words were calculated to convey, and which induced them to urge their journey with the utmost speed, pressing horses in the Queen's name, when those on which they rode became unfit for service.

Chapter Sixteen

The death-bell thrice was heard to ring,
An aerial voice was heard to call;
And thrice the raven flapped its wing,
Around the towers of Cumnor-hall.
MICKLE

WE ARE NOW to return to that part of our story where we intimated that Varney, possessed of the authority of the Earl of Leicester, and of the Queen's permission to the same effect, hastened to secure himself against discovery of his perfidy, by removing the Countess from Kenilworth Castle. He had proposed to set forth early in the morning, but reflecting that the Earl might relent in the interim, and seek another interview with the Countess, he resolved to prevent, by immediate departure, all chance of what would probably have ended in his detection and ruin. For this purpose he called for Lambourne, and was exceedingly incensed to find that trusty attendant was abroad on some ramble in the neighbouring village, or elsewhere. As his return was expected, Sir Richard commanded that he should prepare himself for attending him on an immediate journey, and follow him in case he returned after his departure.

In the meanwhile, Varney used the ministry of a servant called Robin Tider, one to whom the mysteries of Cumnor-Place were already in some degree known, as he had been there more than once in attendance on the Earl. To this man, whose character resembled that of Lambourne, though he was neither quite so prompt nor altogether so profligate, Varney gave command to have three horses saddled, and to prepare a horse-litter, and have them in readiness at the postern-gate. The natural enough excuse of his lady's insanity, which was now universally believed, accounted for the secrecy with which she was to be removed from the Castle, and he reckoned on the same apology in case the unfortunate Amy's resistance or screams should render such necessary. The agency of Anthony Forster was indispensible, and that Varney now went to secure.

This person, naturally of a sour unsocial disposition, and somewhat tired, besides, with his hasty journey from Cumnor to Warwickshire, in order to bring the news of the Countess's escape, had early extricated himself from the crowd of wassailers, and betaken himself to his chamber, where he lay asleep, when Varney, completely equipped for travelling, and with a dark lantern in his hand, entered his apartment. He paused an instant to listen to what his associate was murmuring in his sleep, and could plainly distinguish the words, "*Ave Maria—ora pro nobis*—no—it runs not so—deliver us from evil—ay, so it goes."

"Praying in his sleep," said Varney; "and confounding his old and new devotions—he must have more need of prayer ere I am done with him.—What ho! holy man—most blessed penitent!—awake—awake!—The devil has not discharged you from service yet."

As Varney at the same time shook the sleeper by the arm, it changed the current of his ideas, and he roared out, "Thieves!—thieves! I will die in defence of my gold—my hard won gold, that has cost me so dear.—Where is Janet?—is Janet safe?"

"Safe enough, thou bellowing fool," said Varney; "art thou not ashamed of thy clamour?"

Forster by this time was broad awake, and, sitting up in his bed, asked Varney the meaning of so untimely a visit. "It augurs nothing good," he added.

"A false prophecy, most sainted Anthony," returned Varney; "it augurs that the hour is come for converting thy leasehold into copyhold—what say'st thou to that?"

"Had'st thou told me in broad day," said Forster, "I had rejoiced—but at this dead hour, and by this dim light, and looking on thy pale face, which is a ghastly contradiction to thy light words, I cannot but rather think of the work that is to be done, than the guerdon to be gained by it."

"Why, thou fool, it is but to escort thy charge back to Cumnor-Place."

"Is that indeed all?" said Forster; "thou look'st deadly pale, and thou art not moved by trifles—is that indeed all?"

"Ay, that—and may be a trifle more," said Varney.

"Ah, that trifle more!" said Forster; "still thou look'st paler and paler."

"Heed not my countenance," said Varney, "you see it by this wretched light—up and be doing, man—Think of Cumnor-Place—thine own proper copyhold—why, thou may'st found a weekly lectureship, besides endowing Janet like a baron's daughter.—Seventy pounds and odds."

"Seventy nine pounds, five shillings and five pence half-penny, besides the value of the wood," said Forster; "and I am to have it all as copyhold?"

"All, man—squirrels and all—no gipsey shall cut the value of a broom—no boy so much as take a bird's nest, without paying thee a quittance.—Ay, that is right—don thy matters as fast as possible—horses and every thing is ready—All save that accursed villain Lambourne, who is out on some infernal gambol."

"Ay, Sir Richard," said Forster, "you would take no advice. I ever told you that drunken profligate would fail you at need. Now I could have helped you to a sober young man."

"What, some slow-spoken, long-breathed brother of the congregation?—Why, we shall have use for such also, man—Heaven be praised, we shall lack labourers of every kind—ay, that is right—forget not your pistols—come now, and let us away."

"Whither?" said Anthony.

"To my lady's chamber—and, mind—she *must* along with us. Thou art not a fellow to be startled by a shriek?"

"Not if Scripture-reason can be rendered for it; and it is written, 'wives obey your husbands.' But will my lord's commands bear us out if we use violence?"

"Tush, man! here is his signet," answered Varney; and, having thus silenced the objections of his associate, they went together to Lord Hunsdon's apartment, and, acquainting the centinel with their purpose, as a matter sanctioned by the Queen and the Earl of Leicester, they entered the apartment of the unfortunate Countess.

The horror of Amy may be conceived, when, starting from a broken slumber, she saw at her bed-side Varney, the man on earth she most feared and hated. It was even a consolation to see that he was not alone, though she had so much reason to dread his sullen companion.

"Madam," said Varney, "there is no time for ceremony—my Lord of Leicester, having fully considered the exigencies of the time, sends you his orders immediately to accompany us on our return to Cumnor-Place. See, here is his signet, in token of his instant and pressing commands."

"It is false!" said the Countess; "thou hast stolen the warrant,—thou, who art capable of every villainy, from the blackest to the basest!"

"It is TRUE, madam," replied Varney; "so true, that if you do not instantly arise, and prepare to attend us, we must compel you to obey our orders."

"Compel!—thou darest not put it to that issue, base as thou art," exclaimed the unhappy Countess.

"That remains to be proved, madam," said Varney, who had determined on intimidation as the only means of subduing her high spirit; "if you put me to it, you will find me a rough groom of the chambers."

It was at this threat that Amy screamed so fearfully, that had it not been for the received opinion of her insanity, she would quickly have had Lord Hunsdon and others to her aid. Perceiving, however, that her cries were vain, she appealed to Forster in the most affecting terms, conjuring him, as his daughter Janet's honour and purity was dear to him, not to permit her to be treated with unwomanly violence.

"Why, madam, wives must obey their husbands,—there's Scripture-warrant for it," said Forster; "and if you will dress yourself, and come with us patiently, there's no one shall lay finger on you while I can draw a pistol-trigger."

Seeing no help arrive, and comforted even by the dogged language of Forster, the Countess promised to arise and dress herself, if they would agree to retire from the room. Varney at the same time assured her of all safety and honour while in their hands, and promised, that he himself would not approach her, since his presence was so displeasing. Her husband, he added, would be at Cumnor within twenty-four hours after they had reached it.

Somewhat comforted by this assurance, upon which, however, she saw little reason to rely, the unhappy Amy made her toilette by the assistance of the lantern, which they left her when they quitted the apartment.

Weeping, trembling, and praying, the unfortunate lady dressed herself,—with sensations how different from the days in which she was wont to decorate herself in all the pride of conscious beauty! She endeavoured to delay the completing her dress as long as she could, until, terrified by the impatience of Varney, she was obliged to declare herself ready to attend them.

When they were about to move, the Countess clung to Forster with such an appearance of terror at Varney's approach, that the latter protested to her, with a deep oath, that he had no intention whatsoever of even coming near her. "If you do but consent to execute your husband's will in quietness, you shall," he said, "see but little of me. I will leave you undisturbed to the care of the usher whom your good taste prefers."

"My husband's will!" she exclaimed. "But it is the will of God, and let that be sufficient to me.—I will go with Master Forster as unresistingly as ever did a literal sacrifice—he is a father at least; and will have decency, if not humanity. For thee, Varney, were it my latest word, thou art an equal stranger to both."

Varney replied only, she was at liberty to chuse, and walked some paces before them to shew the way; while, half leaning on Forster, and half carried by him, the Countess was transported from Saintlowe Tower to the postern-gate, where Tider waited with the litter and horses.

The Countess was placed in the former without resistance. She saw with some satisfaction, that while Forster and Tider rode close by the litter, which the latter conducted, the dreaded Varney lingered behind, and was soon lost in darkness. A little while she strove, as the road winded round the verge of the lake, to keep sight of those stately towers which called her husband lord, and which still, in some places, sparkled with lights, where wassailers were yet revelling. But when the direction of the road rendered this no longer possible, she drew back her head, and, sinking down in the litter, recommended herself to the care of Providence.

Besides the desire of inducing the Countess to proceed quietly on her journey, Varney had it also in view to have an interview with Lambourne, by whom he every moment expected to be joined, without the presence of any witnesses. He knew the character of this man, prompt, bloody, resolute, and greedy, and judged him the most fit agent he could employ in his farther designs. But ten miles of their journey had been measured ere he heard the hasty clatter of horse's hoofs behind him, and was overtaken by Michael Lambourne.

Fretted as he was with his absence, Varney received his profligate servant with a rebuke of unusual bitterness. "Drunken villain," he said, "thy idleness and debauched folly will stretch a halter ere it be long; and, for me, I care not how soon."

This style of objurgation, Lambourne, who was elated to an unusual degree, not only by an extraordinary cup of wine, but by the sort of confidential interview he had just had with the Earl, and the secret of which he had made himself master, did not receive with his wonted humility. "He would take no insolence of language," he said, "from the best knight that ever wore spurs. Lord Leicester had detained him on some business of import, and that was enough for Varney, who was but a servant like himself."

Varney was not a little surprised at this unusual tone of insolence; but, ascribing it to liquor, suffered it to pass as if unnoticed, and then began to tamper with Lambourne, touching his willingness to aid in removing out of the Earl of Leicester's way an obstacle to a rise, which would put it in his power to reward his trusty followers to their utmost wish. And upon Michael Lambourne seeming ignorant what was meant, he plainly indicated "the litter-load, yonder," as the impediment which he desired should be removed.

"Look you, Sir Richard, and so forth," said Michael, "some are wiser than some, that is one thing, and some are worse than some, that's another. I know my lord's mind on this matter better than thou, for he hath trusted me fully in the matter. Here are his mandates, and his last words were, Michael Lambourne,—for his lordship speaks to me as a gentleman of the sword, and useth not the words drunken villain, or such like phrases, of those who know not how to bear new dignities.—Varney, says he, must pay the utmost respect to my Countess—I trust you for looking to it, Lambourne, says his lordship, and you must bring back my signet from him peremptorily."

"Ay," replied Varney, "said he so, indeed? You know all, then?"

"All—all—and you were as wise make a friend of me while the weather is fair betwixt us."

"And was there any one present," said Varney, "when he so spoke?"

"Not a breathing creature," replied Lambourne. "Think you my lord would trust any one with such matters, save an approved man of action like myself?"

"Most true," said Varney; and, making a pause, he looked forward on the moonlight road. They were traversing a wide and open heath. The litter, at least a mile before them, was both out of sight and hearing. He looked behind, and there was an expanse, lighted by the moonbeams, without one human being in sight. He resumed his speech to Lambourne: "And will you turn upon your master, who has introduced you to this career of court-like favour—whose apprentice you have been, Michael—who has taught you the depths and shallows of court intrigue?"

"Michael not me," said Lambourne, "I have a name will brook a *master* before it as well as another; and as to the rest, if I have been an apprentice, my indenture is out, and I am resolute to set up for myself."

"Take thy quittance first, thou fool!" said Varney; and with a pistol, which he had for some time in his hand, shot Lambourne through the body.

The wretch fell from his horse, without a single groan; and Varney, dismounting, rifled his pockets, turning out the lining, that it might appear he had fallen by robbers. He secured the Earl's packet, which was his chief object, but he also took Lambourne's purse, containing some gold pieces, the reliques of what his debauchery had left him, and, from a singular combination of feelings, carried it in his hand only the length of a small river, which crossed the road, into which he threw it as far as he could fling. Such are the strange remnants of conscience which remain after she seems totally subdued, that this cruel and remorseless man would have felt himself degraded had he pocketed the few pieces belonging to the wretch whom he had thus ruthlessly slain.

The murderer reloaded his pistol, after cleansing the lock and barrel from the appearances of late explosion, and rode calmly after the litter, satisfying himself that he had so adroitly removed a trouble-some witness to many of his intrigues, and the bearer of mandates which he had no intentions to obey, and which, therefore, he was desirous it should be thought had never reached his hand.

The remainder of the journey was made with a degree of speed, which shewed the little care they had for the health of the unhappy Countess. They paused only at places where all was under their com-mand, and where the tale of the insane Lady Varney would have obtained ready credit, had she made any attempt to appeal to the compassion of the few persons admitted to see her. But Amy saw no chance of obtaining a hearing from any to whom she had an opportun-ity of addressing herself, and, besides, was too terrified for the pres-ence of Varney to violate the implied conditions, under which she was to travel free from his company. The authority of Varney, often used for similar purposes, during the Earl's repeated private journies to Cumnor, readily procured relays of horses where wanted, so that they approached Cumnor-Place upon the night after they left Kenilworth.

At this period of the journey, Varney came up to the rear of the litter, as he had done before repeatedly during the journey, and asked, "What does she?"

"She sleeps," said Forster; "I would we were home—her strength is exhausted."

"Rest will restore her," answered Varney. "She shall soon sleep sound and long—we must consider how to lodge her in safety."

"In her own apartments, be sure," said Forster. "I have sent Janet to her aunt's, with a proper rebuke, and the old women are truth itself—for they hate this lady cordially."

"We will not trust them, however, friend Anthony," said Varney; "we must secure her in that stronghold where you keep your gold."

"My gold?" said Anthony, much alarmed; "why, what gold have I? —God help me, I have no gold—I would I had."

"Now, marry hang thee, thou stupid brute—Who thinks of or cares for thy gold?—if I did, could I not find an hundred better ways to come at it?—In one word, thy bed-chamber, which thou hast fenced so curiously, must be her place of seclusion; and thou, thou hind, shalt press her pillows of down.—I dare to say the Earl will never ask after the rich furniture of those four rooms."

This last consideration rendered Forster tractable; he only asked permission to ride before, to make matters ready, and, spurring his horse, he posted before the litter, while Varney falling about three-score paces behind, it remained only attended by Tider.

When they had arrived at Cumnor-Place, the Countess asked eagerly for Janet, and shewed much alarm when informed that she was no longer to have the attendance of that amiable girl.

"My daughter is dear to me, madam," said Forster, gruffly; "and I desire not that she should get the court-tricks of lying and scaping—somewhat too much of that has she learned already, an it please your ladyship."

The Countess, much fatigued and greatly terrified by the circumstances of her journey, made no answer to this insolence, but mildly expressed a wish to retire to her chamber.

"Ay, ay," muttered Forster, "'tis but reasonable; but, under favour, you go not to your gew-gaw toy-house yonder—you will sleep to-night in better security."

"I would it were in my grave," said the Countess; "but that mortal feelings shiver at the idea of soul and body parting."

"You, I guess, have no chance to shiver at that," replied Forster. "My lord comes hither to-morrow, and doubtless you will make your own ways good with him."

"But does he come hither?—does he indeed, good Forster?"

"O ay, good Forster!" replied the other. "But what Forster shall I be to-morrow, when you speak of me to my lord—though all I have done was to obey his own orders."

"You shall be my protector—a rough one indeed—but still a protector," answered the Countess. "O, that Janet were but here!"

"She is better where she is," answered Forster—"one of you is enough to perplex a plain head—but will you taste any refreshment?"

"O no, no—my chamber—my chamber. I trust," she said, "I may secure it on the inside."

"With all my heart," answered Forster. "So I may secure it on the outside;" and taking a light, he led the way to a part of the building where Amy had never been, and conducted her up a stair of great height, preceded by one of the old women with a lamp. At the head of the stair, which seemed of almost immeasurable height, they crossed a short wooden gallery, formed of black oak, and very narrow, at the farther end of which was a strong oaken door, which when opened admitted them into the miser's apartment, homely in its accommodations in the very last degree, and, except in name, little different from a prison-vault.

Forster stopped at the door, and gave the lamp to the Countess, without either offering or permitting the attendance of the hag who had carried it. The lady stood not on ceremony, but taking it hastily, barred the door, and secured it with the ample means provided on the inside for that purpose.

Varney, meanwhile, had lurked behind on the stairs, but hearing the door barred, he now came up on tiptoe, and Forster, winking to him, pointed with self-complacence to a piece of concealed machinery on the wall, which, playing with much ease and little noise, raised up a part of the wooden gallery, after the manner of a drawbridge, so as to cut off all communication between the door of the bedroom, which he usually inhabited, and the landing-place of the high winding-stair which ascended to it. The rope by which this machinery was wrought was generally carried within the bed-chamber, it being Forster's object to provide against invasion from without; but now that it was intended to secure the prisoner within, the cord had been brought over to the landing-place, and was there made fast, when Forster, with much complacency, had raised this unsuspected trapdoor.

Varney looked with great attention at the machinery, and peeped more than once at the deep abyss which was opened under the vacant part of the gallery. It was dark as pitch, and seemed profoundly deep, going, as Forster informed his confederate in a whisper, nigh to the lowest vault of the Castle. Varney cast once more a fixed and long look down into this sable gulph, and then followed Forster to the part of the manor-house most usually inhabited.

When they arrived in the parlour which we have often mentioned, Varney requested Forster to get them supper, and some of the choicest wine. "I will seek Alasco," he added; "we have work for him to do, and we must put him into good heart."

Forster groaned at this intimation, but made no remonstrance. The old woman assured Varney that Alasco had scarce eaten or drunken since her master's departure, living perpetually shut up in the laboratory, and talking as if the world's continuance depended on what he was doing there.

"I will teach him that the world hath other claims on him," said Varney, seizing a light, and going in quest of the alchemist. He returned, after a considerable absence, very pale, but yet with his habitual sneer on his cheek and nostril—"Our friend," he said, "has exhaled."

"How! what mean you?" said Forster—"Run away—fled with my forty pounds, that should have been multiplied a thousand fold? I will have Hue and Cry."

"I will tell thee a surer way," said Varney.

"How! which way?" exclaimed Forster; "I will have back my forty pounds—I deemed them as surely a thousand times multiplied—I will have back my in-put, at the least."

"Go hang thyself then, and sue Alasco in the Devil's Court of Chancery, for thither he has carried the cause."

"How!—what doest thou mean—is he dead?"

"Ay, truly is he," said Varney; "and properly swoln already in the face and body—he had been mixing some of his devil's medicines, and the glass mask which he used constantly had fallen from his face, so that the subtle poison entered the brain, and did its work."

"*Sancta Mater!*" said Forster;—"I mean, God in his mercy preserve us from covetousness and deadly sin!—Had he not had projection, think you?—saw you no ingots in the crucibles?"

"Nay, I looked not but at the dead carrion," answered Varney; "an ugly spectacle—He was swoln like a corpse three days exposed on the wheel—Pah! give me a cup of wine."

"I will go," said Forster, "I will examine myself"——He took the lamp, and hastened to the door, but there hesitated, and paused. "Will you not go with me?" said he to Varney.

"To what purpose?" said Varney; "I have seen and smelled enough to spoil my appetite. I broke the window, however, and let in the air— it reeked of sulphur, and such like suffocating steams, as if the very devil had been there."

"And might it not be the act of the Dæmon himself?" said Forster, still hesitating; "I have heard he is powerful at such times, and with such people."

"Still, if it *were* that Satan of thine," answered Varney, "who thus jades thy imagination, thou art in perfect safety, unless he is a most unconscionable devil indeed. He hath had two good sops of late."

"How, *two* sops—what mean you?" said Forster—"What mean you?"

"You will know in time," said Varney;—"and then this other banquet—but thou wilt esteem Her too choice a morsel for the fiend's tooth—she must have her psalms, and harps, and seraphs."

Anthony Forster heard, and came slowly back to the table: "God! Sir Richard, and must that then be done?"

"Ay, in very truth, Anthony, or there comes no copyhold thy way."

"I always foresaw it would land there," said Forster; "but how, Sir Richard, how?—for not to win the world would I put hands on her."

"I cannot blame thee," said Varney; "I should be reluctant to do that myself—We miss Alasco and his manna sorely; ay, and the dog Lambourne."

"Why, where tarries Lambourne?" said Anthony.

"Ask no questions," said Varney, "thou wilt see him one day, if thy creed is true.—But to our graver matter.—I will teach thee a springe, Tony, to catch a pewit—Yonder trap-door—yonder gim-crack of thine, will remain secure in appearance, will it not, though the supports are withdrawn beneath?"

"Ay, marry, will it," said Forster; "so long as it is not trodden on."

"But were the lady to attempt an escape over it," replied Varney, "her weight would carry it down?"

"A mouse's weight would do it," said Forster.

"Why, then, she dies in attempting her escape, and what could you or I help it, honest Tony? Let us to bed, we will adjust our project tomorrow."

On the next day, when evening approached, Varney summoned Forster to the execution of their plan. Tider and Forster's old manservant were sent on a feigned errand down to the village, and Anthony himself, as if anxious to see that the Countess suffered no want of accommodation, visited her place of confinement. He was so much staggered at the mildness and patience with which she seemed to endure her confinement, that he could not help earnestly recommending to her not to cross the threshold of her door on any account whatsoever, until Lord Leicester should come, "Which," he added, "I trust in God, will be very soon." Amy patiently promised that she would resign herself to her fate, and Forster returned to his hardened companion with his conscience half-eased of the perilous load that weighed on it. "I have warned her," he said; "surely in vain is the snare set in the sight of any bird."

He left, therefore, the Countess's door unsecured on the outside, and under the eye of Varney, withdrew the supports which sustained the falling trap, which, therefore, kept its level position merely through a slight adhesion. They then withdrew to wait the issue on the ground-floor adjoining, but they waited long in vain. At length Varney, after walking long to and fro, with his face muffled in his cloak, threw it suddenly back, and said, "Never, surely, was a woman fool enough to neglect so fair an opportunity of escape!"

"Perhaps she is resolved," said Forster, "to await her husband's return."

"True!—most true," said Varney, rushing out, "I had not thought of that before."

In less than two minutes, Forster, who remained behind, heard the tread of a horse in the court-yard, with a whistle similar to that which was the Earl's usual signal;—and the instant after the door of the Countess's chamber opened—the trap-door gave way—there was a rushing sound—a heavy fall—a faint groan and all was over.

At the same instant, Varney called in at the window, in an accent and tone which was an indescribable mixture betwixt horror and raillery, "Is the bird caught?—is the deed done?"

"O God, forgive us!" replied Anthony Forster.

"Why, thou fool," said Varney, "thy toil is ended, and thy reward secure. Look down into the vault—what seest thou?"

"I see only a heap of white clothes, like a snow-drift," said Forster. "O God, she moves her arm!"

"Hurl something down on her—thy gold chest, Tony—it is an heavy one."

"Varney, thou art an incarnate fiend!" replied Forster;—"There needs nothing more—she is gone!"

"So pass our troubles," said Varney, entering the room; "I dreamed not I could have mimicked the Earl's call so well."

"Oh, if there be judgment in heaven, thou hast deserved it," said Forster, "and wilt meet it!—Thou hast destroyed her by means of her best affections—It is a seething of the kid in the mother's milk."

"Thou art a fanatical ass," replied Varney; "let us now think how the alarm should be given,—the body is to remain where it is."

But their wickedness was to be permitted no longer;—for, even while they were at this consultation, Tressilian and Raleigh broke in upon them, having obtained admittance by means of Tider and Forster's servant, whom they had secured at the village.

Anthony Forster fled on their entrance; and, knowing each corner and pass of the intricate old house, escaped all search. But Varney was taken on the spot; and, instead of expressing compunction for what he had done, seemed to take a fiendish pleasure in pointing out to them the remains of the murdered Countess, while at the same time he defied them to shew that he had any share in her death. The despairing grief of Tressilian, at viewing the mangled and yet warm remains of what had lately been so lovely and so beloved, was such, that Raleigh was compelled to have him removed from the place by force, while he himself assumed the direction of what was to be done.

Varney, upon a second examination, made very little mystery either of the crime or of its motives; alleging, as a reason for his frankness, that though much of what he confessed could only have attached to him by suspicion, yet such suspicion would have been sufficient to deprive him of Leicester's confidence, and to destroy all his towering plans of ambition. "I was not born," he said, "to drag on the remainder of life a degraded outcast,—nor will I so die, that my fate shall make a holiday to the vulgar herd."

From these words it was apprehended he had some design upon himself, and he was carefully deprived of all means, by which such could be carried into execution. But like some of the heroes of anti-quity, he carried about his person a small quantity of strong poison, prepared probably by the celebrated Demetrius Alasco. Having swal-lowed this potion over-night, he was found next morning dead in his cell; nor did he appear to have suffered much agony, his countenance presenting, even in death, the habitual expression of sneering sar-casm, which was predominant while he lived. The wicked man, saith Scripture, hath no bonds in his death.

The fate of his colleague in wickedness was long unknown. Cumnor-Place was deserted immediately after the murder; for, in the vicinity of what was called the Lady Dudley's Chamber, the domestics pretended to hear groans and screams, and other supernatural noises. After a certain length of time, Janet, hearing no tidings of her father, became the uncontrouled mistress of his property, and conferred it with her hand upon Wayland, now a man of settled character, and holding a place in Elizabeth's household. But it was after they had been both dead for some years, that their eldest son and heir, in making some researches about Cumnor-Hall, discovered a secret passage, closed by an iron door, which, opening from behind the bed in the Lady Dudley's Chamber, descended to a sort of cell, in which they found an iron chest containing a quantity of gold, and a human skeleton stretched above it. The fate of Anthony Forster was now manifest. He had fled to this place of concealment, forgetting the key of the spring-lock; and being barred from escape, by the means he had used for preservation of that gold, for which he had sold his salvation, he had there perished miserably. Unquestionably the groans and screams heard by the domestics were not entirely imagi-nary, but were those of this wretch, who, in his agony, was crying for relief and succour.

The news of the Countess's dreadful fate put a sudden period to the Pleasures of Kenilworth. Leicester retired from court, and for con-siderable time abandoned himself to his remorse. But as Varney in his last declaration had been studious to spare the character of his patron, the Earl was the object rather of compassion than resentment. The Queen at length recalled him to court; he was once more distin-guished as a statesman and favourite, and the rest of his career is well known to history. But there was something retributive in his death, if, according to an account very generally received, it took place from his swallowing a draught of poison, which was designed for another person.

Sir Hugh Robsart died very soon after his daughter, having settled his estate on Tressilian. But neither the prospect of rural independ-ence, nor the promises of favour which Elizabeth held out to induce him to follow the court, could remove his profound melancholy. Wherever he went, he seemed to see before him the disfigured corpse of the early and only object of his affection. At length, having made provision for the maintenance of the old friends and old servants who formed Sir Hugh's family at Lidcote-Hall, he himself embarked with his friend Raleigh for the Virginia expedition, and, young in years but old in griefs, died before his day in that foreign land.

Of inferior persons it is only necessary to say, that Blount's wit grew brighter as his yellow roses faded; and that, doing his part as a brave commander in the wars, he was much more in his element, than during the short period of his following the court; and that Flibberti-gibbet's acute genius raised him to favour and distinction, in the employment both of Burleigh and Cecil.

The outlines of this melancholy tale may be found, at length, in Ashmole's Antiquities of Berkshire, and it is alluded to in many other works which treat of Leicester's history. The ingenious translator of "Camoens," William Julius Mickle, has made the Countess's tragedy the subject of a beautiful elegy, called Cumnor-Hall, which concludes with these lines:

> The village maids, with fearful glance,
>   Avoid the ancient moss-grown wall,
> Nor ever lead the merry dance
>   Among the groves of Cumnor-Hall.
>
> And many a traveller has sigh'd,
>   And pensive mourn'd that lady's fall,
> As wandering onward he has spied
>   The haunted towers of Cumnor-Hall.

THE END

KENILWORTH;

A ROMANCE.

BY THE AUTHOR OF " WAVERLEY," " IVANHOE," &c.

No scandal about Queen Elizabeth, I hope?
The Critic.

IN THREE VOLUMES.

VOL. I.

EDINBURGH:
PRINTED FOR ARCHIBALD CONSTABLE AND CO.;
AND JOHN BALLANTYNE, EDINBURGH;
AND HURST, ROBINSON, AND CO.,
LONDON.

1821.

ESSAY ON THE TEXT

1. THE GENESIS OF *KENILWORTH* 2. THE COMPOSITION OF
KENILWORTH: the Manuscript; changes between Manuscript and First
Edition 3. THE LATER EDITIONS: Second Edition; octavo *Historical
Romances*; duodecimo *Historical Romances*; eighteenmo *Historical
Romances*; the Interleaved Set and the Magnum 4. THE PRESENT
TEXT: punctuation and capitalisation; verbal emendations [misreadings,
wrong insertions and omissions, wrong substitutions, mechanical elim-
ination of repetitions, faulty corrections, problems with names, miscel-
laneous].

The following conventions are used in transcriptions from Scott's
manuscript: deletions are enclosed ⟨thus⟩ and insertions ↑thus↓; an
insertion within an insertion is indicated by double arrows ↑↑thus↓↓;
superscript letters are lowered without comment; the letters 'NL' (new
line) are Scott's own, and indicate that he wished a new paragraph to be
opened, in spite of running on the text, whereas the words '[new para-
graph]' are editorial and indicate that Scott opened a new paragraph on a
new line. The same conventions are used as appropriate for indicating
variants between the printed editions.

1. THE GENESIS OF *KENILWORTH*

IN his *Memoirs of the Life of Sir Walter Scott* J.G.Lockhart, Scott's
son-in-law and biographer, tells how *Kenilworth* began:

For reasons, as we have seen, connected with the affairs of the
Ballantynes, Messrs Longman published the first edition of The
Monastery; and similar circumstances induced Sir Walter to
associate this house with that of Constable in the succeeding novel.
Constable disliked its title, and would fain have had *the Nunnery*
instead: but Scott stuck to his *Abbot*. The bookseller grumbled a
little, but was soothed by the author's reception of his request that
Queen Elizabeth might be brought into the field in his next
romance, as a companion to the Mary Stuart of the Abbot. Scott
would not indeed indulge him with the choice of the particular
period of Elizabeth's reign, indicated in the proposed title of *The
Armada*; but expressed his willingness to take up his own old
favourite, the legend of Meikle's ballad. He wished to call the
novel, like the ballad, *Cumnor-hall*, but in further deference to
Constable's wishes, substituted "Kenilworth." John Ballantyne
objected to this title, and told Constable the result would be
"something worthy of the kennel;" but Constable had all reason to
be satisfied with the child of his christening. His partner, Mr
Cadell, says—"his vanity boiled over so much at this time, on
having his suggestion gone into, that when in his high moods he
used to stalk up and down his room, and exclaim, 'By G—, I am all

but the author of the Waverley Novels!'" Constable's bibliographical knowledge, however, it is but fair to say, was really of most
essential service to Scott upon many of these occasions; and his
letter (now before me) proposing the subject of *The Armada*, furnished the Novelist with such a catalogue of materials for the
illustration of the period as may, probably enough, have called forth
some very energetic expression of thankfulness.[1]

Lockhart's information about the origins of *Kenilworth* is especially
valuable (though its accuracy cannot now be tested) since there is so
little evidence from other sources about the genesis of this novel.
William Julius Mickle's 'Cumnor Hall' was first printed in Thomas
Evans's *Old Ballads* in 1784, and Lockhart records the young Scott's
delighted response to it: the Elizabethan period suggested by Archibald Constable was well-known to Scott because of his scholarly work
in editing various collections of papers and tracts of the period, and the
appropriateness of a favourite literary ballad was a happy imaginative
bonus.[2] Constable must have written towards the end of 1819 or the
beginning of 1820, 'proposing or suggesting a new romance or novel,
"Kenilworth," of the age of Elizabeth'; Scott replied on 12 January
1820: 'I will consider your hint about the subject and when we meet I
will tell you the *pro's* and *con's*'.[3] In John Ballantyne's journal—John
was brother of Scott's printer and partner James, and acted as Scott's
literary agent—there is a copy of an agreement dated 18 January 1820
between Constable and the Ballantynes for 12,000 copies of Scott's
'next work of Fiction in 4 volumes (the title of which shall be decided
& indorsed hereon in the course of one month from this date—the
work to be published about the end of June 1820)': John Ballantyne
makes it clear that the agreement refers to *Kenilworth*.[4] In a revised
agreement of 17 February (f. 105 v) the work is still to be in four
volumes, but the 12,000 is divided between a first edition of 10,000
and a second of 2000, which were indeed the numbers eventually
printed. John Ballantyne noted on 18 February 'Sold last night the
Copies Kenelworth to Constable & Co' (f. 1 v). Constable's usual practice was to seek a co-publisher in London, and to sell on to them a
substantial proportion of the imprint. Negotiations with Longmans
seem to have broken down in October 1820,[5] and Hurst, Robinson
and Co. were chosen in their place, thus confirming the fateful associ-
ation that was to lead to Scott's insolvency in 1826.

In January 1820 Constable, on business in London, asked his son
David to look out materials for Scott's use:

> I wish you would look out any books we have of Elizabeth's reign,
> and get from the Advocates' library any books on the history of
> Berkshire that describe Cumnor Hall. Perhaps you would step in
> there and examine. Look into Gough's Topographical Views; it
> may be in Burke's Views, or some other such book. Get Bank's
> Extinct Peerage of England. . . .

I think Birch's Memoirs of Elizabeth should be got from the Library, if we have it not in Park Place.[6]

In fact, during the first part of 1820 Scott was occupied with *The Abbot*, and he did not begin to write the new novel until September, though no doubt it was taking shape in his mind as the manuscript shows no major stumblings in the conduct of the plot. In a letter dated by H.J.C.Grierson 1 August he asserted to James Ballantyne: 'As to Kenilworth I mean to go on with it but as one must have some breathing it is possible there may be intervals'; and on 30 August he wrote to Constable: 'Many thanks for the books & K. I intend to set toughly & instantly to work so soon as Septr commences'.[7] The books referred to may well have been, or have included, those borrowed from the Advocates' Library on Scott's behalf by Archibala Constable's son David.[8] Scott evidently pushed work forward rapidly during the autumn as anticipated, but there is little evidence for the exact progress of composition. On 10 September he wrote to Constable:

> There was a book publishd some years ago calld I think Clavis Calendaria being an account of the Calendar and the usages and customs on particular Saints days & holidays. I should wish much to have it The Progresses are doing me yeomans service for I am in *progress* myself I have a question to ask you which pray answer as soon as you can. What was the name of Dudley Earl of Leicesters first wife whom he was supposed to have murderd at Cumnor hall in Berkshire I know it occurs in the Sidney papers & probably in the common genealogies but I have no book here which contains the information—In Lysons Magna Britannia or some such name there is something about this same Cumnor Hall I wish you would have it copied out for me & should like indeed to know any thing that occurs to you about the village of Cumnor its situation &c. I like to be as minutely local as I can.
>
> Please not to say a word about K. the very name explains so much that some knowing fellow might anticipate the subject.[9]

On 6 October Scott wrote to Constable saying that Ashmole's *Antiquities of Berkshire* would be 'most welcome', and added 'I am advancing fast and with some confidence. I have littel doubt we will be out by Xmas'.[10] In an undated note of late October or early November he told James Ballantyne: 'I will be in town Monday sennight but I will send much copy before that. I send some with the proofs. I am glad you like what is done but am most anxious you should give your opinion on Queen Bess'.[11] Back in Edinburgh and attending court (the law-term that year opened on Monday 13 November), Scott wrote to James Ballantyne in an undated note: 'I fear that cut up as my time is by the Session work I must stick to K. Send tonight for copy'.[12] On 27 December John Ballantyne was able to note: 'Kenilworth finished writing this day. Esteemed at present the first work of the author: I do not think so'.[13]

While Scott was busy with the composition of the novel, preparations were going ahead for its printing. In September and October, paper in post size (15.25×19 inches) was ordered from the firm of Joseph Bonsor of London. Negotiations began on 7 September with a request for 300 reams at once, 500 in a month, and more thereafter; a further order for 500 reams followed on 18 September. The first batch of 400 reams was required 'towards the end of Octr' and the rest (another 900 or so) 'sometime in Nov'; Bonsor apparently had difficulty fulfilling this demand, and a supplementary order for 100 reams, with possibly another 200 or 300 to follow, was placed with Alexander Cowan of Penicuik on 7 October.[14] On 11 November Robert Cadell wrote to his partner, Constable: 'I have seen Bonsor to day he has sent off in whole about 835 reams paper—and will send in a few days about 150 more, this with Cowans &c will more than do'.[15] Printing presumably began in late October as planned, for on 2 November Constable notified Mrs Mackenzie of Edinburgh: 'I am at present engaged in a new work of the Author of Waverley to be out early in the month of January',[16] and on 13 November Cadell informed Constable that 'the book is going on—and every chance of being finished'.[17] On 20 November he wrote further that 'K. is going on so well that our risk on it gets less every day'.[18] Printing was complete by 5 January 1821, and the main batch of bales containing the unbound sheets was despatched from Leith to London on 9 January. A letter of 5 January from Cadell to William Jerdan in London, editor of the *Literary Gazette*, gives a vivid picture of the hazards of shipping at that time of year:

I am very much obliged by your favor of   Decr—I hope you may find my anticipations of Kenilworth not too sanguine—you now have a copy of said book with the best compt of the Publishers— when I send it however I cannot but express some doubts about the date of Publication we ship on the 9th Inst *from Leith* and if wind and weather were favorable the bulk might be in London by the following Saturday or Monday—the 13th or 15th—but this is uncertain—and I state it thus candidly to you—were the book to get up so as to be out on the monday—your announcement might appear on the Saturday preceding that is the 13th, but if any ice in the River or contrary winds come in the way of this the announce- ment of the 13th would play the devil—under this uncertainty I now write—and I do not see easily how to make the matter more certain.[19]

There does not appear to be any specific surviving evidence as to the proportion of the 10,000 run which was sent to London, but it was probably around half.[20]

A letter from the bookseller John Miller to Carey & Son of Phila- delphia in the Lea & Febiger Collection of the Historical Society of Philadelphia, dated 18 January 1821, states that *Kenilworth* was pub- lished that day in London. In Edinburgh the *Edinburgh Weekly Journal* announced it for publication on 15 January, and by 17 January it had assumed 'This day published' status in the same paper, so that Monday 15 January 1821 may be regarded as the Edinburgh publication date.[21] The price was one and a half guineas (£1.57½).

2. THE COMPOSITION OF *KENILWORTH*

The Manuscript. The original manuscript of *Kenilworth* consisted of 186 main leaves numbered by Scott, the first two volumes both running from 1 to 61, the third volume from 1 to 64. The greater part of it (160 numbered leaves beginning with leaf 16 of the first volume, along with ten whole or reduced leaves bearing insertions) is in the British Library, London (MS Egerton 1661).[22] Eleven leaves from near the beginning of the first volume, numbered 3 to 13 by Scott, are in Edinburgh University Library (MS La. III. 498/1, ff. 1–11).[23] The two leaves presumably numbered 14 and 15 (the binding obscures the numbers) linking the Edinburgh portion of the manuscript and that in the British Library are in the Karpeles Manuscript Library, Santa Barbara, California. Two unnumbered leaves and a 'paper apart' are in the National Library of Scotland (MS 3653, ff. 32, 129, and 130).[24] Thirteen of the main leaves are missing.[25]

Scott followed his usual practice of covering each recto densely; there is no space at the top or at the bottom or at the right, and only the narrowest of margins at the left. On average there are about 1200 words per leaf. Scott used the verso of the previous leaf for corrections and for insertions varying from a single word to substantial passages. The evidence of pens and ink suggests that most of the alterations were made at the time of composition, but that some were introduced after the relevant portion of the main text had been composed, perhaps at the beginning of the following day's task.[26] To preserve the author's anonymity, the manuscripts of all the novels to 1827 were transcribed for the press, and to judge from the folding of the manuscript, copy was sent to the transcriber frequently in small batches, so that the few manuscript revisions in different pens from the main text could not usually have taken place long after initial composition. Although the main text on the rectos may appear at first sight to be relatively free from corrections, a close examination shows that a typical folio contains some thirty corrections or visible hesitations where Scott has begun a word and stumbled, or changed his mind.

With so many minute and often illegible alterations it would be impossible to quantify or classify at all satisfactorily the different types of changes made on the rectos, or to describe them in detail, but many of them clearly anticipate the types of alteration which Scott, and in some cases his intermediaries, made at later stages, the most pervasive and least interesting being innumerable clarifications and the introduction of 'said so-and-so' phrases and new paragraphs. Other characteristic changes in manuscript may be divided for convenience into eight categories.

1] Some of the repetitions of words in close sequence are eliminated. Such repetitions are sometimes caught in the act of coming into being. The manuscript version of 7.1–2 reads: '"By my credit ↑friend↓ Mike said young Laurence Twineall the cutting ⟨you⟩ mercer of Abingdon . . ."'. Scott has here caught the repeated 'young' before it is fully formed.

A considered rejection of a more widely separated repetition can be found in the manuscript version of 128.6–14:

> . . . most of them attempted to satisfy their customer by producing some substitute which when rejected by Wayland as not being what he had askd for they maintaind possessd in a superior degree the selfsame qualities and in general displayd some curiosity concerning the purpose for which he wanted it. One old meagre chemist to whom the artist put the usual question in terms which Tressilian neither understood nor could recollect answerd frankly there was none of the drug in London unless Yoglan the Jew chanced to ⟨be possessd of it⟩ ↑have some of it upon hand↓.

The final phrase is substituted on the facing verso to avoid repeating 'possessd'.

2] Scott frequently improves the rhetorical movement of speeches, either by attending to the rhythm or by developing some of the concepts and images further, or by doing both simultaneously. A small improvement made as Scott wrote can be found in the manuscript version of Tressilian's speech at 33.26–29:

> "With thy will—thine uninfluenced free & deliberate will Amy thou canst not chuse this state of slavery and dishonour—thou hast been bound by some spell—⟨by so⟩ entrapd by some art—art now detaind by some compelld vow . . ."

The insertion of 'entrapd' improves the movement of this passionate speech.

A good example of a double improvement comes at the end of the fifth chapter of the first volume (45.21–26). Varney's speech ends thus on the recto in the manuscript:

> ". . . I must work an interest in her either through love or through fear—and who knows but I may yet reap the sweetest and best revenge for her former scorn.—that were indeed a masterpiece of courtlike art"—

Scott inserted on the facing verso before the concluding quotation marks and dash

> Let me but once be her counsel-keeper—let her confide to me a secret did it but concern the robbery of a linnets nest and fair Countess thou art mine own.

3] The substitution of a more vivid or simply more appropriate word can be observed on many occasions. A striking instance occurs at the end of one of Lambourne's speeches (36.13–14): 'The Black Bear ⟨waits⟩ ↑growls↓ for us'. Other examples include: 'such small ⟨fly⟩ ↑butterflies↓ as Goldthread' (19.3); 'my noble master was then under ⟨charge⟩ ↑dominion↓ of a leech' (146.11–12); 'features which are both ⟨plain⟩ ↑homely↓ and irregular' (206.20); and 'I would I knew by what charm you ⟨subdued⟩ ↑muzzled↓ yonder old bear?' (266.39–40).

4] The narrative is often enlivened by details of setting or other vivid touches that can be seen coming in during writing or shortly afterwards. Among noteworthy passages added to the original conception are 109.33–42 (Pinniewinks) and 112.30–113.1 (time at a standstill at Lidcote Hall). The added detail in the following sentence (243.31–35) enhances the memorability of the narrative:

> At such a pace they ascended the gentle hill we have mentiond and looking from the top had the pleasure to see the party which had left Doddington before them were in ⟨a⟩ ⟨brook betwe⟩ ⟨and where⟩ ↑the little valley or bottom on the other side where the road was traversed by a rivulet beside which was a cottage or two. In this place↓ they seemd to have made a pause ...

Similarly Forster's gateway is made more impressive by the phrase added to the following clause: 'which was closed by two huge oaken leaves ↑thickly studded with nails↓ like the gate of an old ⟨fashiond⟩ town' (21.17–19).

Elaborate descriptive passages were liable to be especially hard-worked, as in the account of Amy's apartment (47.32–38):

> It was carpeted so thick that the heaviest step could not have been heard and the bed richly heapd with down ⟨and⟩⟨ ↑with↓ ⟩ ↑was↓ spread with ↑an ample coverlet of silk and gold ↑↑from↓↓ under which peepd forth↓ cambrick sheets and blankets as white as the lambs which yeilded the fleece that made them.
> ↑The curtains were of blue velvet liond with crimson silk ⟨and⟩ deeply festoond with gold and embroiderd with the loves of Cupid and Psyche.↓

In this case the two longer insertions were added on the opposing verso.

The ballad-like exchange between Forster and Varney before the catastrophe is another telling addition (380.36–40):

> ↑"Is that indeed all?" said Foster "thou lookst deadly pale and thou art not moved by trifles—is that indeed all?" "Aye that and may be a trifle more" said Varney "Ah that trifle more" said Foster "still thou lookst paler and paler↓.

5] The most interesting of the alterations obviously made *currente calamo* show that Scott had a later part of a sentence in mind as he was writing the earlier part. At the beginning of the description of Lidcote Hall he wrote: 'The ⟨moated⟩ old mansion was a low venerable building occupying a considerable space of ground which was surrounded by a deep moat', suggesting the predominance of the moat in his mental picture (112.25–27). Similarly, he often deleted inverted commas at the end of direct speech and expanded the original material: Lambourne's speech on 28.31–40 was originally planned to be much shorter, ending at 'the devil quote Scripture' (28.33); Tressilian's speech at 36.24–27 was an afterthought; and Varney's long utterance on 64.31–65.11 might have finished at 'spur' (64.38) or at 'score' (64.40).

6] Although there are no major changes of plan evident in the manuscript, there are a few indications of lines of thought that Scott did not choose to take up. Thus in the second volume Alasco's descent from the turret chamber is a second thought, replacing the arrival of the famous Dr Allan; Varney says:

> "...⟨Allan waits my Lord is it your pleasure to see him"——"Let him enter" said Leicester⟩ ↑ "Has your lordship further commands for the night?" ...↓

A few lines later Scott tries again:

> It was some minutes ere Varney returnd which Leicester spent in unlocking the steel casket which was now placed before him and taking from thence first a parcel of gold coins and secondly a parchment scribbled over with planetary signs with the lines and calculations used in framing horoscopes. As he lookd on this with a sad and anxious eye Varney introduced in to the apartment a little old man dressd in black and bowing silently again withdrew and left the visitor alone with the Earl. NL. The Astrologer

Scott deletes all of this and inserts 185.16–30 on the facing verso.

7] Occasionally a chapter ending was altered in manuscript. The last sentence of Volume 1, Chapter 7 (76.16–21) was an afterthought; so was the chapter division at Volume 1, Chapter 11 (102). The last two paragraphs of Volume 2, Chapter 9 (208.32–209.24) were a verso insertion, probably written after Scott had started the next chapter; an already striking ending for Volume 2 was converted and made more explicit with the addition of the final brief paragraph in a new pen (257).

8] The mottoes of eighteen of the forty-one chapters were added after the composition of the main text.[27]

Changes between Manuscript and First Edition. To preserve Scott's anonymity the manuscript of *Kenilworth* was transcribed for the press by one of his most regular amanuenses, George Huntly Gordon, though it is possible that another transcriber was also involved.[28] Gordon's transcript passed in batches through the hands of the compositors and other staff of the Ballantyne firm. No proofs of *Kenilworth* are known to have survived, but no doubt the same processes as are described in the General Introduction were followed: the compositors would have set the text and at the same time supplied punctuation, standardised spelling and corrected minor errors, in conformity (theoretically) with a series of standing orders discussed below; the first proofs would have been read against Gordon's copy; James Ballantyne would have edited second proofs and sent them on to Scott; Scott would have been sent revises if required, but otherwise Ballantyne would have been left to supervise the translation of Scott's revisions and corrections into print. Between the manuscript and first edition of *Kenilworth* some 3000 verbal changes, in single words and groups of words, were made, as well as some 50,000 other changes. (These figures include an allowance for the missing leaves, and like all such figures in this essay they should be regarded as indicative rather than precise, given that there is inevitably a degree of arbitrariness in such categorisations and reckonings.)

Since no proofs of *Kenilworth* are known to have survived, the only external evidence to suggest what sort of alteration was made at what stage of proof comes from certain American editions whose final pages (from 344.32 in the present edition to the end of the work) were set from uncorrected second-stage proofs.[29] The major part of the American editions published in 1821 derived from fully corrected first-edition sheets, but in order to expedite publication the American publishers were supplied for this final portion with proofs that had not yet been revised and corrected by Scott. These pages show that some 140 verbal changes were made by the intermediaries to the manuscript text, consciously and unconsciously, before the American (or second proof) stage, and of these rather less than half may be judged to be acceptable executions of Scott's standing orders. Forty of them involve putting right clear errors, usually either the wrong word or (in some twenty cases) words simply omitted. Some fifteen alterations are designed to improve the style, principally by eliminating repetitions, correcting grammatical lapses, and substituting nouns for pronouns. Less acceptably, some twenty valid idioms are missed, more than ten synonyms are unnecessarily substituted in another ten or so cases, and there are some 45 misreadings of the manuscript or omissions of words.

Between the uncorrected second proofs and the first edition Scott, with some continuing input from intermediaries, made a further 200 or so verbal alterations (which do not appear in the earliest American editions). Of these some seventy were made for the sake of clarity and precision (including substituting nouns for pronouns, and more appropriate words for less appropriate ones), another fifty or so for idiomatic or stylistic reasons (including the anglicising of a few Scotticisms), and some thirty to eliminate repetitions not caught at earlier stages; there were some twenty changes to the sense, and ten 'said so-and-so' phrases. A handful of passages were altered, sometimes substantially, for the sake of plot business, and seven new paragraphs were introduced. After correction of the second proofs, and after subsequent proof stages (to all of which the intermediaries, notably James Ballantyne, would have continued to contribute), there would have been a final in-house polishing in Edinburgh before the first-edition sheets were printed.

The first edition shows some 2750 verbal differences from the extant portions of the manuscript. Some 700 of these occur in the first volume, 1100 in the second, and 950 in the third. The second volume is thus the most heavily revised and the first the least. Although some of the categories suggested below are fluid, an attempt to break down the majority of these 2750 verbal alterations may be helpful.

1] Over 450 alterations were made for the sake of clarity or precision, often substituting a name for a pronoun (especially after the creation of a new paragraph) or introducing an explanatory phrase. One of the most telling substitutions clarifies an essential point memorably in the encounter between Leicester and Shakespeare (168.30-32), where the manuscript reads:

> The Player bowd and Leicester ↑ nodded and passd on—so that age would have told the tale—in ours perhaps we might say the ⟨Mortal ha⟩ Immortal had done homage to the mortal. . . . ↓

In the first edition and the present text this begins: 'The *player* bowed, and the Earl nodded and passed on'.

2] More than 300 changes may be classed as generally stylistic, often involving the recasting of sentence structure. Thus the manuscript version of 210.22–26 runs:

> She was the nursing-mother of her people but she was also the true daughter of Henry VIII and early sufferings & an excellent education had repressd & modified but had not altogether destroyd the hereditary temper of that "hard-ruled King."

In the first edition and the present text this reads more convincingly:

> She was the nursing-mother of her people, but she was also the true daughter of Henry VIII.; and though early sufferings and an excellent education had repressed and modified, they had not altogether destroyed, the hereditary temper of that "hard-ruled King."

The first two lines of the motto to Volume 2, Chapter 2, Scott's own composition, were altered in proof from 'This is rare news thou tellest me goodfellow/ There were two bulls were battling on the green' to the present 'This is rare news thou tell'st me, my good fellow;/ There are two bulls fierce battling on the green'.

3] Another 300 changes were made to avoid the repetition of words (or occasionally sounds) in close conjunction, though a few alterations made for other reasons resulted in the inadvertent introduction of such repetitions. This procedure continues the process begun in the course of composition, and it is particularly interesting when the repeated word points to the importance of a certain concept in Scott's mind at that part of the narrative. Thus the manuscript version of 269.3–9, describing Tressilian at Kenilworth, runs:

> He himself became sensible of the necessity of forcing other objects upon his mind and for this purpose he left the Pleasance in

order to mingle with the busy croud upon the walls & view the
preparation for the pageants. But as he left the garden ↑ heard the
busy hum mixd with music and laughter which floated around
him ↓ he felt an uncontroulable reluctance to mix with society
whose feelings were in a tone so different from his own . . .

The first edition and, following it, the present text have a number of
alterations, and the deletions are of interest, but the crucial feature here
is the repeated 'busy'. On its second appearance the echo of Milton's
'L'Allegro' is evident, and Tressilian is clearly cast in the role of Il
Penseroso. The first 'busy' becomes 'noisy' in revision, but the double
manuscript occurrence stresses the pervasiveness of the Miltonic allusion in original conception and verso insertion.

4] Some 300 changes were made to correct obvious errors, most frequently quite wrong words where Scott's attention slipped, and on
eighty or so occasions more vivid or appropriate words were substituted
for less satisfactory ones. To this latter process we owe the 'spitchcock'd' rather than 'fried' eels of 9.27 and the crucial substitution of
'hushed' for 'asleep' in the description of the atmospheric moonlight
scene at 304.7.

5] On some 270 occasions Scott accidentally omitted words: usually
the missing word is obvious, but occasionally he broke off before the end
of a sentence and an intermediary (or perhaps the author himself in
proof) had to supply the gap. The most striking example of this occurs at
286.36–287.2, where the manuscript reads:

The ladies of the court who rode be⟨side⟩side her had taken
especial care that their own ↑ external ↓ appearance should not be
more glorious than their rank and the occasion altogether
demanded so that no inferior luminary might appear to approach
the orbit of ⟨the⟩ royalty. But their personal charms and the
⟨necessa⟩ magnificence by which under every prudential restraint
they were necessarily distinguishd

When Scott encountered this in proof he took the opportunity not just to
finish the sentence but to add another, so that the first edition and
present text runs on thus:

. . . necessarily distinguished, exhibited them as the very flower of a
realm so far famed for splendour and beauty. The magnificence of
the courtiers, free from such restraints as prudence imposed on the
ladies, was yet more unbounded.

6] Some 230 alterations were made to correct or standardise idioms
and grammar, the most frequent being the substitution of 'as' for the
older idiom 'so' in phrases such as 'so soon as'.

7] Alterations of the fundamental sense of a sentence or passage are
less frequent than one might expect, only some 150 cases in the entire
novel, not many of them involving really radical surgery and some of
them making sense of confused passages. One of the most striking
changes in sense occurs at 40.38–40, where the manuscript reads:

"Aye said Foster sullenly when you⟨r⟩ have work in hand it is our
fortunes you speak of but your own you think of I must take the
risque of all"—

In the present text, based on the first edition, this runs:

"Ay, ay," said Forster, sullenly, "this it is to be leagued with one
who knows not even so much of Scripture, as that the labourer is
worthy of his hire. I must, as usual, take all the trouble and risk."

The revised version is perfectly acceptable, but in this case it is not clear
why an effective original version has been so radically changed. Wayland's account of his sighting of Demetrius is fundamentally altered and
expanded in the first edition and present text. The manuscript has
simply: "'I have seen my old master" said the artist "in the vaul ↑ ted ↓
⟨p⟩ passage from the stables to the buttery I met him full in the face—
He was anticly habited' (compare 181.5–12).

8] On some 140 occasions 'said so-and-so', or a similar phrase, is
added, occasionally with an indication of how the speech is delivered.

9] Among the most attractive and least routine alterations are some 120
imaginative rhetorical additions or re-workings, mostly in dialogue.
These may involve only the addition of one word: 'if I have not my share
of such ↑ glittering ↓ dew-drops, may my sword melt like an icicle!'
(37.5–6); 'It is thine own fault, thou sullen ↑ uninventive ↓ companion' (38.39: 'companion' is 'knave' in the manuscript). They may involve purely rhetorical upgrading: 'there are many who will tell you
England will have a king, and ↑England's↓ Elizabeth↑, God save her,↓
a husband, ere the Progress be over' (204.19–21). Some of the finest
phrases and sentences in the novel came in at proof stage: 'so soon as
all is over, ↑ we will lay our noble lord in a noble green grave, have a
blow at those who have hurried him thither, if opportunity suits, and
then ↓ sail for the Indies with hearts as light as our purses' (134.22–25:
the manuscript has 'with an heart as light as their purses'); 'the art of
↑ clashing rhymes and meting out ↓ hexameters' (135.17: the manuscript reads 'of writing hexameters'); 'to which these ↑northern
blinkers ↓ are but farthing candles' (196.21); 'if I should cut his hams
↑ and smoke them for bacon ↓' (197.20–21). The most telling of these
essentially rhetorical insertions is Forster's speech at the catastrophe,
added at proof stage:

↑ "Oh, if there be judgment in heaven, thou hast deserved it," said
Forster, "and wilt meet it!—Thou hast destroyed her by means of
her best affections—It is a seething of the kid in the mother's
milk." ↓ (390.15–17)

10] Also with a significance beyond their number are additions of detail
on some 45 occasions. The details are sometimes minor (which need
not imply that they are unmemorable): 'see how his villainous tailor hath
apparelled him—in blue, green, and crimson, with carnation ribbons,
↑ and yellow roses in his shoes! ↓' (282.33–35: the final phrase re-

places the manuscript's 'by the love of heaven'). Other important details are more extensive:

> These prevailed all through the crowded roads and fields, and especially beyond the gate of the Chace, where the greater number of the common sort were stationed ↑ ; when, all of a sudden, a single rocket was seen to shoot into the atmosphere, and, at the instant, far-heard over flood and field, the great bell of the Castle tolled.
>
> Immediately there was a pause of dead silence, succeeded by ↓ a deep hum of expectation . . . (285.10–17)

11] There is no evidence of radical plot change between manuscript and first edition, any more than in the manuscript itself, but there are some twenty occasions where alterations are made for the sake of plot business: some of them are merely for local tidiness, but a handful are more striking. All of the end of Volume 2, Chapter 7 from 'slowly towards the door' is a proof insertion, substituted for 'to make preparations for his early journey' (194.42–195.7). The important sentences 'I will have a look . . . make or mar me' at 356.36–39 are a proof insertion, as is 'Once, indeed . . . his disguise' (370.10–16).

12] Scott rarely deletes material, but at some thirty points he eliminates tautology or tightens up his expression by shedding a few words. Such a rare pruning took place in one of the descriptions of Blount's braveries. The somewhat tormented manuscript version of 283.1–8 runs:

> Tressilian thus appeald to lookd on them both and ⟨being⟩ ↑ was immediately ↓ sensible ↑ at a single glance ↓ that honest Blount had taken upon trust the pied garments which the tailor had chosen to make and was as much embarassd by the quantity of points ribbands laces and buttons with which his ⟨coat⟩ doublet and cloak were gaurded flounced and garnishd ↑ as a clown is in a holiday ⟨cl?⟩ suit ↓ While the dress of Raleigh was ⟨that⟩ ⟨on him⟩ a well fanc[ie]d and rich suit which the wearer bore as a garb which was too ⟨familiar with⟩ ↑ well adapted to ↓ his elegant person to attract particular attention.

There may be something to regret in the paring down (though not in the tidying up) of that passage, but other proof trimmings are unlikely to raise doubts: 'inferring, however, too surely ⟨in his own mind⟩' (273.25–26); 'the Countess felt at first as if each rocket shot close by her eyes, and ⟨almost as if it⟩ discharged its sparks and flashes so nigh that she could feel a sense of the heat' (309.5–7: the manuscript has 'close' for 'nigh').

13] The manuscript shows that not all the characters or places were conceived complete with their final names, or the final versions of their names: thus one finds Cumnor Manor and Cumnor Hall for the first edition's Cumnor Place, Sir Hubert or Sir Pierce for Sir Hugh Robsart, Haxidence for Holiday, Paulet for Paget (both Paulet and Paget were names of historical characters), and Bolton for Staples.[30] This matter is discussed further in the section 'The Present Text' below.

[14] Finally, there are numerous occasions where the manuscript has been misread or has generated mistakes: these are discussed in the section 'The Present Text' below, and listed in the emendations to the base-text.[31]

3. THE LATER EDITIONS

As shown in the accompanying stemma, or family-tree of editions, the main line of development in the printed text of *Kenilworth* runs from the first edition, through the octavo (8vo) *Historical Romances* which was used as the basis for the Interleaved Set emended and annotated by Scott in 1829–30, to the Magnum Opus edition in which this novel appeared in 1831. The second edition, and the duodecimo (12mo) and 18mo *Historical Romances* are textual dead ends.

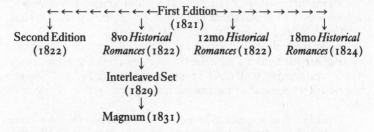

```
 ← ← ← ← ← ← ← ←First Edition→ → → → → → → →
    ↓                  ↓        (1821)       ↓               ↓
Second Edition    8vo Historical    12mo Historical    18mo Historical
  (1822)         Romances (1822)   Romances (1822)    Romances (1824)
                         ↓
                 Interleaved Set
                    (1829)
                         ↓
                  Magnum (1831)
```

The Second Edition. As noted in the first part of this essay, a small second edition of *Kenilworth* was planned almost from the outset. Orders from London were such that by 26 January 1821 Constable was telling Cadell that 1000 extra copies of the first edition had been shipped, and that the novel must go to press again immediately,[32] and his firm wrote to James Ballantyne on 30 January: 'May I beg of you to use all possible exertions to complete the new Edition of Kenilworth 2000 Copies within *three Weeks* as I fear we shall be entirely out of books before it can be ready'.[33] It is probably this new edition which was intimated to John Cumming of Dublin on 27 February as having been completed 'yesterday'.[34] The *Edinburgh Evening Courant* announced the new edition on 3 March.

The second edition generally preserves the pagination and lineation of the first. It has approximately 600 variants from the first, of which ninety are verbal. The variants are fairly evenly distributed, with roughly 200 in each volume. The non-verbal variants are headed by additions (98) and deletions (65) of commas, by changes in spelling (64), and by substitution of semicolons for commas (38). There is a tendency to make the punctuation more formal. The semicolons are often helpful in dividing up sentences, but the effectiveness of the addition and deletion of commas varies. The alterations of spelling are of no importance.

There are many changes affecting dashes, and combinations of punctuation marks including dashes of almost every possible permutation, but these are so isolated as to have no overall effect. Additional areas where the punctuation tends to become a little heavier are the conversion of full stops to question marks (14: two reverse this) or to exclamation marks (seven: one reverses this), and the introduction of new sentences, or capital letters for new clauses (13: two reverse this). Elsewhere there is a rough balance between hard hyphens added (20) and deleted (25, several of these occurring in the course of a determined effort to fillet 'Cumnor-Place' in the final pages); and between raising (17) and lowering (21) of initial letters.

Thirteen of the ninety verbal variants involve words substituted so as to avoid repetitions or, in one case, a recurrent sound, in close proximity. Some eighteen variants result from grammatical or idiomatic correction or standardisation, mostly rather fussy, in line with the move towards formal grammatical punctuation noted above. The remaining verbal variants (apart from a handful of obvious mistakes) are miscellaneous. There are some intelligent corrections, several of which recover the manuscript reading: thus the first word of 'the degrees in the arts' becomes 'thy' as in the manuscript (43.5), and at 329.37–38 the second edition reverts to 'Richard Varney' in place of 'Sir Richard Varney' which is of doubtful appropriateness at that moment. It is quite possible that such readings were recovered spontaneously, but it may be that someone spotted a problem and went back to the manuscript, or the transcript, to resolve the matter. Scott is unlikely to have been involved in these emendations, none of them being beyond the capabilities of a competent intermediary.

The Octavo *Historical Romances*. In a letter of 15 August 1821, Constable suggested to Scott the desirability of a six-volume octavo set, to follow up the success of the *Novels and Tales* and to comprise *Ivanhoe*, *The Monastery, The Abbot*, and *Kenilworth*: 5000 sets would be printed. The title *Historical Romances* was also Constable's suggestion.[35] Scott had no hesitation in accepting on 30 September Constable's offer of £5000 for the copyright of the four novels.[36] Hurst, Robinson and Co. agreed on 19 October to purchase 2700 of this octavo edition, as well as 1620 copies of a duodecimo edition and 5000 copies of an 18mo.[37] On 6 November a memorandum from Constables to James Ballantyne asked for an estimate for 3000 and 3500 octavo and 2000 and 2500 duodecimo, both to be published in March 1822.[38] Actual printing was certainly in progress by 10 January 1822, when Constables rebuked Ballantyne's foreman, Daniel McCorkindale, for using the wrong paper: Ballantynes would just have to 'pay for this blunder of 25 Reams

Paper *spoiled*'.[39] The printing of the octavo edition was too slow for Constables' liking, and on 31 January Cadell wrote intimating that Volumes 5 and 6 would be set and printed elsewhere:

> It is as great a *pang* to me as it must be to you to take any volumes from you—they are done so much to our wish with you—but our book is wanted & must be done—*wherever* it is done—you shall have something else for them during the season that does not call for so urgent dispatch—we are bound to get 8vo Edition out in *March*—you will therefore send me by the bearer Vol V & VI that is to say Abbot all but 31 Pages of 3ᵈ & I shall set it to work forthwith—[40]

Accordingly Volumes 5 and 6 bear the imprint of Walker & Greig, and George Ramsay and Company respectively. Although 3500 copies of the octavo edition were printed[41] vexatious delays continued. On 6 April Cadell wrote to James Ballantyne: 'Do push on the Romances 8vo they are much wanted. the smaller size must be printed so soon as the 8vo is out of your hands—the public are looking anxiously for both of them'.[42] On 24 May Cadell was able to announce to Constable that the octavo edition would be despatched to London the following week.[43] The *Edinburgh Evening Courant* announced the set in 'This day was published' terms on 6 June; the price was £3.12s.

Kenilworth occupies the second half of the fifth volume and all of the sixth and final volume of the octavo *Historical Romances*. At least three compositors can be observed at work. The portion of *Kenilworth* which occupies the second half of the fifth volume, printed by Walker & Greig, of the octavo *Historical Romances* is heavily revised in non-verbal matters, usually in the direction of a more grammatical, rule-based style of punctuation. Many commas are deleted, many others added, and commas are replaced by semicolons. In the first part of the sixth volume, printed by George Ramsay, (up to around page 80, or 175 in the present edition) a different compositor has followed the first edition almost slavishly, with only a handful of variants. In the final part of that volume, there is a return to something approaching the level of variation observable in the fifth volume, with a similar tendency towards the grammatical; but this compositor substitutes a semicolon for a comma only once and prefers the spelling 'enquire' to 'inquire'.

There are rather over 500 variants in all between the first edition and the octavo *Historical Romances* text of *Kenilworth*. All except 17 of these are non-verbal. Some 77 commas are added and 116 deleted; 30 commas become semicolons. Seventeen lower-case letters raised are balanced by 20 upper-case lowered, and 24 hyphens added by 32 deleted. There are some 89 changes in spelling, apostrophes, and other verbal forms. The various permutations of punctuation involving dashes are changed somewhat, without any clear pattern.

Six of the 17 verbal variations are clear errors. Most of the rest involve minor variations in expression, which might be considered tidying up or might be thought of as conventionalising of idiom. Nowhere is Scott's hand to be discerned, though there is a verbal change in the motto at Volume 3, Chapter 4, where 'several courses' becomes 'different courses'. This motto does not appear in the manuscript, and there is no obvious reason for the change.

The Duodecimo *Historical Romances*. The delay afflicting the octavo edition of the *Historical Romances* continued to hold up the duodecimo. On 14 June 1822 Constable told Cadell that he would complain to Ballantyne about this.[44] On 25 June Cadell reported that it was 'very nearly done', having been held up somewhat by *Halidon Hill*.[45] The set featured in an omnibus announcement in the *Edinburgh Evening Courant* on 12 October. The price was three pounds.

There are some 850 variants between the first edition and the duodecimo edition of *Kenilworth*, of which 72 are verbal. In spite of this large number of verbal variants, there is no clear internal evidence of Scott's involvement. The verbal variants are almost all niggling attempts at securing greater smoothness and grammatical correctness. There is a tendency to omit repeated prepositions, and to substitute 'a' for 'an' or vice-versa. Many of the verbal changes seem arbitrary, with no observable gain: 'upon' for 'on' (19.24); 'plighted' for 'pledged' (274.36). There is a handful of undeniable corrections. None of the new readings in the duodecimo text could be described as inspired or creative. The nearest one comes to creativity is the substitution of 'running' for 'so willing to rush' (91.22), to avoid an anticipation of 'so willing' three lines later.

The non-verbal changes are headed by 250 alterations in spelling or in apostrophes within words. The spelling changes include repeated alterations of 'chuse' to 'choose', 'faulter' to 'falter', and 'groupe' to 'group'. The apostrophes in such words as 'did'st' and 'may'st' usually disappear. Commas are the most common mark of punctuation to be altered (139 are added, and 81 deleted), and there are the usual changes to hard hyphens (45 added and 14 deleted), and capitals (37 initial letters raised and 15 lowered). On 53 occasions a dash following closing quotation marks in direct speech is made to precede them. A hallmark of this edition is the changing of sixteen commas to exclamation marks, and there are the usual apparently random changes affecting combinations of punctuation marks including dashes.

The 18mo *Historical Romances*. From the outset it was planned to print 5000 of the 'miniature edition', the 18mo.[46] This intention was confirmed on several occasions and on 11 July 1822 Constable wrote to Scott stating that 5000 copies were to be printed by 1 October 1823.[47] But there were further delays, so that it was not until 22 January 1824 that the *Edinburgh Evening Courant* announced the set as '*Nearly ready*'. Although the first three volumes were printed by Ballantyne, the last three were given to J. Moyes of London, who had problems in obtaining the new type necessary.[48]

The 18mo text shows some 2600 variants from the first edition. This large number is principally accounted for by the systematic lowering of the upper-case initial letters of words such as 'Earl' and 'Queen', which accounts for almost exactly half the variants. Some 176 commas are added and 227 deleted. There are some 290 changes of spelling, on the same lines as the 12mo edition. Forty-eight commas are changed to exclamation marks, and even more strikingly 164 commas become semicolons (21, 52, and 91 in the three volumes respectively). Twenty-six hyphens are added and 78 deleted. There are only 32 verbal changes; none are of any originality, most being minor adjustments ('a' to 'an' and vice versa is the most frequent), and some are clear errors. The usual scattered changes affecting combinations of punctuation involving dashes and other punctuation marks can be observed.

The Interleaved Set and the Magnum. The full story of the making of the Magnum Opus is told in Jane Millgate's *Scott's Last Edition* (Edinburgh, 1987), and the Interleaved Set of the Waverley Novels in which Scott wrote all his notes and textual revisions for the final edition to be published in his lifetime is described in *Scott's Interleaved Waverley Novels*, ed. Iain G. Brown (Aberdeen, 1987). For *Kenilworth* it was a copy of the octavo edition of *Historical Romances* which was interleaved for Scott's use. Scott had revised *Kenilworth* in this set by January 1830, and Robert Cadell transcribed his emendations (and no doubt did a good deal of revising—his term—of his own) between 26 April and 25 May. Scott added further details during the summer of that year before the two volumes (23 and 24) were stereotyped. They were published on 1 March and 1 April 1831.[49] The variants noted above as characteristic of the octavo edition mostly persist from the Interleaved Set into the Magnum. Apart from new notes (both footnotes and notes designed to appear at the end of chapters), Scott makes some 160 alterations, mostly verbal. Between the Interleaved Set and the Magnum some 2200 other alterations were made, approximately 380 of them verbal.

Of Scott's alterations in the Interleaved Set[50] roughly one third appear to have been made in the interests of greater clarity, accuracy, or logic: so, he changes 'a Cornish flaw' into 'a Cornish flaw ↑ of wind ↓' (34.2–3); the Cumnor-Hall curtains now prevent 'the ↑ slightest gleam of↓ radiance from being seen without' (46.16); Elizabeth asks 'Is this a royal garrison, my Lord of Sussex ↑ that it holds so many pikes and calivres ↓?' (149.32–33); and 'the constant hope and theme of all enemies to Elizabeth' becomes 'the constant hope and theme of ↑ encouragement to↓ all enemies to Elizabeth' (167.17–18). Some 25 alterations were made to eliminate verbal repetitions in the usual way, and some fifteen involve grammatical corrections, including the alteration of 'we (I) will' to 'we (I) shall' in speech—applying a distinction that belongs to the period of the compositors rather than the characters (165.26; 276.42). There are a dozen additions of the 'said so-and-so' type, with and without characterisation, and a handful made in the interests of stylistic improvement or vividness. Among the most effective of the latter is the alteration of 'he minded his whine' to 'he minded the poor tyke's whine' (113.34). Alterations of the sense are very rare. One such occurs at 134.25 where 'with hearts as light as our purses' becomes 'with heavy hearts and light purses', and the 'Yes' at 234.11 becomes 'No'. The most interesting changes are those where Scott adds substantially to the octavo text. The added notes will appear in full in the final volumes of the Edinburgh Edition, but there were, as well, several significant additions to the Interleaved Set text. For instance, at 50.1–2, Amy's features 'had been sometimes censured ↑ (as beauty as well as art has her minute critics) ↓ for being rather too pale'. After 'mine own.' (65.11) Scott inserts:

—What was ⟨Tom⟩ Thomas Cromwell but a smith's son and he died my Lord—on a scaffold doubtless but that too was in character—And what was Ralph Sadler but the clerk of Cromwell and he has gazed ⟨eihgh⟩ eighteen fair Lordships—via! I know my steerage as well as they

A paragraph based on material furnished by William Hamper was inserted in the description of Kenilworth, following 'the occasion.' (302.33):

The livery cupboards were loaded with plate of the richest description and the most varied some tasteful some perhaps grotesque in the invention and decoration but all gorgeously magnificent both from the ⟨beauty of th⟩ richness of the work and value of the materials Thus the chief table was adornd by a salt ship-fashion made of mother of pearl garnishd with silver and divers warlike ensigns and other ornaments anckors sails sixteen pieces of ordnance. It bore a figure of fortune placed on a globe with ⟨two⟩? a flag in her hand Another salt was fashiond of silver in the form of a swan in full sail. That chivalry might not be omitted amid this splendour a silver Saint George was presented mounted and equipd in the usual fashion in which he bestrides the dragon. The figures were moulded to be in sort useful. The horse's tail was managed to hold a case of knives while the breast of the dragon presented a similar accomodation for oyster knives

An added sentence after 'withdrew me.' at 332.37 adds to Amy's deathward inclination: 'Then—have but a little patience and Amy's life will not long darken your brighter prospects'. A sentence describing the Kenilworth entertainment is substantially expanded: 'They then marched completely round the hall, in order the more fully to display themselves, ↑ regulating their steps to Organs shalms hautboys & virginals the loud music of the Lord Leicesters household At length the

four quadrilles of masquers ↓ ranging their torch-bearers behind them
...' (350.4–6).

Scott was prompted to introduce a handful of non-verbal alterations
into the Interleaved Set text: he italicises 'can' at 29.35 and possibly
'thou' at 225.7; he changes a full stop to a question mark in 'You have
this day seen Tressilian?' (53.4–5) and in 'I may secure it on the
inside?' (386.31–32), and possibly (the ink is strange) a comma to a
question mark plus dash to make 'Why—why?—' (225.10: Magnum
rejects the dash). Commas become dashes on two occasions: in
'"Millenium is the reign of the Saints—" said Foster, somewhat doubtfully' (228.13–14: Magnum has a comma before the quotation marks
and a dash after them); and in '"It might, indeed, so have been—" said
the Earl, with an involuntary sigh' (303.39–40). A dash is added to a
semicolon in 'Be still, these loud strains suit me not;—and the voice of
the meanest peasant...' (309.37–38: Magnum rejects the dash). Scott
inserts a new paragraph at 202.14: 'It was'.

No proof sheets of the Magnum version of *Kenilworth* are known to
have survived, but there are 380 or so verbal variants in the Magnum as
against the Interleaved Set. These alterations were probably made in the
proofs. It is not known to what extent, if at all, Scott was involved in the
processing of the Magnum text after the Interleaved Set, but it is almost
certain that Robert Cadell was much involved in proof-reading tidying.
There is a sharp diminution in the number of these changes in the final
volume: some 160 in the first volume, some 130 in the second, and only
some 90 in the third. This, like the similar diminution in the verbal
changes in first edition proofs noted above, may suggest a weariness or
hastiness as the task approached its close. The nature of many of the
verbal alterations corresponds closely to that of the Interleaved Set
variants. Over a quarter may be categorised as grammatical, of the usual
sort. Roughly eighty are designed to eliminate repetitions. Some 25
result in increased clarity, accuracy, or logic, and the same number
involve clear corrections. There is a handful of stylistic improvements. A
large number of this set of verbal variants is accounted for by the systematic introduction of preferred forms of words: e.g. 'folk' for 'folks',
'whatever' for 'whatsoever', 'towards' for 'toward', and 'besides' for
'beside'. Here at any rate the hand of Cadell the tidier may be discerned
with reasonable certainty.

Over 1800 non-verbal variants were introduced in the Magnum.
Some 650 of these were preferred spellings: e.g. 'antechamber',
'dependent', 'dost', 'enquire', 'group', 'mayst', and 'show'. Over 100
commas were deleted, but more than 350 were added, making the
Magnum the most heavily punctuated edition of this novel, moving
strongly in the direction of a more formal style of punctuation. Some 55
hard hyphens were added, mostly in place names, and some 165 deleted. Approximately 120 exclamation marks were added, mostly in

place of full stops (90) and commas (25). Raisings and lowerings of initial letters roughly balanced each other, and there was the usual bewildering variety of alterations involving punctuational combinations including dashes.

Although variants from the second edition and from the duodecimo and 18mo *Historical Romances* occasionally reappear in the Magnum, there is no reason to suppose that this is other than coincidental. The Magnum is the product of a clear, if unreliable, line of transmission running from manuscript through proof and first edition to the octavo *Historical Romances*, then to the Interleaved Set and the Magnum proofs.

4. THE PRESENT TEXT

Just over four months elapsed between Scott's writing the first words of *Kenilworth* and its publication. Transcriber or transcribers, compositors and other printing house staff, and James Ballantyne were working under considerable pressure, and no doubt (for it was autumn) often in dubious light. It was inevitable that these intermediaries should make many mistakes, and since Scott was also working under pressure correcting proofs as well as continuing to write the novel (not to mention his numerous other activities) it was inevitable also that many of those mistakes should go uncorrected, or be corrected imperfectly. The aim of the present editorial process is to produce a text as close as possible to what Scott and his intermediaries would have achieved had they been able to devote the requisite time to the task.

Punctuation and Capitalisation. The most pervasive contribution of the intermediaries was the translation of Scott's manuscript punctuation, sentence structure, and orthography into an acceptable printed system. This was mainly the job of the compositors, although others would have been involved, and in the case of *Kenilworth* they executed their task with considerable skill. What they achieved in narrative is almost entirely acceptable, and it is only in direct speech that their punctuation at times distorts the rhetorical shaping suggested by Scott himself. In the main, the present edition accepts their work, which involved something of the order of 50,000 tiny changes to the manuscript, most notably the insertion of punctuation marks. It gives a text which is very much of its time in its mixture of grammatical and rhetorical elements. It is more fluid and less rigid than the Magnum or, still more, the Victorian editions deriving from the Magnum, and thus may be held to be ultimately truer to Scott's minimally punctuated manuscript than the texts which have been generally read over the last hundred years. Readers of the present edition should follow contemporaneous practice and treat the punctuation as indicative rather than prescriptive.

Notwithstanding the Edinburgh Edition's policy of accepting first-edition punctuation in general, every punctuational sign and sentence division in the first-edition text has been examined to ascertain that it does not distort or unnecessarily restrict Scott's apparent intention as evidenced in the particulars of the manuscript. Although the intermediaries clearly had authority to lower or raise initial capital letters, on some fifty occasions one of Scott's numerous manuscript initial capital letters lowered in the first edition has been restored in the present text where it is clear that something has been lost: thus, the 'Guilty' at 31.34 parodies the majesty of the law; the 'great Magician Love' (48.37) conveys rather more than the 'great magician Love'; the 'City' of London is different from the 'city' (127.27, 147.32); the clutch of capitals employed by Lambourne, 'let Leicester be King if he will—good—and Varney, Villain Varney, grand Vizier—why, excellent,—And what shall I be then? —Why, Emperor—Emperor Lambourne' (207.36–39), is indicative of his ruffling manner; and certain prominent personifications such as 'Truth' at 53.42 would appear to require Scott's initial capital for their full effect. On a handful of occasions eccentric manuscript capitals which survived into the first edition have been lowered.

More importantly, in nearly 500 cases the first edition altered sentence divisions, as indicated by full-stops and/or capital letters; in these cases either the manuscript reading itself has been restored, or the editors have produced a reading which the intermediaries would have arrived at if they had interpreted the manuscript a little more sensitively and faithfully. The main issue involved may be illustrated by reference to a speech of Sir Hugh Robsart (116.13–15). In manuscript this begins:

> "True true old friend" said Sir Hugh "and we will bear our trials manfully—we have lost but a woman—see Tressilian"—he drew from his bosom a long ringlet of fair hair—"See this lock—I tell thee ..."

In the first edition this is punctuated thus:

> "True, true, old friend," said Sir Hugh, "and we will bear our trials manfully—We have lost but a woman.—See, Tressilian,"—he drew from his bosom a long ringlet of fair hair,—"see this lock!—I tell thee ..."

In general the intermediary has done a competent job here. The added commas are in the heavily punctuated public style of the period and the exclamation mark after 'lock' is acceptable heightening. The reversal of the manuscript lower and upper case to read 'See ... see' is also acceptable, indicating the change of addressee. However, significantly, and quite unnecessarily, the alteration of 'we' to 'We' changes the movement that Scott must have heard with his inner ear as he wrote. When something of this sort has been lost, the present edition normally restores the manuscript punctuation. A

further example may be given. At 95.7–10 Dickie Sludge says to Tressilian in the manuscript version:

> "Me fear him!" answerd the boy "if he were the devil folks think
> him I would not fear him but ↑ though there is something queer
> about him ↓ he's no more a devil than you are And thats what I
> would not tell to everyone."

The first edition reads 'you are, and', failing to retain the force of the
separate final utterance which appears in the present text as a new
sentence.

When an intermediary has failed to observe a significant manuscript
indicator of the movement of Scott's prose, but has still provided an
acceptable punctuation mark such as a question mark or an exclamation
mark, the present edition adopts a composite reading. Thus at
68.34–36 Scott writes in the manuscript:

> "That were ruin" said Foster his brow darkening with apprehen-
> sion "and all this for a woman—had it been for his souls sake it
> were something …"

In the first edition this becomes:

> "That were ruin," said Foster, his brow darkening with apprehen-
> sion; "and all this for a woman!—Had it been for his soul's sake, it
> were something …"

The exclamation mark is acceptable heightening, but the capitalising of
'Had' spoils the continuity of speech that Scott evidently intended: the
present text reads 'woman!—had'. At 12.35–37 the manuscript version
of Lambourne's speech runs:

> "What so they hung poor Pranc high and dry—so much for loving
> to walk by moonlight—a cup to his memory my masters All merry
> fellows like moonlight …"

The first edition interprets this as follows:

> "What, so they hung poor Prance high and dry? so much for loving
> to walk by moonlight—a cup to his memory my masters—all merry
> fellows like moonlight …"

This is generally effective, but the inserted dash before 'all' does not
quite suggest the pledge as the manuscript does. In this case the present
edition retains the first edition dash and restores the manuscript 'All'. In
narrative the first edition punctuation is normally entirely satisfactory: it
is only in speech that such distortions become significant. Similarly,
changes of case between upper and lower when speeches are resumed
after 'said so-and-so' are not usually felt to be unfaithful to Scott's
implied movement. On a handful of occasions it has been felt to be
preferable to leave a slight distortion in the base-text rather than risk
disrupting a carefully constructed first-edition punctuational hierarchy.

Verbal Emendations. It is clear that the intermediaries were expected
to make many changes in addition to punctuation. They were instructed
to operate a set of standing orders involving the following procedures:

changing words repeated in close proximity to each other; elimination of Scotticisms in narrative and in the speech of non-Scots; correction of clear grammatical errors; substitution of nouns or proper names for pronouns (particularly at the beginning of paragraphs); insertion of speech indicators; and addition of appropriate (usually single) words to fill obvious lacunae left by Scott in his haste. When correcting proofs Scott continued these procedures as well as introducing substantial changes to the sense and many additional passages (passages were rarely deleted), stylistic improvements, major clarifications of narrative business, and additional 'said so-and-so's for unallocated speeches.

Author's proofs, when they survive, provide an invaluable basis for determining what the intermediaries did between receiving the parcels of manuscript and sending Scott the proofs incorporating in-house corrections. One can see what Scott himself changed in those second proofs; occasionally revises are extant and make it possible to follow his further corrections and revisions with some certainty.

In general the Edinburgh Edition accepts changes to the manuscript resulting from the application of standing orders, though in the not infrequent cases where the rules have been applied mechanically or pedantically, or where their use has created unforeseen problems (such as generating new repetitions), the manuscript reading is restored. Scott's own changes in proof are of course accepted except in a handful of cases where his intervention resulted in problems that he did not notice. Changes made by intermediaries which are not in accordance with the presumed standing orders are normally rejected, as are those which result from their mechanical and insensitive application.

In the case of *Kenilworth*, no proofs are known to survive. However, as observed above, the early American editions provide the equivalent of uncorrected second proofs for the final ninth of the novel. Analysis of the American text makes it clear that the same procedures which operated in novels with surviving proofs were applied to *Kenilworth*. Of the 120-odd verbal changes introduced before American/second-proof stage, roughly half are in accordance with standing orders and most of these are accepted in the present text, whereas half appear to result from a misreading of the manuscript or from unjustifiable attempts to correct it. It is possible by examining the differences between manuscript and first edition in the rest of the novel to judge with a reasonable degree of assurance and confidence which changes are likely to have been made by Scott himself, or by intermediaries acting in accordance with standing orders, and which have been introduced without authority or simply as the result of error.

In addition to the 550-odd emendations to punctuation and capital-isation, 1500 verbal emendations to the first-edition base-text have been made. Inevitably, some of these emendations will inadvertently restore manuscript readings changed by Scott in the lost proofs; but the number will be small, and the reader may be confident that the present text is much closer to Scott's ideal in 1821 than any hitherto achieved. The emendations may be divided for convenience into seven classes.

1] *Misreadings.* The most obvious reason for emendation is that the transcriber has misread a word in the manuscript. In Scott's hand certain small words are difficult to distinguish from each other: 'in'/'on', 'these'/'those', 'the'/'this', 'when'/'where', 'the'/'her'/'his', and so forth. The restoration of Scott's intended word in some 70 such cases is usually a minor matter, but occasionally the effect can be telling: most notably, Lord Hunsdon's centinel 'would rather keep watch in [not 'on'] a snowdrift, in the wastes of Catlowdie' (329.24–25). The other persistent cause of minor misreadings is the omission or addition of final '-s', accounting for over 60 emendations.

A rather larger number of cases involve more significant misreadings of individual words: the Cornish proverb is not 'south' but 'sooth' (11.22); Cicely is not a 'light' girl but a 'tight' one (19.43); Lambourne proposes to pass not a 'trick' but a 'carreer' (badly formed in manuscript) on Tony (20.29); Forster advises him to wear his falling band 'unrufled' ('without ruffles'), not 'unrumpled' (30.10); it is Lambourne's 'cue' (badly formed), not his 'duty' to say ay (71.20); on his first appearance Dick Sludge comes 'tumbling', not 'stumbling' into the room (92.35); Wayland is 'besmirchd', not 'besmeared' with soot and charcoal (125.22); Elizabeth 'chimd' rather than 'cap'd' verses with Raleigh (151.12); Amy's veins swell through the hurried impulse of 'the circulation', not 'her articulation' (220.31); Varney's doings would have 'gaind', not 'given' him the preferment of a gallows (222.27); Lambourne speaks proprietorially of 'our', not 'your' old haunted room at Kenilworth (274.9); in the motto from *The Winter's Tale* (334.16) Scott correctly wrote 'She's an adultress', but this was misread as 'This is' and the misreading persisted through to the Dryburgh edition;[51] Leicester, deceived by Varney, calls Amy not 'woman' but 'wanton' (339.15); Tressilian's masquing mantle is not 'short' but 'sheer' (352.18); Leicester experiences not 'sense' but 'scenes' of meditated cruelty, with more powerful effect (354.5); and Forster is invited to endow not a 'lecture-shop' but a prosaic 'lectureship' (380.43–381.1).

2] *Wrong insertions and omissions.* Since Scott often inadvertently omits single words and it was one of the functions of the intermediaries to fill the gaps, it is hardly surprising that they sometimes imagined gaps where none existed, usually as a result of failing to recognise idioms. The editorial team has constantly been surprised to find support in the *Oxford English Dictionary* for unusual idioms, often obsolete in Scott's time and employed as part of the period effect by an author steeped in the vernacular of the Elizabethan and Jacobean periods. Restoration of such idioms, especially when they occur in speech, adds considerably to the novel's stylistic vividness. The intermediaries also frequently

omitted words for no apparent good reason, usually either through simple eye-slip or again because of failure to recognise idioms. The total number of occasions when words have been unnecessarily added or deleted, together with other examples of unrecognised idioms, is approximately 250: in each case the present text restores the manuscript reading.

In the following examples one or more words were inserted unnecessarily, probably because of failure to recognise an idiom: 'every lash which he laid on ↑ thee, ↓ he always was wont to say↑, he ↓ spared the hangman a labour' (8.4–5); 'to pledge ↑ him to ↓ a sentiment' (17.1); 'think'st thou I am ↑ an ↓ infidel...?' (20.7); 'I will not have my child's soul committed ↑ to peril↓ either for your pleasure or my lord's' (40.11–12); 'it is not the shutting thy doors and windows to keep her from flying off, that may deserve ↑ it↓' (41.11–13); 'Look out at ↑ the ↓ window' (44.36); 'I wish him not ↑ to↓ be judge' (56.3–4); 'they approached the ↑ chair of↓ state' (57.30); 'can this madman ... ↑ know↓ aught like good skill of his trade?' (91.41–42); 'it avails not to deny ↑ it↓' (223.8); 'to hang me as high as ↑ St↓ Paul's' (239.28); Amy's 'heart, unaccustomed to such splendour, sank as if died within ↑ her↓' (257.1–2); 'Madam, I speak it ↑ in↓ earnest' (330.38); 'they should all ↑ do↓ homage' (351.15); 'too eager to rid ↑ me of↓ this obstacle' (355.24).

The unnecessary addition of words can impair the sense or style in ways other than idiomatic, as in the following examples: 'piles of withered brushwood, which had been lopped from ↑ the ↓ trees cut down in the neighbouring park' (21.34–36); 'a sense that ↑ the↓ countenance shown to any one of Sussex's household, was, in fact, a triumph to the whole' (180.13–15); 'the patron who had ↑ at↓ first employed him in her service' (265.9).

In the following examples, one or more words were unnecessarily omitted, probably because of failure to recognise an idiom: 'Mr Melchisidec Maultext ... illustrated the ⟨use of the⟩ same by the conduct of an honourable person present, meaning me' (28.26–30); 'It has cut ⟨a⟩ many' (38.10); 'it is ⟨a⟩ chance if he knows you' (114.8); 'left the Queen's barge to go on board ⟨of⟩ my Lord Burleigh's' (173.2–3); 'we have beheld ⟨a⟩ many' (174.42); 'I had never more need ⟨than⟩ that the heavenly bodies should befriend me' (185.5–6); 'grudge not ⟨at⟩ a little seclusion' (188.23); 'were I myself in such ⟨a⟩ perplexity' (213.35–36); 'she must have friends within the castle, ⟨to⟩ whose advice and assistance she could safely trust' (248.31–32); 'with what ⟨a⟩ grace she took the fair-wrought purse' (253.16–17); 'first take ⟨the⟩ farewell of Richard Varney' (345.10).

Deterioration of a non-idiomatic kind resulting from omissions can be observed in the following: 'he must have ruffling swordsmen, who would fight the devil when he is raised and at the wildest—And above all, ⟨but⟩ without prejudice to ⟨the⟩ others, he must have such godly, innocent, puritanic souls as thou' (42.25–28); 'barring only those requests which I cannot and dare not ⟨now⟩ grant' (67.15–16); 'I know ⟨him—⟩ his dotage on one face is as brief as it is deep', where the status of the following clause is also affected (68.11–12); 'patients and disciples, who doubtless thought his long and mysterious absences from his ordinary residence in the town of Farringdon were occasioned by his progress in the mystic sciences, and ⟨facilitated by⟩ his intercourse with the invisible world' (104.5–9); 'My debtors would not pay me money ⟨perhaps⟩, . . . but my creditors of every kind would be less easily blinded' (105.28–30); 'the ⟨most⟩ constant use of violent exercise' (114.40–41); 'Wayland Smith . . . felt the temples of the Earl slightly, from time to time, attending ⟨also⟩ particularly to the state of respiration' (137.16–18); 'The Earl and his follower bowed low, and raised their heads ⟨slowly⟩, without daring to look at the Queen, or at each other' (165.31–32); 'I will, with her Majesty's leave, relinquish for an hour, that which ⟨all⟩ her subjects hold dearest, the delight of her Highness's presence' (172.30–32); 'The verses were not probably new to the Queen, for when was ever such elegant flattery ⟨so⟩ long in reaching the royal ear to which it was addressed?' (176.40–42); 'if ↑I↓ give thee not a Rowland for thine Oliver, ⟨say⟩ my name is not Dickon Sludge' (248.12–13); 'the happiness of those who ⟨can⟩ enjoy a humble lot in virtuous contentment' (255.13–14); 'I require no aid, ⟨Master⟩ Tressilian' (269.39, where Amy's unusually formal mode of address suits her feeling at that moment).

Even the inadvertent inclusion of a deleted 'and' could have serious consequences. The catastrophe (389.39–43) reads as follows in the manuscript:

> In less than two minutes Foster who remaind behind heard the tread of a horse in the courtyard with a whistle similar to that which was the Earls usual signal & the instant after the door of the Countess's chamber opend ⟨and⟩ the trap-door gave way—there was a rushing sound—a heavy fall—a faint groan and all was over

In the first edition the passage was rendered as follows:

> In less than two minutes, Foster, who remained behind, heard the tread of a horse in the courtyard, and then a whistle similar to that which was the Earl's usual signal;—the instant after the door of the Countess's chamber opened, and in the same moment the trap-door gave way. There was a rushing sound—a heavy fall—a faint groan—and all was over.

The transcriber inadvertently included the deleted 'and'. It is probable that Scott saw the resulting sentence as unsatisfactory and inserted in proof (it does not appear in the early American editions) 'in the same moment' before 'the trap-door', deleted the 'and' before 'the instant', and changed the earlier 'with' to 'and then', so that this crucial scene lost much of the force that it has in the manuscript. The parallel phrases, separated only by a dash, present Amy's death in a starkly simple way; the effect is destroyed by the more complex grammar of the first edition.

In a handful of cases phrases or complete manuscript sentences were omitted without any apparent good reason: passages restored in the present text are reproduced in the emendation list for 22.28, 41.19–20, 108.43–109.5 (where the eye has jumped to the second 'withal'), 178.19–21, 224.24–25, 337.22 (making sense of a passage where the eye jumped to the second 'Leicester'), and 360.13. Further, a few passages which seem to have been cut deliberately for a non-literary purpose have been restored; for instance, at 88.15 Erasmus Holiday added, after *'fœnum habet in cornu'*, 'oats shall also be forthcoming', a typically pedantic utterance, but one which may well have suggested an unconscious *double entendre* to James Ballantyne, who was sensitive to such matters on the reader's behalf.

3] *Wrong substitutions.* Idioms were sometimes lost through the substitution of words rather than insertion or omission: 'connect myself ⟨with⟩ ↑in↓ a matter of this dark and perilous nature' (84.34–35); 'answer, ⟨at⟩ ↑in↓ a word and in English' (88.2–3); 'I think ... that ⟨so a poor⟩ ↑when so poor a↓ man does his day's job, he might be permitted to work it out after his own fashion' (99.28–31); 'about three years ⟨hence⟩ ↑since↓' (100.42–43); 'attended ⟨with⟩ ↑by↓ two or three ladies' (143.35); 'I will not be elbowed out ⟨on⟩ ↑of↓ it' (151.14–15); 'the happy period shall be ⟨approachd⟩ ↑brought↓ nearer to us' (227.42–43); 'she weighed them for a second in her hand, as ⟨who should⟩ ↑she would↓ say, I hope they be avoirdupois' (253.20–22); 'Tressilian ... looked ⟨on⟩ ↑at↓ them both' (283.1); 'a distinguished ornament ⟨to⟩ ↑of↓ the rank which she held' (332.12–13); 'Leicester threw ⟨from⟩ his tablets ↑from him↓' (335.27).

The intermediaries frequently changed words for synonyms or near synonyms. The reason was usually to eliminate verbal repetitions, but quite often there is no obvious purpose. Such cases have been restored to the manuscript readings, a handful of which are particularly noteworthy: 'he observed the ⟨deadly paleness⟩ ↑emotion↓ of his countenance' (180.39–40); 'I will see these revels—these princely ⟨pleasures⟩ ↑revels↓' (233.26–27); 'He ascended as [MS: so] high as the suspicious spot—there was no shadow on the wall—he ascended a few ⟨steps⟩ ↑yards↓ higher—the door was still ajar' (277.16–18, where the intermediary has had problems with the spiral staircase). These substitutions, together with other cases where the first-edition readings are so clearly inferior to those of the manuscript that an intermediary's unfortunate intervention is highly likely, account for some 150 emendations.

On a handful of occasions a word was found too particular or difficult, or perhaps even incomprehensible. 'Cumber' and 'cumbering' were changed to 'Concern' and 'busying' (20.3, 39.29)[52] and 'close' yielded to 'struggle' (35.40). In the manuscript and the present text Varney pursues 'courses' rather than 'projects' (50.22); Amy talks of her own 'seem[i]ng', not her 'person' (57.29); Varney says Lambourne will 'abye' rather than 'repent' a possible deception (70.14); Holiday characteristically uses the verb 'concording' rather than the usual 'according' (90.25); Dickie Sludge talks of an orchard of 'pippins', not 'apples' (97.40); in a famous utterance Sir Hugh Robsart says that 'This grief is to my bewilderd mind what the church of Lidcote is to our South wood', not 'to our park', at once more touchingly specific and more appropriate to the following 'briars and thickets' (116.36–38); Tressilian presents a 'placet' rather than a 'Supplication' to the Queen (151.39); Sussex does not refer to the 'Bear-garden' in general but to the specific 'Parish-garden' in Southwark (174.28); Lambourne's oath is not 'odds blades and poniards' but 'oddspittikins' (193.40–41: MS 'oddspitlekens'); Gosling says not 'marvel' but 'marle', which Scott has written with great deliberation (201.20); Varney talks of Forster's leasehold being 'transmewd' not 'transmuted' into a copyhold (227.2); and Leicester's head can fall only by the 'censure', not the 'sentence' of his peers (322.22).

In addition to these substituted words there are some fifty examples where Scott's preferred forms of particular words (which are not always consistent) are changed: 'amongst' to 'among', and permutations of the alternative forms of '(a)round', '(in)to', 'toward(s)', 'forward(s)', and so forth. Changes between 'thou' and 'you' have normally been rejected: Scott was at best a quarter-hearted reviser in this area, often prompted by James Ballantyne to make unnecessary changes.

There will no doubt be occasions where, in the absence of dictionary support, an intermediary's substitution or addition has been unnecessarily accepted and a valid idiom lost. A few examples where the base-text has been accepted in the absence of such confirmation will indicate the type of readings involved in such cases: 'he was wont to boast ⟨on⟩ ↑of↓ it' (13.11–12); 'he took ↑a↓ final farewell' (67.18); 'an the master be like ↑the↓ men' (74.35–36); 'Fill ↑the↓ flaggon, Master Tapster' (198.42–43); 'the Earl started from his seat, and ran to the window, ⟨with⟩ ↑in↓ the momentary purpose of recalling the unworthy commission' (215.6–8); 'all the additional security she could think ↑of↓' (310.6–7); 'to pick up the unfortunate warriors↑, and convey them↓ to the dry land' (364.34–35).

4] *Mechanical elimination of repetitions.* The elimination of ugly repetition was one of the standing orders, but sometimes this was done mechanically, so that effective rhetorical repetition disappeared. An example can be found in Varney's speech at 184.3–7 which reads in manuscript:

"... Had Mary had the hap to have wedded a noble Earl once
destind to Share her throne she had found a husband of different

> metal and her husband had found in her a wife as complying and
> loving as the mate of the meanest squire . . . "

The first edition substitutes 'experienced' for the first 'found', diminishing the effect. A narrative example occurs at 195.23–26, where the
manuscript has:

> A lively bustling arch fellow whose pack and oaken *ell-wand*
> studded duly with brass points denoted him to be of Autolycus's
> profession occupied a good deal of the attention and furnishd a
> good deal of the amusement of the evening.

The first edition changes the second 'a good deal' to 'much', missing the
rhetorical point. Sometimes repetitions appeared between manuscript
and first edition, and these are eliminated in the present text. Decisions
to restore repetitions in order to recover rhetorical effect have been
carefully weighed, but some 200 emendations of this kind have been
accepted nonetheless.

5] *Faulty corrections.* When the intermediaries were confronted with
error in the manuscript or subsequent versions of the text they often
coped well, but inevitably they sometimes failed to correct the error
satisfactorily, on some occasions introducing further error, or acting less
economically than they ideally should have done. At 59.33–35 Scott
wrote: 'I gave the most unbounded order and methinks they have been
indifferently well obeyd'. The intermediary changed 'they have' to 'it
has' rather than making 'order' plural, a more economical procedure
that has the additional advantage of preserving Scott's second thought in
the process of composition. The manuscript version of 102.5–7 reads:
'But will you not taste a stoup of liquor, I promise you that even in this
poor cell I have in store'. Here the intermediary changes the comma to a
question mark and inserts 'some' before 'in', rather than keeping the
comma and reading 'liquor, which I promise you', again a more economical procedure retaining more of Scott's manuscript version. An
intermediary was faced with a gap on 132.29–30 where the manuscript
reads: 'the unhappy Dudley Duke of Northumberland—executed on
Towerhill in   '. The first edition reads 'Tower-Hill, August 22,
1553'. This precise date is out of place, and all that was necessary was
for '1553' to be inserted. At 308.23–25 the manuscript has: 'The
fatigue of body which she had lately undergone joind the agitation of
mind natural to so cruel a state of uncertainty began by degrees ⟨strog⟩
strongly to affect her nerves'. Here the intermediary has substituted
'with' for 'joind', but in this case he has been too economical, since Scott
clearly intended his text to read 'joined with'. The manuscript reads at
386.37–40: 'they crossd a short wooden gallery . . . at the farther end of
which was a strong oaken door which opend admitted them into the
misers apartment'. The intermediary inserted 'and' after 'opend', producing an odd picture of a self-opening door. The manuscript as it
stands is conceivable but hardly what Scott intended, and the preferred

solution is therefore to print 'which, when opened, admitted them'. A few lines later (387.1–2) Scott wrote 'without either offering or permitting the attendance of the had who had carried it'. He clearly intended to write 'hag' for the first 'had', but the intermediary substituted 'old woman'.

6] *Problems with names.* Scott often had trouble with the names of his characters. Sometimes he changed the names completely. It seems likely that in several cases the choice of an actual spelling was made not by Scott but by an intermediary. On his early appearances the Queen's physician Master is spelt correctly in the manuscript, but he appears as 'Masters' from the outset in the first edition. Scott eventually adopts this spelling, presumably to avoid having to revise those earlier parts of the text which were already printed; the present edition restores the historically correct spelling. Forster alternates between that historically correct form and 'Foster' in the early pages of the manuscript, and it is probable that an intermediary made the wrong choice which Scott then followed; 'Forster' is restored in the present text. Although Goldthread was originally 'Twineall', one can detect in the early occurrences of the new name a preference for 'Goldthread' rather than the printed 'Goldthred'. Scott prefers the spelling 'Laurence' to 'Lawrence', which is here restored for the Christian names of Goldthread and Staples. The early appearance of 'Mumblazon' suggests that Scott's predominant concept was of a name ending in '-on' rather than the first edition's '-en'.

7] *Miscellaneous.* Further errors, of a more miscellaneous nature, made by intermediaries and corrected in the present text may be observed in the list of emendations. They include: transposition of words; unnecessary alteration of tenses; inappropriate italicisation, though italicisation for emphasis is normally accepted as part of the standing orders; and a handful of spelling changes where there is deterioration of the sense in the first-edition base-text.

In a very limited number of cases the present text corrects clear errors of fact either for the first time, or at the prompting of editions subsequent to the first. Richard Laneham becomes Robert at 245.5 as he is correctly elsewhere. Mervyn's tower is at the north-west corner of the castle, not the north-east (263.14). Since the dukedom of Rutland was not created until 1703 the Countess of Rutland, correctly designated on her first appearance (150.31), is not permitted in the present text to assume the title of Duchess in the course of the novel (300.34, 301.1 etc., as in the emendation list). Elizabeth was never Leicester's 'host' in his own castle: 'guest' is clearly required (375.18).

A small number of emendations have been introduced to solve particular problems. Scott's additions in manuscript gave rise to some of these. At 91.20 a verso addition 'But the interruption pleased not the Magister' has been taken into the text too early before 'O cæca mens hominum!'; it reappears at 91.28–29, occasioning a further addition in proof. A simple return to the manuscript solves this problem. Scott's decision to introduce a chapter break at 102.15–16 after composing part of what turned out to be the new chapter has led to Volume 1, Chapter 11 beginning 'The artist resumed his narrative'; after inserting on the opposing verso the final two paragraphs of Chapter 10 and the motto from Chaucer for the new chapter, Scott forgot that Wayland, unlike the author, had not yet begun his story. This is easily rectified by omitting the words 'his narrative'. At 140.11–12 Scott decided that Blount should take both Raleigh 'and Tracy' with him to court, and this decision is confirmed in the manuscript version of 140.21. Thereafter Tracy simply disappears from view in the manuscript, though at 143.31 there is probably a reference back to Blount addressing his 'associates' (the final '-s' is doubtful). The first edition keeps up appearances by inserting Tracy at 141.1–2, and this no doubt encouraged Magnum to mention him twice later in the chapter, though he is inactive throughout. The simplest solution to this problem, short of letting Tracy disappear gradually, has been adopted in the present edition: the two references to Tracy's participation, and the retrospective reference, in the manuscript and the additional one in the first edition have been excised. At 174.33–39 Sussex becomes caught up in an excited account of a bear-baiting and employs a dramatic future tense. Scott continues this into the second sentence but omits the 'shall' before 'another mastiff'. This has led an intermediary to change the tenses to the dramatic present, somewhat impairing the flow. It might be thought enough simply to restore the infinitives and leave the 'shall' to be understood, but Scott may well have intended to insert 'shall', and if he did not he was asking too much of most readers, so the auxiliary is supplied in the present text. No attempt has been made in this edition to determine the precise colour of Amy's hair, which is uncertain at first (15.25), then brown and dark-brown (49.25, 49.40), then fair (116.15), then paler than gold (though Varney may be lying: 161.1–2), three times light-brown (219.8, 324.20, 367.27), and finally fair again (377.29).

In conclusion, three unusual matters arising from the early American editions call for comment. At 345.40–41 the manuscript reads: 'the Earl held his hand fast compressd his lips heard and seemd as if he labourd to catch . . .'. In the part of the American editions derived from uncorrected second proofs, this appears as 'hard and round', the last word having been misread by the transcriber. In proof Scott, who did not consult his manuscript to resolve misunderstandings, probably changed it to 'hard, and frowned'. The manuscript's 'seemed' is restored in the present edition. At 346.13 the manuscript reads: 'untill those shall be devised'. The transcriber could not read the last word, which is awkwardly formed, and left a blank. So rushed were the American publishers that some of them simply left a gap, while others inserted a dash. In proof correction 'found' was supplied: the present text restores the slightly stronger manuscript word. The final, and most spectacular, example again demonstrates that Scott's activities in proof are not to be regarded as sacrosanct in every case. At 387.5–10 the manuscript reads:

> Lambourne meanwhile had lurkd behind on the stairs but hearing the door bard he now came up on tiptoe and Foster winking to him pointed with self-complacence to a piece of conceald machinery on the wall which playing with much ease ↑ and noise ↓ raised up ⟨about⟩ a part of the wooden gallery after the manner of a drawbridge . . .

The intermediaries rightly changed 'Lambourne' to 'Varney' and inserted 'little' before 'noise'. At proof stage it unfortunately occurred to Scott (or more likely was suggested to him by James Ballantyne) that since the trap-door was to fall under Amy this raising was out of place. Scott mechanically substituted 'dropped' for 'raised up' and made a similar change at the end of the paragraph. But he left the drawbridge image intact, thus making nonsense of the passage. In fact the manuscript is correct. It is true that the precise nature of the 'machinery' is obscure (presumably it involves pulleys, and the intermediaries were probably wrong to change 'on the wall' to 'in the wall', which in any case may have been a typical transcriber's misreading). But it makes sense for Forster to have contrived, and now to raise, a defensive drawbridge, and it is Varney's wicked ingenuity which conceives the idea of withdrawing the supports and converting the drawbridge into a falling trap. Readers of the present edition will be the first since Scott (and that at the time of composition only) to savour to the full this truly diabolical ingenuity.

NOTES

All manuscripts referred to are in the National Library of Scotland unless otherwise stated. For the shortened forms of reference employed see pp. 481–82.

1 Lockhart, 5.27–28.

2 For the scholarly activities see Historical Note. Lockhart, 1. 134–35. Scott had reviewed the revised version of Thomas Evans's *Old Ballads* containing Meikle's poem in the *Quarterly Review*, 3 (May 1810), 481–92. He included the whole ballad at the end of his introduction to the Magnum edition of *Kenilworth*, taking as his text the modernised version in the 1810 edition of Evans (published, like the first edition, in four volumes at London, and revised by R. H. Evans).

3 *Letters*, 6.111.

4 MS 1812, ff. 103v–104r: this is a photocopy of the original journal in the Pierpont Morgan Library, New York. A month earlier, John Ballantyne had noted in his journal for 27 December 1819 (f. 34r): 'Tales of the Times are to be managed by Constable', and he was to endorse this (perhaps a year later, since the 1820 entries are made parallel to those for 1819

on the same page) 'The idea of this work given up & supplied by Kenelworth'. These *Tales of the Times* are otherwise unknown. The agreement
for *The Pirate*, 20 December 1820, contains the curious statement: 'If a
Romance to be in 3 volumes & if a novel in 4' (f. 105v).

5 MS 323, f. 135r, Cadell to Constable, 30 October 1820.

6 MS 23234, pp. 59–60. Richard Gough, *British Topography; or, An Histor-
icalAccount of What has been Done for Illustrating the TopographicalAntiquities
of Great Britain and Ireland*, 2 vols (London, 1780) is a bibliographical
guide with little detailed information of its own. T. C. Banks, *The Dormant
and Extinct Baronage of England*, 5 vols (London, 1807–37) has only a bare
outline of Leicester's career. 'Burke's Views' has not been identified.
Thomas Birch, *Memoirs of the Reign of Queen Elizabeth, from the Year 1581
till her Death*, 2 vols (London, 1754: *CLA*, 243) covers the second half of
Elizabeth's reign and so can have been of little use to Scott.

7 *Letters*, 6.251, 262. The second letter is here quoted from MS 23117, f.
188r. The abbreviation 'K' resulted from a desire to keep the name of the
new novel secret. James Ballantyne wrote on the title page of the manuscript: 'The Proprietors of the Work do not wish the Name of it to be made
public' (MS 3653, f. 32r). It is not clear what 'K' refers to here: perhaps
Scott intended to write 'for K' rather than '& K', but it might conceivably
mean the lavish volume *Kenilworth Illustrated*. This had been published in parts, and on 28 December 1820 Constables informed its publishers, Merridew of Coventry, that they had sent Scott 'a copy of the first
number im[mediate]ly on its appearance' (MS 791, p. 210), and making it
clear that *Kenilworth* had been in train long before Scott received the first
part.

8 On 5 March 1822 David noted to his father that he had 'not recd. the books
which were borrowed from the Advtes Liby in my name for Kenilworth'
(MS 679, f. 250r). The books may have included one or more of those
referred to in Scott's letter of 10 September below and perhaps Dugdale's
Antiquities of Warwickshire, which does not appear in *CLA*.

9 *Letters*, 6.265–66: here quoted from MS 23117, f. 190r–v. Daniel and
Samuel Lysons, *Magna Britannia: Being a Concise Topographical Account of
the Several Counties of Great Britain*, 6 vols (London, 1813) is in fact not
very informative about Cumnor Hall (1.270–71). John Brady's *Clavis
Calendaria; or, A Compendious Analysis of the Calendar*, 2 vols (London,
1812: *CLA*, p. 254) does not contain anything that is likely to have assisted
in the composition of *Kenilworth*.

10 *Letters*, 6.272.

11 *Letters*, 6.288.

12 *Letters*, 6.266.

13 MS 1812, f. 34r. On 25 December he had written: 'Kenilworth will be
finished writing to morrow: It has great promise; How will it perform?' (f.
33v).

14 MS 791, pp. 142, 150, 162, 165, 167.

15 MS 323, f. 156r.

16 MS 791, p. 177.

17 MS 323, f. 157r.

18 MS 323, f. 165v.

19 MS 791, pp. 217–18.

20 5,500 *Ivanhoe* and 7,500 *Fortunes of Nigel* were shipped at a similar stage in
    1819 and 1822 respectively (MS 319, f. 276v; MS 323, f. 263r); there
    were 52 bales of *Kenilworth* (MS 792, p. 222), and in the case of *Ivanhoe*
    each bale had contained 90 copies (MS 790, p. 717).

21 The date is confirmed by the *Edinburgh Evening Courant*, 8 January 1821.

22 The quarto-type leaves of the manuscript measure approximately 26.5 by
    20.5 cm and are mostly formed by the folding in two of two sets of folio-
    type leaves watermarked respectively with a horn device (compare Hea-
    wood 2774) and the date 1817, and 'VALLEYFIELD' and the same date.
    The chain lines are 2.4 cm apart. The portion of Volume 1 in the British
    Library manuscript begins with a leaf numbered 16 by Scott, 'courtier'
    (30.18 in the present text) and continues to f. 23, numbered 37 (76.12
    'new'): the foliation includes one sheet with a blank recto but insertions on
    the verso (f. 14), which presumably indicates that the preceding leaf had
    been sent to the transcriber, or for some other reason was not to hand at the
    time of composition. (Some, but not all of the anomalous leaves are im-
    mediately preceded by leaves displaying signs of having been the outside
    sheets in packets.) The next three leaves (Scott's 38, 39, and 40) are miss-
    ing, though there are insertions for Scott's 38 on the verso of f. 23. The
    manuscript resumes with Scott's 41 (f. 24) at 82.27 'rather' and continues
    to 58 (f. 42) at 119.40 'by': the foliation includes one leaf with insertions on
    the recto as bound and a blank verso (f. 36). The leaves originally num-
    bered 59 and 60 are missing (there are insertions for 59 on f. 42v), but the
    final leaf of the volume numbered 61 is present (f. 43): this begins at
    123.20 'therefore' and ends half way down the page with 'End of Volume
    Ist'. The verso of this leaf has a full range of insertions for the first leaf of
    the next volume. The misbound f. 44 is discussed below. Volume 2 is
    present from the outset (f. 45, numbered 1) to Scott's 14 (f. 60), 154.38
    'sworn': the foliation includes a leaf with a blank recto but an insertion on
    the verso (f. 48) and a paper apart (f. 59) carrying 152.25 'The Earl' to
    153.9 'command'. The leaves originally numbered 15 to 18 are missing,
    though there are insertions for 15 on f. 60v. The manuscript resumes with
    19 (f. 61) at 164.3 'answered' and continues to the end of the second
    volume without a break, the final leaf being numbered by Scott 61 (f. 106):
    the foliation includes a paper apart with insertions on the recto as bound
    and a blank verso (f. 67), and two full leaves with blank rectos and one or
    more insertions on the verso (ff. 72, 82). The first two leaves of Volume 3
    are missing, and the third is misbound as f. 44 (there are insertions for it on
    f. 43v): it begins at 263.17 'part' and continues to 265.17 'revels'. The rest
    of the volume is bound in its correct place, beginning with the leaf originally
    numbered 4 (f. 107) and ending with 64 (f. 170): the foliation includes two
    leaves with blank rectos and insertions on the verso (ff. 118, 165), and one
    with insertions on the recto as bound and a blank verso, f. 154. The
    numbering is obscured by the binding on several of the folios.

23 The EUL MS begins at 4.28–29 'to recollect'.

24 MS 3653 includes (f. 32) a leaf bearing the inscription in Scott's hand
    'Kenilworth / Vol 1.' and a note by James Ballantyne on the recto, and on
    the verso two brief insertions for the opening pages of the novel. The same

manuscript also contains two fragments of text. The first of these (f. 129) is a slip with the watermark 1817, but unlike the normal *Kenilworth* paper it bears 'D & A C O W [A N]' and no chain lines. It is evidently a 'paper apart' carrying an insertion of some 70 words for the British Library's f. 104 (254.21–27) with antiquarian details in the description of Kenilworth Castle. It also has another, short, insertion, ' "time-honourd Lancaster—' (254.33). BL f. 103v is a normal verso with insertions for f. 104, and shows no signs of having been the end of a batch (as described in the following paragraph). There is ample room on the verso for the material on the slip, so Scott would appear to have noted the details from his source on this scrap of paper: perhaps on returning to the main manuscript he took the opportunity to add the Shakespeare quotation when attaching the slip. The other fragment in MS 3653 is part of a normal *Kenilworth* leaf: on its recto, which was presumably originally the verso, there is an insertion of some 90 words of plot business for the British Library's f. 158 (369.35–42). In this case BL f. 157v is blank, and was evidently the last of a batch, showing folds and dirt; f. 158 has three marginal insertions, but Scott must have decided to use a full extra leaf when he added the plot business.

25   Only the manuscript as it now exists (excluding the fragments in the National Library of Scotland) is recorded in the 'Inventory of Manuscripts by the Author of Waverly, deposited with Thomas Thomson . . . till the right of property in them is determined' (MS 683, ff. 82–83 : 2 June 1827); indeed, that inventory notes that the third folio of Volume 3 is also missing, the one misbound in the British Library.

26   Representative examples of later insertions may be found at ff. 11v/12r, 14v/15r, and 26v/27r.

27   Volume 1, Chapter 3; Volume 1, Chapter 4 (absent from manuscipt); Volume 1, Chapter 9 (on opposing verso); Volume 1, Chapter 12 (on opposing verso); Volume 2, Chapter 1 (on opposing verso, replacing the 'Old Play' motto transferred to the next chapter, which suggests that Volume 2, Chapter 1 grew beyond its envisaged scope); Volume 2, Chapter 3 (on opposing verso, replacing lines from *Romeo and Juliet*, 4.3.21, 24: 'What if *this mixture* do not work at all/ What if it be a poison', which apply only to the opening pages of the chapter); Volume 2, Chapter 4 (on opposing verso); Volume 2, Chapter 6 (absent from manuscript); Volume 2, Chapter 7 (absent from manuscript); Volume 2, Chapter 8 (on opposing verso); Volume 2, Chapter 12 (absent from manuscript); Volume 2, Chapter 13 (absent from manuscript); Volume 3, Chapter 3 (on opposing verso); Volume 3, Chapter 4 (absent from manuscript, the *Virgin Queen* motto here being transferred to the next chapter, again suggesting an unforeseen extension of the scope of the fourth chapter of this volume); Volume 3, Chapter 6 (on opposing verso); Volume 3, Chapter 7 (on opposing verso); Volume 3, Chapter 10 (absent from manuscript); and Volume 3, Chapter 14 (on preceding folio). Volume 1, Chapter 2 originally began with the motto followed immediately by Goldthread's song.

28   *Letters*, 6.251; MS 1812, f. 24r. A few words are transcribed from opposing versos to rectos in Gordon's hand (BL ff. 91, 146, 151).

29   The American editions in question (all dated 1821) are the [first] and 'second' American editions published at Philadelphia by M. Carey & Son,

the 'third' American edition published in the same city by Edwin T. Scott, an edition printed at New York by J. Seymour (vol. 1) and J. & J. Harper (vol. 2), another New York edition published by E. Duyckinck, and an edition published at Hartford by S. G. Goodrich. These five editions are listed in Richard H. Shoemaker, *A Checklist of American Imprints for 1821* (Metuchen, New Jersey, 1967) as numbers 6750 (conflating the two Carey editions), 6749, 6748, 6747, and 6746. Two editions of *Kenilworth* appeared in Paris in 1821, one published by Amyot and Baudry, the other by Galignani. They derive independently from the first edition, and have no textual significance: the Amyot and Baudry is very faithful in verbals and non-verbals; the Galignani is freer, but its verbal variations are entirely compositorial in nature.

30 Twineall, EUL f. 2r: compare 7.1, 7.21, 8.4; Cumnor Manor, EUL f. 11r: compare 26.19–20; Cumnor Hall, Karpeles f. 1r: compare 27.30; Sir Hubert, BL ff. 19, 33: compare 66.1, 102.36; Haxidence: f. 25r: compare 86.29–35; Paulet, f. 68r: compare 179.6,9; Bolton, ff. 113r, 115r: compare 279.9, 281.20.

31 The first edition of *Kenilworth* is remarkably stable textually, though its press-figures are unusually unstable. Only one of the variations in press-figures appears to be linked with a change in the text, and that a purely typographical one: at 2.338.16–17 (257.26 in the present edition) some copies split 'ha-ving' at the line-end, whereas in others it has been completed in line 16; the first state of this gathering has no press-figure, whereas the second has the press-figure 6. The only textually significant variant within the first edition is the presence in one copy (as it happens, that owned by the Edinburgh Edition and used as the standard of collation) of the manuscript dash after 'Hebrew' (2.58.10: 146.37 in the present text): the dash has dropped out in all the other 24 copies examined.

32 MS 319, f. 282r. However, on 29 May 1823 Cadell was to write to Constable: 'look at the numbers of Kenilworth & Ivanhoe unsold and it will be clear that we ought never to have gone beyond 10,000—even with them' (MS 323, f. 415v).

33 MS 791, p. 232.
34 MS 791, p. 255.
35 MS 677, ff. 38r–39v.
36 *Letters*, 7.3.
37 MS 326, f. 60r. Cf. MS 677, f. 39v.
38 MS 791, p. 403.
39 MS 791, p. 466.
40 MS 791, p. 487.
41 MS 23232, f. 61v: Constable's memorandum of 26 February 1822.
42 MS 791, p. 528.
43 MS 323, f. 264r.
44 MS 320, f. 32r.
45 MS 323, f. 291v.
46 MS 677, f. 39v.
47 MS 677, f. 72v.
48 MS 792, pp. 260–61.

49 MS 21020, ff. 19v–23v; Jane Millgate, *Scott's Last Edition: A Study in Publishing History* (Edinburgh, 1987), 24.

50 Interleaved Set additions are given in their original (MSS 23017–18) rather than final Magnum form, and the references are to Volumes 5 and 6 of the 8vo *Historical Romance* texts used by Scott.

51 This persistent misreading was pointed out with disgust by Edward Bensley, 'Notes on Scott's "Count Robert of Paris"', *Notes and Queries*, 167 (15 December 1934), 425.

52 'Cumber' was however accepted on five other occasions: 40.23, 99.32, 156.17, 204.25, 264.13.

EMENDATION LIST

The base-text for this edition of *Kenilworth* is a specific copy of the first edition, owned by the Edinburgh Edition of the Waverley Novels. All emendations to this base-text, whether verbal, orthographic, or punctuational, are listed below, with the exception of certain general categories of emendation described in the next paragraph, and of those errors which result from accidents of printing such as a letter dropping out, provided always that evidence for the 'correct' reading has been found in at least one other copy of the first edition.

The following proper names have been standardised throughout on the authority of Scott's preferred usage as deduced from the manuscript (see 425): Doddington (in the second volume) in place of Donnington; Forster / Foster; Goldthread / Goldthred; Laurence / Lawrence; Master / Masters. Inverted commas are sometimes found in the first edition for displayed verse quotations, sometimes not; the present text has standardised the inconsistent practices of the base-text by eliminating such inverted commas, except when they occur at the beginnings or ends of speeches. The typographic presentation of mottoes, volume and chapter headings, letters, and the opening words of volumes and chapters, has been standardised. It is clear that James Ballantyne and Co. had only one italic ligature for both '*œ*' and '*æ*'; the two are differentiated in this edition. Ambiguous end-of-line hyphens in the base-text have been interpreted in accordance with the following authorities (in descending order of priority): predominant first edition usage; second edition (which, however, usually follows first edition lineation); octavo *Historical Romances*; Magnum; MS.

Each entry in the list below is keyed to the text by page and line number; the reference is followed by the new, EEWN reading, then in brackets the reason for the emendation, and after the slash the base-text reading that has been replaced.

The great majority of emendations are derived from the manuscript. Most merely involve the replacement of one reading by another, and these are listed with the simple explanation '(MS)'. But in the final portion of the novel, '(MS*)' indicates that the MS reading was altered by an intermediary before the second proofs (from which the earliest American editions derive their closing sections) had been corrected by Scott.

The spelling and punctuation of some emendations from the manuscript have been normalised in accordance with the prevailing conventions of the base-text. And although as far as possible emendations have been fitted into the existing base-text punctuation, at times it has been necessary to provide emendations with a base-text style of punctuation. Where the manuscript reading adopted by the EEWN has required

433

editorial intervention to normalise spelling or punctuation, the exact manuscript reading is given in the form: '(MS actual reading)', or '(MS* actual reading)'. Where the new reading has required editorial interpretation of the manuscript, in the provision of punctuation for example, the explanation is given in the form '(MS derived: actual reading)'. Occasionally, some explanation of the editorial thinking behind an emendation is required, and this is provided in a brief note.

The following conventions are used in transcriptions from Scott's manuscript: deletions are enclosed ⟨thus⟩ and insertions ↑thus↓; an insertion within an insertion is indicated by double arrows ↑↑thus↓↓; superscript letters are lowered without comment; the letters 'NL' (new line) are Scott's own, and indicate that he wished a new paragraph to be opened, in spite of running on the text, whereas the words '[new paragraph]' are editorial and indicate that Scott opened a new paragraph on a new line.

In spite of the care taken by the intermediaries, some local confusions in the manuscript persisted into the first edition. When straightening these, the editor has studied the manuscript context so as to determine Scott's original intention, and where the original intention is discernible it is of course restored. But from time to time such confusions cannot be rectified in this way. In these circumstances, Scott's own corrections and revisions in the Interleaved Set have more authority than the proposals of other editions, but if the autograph portions of the Interleaved Set have nothing to offer, the reading from the earliest edition to offer a satisfactory solution is adopted as the neatest means of rectifying a fault. Readings from the later editions and the Interleaved Set are indicated by '(Ed2)', etc., '(ISet)' or '(Magnum)'. Emendations which have not been anticipated by a contemporaneous edition are indicated by '(Editorial)'.

1.30	Bonny (Editorial) / bonny
	The manuscript is not extant for the opening of the novel, but elsewhere (as at 9.20) Scott writes 'Bonny Black Bear', or just 'Black Bear' for short, never 'bonny Black Bear'.
2.8	Bonny (Editorial) / bonny
4.29	What (MS) / what
5.29	host, "and (MS derived: host and) / host;—"and
5.30	earnest?—nay (MS derived: earnest—nay) / earnest? Nay
5.35	jests—keep (MS) / jests. Keep
5.38	and travelled (MS) / and has travelled
5.40	need, for I (MS) / need to travel for. I
5.41	believing (MS beleiving) / crediting
6.4	vengeance—but (MS) / vengeance.—But
6.13	head (MS) / heads
6.16	himself (MS) / himself,
6.27	minutes (MS) / minute's
7.8	they will catch (MS) / they catch
7.21	Goldthread—tempt (MS Twineall tempt) / Goldthred. Tempt
7.28	gull (MS) / gulls
7.35	the ferule (MS) / the schoolmaster's ferule

8.1   these (MS) / These
8.1   My (MS) / my
8.4   on he (MS) / on thee, he
8.5   say spared (MS) / say, he spared
8.7   clerk. "And (MS derived: clerk "And) / clerk; "and
8.13   masters—All (MS masters All) / masters—all
8.17   point (MS) / points
8.36   guest! And (MS guest And) / guest! and
9.5   and seemed (MS and seemd) / and which seemed
9.20   Bonny (MS) / bonny
9.23   knight (MS) / Knight
9.27   ere (MS) / ever
9.42   rarest (MS) / sweet
10.3   bonnet. (MS) / bonnet?
10.7   guests (MS) / thoughts
        The vivid MS reading was probably changed to avoid a repetition at line
        10, but 'thoughts' repeats lines 2 and 4.
10.19   not you scowl (MS) / not scowl
10.20   Devil (MS) / devil
10.35   his (MS) / the
11.1   hair (MS) / hair,
11.11   feast? is (MS) / feast? Is
11.22   sooth (MS) / south
11.28   these (MS) / those
12.1   in (MS) / on
12.20   yet—But (MS) / yet—but
12.28   to it to boot (MS) / to boot
12.28   here's to (MS heres to) / here's one to
12.36   masters—All (MS masters All) / masters—all
13.4   call (MS) / called
13.5   faggots (MS) / pile
13.8   host, "but (MS derived: Host "but) / host.—"But
13.22   purpose (MS) / purchase
13.42   folks (MS) / men
14.6   You (MS) / you
14.10   it (MS) / It
14.17   dame—ah (MS) / dame. Ah
14.26   'What d'ye lack' (MS "What d'ye lack") / what d'ye lack,
14.26   of countenance (MS) / of a countenance
14.27   turkey (MS) / Turkey
14.34   and thy sarsenet (MS) / and sarsenet
14.36   Nay, nay, (MS) / Nay, my
15.20   minute description (Ed2) / conversation
        The phrase 'who had shewn some impatience during this conversation'
        was inserted in proof, and as sometimes happened the insertion fails to
        connect correctly with the original text. Ed2 suggests a neat solution.
16.2   Lambourne. "What (MS Lambourne. What) / Lambourne; "what
16.6   fairest (MS) / rarest
16.15   ever (MS) / even
16.17   the (MS) / thee
16.38   drink success (Ed2) / drink to success
17.1   pledge a (MS) / pledge him to a
17.11   themselves (MS) / the company
17.19   and, by (MS and by) / and whenever I do, by
17.31   upon (MS) / on

18.4   awaked (MS) / awoke
18.16   hath (MS) / has
18.28   Here (MS) / There
18.28   Natural Affection (MS derived: natural Affection) / natural affection
18.32   Bonny (MS) / bonny
18.37   this town (MS) / the town
18.39   would (MS) / may
19.4   sobeit thou wilt listen (MS) / so thou wilt but listen
19.21   has had sulky (MS) / has sulky
19.23   like (MS) / likely
19.24   thrusts (MS) / thrust
19.27   assured (MS) / answered
19.28   short, bestowed (MS) / short, he bestowed
19.34   Cicely (MS) / Cicily
          The second vowel is ambiguous in MS, but it is marginally more like 'e'
          than 'i', and it is so interpreted by Ed1 at 70.18, 72.4–9, 84.1, and
          195.38.
19.41   Cicely (MS) / Cicily
19.41   thee (MS) / you
19.43   tight (MS) / light
20.1   Cicely (MS) / Cicily
20.3   Cumber (MS) / Concern
20.3   Cicely (MS) / Cicily
20.7   am infidel (MS) / am an infidel
20.10   have—true (MS) / have. True
20.12   Eden—I (MS) / Eden. I
20.13   thee. But (MS) / thee.—But
20.26   times—the (MS) / times. The
20.28   reverend (MS) / reverence
20.29   pass—Care (MS pass Care) / pass, care
20.29   career (MS) / trick
20.37   on (MS) / in
21.21   gateway, "if (MS gateway if) / gateway and gate, "if
21.35   from trees (MS) / from the trees
22.28   fellow . . . myself. And (MS fellow and gallant picaroon such as I have
          ever shewn myself And) / fellow. And
22.39   Law (MS) / La
23.9   it—And (MS) / it; and
23.12   forsooth—the (MS) / forsooth? The
23.21   is a chance she (MS) / is chance that she
25.41   his (MS) / the
26.9   for (MS) / from
26.22   chances. (MS) / chances—
26.30   have a (MS) / have in me a
26.33   pillows and puts (MS) / pillows, and who puts
26.34   play (MS) / stage-play
26.37   entered; then (MS enterd then) / entered it; then
27.1   my (MS) / mine
27.2   more brass at every port I stopped at in (MS more brass at every port I
          stopd at in) / more of brass at every port where I touched in
          The alteration creates a repetition with 'touching' at line 5.
27.30   Cumnor Hall (MS) / Cumnor-Place
27.31   of yet greater (MS) / of greater
27.33   same, (MS same) / same wood,
28.10   such commodities (MS) / such learned commodities

28.12   answered (MS) / anwered
28.29   the use of the same (MS) / the same
28.33   Scripture. And (MS scripture And) / Scripture; and
29.9   you have (MS) / you must have
29.25   proposal in thee thus (MS) / proposal—thus
29.27   whelp." (MS) / whelp.'
30.2   mending (MS) / amending
30.10   unruffled (MS) / unrumpled
30.17   describest (MS) / hast described
30.21   Antoline's (MS Antolines) / Antonie's
30.25   English; and (MS English and) / English world; and
30.30   firm—well (MS) / firm?—Well
30.35   patron (MS) / person
31.20   parent (Magnum) / parents
         The Magnum correctly remembered that Amy's mother died in her
         daughter's infancy.
31.34   Guilty (MS) / guilty
32.10   dispatches (MS) / dispatched
32.11   the pain (MS) / his pain
32.15   find him alive (MS) / restore him to health
32.18   place—go (MS) / place. Go
32.19   hence—go (MS) / hence. Go
32.20   well— (MS) / well,
32.25   it (MS) / the loss
32.27   Amy?—do (MS) / Amy?—Do
32.30   prisoner—otherwise (MS prisoner otherwise) / prisoner. Otherwise
32.32   girl (MS) / maiden
         As with the change at 49.30 below, it is likely that James Ballantyne, with
         his exaggerated sense of propriety, was responsible.
32.33   forgiven—fear (MS) / forgiven. Fear
32.35   lives—come (MS) / lives—Come
32.38   more (MS) / farther
32.39   other—and (MS) / other and
33.4   Tressilian!—he (MS Tresilian—he) / Tressilian!—He
33.8   me!—go (MS derived: me—go) / me! Go
33.39   bounds?—retire (MS bounds—retire) / bounds?—Retire
34.3   Indies—make (MS Indies make) / Indies. Make
34.8   What (MS) / what
34.10   Tressilian—be (MS) / Tressilian, be
34.17   courtesies—You (MS courtesies You) / courtesies—you
34.20   draw (MS) / Draw
34.26   meanwhile, pursued with hasty steps the (MS meanwhile pursued with
         hasty steps the) / meanwhile, with hasty steps, pursued the
34.35   recollection (MS) / recollections
34.40   on (MS) / in
34.41   the country (MS) / his country
34.42   intelligence." (MS) / intelligence.'
35.11   you where (MS) / you here, where
35.17   laid hand (MS) / laid his hand
35.40   close (MS) / struggle
36.6   your last look of thy (MS) / the last look of your
36.15   shaking (MS) / striking
36.17   Abject? Abject? (MS) / Abject! abject!
36.19   see— (MS) / see,
37.2   Varney, "I (MS Varney "I) / Varney; "I

37.2   Eldorado. By (MS) / Eldorado—By
38.10   cut a many (MS) / cut many
38.19   rich string (MS) / neck-string
38.21   these—and (MS) / those—And
38.24   but (MS) / But
38.24   brave—My (MS) / brave, my
38.31   dignity—well (MS) / dignity.—Well
38.41   force—canst (MS) / force.—Canst
38.42   toys?—canst (MS toys—canst) / toys? Canst
38.43   goblins?—thou (MS goblins—thou) / goblins?—Thou
39.29   cumbering (MS) / busying
40.7   good—can'st (MS good—canst) / good.—Can'st
40.7   any (MS) / an
40.12   committed either (MS) / committed to peril either
40.18   her. (MS her—) / her?
41.4   wages (MS) / wage
41.13   deserve—remember (MS) / deserve it. Remember
41.14   fivepence (MS) / five-pence
41.17   boots—get (MS) / boots.—Get
41.19   temper. I trust...and me." (MS temper. I trust by skillful teaching she
        may learn to whistle that to our good lord shall advantage both thee, and
        me." [comma doubtful]) / temper."
41.27   they left (MS) / they were left
41.29   methinks (MS) / methinks,
41.36   understand and profit (MS) / understand, and to profit
42.5   debauchees (MS) / debauchers
42.6   Tider (MS) / Tidesly
42.8   murther (MS) / murder
42.14   all sorts (MS) / each sort
42.20   subtile (MS) / subtle
42.27   all, but without prejudice to the others (MS all but without prejudice to
        the others) / all, without prejudice to others
43.5   thy (MS) / the
43.7   in such sort (MS) / into such fashion
43.11   Anthony," (MS) / Anthony,"
43.37   Milan (MS) / Spanish
44.6   ceremony callest (MS) / ceremony—which callest
44.28   world—the (MS) / world—The
44.30   all outward (MS) / all the outward
44.36   at window (MS) / at the window
44.42   Tressilian—admit (MS Tressilian "admit) / Tressilian—Admit
45.4   the soliloquy (MS) / his soliloquy
45.11   lord!—and (MS Lord—and) / lord!—And
45.19   and I (MS) / and besides I
45.27   filled (MS) / filled,
46.5   to observe or speculate (MS) / from observing or speculating
46.10   attaching much credit (MS) / much credit being attached
46.36   furnitures (MS) / furniture
47.11   fairest (MS) / finest
47.13   step from (MS) / step or two from
47.24   on (MS) / in
48.37   Magician (MS) / magician
49.1   hangings!—how (MS hangings—how) / hangings!—How
49.2   life!—how (MS life—how) / life!—How
49.27   vine—my (MS) / vine—My

49.30   breast (MS) / bosom
       See note to 32.32 in this list.
50.1   were (MS) / had been
50.19   and his patron (MS) / and patron
50.21   but (MS) / But
50.22   courses—and (MS) / projects—And
50.25   well—it (MS) / well. It
50.31   which makes men tremble when they look on it. I (MS derived: which
       men tremble when they look on it. I) / which men tremble when they
       look on—I
51.15   afterwards (MS) / after
51.26   it—it (MS) / it—It
52.17   crown, and (Editorial: MS crown and) / crown; and
52.18   necessary—— (MS derived: necessary—) / necessary,
       The phrase is incomplete: it appears that Forster breaks off in mid-
       sentence. Ed1 improves the grammatical sense but generates a nonsen-
       sical explanation for his leaving the room.
52.23   apartment—Out (MS) / apartment; out
52.23   if (MS) / in case
52.28   embroidering (MS embroiderng) / embroidery
52.31   light upon (MS) / find
52.31   the cushions (MS) / the pile of cushions
52.36   husband— (MS) / husband;
52.40   purpose—it (MS) / purpose. It
52.42   honoured (MS honourd) / noble
53.9   not?—to (MS not—to) / not?—To
53.13   sudden— (MS) / sudden;
53.16   he (MS) / He
53.20   my (MS) / My
53.30   this world (MS) / the world
53.30   But Tressilian (MS) / But touching Tressilian
53.31   thou— (MS) / thou.—
53.35   him—for (MS) / him—For
53.42   Truth (MS) / truth
54.3   upon you a falsehood so soon detected (MS) / upon your ladyship a
       falsehood, so soon to be detected
54.22   openness your ladyship," said Varney, "will (MS openness your lady-
       ship" said Varney "will) / openness," said Varney, "your ladyship will
54.24   world—that (MS world that) / world, and that
54.25   you. (MS you—) / you?
54.26   Unquestionably it (MS) / Unquestionably. It
54.27   he said (MS) / Tressilian said
54.39   and then, after (8vo: MS and then after) / And, then after
55.8   Forster—consider (MS Foster—consider) / Foster. Consider
55.13   it—but (MS) / it. But
55.17   suppose (MS) / Suppose
55.39   bears (MS) / endures
56.4   not be (MS) / not to be
56.6   concerns?—no (MS concerns—no) / concerns?—No
56.15   these (MS) / the
56.17   But (MS) / But,
56.19   ruin— (MS) / ruin?—
56.20   prejudice— (MS) / prejudice?—
56.23   me—content (MS) / me—Content
57.9   Great (MS) / great

57.18 ornament (MS) / ornaments
57.23 towards (MS) / toward
57.29 seeming (MS) / person
57.30 the state (MS) / the chair of state
57.32 Earl. "If (MS Earl If) / Earl, "if
58.1 aspiring (MS) / aspi-ing [end-of-line hyphen]
58.23 after (MS) / about
58.38 He (MS) / he
58.40 to court gales of favour (MS) / to gales of court-favour
59.12 owing (MS) / owning
59.17 vestments. For (MS) / vestments; for
59.34 orders ... they have (MS derived: order ... they have) / order ... it has
59.39 desert—but (MS) / desert. But
59.40 arises not (MS) / arises neither
59.42 but by her (MS) / but which is attached to her
60.1 day—" said her husband, "yes (MS derived: day—" said her husband
       "yes) / day?" said her husband,—"Yes
60.19 pause, soon we (MS pause soon we) / pause sooner, we
60.22 ruin—but (MS) / ruin. But
60.38 you. And (MS you And) / you; and
60.41 Earl. "She (MS Earl "She) / Earl; "she
60.42 unrewarded—come (MS) / unrewarded—Come
61.3 forwards (MS) / forward
61.19 and so I think ... sincerity I (MS and so I think is your father In sincerity
       I) / and I think your father is of the same congregation in sincerity. I
61.22 ornaments (MS) / ornament
61.24 at—e'en (MS derived: at e'en) / at. E'en
61.38 counsel (MS) / council
62.9 they (MS) / the company
62.37 had been (MS) / was
63.22 that to (MS) / that in order to
63.31 retreat?—it (MS retreat—it) / retreat?—It
63.41 some of (MS) / some one of
64.6 hawking, and drinking (MS hawking and drinking) / hawking, drinking
64.7 Sheriff"—— (Editorial) / Sheriff"—
64.11 settled—A (MS) / settled—a
64.12 hob (ISet) / Hob
64.13 you then (MS) / You then
64.33 tire if thou (MS) / tire as thou
64.35 Ambition (MS) / ambition
65.4 hand this (MS) / hand on this
66.4 head?" (MS head—") / head?'
66.21 intermingled (MS) / intermingle
66.27 if (MS) / If
66.36 lord," (Ed2: MS lord") / lord?"
66.37 man whom (MS) / man, of whom
67.2 privacy ... private, were (MS privacy and meddles with that which it
       concerns me to keep private were) / privacy, were
67.4 Bear (MS) / bear
67.8 early days (MS) / early day
67.16 not now grant (MS) / not grant
67.25 been already (MS) / already been
67.39 the apartment (MS) / her apartment
68.11 know him—his (MS know him his) / know his
68.12 deep—his (MS) / deep. His

68.15   Janet?—who (MS Janet—who) / Janet?—Who
68.19   daintily for him to (MS) / daintily to
68.27   thou? is (MS thou is) / thou? Is
68.32   accompt (MS) / account
68.35   woman!—had (MS woman—had) / woman!—Had
69.5   farewell (MS) / Farewell
69.8   master (MS) / lord
69.18   life—the (MS) / life. The
70.2   park, and, alighting at . . . Bear, desired (MS park and alighting at . . .
        Bear desired) / park. The latter alighted at . . . Bear, and desired
70.9   more (MS) / so
70.10   ran (MS) / saw
70.12   how (MS) / where
70.14   abye (MS) / repent
71.20   cue (MS) / duty
71.20   life, honour (MS life honour) / life and honour
71.27   it. (MS derived: it—) / it?
71.35   stable?" (MS stable—") / stable?'
71.42   mine honest host (MS) / mine host
72.4   as dost (MS) / as thou dost
72.4   thine (MS) / thy
72.7   go (MS) / Go
72.12   to converse such gallants as you. (MS) / to please such critical gallants as
        yourself.
72.14   courtiers as yourself, my (MS courtiers as yourself my) / courtiers, my
72.16   We (MS) / we
72.19   host. "You (MS host Giles Gosling "You) / host—"you
72.26   of horse (MS) / of the horse
72.28   precluded (MS) / prevented
73.10   all well with (MS) / all with
73.23   you will depend (MS) / thou wilt depend
73.23   horse—thou (MS Horse—thou) / horse—Thou
73.24   which (MS) / that
73.28   will raise (MS) / may raise
73.30   answered (MS answerd) / replied
73.34   was very (MS) / was then very
74.3   lord we (MS) / lord, whom we
74.4   readers (MS) / readers,
74.35   princoxes!—an (MS princoxes—an) / princoxes! An
74.40   Harry!—he (MS Harry—he) / Harry! He
75.33   of their petition, and (MS of their petition and) / of the petition of the
        inhabitants, and
75.36   something (MS) / somewhat
76.34   Varney (Magnum: MS missing) / his old friend and associate Foster
83.13   favourite—he (MS) / favourite.—He
83.13   puritans—he (MS) / puritans—He
83.22   dozen of courtiers (MS) / dozen courtiers
84.4   but that at (MS) / but at
84.5   she cannot grace (ISet) / they cannot fill [MS as Ed1]
84.6   mine (MS) / my
84.10   you? (MS) / you.
84.19   more—let (MS) / more. Let
84.20   all that I (MS) / all I
84.25   that (Magnum) / those [MS as Ed1]
84.35   with (MS) / in

84.42   county (MS) / country
85.6   his (MS) / its
85.12   token—and (MS) / token.—And
85.13   short time (MS) / short a time
85.16   boards—no (MS) / boards.—No
85.17   when (MS) / where
86.7   horse tired and deprived (MS) / horse deprived
86.25   refresh himself and his horse. (MS) / refresh his horse?
86.25   with peculiar (MS) / with a peculiar
86.38   His (MS) / his
86.40   Hundred (MS) / hundred
87.6   ferula stuck (MS) / ferula was stuck
87.14   *Linguæ latinæ* (Editorial) / *Linguæ latinæ*
        For this and subsequent corrections of æ/œ ligatures see the note at the
        beginning of this list.
87.34   smith. (MS) / smith?
87.36   learning"—the (Editorial: MS learning" the) / learning," the
87.38   *cæca* (Editorial) / *cœca*
88.2   at a word (MS) / in a word
88.7   be (MS) / is
88.10   mine (MS) / my
88.15   *fœnum* (Editorial) / *fænum*
88.15   *cornu;* oats shall also be forthcoming, and (MS *cornu*—oats shall also be
        forthcoming and) / *cornu;* and
88.17   cost *ne* (MS) / cost you *ne*
88.30   with learned (MS) / with the learned
88.39   porker (ISet) / partner
        In ISet Scott presumably recovered what he had originally meant to
        write; he also added 'litter' after 'which'.
89.1   *camicæ* (Editorial) / *camicæ*
89.23   of poor Erasmus (MS) / of Erasmus
89.29   Buikerschochius (MS) / Buckerschockius
89.32   "May it long be (MS) / "Long may it be
89.37   him (MS) / himself
90.5   Demetrius Doboobius (MS) / Demetrius
        The deletion of 'Doboobius' here makes nonsense of 'so he wrote
        himself when in foreign parts'.
90.9   gibberish (Ed2) / *gibberish*
90.25   concording (MS) / according
90.32   *cæteris* (Editorial) / *cæteris*
91.2   helleborum (Ed2) / Helleborum
91.3   examen (Ed2) / Examen
91.5   doest (MS) / doth
91.11   clem (MS) / swarf
91.13   Demetrius Doboobie (MS) / Demetrius or Doboobie
91.19   presently." [new paragraph] "*O, cæca* (MS derived) / presently." [new
        paragraph] The interruption pleased not the *Magister*, who exclaimed,
        "*O, cæca*
        This emendation and the next two are discussed in the 'Essay on the
        Text', 425–26.
91.29   the interruption (MS) / this interruption
91.29   magister. (MS Magister) / magister, more than that of the traveller.
91.31   *Sufflamina* (12mo) / *Suflamina*
91.42   "aught (MS) / "know aught
92.11   guest. "A' (MS guest A) / guest; "a'

92.16   furth (MS) / forth
92.17   pupil. *Heus Ricarde* (MS) / pupil. *Ricarde*
92.23   but go (MS) / go but
92.31   to this (MS) / towards this
92.33   *quæso* (Editorial) / *quæso*
92.35   tumbling (MS) / stumbling
93.9   Sludge. "And ye (MS Sludge And ye) / Sludge, "and you
93.10   send (MS) / sent
93.13   *nugæ* (Editorial) / *nugæ*
93.16   fiends (MS) / fiend
93.30   rescue as (MS) / rescue of her chicken as
93.34   *Sufflamina* (12mo) / *Suflamina*
93.38   urchin and prevent (MS) / urchin, and to prevent
94.14   unconcernedly (MS) / unconsciously
94.23   *Faerie* (MS) / *Faery*
94.29   Domine (MS) / Dominie
94.32   be." (MS) / be.''
94.35   now (MS) / Now
94.37   Domine (MS) / Dominie
95.6   whom we (MS) / whom you
95.9   are. And (MS are And) / are, and
95.18   me. But (MS me But) / me—but
95.24   hen-roost (MS) / roost
95.26   Domine (MS) / Dominie
95.29   other his (MS) / other has his
95.31   Domine (MS) / Dominie
95.34   whereabouts (MS) / whereabout
95.37   Domine (MS domine) / Dominie
95.41   eggs (MS) / egg
96.3   has (MS) / hath
96.11   the great (MS) / a great
96.21   that flat (MS) / that other flat
96.29   hark (MS) / Hark
96.43   pursuit entirely with (MS) / pursuit with
97.2   had planted (MS) / had, as formerly, planted
97.10   having (MS) / pursuing
97.20   me, I (MS me I) / me without my consent, I
97.28   stance in (MS) / stance with
97.40   pippins (MS) / apples
97.41   thy silver (MS) / the silver
97.42   Whistle (MS) / whistle
97.43   and I give (MS) / and give
98.3   will (MS) / may
98.8   you (MS) / thou
98.37   while (MS) / time
98.38   time (MS) / space
98.40   space which (MS) / space of time which
99.12   Flibbertigibbet," said (MS derived: Flibbertigibbet said) / Flibberti-
        gibbet?" said
99.24   follow to (MS) / follow me to
99.27   here. You (MS) / here, you
99.29   that so a poor man (MS) / that when so poor a man
99.40   will (MS) / would
100.9   voice, as if issuing (MS voice as if issuing) / voice, issuing
100.21 sword drawn (MS) / drawn sword

100.41 and to address (MS) / and address
100.43 hence (MS) / since
101.33 pursued (MS) / proceeded
101.42 illumined (MS) / illuminated
102.6   liquor, which I (MS derived: liquor, I) / liquor? I
        This and the following emendation are discussed in the 'Essay on the
        Text', 424.
102.6   have in store? (MS have in store—") / have some in store.
102.25 resumed in (Editorial) / resumed his narrative in
        This emendation is discussed in the 'Essay on the Text', 426. Magnum
        has 'commenced his narrative in'.
102.26 was (MS) / WAS
103.1   whatever (MS) / whatsoever
103.38 auri (MS) / aure
103.41 as (MS) / who
104.8   and facilitated by his (MS) / and his
104.12 for (MS) / and
104.17 procured a (MS) / procured me a
104.25 would (MS) / should
104.31 ado (MS) / to do
104.39 carry (MS) / bring
105.2   amongst (MS) / among
105.2   fears. And (MS fears And) / fears, and
105.26 stand little (MS) / stand in little
105.28 money perhaps, (MS) / money,
105.30 blinded—and (MS derived: blinded and) / blinded. And
105.34 lingering an (MS) / lingering for an
105.37 besides the (MS) / besides that the
105.38 his nag (MS) / a nag
106.8   Domine (Editorial) / Dominie
        Scott, unlike Ed1, usually remembered to use the English form
        'Domine' for Holiday, but he slipped here.
106.12 ye (MS) / you
106.25 way from hence (MS) / way hence
107.43 tongue, yet the (MS tongue yet the) / tongue, the
108.5   mysell (MS) / myself
108.39 didst get (MS) / didst thou get
108.43 withal. So . . . ailment withal. (MS So I laid my bit of a scroll on a flat
        stean wi' a good harry groat to keep it firm and I waited my time aneath
        some bit pickle of gorse when lo ye the earth shook and trembled and
        after a while I was wishd by the slip of a boy to venture to the place And
        lo ye gone was my groat and in its place was my packet which I was to
        cure nag's ailment withal.) / withal.
109.6   nag?" was (MS nag" was) / nag, Jack Hostler?"—was
109.8   hostler. "Simply (MS derived: Ostler "Simply) / hostler; "simply
109.10 But (MS) / but
109.18 this (MS) / the
109.26 you (MS) / ye
109.41 Pinniewinks's (Ed2: MS Pinniewinks) / Pinniewink's
110.10 handle a text like (MS) / handle such a text as
110.14 them (MS) / un
110.21 Wayland began (MS) / Wayland Smith began
110.43 Crane (MS) / Crank
111.5   of the (MS) / of his
111.9   wish that the (MS) / wish the

111.10 this same Wayland (MS) / this Wayland
111.12 distinction Satan (MS derived: distinction the devil) / distinction that
        Satan
111.26 but (MS) / saving
111.28 worship (MS) / worshipful
111.38 ate (MS) / sat
112.8   crave hasty travelling (MS) / crave travelling
113.31 time. But (MS) / time; but
113.32 trowling (MS) / towling
113.34 But (MS) / but
113.42 And see as he (MS derived: And sees he) / and see that he
114.8   is a chance (MS) / is chance
114.40 the most constant (MS) / the constant
115.26 enough—but (MS) / enough. But
115.29 it was (MS) / It was
115.32 Hugh. "It (MS Hugh "It) / Hugh, "it
115.37 me—it (MS) / me. It
115.41 Out (MS) / out
115.41 And (MS) / and
115.42 me"—— (MS me"—) / me."——
116.2   primo (MS) / Primo
116.4   but (MS) / But
116.14 manfully—we (MS) / manfully—We
116.27 world—and (MS) / world—And
116.37 south wood (MS) / park
117.4   their (MS) / these
117.27 tertio Mariæ (MS) / *Tertio Mariæ*
117.38 patonce (Editorial: MS patoneé) / patonee
118.3   *laquei* (MS) / *laqueæ*
118.22 said—But (MS) / said,—but
118.24 mine (MS) / my
118.27 *cælebs* (Editorial) / *cælebs*
118.28 than (8vo: MS that) / then
118.38 Leicester. But (MS) / Leicester; but
119.6   company. But (MS derived: company But) / company, but
119.9   south wood (MS derived: southwood) / South wood
119.11 face. They (MS) / face,—they
119.11 my step (MS) / me
119.19 his (MS) / her
119.28 syren (Ed2) / Syren [MS as Ed1]
        Scott must have intended to refer to the serpent in heraldry here, so Ed1
        was wrong to retain his MS capital. 18mo and Magnum give 'siren'.
119.37 hast then (MS) / hast thou then
120.1   ailments (MS) / ailment
120.3   groom—and (MS derived: groom" said the Curate "and) / groom—
        And
120.19 besides I (MS) / besides that I
123.26 hastiiy forward (MS) / forward hastily
123.32 affirmative, he hastily (Magnum) / affirmative, replied. [new para-
        graph] Stevens then hastily
        The Magnum suggests a sensible solution to the confusion in Ed1: MS
        is as Ed1 but without the new paragraph.
123.33 perspirations (MS) / perspiration
123.39 too—My (MS too My) / too—my
123.41 frowning. "We (MS frowning We) / frowning, "we

125.14 suspicious (MS) / conspicuous
125.22 besmirched (MS besmirchd) / besmeared
126.6 man." (18mo) / man.
126.19 Domine (Editorial) / Dominie
See comment on 106.8: here MS has 'mast', for 'master', but that would repeat line 16.
126.30 victory (MS) / Victory
126.41 the unusual alertness (MS unuasual) / the alertness
127.7 MacMahon (MS) / MacMakon
127.17 secrecy and rapidity (MS) / rapidity and secrecy
127.27 City (MS) / city
127.31 retainer to (MS) / retainer, as to
127.35 enter such chemists' or apothecaries' shops as (MS enter such chemists or Apothecary's shops as) / enter the shops of such chemists or apothecaries as
127.38 walked into (MS walkd into) / walked successively into
127.43 he (MS) / Wayland
128.5 the unlearned (MS the unlearnd) / crazy alchemists
The MS reading was probably not understood by an intermediary: it seems more likely that chemists would suggest that Wayland was ignorant than that he was a crazy alchemist.
128.13 the (MS) / that
128.19 apaid (MS) / repaid
128.30 window; a (MS window a) / window—but a
128.36 looked (MS) / look
129.2 well-refined I (MS) / well-refined—I
129.2 it (MS) / It
129.33 of which (MS) / of what
130.7 returned (MS returnd) / answered
130.8 noting (MS) / nothing
130.8 you—but (MS) / you.—But
130.11 you (MS) / You
130.22 may (MS) / May
130.22 do!—had (MS do—had) / do!—Had
130.37 dealings (MS) / dealing
130.40 hast now made (MS) / hast made
131.37 city (MS) / fort
132.2 the period (MS) / that period
132.7 of state (MS) / of the state
132.8 perhaps her (MS) / perhaps as her
132.17 but (MS) / yet
132.30 Tower-Hill in 1553. (MS derived: Towerhill in [space]) / Tower-Hill, August 22, 1553.
This emendation is discussed in the 'Essay on the Text', 424.
133.31 reclined in (MS) / reclined nearly in
133.37 such similar articles as (MS) / the similar articles which
133.41 her own (MS) / his own
134.5 the household (MS) / this household
134.14 he does (MS) / which the fiend does
134.20 dock (MS) / Dock
134.37 news—are (MS) / news. Are
134.42 sway, (Ed2: MS sway) / sway;
135.4 in (MS) / with
135.15 "that the devil (MS) / "the devil
135.24 the moment (MS) / a moment

135.36 that (MS) / That
135.40 Pass his (MS) / Pass over his
135.42 secretary, "and (MS Secretary "and) / secretary. "And
136.29 experiment—But first call in my (MS) / experiment; but first call my
136.34 believing (MS) / in regard I believe
137.17 attending also particularly (MS) / attending particularly
137.27 Even Beauty (MS) / Even a beauty
137.31 who had kept (MS who ↑had↓ kept) / who kept
137.32 and mingled (MS) / and which mingled
138.17 multiplying it." (MS multiplying it"——) / multiplying."
138.29 on (MS) / at
138.29 grassy (MS) / earthy
138.34 this (MS) / thy
138.36 but (MS) / just
139.6 did you (MS) / didst thou
139.14 for (MS) / over
139.21 undeniably, Master (MS undeniably Master) / undeniably, Doctor
          Masters
139.24 Then off flies (MS) / Thus, then, off fly
139.26 younger, (MS younger) / younger brother,
139.29 colouring. "Not (MS colouring "Not) / colouring, "not
139.30 waves—the (MS waves the) / waves. The
139.31 Britain bold (MS) / Britain contains bold
139.37 both make and (MS) / either make or
140.2 around (MS) / round
140.10 bade (MS) / commanded
140.10 instantly take (MS) / instantly to take
140.12 Walter with (Editorial) / Walter and Tracy with
          This emendation, together with those at 140.21, 141.1, and 143.31 are
          discussed in the 'Essay on the Text', 426.
140.21 me, Master (Editorial) / me, Tracy, and come you too, Master
140.26 Let (MS) / let
141.1 two such poor caitiffs as thyself and me upon (MS) / three such poor
          caitiffs, as thyself, and me, and Tracy, upon
141.14 river, with two (MS river with two) / river, and along with it two
141.15 on her person (MS) / on the royal person
141.21 early (MS) / untimeously
          The Ed1 change was made to avoid repeating 'early' from line 19, but
          'untimeously' is quite wrong for Blount.
141.30 reluctantly (MS) / with reluctance
141.33 They (MS) / The gentlemen
142.5 these (MS) / this
142.7 womanhood and full (MS) / womanhood, and in the full
142.8 beauty and would (MS) / beauty, and who would
142.8 been a (MS) / been truly judged a
142.11 distinguishing (MS) / distinguished
142.28 amongst (MS) / among
142.43 shall (MS) / will
143.31 associate (Editorial) / associates
143.35 with two (MS) / by two
143.38 her attendants (MS) / the attendants
144.2 muddied (MS) / mudded
144.6 was both unusual (MS was both unusuall⟨y⟩) / was unusual
144.12 man—Your (MS man Your) / man, your
144.17 hesitating. "It (MS hesitating "It) / hesitating, "it

144.21 We shame (MS derived: Whe shame) / I take shame
144.25 may be—it (MS may be it) / may be—It
144.31 garments? what (MS garments what) / garment? What
144.37 answered (MS answerd) / said
144.42 lords?—the (MS lords—the) / lords? The
145.15 culvers (MS) / culverins
145.19 and such (MS) / and some such
145.22 He whom the speech was addressed to, (MS) / He to whom the speech
        was addressed,
145.33 He (MS) / The noble Earl
145.35 he knew (MS) / his lordship knew
145.37 until this (MS untill this) / until after he awoke this
146.18 awaked (MS) / awakened
146.18 only sound sleep (MS) / only sleep
146.21 these (MS) / this
146.25 that Holy (MS) / the Holy
146.25 In (MS) / in
146.26 safety'?" (Editorial: MS safety——") / safety?" "
146.31 Lincoln? hath (MS Lincoln hath) / Lincoln? Hath
146.35 word"—— (MS) / word, being"——
147.8   was due (MS) / is due
147.16 known—and (MS) / known. And
147.23 her, to (MS her to) / her, how to
147.24 the personal (MS) / her personal
147.32 City (MS) / city
147.39 purport. "Your (MS) / purport. [new paragraph] "Your
147.43 councillors. And (MS) / councillors; and
148.3   received (MS) / reserved
148.12 go before in (MS) / go in
148.20 her (MS) / her,
148.27 scarcer (MS) / scarce
148.29 Rhenish— (MS) / Rhenish;—
148.32 meat (MS) / meats
148.33 hall—But (MS) / hall! but
148.33 *galère* (Magnum) / *galere*
148.36 may (MS) / May
148.37 amidst (MS) / amid
149.1   the custom (MS) / the Queen's custom
149.22 achievement (MS) / achievements
150.1   no further excuse (MS) / no excuse
150.3   will relieve (MS will releive) / will speedily relieve
150.4   own—something (MS own something) / own. Something
150.13 behind her. (MS) / behind.
150.22 attend at court (MS) / attend court
150.24 us—this (MS) / us. This
150.30 shop rather in (MS) / shop in
150.30 Alley, Madam (MS Alley Madam) / Alley rather
151.1   "that (Magnum) / that [MS as Ed1]
        MS has no initial inverted commas to match the closing pair at line 4.
        Giving final compositional thoughts priority, the present text follows
        Magnum in supplying the initial commas rather than deleting the later
        pair.
151.12 she (MS) / She
151.12 chimed (MS chimd) / cap'd
151.13 and all such (MS) / and such

151.15 on it (MS) / of it
151.39 placet (MS) / Supplication
151.41 channel—methinks (MS channell—methinks) / channel. Methinks
152.19 where methinks we (MS) / where, methinks, we
152.22 quarrels (MS) / quarrel
153.13 apprehensions (MS) / apprehension
153.21 shot or long (MS) / shot, or with long
153.38 on (MS) / in
153.40 the gentlemen (MS) / such gentlemen
153.40 train (MS) / train,
154.5   lordly (MS) / lofty
154.38 newly a (MS) / newly admitted a
156.42 you." Yet (MS derived: you"—yet) / you." [new paragraph] Yet
164.25 marriage!—have (MS marriage have) / marriage!—Have
164.28 ourselves (MS) / ourself
165.31 heads slowly, without (MS heads slowly without) / heảds, without
166.8   syren (MS) / Syren
166.9   Ambition (MS) / ambition
166.13 It (Editorial) / "It
166.14 now, he thought, after (MS derived: now he thought after) / now," he
        thought, "after
166.19 compeers. (MS) / compeers."
166.21 maintaining (MS) / preserving
166.29 he must be (MS) / He must be
167.2   on that day in council (MS on that day in counsill) / in that day's
        council
167.26 for (MS) / of
167.40 follower of his fortunes throbbed (MS follower of his fortunes throbd)
        / follower throbbed
168.4   court; and courtiers, from high to low, acted (MS [unpunctuated]) /
        court and courtiers, from high to low; and they acted
168.5   return with (MS) / return the general greeting with
168.8   men." For (MS men. For) / men." [new paragraph] For
168.8   he (MS) / the favourite Earl
168.15 daughter?—why (MS daughter—why) / daughter? Why
168.27 pillow!—we (MS pillow—we) / pillow! We
168.30 Player (MS) / *player*
169.3   wit (MS) / Wit
169.7   cheeks (MS) / cheek
169.9   addressed himself (MS addressd himself) / approached
169.42 irreverend (MS) / irreverent
170.18 hastily—"come (MS derived: hastily "come) / hastily. "Come
170.25 staff (MS) / staff of office
170.33 just (MS) / thus
171.4   I will (MS) / I may well
        The MS reading may be either 'will' or 'well'.
171.26 in the bow (MS) / on the bow
171.29 on the (MS) / in the
171.31 to one to whom (MS) / to those before whom
171.36 those (MS) / the
172.10 his bosom (MS) / he
172.15 honour—for (MS) / honour. As for
172.17 by mine (MS) / by my change of plan, so far as he is concerned
172.26 noble (ISet) / young [MS as Ed1]
        This is Scott's own correction of an obvious error (compare line 29).

172.31 which all her (MS) / which her
173.2 board of my (MS) / board my
174.4 falchion, as I am told, though a (MS unpunctuated) / falchion, though, as I am told, a
174.25 will rather (MS) / should rather
174.28 Parish-garden (MS) / Bear-garden
174.31 adventure (MS) / venture
174.34 in over-courage (MS) / in their over-courage
174.36 then shall another (Editorial: MS then another) / then another
This and the next two emendations are discussed in the 'Essay on the Text', 426.
174.37 catch (MS) / catches
174.38 hang (MS) / hangs
174.42 beheld a many (MS) / beheld many
175.6 Elizabeth. "And (MS Elizabeth And) / Elizabeth; "and
175.13 say they (MS) / say that they
175.13 knaves (MS) / knaves,
175.14 and whose jests (MS) / and jests
175.17 others (MS) / other play artificers
175.32 their earthly (MS) / its earthly
176.5 are in (MS) / are spoken in
The word 'spoken' is awkward in itself, and it repeats line 2.
176.6 besides; beautiful however they (MS besides beautiful however they) / besides; but beautiful they
176.11 shows (MS) / shines
176.11 with taste (MS) / with the true taste
176.12 letters—but (MS) / letters. But
176.41 flattery so long (MS) / flattery long
176.42 recited (MS) / repeated
177.8 wherever (MS) / where-ever
Ed1 repeats the 'e' because of an end-of-line hyphen.
177.12 characters (MS) / character
177.17 manners (MS) / manner
177.21 with delicacy (MS) / in delicacy
177.30 grand (MS) / great
177.40 that now ... golden one. (MS derived: "that now ... golden one.) / that "now ... golden one."
178.19 palace ... departure. It (MS palace and continued to amuse themselves with various conversation untill the Queen gave the signal for departure It) / palace; and it
178.25 a pavilion (MS a ⟨small⟩ pavilion) / a small pavilion
178.29 mantle—come (MS) / mantle. Come
178.37 over with deliberation, once to (MS over with deliberation once to) / over, once with deliberation to
178.40 task—It (MS derived: task—it) / task. It
The movement of the MS is recovered in the present text, but Ed1's new sentence is accepted because the parenthetic pair of dashes which follow would otherwise seem confusing.
179.6 sacrifice of no one can be so (MS) / incense of no one can be more
179.10 Nine—Yet (MS Nine Yet) / Nine—yet
179.28 toward (MS) / towards
179.29 aid she (MS) / aid which she
179.32 without delay transmitted (MS) / transmitted without delay
180.9 intimated he (MS) / intimated that he
180.14 that countenance (MS) / that the countenance

180.22 as any (MS) / as do any
180.27 fair faces (MS) / fine faces
180.33 has (MS) / is
180.39 deadly paleness (MS) / emotion
180.43 basilisk—thank (MS) / basilisk.—Thank
181.26 let the sewer (MS) / Let the sewer
182.19 has at least (MS) / has, at least,
182.20 a (MS) / the
183.15 he saw (MS) / the confidant saw
183.27 an open avowal (MS) / an avowal
183.36 what (MS) / *what*
        This, and the following intensification, typical of James Ballantyne's
        work, would normally be accepted, but here they devalue 'King of
        England'.
183.38 King (MS) / KING
183.39 boot!—it (MS boot—it) / boot!—It
183.39 so, since it (MS so since it) / so. It
184.4   once (MS) / *once*
184.5   found (MS) / experienced
184.8   lord's (MS lords) / husband's
184.11 woman (MS) / women
184.15 her—she (MS) / her.—She
184.23 husband—her (MS) / husband. Her
184.37 Yet (MS) / yet
184.37 Kenilworth; Elizabeth (18mo: MS Kenilworth Elizabeth) / Kenil-
        worth, Elizabeth
185.5   need than that (MS) / need that
185.15 courts. [new paragraph] With (MS courts—NL. ↑With...↓) / courts.
        With
186.9   viewing (MS) / reviewing
186.26 proceed, father (MS proceed father) / proceed farther
186.35 man; "the (MS man "the) / man. "The
187.10 black (Ed2) / white [MS as Ed1]
        The Ed2 correction is preferred to 18mo and Magnum 'dark' since it is
        closer in time to the MS.
187.25 dignity. "You (MS dignity "You) / dignity, "you
187.30 calculations (MS) / calculation
187.32 And (MS) / and
187.36 earth—if (MS) / earth. If
188.3   erred—not (MS) / erred. Not
188.13 than (MS) / save
188.22 Obey (MS) / obey
188.23 not at a (MS) / not a
188.32 it, and (Editorial: MS it and) / it; and
189.37 And (MS) / and
190.3   thee—If (MS thee If) / thee—if
190.10 said (MS) / replied
190.28 Hal (MS) / Hall
190.36 and of reason (MS) / and reason
190.40 I have travelled (MS) / I travelled
190.40 into (MS) / in
191.1   so, there (MS so there) / so, and if there
191.4   production (MS) / productions
191.5   cradle—One (MS) / cradle—one
191.8   world—to (MS) / world—if this be all so, is it not reasonable that to

This emendation follows from the change at 191.1.

191.13 countenance. "Yet (MS countenance "Yet) / countenance; "yet
191.23 not, think'st thou, Art the (MS not thinkst thou Art the) / not Art, think'st thou, the
191.38 sequestered (MS sequestred) / sequestrated
191.42 Great Secret forever (MS) / great secret for ever
191.43 mankind—do not on humanity (MS) / mankind.—Do not humanity
192.3 time (MS) / life-time
192.5 jackanape!—hast (MS Jackanape—hast) / jackanape! Hast
192.13 green wood (MS) / green-wood [end-of-line hyphen]
193.3 among (MS) / amongst
193.6 hence (Ed2) / thence
        The MS is obscure here, possibly reading 'Whenc': Ed2 discerns Scott's probable intention.
193.13 detection. (MS detection—) / detection?
193.17 which (MS) / that
193.20 Varney?—why (MS Varney why) / Varney?—Why
193.38 Michael. "We (MS Michael—We) / Michael, "we
193.39 night (MS) / even
193.40 oddspittikins (MS derived: oddspitlekens) / odds blades and poniards
193.41 in (MS) / on
194.3 at thy pleasure (MS) / at pleasure
194.6 and as (MS) / and exhibiting as
194.13 times—take (MS) / times. Take
194.14 you—use (MS) / you. Use
194.20 remain (MS) / await
194.26 and will not (MS) / and not
195.25 furnished a good deal (MS) / furnished much
195.33 franklin (MS) / Franklin
195.36 Bonny (MS) / bonny
196.5 vogue (MS) / vague
196.9 Out sallied (MS) / Out into the yard sallied
196.10 ushered (MS usherd) / returned, ushering
196.16 insisted (MS) / had insisted much
196.33 Exchequer (MS) / exchequer .
196.38 D'ye (MS Dye) / Dost
197.3 So (MS) / so
197.17 around (MS) / round
197.18 Flower (MS) / flower
197.18 Noble (MS) / noble
197.18 Noble (Editorial) / noble
        The second 'Noble' is part of an insertion in proof.
197.29 and the (MS) / and of the
198.1 hath (MS) / has
198.2 a pretty piece (MS) / as pretty a piece
198.15 huswife's (MS) / housewife's
198.20 a wise man (MS) / wise men
198.26 Your (MS) / your
198.28 the meeter (MS the Meeter) / he who meets him
198.32 swaddled (MS) / raddled
199.8 roof, and (MS derived: roof and) / roof! And
199.22 wagers (MS) / wager
199.27 the place (MS) / The Place
200.3 as the (MS) / as being the
200.5 ingenuous (MS) / ingenious

200.6 whistle—and (MS whistle and) / whistle—And
200.16 flat (ISet) / fleet
The word is part of an insertion in proof.
201.3 discontent (MS) / discontented
201.20 marle (MS) / marvel
201.25 mine. You (MS mine You) / mine; you
201.26 incurred (MS incurrd) / encountered
201.32 the baggage (MS) / their baggage
202.13 apartment (MS) / apartments
202.17 *jouring* (MS) / *jowring*
202.21 moine (MS) / mine
202.31 But (MS) / but
202.31 them?—stay (MS them—stay) / them?—Stay
203.9 hath (MS) / has
203.11 pray (MS) / Pray
203.43 that head (MS) / That head
204.4 sweet-bags (MS) / sweet bags
204.9 occupation, "but (MS occupation but) / occupation. "But
204.12 arisen (MS) / risen
204.25 who cumbers (MS) / who would cumber
204.33 this the (MS) / this time the
205.5 me?—Who (MS me—Who) / me?—who
205.9 and have (MS) / and I have
205.14 in the mind (MS) / on the mind
205.26 this medicine (MS) / the medicine
205.36 She then cast (MS) / The Lady then piled
207.9 remain partially (Ed2) / remain long partially
The word 'long' should have been deleted when 'for many hours' was
inserted as part of a set of changes to this passage in proof.
207.9 it (MS) / it,
207.24 what (MS) / whatever
207.28 Villain (MS) / villain
207.37 King (MS) / king
207.37 Villain (MS) / villain
207.38 Vizier (MS) / vizier
207.38 And (MS) / and
207.38 Why, Emperor (MS Why Emperor) / why, emperor
207.39 have this (MS) / see this
207.42 Earl?—Answer (MS Earl—Answer) / Earl?—answer
207.43 boy. You (MS boy You) / boy, you
208.2 you (MS) / You
208.6 astrologer—"it (MS Astrologer "it) / astrologer. "It
208.17 me!—and (MS me—and) / me! And
208.31 her. [new paragraph] Neither (MS) / her. Neither
208.33 He had felt (MS) / He felt
209.5 Marriage (MS) / Her marriage with the Earl
209.8 favourite Earl's power (MS favourite Earls power) / favourite's
power
209.16 Anthony (Editorial) / Antony
Ed1 repeats the MS mis-spelling
209.32 proposed (MS) / prepared
210.10 momentarily (MS) / at every turn
210.11 He (MS) / Leicester
210.37 and depended (MS) / and who depended
210.42 in her judgment, not in (MS in her judgement not in) / on Elizabeth's

solid judgment, not on
The misreading of 'in' as 'on' probably suggested the 'solid', and 'Elizabeth's' here is a pedantic application of the principle concerning the clarification of pronouns.

210.43 355–356, 362 (Editorial) / 355, 356–362
        MS has '355. 356. 362'. Ed1's interpretation is incorrect.
211.3   predilections (MS) / predilection
211.15 with safety (MS) / in safety
211.17 with bitterness (MS) / in bitterness
211.24 England—all suggest (MS) / England. All things suggest
211.37 universe! and (MS universe and) / universe! And
211.42 what—methinks (MS) / what. Methinks
212.4   desire,—She (MS desire, She) / desire,—she
212.9   upon (MS) / for
212.25 thrown such impediments (MS) / thrown every such impediment
212.26 revels (MS) / revels,
212.26 could even (MS) / could propound even
212.29 yourself—On (MS) / yourself. On
212.30 Kenilworth—we (MS) / Kenilworth—We
212.32 Robsart—we (MS) / Robsart. We
212.41 sirrah! My (MS Sirrah My) / sirrah! my
213.12 methinks (MS) / Methinks
213.19 her?—such (MS her—such) / her? Such
213.36 such a perplexity (MS) / such perplexity
214.6   and consider their wishes (MS) / and to consider that other's wishes
214.7   conveniences (MS) / conveniencies
214.15 such a confinement (MS) / such confinement
214.22 post to (MS) / post for
214.37 after (MS) / afterwards
215.11 before him (MS) / before Leicester
215.18 fate! the (MS fate the) / fate! The
215.21 go—the (MS) / go. The
215.23 kingdom?—that (MS kingdom—that) / kingdom? That
215.35 he desired (MS) / he had desired
216.4   assigned (MS) / sssigned
217.11 respect, but little (MS respect but little) / respect; but with little
217.22 haunt almost constantly those (MS) / haunt those
218.7   up here like (MS) / up like
218.13 happier to (MS) / happier than I now am, to
218.20 Market-place yesterday— (MS market-place ↑yesterday ... ↓) /
        Market-place—
218.25 *to its Purgation* (MS) / *to Purgation*
218.26 *Firebrands*'—what (MS Firebrands" what) / *Firebrands'*—What
218.42 castle (MS) / mansion
        Ed1 retains Scott's idiomatic use of 'castle' for Cumnor Place at 62.29
        and 387.23, and it should have done so here also.
218.43 that (MS) / That
219.3   pshaw!—but (MS pshaw—but) / pshaw!—But
219.10 with an anxious (MS) / with anxious
219.13 court, and the (MS court and the) / court, the
219.17 yet hath (MS) / hath yet
219.18 the tidings (MS) / his tidings
219.20 he is ill. (MS he is ill—) / is he ill?
219.27 ears (MS) / ear
219.41 others—pray (MS) / others. Pray

219.43 brewing—God (MS) / brewing. God
220.1   bodes no (MS) / bodes us no
220.14 you!—undo (MS you—undo) / you!—Undo
220.19 ope (MS) / open
220.20 traitor!—use (MS traitor—use) / traitor!—Use
220.31 the circulation (MS) / her articulation
220.35 so much beauty (MS) / such beauty
221.8   throat!—he (MS throat—he) / throat! He
221.15 Janet—he (MS) / Janet. He
221.23 just claims (MS) / just claim
222.6   plan—thus (MS) / plan. Thus
222.9   to (MS) / in
222.25 darkness—have (MS) / darkness. Have
222.25 oblivion?—do (MS oblivion—do) / oblivion? Do
222.27 gained (MS gaind) / given
222.28 minutes—it (MS derived: minutes it) / minutes! It
222.30 tell (MS) / Tell
223.3   library with (MS) / library; with
223.8   deny the (MS) / deny it. The
223.20 another—lead (MS) / another. Lead
223.29 in pursuit (MS) / in the pursuit
224.4   slave!—but (MS slave—but) / slave!—But
224.24 [additional paragraph] "Speak not...not be." (MS "Speak not of him
        Janet—replied the lady "for thy sake I have striven to fear him less but it
        will not be"—)
        The transcriber's eye has dropped from one line to the next.
225.12 get (MS) / Get
225.18 prejudice—father (MS) / prejudice. Father
225.34 Forster? perhaps (MS Foster perhaps) / Foster? Perhaps
225.36 drink (MS) / Drink
226.12 hope (18mo) / Hope [MS as Ed1]
226.17 I return (MS) / I will return
226.31 matter?—wert (MS matter—wert) / matter? Wert
226.32 as a woman puts (MS derived) / as woman puts
        MS reads 'as women put', and this had to be changed to agree with the
        rest of the sentence, but the present solution is more idiomatic than that
        adopted by Ed1.
227.2   transmewed (MS transmewd) / transmuted
227.5   tend; but (MS tend but) / tend to; but
227.10 city (MS) / City
227.13 contents (MS) / content
227.24 the Apocalypse (MS) / the Christian Apocalypse
227.27 Nature's (MS) / nature's
227.29 summer (MS) / summer's
227.32 doubtfully—"And (MS) / doubtfully; "and
227.34 abomination or frame (MS) / abomination, or who frame
227.42 approached (MS approachd) / brought
228.22 You did (MS) / Thou didst
229.6   patient—the (MS) / patient. The
229.7   win bread (MS) / win my bread
229.28 arms, which were crossed upon a table that (MS arms which wer [or
        badly-formed 'was'] crossd upon a table that) / arms, and these crossed
        upon a table which
229.34 and a cheek (MS) / and cheek
229.37 you—rise (MS) / you. Rise

230.1 what (MS) / What
230.6 rise (MS) / Rise
230.7 let (MS) / Let
230.7 poison—so—now feel you not that (MS) / poison!—So; feel you not now that
230.16 wicked—believe (MS wicked—beleive) / wicked. Believe
230.17 on (MS) / in
230.30 clear in (MS) / clear on
230.35 body?—have (MS body—have) / body?—Have
230.36 mind?—can (MS mind—can) / mind?—Can
230.38 mind—the (MS mine—the) / mind. The
231.1 your (MS) / thy
231.4 may (MS) / May
231.10 of Master (MS) / to Master
231.11 has (MS) / is
231.21 with jewels which (MS) / of jewels, which
231.22 some emergency (MS) / some future emergency
231.23 her own dress (MS) / her dress
231.39 she was (MS) / the daughter of Foster was
231.40 would (MS) / should
233.5 unto him?' And (MS unto him—And) / to him?' and
233.7 discourse, for (MS discourse for) / discourse; but
233.12 their first (MS) / the first
233.23 restores (MS) / restore
233.27 pleasures (MS) / revels
234.14 assigned me (MS assignd me) / assigned for me
234.16 to (MS) / To
234.21 and to own (MS) / And to own
235.18 me—they (MS) / me. They
235.19 pleasure—it (MS) / pleasure—It
235.21 will cease (MS) / shall cease
235.38 cheney (MS) / chency
235.43 beseems (MS) / becomes
236.23 disturbed—fear (MS) / disturbed.—Fear
237.8 while, Wayland (Magnum: MS while Wayland) / while Wayland,
237.9 hand (MS) / hand,
237.13 mists (MS) / mist
237.25 observing the (MS) / observing, that
237.29 from my anvil (MS) / from anvil
237.30 advanced. But (MS advanced but) / advanced on our way. But
237.32 folks' (MS) / folks
237.42 unsurmountable (MS) / insurmountable
238.17 lout of (MS) / lout, seemingly
238.39 boide ye—boide (MS boide ye—boid) / bide ye—bide
239.21 Robbery! Robbery! (MS Robbery Robbery) / Robbery! robbery!
239.28 as Paul's (MS as Pauls) / as St Paul's
240.7 ejaculating "Stop! stop!", (MS ejaculating "Stop stop") / ejaculating, "Stop! stop!"
240.7 seemed however rather (MS seemd however rather) / seemed rather
240.16 such," when the mercer recovered (MS derived) / such." [new paragraph] When the mercer had recovered
    The MS is confused here: this and the following two emendations are designed to repair it as economically and faithfully as possible. MS reads: 'Varney had just time to caution the Lady not to be alarmd adding "this fellow is a gull and I will use him as such" when the mercer had

recoverd breath and audacity enough to confront them and order Wayland in a menacing tone to deliver up his palfrey.'

240.17 them and order (MS) / them, he ordered
240.18 him (Editorial) / Wayland [MS as Ed1]
240.29 spoil (MS) / despoil
240.32 leap on (MS) / leap forth on
240.40 Shottesbrook (MS) / Shottesbrok
241.17 rash, taffeta (MS Rash, taffata) / rash-taffeta
241.17 paropa (Editorial: MS [probably] paropee) / parapa
241.21 bayard (MS) / Bayard
241.28 "yonder (MS) / yonder
242.1 of Master Goldthread (MS Master Goldthred) / of Goldthred
242.39 company (MS) / party
243.36 Wayland hopes of joining with them (MS derived: Wayland the ⟨pleasant pr⟩ hopes of joining with them) / Wayland the hope of joining them
243.39 look deadly pale, so that (MS look deadly pale so that) / look so deadly pale, that
244.2 disorder; the (MS) / disorder. The
245.4 *Sybillæ* (Editorial) / *Sybillæ*
245.4 speaker. "She (MS derived: speaker "She) / speaker, "she
245.5 Robert (Editorial) / Richard
245.8 and woman (MS) / and a woman
245.20 needed—and (MS needed and) / needed—And
246.3 hit, (MS hit) / hit it,
246.4 forth with (MS) / forth of bounds, along with
246.26 do (MS) / love
247.7 tended (MS) / attended
247.13 desire in the Countess of Leicester to (MS) / desire on the Countess of Leicester's part to
247.19 down (MS) / downwards
247.26 miles—But (MS) / miles,—but
247.27 up—although (MS) / up; although
247.28 carriage (MS) / carriages
247.29 which is (MS) / which last is
248.9 shouldst (MS) / should
248.13 Oliver, say my (MS Oliver say my) / Oliver, my
248.16 on the pretext (MS) / on pretext
248.31 castle, to whose (MS Castle to whose) / castle, whose
249.12 upward (MS) / upwards
249.21 had ever been accustomed to express (MS had ever been accustomd to express) / had only been accustomed to form and to express
249.23 of experience and presence of mind, and utterly unable to (MS of experience and presence of mind & utterly unable to) / of presence of mind, and of ability to
250.2 instantly, and (MS instantly and) / instantly ready, and
250.7 she said (MS) / said she
250.10 wishes—the (MS) / wishes. The
250.10 Kenilworth—it (MS) / Kenilworth. It
250.13 unknown (MS) / Unknown
250.23 assure (MS) / ensure
250.24 it *me* (MS it ⟨t⟩ *me*) / it to *me*
250.35 done—thou (MS) / done. Thou
251.20 as the direct (MS) / as direct
251.21 such was (MS) / such and so great was
251.32 sending in large (MS) / sending large

251.38 provisions (MS) / provision
252.1 head (MS) / heads
252.2 There were (MS There was) / Here were
252.19 inconveniences (MS) / inconveniencies
252.23 jollity; the (MS) / jollity. The
252.42 into it (MS derived: into to) / into the high road
253.8 intermixture (MS) / mixture
253.13 to Aglionby, 'Little Master Recorder (MS to Aylionby "Little Master Recorder) / to little Aglionby, 'Master Recorder
253.16 and then (MS) / And then
253.16 what a grace (MS) / what grace
253.21 who should (MS) / she would
253.29 she is (MS) / She is
253.29 she gave (MS) / She gave
253.39 Meantime (MS) / Meanwhile
254.36 princes (MS) / princely
255.13 who can enjoy (MS) / who enjoy
255.41 under direction (MS) / under the direction
256.19 waiting?—come (MS waiting—come) / waiting? Come
256.23 him, and, only (MS him and only) / him, while only
Ed2 and Magnum correct the punctuation error in Ed1; the 'while' repeats line 21.
256.28 entrance (MS) / admission
256.31 in (MS) / or
257.1 poor Amy's (MS) / her
257.2 within, and (MS within and) / within her, and
257.6 give—name (MS derived: yeild name) / give. Name
257.11 well—he (MS) / well! He
257.21 him; "do (MS him, "do) / him; "Do
263.14 north-west (Editorial) / north-east
The manuscript is missing. The Ed1 direction here is wrong factually, and according to all of Scott's known sources.
263.36 these (MS) / those
264.8 tresses. (MS) / tresses, secured by what is called a true-love knot.
The additional words, probably inserted by Scott in proof, inadvertently led to a repetition of 'secured'.
264.14 me—but (MS) / me. But
264.27 journal (MS) / journey
265.9 had first (MS) / had at first
265.10 can (MS) / am
265.11 to Leicester (MS) / to my Lord of Leicester
265.17 its (MS) / their
265.24 find any (MS) / find out any
265.31 where (MS) / when
266.20 so as (MS) / in order
266.24 miller's (Magnum) / millar's
266.40 bear. (MS bear—) / bear?
266.42 will—however (MS) / will. However
267.1 which (MS) / that
267.2 withal (MS derived: with) / which
267.23 you (MS) / ye
267.28 one—fare (MS) / one.—Fare
268.6 where (MS) / when
268.11 toward (MS) / towards
268.33 moorlands (MS) / moorland

269.35 is (MS) / be
269.39 aid, Master Tressilian (MS aid Master Tressilian) / aid, Tressilian
269.40 kindness (MS) / kindnes
270.4 with (MS) / With
270.6 consequence (MS) / consequences
270.8 that naturally (MS) / that had naturally
270.24 apartment?—it (MS apartment—it) / apartment? It
270.27 voice (MS) / tone
270.30 You do (MS) / You *do*
270.31 you do (MS) / you *do*
270.33 this (MS) / the
270.35 towers (MS) / halls
270.41 generous. Grant (MS) / generous—Grant
271.1 do with (MS) / do for me with
271.5 limit (MS) / Limit
271.15 And (MS) / and
271.32 interference more (MS) / interference on his part more
271.38 on her (MS) / in her
272.8 me?—do (MS) / me? Do
272.10 speech or (MS) / speech nor
272.11 interference?—will (MS interference—will) / interference?—
       Will
272.21 the twenty-four (MS the twenty four) / the next twenty-four
273.13 mean (MS) / meant
273.13 thee (MS) / you
273.24 have (MS) / Have
273.35 Only (MS) / only
273.40 and some (MS) / and that same
274.4 that." He (MS that" he) / that." [new paragraph] He
274.6 hearing. "I (MS hearing "I) / hearing. [new paragraph] "I
274.7 that, Master (MS that Master) / that, my Master
274.9 our (MS) / your
274.20 looks, e'en cut (ISet) / e'e, uncut
       This motto is not present in the MS. Presumably Scott's addition was
       misread and he did not spot this until the ISet.
274.29 request. Dependant (MS request. Dependent) / request,—dependant
274.30 Varney, such (MS) / Varney? Such
274.30 reasoning, the (MS reasoning the) / reasoning. The
274.31 her not driving him (MS) / his not driving her
274.33 that man (MS) / Varney
275.22 this is no (MS) / this no
275.23 this (MS) / these
275.26 of Leicester (MS) / of my Lord Leicester
275.27 into (MS derived: enter) / under
275.42 indeed!—no (MS indeed—no) / indeed! No
276.11 did he (MS) / did Wayland
276.16 immense (MS) / stately
276.20 fury!—then (MS fury—then) / fury!—Then
276.33 those (MS) / these
276.38 after—perhaps (MS) / after.—Perhaps
276.40 trow—But (MS) / trow; but
276.43 road—via!" (MS road—via"——) / road."
277.17 wall—He (MS) / wall—he
277.18 steps (MS) / yards
277.20 wide, (MS) / wide open,

277.22 Castle?—march (MS castle—march) / Castle? March
277.24 certain (MS) / timid
277.37 wert (MS) / art
277.37 tower?—thy (MS tower—thy) / tower? Thy
277.41 Upon (MS) / upon
277.43 amongst (MS) / among
278.1 commodities—this (Magnum: MS commodities—Hark thee sirrah—
        this) / commodities.—Hark thee, sirrah—This
        Scott apparently forgot to delete 'Hark thee, sirrah' when he developed
        a new thought with 'Hark ye fellow'. The Magnum's elimination of this
        repetition is accepted.
278.4 on (MS) / in
278.30 felt a deep (MS) / felt deep
279.3 Little-ease, my (MS Little-ease my) / Little-ease. My
279.4 Kenilworth. Know (MS derived: Kenilworth—Know) / Kenilworth,
        know
279.8 come (MS) / came
279.15 let (MS) / Let
279.16 out—if (MS) / out. If
279.21 hearing (MS) / answer
279.29 Ye (MS) / You
279.39 murther (MS) / murder
279.40 ward!—you (MS ward—you) / ward!—You
280.2 untenable (MS) / untenantable
280.2 years—and (MS) / years. And
280.13 go (MS) / Go
280.18 supernatural, "Thou (MS supernatural—"Thou) / supernatural. [new
        paragraph] "Thou
280.22 sets you in (MS) / sets in
280.32 and—in short— (MS) / and, in short,
280.37 and moon (MS) / and the moon
281.8 V—and (MS) / V. and
281.9 hell—And (MS) / hell; and
281.11 'when (12mo) / "when
281.12 sever,' (12mo) / sever,"
281.15 hand (MS) / Hand
281.29 it (MS) / It
281.32 Laurence, but (MS Laurence but) / Lawrence. But
282.24 gentlemen—whence (MS) / gentlemen. Whence
282.26 must multiply (MS) / are fain to multiply
282.27 suits—And (MS) / suits; and
283.1 on (MS) / at
283.8 He said (MS) / Tressilian said
283.39 Bartholomew-fair—we (MS) / Bartholomew-fair. We
283.40 women making moppets (MS) / women moppets
284.10 forwards (MS) / forward
284.31 amongst these (MS) / among these
284.33 amongst the (MS) / among the
285.2 upon (MS) / on
285.25 at (MS) / of
286.2 *fatidicæ* (Editorial) / *fatidicæ*
286.6 *pertæsa barbaræ loquelæ* (Editorial) / *pertæsa barbaræ loquelæ*
286.9 this world will (MS) / will this world
286.12 around (MS) / round
286.14 within it that (MS) / within that

286.27 fast!" [new paragraph] Onward (MS fast" ↑NL↓ Onward) / fast!"
Onward

287.20 these (MS) / those

287.23 but the feelings (MS) / but feelings

287.25 and expressed (MS and expressd) / and they expressed

287.32 amongst (MS) / among

287.35 very few—moral (MS) / very few moral

287.40 he felt (MS) / his lord felt

288.21 his secret ally (MS derived: his ally) / the gigantic warder's secret ally
The change is likely to have been made by Scott in proof, but he failed to
notice the recurrence of 'gigantic' at lines 28 and 33. The present text
compromises by retaining 'secret' but avoiding the 'gigantic'.

288.38 law. [no space] Yet (MS law—[no space] Yet) / law. [line space] Yet

288.44 keys (MS) / key

290.14 Mortimers, and the (MS Mortimers and the) / Mortimers, the

291.6 flight and shot (MS flight & shot) / flight-shot

291.19 under the discharge (MS) / under discharge

291.27 this (MS) / the

293.23 is to (MS) / was to

293.24 most learned (MS most learnd) / wisest

294.10 complacence (MS) / complacency

294.11 to—it (MS) / to. It

294.22 his (MS) / His

294.32 he dared not (MS) / for neither did he dare

295.17 have fair (MS) / have a fair

295.24 they (MS) / it

295.35 desirous (MS) / anxious

295.36 occasion (MS) / reason

295.39 evidences (MS) / evidence

296.42 forwards (MS) / forward

296.42 the robe (MS) / her robe

297.3 request!—decide (MS request—decide) / request! Decide

297.4 hastily—give (MS hastily—grant) / hastily. Give

297.6 to a demonstration (MS) / to demonstration

297.17 fool—what (MS fool what) / fool. What

297.36 worse; for (MS worse for) / worse for him; for

297.38 restraint. We (MS) / restraint.—We

298.9 quiet—only (MS) / quiet. Only

298.25 codshead—for (MS) / codshead.—For

299.24 troublesome guest (MS) / troublesome one

299.36 methinks (MS) / methinks,

300.22 lineage—"Only (MS) / lineage, "only

300.23 and then (MS) / And then

300.34 Countess (Editorial) / Duchess [MS as Ed1]
This emendation is discussed in the 'Essay on the Text', 425.

300.35 to have named (MS) / would have named

300.36 to have enabled (MS) / would have enabled

300.37 this (MS) / his

300.37 waited till the Queen assented (MS derived: waited the Queen
assented) / waited the Queen's assent

301.1 Countess (Editorial) / Duchess [MS as Ed1]

301.15 with (MS) / of

301.31 broad side (MS) / broadside

301.34 amble, and, with a mixture (MS amble and with a mixture) / amble; and
the implied mixture

302.7 Countess (Editorial) / Duchess [MS as Ed1]
302.12 said (MS) / replied
302.12 Countess (Editorial) / Duchess [MS as Ed1]
302.21 Countess (Editorial) / Duchess [MS as Ed1]
302.36 *très* (18mo) / *tres*
303.9 acclamation (MS) / acclamations
304.20 wisdom (MS) / Wisdom
304.37 be misled (MS) / be at present misled
305.30 ever (MS) / soever
305.32 hundredth knows (MS) / hundredth man knows
305.41 and in (MS) / and I believe in
306.1 because astrologers (MS because Astrologers) / because the astrologers
306.8 And (MS) / and
306.13 beside, "go (MS beside "go) / beside him, "go
306.14 not murther (MS) / not do murther
306.18 ill—and (MS) / ill. And
306.20 mortal. (MS) / mortal?
306.22 Away! Away! (MS Away Away) / Away! away!
306.26 brain (MS) / brains
306.27 might (MS) / may
306.29 But, grant (MS But grant) / But God grant
306.30 so, I (MS so I) / so. I
306.36 to the husband conjoining (MS) / to prevent the husband from con-
        joining
306.37 to (MS) / with
307.8 clew (MS Clew) / clue
307.17 thou?—there (MS thou—there) / thou? There
307.36 means (MS) / mean'st
307.39 'Tis (MS Tis) / It is
308.17 me—he (MS) / me. He
308.19 expect; and (MS expect and) / expect him; and
308.23 joined with the (MS derived: joind the) / with the
308.27 before. (MS) / before her.
308.31 each mental and bodily resource (MS) / such mental and bodily
        resources
309.20 are—Great God! And (MS are—Great God And) / are. Great God!
        and
309.25 life—Can (MS) / life, can
309.26 Magician (MS) / magician
309.33 wailed (MS waild) / would melt
310.40 on (MS) / from
311.1 me (MS) / *me*
311.1 me!—a (MS me—a) / me! A
311.6 hasting (MS) / hastening
311.7 had yet the (MS) / had the
311.17 this (MS) / the
311.34 mimicking (MS) / in mockery of
311.39 best...as this is, where (MS best—for rubs in the road of pleasure are
        —like ↑ (he made a step towards her and staggerd) ↓ —like ⟨such⟩ a⟨n⟩
        ↑ damnd ↓ uneven floor as this is where) / best—like thy present as little
        —(he made a step towards her, and staggered)—as little as—such a
        damned uneven floor as this, where
312.1 nearer me (MS) / nearer to me
312.14 damn (MS) / Damn
312.22 What devil's (MS what ⟨the⟩ devils) / What the devil's

312.30 good under (MS) / good prisoners under
312.38 seized (MS) / raised
313.23 wench! where (MS wench where) / wench! Where
313.25 her—that (MS) / her. That
313.29 ay! it's (MS aye its) / ay! It's
313.32 hatches—the (MS) / hatches. The
314.2 and to get (MS) / and get
314.5 impress (MS) / imprint
314.5 keys (MS) / key
314.5 an imprint (MS) / a mark
314.15 Ay (MS Aye) / ay
314.20 lamentation (MS) / lamentations
314.30 amongst (MS) / among
314.31 be (MS) / lie
314.37 letter—even (MS letter even) / letter. Even
315.9 into that (MS) / to that
315.18 her travelling (MS) / her own travelling
315.30 possible, (Editorial [MS punctuation obscure]) / possible;
316.25 habit (MS) / habits
316.33 presented. (MS) / represented or wore.
316.34 with (MS) / and
316.43 Countess (Editorial) / Duchess [MS as Ed1]
317.4 Countess (Editorial) / Duchess [MS as Ed1]
317.5 conclusions (MS) / conclusion
317.9 anticipate (MS) / anticipated
317.10 mingle (MS) / mix
317.29 people—other (MS) / people. Other
317.30 no (MS) / No
317.31 were (MS) / Were
317.32 But (MS) / but
317.32 be—delay (MS) / be.—Delay
317.37 repeated—go (MS) / repeated. Go
317.41 Were it *but* (MS Were it but) / were it *but*
317.41 But no (MS) / but no
318.2 but yet (MS but ↑yet↓) / yet but
318.30 hands (MS) / hands,
319.6 instinctively she (MS) / she instinctively
319.16 Enchanter (MS) / enchanter
319.24 What (MS) / what
320.15 father?—thou (MS father—thou) / father? Thou
320.16 thy (MS) / the
320.16 inches—thou (MS) / inches—Thou
320.22 make (MS) / take
320.26 mercy!—I (Editorial: MS mercy woman—I) / mercy! woman—I
        Ed1's punctuation probably indicates an unfulfilled intention to delete
        'woman' because of its occurrence in lines 28 and 30.
320.31 thou? speak (MS thou speak) / thou? Speak
320.31 thou wert (MS) / Thou wert
321.12 that (MS) / when
321.19 they wont (MS) / they were wont
321.27 was light (MS) / is light
321.28 was to (MS) / were to
322.3 that summons (MS) / that is to summon
322.22 censure (MS) / sentence
322.24 around. "We (MS around—"We) / around, "we

322.26 England—Attach (MS derived: England Attach) / England, attach
322.33 noble, from . . . Boleyns accustomed (MS noble from . . . Boleyns accustomd) / noble, who, from . . . Boleyns, was accustomed
323.24 Elizabeth, while Varney (MS Elizabeth while Varney) / Elizabeth. [new para-
graph] Varney
323.27 pardon!—Or (MS pardon—Or) / pardon!—or
324.34 with (MS) / for
325.2 whom (MS) / which
325.20 hither?—why (MS hither—why) / hither? Why
325.24 could (MS) / can
325.25 when (MS) / who are
325.26 malady—he (MS) / malady. He
327.24 launch out (MS) / launches forth
327.35 is now indeed (MS) / is indeed
328.4 villain—And (MS) / villain; and
328.10 Earl. "For (MS) / Earl; "for
328.17 Leicester sighed, and (Ed2: MS Leicester sighd and) / Leicester, sighed and
328.17 replied, "Varney (MS replied Varney) / replied. [new paragraph] Varney
328.37 she but truly (MS) / she truly
328.38 shall (MS) / *shall*
329.4 of thy (MS) / of the
329.13 him—fetch (MS) / him. Fetch
329.17 apartment (MS) / apartments
329.25 in a (MS) / on a
329.39 effected in (MS) / effected on
330.7 those (MS) / these
330.23 not come hither contrary (MS derived: not hither contrary) / not here contrary
330.38 it earnest (MS) / it in earnest
330.41 a cause (MS) / one
330.42 his—but (MS) / his. But
331.1 mine—may (MS) / mine. May
331.10 have (MS) / has
331.14 you—you (MS) / you. You
331.32 house!—when (MS house.—when) / house!—When
332.11 would, had fate allowed, have rendered her a (MS would had fate allowd have renderd her a) / would have rendered her, had fate allowed, a
332.12 ornament to (MS) / ornament of
332.17 comply—this (MS) / comply. This
332.30 hand—lead (Editorial: MS hand lead) / hand, lead
332.31 throne—say (MS throne say) / throne—Say
333.6 wife?—for (MS wife—for) / wife? For
333.8 dangers (MS) / danger,
333.8 that, like so many scare-crows (MS derived: that so many scarecrows) / that, like scare-crows
333.14 sacrifice—fear (MS sacrifice fear) / sacrifice. Fear
333.19 state!—there (MS state—there) / state! There
333.42 perish (MS) / *perish*
334.7 this (MS) / that
334.16 She's (MS) / This is
334.22 Varney, partly (MS Varney partly) / Varney, and partly
334.29 command Wales (MS) / have authority in Wales
334.30 I command the (MS) / I lead the

334.32 following (MS) / followers
334.39 assumed (MS) / resumed
335.4 you think (MS) / thou thinkest
335.9 by reflected (MS) / by the reflected
335.27 threw from his tablets (MS) / threw his tablets from him
335.40 treason. But (MS treason But) / treason, but
335.41 answered (MS) / said
336.3 that which (MS derived: which) / what
336.6 in (MS) / on
336.24 lord—you (MS) / lord. You
337.16 it had rested (MS) / it rested
337.19 the castle. And (MS) / Cumnor-Place; and
       See note to 218.42.
337.22 Leicester with the circumstances . . . the astounded Leicester (MS with
       the circumstances attending Tressilians visit at Cumnor Place when he
       made use of the agency of Lambourne to make his way into the place of
       Amy's residence. He pointed out to the astounded Leicester) / Leices-
       ter how
       This sentence was clearly omitted accidentally, the transcriber's eye
       dropping from one 'Leicester' to the next.
337.28 and seen (MS) / and had seen
337.32 Tressilian had (MS) / Tressilian at Cumnor-Place, had
337.35 ye—in (MS) / ye—and in
338.1 Thou art (MS) / You are
338.10 sends (MS) / sent
338.15 conference (MS) / conferences
338.28 never—the (MS) / never.—The
338.35 lord—you (MS Lord you) / lord. You
338.40 disguise. But (MS derived: her note But) / disguise; but
       The words 'in disguise' were inserted in proof.
339.15 wanton (MS) / woman
339.19 said—besides (MS) / said. Besides
339.27 Varney—So (MS) / Varney, so
339.29 trusty and faithful (MS trusty & faithful) / trusty, my well-beloved
339.30 life. (MS derived: life—) / life?
339.35 Leicester. "Yet (MS Leicester "Yet) / Leicester; "yet
339.38 has such (MS) / can have no such
339.41 has been (MS) / hast been
339.42 me!—Thy (MS me—Thy) / me! Thy
339.43 piercing—may (MS piercing may) / piercing—May
339.43 innocent?—prove (MS innocent—prove) / innocent? Prove
340.41 fury (MS) / force
340.41 jewels!—force (MS jewels force) / jewels!—Force
341.13 ever!—Speak not for her, Varney—She dies! (MS ever. Speak not for
       her Varney She dies——) / ever!—Tell me not of forgiveness, Varney
       —She is doomed!
341.19 those (MS) / these
341.21 forgotten, when (MS forgotten when) / forgotten. when
341.21 Well is he has an (MS) / Well, he has no
342.7 different totally (MS) / totally different
342.10 military, had seemed (MS military had seemd) / military, seemed
342.10 sphere; while (MS sphere while) / sphere; and while
343.5 interruptedly (MS) / interrupted
343.41 ourselves (MS) / ourself
344.16 evening. And (MS evening And) / evening, and

344.20 Tressilian!—no (MS Tressilian—no) / Tressilian!—No
344.35 incontroulable (MS*) / uncontroulable
For the significance of the American editions denoted by the asterisk see 403.
345.4 but master (MS) / but be master
345.5 shame (MS) / am shamed
345.10 But first take the farewell (MS*) / but first take farewell
345.15 passion—Him (MS*) / passion, him
345.18 this (MS*) / thus
345.30 love—the (MS*) / love? The
345.32 misused? and (MS* misused and) / misused? And
345.35 having ever (MS*) / ever having
345.37 *fiat* (MS*) / fiat
345.38 Being (MS*) / being
345.38 Justice (MS*) / justice
345.41 seemed as (MS* seemd as) / frowned, as
This emendation is discussed in the 'Essay on the Text', 426.
346.13 devised (MS*) / found
This emendation is discussed in the 'Essay on the Text', 426.
347.27 the evening (MS*) / this evening
347.40 of Angelo (MS*) / of Michael Angelo
347.40 Chantrey (1Set) / Chauntry
348.25 him rid (MS*) / them rid
348.29 is a pity (MS*) / is pity
348.33 shape (MS) / one
348.38 wax work for (MS*) / wax for
349.23 part (MS*) / parts
349.27 entrenched (MS) / trenched
349.39 hand (MS*) / hands
350.11 galleries (MS*) / gallery
350.21 amongst (MS) / among
350.37 thrust into (MS*) / thrust themselves into
351.8 around, and (MS* around and) / around him, and
351.15 all homage (MS*) / all do homage
351.30 by direction (MS*) / by the direction
352.5 noticed (MS*) / mentioned
352.18 sheer (MS*) / short
352.24 replied (MS*) / answered
352.31 turned (MS* turnd) / hurried
353.17 Tressilian of Cornwall require (MS*) / Tressilian require
353.23 may (MS*) / May
353.26 own. We (MS*) / own—We
353.28 distemperature—the (MS*) / distemperature. The
353.30 period (MS*) / time
354.5 scenes (MS*) / sense
354.17 But (MS*) / but
354.19 Countess (Editorial: not present in MS) / Duchess
354.23 lord?—we (MS* Lord—we) / lord?—We
355.7 horse-litter. (Editorial: MS horse-litter—") / horse-litter."
355.12 do (MS*) / Do
355.15 Sir Richard departed, and (MS* Sir Richard and) / Sir Richard Varney departed and
The MS is defective here, but the intermediary only needed to insert 'departed' after 'Sir Richard'.
355.22 pressing—he (MS*) / pressing—He
355.23 them—if (MS*) / them. If

355.24 rid this (MS*) / rid me of this
355.30 up (MS*) / upon
355.31 Varney—We (MS*) / Varney, we
356.2 round (MS*) / around
356.9 suit Richard (MS*) / suit Sir Richard
356.19 where (MS) / in which
357.5 small postern-door (MS* small ⟨secret⟩ postern door) / small secret postern-door
357.13 has thus disgraced (MS*) / has this day disgraced
357.15 me?—no (MS* me—no) / me? No
357.16 life—in (MS*) / life. In
357.17 broken—kingdoms (MS*) / broken. Kingdoms
357.28 illumed (MS*) / illumined
358.26 of (MS*) / with
359.1 proceed—you (MS*) / proceed. You
359.21 say her (MS) / speak of her
360.3 villain (MS*) / Villain
360.26 guard, with their halberds in their hands, passed (MS* guard with their hallbards in their hands passd) / guard passed
361.12 to end (MS*) / to an end
361.27 yours—Some (MS*) / yours. Some
361.29 away—I (MS*) / away. I
361.31 head—And (MS*) / head; and
362.11 those (MS*) / these
362.24 this (MS) / his
362.32 blows (MS*) / blows;
362.36 1002 (Editorial) / 1012
         Scott's date is wrong: so is 'Hock-tide', but this may be a traditional association.
362.39 interest (MS*) / influence
363.8 pastime (MS*) / pastimes
363.12 passed (MS* passd) / pressed
363.17 dresses, to (MS dresses to) / dresses, resembling knights, in order to
         This change was made in proof, but it creates a repetition of 'resembling . . . resemble'. The present text adopts the most elegant solution.
364.6 not (MS*) / never
364.9 could (MS) / should
         The early American editions have 'would'.
365.1 subjected—Captain (MS* subjected Captain) / subjected to—Captain
365.12 readers' (MS*) / reader's
365.19 Elizabeth's (MS*) / Elizabeth
365.20 the rude imitation (MS*) / the imitation
365.28 for of withdrawing (MS*) / for withdrawing
366.12 interruption," laid (Ed2: MS interruption laid) / interruption,' laid
366.18 lordship dared (MS) / lordship has dared
366.28 amongst (MS) / among
366.38 bade (MS*) / bid
367.2 slave?—die (MS* slave—die) / slave?—Die
367.13 with (MS*) / in
367.31 with a faultering (MS*) / with faultering
368.21 through (MS* ⟨by⟩ ↑through↓) / by
368.25 boy! Why (MS* boy Why) / boy, why
368.26 it (MS) / the bearer
368.28 bearer (MS) / messenger
368.37 Varney!—And (MS* Varney—And) / Varney!—and

368.41 But (MS*) / but
368.43 she must (MS*) / she *must*
368.43 I must (MS*) / I *must*
369.1   safety—my (MS*) / safety. My
369.1   lord—But (MS*) / lord; but
369.19 acknowledged, and (MS* acknowleged and) / acknowledged in
369.26 page (MS*) / boy
370.8   features and meanness (MS*) / features, and the meanness
371.12 still in (MS*) / still habited in
371.24 here you come with this (MS) / hither you come with a
371.38 must come immediately (MS* must come immediatly) / must immedi-
        ately
372.12 Fens (MS*) / fens
372.13 didst learn (MS*) / didst thou learn
372.14 web-feet (MS*) / webbed feet
372.24 to (MS*) / into
372.28 in presence (MS*) / in the presence
373.21 these wild storms (MS*) / this wild storm
        In MS the first word is ambiguous, but 'storms' is clear.
373.30 statesman (MS) / statesmen
373.41 but seem (MS) / rather than seem
374.19 dignity, her (MS* dignity her) / dignity, and her
374.19 usual (MS) / wonted
374.34 any thing which she could visit upon (MS*) / any thing on account of
        which she could vent her wrath upon
375.8   confession (MS) / confesion
375.18 guest (Editorial) / host
376.14 this secret (MS*) / this a secret
376.15 surprise with (MS* surprize with) / surprise us with
377.36 rose (MS) / could rise
377.40 amusement (MS*) / amusements
378.2   pleasure shewing (MS* pleasure showing) / pleasure in shewing
378.20 his small (MS*) / a small
378.31 countenance (MS*) / countenence
379.3   desiring to (MS*) / desiring him to
379.10 those on which (MS*) / those which
379.26 that trusty (MS) / that his trusty
380.5   his hasty journey (MS*) / his journey
380.12 no (MS*) / No
380.12 ay (MS*) / Ay
380.14 he (MS*) / He
380.15 penitent!—awake (MS* penitent—awake) / penitent!—Awake
380.20 Janet?—is (MS* Janet—is) / Janet?—Is
380.28 what (MS*) / What
380.41 Varney, "you (Ed2 : MS Varney you) / Varney, 'you
380.42 light—up (MS*) / light. Up
380.43 why (MS*) / Why
380.43 lectureship (MS*) / lecture-shop
381.9   ready—All (MS* derived: ready All) / ready, all
381.16 kind—ay (MS* kind—aye) / kind.—Ay
381.17 come (MS*) / Come
381.33 ceremony—my (MS* ceremony my) / ceremony. My
382.22 Cumnor (MS*) / Cumnor-Place
382.26 left her (MS*) / left with her
382.43 sacrifice—he (MS*) / sacrifice. He

383.38 this (MS*) / his
383.43 Lambourne (MS*) / Lambourne's
384.11 trust you (MS*) / trust to you
384.14 wise make (MS*) / wise as make
384.16 any (MS*) / no
384.16 he (MS) / my lord
This change was made in proof, in accordance with the principle that pronouns should be clarified, but it has led to repetition in the following speech.
384.22 litter, at (MS litter at) / litter being at
384.34 time in (MS*) / time held in
385.19 conditions (MS*) / condition
385.20 often used . . . private (MS* often used for similar purposes during the Earls repeated private) / often so used, during the Earl's private
The MS is sound here, but 'repeated' is rightly cut because of repetition at line 25. (The American editions have 'often, during'.)
385.31 apartments, be (MS* apartments be) / apartments to be
385.36 gold? (MS*) / gold!
385.38 Who (MS*) / who
385.39 if (MS) / If
385.43 those (MS*) / these
386.4 behind, it remained (MS behind it remain) / behind it, it remained
386.33 Forster. "So (MS* Varney "So) / Foster, "so
386.39 which when opened admitted (MS* derived: which opend admitted) / which opened and admitted
387.1 hag (MS* derived: had) / old woman
387.8 on (MS*) / in
387.9 raised up (MS) / dropped
This and the next four items are discussed in the 'Essay on the Text', 427.
387.17 raised this (MS) / dropped the
387.20 at (MS) / down
387.20 under the vacant part of the gallery (MS) / by the fall of the trap-door
387.26 have often mentioned (MS* have often mentiond) / have mentioned
388.8 he had been (MS*) / He had been
388.11 *Mater* (MS* Mater) / *Maria*
388.13 you?—saw (MS* you—saw) / you? Saw
388.15 He (MS*) / he
388.30 Forster—"What (MS* Foster—"What) / Foster—"what
388.41 We (MS*) / we
389.3 Yonder (MS*) / yonder
389.20 door (MS) / room
389.30 through (MS) / by
389.30 They then withdrew (MS) / They withdrew
389.33 Never, surely, (MS* Never surely) / Surely never
389.40 with (MS) / and then
This and the next four items are discussed in the 'Essay on the Text', 421–22.
389.41 signal;—and the (MS signal & the) / signal;—the
389.42 opened—the (MS opend ⟨and⟩ the) / opened, and in the same moment the
389.42 way—there (MS*) / way. There
389.43 groan and (MS*) / groan—and
390.3 caught?—is (MS* caught—is) / caught?—Is

390.9   her—thy (MS*) / her.—Thy
390.22 Tider and Forster's servant (Magnum: MS the servants) / Tider and
        Foster's servants
        The MS reading was changed in proof, but imperfectly, retaining the MS
        plural 'servants'. Only one servant (389.15) is involved along with
        Tider: the Magnum completed the correction.
390.30 at (MS*) / on
391.31 Pleasures (MS*) / pleasures
391.31 for considerable (MS*) / for a considerable

END-OF-LINE HYPHENS

All end-of-line hyphens in the present text are soft unless included in the list below. The hyphens listed are hard and should be retained when quoting.

1.18	six-hooped	177.10	high-mettled
6.11	school-companion	183.3	night-robe
12.33	tenpenny-worth	189.7	turret-chamber
20.5	cater-cousins	193.30	witch-monger
21.22	linsey-wolsey	194.21	aqua-vitæ
22.16	manor-close	198.11	parti-coloured
23.5	quick-stirring	199.23	ale-house
23.9	scant-of-grace	203.30	cherry-coloured
23.41	flower-gardens	204.42	turkey-bean
24.14	sour-visaged	206.18	well-formed
26.19	Cumnor-Place	206.41	garden-house
30.20	dame-citizen	207.1	summer-house
34.41	heart-breaking	207.19	Fire-the-Faggot
37.16	entrance-door	208.14	dark-seeking
39.4	church-yard	218.29	play-books
47.16	seed-pearl	219.31	withdrawing-room
48.11	dressing-rooms	240.28	Maiden-castle-moor
50.7	hand-maiden	251.19	bye-roads
52.38	cross-stitch	251.24	bye-paths
53.14	hunting-field	252.12	hob-nailed
68.27	play-thing	252.27	shuttle-cock
73.7	spending-money	260.23	arch-way
74.5	court-yard	261.14	mantle-piece
81.18	inn-keeper	261.34	tilt-yard
97.23	ready-witted	266.30	jolter-headed
100.5	trap-door	277.35	Weatherly-bottom
100.29	horse-shoes	278.23	sally-port
101.39	three-footed	280.1	prison-house
102.26	black-thumb'd	282.36	cross-legged
110.24	dog-hostlers	284.29	riding-suit
114.12	to-morrow	289.38	watchet-coloured
116.40	to-morrow	290.6	well-penned
119.17	church-yard	293.25	smooth-tongued
139.42	over-watched	297.13	four-and-twenty
143.1	foot-cloth	308.27	over-indulgent
144.23	self-destruction	310.39	stag-hunting
149.21	broad-shouldered	311.42	posture-master
151.20	god-send	320.10	Lidcote-Hall
153.41	court-yard	322.11	flag-stones
161.24	presence-chamber	325.20	safe-keeping
168.24	to-morrow	329.4	livery-cloaks
168.35	one-third	333.8	scare-crows
175.30	foul-mouthed	346.36	Presence-hall
175.37	Bear-gardens	353.9	water-brooks

HISTORICAL NOTE

Sources. *Kenilworth* has two centres of historical interest: Leicester's entertainment of Queen Elizabeth at Kenilworth Castle, and the seclusion and death of Amy Robsart at Cumnor.

The public activities at Kenilworth were well attested in two reasonably reliable Elizabethan sources available to Scott: Robert Laneham or Langham's undated and anonymous *Letter*[1] and George Gascoigne's *Palace of Princely Pleasures.*[2] These documents were included in the fascicle covering 1575 in the first volume of John Nichols's *The Progresses and Public Processions . . . of Queen Elizabeth.*[3] The entertainments described in the novel are mostly based on these two documents, and there are many verbal echoes, though the masque at the end of the twelfth chapter of the final volume is apparently Scott's own invention.[4] The Lambourne Arion/Orion incident (290) is recorded in a footnote in Nichols (1 (1575 fascicle), 69). For the castle itself, Scott had personal observation to draw on: he visited it (not for the first time) on his journey back from France in 1815, asking searching questions and spending a couple of hours in contemplation.[5] He was also able to draw again on Langham's *Letter* and on a detailed history, along with a ground plan and drawings of the castle before its partial destruction around 1649, in William Dugdale's *Antiquities of Warwickshire.*[6] The plan and drawings are reproduced on page 479 of the present edition. Dugdale's description, along with Langham's *Letter*, the Gascoigne material, and new descriptions of the various parts of the castle appeared in 1821 as *Kenilworth Illustrated.*[7] This exceedingly handsome volume includes fine plates individually dated from 1 February 1820 to 1 December 1821: Scott is named in the list of subscribers to the volume, and he may have received the early plates while he was planning and writing *Kenilworth*. His general picture of the castle is accurate, but he renamed the Strong Tower Mervyn's Tower and was apparently the first to call the south wing of the Great Hall the Saintlowe Tower.[8] This name, unlike the coinage Mervyn's Tower, has survived. Scott has also added private passages, deep foundations for Mervyn's Tower, and a balcony, and he has enlarged the Pleasance from the small triangular plot which it actually occupied to include details more appropriate to the main Garden.[9]

For the story of Amy Robsart and the Cumnor setting Scott's main source was Elias Ashmole's *Antiquities of Berkshire*,[10] which drew substantially on the anonymous *Secret Memoirs of Robert Dudley, Earl of Leicester*, usually known as *Leicester's Commonwealth*, produced in 1585 by the earl's Roman Catholic enemies.[11] The exact circumstances of Amy's death will probably never be known, but much modern historical opinion regards the accusations against Leicester as largely unfounded.

473

It is thought likely that Amy suffered from cancer of the breast, and that this brought about a spontaneous fracture of the neck bones.[12] Victorian investigations are listed and briefly characterised in J. C. Corson's *Bibliography of Sir Walter Scott*,[13] and their conclusions are neatly sum med up in an anonymous article 'The Death of Amy Robsart' which appeared in *Macmillan's Magazine* in 1885.[14] The most vivid physical detail in the generally vague descriptions of Cumnor Place, Forster's drawbridge, seems to have had a source in the building operations at Abbotsford. On 3 May 1817, Scott had written to Constable (National Library of Scotland, MS 23117, f. 98r):

> I have access to my spare rooms which I had not the last time John [Ballantyne] was here so do not let his report terrify you. To be sure the access resembles the old feudal accomodation of a draw bridge but I'll warrant it secure.

Scott had read widely in source material for the Elizabethan period in preparing editions of Robert Carey's *Memoirs* and Robert Naunton's *Fragmenta Regalia* ('a source from which our historians have drawn the most authentic account of the court of the Virgin Queen'),[15] the Somers Tracts,[16] and Samuel Rowlands's *The Letting of Humours Blood*.[17] He was able to draw on this reading for telling details. Thus Naunton provided him with an anecdote about Bowyer as Black Rod, and a phrase for Sussex (as indicated in the present edition in the notes to 152.2–3 and 154.31); Thomas Fuller's *Worthies of England* gave him the famous incident of Raleigh's cloak and the couplet begun by Raleigh and completed by Elizabeth;[18] Holinshed suggested the scratching on the window with a diamond;[19] William Camden's *Britannia*, first published in Latin in 1607 and translated into English in Scott's own time by Richard Gough, and Daniel and Samuel Lysons's *Magna Britannia* of 1813 furnished *inter alia* details of Wayland's Smithy, the Pusey Horn, Abingdon, and Cumnor.[20] Various aspects of Scott's debts to his source material in this novel have been explored by James Anderson, who rightly points out that above all he was steeped in the literature of the Elizabethan-Jacobean period, and especially in its dramatic literature:[21] Scott stated in the introduction to his edition of Rowlands (page iii) that 'the various affectations of the retainers of Sir John Falstaff, as well as those of the Bobadil, Stephen, and Master Matthew of Jonson, and of the various comic characters pourtrayed by Beaumont and Fletcher, were not, as modern readers might conceive them, the fantastic creatures of the poet's imagination, but had in reality their prototypes upon the great scene of the world'. The explanatory footnotes to *The Ancient British Drama*, with which Scott was associated,[22] elucidate many words and expressions that reappear in *Kenilworth*: the most significant of these are indicated in the Explanatory notes below. In addition, many of the proverbial utterances in the novel may be found in the drama of the period.[23] The notes to the present edition attempt to give some idea of this indebtedness, particularly in the area of vigorous, zestful speech, and much illumination of Scott's period language may be gained from Graham Tulloch's work.[24] P. Sidney's 1901 investigation of the circumstances of Amy Robsart's death has a useful list of Scott's departures from literal historical accuracy,[25] and M. Wolf's Leipzig thesis may be consulted particularly for its list of parallel passages.[26] In addition to works already mentioned the library at Abbotsford contains several general historical surveys of (or including) the Elizabethan period from which Scott would have been able to derive the public events alluded to in his narrative.[27] Samuel Jebb's 1727 life of Leicester has a vivid picture of the armed rivalry between Leicester and Sussex, and he also seems to have suggested the noteworthy image of Leicester struck as with a thunderbolt at Elizabeth's words on page 321.[28]

Scott's pervasive debt to Shakespeare (especially *Macbeth* and *Othello*) in several of the scenes of *Kenilworth* has been explored in two articles by R. K. Gordon.[29] Goethe was aware of the imitation in Volume 1, Chapter 7 of Act 3 Scene 2 of his drama *Egmont*.[30] Coleridge's translation of Schiller's *Wallenstein* furnished not only the motto for Volume 2, Chapter 6, but much of the astrological goings-on in that chapter.[31] Jerome Mitchell has shown how pervasive are motifs from Chaucer and medieval romance.[32]

David Daiches's judgment, which is likely to stand the test of time, is that 'even though it is conceded that this novel lacks the deeper inward quality of the best of the Scottish novels, it does succeed quite remarkably in creating the atmosphere of combined suspicion and pageantry, of national exuberance and personal ambition, of merry England and court intrigue, of aesthetic sensitivity and physical brutality, which is peculiarly Elizabethan'.[33]

Principal characters. A number of Scott's characters would appear to be wholly imaginary. One such is Nicholas Blount, who shares his surname with Sir Thomas Blount, the historical principal officer of Dudley's household who was prominent in the investigations into Amy's death.[34] Other apparently imaginary characters are: Flibbertigibbet; Janet Forster; Laurence Goldthread; Giles Gosling; Michael Lambourne (whose surname is derived from the Berkshire village); Edmund Tressilian;[35] and Wayland Smith, who begins by being associated with a local legendary manifestation of a Scandinavian hero. Alasco is also essentially imaginary. The name is taken from the Polish prince Albert Laski (Albertus Alasco), whom Leicester introduced to Dr John Dee. Dee appears to have been a partial model for the occultist, along with Leicester's adherent and alleged poisoner the Dr Julio of *Leicester's Commonwealth*, properly Giulio Borgarucci, who died around 1581.[36]

Of the historical characters, by far the most fanciful are Anthony Forster (*c.* 1510–72), Richard Varney, and Amy Robsart. Scott represents Forster as the son of the Abbot's reeve, and a widower, with an only child Janet in 1575; in fact he was descended of a good family, and died without any of his children surviving him in 1572, his widow surviving until 1599. His character as portrayed in the novel is largely imaginary: he was indeed a zealous Protestant, but he was a man of some culture.[37] Varney's name and the basis for his role in Amy's death are found in *Leicester's Commonwealth*;[38] his character is wholly imaginary.[39] The facts of Amy's life are given in the table of dates. Her character in the novel is imaginary. Derek Wilson speculates about her real nature: until her illness, she was gay and fond of luxury; in spite of inevitable separations, her marriage with Leicester was harmonious, and she paid several well-attended visits to London.[40]

Of the four major historical characters, Thomas Radcliffe (1526?–83), third Earl of Sussex, is the least fully defined in the novel, so that it is difficult to compare his character with that recorded by history. Most of the facts given are accurate, but in 1575 he was actually married, to Frances Sidney, founder of Sidney Sussex College, Cambridge (contrast 150.33). The character of Walter Raleigh (1552?–1618) as depicted in the novel is compatible with that of the historical Raleigh, but he was never a retainer of Sussex, and he did not frequent the Court until after 1575.[41] Scott adopts the scurrilous rumours against Robert Dudley, Earl of Leicester, including the accusations of his proneness to poison his enemies, but important elements of his character are historical: for example his vanity, charm, profligate expenditure, patronage of the arts, and prominence as a leader of the Protestant party.[42] Scott's portrayal of Queen Elizabeth is generally accurate, but some modern historians would want to emphasise the coarser side of her nature more than Scott does, and they would doubt if she was as much in command of matters as the novel suggests.

Table of dates. The action of *Kenilworth* is set in 1575. Scott violates chronology freely, and often obviously, to bring historical characters and events within range of this date. The table, taken along with the birth and death dates of the characters, will enable the reader to judge the extent of his temporal licence.

c. 1510 Anthony Forster born
1532   Robert Dudley born
1532/3   Amy Robsart born, only daughter of Sir John Robsart of Syderstone, Norfolk
1549   Lord Robert Dudley publicly marries Amy Robsart
1554   Sir John Robsart, Amy's father, dies
1560   Amy dies
1561   Anthony Forster, having before only been a tenant, purchases Cumnor from William Owen
1563   Queen Elizabeth gives Lord Robert Dudley Kenilworth Castle and makes him Earl of Leicester
1566   Debate in Privy Council about Leicester's marriage to Elizabeth
1570   Forster elected to represent Abingdon in Parliament
1572   Forster dies, leaving Cumnor to his patron Leicester
1573   Leicester secretly marries Lady Douglas Sheffield
1575   Leicester entertains Elizabeth at Kenilworth
1578   Leicester abandons Lady Douglas and secretly marries Lettice, Countess of Essex
1588   Leicester dies

For the shortened forms of reference, see pp. 481–82.

1 Robert Langham, *A Letter*, ed. R. J. P. Kuin, Medieval and Renaissance Texts, 2 (Leiden, 1983). Kuin conjectures (18) that the *Letter* was first printed a year or two after 1575.

2 Originally published as *The Princely Pleasures at the Courte at Kenelworth* (London, 1576). The earliest printing still extant is in Gascoigne's *Whole Woorkes* (London, 1587).

3 See p. 481 below.

4 Rudolf Brotanek, *Die englischen Maskenspiele*, Wiener Beiträge zur englischen Philologie, 15 (Vienna and Leipzig, 1902), 328.

5 Lockhart, 3.373; *The Journal of Sir Walter Scott*, ed. David Douglas (Edinburgh, 1890), 2.153n.

6 *The Antiquities of Warwickshire Illustrated* (London, 1656), 159–68. A copy of this edition was in the Signet Library, Edinburgh in 1820, and so would have been available for Scott to use when composing *Kenilworth*: the *Catalogue of the Society of Writers to the Signet* (Edinburgh, 1837) lists it in the second of its four parts, an 1826 reprint of an 1820 catalogue. The copy of the 1730 edition which was in the Advocates Library (*A Catalogue of the Library Belonging to the Faculty of Advocates, Edinburgh, Part 2* (Edinburgh, 1776)) also contains the ground plan but not the drawings.

7 *Kenilworth Illustrated; or, The History of the Castle, Priory, and Church of Kenilworth with a Description of their Present State* (Chiswick, 1821: *CLA*, 242).

8 M. W. Thompson, *Kenilworth Castle* (London, 1977), 11.

9 Langham, lines 1266–87, 1379–1400.

10 3 vols (London, 1719: *CLA*, 245).

11 See p. 482 below.

12 Ian Aird, 'The Death of Amy Robsart', *English Historical Review*, 71 (1956), 69–77; Derek Wilson, *Sweet Robin: A Biography of Robert Dudley, Earl of Leicester 1533–1588* (London, 1981), Ch. 7.

13 James Clarkson Corson, *A Bibliography of Sir Walter Scott: A Classified and Annotated List of Books and Articles Relating to his Life and Works 1797–1940* (Edinburgh and London, 1943), 242–43.

14 53 (December 1885), 131–40.

15 See p. 481 below.

16 *A Collection of Scarce and Valuable Tracts ... Selected from ... Libraries, Particularly that of the Late Lord Somers*, 2nd edn, ed. Walter Scott, 13 vols (London, 1809–15: *CLA*, 29). This collection also contains Naunton's *Fragmenta Regalia* (1.251–83).

17 *The Letting of Humours Blood in the Head Vaine etc.*, ed. Walter Scott (Edinburgh, 1814: *CLA*, 117). (Originally published 1600: Scott's edition is a facsimile of the 1611 edition.)

18 Thomas Fuller, *The History of the Worthies of England*, ed. John Nichols, 2 vols (London, 1811: *CLA*, 29), 1.287.

19 Raphael Holinshed, *Chronicles of England, Scotland, and Ireland, to 1587 Inclusive*, new edition, 6 vols (London, 1807–08: *CLA*, 29), 4.133.

20 William Camden, *Britannia; or, A Chorographical Description of ... England, Scotland, and Ireland etc.*, trans. Richard Gough, 2nd edn, 4 vols (London, 1806: *CLA*, 232), 1.214, 221, 224; Daniel and Samuel Lysons, *Magna Britannia; being a Concise Topographical Account of the Several Counties of Great Britain*, 6 vols (London, 1806–22) 1.213–26, 270, 326.

21 James Anderson, *Sir Walter Scott and History* (Edinburgh, 1981), 79–80.

22 See p. 482 below. Scott's involvement with this edition is investigated in Bill Ruddick, 'Scott on the Drama: A Series of Ascriptions', *Scott Newsletter*, 14 (Spring 1989), 2–6.

23   See p. 481 below.
24   Graham Tulloch, *The Language of Walter Scott* (London, 1980).
25   P. Sidney, *Who Killed Amy Robsart? Being Some Account of her Life and Death. With Remarks on Sir Walter Scott's 'Kenilworth'* (London, 1901).
26   *Walter Scott's Kenilworth: eine Untersuchung über sein Verhältnis zur Geschichte und zu seinen Quellen* (Leipzig, 1903).
27   See especially *CLA*, 24 (Forbes), 28 (Grafton, Hume), 232 (Speed, Lewis), 236 (Strype), 243 (Birch), 249 (Kennet), and 251 (Goldsmith).
28   Samuel Jebb, *The Life of Robert Earl of Leicester* (London, 1727: *CLA*, 258), 26–28, 107.
29   R. K. Gordon, 'Shakespeare and Some Scenes in the Waverley Novels', *Queen's Quarterly*, 45 (1938), 478–85; 'Scott and Shakespeare's Tragedies', *Transactions of the Royal Society of Canada*, 3rd series, 39, section 2 (May 1945), 111–17.
30   Johann Peter Eckermann, *Gespräche mit Goethe*, ed. Eduard Castle, 2 vols (Berlin, [1916]), 1.62.
31   W. Macintosh, *Scott and Goethe: German Influence on the Writings of Sir Walter Scott* (Galashiels and Glasgow, [1925]), 111–12.
32   Jerome Mitchell, *Scott, Chaucer, and Medieval Romance: A Study in Sir Walter Scott's Indebtedness to the Literature of the Middle Ages* (Lexington, Kentucky, 1987), 146–50.
33   *Kenilworth*, intro. David Daiches (New York, 1966), viii.
34   Wilson, 119–22. Wolf says (49) that Nicholas Blount 'ist historisch bekannt als Leicester's Cousin', but it is clear that he is referring to Sir Thomas.
35   The surname 'Tresilian' occurs in a list of extinct Cornish families in Lysons, 3.clix. Tressillian (various spellings) is in *Sir John Froissart's Chronicles . . . translated . . . by John Bourchier, Lord Berners*, 2 vols (London, 1812), 2.278, 285–87, and index (*CLA*, 29) (Corson).
36   Meric Casaubon, *A True & Faithful Relation of What Passed for Many Years between Dr. John Dee . . . & Some Spirits* (London, 1659: *CLA*, 208), Preface, D2; C.O. Parsons, *Witchcraft and Demonology in Scott's Fiction* (Edinburgh and London, 1964), 89–90; *Leicester's Commonwealth*, 274–76.
37   A. D. Bartlett, *An Historical and Descriptive account of Cumnor Place, Berks, with Biographical Notices of the Lady Amy Dudley and of Anthony Forster* (Oxford and London, 1850), 83–104. Scott acknowledged this difference between his character and the historical Forster in a letter of 17 August 1830 to Charles Kirkpatrick Sharpe (*Letters*, 11.386).
38   Peck, 81, 90.
39   Walter Rye (*The Murder of Amy Robsart: A Brief for the Prosecution* (London, 1885), 53–55) believes that the Varney of the murder was not Sir Richard Verney (d. 1567), of Compton Verney, in 1561 High Sheriff for Warwickshire (as asserted by J. E. Jackson, 'Amye Robsart', *Nineteenth Century*, 11 (March 1882), 414–34 (419)), but a plain Richard Verney of Buckinghamshire and Hertfordshire, appointed Marshal of the King's Bench in 1572, and dead by November 1575. In truth, the evidence is insufficient for any certain identification.
40   Wilson, 92–95.
41   Willard M. Wallace, *Sir Walter Raleigh* (Princeton, New Jersey, 1959), 20–21.
42   Wilson, *passim*.

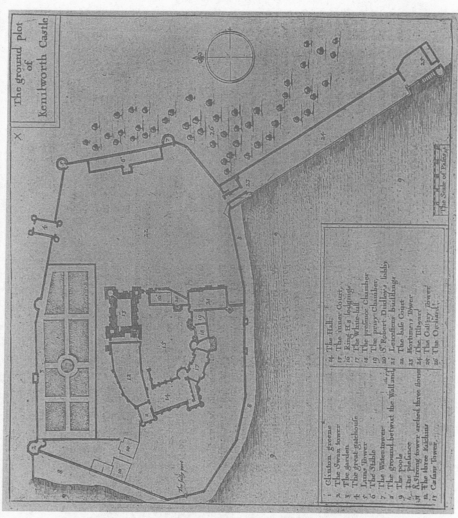

Ground plan and (overleaf) drawings of Kenilworth Castle from William
Dugdale's *The Antiquities of Warwickshire Illustrated* (London, 1656).

EXPLANATORY NOTES

In these notes a comprehensive attempt is made to identify Scott's sources and all quotations, references, historical events, and historical personages, to explain proverbs, and to translate difficult or obscure language. (Phrases are explained in the notes while single words are treated in the glossary.) The notes are brief; they offer information rather than critical comment or exposition. When a quotation has not been recognised this is stated: any new information from readers will be welcomed. References are to standard editions, or to the editions Scott himself used. Thus proverbs are identified both by reference to the third edition of Ray's *A Compleat Collection of English Proverbs*, and to *The Oxford Dictionary of English Proverbs*. Books in the Abbotsford Library are identified by reference to the appropriate page of the *Catalogue of the Library at Abbotsford*. When quotations reproduce their sources accurately, the reference is given without comment. Verbal differences in the source are indicated by a prefatory 'see'. Biblical references are to the Authorised Version. Plays by Shakespeare are cited without authorial ascription, and references are to *William Shakespeare: The Complete Works*, edited by Peter Alexander (London and Glasgow, 1951, frequently reprinted).

The following publications are distinguished by abbreviations, or are given without the names of their authors, in the notes and essays:

ABD   *The Ancient British Drama*, [ed. Dodsley, rev. Walter Scott,] 3 vols (London, 1810): *CLA*, 43.

CLA   [J. G. Cochrane], *Catalogue of the Library at Abbotsford* (Edinburgh, 1838).

The Alchemist   Ben Jonson, *The Alchemist* (1612), ed. G. R. Hibbard (London, 1977).

The Canterbury Tales   Geoffrey Chaucer, *The Canterbury Tales* (written c. 1387–1400), in *The Riverside Chaucer*, 3rd edn, ed. Larry D. Benson (Oxford, 1988).

Child   Francis James Child, *The English and Scottish Popular Ballads*, 5 vols (Boston and New York, 1882–98).

Dent   R. W. Dent, *Proverbial Language in English Drama Exclusive of Shakespeare, 1495–1616: An Index* (Berkeley, California, 1984).

The Faerie Queene   Edmund Spenser, *The Faerie Queene* (written 1579–96), ed. J. C. Smith, 2 vols (Oxford, 1909).

Langham   Robert Langham, *A Letter*, ed. R. J. P. Kuin (Leiden, 1983).

Letters   *The Letters of Sir Walter Scott*, ed. H. J. C. Grierson and others, 12 vols (London, 1932–37).

Lockhart   J. G. Lockhart, *Memoirs of the Life of Sir Walter Scott, Bart.*, 7 vols (Edinburgh, 1837–38).

Minstrelsy   Walter Scott, *Minstrelsy of the Scottish Border*, ed. T. F. Henderson, 4 vols (Edinburgh, 1902).

Naunton   *Memoirs of Robert Cary, Earl of Monmouth . . . and Fragmenta Regalia . . . by Sir Robert Naunton*, ed. Walter Scott (Edinburgh, 1808): *CLA*, 231.

Nichols   John Nichols, *The Progresses and Public Processions . . . of Queen Elizabeth*, 2 vols (London, 1788): *CLA*, 265–66.

OED   *The Oxford English Dictionary*, 12 vols (Oxford, 1933).

ODEP   *The Oxford Dictionary of English Proverbs*, 3rd edn, rev. F. P. Wilson (Oxford, 1970).

Peck   *Leicester's Commonwealth*, ed. D. C. Peck (Athens, Ohio, 1985).
Ray   John Ray, *A Compleat Collection of English Proverbs*, 3rd edn (London, 1737): *CLA*, 169.
Tilley   Morris Palmer Tilley, *A Dictionary of the Proverbs in England in the Sixteenth and Seventeenth Centuries* (Ann Arbor, Michigan, 1950).

All manuscripts referred to in the notes are in the National Library of Scotland. Information derived from the notes of the late Dr J. C. Corson is indicated by '(Corson)'. The following editions of *Kenilworth* have proved most helpful: The Dryburgh Edition, 25 vols (London, 1892–4), vol. 12; an anonymous edition published by Macmillan (London, 1902); ed. William Keith Leask (London, 1904); ed. Oliphant Smeaton (London, 1905); ed. A. D. Innes (Oxford, 1911); and ed. J. H. Flather (Cambridge, 1904). For legal matters the notes by D. E. C. Yale (MS 23082) have been useful.

title page   *Waverley* (1814) was Scott's first novel. His eighth novel, *Ivanhoe* (1820), was the first to be called a 'romance': it inaugurated Scott's movement into pre-17th-century and non-Scottish subject areas, and (along with *The Monastery* and *The Abbot*, both 1820, and *Kenilworth*) appeared in the collected *Historical Romances* in 1822. The epigraph is taken from Richard Brinsley Sheridan, *The Critic* (1781), 2.1.20. Lady Louisa Stuart wrote to Scott on 4 December 1820: 'Mr Morritt [J. B. S. Morritt of Rokeby] whispers the name of Kenilworth Castle and with Mr Sneer in the Critic "hopes no scandal of Q. Elizabeth?" I hope so too' (MS 867, f. 94r).
1.4–9   motto   Ben Jonson, *The New Inne* (1631), 1.1.20–24.
1.14   in some sort   to some extent.
1.17   Patronized   encouraged; with word-play on e.g. French *patron* and Italian *padrone* ('innkeeper').
1.18–19   six-hooped pot   quart wooden drinking-vessel, with bands at equal intervals, to mark the amount each person should drink.
1.22   the eighteenth of Queen Elizabeth   strictly, Elizabeth's eighteenth regnal year, 17 November 1575 to 16 November 1576, but here probably used loosely for 1575.
1.24   somewhat a round belly   applied by Falstaff to himself: see *2 Henry IV*, 1.2.176.
1.27   old Harry Baillie . . . Southwark   the host at the Tabard Inn in *The Canterbury Tales*.
1.30   the Bonny Black Bear   the inn is fictitious, though as a result of the popularity of *Kenilworth* the landlord of The Jolly Ringers in Cumnor changed the name of his establishment to 'The Black Bear' of the first edition (MS 3892, f. 41r).
2.9–10   What, ho! . . . Hostler   see *1 Henry IV*, 1.1, *passim*, especially 46–47: 'What, ho! chamberlain! . . . At hand, quoth pick-purse'. A *tapster* is a barman; a *hostler* or *ostler* is one who attends to horses at an inn.
2.16   Beshrew my heart   frequent jocular Shakespearean expression: *literally* curse my heart (e.g. *A Midsummer-Night's Dream*, 5.1.282).
2.17–18   convince . . . convince   vanquish . . . overcome by argument.
2.24–25   have at you . . . consequence   attack you with a plain logical conclusion. See *2 Henry VI*, 2.3.89.
2.26–27   The horse . . . sack   see Langham, lines 1660–61: 'Set my hors up to the rak, and then lets have a cup of Sak'. The first line refers to a stable-rack holding fodder, the second to mulling dry wine.
2.31   accidents   the science of the inflexions of words, the first part of Latin grammar learned by beginners. This form of the modern 'accidence' was in use up to the early 17th century.

2.37–38 **Mars…Minerva** Roman god of war and goddess of wisdom and handicrafts.

3.21 **turn off** discharge.

3.27 **e'en drink as you have brewed** proverbial (see Ray, 3, 179, 299, and *ODEP*, 85).

3.30–31 **the Three Cranes, in the Vintry** a celebrated London hostelry in Upper Thames Street, so called from the three cranes on the neighbouring Vintry wharf used for lifting casks of wine. *ABD*, 1.93; 2.381.

3.32 **Sheres** Jerez de la Frontera, in SW Spain, famous for the sherry wine to which it has given its name.

3.32–33 **I would I may never touch either pot or penny more** proverbial (see Ray, 274: 'If you touch pot you must touch penny', i.e. pay for what you take, and *ODEP*, 833).

3.37 **neat and comfortable** clear, undiluted, or tasty; and delightful, strengthening, or satisfactory.

3.40–42 **bastard … pottle-pot** see *1 Henry IV*, 2.4.25, 70; *2 Henry IV*, 2.2.72; 5.3.63. See also *ABD*, 1.532; 2.464.

3.41 **the Groyne…Port St Mary's** Corunna in NW Spain…Puerto de Santa Maria in the Bay of Cádiz.

4.8–9 **the Virginia voyage** Sir Walter Raleigh's attempts (1584–89) to establish a colony in the present North Carolina, which he named Virginia in honour of Queen Elizabeth.

4.12–15 **Troth, sir … dead and gone** this speech echoes the conversation between Shallow and Silence in *2 Henry IV*, 3.2.1–50.

4.13 **the siege of the Brill** the revolt of the Dutch against Spain, by which The Netherlands eventually won independence from Spanish Hapsburg rule in 1648, broke out at Brill, a small port south of the Hague, which was seized by them in 1572.

4.20–21 **wild slip** wild young person. There is also a word-play on pruning a plant.

4.21 **the last year of Queen Mary** 1558, Mary Tudor's last regnal year extending from 25 July to her death on 17 November.

4.22 **better lost than found** see the parable of the Prodigal Son, Luke 15.32, and compare 6.3–6 below.

4.30 **the siege of Venlo** Venlo, a town in SE Holland, was besieged unsuccessfully by the Spanish in 1578.

4.31 **Grave Maurice** Grave (i.e. Count) Maurice of Nassau (1567–1625), Prince of Orange, aided by Leicester and Sidney in his role as commander of the Dutch forces against the Spaniards in the 1590s.

5.11 **taking in of a sconce near Maestricht** capturing a small fort or block-house (*ABD*, 3.78); Maestricht (now Maastricht) was a fortress on the Meuse in E Holland, sacked by the Spaniards in 1579.

5.24 **Dame Snort of Hogsditch** both character and place are apparently fictitious, but there is a London street Houndsditch.

5.33–34 **stamped thee with a cold iron** i.e. instead of a hot iron used by the common executioner for branding criminals.

5.35 **truce with** enough of; have done with.

6.3–6 **This may be called…no welcome** see the parable of the Prodigal Son, Luke 15.11–32.

6.16 **demeaned himself** behaved.

6.28 **the Hare and Tabor** the hare playing on the tabor (a small drum), here depicted on an inn-sign, was a common side-show at fairs. Trying to catch a hare by using a tabor was proverbial for an impossible task (Ray, 195; *ODEP*, 393).

6.37 **rip up** open up (as, proverbially, old sores: Ray, 204; *ODEP*, 678).

6.40   the Eldorado   the golden land (or city): at first the name of an imaginary country of fabulous riches which Spanish travellers professed to have found in America; later a general term for Central and South America.

6.41   cherry-pit   a child's game, in which cherry-stones are thrown into a small hole.

7.1–2   the cutting mercer of Abingdon   *cutting* means 'swaggering', with a pun on the tailor's profession.

7.6   bears the pack   carries the pedlar's pack.

7.22   cards and cockatrices   gambling and whores. *ABD*, 1.391, 542; 2.491.

7.23   bide a banging   suffer a thumping (because of storms at sea).

7.24   the Spittal   the hospital; specifically St Mary's hospital, Spitalfields, London.

7.25   Lombard Street   a street principally given over to bankers, extending from the Mansion House to Gracechurch Street in the City of London. The Lombards (from Lombardy in N Italy) were famous as merchants and bankers from the 13th to the 16th century.

7.28 take no snuff in the nose   do not be annoyed.

7.35–36   striking up thy father's crutches   presumably Lambourne knocked or kicked away his father's crutches while the old man was leaning on them.

7.36–37 it is a wise child . . . father   proverbial (Ray, 86; *ODEP*, 899).

7.37   Dr Bricham   an imaginary figure, the name derived from *breech* ('flog').

7.43–8.1   Morior . . . mori   *Latin*   I die—I have died—to die.

8.9   Voto a dios!   *Spanish*   I vow to God, i.e. By God.

8.10 slouched hat   soft felt hat with a broad brim hanging over the face.

8.13–14   under the rose   in confidence.

8.19   falling foul   quarrelling.

8.23   spoil your Sunday's quavering, Sir Clerk   the clerk led the congregational responses to the priest in Church of England services.

8.26–27   I will have no swaggering here   see *2 Henry IV*, 2.4.77–100 (Mistress Quickly).

8.34   prince royal   eldest son of a reigning monarch.

9.15   a Jesuit, or seminary priest   a priest from one of the seminaries at Douai and Rheims in France, Valladolid and Seville in Spain, and Rome, which trained Roman Catholic missionaries for England from *c.* 1580.

9.22–23   the wealthy squire at Bessellsley   the squire in 1575 was John Fettiplace.

9.23   the old knight at Wootton   Scott is not known to have had a particular person in mind.

9.25   on Friday   Roman Catholics abstained from meat on Fridays.

9.27   the Isis   name given to the Thames at Oxford.

9.34   the credit of his house   the reputation of his inn.

9.38   ill tongues   people given to malevolent speech.

9.39   put an evil mark on   speak ill of.

9.40   pull their hat over their brows   cover up and are silent. See *Macbeth*, 4.3.208: 'What, man! ne'er pull your hat upon your brows;/ Give sorrow words'.

10.8   Father Bacon   Roger Bacon (1214–94), a Franciscan friar who taught science and philosophy at Oxford. Ignorance and superstition attributed his discoveries to magic.

10.15–17   their pouch . . . dancing in it   their purses will be empty of coins bearing crosses, and thus the sign of the cross will not be present to keep Melancholy away like other devils. Compare the proverb: 'He hath never a cross to bless himself withal', i.e. no money (Ray, 184; *ODEP*, 156).

10.20 the Devil looking over Lincoln proverbial, referring to a stone figure either on Lincoln Cathedral or at Lincoln College, Oxford, or to the Devil himself looking at Lincoln Cathedral with envy (Ray, 224; *ODEP*, 183).

10.43 letter of change bill of exchange, a written order to pay cash to a designated person.

11.4 flat cap a round cap with a low, flat crown typical of 16th and 17th-century London citizens. *ABD*, 1.537.

11.5 breaking parks trespassing on estates, for poaching and so forth.

11.7 betwixt Hounslow and London Hounslow Heath on the great western road was a noted neighbourhood for highwaymen.

11.14 a desperate Dick a reckless fellow.

11.23–24 By Pol ... Cornish men proverbial (see Ray, 237 and *ODEP*, 836–37). 'Pol', 'Tre', and 'Pen' are the first syllables of the most distinctive Cornish names.

11.28–29 Saint Michael's Mount island near Penzance in Mount's Bay, Cornwall.

11.36–37 motto *The Merchant of Venice*, 2.2.42.

12.15 match me this catch join in this sung round by catching at my words; provide a catch to match this one of mine. For lines 1–3 compare Epigram 20 in S. Rowlands, *The Letting of Humours Blood in the Head Vaine etc.*, ed. Walter Scott (Edinburgh, 1814; originally published 1611: *CLA*, 117): 'And when you see him stagger, reele, and winke,/ He is a man and more, I by this Drinke'.

12.28 to boot into the bargain.

12.28 Do me right see *2 Henry IV*, 5.3.72.

12.31 Prance of Padworth the name was perhaps suggested by Miles Prance, whom Scott refers to in his edition of *The Works of John Dryden*, 18 vols (London, 1808), 9.382, 383 and note (Corson).

12.33 Oxford Castle the castle incorporates a prison.

12.33 Goodman Thong the hangman.

12.36 walk by moonlight practise highway robbery. Much play is made with the idea in *1 Henry IV*: e.g. 1.2.12–14.

12.40 Hempseed gallows-bird. See *2 Henry IV*, 2.1.54.

12.42–43 the Duke of Norfolk's matter Thomas Howard (1536–72), fourth Duke of Norfolk, was the leader of the Roman Catholic party in the early years of Elizabeth's reign. Without Elizabeth's knowledge he planned to marry Mary Queen of Scots (1568) after she took refuge in England. His intrigue with Spain led to the belief that he intended to re-establish the Roman Catholic religion. Elizabeth refused to allow him to marry Mary, and he was sent to the Tower (1569). On his release he was concerned in the Ridolfi Plot (1571), which had for its objects his marriage with Mary and a general rising of the Roman Catholics against Elizabeth. The plot was discovered, and Norfolk was executed for high treason.

13.5 to kindle the faggots round Latimer and Ridley Hugh Latimer (1485?–1555), Bishop of Worcester, and Nicholas Ridley (1500?–55), Bishop of London, were burned at the stake in Oxford on 16 October 1555 for their Protestant beliefs.

13.10 brook the stab suffer death by stabbing.

13.22 whose exchequers lie in other men's purpose whose incomes depend upon other men's aims.

13.39–40 as bitter a precisian ... Lent Puritans rejected abstinence from meat during Lent as a popish practice, although it continued to be enjoined by the Church of England after the Reformation.

13.42 keep such a coil make such a fuss.

14.5   mewed up   confined, like a hawk at moulting time. See e.g. *The Taming of the Shrew*, 1.1.87, 178 and *Romeo and Juliet*, 3.4.11.

14.14–15   pinked out with cloth of gold   punched or slashed with ornamental holes to show cloth of gold beneath.

14.26   'What d'ye lack'   the cry of the London tradesmen or their apprentices to the passers-by. Proverbial (Tilley, L20).

14.27   a gilded brooch   set in the hat by way of ornament.

14.34   sarsenet   resembling sarsenet (thin silk) in softness. See *1 Henry IV*, 3.1.252.

15.13   laid down and guarded ... silver   with woven braids applied to the surface (*laid down*), in particular as decorative borders along the edge of a garment (*guarded*).

15.32   a jackanape, simpering at a chesnut   a coxcomb, smiling foolishly at a stale joke.

16.16   hold stakes ... stake down   keep the sums being wagered ... deposit such a sum.

16.18   Good now   interjection, here denoting entreaty.

16.20–21   lay you up in lavender   have you put comfortably out of the way (lavender being laid with cloth as a preservative).

16.22–28   town-stocks ... pinfold ... shelled pea-cod   see *King Lear*, 1.4.192; 2.2.8, 120–34.

16.28   Lindabrides   the heroine of *The Mirror of Knighthood*, a romance of Spanish origin translated into English at the end of the 16th century by Richard Percival (1550–1620), here used allusively for 'mistress', as in e.g. *ABD*, 2.471.

17.3   chop logic   argue contentiously.

17.5   galloon lace   narrow ribbon or braid, of gold, silver, silk, or woollen thread, used for trimming clothes.

17.19   Saint Julian   the patron saint of hospitality and travellers.

17.39   Solomon   king of Israel in the 10th century BC, proverbial for his wisdom (*ODEP*, 751), and traditionally believed to have been the author of the book of Proverbs. Gosling is probably citing Proverbs Chs 5–7.

18.2   the Three Cranes in the Vintry   see note to 3.30–31.

18.7–11   motto   not identified: probably by Scott.

18.7   hold touch   keep faith.

18.27–31   You have spoken ... Justice   the opening of this speech echoes *The Merchant of Venice*, 2.2.1–27. Compare note on 11.37.

18.36   scot and lot   a tax levied by civic authorities.

18.38–39   six-hooped pot   see note to 1.18–19.

18.40   a desperate Dick   a reckless fellow.

19.1   the seven damnable sciences   set of vices opposed to the seven liberal arts or sciences (Grammar, Logic, Rhetoric, Arithmetic, Music, Geometry, Astronomy). Gosling may be thinking of the seven deadly sins in general, or of such contemporary interpretations as that found in Thomas Dekker, *The Seven Deadly Sinnes of London* (1606) where the sins are 'Politike [premeditated and fraudulent] Bankeruptisme, Lying, Candle-light, Sloth, Apishnesse [foolish imitation], Shauing [cheating], and Crueltie'. In Thomas Randolph, *The Muse's Looking-Glass* (printed 1638), Mrs Flower says: 'I have heard our vicar/ Call play-houses the colleges of transgression,/ Wherein the seven deadly sins are studied' (*ABD*, 2.401).

19.4   forewarned, forearmed   proverbial (*ODEP*, 280; compare Ray, 279).

19.7   passed my word   given my word in pledge.

20.5–6   cater-cousins   cater-cousins were persons on terms of cousinship or familiarity with each other, who were not cousins by blood. Gosling plays upon the proverbial sense of 'good friends' (Ray, 181; *ODEP*, 111; *The Merchant of Venice*, 2.2.119).

20.10   true, thou art ... my Eden   see Genesis 3.1–15.

20.18   country-breeding   rusticity. People from the country were bywords for ignorance among the sophisticated.

20.29–30   Care killed a cat   proverbial (see Ray, 84 and *ODEP*, 103).

20.29   pass the career on   charge (as in a tournament).

21.12–13   the ruins may be still extant   H. U. Tighe wrote in 1821, the year of *Kenilworth*'s first appearance: 'A heap of stones, and the foundations, now scarcely discernible, are all that remain of that venerable structure' (*An Historical Account of Cumner* (Oxford, 1821), 15). The mansion had been demolished in 1810, and some fragments were incorporated in the rebuilding of the church at Wytham nearby four years later.

21.20   finely holped up   in a real fix: an ironical use of a phrase meaning 'well helped over an obstacle'.

22.7   as dark as a wolf's mouth   proverbial (*ODEP*, 167–68).

22.18   played fast and loose   irresponsibly played a cheating game.

22.19   White-friars   a precinct designated as a sanctuary for lawbreakers, between Fleet Street and the Thames, the Temple walls and Water Lane. It figures in *The Fortunes of Nigel* under its well-known appellation of Alsatia.

22.23–24   grudged ... mill   proverbial (compare Ray, 136, 285 and *ODEP*, 201).

22.32   humour jumps   disposition agrees. See *1 Henry IV*, 1.2.67–68.

22.39   Law you there now!   goodness me!

23.4–5   put the change on   deceive.

23.7   makes it good   proves it.

23.12–13   curiously balanced   carefully weighed.

23.23   the philosopher's stone   the philosopher's stone was reputedly a solid substance or preparation supposed by the alchemists to possess the property of changing other metals into gold or silver, the discovery of which, sometimes along with spiritual enlightenment, was the supreme object of alchemy. Being identified with the Elixir, it had also, according to some, the power of prolonging life indefinitely and of curing all wounds and diseases. For the term see *2 Henry IV*, 3.2.308.

24.4   Sampson   Samson, the Hebrew champion. See Judges Chs 13–16.

24.6   this garden of the sluggard   see Isaac Watts, 'The Sluggard', *Divine Songs for the Use of Children* (London, 1715), lines 9–10: 'I pass'd by his Garden, and saw the wild Brier,/ The Thorn and the Thistle grow broader and higher'. Watts's poem is based on Proverbs 20.4, 24.30–31.

24.20   make that good   substantiate that.

24.23–24   go on ... come off   advance ... extricate himself from the engagement.

26.15   Tyburn tippet   hangman's rope. Tyburn, in Elizabethan times a village N of Westminster, was the place of execution for Newgate prisoners.

26.33–34   who hides halters ... play says   see *King Lear*, 3.4.52–54.

26.43   Uds daggers!   meaningless oath (God's daggers). See John Webster and Thomas Dekker, *Westward Ho* (1607), 5.3.23.

27.7   Corinthian   rogue, game fellow. See *1 Henry IV*, 2.4.11.

27.13   come to   probably an allusive use of the nautical phrase meaning 'come to a fixed position', i.e. fall in with us, become like us.

27.14–15   cocks of the game   leaders or victors in the game.

27.25–29   motto   not identified: probably by Scott.

27.25   Not serve two masters   see Matthew 6.24 and Luke 16.13.

28.6   yeoman's service   faithful service. *Hamlet*, 5.2.36.

28.24–25   the gall of bitterness and bond of iniquity   see Acts 8.23.

28.25 my ways common biblical expression.

28.26 Melchisidec the priest-king of Genesis Ch. 14: 16th and 17th-century Protestants typically used such Old Testament names.

28.27–28 the Apostle Paul ... Saint Stephen see Acts 7.57–60.

28.32–33 the devil quote Scripture proverbial (see Tilley, D230 and *ODEP*, 180). See Matthew 4.6 and *The Merchant of Venice*, 1.3.93.

29.2–3 The hope ... Kingston the allusion has not been traced: Scott first wrote 'Stirling'.

29.7 dance in a net act with practically no disguise or concealment, while expecting to escape notice. Proverbial (see Ray, 5; *ODEP*, 166).

29.14 Covetousness bursts the sack proverbial (see *ODEP*, 150).

29.18 at view *hunting* by sight (as compared with e.g. by smell); but the use with 'kill' here might suggest 'at sight' or 'on sight'.

29.29–30 keep thee well from me ... has it be on your guard against me. This and similar phrases appear several times in Sir Thomas Malory (d. 1471): see e.g. *The Works of Sir Thomas Malory*, ed. Eugène Vinaver (London, 1954), 4.9; 9.41, 42.

29.38 starting at scruples feeling startled by (or being troubled by) scruples (in such a way as to incapacitate him for service).

29.41 Milan visor face-piece of a helmet made of fine steel from Milan in N Italy.

30.1 the Seven Sleepers seven noble Christian youths of Ephesus who, after taking refuge in a cave to escape persecution, were believed to have slept for 187 years.

30.9 wear your cloak on both shoulders it was the fashion for a gallant to wear his cloak hanging only on one shoulder. Lambourne must eschew fashionable modes of dressing in line with the Puritan practice of Leicester's party.

30.10 falling band a turned-down collar, at first attached to the shirt but from *c.* 1585 a separate item. It was an alternative to the ruff which it replaced by the 1630s. *ABD*, 1.530; 2.33, 326.

30.10–11 enlarge the brim of your beaver wear a large-brimmed hat of the type which became associated with the Puritans, although it was not exclusive to them.

30.21 Saint Antoline's or St Antholin's (St Anthony's), a church which stood in Budge Row, Watling Street, London. 'A morning prayer and lecture, the bells for which began to ring at five in the morning, was established ... "after Geneva fashion," in September, 1559.' (Henry B. Wheatley, *London Past and Present*, 3 vols (London, 1891), 1.51). *ABD*, 1.401; 2.387.

30.22 flat-cap'd see note to 11.4.

30.22 take the wall of her walk close to the wall and compel her to turn out into the (muddy) road. See *Romeo and Juliet*, 1.1.12.

30.33 are you there with your bears? are you harking back to the old question? A proverbial phrase (Ray, 177; *ODEP*, 18), said to have originated from a worthy who tried three churches on three Sundays running and each time heard a sermon on Elisha and the bears (2 Kings 2.23–25).

30.35–36 in rerum natura *Latin literally*, in the nature of things, i.e. extant in actual nature.

30.37 sodden-brained see *Troilus and Cressida*, 2.1.42–43: 'thou sodden-witted lord! Thou hast no more brain than I have in mine elbows'.

31.1 the holy Cross of Abingdon a fine market cross set up in Abingdon by the Guild of the Holy Cross; destroyed 1644. There was also a rood cross in St Helen's church.

33.38 Uds precious! God's precious (body, or blood)!

33.41–34.3 before ... acquainted ... hurricanoe see *King Lear*, 3.2.2; 4.6.241.

34.1   cutter's law   i.e. 'when one tall fellow has coin, another must not be thirsty' (*Woodstock*, 1826, 3.66 (Ch. 27)). *ABD*, 2.463.

34.3   flaw   the word means both 'squall' and 'quarrel' in John Webster, *The White Devil* (*c.* 1608), 1.2.56–57 (*ABD*, 3.6).

34.4–5   we'll have you summoned before the Mayor of Halgaver   alluding to a Cornish proverb. 'This is a joculary and imaginary court, wherewith men make merriment to themselves, presenting such persons who go slovenly in their attire: where judgment in formal terms is given against them, and executed more to the *scorn* than *hurt* of the persons.' (Ray, 237; *ODEP*, 786).

34.5–6   before Dudman and Ramhead meet   alluding to a Cornish proverb. 'These are two fore-lands, well known to sailors, nigh twenty miles asunder, and the Proverb passeth for the *Periphrasis* of an impossibility.' (Ray, 237; *ODEP*, 207). Dudman Point is SW of St Austell and Rame Head is the W horn of Plymouth Bay.

34.12   Here is proper gear   *ironical*   here are fine goings-on.

34.17   by blood and nails   oath referring to the Crucifixion.

34.20   draw thy tool   draw thy sword. See *Romeo and Juliet*, 1.1.31.

34.22–23   see him fairly out of Flanders   the reference is untraced, but the phrase clearly means that, having given his word, he will see him off the property without hurting him. There is probably an allusion to the Spanish occupation of the Netherlands, and there may also be a verbal echo of, though not an allusion to, the proverb 'Like Flanders-Mares, fairest afar off' (Thomas Fuller, *Gnomologia* (London, 1732), no. 3229; *ODEP*, 266).

35.43   the games of antiquity   the Olympic Games were held at intervals from 776 BC until *c.* AD 393 and were revived in 1896.

36.13   put up your fox   sheathe your sword.

36.35   broad piece   after the introduction of the guinea in 1633 this name was applied to the old twenty-shilling pieces which were much broader and thinner than the new milled coinage.

36.36   takes earth   finds a hiding-place (like a fox).

36.38   draw on a scent   track game.

37.8–13   motto   by Scott.

37.18   fairly sped   in an awkward situation.

38.20   the daughters of Tyre   see note to 61.17.

38.30   takes state on her   assumes an appearance of grandeur or dignity; gives herself airs.

38.43   goblins ... church-yard   see *The Winter's Tale*, 2.1.25–30: 'A sad tale's best for winter. I have one/ Of sprites and goblins.... There was a man ... Dwelt by a churchyard'.

39.6   Holdforth   the name means 'to preach': 'Do not you know, that the Phrase of *Holding-forth* was taken up by *Non conformists*? about the Year 1642 or 1643, as I remember, (at least I do not remember to have heard it sooner: It might perhaps by the *Dissenting Brethren* be brought with them out of *Holland*) and in contradistinction to the word *Preaching*? and used by them (or some of them) so long and so frequently, till it began to be thought a ridiculous *Affectation*, and did afford matter of Drollery to those that had a mind to be pleasant?' (John Wallis, *A Defence of the Christian Sabbath* (London, 1667), 27–28). The ultimate source of the name is Philippians 2.15–16.

39.6   Saint Antholine's   see note to 30.21.

39.13   Cornish chough   red-legged crow.

39.16   order taken   arrangements made.

39.17   sit down with   put up with.

39.23   a bush over thy door   an ivy bush (sacred to Bacchus, god of wine) was hung as a sign outside taverns.

40.5   stoop to his lure   swoop down to the bait whirled by the fowler to call back his hawk.

40.26   held his hand   restrained him.

40.33   thou shalt live as long as Methuselah   if taken literally, 969 years. See Genesis 5.27.

40.34   amass as much wealth as Solomon   see 1 Kings 10.14–29.

40.39–40   the labourer is worthy of his hire   Luke 10.7.

41.8   leasehold ... copyhold   a leasehold must be given up at the end of a fixed period, whereas a copyhold estate is held in perpetuity.

41.28   gay as a goldfinch   see *The Canterbury Tales*, 'The Cook's Tale', 1 (A), 4367: 'Gaillard he was as goldfynch in the shawe'.

41.30–31   the congregation ... bakers   see Ben Jonson, *Bartholomew Fair* (1614), *dramatis personae*; 1.3.114–20; 1.5.152.

41.33   in the spirit   *either* in a spiritual manner (compare 1 Corinthians 14.2), *or* in the same spirit; or perhaps both.

41.34–35   fling sacred and precious things before swine   see Matthew 7.6: 'Give not that which is holy unto the dogs, neither cast ye your pearls before swine, lest they trample them under their feet, and turn again and rend you.'

41.35–36   he, who is King of the World   Satan. See Luke 4.5–6 and John 14.30.

41.42   dried neats-tongue   dried oxtongue. See *1 Henry IV*, 2.4.235–36 and *The Merchant of Venice*, 1.1.112.

42.6   Tider, Killigrew   Robin Tyder (Tider, or Teuder, a member of the Queen's Guard) and William Killigrew (d. 1622) are named as Leicester's servants in Peck, 92, 93, 202, 211.

42.13   at all points   in every particular.

42.23   licenses for monopoly   licences conferring exclusive rights of trading in certain articles. See note to 168.16–17.

42.24   spice a cup   with the implication of poisoning. See *The Winter's Tale*, 1.2.316–17: 'mightst bespice a cup/ To give mine enemy a lasting wink'.

42.24–25   his cabalists, like Dee and Allan   cabalists were interpreters of the oral law of the Jews, the hidden or inner meaning of the law being declared to have been orally transmitted from generation to generation. John Dee (1527–1608), was a mathematician, astrologer, and alchemist; Thomas Allen (1542–1632), a mathematician and astrologer, was regarded as a magician.

42.31, 37   fulfilled in ... fulfilled of   filled with.

43.7   in such sort   into such a condition.

43.10   the Queen of Sheba   see 1 Kings Ch. 10.

43.13   We build on sand then   see Matthew 7.26.

43.37   Milan steel   see note to 29.41.

44.6   the sacrament or the ceremony   Roman Catholics recognise seven sacraments, of which marriage is one, whereas Protestants accord full sacramental status only to Baptism and the Lord's Supper.

44.8   has you at feud   is hostile to you.

44.10   dark lantern   lantern with a slide or arrangement for concealing the light.

44.27   Ka me, ka thee   one good turn deserves another. Proverbial (see Ray, 126; *ODEP*, 416).

45.11   a true broker   a faithful agent.

45.32–36   motto   William Julius Mickle (1735–88), 'Cumnor Hall', lines 1–4. See 'Essay on the Text', 395–96. Scott included the entire ballad in his Introduction to the Magnum edition of *Kenilworth*.

46.18–19   scale staircase   straight staircase with flights and landings, as opposed to a spiral staircase. A Scottish expression, current from the 17th century.

47.7 **Briareus** in Greek mythology, a giant with a hundred arms.

47.11 **the fall of Phaeton** in Greek mythology, Phaethon was the son of Helios the sun-god. He drove the sun's chariot too near the earth, scorching it, until Zeus killed him with a thunderbolt which hurled him into a river.

47.38 **Cupid and Psyche** in late classical mythology, Cupid (Eros) and Psyche (the human soul) fell in love, incurring the wrath of Cupid's mother Venus (Aphrodite); but her jealousy was eventually appeased and the pair lived happily together.

48.7 **two Books of Common Prayer** the official service book of the Church of England, first issued in 1549, and revised in 1552 and again (slightly) in 1559.

48.10 **Morpheus** in classical mythology, the god of dreams.

49.27 **falling ruff** gathered band, not 'set' into open pleats but allowed to 'fall' down onto the shoulders from a high neckband.

50.18 **keep terms with** continue to have dealings with.

50.35 **keep her in honourable countenance** keep her from being ashamed.

52.10–11 **Heaven...wife** see Ephesians 5.22–24; Colossians 3.18; and 1 Peter 3.1.

53.42–43 **to the very outrance** to the uttermost. See *Macbeth*, 3.1.71: 'come, Fate, into the list,/ And champion me to th'utterance'.

54.9 **country-bred** the ironic overtone of Amy's usage of this term is brought out by a comparison with 20.18 and the corresponding editorial note.

56.29–35 **motto** not identified: probably by Scott.

57.13–14 **many a poor blade...scabbard** see Ben Jonson, *Every Man in his Humour* (1598), 2.4.74–76.

58.7 **the English Garter** the Order of the Garter is the highest order of English knighthood. It was founded between 1343 and 1350 by Edward III, allegedly after Joan, Countess of Salisbury, having slipped her garter in a dance, her royal partner bound the blue ribbon round his knee, as if it were his own, with the remark, 'Honi soit qui mal y pense' ('Evil be to the one who evil thinks'), which became the motto of the order. The insignia include the George, a gold medallion representing St George and the dragon. The star was not added to the Garter insignia until 1626 (Corson).

58.13–15 **this most honourable Order ... three most noble associates** Leicester was created Knight of the Garter in 1559 along with Thomas Howard (1536–72), fourth Duke of Norfolk, Sir William Parr (1513–71), first Marquis of Northampton, and Henry Manners (d. 1563), second Earl of Rutland.

58.24 **Order of the Golden Fleece** an order of knighthood instituted by Philip of Burgundy in 1430.

58.26 **the King of Spain** Philip II (1527–98), King of Spain 1556–98 and, as husband of Mary Tudor, King of England 1554–58.

58.33 **this same Philip** Philip was in fact seldom in England; and though popular prejudice naturally held him partly responsible for the persecution under Mary, the Spanish influence was, from motives of policy, employed rather against the persecution.

59.2 **Egmont, Orange** Lamoraal (1522–68), Count of Egmond, and William I the Silent (1533–84), Prince of Orange, two of the leaders of the Netherlanders in their resistance to Spain's control of the Netherlands.

59.7–8 **the Order of Saint Andrew ... Scotland** the Order of the Thistle was probably founded by James III around 1470; it was not a fully fledged knightly order but something less pretentious, perhaps just a giving of badges to retainers. If the order survived James III it did not do so for long, and it certainly was not active in the *Kenilworth* period. As an order paralleling the Garter, the Thistle was re-founded by James VII and II in 1687.

59.9–11   the young widow ... crown matrimonial   Mary Queen of Scots was the widow of Francis II of France, who died in 1560. Elizabeth suggested in 1563 that Leicester might marry Mary. A crown matrimonial is one obtained by marriage and not by right of birth.

61.16–17   the vain women of Tyre and of Sidon   probably a conflation of such Old Testament passages as Isaiah 3.16–26 and Ch. 23, and Ezekiel 26.1 to 28.23. Tyre and Sidon are bywords for wickedness in Matthew 11.20–24.

62.15   sat beneath the salt   the principal salt-box stood at the centre of the table; those of rank sat above the salt, retainers below it.

62.43   do on   don (put on).

63.13   What brought my father to the block   John Dudley (1502?–53), Duke of Northumberland, was executed for his plot to place Lady Jane Grey on the throne, with his own son Guildford Dudley as her husband, on the death of Edward VI.

63.18   Dan Cupid   Master Cupid, the Roman god of love. See Chaucer, *The House of Fame* (an unfinished poem, probably written *c.* 1379–80), 1.137.

64.7   the High Sheriff   formerly the king's representative in the shire in judicial, military, and financial affairs. In fact, however, the military control had been transferred from the Sheriff to the Lord Lieutenant in the reign of Edward VI.

64.15   look babies in the eyes   proverbial (*ODEP*, 482).

64.39–40   lest you are called ... score   if you run up a new account, you may have to pay the old one too.

64.43   Burleigh and Walsingham   William Cecil (1520–98), Lord Burleigh, Elizabeth's Treasurer from 1572, and Sir Francis Walsingham (1530?–90), her Secretary of State from 1573.

65.1–2   red and white   the traditional colours of love.

66.34   her father Henry   Henry VIII.

67.4   The Bear   the bear, chained to a ragged staff as in bearbaiting, was Leicester's emblem.

67.19   slouched hat   soft hat, especially one with a brim which hangs down over the face.

68.32–33   called to accompt in Exchequer   made to pay in the financial court for their appropriation of church lands.

69.3–4   He would be ... fruit   the reference is to the dragon which guarded the golden fruit in the garden of the Hesperides. To obtain these apples was one of the labours of the legendary classical hero Hercules.

69.5   thy occupation is ended   see *Othello*, 3.3.361 : 'Othello's occupation's gone'.

69.5   A word to the wise   a word to a wise man is enough (from the Latin proverb 'Verbum sat sapienti', but common in English: see Ray, 170; *ODEP*, 914).

69.17   at a hard pass   in a critical situation.

69.19–20   a whited sepulchre ... bones   see Matthew 23.27: 'Woe unto you, scribes and Pharisees, hypocrites! for ye are like unto whited sepulchres, which indeed appear beautiful outward, but are within full of dead men's bones, and of all uncleanness.'

71.15   no peace beyond the Line   Pope Alexander VI issued a series of bulls demarcating the world for exploration and settlement between Spain and Portugal. These culminated in the Treaty of Tordesillas between the two kingdoms, 7 June 1494. The world was divided by a line from pole to pole, running 370 leagues west of the Azores and the Cape Verde Islands. In 1529 a similar dividing line down the Pacific was agreed by the Treaty of Zaragosa. Other states naturally refused to recognise this arrangement.

71.29   on the square   honestly.

71.37–38 Shooter's Hill a favourite haunt of highwaymen E of Greenwich. The incident is referred to on page 243.

72.7–8 gather grace ... grows the primary allusion here is probably to 2 Peter 3.18 ('grow in grace'), but there is also a punning allusion to the plant known as grace of God.

72.11 a sun-burnt beauty for Elizabethan dislike of well-tanned ladies, see *Troilus and Cressida*, 1.3.281–83: 'he'll say in Troy, when he retires,/ The Grecian dames are sunburnt and not worth/ The splinter of a lance'.

72.11–12 stand out endure.

72.21 halter involving word-play on horse's halter and hangman's noose.

73.1 bear me out back me up, support me.

73.9 by the eye in unlimited quantity.

73.10 jumps all well with my humour entirely suits my disposition. See also note to 22.32.

73.28 at thine own hand on your own account.

73.34–39 Woodstock Woodstock was one of the ancient estates belonging to the crown. Henry I (1068–1135) built the manor-house, where he kept 'Fair Rosamond', the daughter of Lord Clifford, hidden from the jealousy of Queen Eleanor by many secret passages and recesses. Blenheim House is a mansion designed by the architect-playwright Sir John Vanbrugh (1664–1726)—'Vanbrugh' is the usual spelling—and presented by the nation to John Churchill (1650–1722), first Duke of Marlborough, for his victories in the reign of Queen Anne.

74.35–36 an the master be like the men alluding to the proverb 'Like master like man' (*ODEP*, 517).

74.36 the fiend may take all alluding to the proverbial 'The Devil take all' (Dent, D266.1). Compare *The Merry Wives of Windsor*, 1.3.70.

75.16 Sir Thomas Copely Sir Thomas Copley (1534–84) became a Roman Catholic and went into exile *c.* 1570.

76.5 a Staple for wool the Plantagenet kings established a regular *staple* or market at particular towns in England for the chief products of English industry —wool, skins, tin, etc. Only 'merchants of the staple' were allowed to buy these goods for export, and only at the staple towns.

76.9 The freedom of the corporation the right of participating in the privileges of a town, presented as a sign of esteem.

76.23–25 motto see *The Merry Wives of Windsor*, 4.6.6–7.

77.25 as brave as steel the usual proverbial comparison is 'As true as steel' (Ray, 226; *ODEP*, 840).

77.30 dark lantern see note to 44.10.

77.39–40 as close as ever cat watched a mouse proverbial (see Tilley, C128; *ODEP*, 869).

78.4–5 the conjunction ... threatens misfortune in astrology the planet Mars portends bloodshed, Saturn gloom. When they are in the same sign of the zodiac, or adjacent signs, their combined influence is thought to be particularly threatening.

78.5–6 the buckles of your girdle were brought forward i.e. the buckles had been carelessly returned to their normal position after being turned behind the body for ease in combat. There was a proverbial saying: 'If you be *angry* you may turn the buckle of your girdle behind you' (Ray, 175; *ODEP*, 14), alluded to in *Much Ado about Nothing*, 5.1.138–42.

78.12 Under favour by your leave.

78.42 Uds precious see note to 33.38.

79.1 his pretending to ... in right of laying claim to ... by right (or by virtue) of.

79.8   neat's leather   cow-hide. See *Julius Caesar*, 1.1.26 and *The Tempest*, 2.2.67.

79.28–80.7   the battle of Stoke   an impostor named Lambert Simnel claimed to be Edward Plantagenet, Earl of Warwick, nephew of the late King Edward IV, and allegedly the rightful king. He was supported by Margaret, widow of Charles the Bold of Burgundy and sister of Edward IV, who sent German mercenaries commanded by a leader named Martin Schwartz. The rebels were routed by Henry VII at the battle of Stoke, near Newark, on 16 June 1487.

79.28–29   old Sir Roger Robsart   see Historical Note, 476.

79.37–40   He was the flower...remain   see *The Battle of Floddon Field*, ed. Henry Weber (Edinburgh, 1808), lines 1221–24: 'Most fierce he fought at Thallian Field,/ Where Martin Swart on ground lay slain;/ Where rage did reign he never reel'd,/ But like a rock did still remain.'

79.42–80.1   Almains...all frounced with ribbons   German soldiers employed as mercenaries. For their *frounced* ('plaited') garments, see *The Mirror for Magistrates* (1559), 'Lord Mowbray', lines 173–74: 'Their pleyted garmentes herewith well accorde,/ All iagde and frounst, with diuers coloures dekt' (ed. Lilly B. Campbell (Cambridge, 1938), 107–08).

80.1–2   nether stocks   stockings.

80.4–7   Martin Swart...well   see William Wager, *The Longer Thou Livest the More Fool Thou Art* (1569), (with *Enough is as Good as a Feast*), ed. R. Mark Benbow (London, 1968), lines 92–93: 'Martin Swart and his man, sodledum, sodledum,/ Martin Swart and his man, sodledum bell.'

80.12   comes across   occurs to.

80.17–18   Perkin Warbeck   Perkin Warbeck (1474–99) was an impostor who pretended to be Richard Duke of York, the younger of the two princes who were murdered in the Tower, perhaps by order of Richard III. Warbeck landed in Cornwall on the occasion of his last attempt to win the crown from Henry VII in 1497. He was captured in the New Forest and executed in 1499.

83.19   very confident with him   entrusted to a high degree with his secrets; entrusted with his most intimate secrets.

83.39–40   Better ride safe...elbow   no other reference to this proverb has been found. In the Interleaved Set Scott changed 'murderer' to 'cut-throat', suggesting that the saying may have been his own invention.

84.8   keep measure   be restrained.

84.24   case of peepers   set of eyes.

85.2   I will e'en be a madcap   see *1 Henry IV*, 1.2.137.

85.7–9   Varney has interest...cellar   see Philip Massinger, *A New Way to Pay Old Debts* (written c. 1625, published 1633), 4.2.76–80: 'For which gross fault, I here do damn thy licence,/ Forbidding thee ever to tap, or draw./ For instantly, I will in mine own person/ Command the constable to pull down thy sign;/ And do it before I eat.'

85.27–33   motto   John Gay, *Trivia* (1716), 1.251–56.

86.6–7   the vale of Whitehorse...days   the vale takes its name from the colossal figure of a galloping horse on a hill, formed by removal of the turf so as to expose the underlying white chalk. In 871 Ethelred I and his brother Alfred defeated the Danish invaders in a battle at nearby Ashdown. The White Horse traditionally commemorates this event, though it actually dates from c. 100 BC.

86.33   Favete linguis   *Latin*   be silent. Horace, *Odes*, 3.1.2.

86.39   Quid mihi cum caballo   *Latin*   what have I to do with the horse?

87.2   Dionysius   Dionysius the younger, tyrant of Syracuse, retired after his second expulsion in 343 BC, to Corinth, where it is said he earned his living as a schoolmaster.

87.7   Harlequin's wooden sword   in Italian comedy and English pantomime, the figure of Harlequin usually carries a sword or baton of lath.

87.12–13   Salve, domine … latinam? *Latin*   greeting, sir. Do you understand the Latin tongue? See *Love's Labour's Lost*, 5.1.22: 'ne intelligis, domine?'.

87.14–15   Linguæ latinæ … loquor *Latin*   though not altogether ignorant of the Latin tongue, with your leave, most learned sir, I prefer to speak the vernacular.

87.16–17   the effect … trowel   freemasons make themselves known to other members of the order by a special handshake.

87.21–22   tuguria … faber ferrarius *Latin*   cottages … blacksmith.

87.24   compos voti *Latin*   in possession of what you prayed for.

87.29   pauca verba *Latin*   *literally,* few words (i.e. don't chatter so much). See *Love's Labour's Lost*, 4.2.155 and Henry Fielding, *Tom Jones* (1749), Bk 8, Ch. 5.

87.30–31   curetur jentaculum *Latin*   let the breakfast be attended to.

87.33   felix bis terque *Latin*   twice and thrice blest.

87.38   O cæca mens mortalium! *Latin*   O blind is the understanding of mortals!

87.39   numinibus … malignis *Latin*   prayers answered by hostile deities, i.e. granted in order to do harm to the one who prays. *Satire* 10, line 111, by Juvenal, Roman satiric poet, writing *c.* AD 98–128.

88.1   Quinctilian   Marcus Fabius Quintilianus, Roman rhetorician (*c.* AD 35–*c.* 95).

88.2   at a word   immediately.

88.7–8   nostra paupera regna *Latin*   our poor domains.

88.8   no regular hospitium, as my namesake Erasmus calleth it   Erasmus of Rotterdam (*c.* 1466–1536), the leading humanist scholar. *Hospitium* is the normal Latin word for an inn, and it may be that the reference to Erasmus is merely to give Holiday an opportunity to refer to his namesake.

88.15   fænum habet in cornu *Latin*   she has straw on her horn. Horace, *Satires*, 1.4.34: bulls given to goring had their horns bound with hay.

88.17   ne semissem quidem *Latin*   not even half an as (a Roman coin of small value).

88.24   I bear no such base mind   I am not so undignified. A popular tag: see *2 Henry IV*, 3.2.230, 235.

88.36–37   He was born at Hogsnorton … organ   proverbial (Ray, 206, 258; *ODEP*, 376). The reference is properly to the village of Hook Norton, in Oxfordshire, whose inhabitants were said to be extremely boorish. *ABD*, 2.413.

88.38–39   the herd of Epicurus … porker   see Horace, *Epistles*, 1.4.16. Epicurus was a Greek philosopher who gave his name to the school which stood in contrast with the Stoics, as professing the belief that pleasure is the chief good. When Horace described himself as 'pinguem et nitidum … / Epicuri de grege porcum' ('a plump sleek porker from the herd of Epicurus') he adopted a popular interpretation of Epicurus and meant that he was a votary of refined sensual pleasure.

88.41–42   held that great scholar … Oxford   Erasmus spent most of his visit to England, 1499–1500, at Oxford.

89.8   Amsterdam   Erasmus was actually born at Rotterdam (or possibly Gouda) and styled himself *Rotterdammensis*.

89.10   quasi lucus a non lucendo *Latin*   as if it (a grove) were called light because it was not light. The etymology occurs first in Quintilian (*c.* AD 35–*c.* 95) (1.6.34), and thereafter this became the standard example of etymology by opposites. The form 'lucus a non lucendo' is said to have been first used by the late 4th-century grammarian Servius Honoratus Marius.

89.12   Ludi Magister   *Latin*   the master of *ludus* (meaning both 'school' and 'play').

89.24   Parvo contentus   *Latin*   satisfied with a little: Cicero (106–43 BC), *Ad Atticum*, 12.19.1.

89.27   Erasmus ab Die Fausto   Erasmus de Holiday. *Die Fausto* is a literal translation into Latin of *holiday* ('holy day').

89.29   Buikerschochius   the name is apparently fictitious, alluding to Dutch *buik* ('belly').

89.30   the letter Tau   the Greek letter T.

89.30   In fine   in short; to conclude.

89.33   Quid hoc ad Iphycli boves   *Latin*   what has this to do with the cattle of Iphyclus? (i.e. 'Let us return to the subject'). See Homer, *Odyssey*, 11.290. The saying was in use in the 17th century: see the note by John Pickford in *Notes and Queries*, 7th series, 8 (1889), 51.

89.35   Festina lente   *Latin proverb*   hasten slowly; i.e. more haste, less speed.

89.38   Magister artium   *Latin*   Master of Arts.

89.38   in right of   by right (or virtue) of.

89.40   a white witch   one who uses witchcraft for beneficent purposes.

89.40   a cunning man   a 'wise man', one possessing magical knowledge.

90.7–8   Order of the Rosy Cross   Order of Rosicrucians, a secret world-wide brotherhood of obscure origin claiming to possess esoteric wisdom handed down from ancient times and involving the practice of alchemy and magic.

90.8–9   Geber...gibberish   Geber was a famous Arabian alchemist of the 8th century, 'from whose name is derived the vernacular word *gibberish*', as Scott's Latin indicates; the derivation is false.

90.10–12   discovered stolen goods...invisible   'Sticke a paire of sheeres in the rind of a sive, and let two persons set the top of each of their forefingers upon the upper part of the sheeres, holding it with the sive up from the ground steddilie, and aske *Peter* and *Paule* whether A. B. or C. hath stolne the thing lost, and at the nomination of the guiltie person, the sive will turne round.' (Reginald Scot, *The Discoverie of Witchcraft* (London, 1584: compare *CLA*, 123), 262). Right-maddow or meadow-sweet was supposed, if gathered on St John's Day, to reveal a thief. It was supposed that the fern had an invisible seed, and whoever got possession of some could become invisible themselves. See *The Alchemist*, 1.1.95; *1 Henry IV*, 2.1.82–85. The latter reads: 'we have the receipt of fern-seed, we walk invisible.// Nay, by my faith, I think you are more beholding to the night than to fern-seed for your walking invisible'.

90.13   the panacea, or universal elixir   *alchemy* the philosopher's stone, or a drug with properties similar to the stone's: see note to 23.23.

90.19–21   patientia...perpessio   *Latin*   patience is the daily enduring of hardships. See Cicero (106–43 BC), *De Inventione*, 2.163.

90.23   inter magnates   *Latin*   among great people.

90.31   tracing his circles   in astrology a number of circles define the motions and disposition of the stars.

90.31–32   et sic de cæteris   *Latin*   and so on with the rest.

90.34–35   Uno avulso non deficit alter   *Latin*   one being torn away, another appears in its place. See Virgil (Publius Vergilius Maro, 70–19 BC), *Aeneid*, 6.143.

90.40   saltim banqui and charlatani   *Latin*   mountebanks (itinerant quacks) and charlatans.

91.2–3   Diluis...medendi   *Latin*   you're mixing hellebore, and you don't know the proper point to steady the scales? The very essence of the healer's art prohibits this. See Persius (AD 34–62), *Satire* 5, line 100.

91.20   O, cæca mens hominum!   *Latin*   see note to 87.38.

91.31   Sufflamina   *Latin*   stop; be silent.

92.1 **give the devil his due** proverbial (Ray, 97; *ODEP*, 304).

92.1–2 **Mulciber... with all his Cyclops** in classical legend, Mulciber, or Vulcan, had a forge under Mount Etna in Sicily, where the Cyclopes, one-eyed giants, were his assistants.

92.4 **the author of evil** the Devil.

92.11–12 **A' must needs go, when the devil drives** see *All's Well that Ends Well*, 1.3.29. Proverbial (see Ray, 97 and *ODEP*, 560).

92.13 **Do manus** *Latin* I give in. Colloquial phrase particularly used by the comic dramatist Plautus (*c.* 250–184 BC): see *Persa*, line 855.

92.14 **possessed ... with** informed of.

92.17 **Heus Ricarde! Adsis, nebulo** *Latin* Ho Richard! here, you rogue.

92.18 **Under your favour** by your leave.

92.26 **the Septuagint** the Greek version of the Old Testament.

92.26–27 **the Greek Testament** the New Testament.

92.28–29 **I have sown a sprig... doublet** like the rowan or mountain ash, the witch-elm was regarded as a protection against sorcery.

92.33–34 **Ergo, heus Ricarde! ... didascule** *Latin* ho then, Richard! here, prythee, my pupil. The final word is a slip by Scott, or a coinage on the similar and doubtful form 'pedascule' in *The Taming of the Shrew*, 3.1.48. There may be an echo of the Greek διδάσκαλε ('teacher').

93.4 **profecto** *Latin* meaning not 'forthwith', but 'to be sure', 'certainly', 'indeed'.

93.16 **defend the foul fiends** set the foul fiends at defiance. See *King Lear*, 3.4.94–95 ('defy the foul fiend').

93.16 **Eumenides Stygiumque nefas** *Latin* the Eumenides [Furies], and the Stygian [infernal] horror. Lucan (AD 39–65), *Pharsalia*, 6.695.

93.21 **upon his own bottom** independently.

93.43–94.1 **mi anime, corculum meum** *Latin* my soul, my little heart.

94.18–23 **motto** see *The Faerie Queene*, 4.5.34.1–5.

94.29–32 **you might sing ... Tom-fools be** compare *Twelfth Night*, 2.3.16: 'Did you never see the picture of "we three"?'. A note by Steevens in *ABD*, 1.402 explains: 'A common [inn] sign in the time of Shakespeare, &c consisting of two men in fool's coats. The spectator, or enquirer concerning its meaning, was supposed to make the *third*.'

95.12 **another guess** otherguess; another sort of.

95.29–30 **I would have given them the candle to hold** I would have left them with their domestic responsibilities. Compare *Romeo and Juliet*, 1.4.37: 'For I am proverb'd with a grandsire phrase;/ I'll be a candle-holder and look on' (see Ray, 3 and *ODEP*, 100).

95.30–31 **shewn ... a fair pair of heels** see *1 Henry IV*, 2.4.45. Proverbial (Ray, 70, of a bankrupt; *ODEP*, 729).

96.19–27 **you must tie your horse... shod** 'The country people call this place Wayland Smith, from a fabulous tradition, that it was once the dwelling of an invisible smith; and that if a traveller's horse had lost a shoe upon the road, he need only bring his horse to this place, with a piece of money, and, leaving both there for a short time, at his return he would find the money gone, and his horse new shod.' (P. Russell, *England Displayed*, 2 vols (London, 1769), 1.240: Corson). *CLA*, 262.

96.29 **play off** practise, perform.

96.31 **to purpose** effectively.

97.17 **there is a marsh hard by** Wayland's Smithy is on top of the Berkshire downs, a wholly unmarshy area.

97.18 **the Queen's Guard** the Yeomen of the Guard, the sovereign's body-guard, founded by Henry VII in 1485.

97.25 **Leave thy mopping and mowing** see *Hamlet*, 3.2.241 ('leave thy damnable faces, and begin') and *King Lear*, 4.1.62 ('Flibbertigibbet, of mopping and mowing'). Proverbial (Tilley, M1030).

98.12   He may be in the King of France's stables   alluding to a story 'concerning one of the Lord *Duffus* (in the Shire of *Murray*), his Predecessors, of whom it is reported, That upon a time, when he was walking abroad in the Fields near to his own House, he was suddenly carried away, and found the next day at *Paris* in the *French* King's Cellar with a Silver Cup in his Hand' (John Aubrey, *Miscellanies*, 2nd edn (London, 1821: *CLA*, 149), 158).

98.36   played off   performed.

99.12   Flibbertigibbet   *King Lear*, 4.1.61–62.

99.18–21   Who questions ... consume   This is not strictly 'gipsey cant', but a set of alchemical cant terms, difficult to define precisely, or mere impressive nonsense. The Green Lion is 'a spirit of great transmuting power, supposed to be produced by a certain process in alchemy, sometimes identified with the philosophical mercury' (*OED*, see 'lion' 9); the Red Dragon is a name for Satan in Reginald Scot, *The Discoverie of Witchcraft* (London, 1584: compare *CLA*, 123), 437, though there are Welsh and other red dragons. Talpack is untraced. For the final phrase see *A Midsummer Night's Dream*, 5.1.279: 'Quail, crush, conclude, and quell'.

99.20   avoid thee   depart.

99.27   cut boon whids   see *ABD*, 2.356.

100.43   Saint Lucy's Eve   12 December.

101.27–28   I have ... driven the nail to the quick   conflation of the proverbial hitting the nail on the head and touching to the quick (see Ray, 293 and *ODEP*, 374–75, 833–34).

102.6–7   in store   *either* in plenty *or* in reserve.

102.17–24   motto   see *The Canterbury Tales*, 'The Canon's Yeoman's Prologue', 8 (G), 620–26.

102.38–39   the Black Bull, the Globe, the Fortune   the Black Bull is a slip for the Red Bull Theatre, St John Street, London, probably an innyard used for theatrical entertainment, converted to a regular theatre late in Elizabeth's reign; the Globe Theatre, Bankside, Southwark, London, with which Shakespeare was connected, was built in 1599; the Fortune Theatre in the parish of St Giles, Cripplegate, London, was opened in 1601. *ABD*, 2.584.

103.3–4   shewed ... a clean pair of heels   see note to 95.30–31.

103.9   Jack Pudding   a clown attending a mountebank (itinerant quack).

103.25   fix mercury   render mercury solid by combination with another substance.

103.25–26   made a fair hit at the philosopher's stone   see *The Alchemist*, 1.3.79–80. For the stone see note to 23.23.

103.36–39   Si fixum solvas ... potest   *Latin* if you dissolve what is fixed, and make fly what is dissolved, and fix what flies, they will make you live safe. If it bring forth wind, it is worth a hundredweight of gold. The wind bloweth where it listeth—Catch who catch can. See John 3.8 (Vulgate): 'Spiritus ubi vult spirat.'

103.41   Catch as catch can   proverbial (see Ray, 53 and *ODEP*, 111).

104.28   the grand magisterium   the philosopher's stone.

104.35   the transmutation of metals   alchemical conversion, especially of base metals to gold or silver.

105.5   taken up for a wizard   arrested for the criminal offence of practising witchcraft.

105.26   stand little need   stand in little need.

106.13   leading strings   strings for helping children learning to walk.

106.33   Are you avised of that?   *The Merry Wives of Windsor*, 1.4.90.

107.36   excepting one   Arthur Wellesley, first Duke of Wellington (1769–1852).

107.38–39 Ill news fly fast see Ray, 125 and *ODEP*, 400.

107.39 Listeners . . . themselves see Ray, 59 and *ODEP*, 468.

108.12 I skill not *OED* suggests 'I care not', a nonce personalisation of the common impersonal construction 'it skills not' ('it does not matter').

108.21 hop-o'-my-thumb dwarfish, pygmy (Tilley, H613).

108.23–24 My Dame hath a lame tame Crane a round by Matthew White (fl. 1600–30), which can be found in *The New National Song Book*, ed. C. V. Stanford and Geoffrey Shaw (London, 1958 printing), 234.

108.35 palabras words; palavers. See *Much Ado about Nothing*, 3.5.16: 'Comparisons are odorous; palabras, neighbour Verges.' Variants of Spanish *pocas palabras* ('few words') were popular tags. *ABD*, 1.507; 2.357.

108.43–109.2 bit of a scroll . . . bit pickle little scroll . . . small amount.

109.28–30 Every man . . . curry-comb only the first phrase is recorded as proverbial (*ODEP*, 230).

109.35 Pinniewinks the name is an 18th-century form of 'pilliwinks', an instrument of torture for crushing the fingers.

109.36 comprehend *OED* gives 16th and 17th-century examples for 'comprehend' as a physical seizing, but Scott probably intends a malapropism for 'apprehend', following *Much Ado about Nothing*, 3.3.22 and 3.5.42–43: compare note to 108.35.

109.37 poking-awl a sharp tool, here used to see if the prisoner possessed human flesh or not.

109.42 piccadilloe-needle poking stick, used to re-shape fluted ruff.

110.12–13 you yourself are now no text for their handling you yourself are not good-looking enough now to tempt a curate to kiss you.

110.15 set up her throat raised her voice.

110.24 mareschal the meaning 'farrier' did not survive beyond the 18th century.

111.13 hold opinion with agree with.

112.11 Bradford Bradford-on-Avon.

112.16 Lidcote Hall apparently a fictitious estate.

112.18–20 motto see Joanna Baillie, *The Family Legend* (1810), 4.1.

112.21–22 the village of the same name there is no actual village of this name, though there was formerly a Lidcote in Buckinghamshire.

112.23 Exmoor Exmoor is now heath and marshland, but was formerly a natural forest.

113.10 squire of his body a nobleman's attendant. See *1 Henry IV*, 1.2.23.

113.14–15 in flesh and fell in flesh and skin; entirely. See *King Lear*, 5.3.24.

113.24 the dead palsy palsy producing complete insensibility or immobility of the part affected.

113.35 madge howlet barn-owl.

114.8 it is a chance if he knows you it is fortuitous whether he will know you.

114.12 Mount Hazlehurst apparently fictitious.

114.14 rode to cover *hunting* rode to the woods and bushes where game was to be found.

114.24–25 a forked shaft a barbed arrow.

114.25 I swear by salt and bread *ABD* states that it was once customary to eat bread and salt before taking an oath (1.112; compare 1.552 and 2.92).

114.27 winter apple late-ripening apple.

115.17 the tears chasing each other . . . cheeks see *As You Like It*, 2.1.38–40 ('the big round tears/ Cours'd one another down his innocent nose/ In piteous chase'), and Dryden, *All for Love* (1678), 1.1.267–68 ('The big round drops course one another down/ The furrows of his cheeks').

115.27 Edmund. I have cause to weep perhaps echoing *King Lear*, with the character Edmund and Lear's 'I have full cause of weeping' (2.4.281; compare 4.7.71–75).

115.34 bespeak her say that she is.

115.43–116.3 The battle of Bosworth ... natum Henry VII overthrew Richard III at the battle of Bosworth in the year 1485 'after Christ's birth' in Scott's Latin.

116.2 primo Henrici Septimi *Latin* in the first regnal year of Henry VII (22 August 1485 to 21 August 1486).

116.7 hunts counter rides in a direction opposite to that taken by the game.

116.9–10 a composing draught ... our Great Physician a sedative ... God.

116.29–30 C'est l'homme ... conseille *French* it is man who fights and advises.

117.27 in tertio Mariæ *Latin* in the third regnal year of Mary (6 July 1555 to 5 July 1556).

117.35 cell of removal monastery depending on larger house, to which monks might retire, for instance during sickness or plague.

117.38 a cross patonce betwixt four martlets the arms of the Abbey of Abingdon consisted of a cross patonce (that is, with expanding arms terminating in fleurs-de-lys) and four swifts. The manuscript has 'patoneé', and the first edition 'patonee'.

117.43–118.1 Vengeance is mine ... repay it see Romans 12.19.

118.3 laquei amoris, or lacs d'amour *Latin and French* true love knots, a kind of double knot, made with two bows on each side, interlacing each other, and with two ends.

118.27 cælebs and sine prole *Latin* unmarried and without issue.

118.28–29 part, per pale, the noble coat *Latin* divide the coat of arms by a vertical line, showing the husband's arms on one side and the wife's on the other.

119.15 Saint Austen's eve 25 May, the day before the feast sacred to St Augustine, first Archbishop of Canterbury (d. 604 or 605).

119.17 proper handsomely; suitably. There is also an allusion to the heraldic use 'represented in the natural colouring'.

119.20 taken in the manner apprehended in the act.

119.21 that I may thrust conviction down his false throat see *Titus Andronicus*, 2.1.55.

119.27–28 worse heraldry than metal upon metal in heraldry a figure in colour (gules, azure, etc.) may be placed on a metal field (or, argent) or vice versa; but not metal on metal, or colour on colour. See Note G in the Magnum edition of *Ivanhoe* for a discussion of this point.

120.28 truce to enough of; have done with.

120.31 mandragorn the sedative drug mandragora. Scott's form is perhaps derived from a misprint, *mandragoru*, in the First Folio *Antony and Cleopatra*, 1.5.4, or it may be influenced by *mandragon* ('mandrake').

120.40 witch's mark a mole or mark made by the Devil upon his servants. It was believed that, being insensible to pain, it could be located and used to prove sorcery.

121.10–11 she is but a hawk ... wind see *Othello*, 3.3.264–67, where Othello says of Desdemona: 'If I do prove her haggard,/ Though that her jesses were my dear heart-strings,/ I'd whistle her off and let her down the wind/ To prey at fortune.'

121.16 warrant of attorney document giving full powers to a specified person to act in place of the person who signs it.

121.25 pass current be generally accepted.

122.27 hold the end of a feast ... fray proverbial (Ray, 106; *ODEP*, 52).

See *1 Henry IV*, 4.2.74–75: 'To the latter end of a fray and the beginning of a feast/ Fits a dull fighter and a keen guest.'

122.38–40 a silver cognisance . . . degree this badge is apparently fictitious. It does not appear among the badges associated with the Radcliffe family: there are several examples of a hand grasping a dragon, but none of a fire-drake or dragon grasping a brick-bat. Neither 'fire-drake' nor 'brick-bat' is a term normally found in English heraldry.

123.11 Say's Court, near Deptford Say's Court was the ancient mansion-house of the manor of West Greenwich, so called from its having been possessed *c.* 1191–1404 by the family of Saye. In 1487 it was forfeited to the Crown which granted the stewardship to various different people in the 16th century. By 1603 it was in the hands of the diarist John Evelyn's wife's grandfather: it was confiscated from that family in the aftermath of the civil war and bought by Evelyn in 1653. It was replaced by a workhouse in 1759. According to Scott, the Evelyn family was in possession at the time of the novel and lent the mansion to Sussex: see page 131.

123.23–24 The leeches are at a stand the doctors are perplexed, can make no progress.

123.38 the manna of Saint Nicholas '*Aqua Tofana*, which was the same poison, was perhaps known at the time treated of in the novel, but apparently it was at least half a century later that the reputed daughter, Giulia Tofana, of the inventress Teofania di Adamo, sold the liquid at Rome and Naples under the name of "Manna of St. Nicholas of Bari"—a "miraculous oil" held in great esteem in Naples at that time for curing diseases. At any rate, it was much later than Elizabeth's reign that this violation of a sacred name roused the clergy, and finally led to the putting to the rack and the strangulation of the wretched woman who sold the phials of poison.' (C. Nelson Stewart in *Notes and Queries*, 11th series, 3 (1911), 488).

125.4–10 motto see *The Alchemist*, 1.3.75–80.

126.5–6 Ban . . . man see *The Tempest*, 2.2.172–73.

126.17 Quarter Sessions in England, a lower court with limited criminal and civil jurisdiction, held quarterly until 1972 by the justices of the peace.

126.24–25 a sailor whistling in a calm it was a common superstitious practice among sailors to whistle for a wind.

126.30 Alfred's victory see note to 86.6–7.

126.30–31 the celebrated Pusey Horn the manor of Pusey in Berkshire is held by virtue of an ox-horn believed to have been presented to the Pusey family by Canute the Great (994?–1035).

126.31–32 the wild legend of Wayland Smith Weland the Smith is a celebrated hero of Norse legend, but Scott uses only local Berkshire lore.

126.42 note see Historical Note, 474.

127.5 Lord Deputy of Ireland one of the titles borne by the representative of the English crown in Ireland. In 1575 the Lord Deputy was Sir William Fitzwilliam (1526–99).

127.5–6 take the Queen's pleasure ascertain the Queen's will.

127.6–7 Rory Oge MacCarthy MacMahon the name is a combination of such actual rebel names as Donnell MacCarthy More, Brian MacHugh Oge MacMahon, and Rory MacCragh.

127.7–8 an agent of Monsieur . . . Elizabeth the prince standing next to the throne in France was commonly entitled *Monsieur*. At the time of the novel, *Monsieur* was François (1554–84), Duke of Alençon: for some ten years Elizabeth played with the idea of marrying the prince.

127.9–10 the Duke of Medina . . . princess Scott is using the name of either Alonso Pérez de Guzmán (1550–1613), seventh Duke of Medina Sidonia, later commander of the Spanish Armada, or the Duke of Medina

Celi, who in the 1570s commanded a Spanish fleet which took troops to reinforce the Duke of Alva in the Netherlands, arousing some concern in England as
it was feared that his destination might be either Ireland or Scotland. Neither is
recorded as having been an ambassador to England.

127.24   Greenwich   Greenwich Palace, built in 1427, was Elizabeth's birth-
place and her principal summer residence; it was demolished during the
Commonwealth, but rebuilt by Charles II and William III, in whose reign it was
converted in 1694 into the Royal Naval Hospital.

127.36   Fleet Street   the street running west from the foot of Ludgate Hill in
the City of London to the Strand.

129.3   Mount Sinai... Law given forth   see Exodus Ch. 19.

129.7   gaberdine   loose upper garment of coarse material, worn by Jews,
such as Shylock in *The Merchant of Venice*, 1.3.107.

129.9   the castle-ditch at Aleppo   Aleppo, the principal city of N Syria, has
a great citadel (mainly 13th-century). Perhaps suggested by *Macbeth*, 1.3.7 and
Othello, 5.2.355.

129.17   Elias   Elijah, Hebrew prophet. See 1 Kings Ch. 17 to 2 Kings Ch. 2.

129.24   Tokay... Lachrymæ   Tokay and Lachryma Christi are two sweet
wines from Hungary and the Vesuvius district of Italy respectively.

130.10–11   the withered gourd... prophet   see Jonah 4.6–7.

130.14   the Schah-majm   *Hebrew* 'the heavens' (*shāmájm*).

130.15–16   watch therefore, and pray   see Matthew 26.41; Mark 13.33
and 14.38.

130.16   Alchahest Elixir   the philosopher's stone. See note to 23.23.

130.16   Samech   the fifteenth letter of the 22-letter Hebrew alphabet.
Apparently the Jew should attain a higher numbered degree of proficiency in
alchemy before Wayland told him anything.

130.32   the philosopher's stone   see note to 23.23.

130.34–35   Match for match... collier   see *Grim, the Collier of Croydon*
(performed 1600, published 1662), of doubtful authorship: *ABD*, 3.320 ('if
Grim be merry,/ I will make up the match between ye.// There will be a match in
the devil's name!').

130.40–41   made up   completed.

130.43   orvietan   or 'Venice Treacle', a preparation believed to be an antidote to poison, invented by a native of Orvieto in central Italy.

131.10   the famous Bell-Savage   a popular inn in Ludgate Hill, demolished in 1873.

131.19–23   Say's Court... Sussex   see note to 123.11.

131.25–28   the celebrated Mr Evelyn... gentlemen   the *Memoirs* of John
Evelyn (1620–1706), author of *Sylva; or, A Discourse of Forest-trees, and the
Propagation of Timber in His Majesties Dominions* (London, 1664: see *CLA*, 240),
were published in part in 1818. Scott was particularly interested in Evelyn as a
fellow arboriculturist and memorialist.

131.30–36   motto   by Scott.

132.21   the great northern rebellion   the Earls of Northumberland and
Westmoreland led a rebellion with the aim of deposing Elizabeth in favour of
Mary.

132.24–27   The Earl of Sussex... Ratcliffes   the first Earl of Sussex,
Robert Radcliffe (1483–1542) had been second Baron Fitzwalter and first
Viscount Fitzwalter.

132.27   the scutcheon of Leicester   Leicester's grandfather was Edmund
Dudley (1462?–1510), instrumental in carrying out Henry VII's rapacious
fiscal policies and accused of perverting justice for his own ends; he was executed for alleged treason on the accession of Henry VIII. For Leicester's father
John Dudley see note to 63.13.

132.30 Tower-Hill a place of execution for state prisoners outside the walls of the Tower of London.

133.18 The younger for Walter Raleigh see Historical Note, 476.

134.9–10 the very worst... practice for accusations of poisonings made against Leicester in *Leicester's Commonwealth* see Peck, 80–91.

134.17 Tracy, Markham neither Tracy nor Markham is known to have been a historical person, but several Markhams of the period occur in Sir John Harington, *A New Discourse of a Stale Subject, Called the Metamorphosis of Ajax* (London, 1596: *CLA*, 106): see the index in the edition by Elizabeth Story Donno (London, 1962). The letter quoted on page 210 of the novel is addressed to Mr Robert Markham.

134.24–29 the Indies ... the Indian voyage the terms *Indies* and *Indian* could refer to either the East or the West Indies, but the name *Indamira* suggests an eastern beauty: Indamora is the bride of Aureng-Zebe in Dryden's play *Aureng-Zebe* (1676), set in India.

134.25 with hearts as light as our purses compare the proverb 'Light (heavy) purse makes a heavy (light) heart' (see Ray, 130; *ODEP*, 366, 463).

134.33 Amoret Amoret, 'of grace and beautie noble Paragone': *The Faerie Queene*, 3.6 and 12, and 4.7. Her love for Timias, censured by Belphoebe, refers to Elizabeth's displeasure at the relationship of Raleigh with Elizabeth Throckmorton.

134.41–135.2 What man ... decay see *The Faerie Queene*, 7.6.1.1–5. 'Chance' was not corrected to 'Change' in any edition of *Kenilworth* published during Scott's lifetime.

135.15 Blount see Historical Note, 475.

135.15–16 the devil woo'd Eve ... Knowledge see Genesis 2.9, 16–17 and 3.1–5.

135.33 the rascal cook *The Taming of the Shrew*, 4.1.146.

137.12 Stanley Stanley is not known to have been a historical person.

137.21–24 motto *The Taming of the Shrew*, 4.1.109–11.

137.38–40 owls...ivy-tod compare the proverbial 'To look like an owl in an ivy bush' (Tilley, O96; *ODEP*, 604), and see Coleridge, 'The Rime of the Ancient Mariner' (1798, rev. 1800), lines 535–36: 'When the ivy-tod [ivy-bush] is heavy with snow,/ And the owlet whoops to the wolf below'.

138.15–18 the talent ... multiplying it see the parable of the talents, Matthew 25.14–30.

138.27 O base transmutation! see *The Taming of the Shrew*, Induction.2.18.

138.32 hay mow rick or stack of hay.

138.37 Doctor Master Richard Master (d. 1588) was appointed physician to Queen Elizabeth in 1559.

139.34 quicksilver in his veins mercury in the veins would indicate a subtle, busy, ingenious, and eloquent man. Blount is following the usual misinterpretation of a characteristic originally derived from the god Mercury as being to do with metal.

139.40 the Seven Sleepers see note to 30.1.

140.37–38 They were soon launched ... splendour see Alexander Pope, *The Rape of the Lock* (1712–14), 2.1–4: 'Not with more Glories, in th'Etherial Plain,/ The Sun first rises o'er the purpled Main,/ Than issuing forth, the Rival of his Beams/ Launch'd on the Bosom of the Silver *Thames*.'

141.1 the King of Elements the sun.

141.10 take water embark in a boat on the Thames.

141.43 Irish kernes Raleigh would have encountered kernes (members of war-bands) during his service in Ireland in 1580–81. See *Richard II*, 2.1.156 and *2 Henry VI*, 3.1.367. *ABD*, 1.170, 346, 573; 3.77.

142.4 Gentlemen Pensioners the select body-guard of Henry VIII and Elizabeth.

142.10 Lord Hunsdon Henry Carey (1524?–96), first Baron Hunsdon, son of Anne Boleyn's sister and first cousin to Elizabeth.

143.7 in cuerpo *Spanish* without the cloak; naked (*literally* in the body).

143.21 Who the good jere who the pox, or the devil.

145.10 physician in ordinary regular physician.

146.25–26 In the multitude of counsel there is safety see Proverbs 11.14 and 24.6.

146.29 pushed me home pressed me hard, to the root of the matter.

146.42–147.6 your service in Ireland Raleigh served in Ireland 1580–81.

148.28 Yarmouth herrings Great Yarmouth, a town on the Norfolk coast, was the chief centre of the English herring-fishing industry.

148.30 Thomas ap Rice probably fictitious, but possibly the celebrated poet Thomas Price or Prys (1564?–1634).

148.30 Evan Evans no particular historical figure is known to be intended.

148.33 vogue la galère row on the galley; i.e. here goes, come what may (Scott's following phrase is effectively itself a translation). From Alain-René Lesage and d'Orneval, *Le Théâtre de la Foire*, 10 vols (Paris, 1721), Air 98: 'Et vogue la galère tant qu'elle' (the air appears at the end of vols 1–3).

149.41 the very verge of our royal residence an area within twelve miles of the Court, wherever it might be, in which statutory jurisdiction was exercised by the Lord High Steward.

150.16–21 motto *Richard II*, 1.1.15–19.

150.30 Ram's Alley or Ram Alley, off Fleet Street near Whitefriars, a resort of thieves and bad characters, noted for its dirty eating-houses. 'Ram-Alley stinks with cooks, and ale': Lodowick Barry, *Ram Alley; or, Merry Tricks* (1611); in *ABD*, 2.295.

150.31 Countess of Rutland Isabel, whom the third earl Edward Manners (1549–87) married *c.* 1573.

150.32 my Lord of Lincoln Thomas Cooper (*c.* 1517–94) was Bishop of Lincoln 1571–84.

151.11 Knight of the Garter see note on 58.7.

151.16–17 for considerations for reasons of my own.

152.2–3 Were war ... white boys the phrase is found in Naunton (see Historical Note, 474), 246, where it is attributed to Sir John Perrot (*white boys* are 'favourites'): 'Lo, now she is ready to piss herself for fear of the Spaniard; I am again one of her white boys'. The phrase is proverbial (Tilley, B579; *ODEP*, 884–85).

152.4–5 walking rapiers rapiers worn by civilians.

152.5 bear the bell take the first place, as the leader of a flock of sheep, the 'bell-wether', wears a bell. Proverbial (see Ray, 177; *ODEP*, 44).

152.8 a stand of pikes a compact group of pikemen.

153.21–22 the High Sheriff of Kent see note to 64.7.

153.27 Greenwich see note to 127.24.

154.18–19 a peer of older creation than his own the earldom of Sussex was created in 1529, that of Leicester (in Robert Dudley himself) in 1564.

154.22 Usher of the Black Rod the chief Gentleman Usher of the royal household.

154.31 Master Bowyer the name and the story are taken from Naunton (see Historical Note, 474), 179–80.

155.32 mayor of the palace title of the prime ministers (under the later Merovingians the virtual sovereigns) of the Frankish kingdoms, here used ironically in the literal sense 'superintendent of the palace'. Scott is following the version of Naunton in Somers (see Historical Note, 474) where the Bowyer story is headed '*A Major Pallacii*' (1.253).

156.8–9 yonder rebellious Earls in the north see note to 132.21.

156.10 Do you bandy looks and words with me ...? see *King Lear*, 1.4.81.

156.12–15 I say, my lord ... disorderly retinues the general tendency of the legislation of Henry VII and VIII was to prevent the possibility of large bodies of men being raised by the nobles, and to reduce the number of their followers.

156.28 appeal from appeal to any higher authority than.

157.4 Sir Henry Lee (1530–1610), master of the ordnance, and personal champion (ceremonial defender) of Elizabeth 1559–90.

157.7 our Tower fare prison food in the Tower of London.

157.22 Nonsuch an immense palace (so-called because unequalled) which stood between Ewell and Cheam in Surrey, five miles SE of Kingston-upon-Thames. Begun in 1538, it was sold in 1556 by Mary Tudor to the Earl of Arundel, who became High Constable and High Steward in 1558. Elizabeth stayed there in 1559 and 1567. On Arundel's death the palace passed to his son-in-law, Lord Lumley. From this time on, Elizabeth visited the palace nearly every year, as if it were one of her own houses, and in 1592 she accepted it from Lumley in payment of his debts to the crown. It was demolished in 1682–87 and the very site was forgotten until excavation in 1959–60.

158.37 Varney was ... a skilful pilot in extremity compare the portrait of Achitophel (Shaftesbury) in Dryden, *Absalom and Achitophel* (1681), 1.150–62, especially line 159: 'A daring Pilot in extremity'.

160.43–161.1 the golden web wrought by Minerva spinning and weaving were among the Roman goddess Minerva's accomplishments. There may be an allusion to the weaving contest between Minerva and Arachne described at the beginning of Book 6 of *Metamorphoses* by Ovid (43 BC–17 AD).

162.24–25 in her cause ... honour when Elizabeth was sent to the Tower by Queen Mary in 1554, under suspicion of complicity in Sir Thomas Wyatt's rebellion, Lord Robert Dudley was a fellow prisoner; but he had actually been a supporter of Lady Jane Grey (his sister-in-law) as monarch.

163.18 false Cressidas faithless lovers (or wives). Cressida was the wife of Troilus, but left him for Diomedes, one of the Greeks engaged in the war against the Trojans.

163.31–34 Cresseid was your's ... Diomed see *Troilus and Cressida* (written 1602, published 1609), 5.2.152–58.

163.35 my Lord of Southampton probably Henry Wriothesley (1573–1624), Shakespeare's patron, though he became the third Earl of Southampton only in 1581.

165.10 High Treasurer William Cecil, Baron Burghley (1520–98).

165.11 the two famed classic streams the Rhône and the Arar (Saône), described in Julius Caesar (100–44 BC), *De Bello Gallico* (Gallic War), 1.12; but Caesar does not mention the colour of the water in the two rivers.

165.12–13 Master Ascham Roger Ascham (1515–68), a notable classical scholar, had been Elizabeth's tutor.

165.26–27 Paris and Menelaus ... Helen the Trojan war was caused by Helen, wife of the Spartan hero Menelaus, deserting him for the Trojan Paris.

165.38 take the water embark in a boat on the Thames.

166.5–10 motto not identified: probably by Scott.

166.35–36 Scylla ... Charybdis in classical legend, mariners traversing the straits of Messina, between Italy and Sicily, had to sail between the cave of the devouring monster Scylla and the whirlpool Charybdis.

167.3–4 the unfortunate Mary ... currency in May 1568 Mary Queen of Scots had fled to England after her defeat at Langside, and although throwing herself on the mercy of Elizabeth had been virtually a prisoner. The seventh year was actually completed by July 1575.

167.15–16   a vain and unjust pretence to the throne of England   Elizabeth's title to the throne rested on her position as the last surviving child of Henry VIII; but Roman Catholics claimed that she was illegitimate. They refused to recognise the validity of Henry VIII's divorce from Katherine of Aragon, and therefore his subsequent marriage to Anne Boleyn was invalid in their eyes. If Elizabeth was illegitimate, then Mary Queen of Scots could claim the throne as great grand-daughter of Henry VII: his daughter Margaret Tudor (sister of Henry VIII) had married James IV of Scotland.

167.29–30   the Countess of Shrewsbury   during much of her imprisonment Mary was nominally in the charge of George Talbot, Earl of Shrewsbury, but in practice his wife Elizabeth acted as a (friendly) custodian.

168.8   golden opinions from all sorts of men   see *Macbeth*, 1.7.33: 'I have bought/ Golden opinions from all sorts of people'.

168.16   why come they not to court?   see John Skelton, 'Why Come Ye Nat to Courte?' (written 1522).

168.16–17   the Queen will grant no more monopolies   monopolies, or patents conferring exclusive rights of trading in certain commodities, were a cause of grievance throughout the reign, but it was not till 1601 that Elizabeth told the Commons that she would grant no more on her own prerogative.

168.18   Alderman Aylford   Aylford is not known to have been a historical person.

168.19   Queenhithe   a royal property on the north bank of the Thames near London Bridge. Tolls were collected here from half of the vessels discharging cargoes, and formed the Queen's pin-money.

168.20   Master Edmund Spencer ... Lord Treasurer   Spenser spent much of his life in Ireland between 1580 and 1598, and wrote *A Veue of the Present State of Ireland* in 1595–97. Scott probably has in mind the story that Burghley attempted to reduce the pension awarded the poet on the publication of *The Faerie Queene* Bks 1–3 in 1589.

168.26   my nephew, Philip Sidney   the poet Philip Sidney (1554–86) was the son of Sir Henry Sidney and Mary Dudley, Leicester's sister.

168.27   Venus and Adonis   Shakespeare's poem of this title was published in 1593.

168.29   patent ... bears   control over theatrical companies was exercised by a licensing system involving royal patents. For the bears, see 173–76.

168.34   Sir Francis Denning   Denning is not known to have been a historical figure.

169.7–8   good life   assiduous drinking. See *Twelfth Night*, 2.3.34–37.

169.10   Master Robert Laneham   Robert Langham (*c*. 1535–80) was Keeper of the Council Chamber.

169.37   to cote a hare   *hare-coursing*   properly, one dog *cotes* ('passes') another dog, not the hare.

169.42–43   irreverend ... canons   Leicester uses the word *irreverend* to mean 'disrespectful'. Laneham punningly takes it in an ecclesiastical sense: hence the *canons*, or rules of the Church.

170.2   her grandmother, who eat the apple   Eve.

170.20   My wife ... Mystery   i.e. in a mystery play. Compare John Heywood, *The Four P's* (published 1545?), lines 948–49: 'For oft, in the play of Corpus Cristi,/ He hath playd the devyll at Coventry' (*ABD*, 1.18).

170.26   runs wild humours   is in a wild mood. See *Henry V*, 2.1.116, 121.

170.27   wink at their unsettled starts   disregard their fits of turbulent passion.

171.16   your hose are unbraced   see *Hamlet*, 2.1.78, where it is Hamlet's doublet that is *unbraced* ('unfastened'). Hose would be *ungartered* (as in *As You Like It*, 3.2.351) or *untrussed*.

172.2 Esculapius son of Apollo; Greek god of healing.

172.26 Lord Willoughby although much play is made with Lord Willoughby's age in this scene the first mention in the manuscript is of a young man, and this along with his gallantry suggests that Scott probably had in mind Peregrine Bertie (1555–1601), who became Baron Willoughby de Eresby in 1580, and was a distinguished soldier in the Low Countries in the decade thereafter. An older possibility is Sir Fulke Greville, fourth Baron Willoughby de Broke, married in 1553, knighted in 1565, who died in 1606.

173.20 Orson Pinnit this feigned name suggests a pun on Italian *orso* ('bear') on the one hand, and *whoreson* on the other, plus restraining (an animal). Orsin is the bear-warden in Samuel Butler, *Hudibras* (1663).

173.25 the Irish clan MacDonough the MacDonoghs, unlike the MacDonnells, played a very minor role in the Irish rebellions.

173.30–31 We would give ... use see note to 127.24.

174.3–4 single falchion combat using small version of sword with a single-edged blade, the back straight or slightly concave, the edge with a pronounced convex curve.

174.4–6 stood ... daughter see *The Merry Wives of Windsor*, 1.1.100–02. Sir Thomas Lucy (1532–1600), owner of Charlecote near Stratford-upon-Avon in Warwickshire, is traditionally believed to have prosecuted the young Shakespeare for deer-stealing.

174.8 that matter was heard in council see *The Merry Wives of Windsor*, 1.1.31–35, 106.

174.14–15 the gamesome mad fellow ... whoreson poetry see *Hamlet*, 5.1.165.

174.17 sounded to boot and saddle gave the signal to mount.

174.23 matchless mastiffs see *Henry V*, 3.7.130–31: 'That island of England breeds very valiant creatures; their mastiffs are of unmatchable courage.'

174.28 Parish-garden or Paris garden, an Elizabethan bear-garden at Bankside, Southwark. *ABD*, 2.401.

174.39 Sir Talbot Talbot is a dog's name, occurring in *The Canterbury Tales*, 'The Nun's Priest's Tale', 7.3383 (B2.4573). It is also used of hunting dogs and in heraldry.

175.6–7 your cognizance ... staff see note to 67.4.

175.9–10 my brother Ambrose of Warwick Ambrose Dudley (1528?–90), Earl of Warwick.

175.12 fight dog, fight bear fight till one be overcome. Proverbial (Ray, 190; *ODEP*, 256).

175.17 Marlow Christopher Marlowe (1564–93), playwright and poet.

175.24 the Dean of St Asaph's, an eminent Puritan the Dean in 1560–87 was Hugh Evans, but if a Puritan he was far from eminent.

175.38 this new undertaking of his Chronicles Shakespeare's history plays were written in the late 1580s and the 1590s.

176.15 Minerva see note to 160.43–161.1.

176.26–35 That very time ... fancy free *A Midsummer Night's Dream*, 2.1.155–64.

177.40 Lady Derby probably either Mary (d. 1580), widow of Edward Stanley (1508–72), third Earl of Derby, or Margaret, wife of Henry Stanley (1531–93), who became fourth Earl in 1572.

177.42 copper nose red nose caused by disease or intemperance.

178.24 Lady Paget possibly Nazaret, who separated from her husband, Thomas, third Lord Paget, in 1582 and died in the following year in which also her husband fled abroad as a suspect because of his Roman Catholicism.

Alternatively, Thomas's mother Anne (widow of William Paget (1505–63), first Baron Paget), who was still living in 1583.

178.36   Fain would I climb ... fall   see Historical Note, 474.

179.7–10   the ladies of Parnassus ... Nine   the nine Muses, the goddesses of poetry, music, and the other arts, were worshipped at Parnassus, a high mountain in Greece.

179.23–24   with the flight of a lapwing   see *Much Ado About Nothing*, 3.1.24: 'For look where Beatrice, like a lapwing, runs/ Close by the ground, to hear our conference.'

180.17   one swallow a summer   proverbial   see Allan Ramsay, *A Collection of Scots Proverbs*, *The Works of Allan Ramsay*, ed. Alexander M. Kinghorn and Alexander Law, 5 (Edinburgh and London, 1972), 64; *ODEP*, 791; compare Ray, 143.

180.22   chattering gulls   there is a word-play on *gulls* meaning 'sea-birds' and 'fools'.

181.6   the palace clock   there appears to be no record of such a curious clock.

181.14   Tarleton   Richard Tarlton (d. 1588) was a comic actor and jester patronised by Leicester.

182.19   my old master ... devil   see *The Merchant of Venice*, 2.2.19–23, where Launcelot Gobbo (compare Lancelot Wayland) says: '... I should stay with the Jew my master, who—God bless the mark!—is a kind of devil; and, to run away from the Jew, I should be ruled by the fiend, who—saving your reverence!—is the devil himself.'

182.22   the Scotch wild cattle   Scott noted in the Magnum edition (22.342): 'A remnant of the wild cattle of Scotland are preserved at Chillingham Castle, near Wooler, in Northumberland, the seat of Lord Tankerville. They fly before strangers; but if disturbed and followed, they turn with fury on those who persist in annoying them.'

182.32–38   motto   see Schiller, trans. Coleridge, *The Piccolomini; or, The First Part of 'Wallenstein', a Drama in Five Acts* (London, 1800), 179: 'The moment comes,/ It is already here, when thou must write/ The absolute total of thy life's vast sum./ The constellations stand victorious o'er thee,/ The planets shoot good fortune in fair junctions,/ And tell thee, "Now's the time!"'.

183.43   the Crown Matrimonial   crown obtained by marriage with the sovereign.

184.1   Darnley   Henry Stewart or Stuart (1545–67), Lord Darnley, married Mary Queen of Scots in 1565; he was murdered when the house where he was staying at Kirk o' Field, Edinburgh, was blown up.

184.2   a gull, a fool, a thrice sodden ass   see *Henry V*, 3.6.65; *The Tempest*, 5.1.295; *Love's Labour's Lost*, 4.2.20.

184.4–5   the noble Earl ... throne   see note to 59.9–11.

184.18   nil ultra   *Latin*   nothing beyond; thus far and no further.

184.19–20   Cupid and Hymen   Cupid was the Roman boy-god of love and Hymen the Greek and Roman deity of marriage.

185.9   judicial astrology   the supposed science of divining the future from the planets.

185.19   planetary signs   each planet is denoted by a sign, e.g. ♂ for Mars and ♀ for Venus.

186.4–5   Astra regunt homines, sed regit astra Deus   *Latin*   the stars rule men, but God rules the stars. A popular saying quoted in Andrea Cellarius, *Harmonia Macrocosmica* (Amsterdam, 1661), 94: 'Tempora mutantur, nos & mutamur in illis,/ Astra regunt homines, sed regit astra Deus'.

186.10–12   Saturn, being in the sixth House ... sickness   the sky was mapped out into twelve sections or houses. In this horoscope the planet Saturn (denoting Time) is in the House of Health; the planet Mars (denoting War) is in the House of Life, sinking, but at a point in the heavens opposite Saturn. Thus Time is working against Sussex, a warrior, and cutting short his life.

186.14–15   erect another scheme   construct another horoscope.

186.23   those blessed signs   the signs of the zodiac.

186.35–36   the ire of princes is as the wrath of the lion   see Proverbs 19.12 and 20.2.

186.36–37   Venus, ascendant . . . Sol   the planet Venus rises to join the Sun in the first house, denoting a fortunate marriage (with the Queen).

186.40   Augustus   title conferred on Octavian (63 BC–AD 14) when he became the first Roman emperor in 27 BC.

186.41   Haruspices   Etruscan diviners, who foretold future events.

187.10   penthouse   see *Macbeth*, 1.3.20, where the witches chant: 'Sleep shall neither night nor day/ Hang upon his pent-house lid;/ He shall live a man forbid.'

187.34–35   predominant in the horizon   the controlling influence in the visible hemisphere.

187.39   Chaldæa   Babylonia, reputed birthplace of astronomical and astrological knowledge.

188.1   celestial intelligences   *either* spirits governing the heavenly bodies *or* the sciences dealing with them.

188.10–11   the malignant and adverse aspect   ordinary and technical adjectives respectively, denoting a particular angular relationship between heavenly bodies regarded as unfavourable.

189.4   plan or figure   chart or horoscope.

189.14–16   until the daggers . . . ribs   see *Julius Caesar*, 5.1.39–40: 'Villains, you did not so when your vile daggers/ Hack'd one another in the sides of Cæsar.'

189.19–20   Does Hali . . . Life?   do you, Hali, foresee any calamity in your own affairs? Varney is using a jeering diminutive of Alasco's name, possibly with an allusion to Ali ben Aban-Ragel, an Arab astrologer of the 11th century. For the House of Life see note to 186.36–37. An *infortune* is an unfortunate or malevolent planet or aspect, especially referring to Saturn or Mars.

189.36   Ne quisquam Ajacem . . . Ajax   *Latin*   lest anyone except Ajax may be able to conquer Ajax. Ovid (43 BC–AD 17), *Metamorphoses*, 13.390: a tag from Scott's schooldays, the extract being long standard in Scottish schools.

189.38   Rosy Cross   see note to 90.7–8.

190.7   the sign of the ascendant being in combustion   the Earl's astrological sign (in the ascendant when he was born) is being obscured by proximity to the Sun.

190.28   King Hal   Henry VIII.

190.31–32   until the Green Dragon . . . golden-goose   for the cant term 'Green Dragon' compare note to 99.18–21. The legendary 'golden goose' laid golden eggs.

190.41   Tartary   central Asia.

190.43   the Jewish Cabala   see note to 42.24–25.

191.21   a stumbling block to the wise   see 1 Corinthians 1.19–30, especially 23.

191.22–23   he who runs may read   proverbial (John Ray, *A Collection of English Proverbs* (Cambridge, 1670), 191; *ODEP*, 689–90; see Habakkuk 2.2).

191.33   in fumo   *Latin*   in smoke.

192.22   if thou keep'st time and touch   if you regulate matters accurately and act faithfully.

193.12   do my turn   carry out my task.

194.13   by times   betimes; early in the morning.

194.15   pistol him   see *Twelfth Night*, 2.5.34.

194.38   It is from Saint-John's-Berg   it is the white wine from Johannis-berg in the Rhine region.

195.4–5   the room turns round with him like a parish-top   see *Twelfth Night*, 1.3.37–38: 'He's a coward and a coystrill that will not drink to my niece till his brains turn o' th' toe like a parish-top.' A *parish-top* was a spinning-top kept for the use of the parishioners.

195.9–14   motto   see *2 Henry IV*, 5.3.94–99.

195.18   the cutting mercer   see note to 7.1–2.

195.24   Autolycus   the pedlar in *The Winter's Tale*.

196.1   nether stock   stockings.

196.1   Gascoigne hose   wide breeches, in the style of Gascony, France.

196.19   Cancer and Capricorn   the Crab and Goat, two opposite signs of the zodiac.

196.29   stand shot to   pay the whole bill for.

196.33   Mexico and Peru   sources of gold.

196.39–40   as old and withered a chip . . . porridge   compare Ray, 182: 'Like a *chip* in a pottage-pot, doth neither good nor harm'.

196.41   Potosi   a Bolivian town, renowned for its rich silver mines.

197.1   what belongs to falsifying the Queen's coin   forgery of coins was a treasonable offence, for which the penalty was death.

197.17   Skinker   tapster (barman). *ABD*, 3.309.

197.19   does me not reason   does not drink adequately according to my notions.

198.2–3   a pretty piece of man's flesh . . . Berkshire   see *Much Ado About Nothing*, 4.2.76; *Twelfth Night*, 1.5.25–26.

198.6   stand upon   *either* be sparing of *or* be scrupulous or punctilious (of the fact that one is telling lies). Lambourne is using figuratively an expression normally applied to money.

198.9   crying up   extolling.

198.15   shews like a huswife's distaff . . . spun off   see *Twelfth Night*, 1.3.96–98.

198.23   Hang him, a mechanical chuff   expression dismissive of a mean or vulgar boor or clown. See *The Merry Wives of Windsor*, 2.2.249.

198.27   Maiden Castle   the most famous construction so designated is an earthwork two miles SW of Dorchester, Dorset. No Maiden Castle has been located in Berkshire, but the name is liable to be applied to any earthwork. Scott may have been thinking of Uffington Castle, the large Iron Age fort just by the White Horse.

198.31   by cock and pye   *oath literally* by God and the pre-Reformation ordinal, or Church calendar.

198.32–36   he who swaddled Robin Hood . . . stand   a variant of 'The Bold Pedlar and Robin Hood' (Child no. 132), lines 37–40: 'Then Robin Hood he drew his sword,/ And the pedlar by his pack did stand;/ They fought till the blood in streams did flow,/ Till he cried, Pedlar, pray hold your hand!' (*swaddled* and *raddled* both mean 'thrashed').

198.37   Hang him, foul scroyle   expression dismissive of a foul wretch. See *Twelfth Night*, 3.4.111–12.

198.38   there were small worship to be won upon him   there would be little honour to be gained by fighting him.

199.2–3   rails at thee all to nought   abuses thee as worthless.

199.9   a black sanctus   diabolical parody of the Sanctus ('Holy, holy, holy') of the Mass.

199.11   the pottle-pot is uppermost, with a witness   he is drunk, and no mistake.

199.14 **thin-faced gull** see *Twelfth Night*, 5.1.199.

199.16 **false light** blind or imitation window.

199.31 **to save mutton-suet** i.e. to save candles.

199.42 **vinegar aspect** see *The Merchant of Venice*, 1.1.54.

200.1–2 **he disposes of all ... congregation** Forster as one of the elect regards all except strict Protestants as damned.

200.5 **ingenuous** *either* 'ingenious' *or* (ironically) 'honourably straightforward'.

200.5–6 **to whet thy poetical whistle** the normal expression is 'to wet one's whistle (throat)', i.e. 'to take a drink'.

200.16 **flat cap** see note to 11.14.

200.33 **in some sort** to some extent.

200.34 **a limb of Satan** a wicked rascal.

201.22 **I were foully sped** I would be in a sorry plight.

201.24 **take me with you** speak explicitly, so as I can understand you. See *Romeo and Juliet*, 3.5.141.

201.37 **Albumazar** a noted Arab astrologer of the 9th century.

201.39 **Ursa Major** the Great Bear. (This scene is set in the Bonny Black Bear inn.)

202.2–4 **motto** see *The Winter's Tale*, 4.4.212–13. Editions of Scott's time did not divide Scenes 3 and 4.

202.21 **Slocket** the *English Dialect Dictionary* defines *slocket* as 'to commit a petty theft; to pilfer', and gives the word *slochet* for 'to go slowly', which is closer to the sense required here.

202.35–38 **Lawn as white ... noses** *The Winter's Tale*, 4.4.215–18.

203.3 **Dorcas** shepherdess in *The Winter's Tale*.

203.29 **pair of sleeves** in Elizabethan times sleeves could be detachable.

203.30 **drawn out with cyprus** *perhaps, either* with holes made by drawing out threads of cypress *or* extended with cloth of gold.

203.31–32 **is it not of an absolute fancy ...?** is it not a perfect dream, a perfect delight?

204.2 **take off** *probably* lift off, i.e. from the pile of goods.

204.4–5 **casting bottles** vinaigrettes, perfume-sprinkling bottles.

207.26 **al fresco** *Italian* in the fresh air; out of doors.

207.31 **Aha! ... old Truepenny** see *Hamlet*, 1.5.150 (Hamlet to the Ghost: 'Ha, ha, boy! say'st thou so? Art thou there, truepenny?').

207.32–34 **Ay, I should have coperas ... cauldron** see John Webster, *The White Devil* (1612), 5.3.156–62: 'That would have broke your wife's neck down the stairs/ Ere she was poison'd.// That had your villainous sallets—/ And fine embroidered bottles, and perfumes/ Equally mortal as a winter plague —/ Now there's mercury—// And copperas—// And quicksilver—/ With other devilish pothecary stuff/ A-melting in your politic brains'. *Copperas* is a sulphate of copper, iron, and zinc; *hellebore* is a drug prepared from any of a number of plants; *vitriol* is sulphate of metal, especially iron; *aqua fortis* is nitric acid.

208.1 **the book of life** New Testament phrase for the roll of the redeemed (e.g. Philippians 4.3; Revelation 3.5, etc.).

208.11 **Lex Julia** none of the many *Leges Juliae* were against poisoning. The chief Roman law against poisoning was the *Lex Cornelia*, enacted in 81 BC. The mistake probably originated with Suetonius (*c.* 70–*c.* 160), *Nero*, 33.

208.12 **Leyden** the university of Leiden in Holland, founded in 1575.

208.13 **up seyes** or *upsey, upsee, upsy*. A drinking exclamation, from Dutch *op zijn*, 'in his (manner)'.

209.26–28 **motto** see *Macbeth*, 1.7.27–28.

209.38 **Alter Ego** second self.

210.3–4 the Fairy King's superiority . . . could not in the 13th-century romance *Huon de Bordeaux* Oberon has the power of insight into people's thoughts.

210.22 the nursing-mother of her people see Isaiah 49.23: 'kings shall be thy nursing fathers, and their queens thy nursing mothers', a verse associated with English coronation services.

210.26 hard-ruled King difficult to manage. Used by Wolsey of Henry in *Henry VIII*, 3.2.101.

210.26–35, 43 Nugæ Antiquæ this work, whose title means '*Old Trifles*', was by Sir John Harington (1561–1612). Scott owned the 1804 version (2 vols, London) edited by Thomas Park (*CLA*, 190).

210.40 Walsingham Sir Francis Walsingham (1530?–90), Secretary of State 1573–90.

211.12 too great to keep or to resign Samuel Johnson, *The Vanity of Human Wishes* (1749), line 134.

211.25–26 the rabble throw their caps up see *Julius Caesar*, 1.2.242–44.

211.28 prayed for in the Calvinistic churches abroad Leicester's strong Protestant sympathies appealed to the continental reformed churches.

211.37 crown imperial *Henry V*, 4.1.246.

212.2–4 the daughter of Henry . . . desire see Naunton, 176, where it is said of Henry VIII that he 'never spared man in his anger, nor woman in his lust'.

212.8 furens quid fœmina *Latin* what a raging woman (is capable of). Virgil, *Aeneid*, 5.6 (of Dido, Queen of Carthage, who killed herself when Aeneas left her).

212.22–23 the slave in the chariot see Juvenal (writing *c.* 98–128), *Satire* 10, lines 36–42: 'What if he had seen the Praetor uplifted in his lofty car amid the dust of the Circus, attired in the tunic of Jupiter, hitching an embroidered Tyrian toga on to his shoulders, and carrying a crown so big that no neck could bear the weight of it? For a public slave is sweating under the burden; and in order that the Consul may not esteem himself overmuch, the slave rides in the same chariot with his master.'

212.27 to a hazard in jeopardy.

213.43–214.2 those high points of romantic scruple . . . Sidney, writes *The Arcadia* (begun 1580, published 1590) by Sir Philip Sidney.

215.21 the rich Netherlands . . . leader in 1586 Leicester was elected to supreme command as Governor General of the Netherlands to unite the quarrelsome provinces in the face of Spanish advances.

215.22–25 And have I not such a claim . . . house Henry Hastings (1535–95), third Earl of Huntingdon and brother-in-law of Leicester, claimed by his descent on his mother's side from Edward IV's brother, George, Duke of Clarence, to be Elizabeth's successor, in opposition to Mary Queen of Scots; his claim was supported by Protestant nobles. Mary's claim is described in the note to 167.15–16.

216.17–25 motto see lines 25–28, 13–16. For the ballad see 'Essay on the Text', 395–96.

217.2–3 Minerva's labours see note to 160.43–161.1.

218.23–26 A Pair of Snuffers . . . Firebrands of these titles only one has been traced: Philirenes [John Nalson LL. D.], *Foxes and Firebrands; or, A Specimen of the Danger and Harmony of Popery and Separation*, ed. Robert Ware (London, 1682) (*CLA*, 59). With *A Draught of Water* one may compare the Covenanting tract by Robert McWard, *The Poor Man's Cup of Cold Water* (Edinburgh?, 1678).

218.33 Boke of Cookery . . . Lant *A Propre New Booke of Cokery, Declaryng What Maner of Meates Bee Best in Ceason for All Tymes of ye Yere . . . With a New Addicion, R. Lant and R. Bankes* (London, 1545).

218.34 **Skelton's Books** works by the poet John Skelton (1460?–1529).
218.34 **The Passtime of the People** [John Rastell,] *The Pastyme of People: The Cronycles of Dyuers Realmys and Most Specyally of Englond* [1530?]. *CLA*, 28 lists T. F. Dibdin's edition (London, 1811).
218.34–35 **The Castle of Knowledge** Robert Record, *The Castle of Knowledge, Containing the Explication of the Sphere, bothe Celestiall and Materiall* (London, 1556).
219.25 **in the gross** without going into particulars.
220.29 **Pythoness** woman supposed to have a 'familiar spirit' and to utter his words; probably alluding here (in conjunction with the Graces and Fury of lines 34–35) to the Pythia or priestess of Apollo at Delphi.
220.34–35 **Graces ... Fury** in classical mythology the Graces were the three sister goddesses in whom beauty was deified, the Furies the three goddesses of vengeance.
221.35–40 **the patriarch Abraham ... Pharaoh** see Genesis 12.10–20.
222.25 **have I drank of oblivion?** in Roman mythology souls about to be reincarnated drank of the river Lethe ('oblivion') which made them forget their previous existence.
223.9–10 **the Woman and the Devil ... beginning** the usual interpretation of Genesis Ch. 3.
226.35–36 **the Castle of Wisdom** *either* a general term, *or* the Cabala of line 41.
226.40–41 **Tresmigistus** Hermes Trismegistos ('Hermes the Thrice-Greatest') was the Greek name for the Egyptian god Thoth, allegedly the author of astrological and alchemical treatises.
226.41 **the Cabala** see note to 42.24–25.
227.2–3 **leasehold ... copyhold** see note to 41.8.
227.3–4 **your pewter artillery untransmigrated** probably an array of pewter vessels, pewter being a base metal such as alchemists might transmute to gold. The word *untransmigrated* is apparently unique to this novel (compare 281.2): it presumably means 'untransmuted'.
227.6 **in one thing I am bound up** this appears to be a mixed construction, probably meaning 'to one thing I am devoted' or 'I am inseparable from or dependent on one thing'.
227.6 **fall back fall edge** whatever comes. Proverbial (Ray, 189; *ODEP*, 242).
227.10–12 **that happy city ... stones** see Revelation 21.1–2, 10–21 (compare lines 24–25).
227.26 **the Grand Secret** probably the mystical conflation of the Philosopher's Stone, which was supposed to kill base metals and resurrect them into gold according to the terminology of some alchemists, with the spiritual concept of resurrection, or whatever might be the key to the universe, which became the goal of later alchemists. This passage exemplifies the common fusion of alchemical and Christian apocalyptic terminology.
227.32–34 **the Holy Writt says ... lies** see Revelation 21.27.
227.33 **in no sort** not at all.
228.12 **the holy Millenium** see Revelation 20.1–5, describing the thousand years during which Christ will reign in person on the earth.
228.21–22 **burning bricks in Egypt ... Sinai** see Exodus 1.14; 5.7–19; 19.1: as slaves in Egypt or wandering in the desert, the Israelites had not attained the Promised Land.
228.24–25 **as the magicians strove ... Pharaoh** see Exodus 7.19–25; 8.16–19.
229.4–5 **Saint Luke's Hospital** a hospital for the insane which was founded in Old Street Road, London in 1751.

229.17–23 motto not identified: probably by Scott. It is not, as might be thought, from Beaumont and Fletcher's play *Love's Pilgrimage*.

232.41–43 the wicked Ahab ... spoken see 1 Kings 22.11.

233.3–5 the tyrant Naas ... unto him Nahash the Ammonite. See 1 Samuel 11.2.

235.28 the Star-chamber a court of criminal jurisdiction whose function was to control riots and enforce proclamations: riots were broadly defined and included attacks on men in authority.

235.37–38 Philippine cheney, with that bugle lace see Thomas Middleton and William Rowley, *Wit at Several Weapons* (1609), 2.1: '"Twill put a Lady scarce in Philip and Cheyney,/With three small Bugle Laces, like a Chambermaid'. 'Philippine cheney' is a variant of 'Philip and Cheyney', a worsted cloth; bugle lace was ornamented with tube-shaped glass beads.

236.19–20 the wise widow of Tekoa ... mouth see 2 Samuel 14.1-20: the wise woman is instructed by Joab to induce David by means of a parable to fetch home his son Absalom.

237.22 prigged a prancer *thieves' cant* stolen a horse.

238.11–13 motto see *Richard III*, 5.4.7–8.

238.36–39 Beans ... Pease in Scott's time an Edinburgh street cry was 'Whae'll hae my pease and beans—hot and warm!' (*Blackwood's Edinburgh Magazine*, 9 (July 1821), 401).

239.14–15 the Hue and Cry neighbours of one who had suffered from a crime were under a duty to pursue the criminal. There may be a reminiscence of *The Merry Wives of Windsor*, 4.5.83–84, reinforced by the password exchange above (compare *The Merry Wives of Windsor*, 5.2.5–7 and 5.5.186–87).

239.27 Smithfield, or Turnball Street Smithfield market was an open space outside the city walls of London, where horses and other livestock were sold. Turnbull or Turnmill Street, near Clerkenwell, was a resort of low characters. See *2 Henry IV*, 3.2.287, where it is 'Turnbull'. In *The Ancient British Drama* it is first 'Turnbull' (2.306) and then '*Turnbal*, or, as it would be more properly called, *Turnmill-street*' (2.423).

239.28 as high as Paul's as high as (old) St Paul's Cathedral, destroyed in the Great Fire, 1666. The phrase is proverbial (Dent, P118.11).

240.19 in King Cambyses' vein in the ranting manner of Thomas Preston, *A Lamentable Tragedy, Mixed Ful of Pleasant Mirth, Conteyning the Life of Cambises, King of Percia* (1570?). Scott is imitating Shakespeare's imitation of Preston in *1 Henry IV*, 2.4.376.

240.21 Excalibar King Arthur's sword (variously spelt).

240.25 Thou swearest thy Gods in vain see *King Lear*, 1.1.159.

240.28–29 Maiden-castle-moor see note to 198.2.

240.29–30 betake thee to thy weapons presently possibly an echo of *Twelfth Night*, 3.4.210, 220–21, supported by the 'vow' in line 37 below. Compare *Twelfth Night*, 3.4.284.

240.34 most puissant mercer see *Julius Caesar*, 3.1.33: *puissant* means 'powerful'.

240.38 Doddington Scott sometimes writes Doddington, sometimes (presumably by confusion with the village near Newbury which features earlier in the novel) Donnington. He is probably thinking of Deddington, a prominent coaching village on the main road from Oxford to Banbury (see map). In 1809 it had five inns, though none of them was an Angel. The village Donnington just N of Stow-on-the-Wold in Gloucestershire is geographically possible, but too insignificant to be likely.

241.2 Lot's wife see Genesis 19.26, where Lot's wife is changed into a pillar of salt.

241.11 take down diminish.

241.16   damask'd leathern hangings   decorative leather hangings patterned to resemble and act as a substitute for expensive and less durable silks.

241.17–18   rash, taffeta...grogram   see John Taylor, *The Praise of Hempseed, Works* (London, 1630), third section, 64/2: 'Rash, Taffata, Paropa, and Nouato, Shagge, Fillizetta, Damaske and Mockado'. The various materials are defined in the glossary.

242.16–17   A good, but not a gay horse   see *The Canterbury Tales*, 'General Prologue', I (A), 75.

242.31   in some sort   to some extent.

243.3   a hand gallop   an easy gallop.

243.14   put on   go faster (also at line 17).

243.14–15   a poor provant rapier...Toledo   a provant rapier was one of inferior quality issued to common soldiers; a Toledo was a sword of the finest steel from Toledo in Spain. See Ben Jonson, *Every Man in his Humour* (performed 1598, published in an extensively revised folio edition 1616), 3.1.127–51.

243.17–18   he did the great robbery of the west-country grazier   see 71.37–40.

243.26   happy man be his dole   proverbial expression, meaning 'good luck go with him' (see Ray, 116; *ODEP*, 352). See also *The Merry Wives of Windsor*, 3.4.63; *The Taming of the Shrew*, 1.1.135; and *The Winter's Tale*, 1.2.163. *ABD*, 1.18; 3.321.

244.20   designing for   intending to go to.

244.21   Recte quidem, Domine spectatissime   *Latin*   you are right, most honoured sir. *The Alchemist* has the sentence 'This day you shall be *spectatissimi*' (2.1.8).

244.36   Lucina fer opem... tugurium   *Latin*   Lucina, give thine aid. From Terence, *Andria* (produced 166 BC), line 473. Lucina (Juno) was the Roman goddess of childbirth; *tugurium* means 'hut'.

244.37   By Saint George ... Dragon   St George, the patron saint of England, is reputed to have slain a dragon that threatened a town and a maiden.

244.38   in the straw   in childbed.

244.39   for the nonce   for the occasion.

245.1–2   timed her turns so strangely   timed her labour fits so oddly or unfavourably (i.e. so inconveniently).

245.4   Gaudet nomine Sybillæ   *Latin*   she rejoices in the name of Sibyl, or Roman prophetess.

245.14–15   devil major   principal devil.

245.16–19   sage person...wise woman   midwife (*sage woman*), probably with play on the other sense of *wise woman* as 'witch'.

245.21   limb of Satan   wicked rascal.

245.26   Ætna   Mount Etna is a volcano in Sicily.

245.30   as the play says, 'God be with your labour!'   see George Chapman, Ben Jonson, and John Marston, *Eastward Ho* (1605), 3.2.90 (Corson).

245.35   imp   here and below play is made with *imp* meaning 'little devil' and 'lad'.

246.6   at fault   at a loss.

246.7   drew up   came up.

246.19   a sea of troubles   see *Hamlet*, 3.1.59.

246.22   would win the fish out o' the stream   perhaps an Orphean image akin to that in the song 'Orpheus with his lute' in *Henry VIII*, 3.1.3–14. One may compare the proverbial idea of charming birds from trees, and the second stanza of the ballad 'Glasgerion' (Child, no. 67B).

246.31   keep fair weather   be conciliatory.

247.9   the Wife of Bath   one of the pilgrims in *The Canterbury Tales*.

247.16   Rare Gillian of Croydon   this may be a conflation of the perhaps proverbial Gillian of Brentford and either *Grim the Collier of Croydon* (1600), of uncertain authorship, or Tom Collier of Croydon in *Like Wil to Like Quod the Deuel to the Colier* (1568), by Ulpian Fulwell. Scott refers to '*Fair Gillian* of Croyden' in *Minstrelsy*, 3.205.

247.21–22   the princely pleasures of Kenilworth   see Historical Note, 473.

247.33–34   But age has clawed me ... song says   the original song by Sir Thomas Vaux, 'The aged louer renounceth loue', appeared posthumously in *Tottel's Miscellany* (1557–87), ed. Hyder Edward Rollins, 2 vols (Cambridge, Massachusetts, 1965), 1.165. One of the gravediggers sings a stanza from it in *Hamlet*, 5.1.69–72.

247.35   dance the heys   the hay or hays was a country dance. See *Love's Labour's Lost*, 5.1.134.

248.7–8   when the crow's egg ... cygnet   i.e. never.

248.12–13   a Rowland for thine Oliver   tit for tat. A proverbial expression (see Ray, 208 and *ODEP*, 682). Roland was a legendary nephew of Charlemagne, and Oliver was his companion: the two were equally matched.

249.2–10   motto   not identified: probably by Scott.

251.26   The Queen's purveyors   officers whose duty it was to collect provisions in the region where the sovereign was travelling.

251.29   the Board of Green Cloth   the committee of the royal household charged with the duties of finding provisions.

252.4   Palace of Princely Pleasure   see Historical Note, 473.

252.13–14   treading on the kibes ... worship   i.e. pressing so closely upon them as to annoy. See *Hamlet*, 5.1.133. A kibe is an irritated chilblain on the heel.

252.21   that irritable race   see Horace (65–8 BC), *Epistles*, 2.2.102: 'genus irritabile vatum' (i.e. poets).

253.11   Master Griffin the preacher   Griffin is not known to be a historical person.

253.13   Aglionby   Edward Aglionby (1520–87?), recorder of Warwick 1572–87, who made a speech to Elizabeth on her visit there in 1572, reprinted in Nichols, 1 (1572 fascicle), 19–22: Elizabeth's reply is based on a speech on page 23.

253.25   clipt coin   before 1692 coins did not have milled edges and those of gold and silver were gradually clipped away illegally.

254.3   squire of the body to a damosel-errant   a *squire of the body* was an officer charged with personal attendance on a knight-errant (itinerant knight): Scott here coins *damosel-errant* on the basis of Spenser's 'Errant Damzell,' (*The Faerie Queene*, 3.1.24: compare *errant-damozel* at 276.31). Wayland wishes to avoid becoming squire to a female equivalent of a demanding knight-errant.

254.25   Kenelph   Cynewulf, King of the West Saxons (d. 785). He is called Kenulph in Dugdale's account of Kenilworth, 155: see Historical Note, 473.

254.27   the Clintons   Geoffrey de Clinton (dates unknown), chamberlain and treasurer to Henry I, founded Kenilworth Priory, probably before 1126.

254.29   Simon de Montfort   (1208?–65), Earl of Leicester, leader of the Barons who, in the contest with Henry III, was responsible for first summoning representatives from boroughs to sit in parliament. He was killed at the battle of Evesham. Kenilworth, which was in possession of his party, still held out, until the pacification was settled by the agreement known as Dictum de Kenilworth.

254.30–31   Mortimer, Earl of March   Roger Mortimer (1287?–1330) became Earl of March (i.e. of the Welsh border) in 1328. He joined with Isabella, wife of Edward II, in dethroning and murdering that king.

254.33   Old John of Gaunt, "time-honoured Lancaster"   John of Gaunt

(1340–99), Duke of Lancaster 1362–99, so referred to in *Richard II*, 1.1.1.

255.3 fallow deer small yellowish-brownish deer.

255.16 those grey and massive towers Kenilworth is built of pink stone, though in certain lights it can appear grey.

255.41–42 Bear and Ragged Staff see note to 67.4.

257.9–10 Whom God hath joined, man cannot sunder compare 'The Form of Solemnization of Matrimony' in *The Book of Common Prayer*: 'Those whom God hath joined together let no man put asunder.'

259.4–7 motto *A Midsummer Night's Dream*, 1.2.58–61.

259.15 the Heptarchy term referring to the seven kingdoms of Anglo-Saxon England.

259.23–24 Colbrand, Ascapart Colbrand was a Danish giant slain by Guy in the verse romance *Guy of Warwick* (*c.* 1300), stanza 269; Ascapart was a giant killed by Bevis's uncle in the verse romance *Sir Beues of Hamtoun* (late 13th century or early 14th century), A 3884–87. See *CLA*, 103, 105, 217.

259.25 by the altitude of a chopin *Hamlet*, 2.2.407. A *chopin* was a shoe with a high sole of cork worn by actors.

259.26 this son of Anak for this giant see Numbers 13.33.

260.10 Titan in Greek mythology, member of a family of giants.

260.38–39 I know where the shoe pinches proverbial (see Ray, 156, 167; *ODEP*, 725).

261.19 Philistine ... Goliath of Gath see 1 Samuel 17.23.

261.37–38 the Earl of March see note to 254.30–31.

261.39 She-wolf of France *3 Henry VI*, 1.4.111; Thomas Gray, 'The Bard' (1757), line 57.

262.25 Bess of Bedlam wandering female lunatic. Bedlam, or St Mary of Bethlehem, was a hospital for the insane in London: from the 1660s the term was used as a generic name for such institutions.

263.8–9 King Henry's Lodging the buildings erected in Henry VIII's time.

263.11 the Conquest the Norman Conquest of England in 1066.

263.24 Tradition called this prisoner Mervyn this tradition is apparently Scott's invention. Mervyn is called Arthur ap Mervyn at 279.30.

265.19–22 motto see Francis Beaumont and John Fletcher, *The Coxcomb* (performed 1612, published 1647), 2.2.16–22: 'Wee want a Boy extreamely for this function kept under for a yeare, with milke and knott-grasse; in my time I have seene a boy do wonders. *Robbin* the red Tincker had a boy (Rest his soule, he sufferd this time four yeares for two spoones, and a Pewter Candlestick), that sweet man had a Boy as I am Curstend Whore, would have run through a Cat hole, he wold have boulted such a peece of linen in an evening'.

266.24 miller's thumb *literally* a small freshwater fish, the bullhead.

266.26–28 the mouse ... an ass in Aesop's fable of the Lion and the Mouse, where the mouse gnaws asunder the net in which the lion has been trapped.

266.39 a Sheffield whittle a knife made in Sheffield. See *The Canterbury Tales*, 'The Reeve's Tale', 1 (A), 3933.

267.9–10 I promised ... gaberdine see *Coriolanus*, 2.3.108–09 and *The Tempest*, 2.2.36, 103.

267.32 cast a somerset turned a somersault.

269.7 the busy hum Milton, 'L'Allegro' (written 1631?, published 1645), line 118.

272.29–35 motto not identified: probably by Scott.

273.17–18 the porcelain clay of the earth for an exactly contemporary parallel see Byron, *Don Juan*, 4.11 (written 1819–20, published 1821).

273.35   cock their beaver   turn up the brim of their fur hat with an air of pertness.

274.4   I am no dog in the manger   proverbial (see Ray, 186; *ODEP*, 195).

274.7   carry coals   submit to degrading work; endure an insult. A proverbial expression (Tilley, C464; *ODEP*, 104), best known from *Romeo and Juliet*, 1.1.1. *ABD*, 3.306.

274.16   Lindabrides   see note to 16.28.

274.19–23   motto   not identified: probably by Scott.

275.4   verge of the Royal Court   see note to 149.41.

275.42   that were a jest indeed   proverbial (Dent, J41.1). *The Merry Wives of Windsor*, 2.2.101.

276.41   bear a base mind   entertain unworthy sentiments. *2 Henry IV*, 3.2.223, 228.

277.35–36   Weatherly-bottom   apparently fictitious.

277.41   here be truths   *Measure for Measure*, 2.1.127.

278.2–3   broad pieces   see note to 36.35.

278.4–5   give Puss a hint . . . form   see Henry Fielding, *Tom Jones* (1749), Bk 5, Ch. 12: *Puss* is a hare, *form* its lair.

278.5   sheep-biting visage   sneaking face. See *Measure for Measure*, 5.1.352.

278.11   Sister on Adam's side   mistress (because everybody is everybody else's brother or sister by descent from Adam).

278.12–13   thou diest on point of fox   thou diest by the sword. *Henry V*, 4.4.9.

278.14   uds daggers and death   see note to 26.43.

278.16   Arion   semi-mythical Greek poet said to have been saved from drowning by a dolphin.

278.19   Orion   in Greek mythology, a giant hunter who after his death was turned into the constellation with three bright stars known as Orion's belt.

278.43–279.1   Black Joan Jugges of Slingdon   figure and place are both apparently fictitious.

279.2–3   Limbo . . . Little-ease   *Limbo* is prison, and *Little-ease* a narrow place of confinement.

279.6   a hole in this same Tressilian's coat   see *Henry V*, 3.6.80: 'I tell you what, Captain Gower, I do perceive he is not the man that he would gladly make show to the world he is; if I find a hole in his coat I will tell him my mind.'

279.8   go snick up   *contemptuous* go hang. See *Twelfth Night*, 2.3.89. *ABD*, 1.394.

279.11   Liberty and Honour   terms denoting the area under a lord's complete jurisdiction.

279.20   force per force   under compulsion; of necessity.

279.30–33   Arthur ap Mervyn . . . name   see notes to 254.30–31 and 263.24.

279.36   Santo Diavolo   *Italian* Holy Devil.

280.7   Saint Peter of the Fetters   see Acts 12.6–7.

280.24   Body o' me   oath. See *Henry VIII*, 5.2.22.

280.31   began to make some innovation   i.e. some change. See *Othello*, 2.2.35: 'I have drunk but one cup to-night, and that was craftily qualified too, and behold what innovation it makes here.'

280.33   least said . . . soonest amended   proverbial (Tilley, L358; *ODEP*, 472).

280.43–281.1   an humour of sympathies and antipathies   a disposition towards the natural affinities and contrarieties believed in occult science to exist between things.

281.2   transmigrated   apparently Scott's form of 'transmuted', rather than an error of Lambourne's: compare Varney at 227.3–4.

281.11–12 **"when soul and body sever," as the ballad says** the ballad has not been identified.

281.12 **your antecedent will have a consequent** the antecedent is the statement on which any consequence logically depends, and the consequent is the logical result of it.

281.13 **raro antecedentem** *Latin* Horace (65–8 BC), *Odes*, 3.2.31: 'Retribution, though slow, rarely quits the criminal who goes before'.

281.13 **Doctor Bricham** see note to 7.37.

281.14 **Greek to you** nonsense to you. Proverbial (Tilley, G439; *ODEP*, 336). See *Julius Caesar*, 1.2.281.

282.6–13 **motto** not identified: probably by Scott.

283.13–14 **fools of the first head** prime fools.

283.32 **God bless the mark** exclamation of impatient scorn.

283.39 **Bartholomew-fair** fair held in Smithfield, London, on 24 August, the feast of St Bartholomew, until suppressed in 1840.

284.9 **cocked his beaver** see note to 273.35.

284.31 **fierce vanities** *Henry VIII*, 1.1.53.

285.14 **far-heard over flood and field** see Coleridge, 'The Rime of the Ancient Mariner' (1798, rev. 1800), line 201: 'With far-heard whisper, o'er the sea'. The Coleridge passage has had a pervasive influence on this scene.

285.25 **Wittens-westlowe** a Westlowe is mentioned in Elias Ashmole, *Antiquities of Berkshire*, 3 vols (London, 1719: *CLA*, 245), 2.499, quoting the antiquary Thomas Hearne, as a *'Common Field'* near Shottesbrooke.

285.33–34 **owl . . . ivy-tod** see note to 137.38-40.

285.37–39 **An eagle . . . a sun to gaze upon** alluding to the proverb 'Only the eagle can gaze at the sun' (Tilley, E3; *ODEP*, 210). See *3 Henry VI*, 2.1.91–92.

285.40 **Saint Barnaby** St Barnabas was one of the earliest Christian disciples at Jerusalem. The reference is appropriate because 'Barnaby the bright' was the longest any. See Ray, 39 and Spenser, *Epithalamion* (1595), lines 265–66.

286.6–7 **pertæsa barbaræ loquelæ** *Latin* thoroughly sick of these barbarous speeches.

287.39–41 **the fire that is never quenched . . . dieth not** see Isaiah 66.24 and Mark 9.43–48.

288.17 **black jack . . . double ale** large leather beer-jug, coated with tar . . . ale of twice the usual strength.

288.22–23 **short femoral garment** garment reaching to or covering the thighs: femoral is normally a medical term, and is here probably used in a slightly jocular way.

288.35–44 **What stir . . . sight as this** for the porter see Langham, lines 152–67. His speech is based on verses in Gascoigne (Nichols, 1 (1575 fascicle), 59–60).

288.35 **for the nones** poetical tag with no particular meaning.

289.39–40 **bound with a broad girdle . . . phylacteries of the Hebrews** properly, a *phylactery* is a small leather box containing passages of Scripture written on parchment, worn on the arm or forehead by Jews; but Scott appears to be conflating this box, or its contents, with the common but erroneous use of the term to denote the fringe or blue ribbon which the Israelites were commanded to wear in Numbers 15.38–39.

290.7–10 **that famous Lady of the Lake . . . Merlin** Elizabeth's encounter with the Lady of the Lake is based on Langham, lines 185–200. See also lines 772–819 and Gascoigne in Nichols, 1 (1575 fascicle), 60–61 (and Langham, 126–27). See further Thomas Malory (d. 1471), *The Tale of King*

Arthur, The Works of Sir Thomas Malory, ed. Eugène Vinaver (London, 1954), 1.25.

290.13–15   The Saxons ... Plantagenets   Lord Sentloe appears in Gascoigne as the owner of the Castle after the Norman Conquest (Nichols, 1 (1575 fascicle), 61). For Geoffrey de Clinton see note on 254.27; he received Kenilworth from the King *c.* 1120, but his grandson Henry had to exchange it with Henry II at the time of the rebellion of 1173–74. For Simon de Montfort see note on 254.29; Henry III presented Kenilworth to him in 1244, but his son Simon surrendered it in 1266. For Roger Mortimer see note on 254.30–31. The term Plantagenets usually designates English kings between 1154 and 1485.

290.27–36   Arion ... Kenilworth Castle   the incident is based on the performance of one Harry Goldingham (Nichols, 1 (1575 fascicle), 69; Langham, 100).

290.32–33   Cogs bones   *oath* God's bones.

291.4–9   Such ... afraid   the lines are abridged from Nichols, 1 (1575 fascicle), 11; Langham, lines 308–16.

291.11–15 motto   in spite of the attribution, this is probably by Scott. Beaumont and Fletcher have several court scenes, but this is from none of them. There is something like it in *The Spanish Curate*, 3.3.188–93: 'This tastes of passion,/ And that must not divert the course of justice./ ... Break up the court! —/ It is in vain to move me; my doom's passed,/ And cannot be revoked.' The alliterative opening recalls 'More matter for a May morning' (*Twelfth Night*, 3.4.136). The 'wall' metaphor is inauthentic: one gives or takes the wall, but a third person cannot do the giving or taking for one. To 'give the wall' is to yield the superior place.

291.36   as ever blotted paper   see *The Merchant of Venice*, 3.2.254.

291.37–39   Mr Nicholas's ... collection ... vol. I.   for Nichols see Historical Note, 473, and list of abbreviations heading these notes, 481.

291.39   Kenilworth Illustrated   see Historical Note, 473.

293.12   Menelaus   in Greek legend, the husband of Helen who was carried off by Paris to Troy.

293.24–25   those of whom ... the wisest men   *The Canterbury Tales*, 'The Reeve's Tale', 1 (A), 4054. Proverbial (see Ray, 88 and *ODEP*, 126).

293.41   close jerkin   closely-fitting jacket.

296.10   The Earl of Oxford   Edward de Vere (1550–1604) was noted for his extravagance.

296.23   The Earl of Huntingdon   see note to 215.22–25.

296.24   the old Countess of Rutland   the dowager Countess of Rutland, widow of Henry Manners, second Earl of Rutland who had died in 1563, married the Earl of Bedford in 1566 and was thereafter properly known as Countess of Bedford.

296.36–37   when she expelled Essex ... boots   the Queen's sensitivity is frequently alluded to, as is Essex's carelessness in such matters. His most celebrated appearance before her in a filthy state was on his return from Ireland on 28 September 1599, but he was not expelled on that occasion.

297.6   to a demonstration   conclusively.

297.7   false as hell   *Othello*, 4.2.40.

297.10–11   my godson Harrington ... Orlando Furioso   *Orlando Furioso in English Heroical Verse*, by John Harington (London, 1591), i.e. translated from the Italian of Ariosto by Sir John Harington (1561–1612). Compare *CLA*, 185. The title means 'Mad Orlando'.

297.37   Parnassus   Greek mountain associated with the worship of Apollo and the Muses; hence, poetry.

297.37   Saint Luke's Hospital   see note to 229.4–5.

298.10   **at no rate**   by no means.
298.20   **get off**   remove.
298.28   **truckle bed**   low bed running on truckles or castors.
299.8–14   **motto**   not identified: probably by Scott.
299.38–39   **fata Morgana ... rhimes**   see Matteo Maria Boiardo, *Orlando innamorato* (written *c.* 1476–84), 2.4.26, where Fata Morgana (Morgan le Fay) is so described.
299.42   **Saint George**   see note to 244.37.
300.4   **The buckling of the spur ... remain**   a pair of gilt spurs was given to a newly dubbed knight.
300.34   **Countess of Rutland**   see note to 150.31.
302.4   **the Stewarts**   sovereigns from James VI of Scots and I of England to Anne.
302.18   **mopping and mowing**   *King Lear*, 4.1.62: 'Flibbertigibbet, of mopping and mowing' (grimacing).
302.36   **Largesse ... hardis**   *French*   gifts, gifts, most bold knights. From Langham, line 1017.
303.13   **Sir Pandarus of Troy**   see *The Merry Wives of Windsor*, 1.3.69. In Greek legend, Pandarus was a Trojan leader in the Trojan war (Homer, *Iliad*, Bks 4–5), but in Chaucer's *Troilus and Criseyde* and Shakespeare's *Troilus and Cressida* he appears less nobly in the role of pander to which Pistol alludes in *The Merry Wives*.
304.18–20   **Ye distant orbs ... a voice**   see Joseph Addison, 'Ode. The Spacious Firmament on High' (published in *The Spectator*, no. 465, 23 August 1712), stanza 3.
304.34   **Saul among the prophets**   see 1 Samuel 10.11.
305.22   **Put not thy trust in Princes**   Psalm 146.3.
306.34–40   **Have we not known ... Old Testament**   the custom of morganatic or left-handed marriage involved legally valid marriage between a male member of a sovereign, princely, or noble house and a woman of lesser birth or rank, with the provision that she should not thereby succeed to his rank and that the children of the marriage should not succeed to their father's hereditary dignities or property. Essentially a German institution, it was adopted by some dynasties outside Germany, but not by those of France or England. The polygamous practices of the Old Testament period were interpreted as authorising the custom.
307.2–4   **ten times the leisure ... Mary**   see notes to 58.26 and 58.33.
307.6   **your Eleanor and your fair Rosamond**   see note to 73. 34–39.
307.27–28   **seeming-virtuous**   *Hamlet*, 1.5.46.
308.2–8   **motto**   not identified: probably by Scott.
308.5   **Dian**   Diana, Roman goddess of hunting.
310.14–15   **The Indian ... his tortures**   the North American Indian. Scott knew the account of such extraordinary fortitude in William Robertson, *History of America*, 3rd edn, 3 vols (London, 1780), 2.161–63. *CLA*, 204.
311.35   **fair Callipolis**   *2 Henry IV*, 2.4.164. Shakespeare's passage is itself one parody, among several in the Elizabethan period, of George Peele, *The Battle of Alcazar* (published 1594). In this play Calipolis is the wife of the Moorish king, and she was frequently quoted as typical of a sweetheart.
311.36   **Countess of clouts**   mere doll in guise of countess.
311.36–37   **Duchess of dark corners**   keeper of secret assignations. See *Measure for Measure*, 4.3.154: 'If the old fantastical Duke of dark corners had been at home, he had lived.'
312.12–15   **I have heard the sea ... a town stormed**   see *The Taming of the Shrew*, 1.2.196–205, and compare *1 Henry IV*, 3.1.129–30.
312.24   **Saint Peter of the Fetters**   see Acts 12.6–7 and compare 280.7.

312.31   Newgate or the Compter   Newgate was the principal London prison until 1902. The Compters were debtors' prisons.

312.36–37   thou old ostrich . . . keys   alluding to the proverbial 'to digest iron like an ostrich' (Tilley, I97; see *ODEP*, 776). See *2 Henry VI*, 4.10.27.

313.25–27   that filthy paunch . . . history   notably the giant of Mont Saint Michel: *The Tale of the Noble King Arthur* in *The Works of Sir Thomas Malory*, ed. Eugène Vinaver (London, 1954), 5.5. Scott would have known this from e.g. *The Byrth, Lyf, and Actes of Kyng Arthur*, ed. Robert Southey, 2 vols (London, 1817), 1.138–41 (*CLA*, 122).

313.31–32   under the little turn of my forefinger and thumb   under lock and key.

313.32   under my hatches   under restraint in my prison.

313.41   then, element do thy work   see *Hamlet*, 5.2.309.

314.15   the Welch marches   borderland of England and Wales.

315.19   cloak and capotaine hat   see *The Taming of the Shrew*, 5.1.57. A copintank hat was high-crowned, in the form of a sugar-loaf.

315.36–40   motto   see Matthew Prior, 'The Dove' (1717), lines 53–56.

316.23–24   Amazons   legendary race of female warriors.

317.4   look down   subdue by staring.

317.29   the mother of my people   compare line 42 and see note to 210.22.

318.6   Rocking-stones   logan stones, large boulders so poised as to be easily swayed to and fro, formerly objects of superstition.

318.8   Hercules   classical mythological hero of great strength.

318.16   the story of Numa and Egeria   in Roman legend, King Numa Pompilius used to meet the goddess Egeria at a spring and received her counsels in developing Roman institutions.

322.2–3   the last dread trumpet-call . . . judgment seat   see 1 Corinthians 15.51–52.

322.5–6   As at the blast . . . cover them   see Hosea 10.8: 'they shall say to the mountains, Cover us; and to the hills, Fall on us'; also Luke 23.30 and Revelation 6.16.

322.21–22   My head cannot fall . . . peers   a peer could only be tried for treason or felony by the House of Lords or, if Parliament was not sitting, in the Court of the Lord High Steward, in which the verdict was given by a select number of peers.

322.26   My Lord Shrewsbury, you are Marshall of England   George Talbot (1528?–90), sixth Earl of Shrewsbury, succeeded the executed Duke of Norfolk as Earl Marshal of England in 1572, regulating ceremony and order at court assemblies.

322.33   his relationship to the Boleyns   see note to 142.10.

323.12–13   the wrath of kings . . . furnace   compare the descriptions of the wrath of a king and of God in such passages as Proverbs 16.14 and 19.12; Psalm 89.46; and Matthew 13.42 (the parable of the tares).

324.17   lady-birds   see *Romeo and Juliet*, 1.3.3.

326.6–7   Discord, as the Italian poet says . . . families   see Lodovico Ariosto, *Orlando furioso* (1516), 14.76–82.

326.10–11   We will take the lion's part . . . forgive   see Aesop's fable of the lion and the rat, and the version by Robert Henryson (1425?–1505), 'The Lion and the Mous', *Fables*, lines 1503–09, where the lion pardons the mouse for running over him when he was asleep.

326.26   Varium et mutabile   a variable and changing thing (is woman ever). Virgil, *Aeneid*, 4.569.

327.2–7   motto   [John Home,] *Douglas: A Tragedy* (Edinburgh, 1757), 14 (Act 1). *CLA*, 10, 209.

327.32   post it over   pass it off.

328.13–15 the Italians say right...fault the allusion has not been identified.

329.25 Catlowdie village in N Cumberland.

329.28 at a dead pinch in dire straits.

333.14 like Norfolk see note to 12.42–43.

333.23–26 Truth...Wisdom...proof in Renaissance iconography, Truth may hold such symbolic objects as mirror, open book, palm branch, and sun; Wisdom sometimes has armour, spear, and shield. 'Panoply of proof' is a whole suit of armour which has stood or can stand the test of combat.

334.15–20 motto see The Winter's Tale, 2.1.87–91.

334.27–34 Let me see...deposited there this catalogue is based on a passage in Leicester's Commonwealth (Peck, 103–05). Sir Francis Knollys (1514?–96), a consistent supporter of the Puritans, was governor of Portsmouth 1563. Sir Edward Horsey (d. 1583), was a commissioner of the Isle of Wight from 1565, and shortly thereafter captain of the island until his death. For Huntingdon see note to 215.22–25. Henry Herbert (1534?–1601), second Earl of Pembroke, was president of the Council of the Marches and Wales from 1586. Francis Russell (1527?–85), second Earl of Bedford, was a staunch Protestant. For Warwick see note to 175.9–10. Sir Owen Hopton (1533–91), knighted 1561, was Lieutenant of the Tower from c. 1570 to his death.

334.33 at my devotion at my service, disposal.

334.34–36 My father and grandfather...enterprizes see note to 132.27.

335.12 the Prophet's gourd see Jonah 4.6–7, and compare 130.10–11.

335.18 Norfolk see note to 12.42–43.

335.19 Northumberland Thomas Percy (1528–72), seventh Earl of Northumberland, executed after the 1569 rebellion.

335.19 Westmoreland Charles Neville (1543–1601), sixth Earl of Westmorland, in exile from the 1569 rebellion till his death.

335.34 Possess the town's-people with some apprehension either cause the townspeople to feel some fear as to what may happen or give the town's-people some forewarning.

335.35 Pensioners see note to 142.4.

335.36 Yeomen of the Guard see note to 97.18.

338.11–12 Killigrew and Lambsbey for Killigrew see note to 42.6; Lambsbey has not been identified.

338.28 'tis a woman's fault 1 Henry IV, 3.1.241.

338.28 false to me Othello, 3.3.337.

338.37 Carrol Carrol has not been identified as a historical person.

338.43 the Bear and Ragged Staff see note to 67.4.

339.2 They were my own gift see Othello, 3.3.440.

339.29 trusty and faithful servant see Matthew 25.21 (the parable of the talents).

342.2–4 motto Macbeth, 3.4.109–10.

342.11 trick them up adorn them.

345.10 the farewell possibly the payment on quitting a tenancy, here used figuratively.

346.35 What thou doest, do quickly see John 13.27 (Jesus to Judas).

347.40 Angelo Michelangelo di Lodovico Buonarroti Simoni, Italian painter and sculptor (1475–1564).

347.40 Chantrey Francis Legatt Chantrey, sculptor (1781–1841).

348.18 rather hypochondria than phrenesis i.e. the disease is of the melancholy, not the feverish, form: phrenesis, or phrenitis, is brain-fever.

348.33 Juno-like in Roman religion, Juno was the sister and wife of Jupiter: she is usually depicted as being of ample proportions.

349.4 **flourish of trumpets and kettle-drums** see *Hamlet*, 1.4.11.

349.8 **The masque** see Historical Note, 473.

349.18 **Belus** Belenus, Celtic deity sometimes believed (wrongly) to have been a sun-god.

349.34 **Mars** the Roman god of war.

349.41 **Odin** or Woden, one of the principal gods in Norse mythology.

350.24–25 **trumpet was heard ... won** see *The Faerie Queene*, 3.12.1.

350.31 **the fiend-born Merlin** magician, born of a devil and a virtuous maiden, who guides the destinies of King Arthur.

352.10–11 **motto** *Macbeth*, 2.2.58.

353.8–10 **such a thirst ... water-brooks** see Psalm 42.1.

354.8–9 **shifting of trenchers** moving of plates. See *Romeo and Juliet*, 1.5.2.

355.32 **proceed no farther** see *Macbeth*, 1.7.31.

355.34 **safely bestowed** safely disposed of. See *Hamlet*, 4.2.1.

355.36 **think for** expect.

356.32 **a cast of mine office** a job of work done by me.

356.40 **Bayard** name of the magic horse given by Charlemagne to Renaud in medieval romance.

357.9 **a man more sinned against than sinning** *King Lear*, 3.2.59–60.

357.16 **unloosing the cords of life** see Job 30.11 and Ecclesiastes 12.6.

357.18 **oceans roll betwixt us** see Robert Burns, 'Auld Lang Syne' (written 1788, published 1796), line 19.

357.34–35 **sheeted ghosts just arisen from their sepulchres** see *Hamlet*, 1.1.115; 1.4.48.

357.40 **The bird of summer night** see *Hamlet*, 1.1.160.

360.23 **they are tilting here** see *Othello*, 2.3.173.

360.35 **chopping off a hand** this was the penalty for drawing a sword in a court of law; near the royal presence, blood had to be shed for the sentence to be applicable.

361.26 **By gog's-nails** *oath* by God's nails (the nails of Christ's cross).

361.36 **take order** take measures.

362.5 **drinking healths pottle-deep** see *Othello*, 2.3.49–50.

362.19–25 **motto** see Ben Jonson, *The Masque of Owles at Kenelworth. Presented by the Ghost of Captain Coxe mounted on his Hoby-Horse* (performed 1624, published 1640), lines 1–2, 10–13.

362.35 **the general massacre ... 1012** the scene is based on Langham, lines 607–42, where 1012 is a mistake for 1002. Hock Tuesday was the second Tuesday after Easter Day. 'From an early date it has been connected with the Danes: either (as here) with Ethelred's victory in 1002, or with the death of Hardicanute in 1042. In neither case is the date relevant, for Ethelred's victory fell on St Brice's Day (November 13), while Hardicanute died on June 8.' (Langham, 96).

363.11 **an ambrosial breakfast** actually Langham calls the evening meal 'an Ambrosiall Banket' (line 746).

363.20 **hobby-horses** not the child's toy, but a figure of a horse, made of wickerwork, or the like, fastened about the waist of one of the performers in a morris-dance, or on the stage, who executed various antics in the character of a horse.

363.23 **Mr Bayes's tragedy** *The Rehearsal* (performed 1671, published 1672), written probably in collaboration with others by George Villiers, second Duke of Buckingham, in which the leading character is called Bayes; some of the combatants in the concluding battle are mounted on hobby-horses. *CLA*, 218.

363.37 **Captain Coxe** virtually nothing is known of Coxe, or Cox, the bibliophile. See Langham, 97–98, 131–43. The whole scene is based on Langham, lines 693–717.

363.43 saith Laneham see Langham, lines 693–95. Langham's phrase is actually 'cleen trust and garterd abooue the knee', meaning that the hose or breeches were neatly laced on to the inside waistband of the doublet, and that the stockings were tied with garter ribbons above the knee, which was unusual: normally, garters were tied below the knee with the bow to the outside of the leg, unless cross gartering was preferred, in which case the ribbon was tied above and below the knee.

364.2 the siege of Boulogne Boulogne was captured in September 1544, when Henry VIII in alliance with the Emperor Charles V had gone to war with France.

364.6 two-legged hobby-horse see note to 363.20.

364.12 northern bag-pipe there is no evidence for native Danish bag-pipes, but the instrument was known elsewhere in Scandinavia from the middle ages onwards.

364.21–22 as Master Laneham testifies see Langham, lines 702–03: 'ooutragioous in their racez az ramz at their rut'.

364.43 Amadis, Belianis, Bevis, ... Guy of Warwick Amadis is the hero of a 15th-century Spanish or Portuguese prose romance translated into English (1590?) by Anthony Munday and (abridged, 1803) by Robert Southey. Belianis of Greece is the hero of the Spanish romance *Don Belianis de Grecia* (1547, 1579) by Gerónimo Fernàndez. For Bevis and Guy see note to 259.23–24.

365.7 Ben Jonson see note to 362.19–25.

371.5–8 motto not identified: probably by Scott.

371.25 dry nurse a nurse who looks after a child but does not suckle it.

372.14 gulls there is a word-play on *gulls* meaning the birds and 'credulous persons', 'fools'. The gulling and yellow stockings recall Malvolio in *Twelfth Night*.

372.36–37 the Lord Shrewsbury ... England see note to 322.26.

373.29 oriel window window in a large polygonal recess projecting from the outer face of a building.

375.19 gall and wormwood see Lamentations 3.19.

375.43–376.2 His lordship is patriarchal ... left hand i.e. he is like one of the patriarchs, or heads of families in the Old Testament: Solomon, for example, had 700 wives (1 Kings 11.3). For left-handed or morganatic marriage see note to 306.34–40.

376.22–24 Urge not a falling man i.e. do not hasten his fall. See *Henry VIII*, 3.2.333; 5.3.77.

379.12–16 motto 'Cumnor Hall', lines 101–04.

379.32 Robin Tider see note to 42.6.

380.9 dark lantern see note to 44.10

380.11–12 Ave Maria—ora pro nobis *Latin* Hail Mary—pray for us. Phrases from the common Roman Catholic prayer.

380.12 deliver us from evil phrase from the Lord's Prayer (Matthew 6.13; Luke 11.4).

380.13–14 confounding his old and new devotions i.e. confusing or mingling his Roman Catholic and Protestant prayers.

380.30 at this dead hour *Hamlet*, 1.1.65.

381.2 and odds and a few pounds more.

381.21–22 it is written, 'wives obey your husbands.' see Ephesians 5.22; Colossians 3.18; and 1 Peter 3.1.

384.31 my indenture is out an apprentice was bound to a master by an indenture, usually for seven years, at the end of which he could set up in business on his own account.

384.33   quittance   word-play on 'discharge from indenture' and 'recompense'.

387.7–8   a piece of concealed machinery   probably a block and tackle such as was used to raise and lower actors and properties on the stage.

388.4–5   Court of Chancery   Court of the Lord Chancellor, subordinate only to the House of Lords.

388.11   Sancta Mater!   *Latin* Holy Mother!

388.15–16   a corpse three days exposed on the wheel   refers to the exposure of criminals' bodies after they had been executed by tying them to a wheel and breaking their limbs.

388.29   two good sops   appeasing morsels, recalling the sops offered to Cerberus, the dog which guarded the entrance to the Underworld, by the heroes of classical legend.

389.2–3   a springe, Tony, to catch a pewit   proverbial with 'woodcock' (the manuscript reading) rather than 'pewit' (Tilley, S788; *ODEP*, 768). See *Hamlet*, 1.3.115; 5.3.293; and *The Winter's Tale*, 4.3.34. .

389.25–26   surely in vain is the snare set in the sight of any bird   see Proverbs 1.17.

390.17   It is a seething of the kid in the mother's milk   forbidden in Exodus 23.19 and 34.26, and in Deuteronomy 14.21 because it was an alien fertility rite, but here used as an image of gratuitous cruelty.

391.7–8   The wicked man, saith Scripture, hath no bonds in his death   see Psalm 73.3–4: 'For I was envious at the foolish, when I saw the prosperity of the wicked. For there are no bands in their death: but their strength is firm.'

392.6   with his friend Raleigh for the Virginia expedition   Raleigh himself never sailed to Virginia, though he organised a series of expeditions between 1584 and 1602.

392.13   Cecil   Robert (1563?–1612), created Baron Cecil 1603, Viscount Cranborne 1604, and first Earl of Salisbury 1605, son of Burghley (for whom see note to 165.10).

392.15   Ashmole's Antiquities of Berkshire   see Historical Note, 473.

392.16–17   The ingenious translator ... Mickle   Luis de Camoëns (*c.* 1524–80), *The Lusiad; or, The Discovery of India: An Epic Poem*, translated by W. J. Mickle (Oxford, 1776: *CLA*, 195).

GLOSSARY

This selective glossary defines single words; phrases are treated in the Explanatory Notes. It covers archaic and dialect words, and occurrences of familiar words in senses that are likely to be strange to the modern reader. For each word (or clearly distinguishable sense) glossed, up to four occurrences are noted; when a word occurs more than four times in the novel, only the first instance is given, followed by 'etc.' Often the most economical and effective way of defining a word is to refer the reader to the appropriate explanatory note.

a' *pron.* he 92.11

a' *prep.* in 20.4

abate degrade 303.28

abide await 27.19

aboriginal primitive 349.13, 349.19

abutting adjoining 303.43

abye pay the penalty for, make amends for 60.36, 70.14, 146.1

accidens accidents 88.19; see note to 2.31

accidents see note to 2.31

accolade a tap on the shoulders with the flat of a sword 302.21

address skill 35.41 etc.; manner of speaking 3.11, 132.31

ado to do 104.31, 140.22

adventure venture an assault 174.31

affection(s) malady, disease 205.6, 205.12; passion 211.11; disposition 295.5

afrite evil demon in Arabian mythology 260.43

against by the time that, before 204.3, 235.35

agitate discuss 167.2

aiguillette ornamental metal tag 316.23

alembic distilling apparatus 100.31, 223.35

Alicant wine made at Alicante in Spain 41.41

Almain see note to 79.42

ambrosial celestial 363.11

amend surpass 92.2

an, an' if 5.31 etc., that 134.26

anan? eh? what? 123.28

and an it, if it 86.31

angel a gold coin, worth ten shillings (50p) in the Tudor period 16.12, 199.15, 199.22, 203.40

antecedent see note to 281.12

anti-masque grotesque interlude between acts of masque 363.24

antic grotesque, bizarre, uncouth 181.11, 302.26

apaid satisfied, requited 128.19

apprehension see note to 335.34

approach bring nearer, bring 101.39, 227.42

aqua-vitæ spirits, such as brandy 194.21, 282.1

aquafortis nitric acid, a corrosive and solvent 207.33

arcanum great secret of alchemy 120.27, 189.28, 223.29

architrave main lintel beam 322.8

argent *heraldry* silver 121.24

array *noun* militia 153.22

array *verb* prepare 89.22

arrow *English dialect* ever a, any 93.11

artillery see note to 227.3-4

artist artisan, craftsman, medical practitioner, alchemist 100.40 etc.

ascendant *astrology* see notes to 186.36-37 and 190.7

aspect particular angular relationship between heavenly bodies 186.3, 188.11

aspic asp (serpent) 206.31

atheism godlessness, impiety, general lawlessness 287.37

attach arrest 322.27

avise inform, make aware 106.33

avoirdupois the standard system of weight 253.22

aw *English dialect* all 202.21

awful profoundly respectful 292.31

bailiff chief magistrate 74.38 etc.

balance weigh 23.12

baldric warrior's belt or shoulder-sash 316.29

ball bolus, large pill 120.9

ban-dog chained dog, mastiff 56.6

bantling small child, brat 247.12

barbed the breast and flanks covered with armour or ornamental covering 256.10

barbican double tower over a gate 254.43

barrow mound marking ancient burial place 96.12

bases pleated skirt, or imitation of one in mailed armour 365.2

basilisk fabulous reptile whose look was supposed to be fatal 180.43

bastard a sweet Spanish wine, often adulterated with honey 3.40, 19.41

baulk balk, disappointment 12.45

bayard bay horse 241.21

beadle a parish officer or constable 303.5

beadroll long list of names, especially of the dead to be prayed for 12.21

beaver hat of beaver fur 30.11, 93.32, 273.35, 284.9

bedizen dress gaudily 19.15

beeves oxen 285.28

belie tell lies about 160.14, 320.40, 323.9

belike probably, possibly, perhaps 54.34, 274.9, 347.33, 376.33

belt invest with a belt as a signal of knighthood 13.32, 369.6

beshrew curse 2.16 etc.

besognio worthless fellow 193.42

bespeak ask for 74.20; call 115.34

Bess see note to 262.25

bestow dispose of 275.19, 324.5, 355.34

bewray reveal 56.20

bide suffer 7.23

bilboa bilbo, sword noted for temper of blade (originally from Bilbao in Spain) 152.3

billet[1] letter 38.15, 341.8

billet[2] small log 21.39, 232.15

bit see note to 108.43–109.2

bitter virulent 13.39

black-letter Gothic printing-type 364.39

blazonry armorial bearings 121.24

bleed let blood 120.9

bleed-barrel tapster, barman 199.26

blent mingled 186.38

blister raise blisters for medical reasons 120.9

block mould for making a hat 10.13

bloom-coloured rosy 372.1

blow brilliant display, bloom 44.24

bona-roba showy wanton, courtesan 7.7

boot for 12.28, 140.34, 183.39, and 278.20 see note to 12.28

botcher cobbler, tailor who does repairs 41.30

bots animal disease caused by parasitical worms 108.13, 109.12

bottle bundle 88.13

bottom hollow 243.33, 277.36; for 93.21 see note

brass effrontery 27.2

bratchet little brat, child 372.10

brave finely-dressed, handsome 20.13, 38.24, 41.19, 235.40

braveries fine clothes 140.31, 152.6, 283.15

bravery adornment 154.29, 222.36

bravo reckless desperado, daring villain, hired soldier, assassin 8.12

break see note to 11.5

breech flog 248.10

brick-bat piece of brick 95.5, 122.40

broad open 82.35, 115.36, 222.20

broil quarrel 8.30, 165.28, 348.5

broker agent 45.11; retailer, especially dealer in second-hand clothes 5.3

brook suffer, endure, allow 13.10 etc.

brulziement commotion, quarrel 131.34

buckram coarse open-woven fabric of jute, cotton, or linen made very stiff with size 87.4, 198.14, 244.15, 259.18

buff made of buffalo-hide leather 3.16, 25.27

bugle see note to 235.37–38

bump verb denoting the cry of a bittern 97.19

bumpkin loutish, rustic 12.10

buskin tragic actor's boot, boot 103.3, 259.17

buttery-hatch half-door to storeroom, over which provisions were served 263.43

cabala, cabalist, cabalistical for

42.24, 103.32, 190.43 and 226.41
see note to 42.24–25

caco-dæmon evil spirit 266.25

caitiff wretch, villain 36.24, 141.2,
209.16, 278.40

calcine reduce by fire to a powder
194.35

caliver light portable gun 3.24, 4.14

cambric fine white linen 47.35 etc.

camerado comrade 83.30

camiciæ *Latin* shirts 89.1

camlet costly eastern fabric, in 16th
century made of Angora goat's hair
241.1

canon rule of the Church 169.43

capotaine see note to 315.19

caravansary inn 76.30

carder card-player 18.40

career charge, gallop 20.29 etc.

carman carter 252.21

carnal bloody, bodily as opposed to
spiritual 30.15, 227.23, 233.2

carrion-crow crow that feeds on dead
flesh 35.14

carry take 104.39, 108.17, 354.19,
369.18

cartel written challenge, letter of defiance 140.17

case position 192.33

cast *verb* turn 267.32

cast *noun* see note to 356.32

castellate furnish with battlements
254.14, 263.11

catch see note to 12.15

cater-cousins see note to 20.5–6

caudle sweet spiced gruel 5.24, 42.24

censure condemnatory judgment
322.22

certes assuredly 354.15

chace, chase unenclosed land
reserved for breeding and hunting
wild animals 74.13 etc.

chafe *verb* be angry 280.15

chafe *noun* passion, fury 199.15

chamberlain room steward, waiter
3.2, 17.7

change see notes to 10.43 and 23.4–5

changes undergarments 202.25

chargeable burdensome, costly
299.24

cheney see note to 235.37–38

cherry-pit see note to 6.41

chesnut stale joke 15.32

chime recite 151.12

chip flavourless fragment 196.39

chirurgeon surgeon 110.37

chop see note to 17.3

chopin actor's high shoe 259.25

chough see note to 39.13

chuff clown, surly fellow, boor 23.22,
198.23

circle see note to 90.31

clary sweet liquor, a mixture of wine,
clarified honey, and various spices
7.26

clem starve 91.11

clerk for 7.42, 8.7, 8.20 and 8.23 see
note to 8.23

clew ball of thread to guide through a
maze 307.8

close *adj.* close-fitting 209.12,
259.28, 293.41; strictly confined
156.38

close *noun*[1] enclosed field 285.25

close *noun*[2] a closing in fight,
struggle 35.40

clout see note to 311.36

clown boor 3.35 etc.

cock *noun*[1] leader 27.14

cock *noun*[2] see note to 198.31

cock *verb* for 273.35 and 284.9 see
note to 273.35

cockatrice prostitute 7.22

codling unripe apple 4.16

codshead blockhead 298.25

Cog God 290.32

cognisance, cognizance *heraldry*
device borne as a distinguishing
mark by the retainers of a noble
house 122.40, 175.10, 256.35

cogsbones *oath* God's bones 356.31

cogswounds *oath* God's wounds 70.9

coif close-fitting cap 65.20, 156.15,
202.19

coil fuss, to-do 13.42, 139.16, 140.35,
260.32

collar ornamental chain forming part
of the insignia of orders of knighthood 59.5

collogue chat, confer 196.25, 196.27

colour cloak 346.23

combust *astrology* in or near conjunction with the sun 190.7, 304.41

comely proper, seemly, decorous
1.16, 9.29, 118.10

comfortable strengthening, cheering,
sustaining, reassuring, causing comfort, self-satisfied 3.37 etc.

commit endanger, compromise 40.12,
118.35

companion fellow, rascal 38.39, 39.30

compassionate pity 314.42

compeer equal 166.19, 342.27

complacence pleasure, delight 294.10

complacency self-satisfaction 387.17

complacent obliging in manner 217.14

comprehend see note to 109.36

Compter debtors' prison 312.31

compulsory coercive 83.2

concernment affair 30.35, 30.40

concord agree 90.25

condition *noun* rank 268.19

condition *verb* stipulate 136.14

conditions state, condition 6.31, 91.23

confessor one who adheres to their own religious faith in time of persecution 115.5

confident see note to 83.19

confound fail to distinguish, mix together 110.35, 380.13

congé bow 130.18

conjoin see note to 186.36–37

conjunction *astrology* an apparent proximity of two heavenly bodies 78.4, 186.3

conjure implore 186.33, 368.14, 382.11

conscionable conscientious, scrupulous 41.16

consequent see note to 281.12

consider requite, recompense 188.24, 228.40

considerate deliberate 26.36; careful, prudent 300.24

consideration see note to 151.16–17

construe translate, interpret 89.25, 360.40

contents satisfaction 227.13

conversation social intercourse 178.20

convince see note to 2.17–18

copartnery joint partnership 30.28

cope vault 353.26

coperas sulphate of iron 207.32

copyhold for 41.8 etc. see note to 41.8

coragio *Italian* courage 83.23

cordage ropes of ship's rigging 7.15

cordovan of Cordovan or good quality leather 14.25

Corinthian dissipated idler 27.7

corporation see note to 76.9

corslet piece of defensive armour covering the body 255.37

coruscant sparkling, glittering 291.5

cote see note to 169.37

coucher evening reception 303.22

countenance favour, approbation 26.14 etc.; favourable demeanour 377.24

counter see note to 116.7

countervail counterbalance 176.2

country-breeding rusticity 20.18

couples braces or leashes 317.15

course hunt 169.37

courses proceedings, ways of action especially if reprehensible, goings on 50.16, 50.22, 64.39

coxcomb simpleton, showy person 34.18 etc.

cozen(er) dupe 99.23, 345.9, 345.30

credit reputation 9.34, 20.43, 118.31, 294.36

crib narrow room 169.26

cricket low wooden stool 101.41

crisp crimp 49.15

crop sow crops 108.10

cross see note to 10.15–17

cross-stitch decorative needlework consisting of stitches crossing each other 52.38

croupe rump 257.17

crow-trodden ignominiously treated 111.29

crown coin worth five shillings (25p) 10.43 etc.

culiss strong clear stock made of beef, chicken etc. 18.21

culminate reach its greatest height 304.39, 347.17

culver culverin, hand-gun 145.15

cumber trouble 20.3 etc.

curious *adj.* careful, interesting, ingenious 23.12 etc.

curious *noun* a connoisseur 181.7

curry-comb comb for rubbing down horse 109.30

curvet leap 266.14

cutter bully, cut-throat 27.7, 34.1 (see note)

cutting for 7.2, 195.18 and 242.5 see note to 7.1–2

cymar light loose garment for women 65.18

cypress, cyprus name for various expensive fabrics, e.g. gold, satin or crêpe 7.3, 202.36, 203.30

dainty handsome, fine 93.10

dam mother 245.1

damasked inlaid or woven with an ornamental design 241.16, 299.34

damosel-errant see note to 254.3

Dan Master, Sir 63.18

dandieprat urchin 261.8

danger power to harm 91.25, 174.31

dangerous difficult to deal with or please, particular, fastidious 8.17

deboshed disreputable 30.6

decoct boil so as to extract the soluble parts 7.13, 7.20

defend repel 93.16

defoul defile 18.30

demean see note to 6.16

deputy-marshal's-man deputy to one of the officers of the royal household preceding the sovereign in processions 251.43

design be bound 244.20

despite indignation arising from offended pride 335.28

devoir duty 2.35

devotion service, disposal 210.3, 334.33; extreme deference 129.32

diablotin little devil, imp 245.12

dicer gambler with dice 19.1

Dick fellow 11.14

diffidence want of faith 188.2

dink *Scots* trim, finely dressed, prim, haughty 252.12

dirl *Scots and northern English* reverberate 329.24

discharge forbid 104.20

disclamation repudiation 172.22

discompose ruffle, agitate 353.27

discover reveal 100.5, 213.2, 315.8

dish-clout dishcloth 88.23

dishabille negligent dress 284.32

disperse distribute, spread about 170.30

distemperature uneasiness, disturbance of mind or temper 324.34, 353.28

divertisement diversion, recreation, amusement 165.38

dog-hostler wretched hostler 110.24

dollar German thaler, Spanish piece of eight 130.31, 207.19

domine schoolmaster 92.20 etc.

doublet close-fitting body garment 5.26 etc.

doubt fear, suspect 5.13 etc.

douse dull heavy blow 288.25

drab-de-burée drap-de-Berry, woollen cloth from Berry in France 143.2

drachm one-eighth of an ounce apothecaries' weight 130.4

drawer one who draws beer or fetches liquor in a tavern 17.40, 20.22, 20.27

drench liquid medicine, especially for an animal 120.9

drive exercise 99.15

ducat gold or silver coin of varying value 189.22, 196.41

dun person pressing for money, especially money owed 139.5

elaboratory laboratory 104.4, 104.20, 190.26, 194.17

Eldorado for 6.40, 7.26, 37.2 and 37.3 see note to 6.40

electuary medicine, being a powder or other ingredient mixed with honey, jam, or syrup 131.17

elf malicious or mischievous creature 237.31, 267.20

elf-locks a tangled mass of hair 25.10

elixir medicine 226.37; for 90.13 and 130.16 see notes

ell-wand ell measure (in England 45 inches or 114 cm) 195.23

empiric quack, charlatan, untrained practitioner in medicine or surgery 146.15, 378.22

engross monopolise 29.12

enow enough 109.27, 152.8

ensure convince, assure 5.13, 93.14

envious odious 38.3

equal unruffled, indifferent 223.5, 353.28

erect elevate, set up 76.5, 186.14

ermine stoat 53.34

errant itinerant 235.42

errant-damozel for 276.31 see note to 254.3

eruct belch out 245.25

espalier fruit-tree trained on stakes 23.38

exchequer private fortune, income 13.22

Exchequer department or court dealing primarily with royal revenue 68.33, 196.33

exhale evaporate 387.39

fair-favoured good-looking 372.11

fairly see note to 37.18

faitour impostor 377.5

falchion see note to 174.3–4
fallow see note to 255.3
fancy see note to 203.31–2
farcy chronic glanders, a disease chiefly of horses 237.23
farewell see note to 345.10
fatidicæ *Latin* prophetesses 286.2
fell skin 113.15
felly fiercely 313.10
femoral see note to 288.22–23
fence *noun* defence 363.34
fence *verb* protect, fortify 385.40
ferrateen ferreting or ferret, silk or cotton tape 240.27
ferula, ferule rod, cane 7.35, 87.6
fiduciary trustee 118.23
fierce proud 284.31
figure chart, horoscope 189.4
fillagree filigree 47.39
finger lay hands on 170.28
fire-drake fiery dragon 122.40
fix render solid by combination with another substance 103.25
flashing showy 39.32
flat-cap'd for 30.22 see note to 11.4
flavour smell 208.12
flaw squall, quarrel 34.3, 134.31
fleer mock 262.35
foil *wrestling* almost a throw 151.23
foot-cloth cloth to set feet on, carpet 143.1; richly-ornamented cloth on horse's back, reaching to ground 365.3
foot-post messenger travelling on foot 104.17
forepart stomacher, ornamental bodice 15.10
form lair 278.5
foul choked with weeds, barren 138.25
founders founder, inflammation of horse's foot, usually caused by over-work 126.26, 237.24
four-nooked square 276.19
fox sword 36.13, 278.13
frame mental or spiritual state 7.43
franklin freeholder 195.33, 296.12
freedom see note to 76.9
freehold property held free of duty except to the monarch 38.22, 41.5, 306.34
freestone easily worked building stone 357.29
frippery tawdry finery, second-hand clothes 5.3
front face 51.17, 358.23

frontless shameless 360.1
frounce pleat, gather 80.1
furth forth 92.16
fusille *heraldry* fusil, elongated lozenge 58.21
gaberdine loose upper garment 129.7, 224.35, 241.43, 267.10
Gaffer rustic title for man below rank of 'Master' 108.16 etc.
gainsay oppose, hinder 32.8
galliard lively, brisk, as in the galliard dance 97.28
galloon see note to 17.5
gallows-bird one who deserves to be hanged 26.12
gambade leap or bound of horse 364.5
game-cock cock bred for cock-fighting 360.34
gamesome sportive, merry 18.9, 173.17, 174.15
Gammer female equivalent of 'Gaffer' 86.34 etc.
garniture appurtenances, trappings, dress 198.12, 204.1, 238.20
gay brilliantly good, shewy, richly attired 4.39 etc.
gaze-hound species of dog which hunts by sight 29.17
gear rubbish 218.26; for 34.12 see note
genethliacally by calculating birth-days 103.23
gentle noble, generous 53.20, 269.2, 301.6; well-born 51.31
gentles gentlefolks 14.28, 273.17
gentry polished manners 20.29
gew-gaw gaudy 386.16
gharn *English dialect* garden 202.22
gie *English dialect* give 120.9
gimcrack knick-knack 361.33; mech-anical contrivance 389.3
gog's-nails see note to 361.26
Gogsnouns *oath* God's wounds 72.6
gossip chum 26.1, 247.9, 372.11; godfather or godmother 244.40
grace show favour to 38.25
grace-cup cup from which last drink is taken at night 114.12
gramercy thank you 4.4, 301.5
grand great, principal 177.30
grandee nobleman 3.21
grateful agreeable 303.27
grazier one who pastures cattle and raises them for the market 71.38, 243.18

griffin imaginary animal, part eagle, part lion, vulture 119.29

gripe grip 230.25, 360.37

groat coin worth four pre-decimal pence (1.66p) 23.22 etc.

grogram coarse cloth of silk and mohair 241.18

ground-baits bait dropped to the bottom to attract fish 23.28

grudge complain 188.23

guard see note to 15.13

guerdon recompense 8.39 etc.

gules *heraldry* red 217.43

gull *noun* credulous person, fool 7.28 etc.

gull *verb* deceive 83.4, 189.37

gullery trickery, deception 205.5

gum-mastick gum from the bark of a number of trees 103.16

habit dress, appearance 9.6 etc.

hackney ordinary horse 243.2

halberd, halbert weapon combining spear and battle-axe 141.17, 141.24, 360.26

halt limp 108.21, 163.36, 174.4

halter hangman's noose 26.33, 72.21 (see note), 275.24, 383.28

handsel present given e.g. on first wearing new clothes 198.42

hang-dog despicable fellow 8.36

hap fortune 58.14, 184.4

hard-ruled difficult to manage 210.26

harness body-armour 80.20

haro call for help 240.23

harrotry heraldry 113.29

Harry-noble gold coin of the reign of Henry VI 20.40

hartshorn solution of ammonia in water, formerly obtained from antlers 109.11

hazard game of chance, risk or stake 20.36; for 212.17 see note

hazard-table gambling table 18.11

headborough officer performing administrative and policing duties in a parish 9.13 etc.

heart-spone heart-spoon, midriff 208.16

hellebore name for various poisonous and medicinal plants, drug prepared from them 91.5, 207.32

hence since, ago 100.43

Heptarchy see note to 259.15

her *English dial.* she 202.22

herd go in company 243.24

hermetic alchemical 189.26

heys country dance 247.35

high-trussed see note to 363.42

hilding good-for-nothing 236.14

hilts handle of sword or dagger 138.32

hind servant, underling 39.17, 385.41

hit hit the mark 246.3

hob-nailed rustic, boorish 189.22

hobby-horse for 363.20 etc. see note to 363.20

hogshead large cask 251.37

hoise hoist 7.17

Hollands linen fabric 16.11, 198.39, 199.1

hollo halloo, shout (to) 97.11

homage do homage 351.15

honour see note to 279.11

hop-o'-my-thumb see note to 108.21

hop-the-gutter gutter-snipe 266.29

hopeful promising 7.30, 88.18, 212.2, 245.28

horn side of a lantern made of translucent horn 30.40

horse-courser jobbing dealer in horses 239.27

horse-litter curtained couch carried between two horses 355.7, 379.37

hospitium hospice, house of rest and entertainment for strangers 88.8

hostler man who attends to horses at an inn 2.6 etc.

House for 186.11, 186.12, 186.37, and 189.20 see note to 186.10−12

house-keeping hospitality, keeping a good table 84.42

humour temperament, habitual frame of mind, mood, state of mind 1.16 etc.

humourist fanatical or whimsical person 363.37

Hundred subdivision of county or shire, with its own court 86.40, 109.34

hurricano(e) hurricane 34.3, 326.28

huswife housewife, hussy 198.15

ield reward 202.21

import concern 44.41

incontinent immediately 200.17

Indian *noun* North American Indian 310.14

Indian *adj.* for 134.29 see note to 134.29

Indies West Indies 34.3; for 134.24 see note

infer imply 9.5, 306.18; involve 17.1, 55.1

infractor violator 208.11

ingenuous see note to 200.5

ingle properly a homosexual partner, but used by Scott to mean 'chum' 25.40, 199.28, 246.9

ingrate ungrateful person 229.22

inmate lodger, one sharing a house 1.14 etc.

innovation see note to 280.31

intelligence see note to 188.1

intelligencer informant 85.4, 150.27, 197.14

interfere take part, intervene 13.36, 297.42, 314.23

interlude stage-play 247.16

inveteracy hostility, prejudice 361.16

irregular disorderly 30.6

ivy-tod ivy-bush 137.40, 285.34

jack fellow, jack-fish or pike 23.28

jackanape impudent fellow, coxcomb 15.32, 192.5, 360.22

jade trick 388.28

jealous vigilant, suspicious 84.8 etc.

jolterhead blockhead 95.4, 266.30

jouring *English dialect* muttering, grumbling, speaking the (Somerset) brogue 202.17

journal day's journey 264.27

judicial see note to 185.9

jump for 22.32 and 73.10 see note to 22.32

just justly 170.33

justice-book court records 29.38

juvenal youth 244.34

keep make 13.42

kennel street gutter 28.15, 313.17

kerne member of war-band 141.43

kibe irritated chilblain on heel 252.13

kirtle gown, skirt 235.37, 236.3

Lachrymæ *Latin* lachrymae Christi, strong sweet red wine from southern Italy 129.24

lack need 2.33

lap flap 311.20

latest last 8.1

latitudinarian religious liberal 61.23

lawn fine woven linen or cotton 7.3, 198.1, 202.35, 203.26

lay exorcise 10.9

lea-land fallow land 247.32

leasehold for 41.8, 227.2 and 380.27 see note to 41.8

leech doctor 123.24, 139.16, 146.12

legerdemain sleight of hand, hocus-pocus 102.30, 130.39

lemman, leman mistress 115.38, 240.36

levanter easterly wind 326.25

levee morning assembly held by noble 69.42, 75.11

liberty for 279.11 and 286.6 see note to 279.11

lightly nimbly, easily, readily 8.16, 196.37

like likely 19.23 etc.

limber supple, pliant 198.13

limbo prison 279.2

Lincoln-green bright green material made at Lincoln 316.28

linsey-wolsey see note 21.22

linstock stick to hold lighted match for firing cannon 282.8

list wish, choose 6.33 etc.

little-ease dungeon, pillory, stocks, narrow place of confinement 10.19, 279.3

littocks rags and tatters 202.21

livery-cloak uniform-cloak 64.23, 67.19, 329.4

livery-man uniformed servant 74.8

long-breathed long-winded 381.14

loon rogue 237.16

lubbard lubber, lout 106.2, 288.16

lure bait 40.5

lyme-hound bloodhound 29.16, 29.18

Magister Master 87.40 etc.

magisterium for 104.28 and 191.32 see note to 104.28

main important 203.23, 278.15

make-bate breeder of strife 273.33, 337.42

malapert presumptuous, impudent, saucy 147.35

mandragorn see note to 120.31

manna for 123.38 etc. see note to 123.38

marches borderland 314.15

mark see note to 283.32

marle marvel 201.20

marry name of the Virgin Mary, used as exclamation of asseveration, surprise, indignation etc. 2.17 etc.

martialist military man, one skilled in warfare 132.20

mask masked person 352.19, 352.24,

352.31, 353.1

masquer one who takes part in a masquerade 31.32 etc.

mass originally eucharist, used as exclamation 285.24

match see note to 12.15

matters things 381.8

maugre in spite of 14.41

mavis song-thrush 41.18

May-game merry-making 376.17

mayor see note to 155.32

mazed out of his wits 113.21, 140.28, 180.35

mean ignoble, of low degree 4.6 etc.

mechanic handicraftsman 10.42, 59.41, 252.11

mechanical lower-class, vulgar 198.23

medulla *Latin* bone-marrow 90.28

meeting nonconformist service or place of worship 30.12

mercer dealer in textile fabrics 8.21 etc.

meridian full splendour 69.35

mess portion of food 169.26, 267.38; group of four 276.21

messmate companion at meals 1.14

mew confine 14.5, 119.19, 218.7, 275.2

Millenium for 228.12 and 228.13 see note to 228.12

mincing affectedly fastidious 199.6

minikin diminutive person 266.24

minion favourite, darling 171.7 etc.

minish lessen 84.41

mockado common cloth 241.18

momentarily at every moment 210.10

mon *English dialect* man 86.26 etc.

monopoly exclusive right of trading in certain commodities 42.23, 168.17

moonstruck deranged 43.29, 297.34

moppet *contemptuous* gaily dressed or frivolous woman 39.42, 252.16, 283.40

morion helmet without beaver or visor 255.38

mump mumble, mutter e.g. as if toothless, grimace, assume a sanctimonious expression 28.13

murrain plague 74.28, 120.39, 313.15

murrey mulberry-colour, purple-red 15.12

muscadine muscatel, a strong sweet

wine made from the muscat grape 18.18

musquetoon short musket with large bore 199.40

muster assembling or coming together 151.43, 351.43

myrmidon faithful servant 2.8, 364.4

mystery craft, profession, skill, art 20.20 etc.; mystery play 170.20

naiad river nymph 318.17

neat *noun* cow 79.8

neat *adj.* clear, unadulterated, fine 3.37

neats-tongue ox-tongue 41.42

neophyte new convert 27.14

nereid sea-nymph 289.34

nice punctilious 25.5

night-sack bag containing necessities for the night 275.43

nineteenthly the nineteenth head of a sermon 28.14

noble gold coin worth six shillings and eight pence (33p) 13.21 etc.

'noint anoint 74.42

nonage immaturity, minority 8.15, 191.32

nonce occasion 244.39

nones see note to 288.35

nooning noonday meal 181.31

nugæ *Latin* mere trifles, nonsense 93.13

nuncle uncle 196.31

obeisance bow, salutation 37.28, 155.6, 300.2

objurgation scolding 17.40, 383.30

observance deference, dutiful service 44.30, 217.36

occupy practise one's craft 190.31

odds see note to 381.2

oddspittikins *oath* God's blessed pity 193.40

office see note to 356.32

on of 3.20 etc.

on-hanger hanger-on 19.12

oons *oath* God's wounds 239.40

or *heraldry* gold 121.24

order see notes to 39.16 and 361.36

ordinary eating-house 20.21

organization constitution 296.36

orient oriental, hence valuable, precious, lustrous 38.14

orvietan for 130.43 and 181.20 see note to 130.43

outrance uttermost 53.43

owe own 59.12

owzle ouzel, blackbird 98.8

page boy 369.26

pageant piece of stage-machinery 259.17, 289.33

palabra word, palaver 108.35

palter deal crookedly 187.14

paltering babbling 39.9

pan-tile roofing-tile whose cross-section forms an ogee curve 6.42

pandæmonium dwelling-place of the devil and his companions 223.21

pantoufle, pantofle slipper 138.26, 222.36

papestrie, papistrie papistry, popery 30.5, 324.31

parcel in part 15.26, 94.36

Parish-garden see note to 174.28

parish-top see note to 195.4–5

paropa kind of fabric 241.17

paroquet parakeet, parrot 41.11

parterre level space in a garden with flower-beds ornamentally arranged 23.41, 254.11, 316.12

partizan[1] long-handled spear 133.37, 256.34, 284.22

partizan[2] adherent 284.33, 301.36, 358.34

partlet ruff, neckerchief, collar 203.29

pass *verb* pledge 274.27

pass *noun*[1] see note to 69.17

pass *noun*[2] passage, corridor 390.25

passage intimate interchange 159.4 etc.; passage of arms, combat 16.35; incident, occurrence 339.6

passant *heraldry* walking 119.7

pass-devant *probably* fashionable women's dress, dress worn at dances 15.18

pate head 2.18 etc.

patent see note to 168.29

pater *Latin, short for* paternoster, Lord's Prayer 93.15

patientia *Latin* patience 90.19

patonce see note to 117.38

patronize see note to 1.17

paynim pagan 240.25, 282.9

pea-cod peasecod, pea pod 16.28

peeper eye 84.24

pen-fold sheepfold 312.32

pepper-box box for sprinkling pepper, here applied contemptuously to small cylindrical turret 112.32

perdue hidden 288.22

period end 318.4, 391.30

peremptorily without fail 384.12

perquisition thorough search 104.32

persecute importune 211.41, 223.1

personage assumed character 330.32, 347.6

pewit lapwing 389.3

phantasy caprice, whim 82.25

Philippine see note to 235.37–38

phrenesis phrenitis, brain-fever 348.18

phylactery see note to 289.39–40

picaroon pirate, corsair, rogue, knave, thief, brigand 22.28, 206.25

piccadilloe-needle poking stick used to re-shape fluted ruffs 109.42

pickle see note to 108.43–109.2

pied multi-coloured 283.3

pike kind of long-shafted spear 3.24, 152.8, 284.11, 284.22

pile heap of faggots for burnings at the stake 207.36

pinching parsimonious 9.21

Pindaric expressing oneself in the wildly enthusiastic style associated with the Greek lyric poet Pindar 297.35

pinfold place of confinement, pen 16.24

pink for 14.14 and 168.42 see note to 14.14–15

pioneer *literally* one of advance guard who prepare the way by digging trenches 42.20

pize term of imprecation, pox, pest 10.13

place manor-house 199.27

placet placit, petition 151.39

pledge *noun* a toast 11.34

pledge *verb* toast, drink to 3.26 etc.

plenty abundant 7.4, 102.40

plush type of cloth with nap longer and softer than velvet 241.18

poignado poniard, dagger 276.20

poignant sharp or piquant to taste 41.41

point tagged lace or cord for fastening clothes 283.4

poking-awl sharp tool 109.37

poking-iron rod used for re-shaping fluted ruffs 50.32

pole-cat type of weasel 53.35

policy shrewdness, cunning, prudent practice, political sagacity, diplomacy, conduct of public affairs 45.14 etc.

politic political, shrewd 65.3

pomade scented ointment for skin or hair 181.30

poniard dagger 30.19 etc.

portmantle portmanteau 64.24, 85.22

posey posy, motto 38.21

possess see notes to 92.14, 234.29 and 335.34

posset-dish dish for drink of hot milk curdled with ale, wine, or other liquor, often with sugar, spices etc. 47.40

post *noun* messenger 104.40, 265.38

post *verb* travel speedily, travel with relays of horses 214.22, 219.17, 327.13, 386.3; for 327.32 see note

post *adv.* speedily, with relays of horses 93.36, 213.36

post-contract subsequent contract 42.21

postern-door back or private door 14.11 etc.

postern-gate back or private gate 69.27 etc.

postpone regard as inferior to 212.33

posture-master acrobat 311.42

pot pot of or for liquor, liquor 1.19 etc.

potential potent, powerful 215.14

pottle-pot a half-gallon pot 3.42 etc.

powdered preserved, cured, corned 9.26

prancer horse 237.22

prank deck (oneself) out 154.41

pre-contract pre-existing contract 42.21

precise strict, puritanical 30.31 etc.; correct, fastidious 11.4

precisian strict Puritan 13.16, 13.39, 13.40, 61.24

precision puritan demeanour 60.39

predominant see note to 187.34

prepossession preconceived opinion, prejudice 9.17, 359.40

presence demeanour 1.16

present *verb* represent 58.22, 362.31

present *adj.* urgent 355.36

presently immediately, instantly 64.23 etc.

pretend claim (to have) 30.34, 391.12; lay claim (to) 79.1

pricker mounted attendant 304.11, 317.16

prig *thieves' cant* steal 237.22

princox coxcomb 74.35

privy-council(lor) (member of) body advising the sovereign 56.4, 83.29, 165.36, 166.12

probation trial, examination 109.36

process prosecute, proceed with 83.2

profecto see note to 93.4

professor one who makes open profession of religious belief 61.18

progress state journey 75.43 etc.

projection alchemical transmutation of metal into gold 189.26, 228.25, 388.12

proper inherent as a property, belonging to oneself 48.11, 380.43; appropriate 100.30, 210.18, 223.41; for 34.12 and 119.17 see notes

proselyte convert 27.14

provant of inferior quality 243.15

prove make trial of 98.5

provocatives food bringing out the taste of wine 41.42

puckfist empty braggart 193.42, 207.25

puissant powerful, mighty 240.34

puny novice 27.15

purblind totally blind 281.5

purlieus haunts, disreputable regions 18.17, 22.19

purpose see note to 13.22

pursuivant royal or state messenger with power to execute warrants, junior heraldic officer 13.1 etc.

purveyor for 251.26 and 251.43 see note to 251.26

puss hare 278.4

pye see note to 198.31

pyrrhic ancient Greek war-dance 350.13

quack-salver quack, pretender to medical skill 90.15, 193.30

quadrille square dance of French origin 351.25, 352.3

quail-pipe pipe for imitating note of quail to lure birds into net 68.19

qualify designate 169.17, 173.21; modify strength or flavour of 41.40

quarter *heraldry* place (coats of arms) quarterly upon a shield 310.33

quarter-staff fighting or exercise with stout poles, stout pole 174.3, 251.42

quartern quarter pint 16.10

quittance recompense 381.8

quittance see note to 384.33

quotha said he 13.23

rabatine collar 235.36
rack stable-rack holding fodder 2.26
raddle *northern dialect* thrash 198.35
rampant *heraldry* rearing up 119.30
rash smooth fabric of silk or worsted 241.17
rat's-bane rat-poison, especially arsenic 208.10
rebeck early form of violin 101.35
receipt prescription 296.26
receipt-book recipe-book 217.5
receive accept as valid 148.3, 391.38
reckoning bill 6.20 etc.
reclaim *falconry* call back 121.12
reclaimed tamed 192.28
reeve bailiff, steward 13.15
reform convert 235.35
reguardant *heraldry* looking backward 119.14
relish *noun* flavour 194.40
relishing *verb* having or giving a savoury or piquant taste 41.41
remain await 194.20
rencounter, rencontre chance meeting, encounter, casual combat, duel 16.35, 76.29, 360.17
rent income 303.2
retrograde *of planets* moving from east to west 186.11, 304.41
return reply 130.7, 168.5, 380.26
reveillée morning signal 310.38, 326.22
reverence bow, deferential gesture 51.25 etc.
reverend reverent, deeply respectful 20.28; worthy of respect 194.11
Rhenish wine from Rhine region 148.29
riband, ribband ribbon 7.3, 82.24, 283.4, 284.27
rid remove 355.24
rocking-stone large stone so evenly balanced as to be easily swayed to and fro 318.6
Roman Roman Catholic 9.24, 9.29
romantic as part of the romantic tradition of literature 259.14
rood cross 81.30
rose-noble gold coin bearing figure of a rose 23.23
round large 29.4
roundell ornamental circle 203.29
rout company 248.23
rub rough place, impediment 151.19, 311.40, 338.7

ruffle swagger 11.11 etc.
sables sable fur 63.2, 149.17
sack general name for a class of white wines from Spain and the Canaries 2.27 etc.
sad-coloured dark or sober-coloured 20.15
sage see note to 245.16–19
salamander lizard or spirit supposed to live in fire 309.4
sally-port gateway for making sallies, postern 268.9, 278.23, 278.28
salver quack, pretender to medical skill (compare quack-salver) 90.15, 103.10
sarsenet *noun* fine soft silk material 8.25
sarsenet *adj.* soft 14.34
savin drug derived from a species of juniper 109.11
'sblood *oath, short for* God's blood 196.41, 199.37
scald skald, ancient Scandinavian poet 349.41
scant-of-grace *Scots dialect* reprobate 23.9
scape escape 386.9
scathe injure or destroy by fire, blast 126.19
scheme chart of the heavens, horoscope 186.15
sconce[1] candlestick 46.27, 46.39
sconce[2] small fort or earthwork 5.11
scroyle wretch 198.37
scruple a small unit of weight in apothecaries' weight 23.13
sculler boat propelled by sculling 180.34
scutcheon shield-shaped surface, or funeral hatchment, with armorial bearings 132.27, 254.27, 261.37, 310.29
'sdeath *oath, short for* God's death 373.41
secretary-office office of state 374.39
seeming appearance 57.29
seethe stew 390.17
seiant *heraldry* sitting 119.7
self-complacence self-satisfaction 387.7
seneschal steward 56.8, 225.10
sequestrated secluded 191.38
seraphs the highest class of angels 388.34
sewer officer superintending service

at table 181.27 etc.

shag velvet cloth of worsted or silk 241.17

shag-headed having shaggy hair 141.43

shambles slaughter-house 313.18

shame be ashamed 345.5

sheep-biting sneaking 278.5

sheer thin, diaphanous 352.18

shift stratagem, expedient 103.5, 237.21, 250.40

shog go away 36.20

shorten hold (sword) nearer to middle, so as to strike more effectively 35.37

shot share of the reckoning 8.34, 196.29 (see note)

shot-window casement 240.42

shovel-board game resembling shove-halfpenny 46.31, 113.28

sign see notes to 185.19, 186.23 and 190.7

signal remarkable 192.24

simple medicine composed of one plant or herb, medicinal plant 103.24, 131.6

six-hooped for 1.18 and 18.38 see note to 1.18–19

skene dagger 173.25

skill see note to 108.12

skinker one who serves liquor 197.17

skirts lower part or tail of coat or similar garment 197.3, 199.10

slate-shivers fragments of slate 207.19

sleuth-hound bloodhound 36.39

slip young person for 4.21 and 150.2 see note to 4.20–11

slocket see note to 202.21

slop-pouch pocket of baggy trousers or hose 29.5

slouched for 8.10, 35.5 and 67.19 see note to 8.10

slough outer layer, coat 283.33

sluggard habitually inactive or lazy person 24.6

sly surreptitious, illicit 197.40

smock-faced having a pale, smooth face 128.33

smock-frock coarse, loose-fitting garment worn by farm-labourers 241.43

'snails oath, short for God's nails 239.39

snake wretch, drudge 90.29

sobeit provided 19.4

sodden dull, stupid 30.37, 184.2

somerset somersault 267.32

sort for 1.14, 200.33, 227.33 and 242.31 see notes

sort manner 30.23; condition 43.7

special particularly 15.23

specific remedy for particular condition 206.36

sped see notes to 37.18 and 201.22

spiggot a small wooden peg used to stop the vent-hole of a barrel 2.10, 80.13, 201.334

spitchcock'd cut into short pieces, tossed in bread-crumbs and chopped herbs, and grilled or fried 9.27

Spittal see note to 7.24

spoil despoil, rob 27.38, 240.29

sponsor surety 188.42

springe snare 389.2

square see note to 71.29

squire escort 30.20

stab see note to 13.10

stamp character, kind 1.23, 30.4, 37.3

stand see note to 152.8

Staple see note to 76.5

start *verb* discharge, pour out 27.3; for 29.38 see note

start *noun* see note to 170.27

startup rustic boot 238.18

state appearance of grandeur or dignity 38.30, 327.17; chair of state 57.30

statist statesman 211.29

stave stanza 126.1

stirabout porridge 279.36

stithy anvil 102.28, 184.40

stock for 80.2, 196.1 and 198.10 see note to 80.1–2

stoop lower, bow 38.36; swoop on prey 192.28; for 40.5 see note

stoup drinking vessel 17.20, 102.5, 280.14

strangely unfavourably, inconveniently 245.2

strappadoe torture by hoisting up, then letting the victim fall half way with a jerk 362.12

straw see note 244.38

stricture tight closure 191.36

suburb-wench prostitute 222.35

supplication formal written petition 177.6, 336.43

supply furnish a substitute for 144.14

suspected suspect 346.17
swaddle beat soundly 198.32
swagger behave or talk blusteringly, quarrel, stagger 8.26
swart-faced black-faced 102.27
swash bluster, swagger 12.22, 18.40, 30.14
sway inclination 22.26
sweet-bag small bag filled with aromatic substance for perfuming 204.4
sybil sibyl, female fortune-teller 286.2
sylph spirit inhabiting the air 269.27, 309.5
syren *heraldry* imaginary species of serpent 119.28; *classical mythology* monster (part woman, part bird) who lured sailors to destruction by singing 166.8
tablets pocket book for memoranda 334.21, 335.27
tack *noun* sound of a sharp tap 98.28
tack *verb* attach 12.22
taffeta thin silk material 15.12, 15.15, 241.17
take ascertain 127.5
taking state, plight 109.28
talismanical magical, occult 103.31
tall bold, brave, strong 80.36, 198.29; *ironic* handsome, fine 39.31
tamper try to enter into secret dealings, scheme, plot 187.24, 336.23, 383.40
taper tapering 248.6
tapster barman 2.9 etc.
target light round shield or buckler 174.19, 363.35, 364.23
Tau Greek letter T 89.30
tear-cat bully, swaggerer 122.25
tell count 96.15, 96.25, 198.21
tempt attempt, risk the perils of 7.21, 63.16
tend attend 247.7
tent(-stitch) kind of embroidery stitch, petit point 52.38
tergiversation equivocation, prevarication 332.41
term see note to 50.18
termagant virago, violent overbearing woman 223.11
testimonial testimony 295.9, 297.27
thewes muscles 259.22
thieves'-latin thieves' cant or slang 280.43
three-piled with a pile of treble thick-

ness 235.39
thriftless worthless 6.15
throw start, turn sharply 335.27
tight *general term of commendation* competent, lively, neat 19.43
tightly soundly, vigorously 170.28, 198.32
tincture pigment 121.24, 122.15
tippet hangman's rope 26.15
tiring-room dressing-room 37.37, 38.24
tit small horse 105.13, 122.38, 126.25
toilet toilet-table, dressing-table 47.39
toils net(s), trap 165.33, 193.21, 266.26
Tokay sweet Hungarian wine 129.24
Toledo superior sword made at Toledo in Spain, or the like 243.15
tool sword 34.20
toper hard drinker 2.34, 22.26, 196.30
touch *verb* mention 174.18
touch *noun* see notes to 18.7 and 192.22
Tower Tower of London 157.7, 214.16, 322.36
Tower-Hill see note to 132.30
trammels fetters 332.27
transmewed transmuted, changed 227.2
transmigrate transmute 281.2
transmutation alchemical conversion 104.35
transpire become known 9.12, 178.1, 180.9
travel-toiled weary with travelling 247.29
traverse thwart, oppose 29.31
trencher plate 354.9
trick dress 342.11
trinket intrigue 92.16, 339.15
triton sea deity or monster 289.34
trowl troll, pass round 12.4; toll 113.32
truce for 5.35, 120.28 and 246.10 see note to 5.35
truckle-bed a low moveable bed 298.28, 298.41
trunk-hose full bag-like breeches covering hips and upper thighs 30.11
tucket flourish on a trumpet 282.7
turkey-bean the scarlet runner-bean 204.42

turmerick name for various plants used medicinally or as a condiment 103.16

turn trick 22.43

turns going into labour 245.2

typically symbolically, emblematically 227.26

ud God 26.43, 33.38, 78.42, 278.14

un's *dialect* his 92.29

un¹ *dialect* him, he 86.26 etc.

un² *dialect* one 87.27, 119.42

unadvised rash 84.34

unbraced with clothing unfastened 11.2, 135.20, 171.16 (see note)

undress incomplete or informal dress 289.25, 303.21

unguent ointment 181.30

unkindly lacking proper affection or respect 196.22

unruffled without frills 30.10

untenable uninhabitable 280.2

unthrift spendthrift, prodigal 22.20, 296.10

untransmigrated untransmuted 227.3

urge accelerate the pace of 376.22, 379.8

vail gratuity, tip 341.26

vanity vain thing, inanity 284.31

vantage advantage 37.12

vapour boast, swagger 6.34, 11.3

vapours depression, noxious bodily exhalations 205.1, 205.13

varlet groom, attendant, valet 273.28

varlet rogue 97.15, 146.15, 293.26

vengeably intensely, greatly 291.9

verge for 149.41 and 275.4 see note to 149.41

veriest most outright 168.28, 327.30

via onward, never mind 276.43, 281.2

vindicate claim, as properly one's own 3.14, 333.29

virgin-silver pure, unadulterated silver 6.43

vitriol sulphate of metal, e.g. iron 207.32

vivat acclamation wishing long life 303.6

vizard mask 244.25, 259.17, 290.32, 352.18

vizier chief minister of a sovereign 207.38

viznomy physiognomy 95.4

votary zealous worshipper 329.28, 342.9

voto *Spanish oath* I vow (to God) 77.5

waggery mischief 96.30

waggish mischievous, droll 246.12, 246.13

wainscot to line a wall with wooden panel-work 46.22

ward prison, division of prison 279.40, 279.43, 312.22

warp twist, entwine 217.39

wassail riotous festivity 356.16

wassailer reveller 380.7, 383.14

watchet-coloured light blue 289.38

water-dog dog trained to retrieve water-fowl 11.2

weal well-being 54.43, 165.22, 167.25

web a piece of weaving 7.20, 161.1, 161.11

weeds clothes 316.27

well-fancied tasteful 283.6, 284.7

whistle see note to 200.5–6

whittle knife 266.39

wicket small gate 279.19 etc.

wight creature 13.31

win catch 246.22

wind inveigle, entice 69.11

wine-skin bag for holding wine, made out of skin 282.2

wink sleep 12.16

wink (at) seem not to see 19.2, 170.27

wise see note to 245.16–19

witch-monger one who deals with witches 193.30

withal with 34.24 etc.

without outside 2.12 etc.

wittol contented cuckold 340.23, 345.8

won dwell 108.7

wood-nymph semi-divine being, imagined as maiden living in woods 269.26

worship honour 57.30 etc.

wot know 11.15 etc.

wyvern *heraldry* winged dragon with eagle's feet and serpent's tail 119.29

yield reward 88.20

younger younger or junior member of family 139.26

zany mountebank's assistant 90.34, 90.42

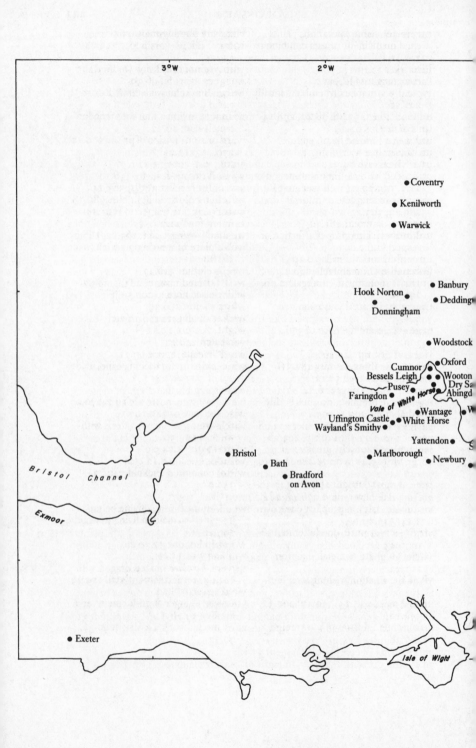

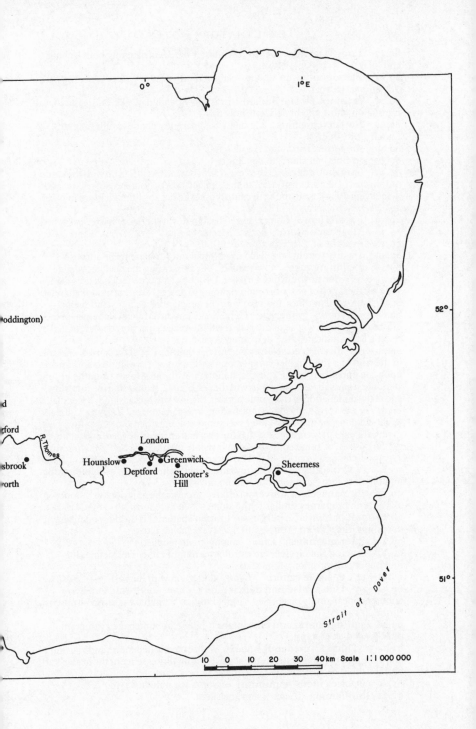

0°   1°E

52°

oddington)

d

ford

sbrook

orth

R.Thames

Hounslow

London

Deptford

Greenwich

Shooter's
Hill

Sheerness

51°

Strait of Dover

10   0   10   20   30   40 km Scale 1:1 000 000